DEFIANCE OF THE FALL 1

aethonbooks.com

DEFIANCE OF THE FALL

Aethon Books
www.aethonbooks.com

Print and eBook formatting by Steve Beaulieu.

Published by Aethon Books LLC.

ALSO IN SERIES

DEFIANCE OF THE FALL

BOOK ONE

BOOK TWO

BOOK THREE

BOOK FOUR

BOOK FIVE

BOOK SIX

BOOK SEVEN

BOOK EIGHT

BOOK NINE

BOOK TEN

BOOK ELEVEN

PROLOGUE – WELCOME TO THE MULTIVERSE

Information is power. It can both be the sword with which you impale your enemy, or the sword you impale yourself upon. That was what was going through Zac's head as he walked through the woods, a small hatchet in his hand and his face glowing with a sheen of perspiration and irritation.

He was still unsure of how a short mention about spending time in his family's cabin as a child turned into him being tasked with bringing firewood back to the campsite. He pushed some intrusive shrubbery out of the way as he ventured further into the woods. Maybe his friends were laughing it up as they stayed by the fire in their cozy chairs with a few beers while he was living the age-old scenario of man versus nature.

Swinging his hatchet, he chopped off a small twig, but immediately saw that it would make terrible firewood due to how fresh it was. What the hell did he know about gathering firewood anyhow? It had always been his dad gathering it for their cabin, and Zac was pretty sure that he had actually bought it rather than cutting down trees.

It was a sweltering day in May, with high humidity, even

though not a cloud was in sight, probably from yesterday's drizzle. This, along with it being spring, made Zac seriously doubt whether any of these trees made for a decent fire if chopped down. The humidity and moisture in the wood would turn the campsite into an inferno of tear-inducing smoke at the first lick of fire. If it was even possible to light the fire at all.

Besides, this whole area was part of a nature reserve, and he was not really sure if there were legal ramifications to cutting anything down. Still, he trudged on, brushing his now sticky hair out of his face as he surveyed the surroundings.

For exactly what, Zac still didn't know. He was still half-hoping to run into a neatly stacked pile of firewood secured under a tarp, left behind by some more adroit forester. Zac had been walking around aimlessly now for fifteen minutes, and he wasn't really cut out for this, so he could really use the backup.

Which was sort of ironic, as his appearance would usually indicate someone who has a good command of the great outdoors. Standing at five feet eleven with a set of broad shoulders, sporting a flannel shirt with the arms rolled up to his elbows, he at least somewhat looked the part. But the slightly too even beard, the pudge at his belly, and the lack of wiry muscles coming from manual labor were signs of a far more sedentary lifestyle.

He was actually just a marketing consultant who jumped onto the bandwagon and got the slightly grizzly look, as it seemed pretty popular at the moment. And it did actually pay dividends. This trip was arranged with his new girlfriend, Hannah, and three of her friends.

Truth be told, had it not been for the heat and the humidity, he wouldn't really have minded this solo trip into the woods. It is always a weird situation, being a new addition to a group that has years of history together. To figure out the dynamics and personalities of everyone while keeping up with conversations where half the content is inside jokes and stories from before you were in the picture.

Of course, Hannah's friends mostly seemed like decent people. David was open and cheerful, and the trip would likely have lost much of its energy had he not been there. Unfortunately, David's interests diverged with Zac's, him being into soccer and hockey, and Zac into video games and art. This made it a bit harder to find things to talk about during the long trip up into the woods.

But he was still a guy Zac wouldn't mind having a beer with.

David's girlfriend, Izzie, was a harder pill to swallow, with her unceasing grandstanding about whatever issue she could insert into the conversation, be it veganism, environmental conservation, or social issues. Of course, Zac generally agreed with her points of view, but it did get tiring to be constantly preached to.

It's ironic, he thought. *It's often the kids of the elite who get like this.*

He had heard from Hannah that Izzie's father was some sort of manager at a hedge fund, and her mother was a partner at a high-end law firm. Apparently, a complete lack of supervision and unlimited funds leaves one with a surplus of energy that needs to be directed somewhere. And in her case, it was usually a crusade against "the Man" and the corporate machine. Still, it was hard to stay annoyed forever with her, as her bubbling energy was somewhat infectious.

Which left Tyler. Or *the Snake*, as Zac renamed him in his head. He seemed like a charismatic enough guy and had those annoyingly clean-cut good looks. Had he been in a movie, he'd be cast as the good-looking jerk the heroine was dating before she found her true love, which was somewhat his situation here. Not that Tyler and Hannah had ever been a couple, but most people had probably expected them to sooner or later get together considering how often they hung out with David and Izzie in some sort of faux-double-date-fashion. Zac was not overly surprised with the hidden hostility he'd gotten from Tyler since the day they first met two months back.

Tyler probably felt that I sabotaged the grand plan of the universe when I came along and inserted myself into Hannah's, and by extension his, life, Zac thought with a snicker.

"Maybe I should get back after all…" he mumbled, a slight unease at the situation lingering, adding to his general irritation of being stuck in the woods, waving around a hatchet like an idiot. He wasn't really a jealous guy, but also not a huge fan of leaving his girlfriend with a vulture circling around. And it wasn't like he would magically produce some firewood by walking around in this forest any longer. He adjusted his grip on the axe and once again readjusted his bangs, which by now were a walnut mess of wax and sweat, and started veering back towards camp.

He had trekked in somewhat of a semicircle and should return back to the vicinity of the camp, or at least the road they took to get here, if he just kept veering right. After walking along for another five minutes, battling the constant threat of shrubbery and mosquitoes, Zac came up to a small clearing.

Insidious shrubbery and intrusive twigs gave way to rustling grass and patches of bloodroot and cardinals. Somehow it felt like an oasis, with a noticeable lack of things to scratch him, and the sounds of wildlife felt somewhat subdued.

Not a bad place for a camp should we decide to move it a bit further into the woods, he mused as he walked into the center of the glade, taking a last look around before turning toward the direction of his camp.

But as he prepared to leave, all sounds suddenly stopped without notice, turning to an almost deafening form of silence he hadn't really ever felt before. Just a breath later, the world was darkness.

[Initiating System…]
[Welcome to the Multiverse.]

…

1

ROLL FOR SURVIVAL

[Initiating System…]
[Welcome to the Multiverse.]

A cold, detached voice echoed in Zac's ears. *Or in my head?* he thought while looking around, confused. Nothing in his life had prepared him for his current circumstances, and for a second, he thought there was an extreme solar eclipse happening. All that greeted his eyes was complete and utter darkness. The only thing visible was himself, as if there was an invisible source of light shining just on him, leaving the rest of the world in black.

"Heatstroke?" he muttered hesitantly even though this didn't feel like some heat-induced delirium. But before he could further analyze these baffling events, the monotone voice interrupted his train of thought.

[Planet Earth scanning complete. Low F-grade mass, ungraded energy.]

[Adjusting…]

[Due to insufficient energy and size, planet Earth will be merged with additional planets drafted for initiation. New values: Low D-grade mass, low D-grade energy. Topography readjusted. Spawn points randomized based by cohorts. Wildlife upgraded due to insufficient challenge. Link to the Multiverse System activated.]

"What? Hello?" he shouted, or at least he thought he did, as the utter blackness seemed like a natural dampener, squelching all sound. But the voice seemed unaware or uncaring of his calls.

This was starting to feel less like some extremely elaborate practical joke or heatstroke, as everything felt just too real. Zac pinched himself, and the sting told him he hadn't passed out either.

Trying to glean any meaning the ramblings from the odd voice only made him more confused. It spoke about Earth, but also used some terms that felt like they came out of a sci-fi movie or a video game. However, the voice gave Zac no opportunity to figure the situation out as it heedlessly droned on.

[Initiating Incursions. Spawning Heral–]
[ERROR! Herald occupying same space as you! Adjusting…]

A more blaring version of the same mechanical voice interrupted itself.

The ominous voice and the message quickly accelerated Zac's heartbeat, and he got a sinking feeling. This was all too real in its craziness, and if this was real, he was in deep shit. He was told he occupied the same space as some herald, and no matter how he looked at it, it couldn't be anything good.

Erring on the side of caution, he jumped to the side to avoid whatever would happen, but it was as though he were in space. He made the motions of movement but remained exactly where he was.

[Merge unfeasible. Protocol SL-34572 initiated.]

"Phew." At least he wouldn't be turned into a half human, half herald, whatever that was. But the fact that the voice seemed to be ready to mash him together with another being was extremely unsettling, and his unease was quickly turning into panic.

Zac mentally tried to force himself to awaken, and when that didn't work, he even slapped himself hard in the face. But nothing worked, and he was still stuck in the darkness.

[Roll for survival. Due to the massive power gap between Herald Ur'Khaz and you, odds heavily in his favor.]

"SHIT!" Zac screamed, or rather squeaked. The panic was now full-blown, and adrenaline coursed through his veins. "WHAT THE HELL IS GOING ON?"

But again, the only thing greeting his inquiries was utter silence until there was a break in the darkness. Seemingly from nowhere, a screen popped up in front of him, hovering silently.

The window looked like something taken out of an old video game, blue with white edges and text. The surreal situation made him blank out for a few seconds before registering what the screen actually said.

Ur'Khaz | 1–100,000 | ROLL
Zachary Atwood | 1–100 | ROLL

It resembled a prompt from a video game, and the familiarity actually calmed him down for a second until he reread what it said and realized the implications. At that point his panic threatening to evolve into hysteria.

It looked like the window was a prompt for rolls between him and this herald, but instead of loot, they were rolling for their survival. And the roll ranges were clearly skewed in his opponent's favor, giving Zac abysmal odds for actually surviving.

"Hello? This isn't funny anymore. Let me out!" he screamed, hoping against hope that this was all some insane experiment. But the reality of the situation was starting to set in.

Zac stared numbly at the screen in front of him for a few seconds as if to comprehend what he was seeing.

"This is crazy. Wanting me to gamble with these odds? Why the hell would I roll?" Zac muttered. But the second he said "roll," the screen changed, and the numbers next to his name started to rapidly change.

[Protocol SL-34572 accepted by participant. Rolling…]

"No, no, no, wait, wait. Stop. Let's figure out a different solution!" he shouted, waving his arms in a panicked attempt to stop the proceedings. But no matter what he did, the numbers kept spinning. It was as though they were rapidly counting down his remainder of time on Earth.

Terror was slowly turning into rage in Zac's mind over the messed-up situation he was in. Rage over the complete and utter lack of answers. Rage over the obviously paltry assessment of him by the voice, seeing the obvious disparity in treatment between him and this Ur'Khaz guy. Rage over the scammy way the voice had started the roll, as though it looked for a loophole to proceed.

With a red tint that suffused his otherwise blue eyes, Zac roared and smashed the hovering screen in an effort to vent his fraying emotions. The screen, however, did not acquiesce to his feelings and shatter in a million pieces, but only flickered slightly.

Unheeding of any attempts at a physical catharsis, the numbers once again flashed intermittently, and the spinning started to slow down until it stopped at a final number. Almost as an afterthought, it also added an infuriating line instead of the roll button.

Ur'Khaz | 1–100,000 | ROLL
Zachary Atwood | 98 | Rerolls unavailable

Something about the reroll message sucked the energy out of him. It really wasn't a bad roll. *If this were in a game, I'd definitely have won the loot*, he thought with a morbid sense of humor. But by this point, he was quite aware that this was no game.

He still held out some hope that he was still lying unconscious in the woods from massive heatstroke. But if that were true, he most likely was a goner as well. So, either he was about to be killed by the sun, or by a video-game god. Neither was an ending he had expected or hoped for.

Not knowing whether to laugh or cry, his face settled on a sickly grin as he blankly stared ahead.

Of course, all hope wasn't lost, as the other individual hadn't rolled yet. But it didn't really feel like it mattered when the game was rigged. He once again took a glance at the screen, and his eyes lingered for a second on the roll range of the other entity.

The smile slowly shrank away from his face. A sigh escaped his mouth like a deflating balloon, and he closed his eyes and slumped down to a sitting position. All of Zac's strength and energy were wrung out by the situation and a roller coaster of emotions. Only a bleak sense of despair remained as he realized that this was it.

Dead alone in the woods, never being able to say goodbye to his family and loved ones.

Zac had no epiphanies or huge regrets at this point, the likely end of his life. Except that he wished he had been closer and better to his family. His mind drifted to memories of his past as a solace and escape from the insanity he was experiencing.

Hazy recollections of his mother hugging him, her long brown locks cascading around him in her embrace. His dad giving him a quiet smile as he opened the door of their apartment to head to work, his eyes sad and tired but full of love. Spending most of his youth plastered in front of the computer, largely ignoring his smaller sibling. College years drowned in alcohol and partying. First day at his job, and the humbling realization of how ill-prepared for adult life he was even after seventeen years of school and university.

[Protocol SL-34572 accepted by Herald. Rolling…]

The monotone voice again droned, like an executioner giving final rites.

[Congratulations!]

Zac didn't bother with the voice anymore as memories flashed past in his mind one by one. Friends, family, and events both happy and sad. Not the most exciting of lives, but it was his…

Wait, what, congratulations? His eyes snapped open and refocused on the monitor.

Ur'Khaz | 91 | Rerolls Unavailable
Zachary Atwood | 98 | Rerolls Unavailable

Stunned, he stared blankly at the screen until the voice interrupted his lack of thought.

[Protocol results in the continued existence of Zachary Atwood. Ur'Khaz vanquished. Resuming standard protocols.]

A nauseating explosion of light, color, and sound took over, disorienting him and turning his insides to mush. His body suddenly felt like it was on fire, tearing and scorching him all over. The last things he saw before passing out was the small clearing he disappeared from and a huge red pillar reaching toward the sky.

2

A NEW WORLD

Zac slowly woke up, groggy and disoriented, finding himself face-first on the ground. His body was still aching from whatever had happened to him before. Spitting out a few blades of grass and dusting himself off, he scrambled up and surveyed the surroundings. The glade looked the same as before with its few rocks and flowers, all surrounded by stout leafy trees and dense shrubbery.

His first reaction was that luckily he had just passed out from the heat or exhaustion and woke up. There were some things that gave Zac the foreboding feeling that what had happened was more than just a heat-induced nightmare. First and foremost was the fact that he was currently staring up at two suns, only one of them being the familiar yellow.

He thought he was seeing double for a second, but shaking himself awake had no effect on what he saw. The sun was accompanied by a little brother. He felt something was a bit off with the original one as well. It seemed larger and more intense than he remembered. The other sun was a far smaller star that shone in a piercing aquamarine. It hovered close to the other celestial body and seemed to orbit it like a satellite.

The other unsettling sight was a huge vortex of light and energy reached up towards the sky in the distance, like a grisly red claw reaching up from the ground. It pulsated in an eerie red glow that could only be described as demonic. It looked like it was quite some distance away, but it was hard to tell. This *pillar* was the last thing Zac had seen before passing out, and it greeted him as he woke up as well.

A bestial roar snapped him out of his thoughts, refocusing him on the situation at hand.

"Hannah…" he muttered, a glint of determination filled his eyes as he threw all these inexplicable events to the back of his mind. If this was all real, and that seemed to be the case after looking around, he needed to get back to the camp immediately.

The emotionless voice in the darkness had said something about making the wildlife more dangerous to "improve the challenge." The roar he'd just heard could be a freaking tiger or bear for all he knew, which meant the others were in danger.

For a second, he was even afraid that the others would jump into the car in a panic and leave him stranded here with whatever was roaring. Even though he didn't know what was going on, burning anxiety was already consuming him and urging him to action. He took off in a sprint toward the direction of the camp, heedless of the unfamiliar sounds all around him or the prickly greenery aiming to slow him down.

The surroundings blurred around him as he thundered on through the forest like a runaway train. It was as though he had gotten ten shots of adrenaline, his legs pushing him forward at a breakneck pace.

But something was off. He felt that he was running even faster than an Olympian athlete, and in complicated forest terrain at that. The previously somewhat weighty axe in his hand also seemed weightless, tearing through any branch trying to impede his way with pinpoint accuracy.

Zac had never felt as strong or fast as he did right now. The voice had said it upgraded wildlife. Did his speed and power mean he was considered a part of that? He didn't know whether to be happy with his improved physique, or to be pissed off that the mysterious voice considered him an animal.

Finally, a few minutes after his mad dash started, he recognized a large boulder that a tree had somehow split and grown through. The camp was just a few hundred meters away.

Readjusting his grip on the hatchet, he changed his course to run straight toward the camp when another of the otherworldly roars echoed through the forest. This time, far closer than the others he'd tuned out on his way here.

Panic gave him even greater speed, and he barreled into the camp with a look of frenzy and fear on his face. Familiar sights greeted him; the gray Range Rover, the camper, and the few folding chairs strewn about.

What immediately garnered his attention wasn't this, though, rather the monster rifling through one of the coolers. It was the size of a Great Dane, but this was where the similarities ended since it was an unholy mix of flesh and bone. The beast looked like it had been skinned, then let out in the woods again—an amalgamation of red and white. It sported a thick trunk of a torso with rippling muscles extending down to six stubby legs, each one ending with a paw that reminded Zac more of a bird of prey than a woodland creature.

Two of the pairs aligned at the front of the torso with the last at the back. Each paw was adorned with four ghastly claws with three in the front and one in the back, with the front set of claws seeming slightly larger than the other two pairs. Its head appeared overly large for its body, with a broad base but a long snout, enabling an impossibly large maw. The mouth reminded him of a crocodile's, if a crocodile possessed three rows of teeth. The eyes were small and beady, shining the same color as the pillar he'd seen earlier.

The power of the beast's maw was readily apparent, as it was currently biting through a can of beans like it was nothing, swallowing the metal and contents alike. The strange sight made Zac stop right in his tracks, unable to compute these turns of events. Suddenly, he wished that it had been a tiger roaring in the distance earlier, since that seemed preferable to the monstrosity in front of him.

The beast perked up before Zac could do anything, spotting him standing mutely across the camp. After an enraged roar, it bolted straight toward him with a speed belying its stocky appearance. Zac barely had time to react as the beast was upon him.

Taking an unstable step back, he swung the hatchet horizontally with all the power he could muster. With his shaky stance, there was no real authority behind the blow, but it managed to strike the beast's neck, leaving an ugly gash and pushing the demon aside.

Zac was once again reminded of how he somehow had become a superhuman, as even a crappy swing like that had contained enough power to throw off a large beast. However, the front paws of the monster were latched on to him, and with the combined momentum of Zac's strike and its own, the claws drew a deep gash on his midriff and left leg. Large wounds were ripped open, and blood immediately started pouring out.

A pain like Zac had never experienced before exploded in his mind, clouding his vision and threatening to incapacitate him completely. Any thoughts of combating the monster head-on with his new strength flew out the window, and instead, an intense desire to escape emerged.

He shook his head in an effort to clear his mind. It didn't work.

What the hell do I do? Do I run? His eyes searched frantically for a way to get out of this situation. Primal survival instincts he didn't know he possessed kicked in. The beast had fallen over from the surprising power of the swing but was already clambering back up to its feet.

"Guys! Are you here? Help!" he shouted toward the camper, hoping for backup. But only silence met his pleas. Did the others flee into the forest to get away from this monster?

Out of ideas, Zac hobbled a few steps toward the forest, his left leg now burning and not properly listening to his commands.

But before any plans could form, the beast was barreling towards him, maw in an open snarl, seemingly unheeding of the small stream of blood trickling down its torso to its stumpy legs.

This time, Zac was slightly more prepared, putting weight on his right leg to jump out of the way. He heard a snarl and felt a gust of wind sweeping by him before he unceremoniously landed in a pile three meters away.

Quickly scrambling to his feet, he saw the monster had skidded past his original position in an effort to stop, continuing on for twenty meters.

Zac realized the monster had high speed but low maneuverability, and started to frantically figure out a way to use this to his advantage. With a determination he didn't know he had, Zac abandoned all thoughts of fleeing and returned toward where he came from when running through the forest.

"This had better work…" he mumbled while moving as fast as his pain-racked body could allow.

3

BATTLE TACTICS

Zac took a quick glance behind him and noticed the demonling following. That's what he decided to start calling it in his head. It wasn't dissuaded at all from continuing its pursuit, though it looked slightly disoriented from the previous charge. Or perhaps the still bleeding gash on the neck was starting to have some effect. Its speed was somewhat slowed, though it was still quickly catching up to him.

No longer being able to afford to care about adages such as not putting weight on a hurt leg, Zac ignored the pain and started charging toward the split boulder he'd passed earlier. His wounds split open even further, and his left leg was now completely dyed red. The pain was excruciating as he ran, but the fear of death kept him pushing forward.

He was pretty sure this was his only shot, as the short run managed to up his pain to a terrifying level, and he was starting to get woozy from the blood loss. And who knew what poisons or pathogens a demon dog had on its claws. Zac could only pray that his new superpowers included super white blood cells.

Finally arriving at his goal, he heaved a few raspy breaths and turned around to face the monster, which was now roughly forty meters away from him. Seeing that its prey had stopped moving, it hesitated slightly and stopped. The demonling growled slightly and then hissed in a register that sounded much too low for something its size.

Zac was afraid it would wait for his wounds to worsen his condition even further, or even gather reinforcements. If that happened, his small chance of survival would be completely extinguished. He needed to end this fight quickly in any case, as the pulsating wounds on his legs reminded him that time was limited, with or without backup.

"COME GET IT, PIECE-OF-SHIT DOG!" he hollered, inwardly cursing his limited cursing abilities. He then picked up a small rock and flung it at the demonling with all the force he could muster. It drew a great arc as it zoomed through the air and missed spectacularly by a few meters. Luckily, it seemed the demon dog needed almost no encouragement for mayhem and slaughter, and with a great roar, it started barreling straight towards him again.

"Come on, come on…" Zac whispered, once again readjusting his grip on the hatchet. This was it, do or die time. When the monster was just three meters away from him, he once again dove to the side. This time, the monster was somewhat ready for him and managed to swipe at his calf. It wasn't as deep as his last gashes but still burned like hell.

The momentum of the demonling pushed it forward, straight into the cleft of the split boulder. The space was barely wide enough for it to fit in, and it got stuck when its second set of legs reached the edge of the rock. Gravel and rock chippings flew about from the collision, accompanied by an enraged, but pained, snarl.

Zac knew he couldn't hesitate, and quickly scrambled to his feet. The pain was staggering, but the coursing adrenaline in his

System kept him going. This was the small window he created for himself, and if this didn't work, he had no other recourse.

Mentally praying to the long-lost gods of lumberjacking, he took a two-handed grip on the hatchet and swung with all his might at the lower end of the monster's spine. Hopefully, the anatomy of hell spawns was somewhat similar to normal animals and a cut on the spine would cut important nerves and maybe even nick an artery.

The axe struck true and severed the spine, even digging a bit further. A great spurt of blood and a pained yelp accompanied it. It thrashed wildly from the strike, and one of its four legs managed to hit Zac squarely in the stomach. He was thrown backwards and lost his grip on the handle of the axe.

All the air fled his lungs as he hit the ground hard. He didn't dare take account of his steadily worsening wounds though, and immediately got back to his feet. The world spun for a second as he scrambled up, but he forced himself to stay awake.

The sight meeting him seemed even more positive than he had dared hope. Both its hind legs uselessly slumped down. The wound Zac had managed to inflict must have actually cut a couple of veins, as blood unceasingly poured out of its back wound in far larger quantities compared to the shallow wound on its neck, pooling in the dirt.

There was still some fight left in the monster, however, and it was still trying to extricate itself from the rock with some minor success. It also desperately and incessantly roared, perhaps hoping for some of its brethren to arrive.

Not wanting to wait for that to happen, Zac gingerly stepped forward, gripped the axe, and with a speedy tug ripped it out of the lower back of the monster. He also stepped back a bit in the event of further thrashing. This time, however, only a weak snarl accompanied the action. Blood started gushing out even faster through the open wound, and it looked doubtful that the monster would survive even if left unattended.

Not daring to take any risks, Zac stepped forward and, with a baseball swing, planted the axe in the torso, hoping to hit vital organs and the lungs. A sickening thud sounded, and more blood streamed out. The beast barely moved anymore, and just weak whimpers could be heard. Zac didn't dare stop and kept swinging the hatchet over and over until he himself fell to the ground heaving.

His body felt a burst of warmth, likely caused by the strenuous activity, and by now the whole left side of the monster was a maze of grisly wounds. Its movements had come to a complete stop, and no more roars or whimpers escaped its maw. The head was still between the two halves of the boulder, along with its front two paws. The arms were mangled from the reckless charge into the rock and the subsequent desperate attempts to rip itself free.

While Zac had no idea about the resilience or tricks of a demonling, it looked deader than dead. He sat up and caught his breath. Slowly calming down, he was reminded of the stark reality. He was hurt. Really hurt. By now, he must have appeared to be a homicidal maniac, almost covered in blood from head to toe, and it was impossible to tell which was his and which was the monster's.

It already seemed impossible he was still alive with the amount of blood he had lost, and if nothing was done, he definitely would not make it to tomorrow. Rising to his feet with a groan, he started staggering back toward the camp. He thought about shouting for help again but immediately discarded the idea. He didn't want to lure another monster to the camp by mistake.

Last time the trip between the boulder and the camp took half a minute. This time he dragged his body forward for what felt like an eternity until he once again came upon the ransacked and chaotic campsite. The camper was still standing next to the car but was now dented in places. The cooler they had brought had been knocked over, the water and beers spilled around.

Not having the energy to care about the mess, he moved toward the camper. Its door was wide open. They had actually brought a decent first aid kit with them when traveling, lucky for him. He felt he should probably get to a hospital, but unless someone drove him, he doubted he would make it. At least he could disinfect, tape, and bandage the wounds here. That would hopefully allow him to return to civilization to get properly patched up.

For the first time since he came back, Zac realized there was no blood or body parts in the camp. Though he hadn't dared think about it at the time, he subconsciously worried the demonling killed the others.

If they had been attacked, there should have been some blood at least, as Zac had little confidence in the four being able to fend off that beast and flee. The axe in his possession had been the only real tool that could be used as a weapon in the camp, apart from some small kitchen knives. And even with that, he had only survived with great luck and some quick thinking. His improved physique had helped immensely, but that alone would not have been enough against that monstrosity. That beast had been both faster and stronger than a bear, and unless his friends had gotten the same type of strengthening as him, they would just be food rather than an adversary for it.

He surreptitiously glanced around as he neared the camper. The car stood empty, and no sound came out of the camper either.

"Guys, are you there? Hannah?" he croaked in a subdued voice, still scared a scream would attract more monsters.

Nobody answered. Only silence.

4

ALONE

Zac had an ominous feeling and prepared to search for tracks or signs of where his friends had gone. However, a dizzy spell reminded him of the most pressing issue. Almost falling, he went to the car and brought out the small green box with the first aid kit from the trunk.

He then limped to the camper and hesitantly entered. The interior was completely empty, with no signs of either friend or foe. Scared that the smell of blood would attract more monsters, he firmly closed the camper's door behind himself. Luckily, it was one of the few spots that hadn't been dented by the demonling's rampage. Zac finally slouched down on the sofa, not caring that the blood would stain the fabric.

He put the box on the small dining table, opened it, and grabbed the small bottle of surgical spirit. By this time his face was drenched in sweat from the pain, and his hands were already shaking. Putting all the things he needed next to him, he started to prepare for his treatment.

Slowly and gingerly, he took off his shirt and pants. Luckily, the blood was still wet and hadn't had time to coagulate and stick to his wounds. Still, the pain was a hundred times worse than ripping off a Band-Aid.

The beast's claws had raked a long gash on his waist, and three additional but slightly smaller ones on his left thigh. There was finally the last wound on his right calf. While the injuries looked ghastly, it actually did not seem as bad as he feared. The cuts seemed clean and straight, and the bleeding had slowed to a trickle. He could only hope that meant he was getting better, and not that he was running out of blood.

Knowing what came next, he almost whimpered when grabbing a water bottle and a gauze swab. He carefully poured the water over the wound at his waist to clean out the blood and dirt, and the agony almost made him pass out. Gritting his teeth and blinking away tears, he then grabbed the alcohol solution and poured some in the gashes. The wound didn't look inflamed, but he didn't dare skip this part, even though it felt like he was being ripped in two from the alcohol.

His face was like a beet by now, sweat pouring down and veins throbbing out on his forehead. Finally, he took some surgical tape and taped the wound together, and then wrapped some bandages a few rounds around his waist.

The first part down, Zac sat panting for a while. He closed his eyes, and a wave of exhaustion hit him like a truck. However, there were still wounds to treat, so he slapped his face to rouse himself again.

Zac performed the same procedures on his legs, and by the time he was done, his face had gone from red to a ghastly white. His hands were shaking so bad that he could barely grip the water bottle when he downed the last of its contents in a few big gulps. He was so weak, he barely managed to make it to the bed in the back, and as soon as he hit the pillow, he passed out even though the suns floated high in the sky.

. . .

The suns were still shining brightly through the window when Zac woke up. Was there no longer any night now that there was an additional sun up in the sky?

He stretched a bit and found out that, while far from healed, he did feel much better than he had before. His bandages were red with blood but not wet, so the bleeding seemed to have stopped. He also didn't feel that intense pulsing agony anymore as it was replaced by a lesser throbbing pain. He still had problems keeping weight on his left leg, though, and almost fell when moving toward the fridge.

The second thing he noticed when waking up, besides his wounds improving, was a fiendish hunger as if he hadn't eaten for weeks.

He ambled to the fridge and found out it didn't work anymore. Some food was already starting to spoil. The monster had probably broken something while smashing against the mobile home. He picked up a few sausages they'd prepared yesterday before they ran out of firewood and a couple of slices of bread. Then Zac virtually inhaled the food like a starving bear, washing it all down with a bottle of water.

The others still hadn't returned. Zac feared they had either fled without looking back or were… dead. Both scenarios were grim, though the possibility of the second left a sour taste in his mouth. He took out his phone from his pocket, but it was mangled and bloodied beyond redemption, likely from one of his tumbles.

Luckily, they had prepared an emergency phone in the camper in case something went wrong, and he opened a cupboard and took it out. The phone was in working order, but it had no reception. This was weird since they'd had a decent signal yesterday. Even if they were camping and enjoying the wilderness, they wouldn't stop at a spot with no reception, as no one was ready to go a whole day without surfing on their smartphones.

He also noticed from the time that three whole days, not one, had passed since the world had gone mad. He truly had blacked out hard after tending his wounds. The date only further reduced the chances of his travel mates and Hannah coming back. At least it also probably meant that the monsters kept to their territories and didn't wander around as much as he feared. He wasn't sure he would be able to handle another of those demon dogs at the moment, even with knowing their weaknesses from the last fight.

With food settled and not having any pressing issues, he started to take account of what had happened, and what to do from here. The absurdity of the situation finally hit him, and Zac spaced out with glazed eyes, unsure of how to proceed.

A distant roar brought him back to reality. This was no time to slack off. He was by no means safe, in the middle of the forest surrounded by crazy monsters. And that glowing pillar still shone in the distance, reminding him that more monsters might come.

Perhaps the pillar was a portal to hell or something similar, and demons could keep flooding through from their infernal plane. Or was this an alien invasion? The monsters could be something like Zergs in a popular computer game he'd played back in the day.

Then he finally remembered the weird robotic voice he'd heard earlier, and the confusing things it said before it started its crooked gambling scheme that almost cost him his life.

"Welcome to the Multiverse…" he mumbled. If the TV shows and comic books he had devoured throughout the years were any indicators, a Multiverse was a connection between multiple planets, galaxies, and even dimensions.

If the voice was to be believed, Earth had been introduced to some larger System, and due to this, there were suddenly demons roaming the forests. But that didn't mean that only demons were around. What about other monsters or races? Would he suddenly meet elves jumping around in the trees, shooting arrows at him with pinpoint accuracy?

The voice also said it had initiated incursions. It seemed reasonable that the huge pillar in the distance was the incursion, which would mean he probably wasn't too far off with his demon-portal theory. And when it spawned in the forest, the demons came with it.

But that meant that the monsters wouldn't necessarily spawn next to it, as one had already been in the camp when he came back. It was hard to tell the distance to the huge pillar, but it should take hours on foot to get there. And something called a herald had spawned right on top of Zac, resulting in the largest emotional roller coaster in his life.

Lastly, he had gotten stronger for some reason with all these changes. Both his speed and power saw noticeable improvements from whatever the weird voice did. It almost felt like he had gotten a power-up like in some video game, which made sense after having seen the floating windows in the dark dimension. He still didn't understand why the prompts were designed to look like an old-school RPG.

Was it his mind desperately trying to make sense of an insane situation and adjusting reality for him?

Fantasy monsters, magical portals, and gamelike elements. If some parts of the world were turned into an RPG, did other elements get introduced as well? At least there was no health bar, and the demon had no description or text above its head either. In fact, the only time he had seen any true game elements was when he was in the black space the voice brought him to.

He tried to notice anything in the periphery of his vision, but there was nothing there apart from the vision of the now somewhat bloody and grimy trailer. *Tyler's parents will probably be pretty pissed off when they see the state of their camper,* he thought with a smirk.

If they're even still alive, he then realized somberly. If the world was turned to shit at his location, what about the rest of the planet? Would it be safer or even more messed up? What about his hometown?

Thoughts of his father and younger sister surfaced, and a sense of urgency appeared. If this was a global problem, nowhere was safe. Zac had no idea what was going on, but he would have to figure that out on the way.

He needed to get back home.

5

STRANDED

Driven by a newfound sense of purpose, Zac immediately packed a backpack with food that wouldn't spoil easily and some other necessities, and then made a beeline for the SUV. If a slow shuffle where every step felt like walking on fire could be called a beeline.

He opened the door, relieved that no one had been paranoid enough to lock the car in the middle of nowhere. The electric keys were lying on the driver's seat. With no time to spare, he placed the backpack on the front passenger seat and pressed the button to start the car. A spectacular absence of sound greeted him. The car had no reaction, even after pressing the key increasingly hard accompanied by angry swearing. The focused power of his will had no impact either. The dashboard remained dim and the motor didn't give so much as a whimper in response.

So, the car was broken as well. Or not broken, but out of battery, he surmised after noticing a black smartphone plugged into the outlet in the car. The car had been on when the world turned to shit, and by now the battery had died. *Freaking Tyler*.

It was a weird feeling returning to the camper with his backpack. He felt somehow robbed of his momentum. If the car battery was broken, he was pretty much stuck in the middle of nowhere, at least for now. Either he had to somehow fix the car with his nonexistent knowledge of vehicles, or he had to get back to the nearest town by foot, which was about eighty kilometers away.

Eighty kilometers would take the better part of a day when conditions were good, but with hurt legs and monsters likely lurking in the woods, it was suicide. There was no way he would try that in his current condition. His only option was to wait where he was in order to heal up, and maybe someone would even come and rescue him. Like the military or the police.

To be honest, he didn't hold high hopes of a rescue. First of all, no one really knew he was here. Even if someone did, he was afraid that these changes would have disrupted law and order to the point they couldn't be bothered about a single straggler stuck deep in a demon forest.

He would have to save himself, and for that he needed to recover and figure out a way to get back to civilization.

"If this stupid System could help out a little and tell me what to do, that would be great," Zac mumbled, lost as to what to do now.

Active Quests:

1. **Unlimited Potential (Normal): Reach level 25. Reward: Unlock Class System. (16/25)**

Dynamic Quests:

1. **Demon Slayer (Normal): Kill 10 denizens with demonic alignment, each at least ten levels above you. Reward: +3% All Attributes when fighting enemies of demonic alignment. (2/10) [Note: Only one Slayer title can be attained.]**

2. **Off with their heads (Unique): Kill the four heralds and the general of incursion within 3 months. Reward: 10 E-Grade Nexus Crystals, E-Grade equipment, unique building depending on performance. (1/5)**
3. **Incursion Master (Unique): Close or conquer incursion and protect base from denizens of other alignments for 3 months. Reward: 5 E-Grade Nexus Crystals, outpost upgraded to town, status upgraded to Lord. (0/3)**

A screen flashed in his view just like when he had been transported to the blackness earlier. Zac froze for a second before even registering what was happening. So, there was more to this System and Multiverse as he'd suspected.

The screen slowly hovered in front of him and even moved with him when he turned his head.

It seemed the System could give out quests that would grant different advantages and power-ups. What Zac first took note of was that there were two types of quests, active quests and dynamic quests. From looking at the contents, it seemed that active quests were normal quests that you either automatically got or received from quest givers or something.

Wait, would NPCs spawn around the world, with yellow exclamation points above their heads, giving out quests? Zac's gut feeling said no.

The other type of quest was dynamic quests. All the quests were related to the demons and the red pillar. By now, he was pretty certain the red pillar in the distance was, in fact, the incursion mentioned by the System.

He also noticed that there was a rarity or difficulty in front of each quest. He currently had two types, normal and unique. Normal was pretty straightforward and seemed like normal grinding quests in video games. "Kill x number of y…" or "collect ten ores," which would reward some experience and gold.

In this case, there was no gold, but the unique quests did reward him with something called Nexus Crystals, which might be a currency. The other rewards were a bit more unclear.

He could somewhat guess what the Class System meant. He would probably get to choose Warrior, Magician (if magic was now real, which actually felt like a very real possibility) or something, and get buffs pertinent to that class.

The demon-slaying quest's reward was also somewhat straightforward, although +3% stats did not seem very strong. However, it was better than nothing, and anything that would help him deal with these weird monsters that had popped up was more than welcome.

The last rewards he had no idea what they meant. Upgrade outpost to town? What outpost? And why would he want a town in the middle of nowhere surrounded by monsters? As that quest somehow seemed the hardest to complete, he felt there was something more to it, but couldn't figure out what. As for the benefits of being a Lord of Monstertown or a unique building, he did not have the slightest idea.

"Why is there no explanation of things?" Zac grumbled. "There should be a Tutorial or something."

[User does not qualify for teleportation to Tutorial protocol. Please explore the System of the Multiverse yourself,] a robotic voice echoed in his head.

"WHAT?" Zac shouted. "Why can't I get the Tutorial? Teleport me right now!"

[By accepting Protocol SL-34572, user gained a personalized initiation protocol, a lottery opportunity.]

"OPPORTUNITY? PLAYING A RIGGED GAME IS AN OPPORTUNITY?!" Zac screamed, forgetting he was surrounded by who knew how many beasts. This shitty System actually did not only almost get him killed, but it also skipped a teleportation to a safe zone, which sounded a lot better than a demon-infested forest.

[Affirmative. Please explore the System of the Multiverse yourself,] the voice dully responded and once again went quiet.

Zac fumed but realized he would get no more help from the cosmic douchebag robot. With a few deep breaths, he once again calmed down and realized the implication of what the voice said.

He himself had missed the opportunity to get to the safe zone, but what about others? Unless it was voluntary, then almost everyone should have been teleported to wherever those safe zones were, barring any extremely unlucky instances like his.

[Protocol SL-34572 is a unique opportunity. Congratulations, user,] the System responded as if reading his mind.

"Well, fuck you too."

Once again calming down, he thought of his fellow campers. Hannah and the others might actually still be safe, teleported away somewhere before this forest turned insane. That would explain the lack of blood and mangled body parts at the campsite.

It also meant that his family hopefully still was alive. While not optimal, a safe zone sounded pretty swell compared to his surroundings. He was still worried, though, and wanted to get to them as soon as possible. Both his father and little sister were out there somewhere, and he was afraid the apocalyptic events would lower the inhibitions of less scrupulous people. While his sister was an avid martial arts practitioner, he wasn't confident that would hold up against perverts with guns and other weapons.

Refocusing his thoughts, he realized something he had just glossed over from the quests. The normal quest had a progression of (16/25). Did this mean that there was actually such a thing as levels, and he was level 16?

What the hell was going on?

6

BORN FOR CARNAGE

There was only one way to find out. The quest panel appeared when he asked what he was supposed to do. Maybe there were other panels as well?

"Menu," Zac said into the air, somewhat embarrassed, feeling like those LARP'ers he had once seen running around in the park. Nothing happened, and he imagined the System snickering at him. Not discouraged, he continued to search for some other panels or menus.

"Status."

This time it worked, and a new bar replaced the one with the quests.

Name: Zachary Atwood
Level: 16
Race: Human
Alignment: [Earth] Human

Titles: Born For Carnage, Ultimate Reaper, Luck of the Draw, Giantsbane, Disciple of David, Overpowered, Slayer of Leviathans, Adventurer

Strength: 31
Dexterity: 25
Endurance: 27
Vitality: 27
Intelligence: 29
Wisdom: 29
Luck: 44

Free Stats: 30
Nexus Coins: 5,100

The status screen did indeed look somewhat like what he expected, with levels and stats. There were a few points he did not really understand though. The first was the alignment. Did it need to be specified that it was humans on Earth that he was aligned with? Were there actually humans on other planets or in other dimensions?

He was surprised how much like a game the rest of the screen was. While there didn't seem to be such a thing as HP or mana, stats did exist. He didn't have any framework of what the numbers meant though, apart from higher obviously being better. Ironically, he saw that his highest stat actually was luck, even though he felt very much out of luck.

Strength seemed pretty straightforward, while the other stats might mean different things. Dexterity likely had something to do with movement and reaction speeds. Endurance and Vitality both meant survivability, though he wasn't sure of the difference. He was pretty sure that his stats were higher than a normal human's though, maybe from his level. He couldn't explain his super-human recuperation otherwise. While he still felt pretty banged up, he should be lying on a bed dying now with the wounds he'd sustained, not walking around.

Intelligence and Wisdom should increase mental faculties. If the world actually had magic and wizards now, these stats would probably make them cast spells better. Finally, he had thirty free stats. A quick count showed that he had gained two points per level-up, if he had started at Level 1. He held off trying to allocate any points though, as he still had no idea what he was doing.

The titles, to be honest, sounded pretty badass. They didn't, however, really feel like something that described him too well. He neither felt like he was born for carnage nor overpowered from the last encounter with the demonling.

"Titles," Zac said, hoping for some explanation of the titles and what they meant.

Just as he hoped, a new screen popped up with an explanation.

Born for Carnage: First to kill a monster in world. All stats +10%.

Ultimate Reaper: First to solo kill an Incursion General in world. All stats +5, all stats +10%.

Luck of the Draw: Successful in cheating death in an endeavor against all odds. Luck +5, Luck +20%.

Giantsbane: Solo kill enemy 5 levels or more above you. All stats +1.

Disciple of David: Solo kill enemy 10 levels or more above you. All stats +2.

Overpowered: Solo kill enemy 25 levels or more above you. All stats +3.

Slayer of Leviathans: Solo kill enemy 50 levels or more above you. All stats +5, all stats +10%.

Adventurer: Reach level 10. Rewards: Strength +1, Endurance +1, Intelligence +1.

"Amazing…" Zac whispered. Titles were far more important than just sounding cool. From looking at his status page, he realized that most of his stats came from his titles rather than being strong on his own.

This also gave him a few very important realizations. Almost all titles came from killing things, meaning that the System probably did not wish for a peaceful and harmonious world. It wanted a world of conflict, where people became stronger by walking over the corpses of their enemies.

That didn't bode well for humanity. If the System incentivized killing, who knew if some people would go crazy and start massacring others for strength instead of monsters. Who was to say that there were no titles for killing humans?

He once again realized the urgent need to meet up with his family before some maniac started cutting people down in an attempt to power-level.

The second important point was that there were different types of titles. The first type was the Adventurer title. This was probably a title most people would gain. He did not know how hard it was to gain levels, but since he was already level 16 after three days, it shouldn't take too long. Therefore, the rewards were not too exciting.

The second type was struggling to complete tasks that were extremely hard. Zac had a slew of rewards for killing monsters at a higher level than him. He was a bit confused at first. While it had almost killed him, it did not feel like killing the demonling warranted all these titles. It did not feel like a boss or some monster that was more than 50 levels above himself if he could kill it with some dumb luck, a well-placed rock, and a lumber axe. The only thing he could imagine was that the System had given him the kill credit for out-rolling the unlucky herald and awarded him with the titles.

Those rewards were a lot stronger and gave him all stat boosts, which likely increased his all-around powers. The most difficult titles even gave multiplier bonuses to his stats. Those bonuses would only get stronger and stronger the higher his level went, and the more stats he accumulated.

Having those kinds of titles would almost ensure he would be stronger than an opponent at the same level unless the opponent also had some hidden means.

He now realized what the System meant when it said that the lottery was an opportunity. All odds were stacked against him, but if he survived, he would not only gain a bunch of experience, but also amazing titles that would benefit him forever.

[Protocol SL-34572 is a lottery opportunity. Congratulations, user,] the robot voice once again droned, this time with a tinge of satisfaction discernible in the tone.

"Still fuck you," Zac muttered back, pretty sure he would have declined even if presented the opportunity again. It was only dumb luck he sat here today instead of being vaporized by the System.

The First Kill titles also intrigued Zac. It seemed that being the first in the world to accomplish certain deeds would grant a powerful title as well. Most likely no one else on this planet would be able to gain the Born for Carnage or Ultimate Reaper titles, as he'd taken them.

From these facts, he could somewhat imagine how the world would develop. Everyone would soon realize the possibility of becoming stronger and breaking the limits of the human body. The importance of titles would also soon be public knowledge, at the latest as soon as people started reaching level 10. Maybe the Tutorial in the safe zones had already explained everything.

Those who were willing to take large risks and survive would gain strong titles, which would make them even stronger, enabling them to level faster and gain even more titles. Some would become elites, being far more powerful than normal people.

Maybe some would keep their humanity and help the average citizens, but many would probably become tyrants, domineering everyone with sheer power.

The world had turned into a place where power was paramount. And if he wanted to protect his friends and family, he would have to become one of the elites himself. Luckily, he had a pretty substantial head start. Zac was pretty sure that high-level titles were not easy to obtain, so very few, if any, knew about the amazing power they could bring.

Finally, below the stat points was something called Nexus Coins, and he had 5,100 of them for some reason. If he were to compare the menu to an RPG, then the Nexus Coins would be the in-game currency.

"Nexus Coins," Zac said, hoping to get an explanation similar to the titles, but nothing happened.

"Coins. Currency. Shop. Store," he continued, searching for a correct keyword. But still there was no response.

"System, are you there?" he grumbled up to the heavens. "Can you come and explain the menu for me real quick? Such as the Nexus Coins and stats?"

[By accepting Protocol SL-34572, user automatically declined standardized initiation protocol in favor of lottery opportunity. Please explore the System of the Multiverse yourself. Goodbye,] the System soullessly responded in a mechanical almost word-for-word repeat of what it had said earlier. After this the System didn't respond to Zac no matter what he asked or how he extolled, as though the System earlier somehow was here, but now had left.

After a while, Zac gave up and refocused on the task at hand. He would have to keep his head start going and keep pushing forward to get more benefits in this new world. He also thought about classes. Perhaps the Class System was similar, where some classes were better than others, and some might even be exclusive ones. Lastly, there were the mentions of towns and becoming a Lord. While not something Zac was planning on focusing on now, it seemed that it was something extremely beneficial, seeing how hard it was to attain.

A plan started to form in his head of how to get out of this situation and head back to his family.

First, he needed his weapon.

7

OUTPOST

It had been four hours since Zac had woken up after getting hurt. Even after moving around for all that time, his wounds only throbbed dully, and he once again was amazed by the efficiency of his constitution. If his Endurance and Vitality grew to 100, would he be able to regrow limbs?

He had spent the last hours discreetly surveying the surroundings to come up with a solution to being stranded in the woods. He had made some discoveries during this time, some more shocking than others.

The first thing Zac had done after figuring out the basics of the System was head back to the scene of the fight to retrieve his axe.

When he arrived at the boulder, the monster was still there, and by then a putrid smell had started to emanate from the carcass. This meant that the System would not remove bodies like in a game. What was dead was dead. After looking around the body, even somewhat moving it to look beneath, it also hadn't dropped any items such as gold or equipment.

He still didn't know if that was just bad luck or whether the System was not that convenient and just wouldn't hand items to him in that manner. Perhaps he would have to make do with what already existed, or there were chests strewn around the world.

Judging from the smell and how the beast looked like when alive, it would not be serviceable to eat, even if fresh. The axe lay next to the body, blood caked all over the shaft and the head. Luckily, it hadn't been corroded or rusted yet, and after a good cleaning, the axe was almost as good as new, albeit slightly dulled.

The next realization he made on the way back to the camp. Since the world in a sense had turned into a game, he thought maybe there was some sort of equipment System. But when saying things like "equip," "equipment," and "inspect" provoked no response from the System, he surmised that there probably was no such thing. An axe was just an axe. Maybe there would be magic gear in the future, but at least for now he had no means to distinguish it. He felt that he had missed something though, as one of his quests would reward him with something called "E-grade equipment," whatever that was.

However, he still was no closer to completing that quest now than he was back then. One thing at the time.

His next discovery was that will and determination do not a mechanic make. After popping the hood of the car, he had blankly stared at the engine for a few minutes, hoping something obvious and easily solved would present itself. But he had to simply face reality that he would not be able to drive it back. The battery was well and truly dead.

But the most disturbing discoveries came after. Since discarding the car seemed the only option, Zac had started scouting the road back to see if it was possible to traverse or whether it was teeming with monsters.

He stealthily moved along the road they came from, keeping to trees and bushes, axe at the ready and maintaining a constant vigil for any sign of danger. If he kept this pace going back, the trip would likely take a week, and he didn't cherish the thought of sleeping out in the open.

Before he got further than around a kilometer, the road abruptly stopped, and dense forests gave way to a cliff with a drop of roughly five meters. The road—heck, the whole ground—was simply gone.

The view that greeted him instead was a panoramic view of an *ocean.* At least he thought it was, as he could see no land in sight, and he was still too sore to climb down and test whether it was freshwater or salt water. He guessed it was salt water though from the smell in the air. In either case it was mind-boggling, as the campsite was hundreds of kilometers away from any body of water of that size.

Zac remembered some words the System had said at the start, which he had completely glossed over in his panic. It said it had merged the planet with others and had been somehow randomized.

Just how powerful was the System in the end, to grab multiple planets out in space and mash them together without him noticing anything? That thought was almost scarier than the immediate threat of the demons.

This also made him realize that most of his plans of going back home and finding his family likely had to be scrapped. If the System could drop an ocean in the middle of the country, his family might be on the other side of the planet for all he knew.

Zac had mutely trudged back to camp, this time with far less vigilance than before. Still, it seemed that there were, at least for the moment, no threats in the immediate vicinity.

Which brought him back to now. He sat in one of the camping chairs, at a loss for what to do. He was emotionally and physically wrung out after the day, and the sense of purpose he'd had before had largely vanished. He was still anxious to find his family and friends, but now he didn't even know how to begin looking for them. Were they even together after the teleportations and reshuffling of the world?

For all he knew, he was actually on an island rather than next to a large body of water. Then he would be well and truly stuck in some sort of nightmarish castaway situation. At least he had a camper, which was lucky, as he had no real idea how to build a serviceable shelter. He regretted bloodying it up now though, but hindsight is twenty-twenty.

He knew that finding anyone he knew would likely be a far-off venture now, and he had to focus on surviving this demon forest first. He had already discarded trying to swim towards where the nearest city was before the apocalypse, as he had no idea of how large the body of water was or, even more importantly, what was lurking in its depths. If there were demon dogs in the forest, why not demon sharks in the water? No thanks. He had to put some faith in the fact that the System wasn't a complete maniac and had put some checks and balances in the Tutorial zones, which would keep his family safe.

He once again opened his status page and quest page to see whether there was something he had missed earlier that could help him with his current situation. After a while he gleaned a clue from his quests.

Incursion Master (Unique): Close or conquer incursion and protect base from denizens of other alignments for 3 months. Reward: 5 E-Grade Nexus Crystals, outpost upgraded to town, status upgraded to Lord. (0/3)

There were references to some sort of base building in two of his quests, and it seemed important, almost like the main quest of the area.

"Outpost," Zac said, hoping for some sort of prompt that could guide him further.

[Requirements met to create incursion outpost. Create now?]

This time, he heard no robotic voice; only a prompt showed up, still looking like an old RPG window.

So there was a function like this. Once again a tinge of rage flared up at the System for its chronic inability to properly explain what was possible. How many other things did he not know about due to the System not teleporting him to a Tutorial village?

Zac didn't immediately answer the prompt, leaving it hovering. He was unsure whether this was the correct choice. Was creating an outpost a onetime thing? Would it make him even more stuck to this area? Would it make a loud noise, attracting curious beasts?

Then again, he wasn't sure if he had much of a choice. It was either creating an outpost and hoping that it would somehow help with his situation, or essentially going out into the woods and grinding for levels by killing demons, hoping that he would grow strong enough before getting himself killed. Seeing as his state was pretty pathetic after just one encounter, it didn't feel like an option. What if he met a pack of the demon dogs instead of a lone scavenger?

Gritting his teeth, he decided he just had to go with the flow this time and decisively said, "Yes."

He stood up, eyes fixed on his surroundings, waiting for something to happen. Maybe a medieval town would sprout up around him? At least some rudimentary battlements? He was hunkered down with his axe at the ready, ready to flee at a moment's notice. But the only thing greeting him was the vision of a lush forest and the sounds of birds and insects.

Confused, Zac sighed and was getting ready to try some different commands to create his outpost when a voice suddenly appeared from behind him.

"What are you doing?"

8

ABBY THE EYE

"What are you doing?" a pleasant, decidedly female voice sounded from right behind him.

Zac, whose nerves already were frayed from the past days' events, shrieked in a higher- than-desirable octave and jumped away from the sound before registering the words. Somewhat embarrassed, he turned around while stuttering, "Sorry about tha–" before once more shrieking and falling back after seeing the stranger. His fight-or-flight instincts also failed spectacularly as he dropped the axe while falling.

What had entered his sight was not a beautiful female, as the voice had indicated. His dream of at least having a pretty girl to share this harrowing experience with died as fast as it had flashed to life. In front of him was a floating eye larger than his torso.

At least, he assumed it was an eye. It looked as though a part of the cosmos had been taken and put into an eyeball. The pupil was a black hole, seemingly sucking in Zac's soul as he was looking at it. The monster had no iris, but rather a slowly rotating cosmic cloud, looking like it was slowly being absorbed into the pupil in the middle.

The sclera was not white as with a human, but black studded

with shining lights. It looked like the stars in the night sky. Surrounding the eye was purplish-tinted skin and an eyelid. It, however, had no mouth, making Zac confused how it could make any sounds.

The thing was beautiful and harrowing all at once, and certainly not what Zac expected after hearing the pleasant voice.

"Rude," the eye muttered. "I am lucky enough to get an assignment at a newly initiated world and I get to work with this rube. By the way, you smell."

Zac was still sputtering. Unsure of whether to run, get the axe, or bow down to his new ocular overlord, he compromised by simply staring dumbly with his mouth ajar.

"Oh well. It makes sense that there were no Stargazers on your planet before the initiation, human. We usually only appear where the System sends us. My real name is a bit tricky for you to say with vocal cords but sounds something like Veth-Abarak. I am here to assist you in your endeavors regarding your outpost. You are welcome," the eye continued, somehow making a haughty expression with only the help of an eyelid. "I am sure you have some questions, though the Tutorial should have explained most of what you can do."

"Um… Hello, my name is Zac… er, Zachary Atwood. What do you mean assist me? And how are you talking without a mouth?" Zac responded, still having some problem adjusting to the situation.

The eye, or Stargazer as it called itself, gave a long-suffering sigh, already seeming to have labeled Zac as a mental invalid.

"Did you not listen to the pixies during the Tutorial? I am the assistant assigned to you when you chose this… trailer? Why did you choose a trailer? Anyway, when you chose this trailer to be your outpost while assaulting the incursion. I will help with answers regarding the choices you make, to get the ball rolling, so to speak. As for how I talk, magic of course," the Stargazer answered, a flash of what looked like cosmic mist grandly surrounding herself to accentuate her powers.

"What choices? And no, I didn't listen to any pixies or fairies because the stupid System never sent me to any Tutorial. It left me in this crazy demon forest three days ago while it teleported my friends away." Zac was starting to feel a bit peeved at being looked down on by a floating eyeball.

"Oh, you didn't go to the Tutorial. I guess tha… THREE DAYS? This world was initiated only three days ago? Don't you mean months?" The Stargazer started shaking, the pupil shrinking to a… well, not pinpoint, but from a basketball to a baseball in size. "Stop joking with me. How would you be able to create an outpost after only three days, even if you skipped the month-long Tutorial?" Veth-Abarak shook and hovered closer to Zac's face, the grand mist surrounding it disappearing.

Zac, who had somehow started to get acclimatized to talking with this odd being, sighed and briefly explained his experience, starting when the world turned dark. The eyeball seemed harmless enough and appeared to be on his side. Furthermore, he really needed someone to talk to, both to unload and to make sense of the situation.

"Oh wow, I got assigned to a Defier. I guess I have some good karma after all! No returning in defeat for Abby!" The Stargazer suddenly seemed quite a bit more amiable, virtually shaking with excitement. It almost felt like the creature would start rubbing itself on him if he weren't still generally caked in grime.

"What's a Defier? It doesn't sound great. And wait, Abby? Wasn't your name Veth-something?" Zac questioned, growing more and more confused the more the Stargazer spoke.

"Now, now, don't be so formal. Just call me Abby," Abby answered. Gone was the slightly haughty attitude, replaced with the mild pleasant tone from the beginning. "And I guess some explanations are in order. As you have figured out, some people of your world have been moved to Tutorial towns after your world was integrated into the Multiverse. However, others have some sort of deficiency where they can't naturally absorb Cosmic Energy, and the System deems them worthless. It doesn't bother with these people and leaves them where they are. These people mostly die sooner or later. They are essentially defenseless at the beginning as the System generally vastly increases the danger of the surroundings."

"And these are the Defiers?" Zac interrupted, a bit anxious. "Is it genetic? Do you think my family is stuck somewhere as well?"

"Being a Defier isn't something genetic; it's more like a title. And those left behind aren't all Defiers. These people are generally called mortals. Please let me finish. We have limited time. As far as research shows, it is essentially random who can take in Cosmic Energy and who can't when a world gets integrated. However, in worlds with lower-class energy, mortals are more common.

"The higher the energy, the more common it is to be able to absorb the energy. On B-rank planets and above, almost everyone can absorb Cosmic Energy naturally, from what I've heard. Families with strong genes also have a lot better chance of being naturally endowed."

"When I was in that black space, the System said Earth had sub-F-grade energy, and after the merge, a low D-grade," Zac chimed in, hoping for some additional information.

"Well, sub-F? That's the lowest of the low. I doubt there were people who could fly or use magic before the merge, right?"

Zac nodded affirmatively.

Abby shook her eye and continued, "From what I've heard, only 5–10% of the population turn out to be cultivators in a world like that. And most of those people are younger, as their minds haven't turned too rigid yet. Of course, this is for you humans.

The Multiverse consists of myriad races and civilizations, and many races have natural advantages compared to you humans, who are notoriously average.

"Cultivators are what they call those who can naturally draw the cosmic energies into themselves, by the way. They can be divided further into many types depending on class and skills, but that's for later. D-grade energy is pretty good for a new world, even if it's at the low stage. Most planets end up at E-grade. So, to recap, the world is populated by mortals and cultivators. This might mean your family is safe for now."

"Safe how?" Zac questioned testily. "It sounds pretty bad to me that my family are probably stranded somewhere with monsters spawning just like me, but without the titles."

"Well, if they all are mortals, they haven't been split up. They are probably together in the city you lived in. Also, even if they are mortals, there is strength in numbers. Even if the monsters are normally impossible to kill one-on-one, they should be able to kill the easier monsters using teamwork. And while they can't just get continuously stronger through cultivating, they still get stronger from killing monsters and leveling up like you did," Abby explained patiently.

While not completely comforting, what she said did make some sense to Zac. He could only hope his family was being careful and safe right now.

"Anyway, that brings us to Defiers like you," Abby said. "In extremely rare cases, a mortal gains power far above what's expected, either through luck, some odd talent, or hard work. There is no strict definition of them, rather a 'you know it when you see it' attitude. The name comes from the fact that the System essentially has deemed you trash, but you defy the System and fate, and become strong. Your situation is extreme even for Defiers. I mean an incursion leader spawning on top of you and you get some weird lottery opportunity? Stealing a bunch of exclusive titles? Crazy. It must be the System experimenting with some new functionality." Abby seemed to get excited just thinking about it, happily bouncing up and down in the air.

"Have you never heard of it happening before?" Zac asked curiously.

Abby rolled her eye in response. "No, but what do I know? I'm just a tad better off than you in the grand scheme of things. If it's some experiment the System is running, it might have created the same situation on a few million planets."

"What? Millions of planets?" Zac blurted.

"Oh, right, you missed the Tutorial. Suffice to say the Multiverse is almost infinite, with endless worlds with life on them, most far larger and more populated than your Earth. It has existed for billions of years. And in such an environment, it is still extremely rare for one person to get such a huge head start at the point of an integration. Makes you an aberrant even among Defiers. You, and by extension me, have truly hit the jackpot. "

"So how does it help me?" Zac asked. "I understand that I have a leg up on others with all these strong titles, but I still can't absorb that Cosmic Energy you mentioned. What is that, anyway?"

"Cosmic Energy is the building block of the Multiverse. It is energy, it is magic, and it is life. It is everything. You couldn't really see the effects of it earlier, as your world had so little of it, but you will soon see the effects of it on everything around you," Abby said, almost having a reverent tone mentioning it.

"See how?"

"Some things in nature will be unable to take in the stronger energy and die out. But many things will be like the cultivators, naturally absorbing the energy. Essentially, things will grow big. Both the beasts and nature itself. Many things will also change in unpredictable ways. A tree might gain the properties of metal and be almost unbreakable; a mouse might grow wings and fly or suddenly be able to spit thunder. It's quite spectacular.

"Not being able to cultivate will impede you somewhat, but not as much as you think. You have a massive advantage in the form of titles, strength, and your newly created outpost. In any case, there are so many things to go over, but unfortunately, we are running out of time. I will be summoned back in ten minutes."

9

FORCED TO FIGHT

Zac was gobsmacked.

"You're not here to help out permanently?" he inquired hesitantly. While it took some time to get used to talking to an eyeball, he was pretty unwilling to be stranded alone in the forest again. Besides, there were so many things he still didn't understand about what was happening.

"Unfortunately, no. The System only summons an administrator such as myself for a short while when creating an outpost. Also, we only get summoned the first six months after initiation. Something like an add-on Tutorial. But we got a bit sidetracked here and need to hurry up with your outpost," Abby explained, seeming a bit embarrassed she'd gotten sidetracked from her duty.

"Outposts will evolve into full-fledged towns if you complete certain missions. The difference between a System-sanctioned town and a normal mortal town is that the city leader of a System-sanctioned town can use the System to summon buildings, tax the population, and connect to other city leaders, for example. The difference between an outpost and a town is that an outpost is temporary. Either you manage to turn it into a town by completing your quest, or the incursion over there will stabilize and turn to a town owned by the invading general. And then A LOT more demons will spawn, and unless you're already dead, you will likely die then, titles or not."

Zac nodded, a better picture forming in his head. Remembering the three-month deadline in his quests, he realized that what Abby described would happen in roughly three months. Still, there were some things he was unsure about.

"But do I really need to care about creating an outpost?" he asked. "My goal is to find my family. I can just leave before the demons arrive."

That question managed to elicit a full-body eye roll from the eyeball.

"And go where? Couldn't go to the Tutorial town, so you can't learn skills or choose classes, making you quite weak compared to what you should be. There are monsters everywhere, so you aren't safe anywhere. An outpost can help you get stronger through its facilities, and having a town would be the most effective way to look for your family, compared to manually looking everywhere like a vagabond. You will soon learn just how vast this new planet of yours is." The Stargazer snorted.

"Besides, being the first to create a town has amazing benefits, just like with the titles. The System likes the people in the forefront," Abby added as she went into lecturing mode.

"And if that's not enough, I can also tell you that the System hates cowards. You only get one shot at creating your outpost. If you fail, the System deems you unworthy to be a Lord in the future. If you not just fail, but abandon the mission, the System will also punish you. It would range from crippling you to outright killing you depending on how bad it judges your performance."

"WHAT?" Zac shouted, aghast. "You mean I must complete this quest and kill all the other boss demons or the System might kill me?" The little goodwill Zac had been building toward the System during Abby's explanations was thoroughly erased.

"Well, yes. So, I suggest you improve your outpost as much as possible in order to have a chance at survival," Abby nonchalantly explained, as if risking life and limb fighting demons was completely normal.

"Well, shit. So what do you suggest I build?" Zac hoped to get some guidance in order to create a good foundation for the outpost.

"I'm sorry, I am not allowed to guide your choices of buildings. Building a base properly is also a test from the System. I am only allowed to provide information. The System doesn't want to give too much direction or tips to newly initiated civilizations, as it wants to test their ingenuity."

"Yeah, the System is a real asshole, isn't it?" Zac muttered. Abby's pupil enlarged and looked around nervously. Apparently speaking ill of the System seemed like some sort of blasphemy, which Zac guessed made sense, as the System essentially was a god. Maybe speaking ill of a being that could spawn portals that puked out demons was a bad idea after all, he reflected and vowed to try to keep a lid on his mouth.

"Er… Anyway. If you imagine the words 'outpost base,' a menu will appear with your options. Most of the options are unavailable at the start, but more and more get unlocked as your outpost grows into a town and further. You use the Nexus Coins you have to buy the upgrades, and you can get more coins from various sources. Nexus Coins are the official currency of the Multiverse, and the only one used when trading with the System," Abby said, seemingly eager to change the subject.

This answered the question Zac had about the coins in his status screen. He still wasn't sure why he had 5,100 of them though.

"Wait, is there some connection between Nexus Coins and

Nexus Crystals?" Zac asked, remembering the rewards from his quests.

"Not really. Nexus Crystals are a staple cultivation resource in the Multiverse. Both cultivators and mortals can absorb Cosmic Energy from them. The higher the grade, the more energy it contains, and the faster you can absorb it."

"Okay… I—"

She cut Zac off. "Well, I would normally have time to answer some specific questions about the different buildings, but we're out of time. Good luck, Zac. If you somehow survive this, remember me when you create your town!"

It seemed the time for the Outpost Tutorial was coming to an end. Abby seemed to hesitate a bit but then apparently came to a decision.

"You… You should really try to complete the quests within a month, or at least within two months. That would…" She didn't get any further before a heavy pressure suddenly bore down on the camp. Abby's pupil dilated, and red squirming veins appeared all over the eye. And suddenly she was gone.

Zac wasn't sure, but it didn't feel like this was how she was supposed to disappear, as she'd appeared completely without him noticing. He had been able to sense something that could almost be anger in the pressure that had descended. Had Abby been punished for what she said at the end?

"Complete the quests within a month…" he repeated, trying to glean any hidden meaning. Something obviously had happened because of those sentences. If the System punished her for lying, it could only mean Abby wanted him to run to his death like an idiot. But if it was for unduly helping, it might be an important clue to help him stay alive. That meant something likely happened to the world or the incursion after a month had progressed. Something that was bad for him.

He couldn't figure out why the Stargazer would just help him like that, even risking the wrath of the System, as she had already explained it didn't like her giving undue guidance. Zac couldn't figure out any real reason for that yet and could only put it aside for now. Instead, he followed her instructions and thought, *Outpost base.*

A new window popped up in front of him. But while it still had the blue background and white borders, it reminded him more of a web store than an old-school RPG game. There were multiple categories of buildings and add-ons to choose from to the left and a seemingly unending number of products in the main window.

Zac took a bottle of now tepid water from the cooler the demonling had been rummaging through earlier and retreated to the camper. The suns were starting to set, which was a relief to Zac as it proved that at least the daily cycles remained in the world, giving some normalcy.

Unheeding of the bloody mess inside, he cracked open a tin of beans from the cupboard. Luckily, they had stocked the camper well before the trip, as they had planned to spend a week on the road, and most of it was nonperishables. He still had food and water for at least two weeks unless he gorged himself.

He sat down at the small dining area, and while slowly eating his beans, he started mentally browsing through the shop. Zac noticed that the prices were denominated in Nexus Coins, which he had 10,100 of now. He had gained 5,000 coins during the day, likely from creating the outpost.

If he was going to survive in this new world, it seemed the first step was getting the most out of this outpost of his.

10

PREPARATION

Zac woke up the next morning feeling sore, but his wounds had obviously healed even further. It no longer hurt much to put weight on his wounded leg, and he could actually turn his midriff without a blazing pain erupting.

The smell in the camper was getting pretty bad though, and he knew he had to do something about it if this was going to be his base for the foreseeable future. Gathering the bloody bedsheets he had fallen asleep on when he passed out from his wounds, he put them in a garbage bag. He didn't dare throw it outside yet though, afraid the smell of blood would attract beasts.

He spent another thirty minutes cleaning most of the blood away with some detergent, making the trailer go from looking like the site of a vampire orgy to a serial killer's hideout. The blood had badly stained multiple places, especially around the dining area, and it wasn't something he'd be able to fix in the short run. At least it smelled a lot better now.

Finally, he decided to waste some water for a quick shower in the trailer bathroom, even though the water was limited. After some intensive scrubbing away of the blood caked all over him, the filth was mostly rinsed away.

He stepped out of the shower and donned another set of clothes, feeling like a new man. While showering, he had also noticed that he seemed to have actually gotten more in shape, with most of his gut gone and his muscles seeming, if not bigger, then harder and more compact than before. The stats apparently had some effect on his physical appearance.

Hopefully, an increase in intelligence won't make my head larger and larger, he thought, picturing how ridiculous that would look.

After a quick breakfast, he was finally ready to head out according to plans he had made yesterday after browsing through the shop. There were a dizzying array of possibilities to choose from when building an outpost, even when most of the options were disabled.

Many of them he could understand or at least somewhat intuit the purpose for after a lifetime of playing video games. There were buildings such as an inn, a blacksmith, different types of stores, a bank and so on. Most of these required a town though. There was also something he was extremely keen on getting—the teleporter. If he built that, he might be able to beam back to his hometown in one go.

There was one confusing aspect of the buildings though, which was that there were often hundreds of versions of most of the buildings, especially the commercial ones. Even though they seemed to fill the same function, they were of different designs, with some minor differences in the description.

After a while he could only surmise that the different choices represented different factions or planets. It seemed that creating a store wouldn't actually create some NPC-style beings, but rather move people here from other planets or intergalactic corporations.

A huge number of supporting buildings could also improve the offense, defense, or improve the town in other manners. There even seemed to be some sort of training facility able to slowly improve stat points without leveling. If possible, Zac would have gone on a shopping spree, but he quickly realized the harsh reality that roughly ten thousand Nexus Coins would only be able to buy a few of the most basic buildings.

He needed to explore some more before spending the few coins he had.

Zac had seen a hill the day he had been forced to go out to gather firewood, and he planned to scale it to get a better lay of the land. Donned in a fresh set of clothing and with his trusty hatchet, he once again set out into the woods.

Soon, he reached the hill, hunkered over to not be spotted by any potential threats. Luckily, the hill was filled with lush bushes and even a tall tree at the top, making for some simple protection. Unfortunately, the hill wasn't tall enough to give a complete overview of the surroundings, with the crowns of larger trees still obscuring the distance inland. Still, he could see his trailer and further across the ocean.

He had wanted to see whether he was actually on an island, or if the System had teleported any type of civilization in the vicinity. It would be a bit insane if he lived as a transient mountain man in the trailer if a town was just a few kilometers away.

Swinging the axe and embedding it slightly in the tree, he started climbing it for a better vantage. Zac once again marveled at the improvement of his constitution from his increase in stats. He felt like a gibbon, almost effortlessly dragging himself upwards along the branches with his arms, something that would have been an impossible workout in the past.

Before long, he was almost at the crown of the tree, afraid to continue up any further as the branches seemed inadequate to support his weight. A quick glance around unfortunately realized his fears.

It very much seemed that he was on an island without any civilization in sight. However, he couldn't be completely sure, as there were actually mountains off in the distance. They weren't gargantuan, but still large enough to solidly block any visibility of what was beyond. It would be quite odd to have steep mountains right next to the ocean, but Zac guessed that was what happened when the System pressed the randomizer for a world. The good news was that there was land in sight in the distance, though it looked like a few scattered islands rather than a solid landmass.

The island—as Zac decided to call it until proven wrong—he was on was huge, and he couldn't properly assess the size. He and his trailer were on the far edge of it, while the ever-shining red beam of light was almost on the opposite side, in a vale halfway between the center of the island and the mountains. He guessed that the reason why he still only had encountered one of the demon dogs was that they mainly spawned scattered around the incursion itself.

Zac didn't have time to analyze the situation any further. A branch in the periphery of his sight suddenly exploded into movement and instantly was upon him. Before he had time to adapt to the situation, a brown snake had wrapped itself a few loops around his torso, leaving only the arm he used to hold onto the tree for leverage free. The snake seemed to be over three meters long and slightly thicker than his arm.

He immediately felt an intense pressure on his chest, the air leaving his lungs and the wounds on his side screaming in protest. Zac strained until his face was red with exertion, but was unable to free his trapped arm at all. The snake had him in a vise, and even with his improved strength, he could not get free. Its head slowly rose towards his, hissing.

The air all but squeezed out of Zac's lungs, his consciousness started to get fuzzy, and lights flickered in his sight. Zac knew he was running out of time. It was time for a Hail Mary. He suddenly let go of the tree with his free hand, grabbed the head of the constrictor, and bashed it with all the force he could muster into the tree trunk.

The slam obviously had an effect on the snake, as it slightly released him from its grip. With newfound strength from a ragged breath, he smashed the snake's head twice again into the tree with even more fervor.

However, just as Zac was feeling jubilant about escaping death's grasp, he felt the branch he stood on give way, and both he and the still-entwined snake came crashing down.

11

UPGRADES

Zac woke up with a jerk, which caused a pained groan to escape from his mouth. There was not a single part of his body that didn't feel battered and broken. A quick look around showed that he was halfway down the hill, his whole body full of scratches. The snake lay lifelessly a few meters away from him, seemingly having uncoupled from him somewhere during the tumble downhill.

Not daring to take any chances due to negligence again, he ignored the screaming protests of his body and dragged himself toward the snake. There was a rock roughly the size of a head on the way, which he ripped out of the ground. Finally, he arrived in front of the beast, and with a snarl, grabbed the stone with both hands and slammed it with all the power he could gather right in the forehead of the snake. The long body convulsed slightly but seemed not to react further than that. Zac wasn't done, however, and with guttural grunts from deep within his throat, he kept slamming the stone down again and again, each time eliciting a wet thud. After a few hits, the body's death throes stopped, but Zac kept going until the bloodied stone finally slipped out of his hands. By then, the head and neck were only a mess of broken flesh and brain matter.

The grunts gave way to sobs as Zac collapsed next to the headless snake, his whole body shaking. He had messed up; that had been way too close. Not finding any more demons the last two days had made him complacent, barely looking around for threats. The Stargazer had even warned him just yesterday about the world changing due to absorbing Cosmic Energy, but he hadn't even reflected on what that meant. There shouldn't have been snakes of this size in the woods where he was, but the energy in the world had not only increased its size and strength but made it more aggressive. Had that been a venomous snake instead of a constrictor, he would be a bloated corpse by now.

He finally understood that there was simply no such thing as safety in the wild, and he had to start taking things more seriously. Not even the last near-death experience had really woken him up, as the stats and quests made him subconsciously consider it all a game. But this was life and death, and he had to treat it as such.

Zac shakily got to his feet and started to make his way to the top of the hill again. His hatchet was still left in the tree, and he refused to go anywhere without it again. It felt like he had been hit by a truck, but he could only grit his teeth and trudge on.

At the crest, there were fallen leaves and broken, bloodied branches all over the ground. Luckily, it seemed that the snake had taken the brunt of the damage from the fall; otherwise, he might not even have survived just from the height. He didn't want to linger at such an exposed location, so he quickly ripped the axe out of the tree and made his way back down the hill.

When he reached the snake once again, he hesitated for a few seconds, but then gripped the reptile and wired it around his torso a few turns then put the end up on his shoulder. He had to think like a survivor now, and the snake might both give food and its scales could be fashioned into some sort of protection.

Any other exploration would have to wait. He needed to get back to base. On the way back, he walked with much greater care, trying to avoid stepping on twigs and staying close to the trees for shelter. However, the only sound from the forest was the sleepy rustling of the trees, only occasionally interrupted by a distant roar. After another fifteen minutes, he was finally back in the camp.

He had planned to go over his strategy for the town once more but currently felt intensely unsafe right now, and decided not to drag things out any longer. He brought up the base-building interface and bought an **[F-Grade Small-Scale Illusion Array]** for two thousand Nexus Coins. Suddenly, as if it had always been there, a small wooden box appeared in front of him. Zac opened the box, and inside were eight intricately carved wooden poles. They were each roughly thirty centimeters long and three centimeters thick, with a glossy black coating. One end was sharpened down to a needle point while the other was completely flat. The carvings were in a golden hue, and it seemed they were depictions of intricate fractals rather than words or pictures.

When Zac picked up the poles, suddenly, eight small yellow pillars lit up around the camp. He wasn't surprised at this, as the shop had mentioned the usage method. When holding the poles, or flags as the System had called them for some reason, the System would guide him where to place them. As soon as all the flags had been placed, the formation would activate. There also was a cheaper alternative of the same array, but it didn't have the guidance system, leaving the user to figure out the correct placement according to energy flows and ley-lines. Zac quickly placed down the flags according to the instruction, and suddenly, a translucent dome shimmered into being around the small campsite. It initially looked like uneven glass, distorting the outside, but soon turned invisible. Not sure if it had any effect, he walked outside the camp and took a look.

What met his gaze was just a normal-looking forest, albeit slightly denser than around it. The trailer, campfire, and car were completely gone. Even the bloody smell from the snake was removed, replaced with only the fresh earthy smell of the forest. There were some thorny bushes between the trees, looking almost like a natural wall, which would hopefully encourage nearby enemies to walk around the camp rather than straight through.

That was the disadvantage of the illusion array, and why it was so cheap compared to many other defensive options. Anyone could simply walk through it if they desired, as it provided no stopping power. As soon as someone knew where to look or just was passing by, it simply had no value. Also, it didn't work on stronger individuals, as they could sense something was wrong with the Cosmic Energy in the area. However, it was a cost-effective alternative right now, which left Zac with more coins for other buildings. Later, he would see if he could get some physical bushes transplanted at the edge of camp to dissuade any roving animal or monster from taking a path through the camp even further.

Zac was not done with that, though, and he made another purchase, which spawned a box similar to the first one, but slightly larger. Inside were twelve poles, this time white but still engraved in gold. They were slightly larger than the illusion flags and had a different fractal engraved, but obviously, they had the same purpose – to create an array. It was the **[F-Grade Small-Scale Mother-Daughter Gathering Array]** and cost Zac a whopping 7,500 Nexus Coins, almost cleaning him out. The gathering arrays for sale in the shop were designed to gather Cosmic Energy from the void and increase the density of it within its borders. This would improve the cultivation speed of the cultivators and was likely a must for any town of repute in the Multiverse. This normally was of no use to Zac, as he wasn't a cultivator and instead had to kill monsters to gain levels.

However, the array he had bought had a special function, which was highly desirable to Zac. The Mother-Daughter in its name referred to the fact that it actually was two arrays.

One of them was the normal gathering array, which was referred to as the mother array. The other array was actually a necklace, which looked a bit like a small ship's wheel from a medieval ship attached to a silver chain. The unique function of the Mother-Daughter Gathering Array was that most of the energy that the mother array gathered did not increase the density of Cosmic Energy within the array, but was actually transferred to the daughter array.

As long as Zac wore the amulet and was within fifty kilometers of the mother array, Cosmic Energy would continuously be transferred to the amulet, and from the amulet into Zac. In other words, the array essentially turned him into a cultivator who continuously drew energy into himself, as long as he was on the island.

The downside of this type of array was that the gathering efficiency was far lower compared to a similar F-grade Gathering Array, which would result in a far more sparse concentration of Cosmic Energy in a town. However, this didn't matter to Zac, as he had no citizens that he needed to take into account, at least not for now. He quickly followed the instructions and placed the twelve flags around the camp.

This was Zac's main plan to have a chance to get strong enough to survive against the incursion. He had no experience of combat from his earlier life and needed to gain power from stats and levels to simply be able to overpower his enemies, at least until he gained some actual combat experience.

There were more things Zac wanted to buy, but he simply had run out of coins. Finally, Zac took a look at his status screen once more and saw that even though it had been a harrowing experience, killing the snake had not given him another level.

Name: Zachary Atwood
Level: 16
Race: Human
Alignment: [Earth] Human

Titles: Born For Carnage, Ultimate Reaper, Luck of the Draw, Giantsbane, Disciple of David, Overpowered, Slayer of Leviathans, Adventurer

Strength: 31
Dexterity:25
Endurance: 27
Vitality: 27
Intelligence: 29
Wisdom: 29
Luck: 44

Free Points: 30
Nexus Coins: 600

After checking out the menu, he looked down on his battered and bruised body and felt embarrassed with himself. He had 30 stat points he still hadn't allocated. If he had done that this morning, he might not have been in such a precarious situation as he was.

It was time to upgrade.

12

THE WARRIOR ROUTE

Initially, Zac had wanted to hold out on spending his points until he understood the class system better, maybe even waiting to allocate until level 25. He now realized that such thinking was naïve. He needed every advantage he could get in the coming months if he wanted to survive. He was supposed to kill three more heralds somehow but had almost died *twice* to low-tier monsters at the edge of the island.

Still, he didn't just want to do anything hasty, so he donned the amulet and sat down in a camping chair. Immediately, he felt a warm pulse from the amulet, which entered his chest and spread through his body. Almost his whole torso and large sections of his body were purple from being first strangled and then falling down a tree. It seemed, however, that the amulet actually slowly alleviated his symptoms. Abby the eye had said that Cosmic Energy was *life*, so it made sense that it would not only help with his cultivation.

When choosing stats, one needed to plan for the long term, to make sure it was suitable to his class. The problem was that he had no idea how the class system worked. Could he even decide on a class himself, or would it just be assigned to him?

"System…? Are you there?" Zac once again tried to get some information out of the System, but was met with silence. "Can you tell me about stat points?" he entreated, trying hard to hide the rancor he was feeling toward this unfeeling overlord.

With a lack of answers, he could only make educated guesses and hope that any bad choices wouldn't haunt him in the future. If it were a video game, he would likely dump all the points in the main stat of a class, such as Strength for a Warrior and Dexterity for a Ranger. The difference was that, in a game, he could respawn if dying, whereas here it was game over for real.

If he could choose, Zac would have preferred to be a mage. Then he could just stand safely in the distance, throwing fireballs at unsuspecting monsters until they were burnt to a cinder. Yet he didn't dare go this route. He had no idea if he would be able to use magic even if he got a class, or how to progress in such skills.

He also skipped Ranger-type classes, simply because he had no such weapon. His eyes swept to the hatchet lying down next to his leg. Even after his recent battles, it looked almost as good as new. Luckily, they had bought a fancier model, being a solid piece of metal with a plastic grip. If the handle had been made of wood, it might have snapped by now.

"I guess it's the Warrior route…" Zac muttered and sighed. From the experiences since last week, he was plenty reluctant to choose this class type, but he saw no different option as of yet. Maybe the System would prepare other options he hadn't thought of yet when he reached 25.

Zac brought up and decisively spent his 30 free points. First, he placed 10 points in Strength. In both fights so far, he had been physically weaker, and he needed a boost in that department. What good was his hatchet if he couldn't give more than flesh wounds on his targets? He then spent 5 points in Dexterity in somewhat of a test to see what improved. Five points also went into Endurance. He would be moving and fighting a lot across the island, and he needed a sturdy constitution.

Finally, he put 10 points in Vitality. Vitality wouldn't help killing monsters directly, but he felt that it would help indirectly. He simply was in no condition to fight right now. With increased Vitality and the amulet, he should heal plenty faster compared to before. Secondly, he would be running around and fighting a lot in the coming months. He couldn't take a few days off after every fight to nurse his wounds, or he'd likely never be able to clean out all the demons before the three-month deadline. He also felt that a high Vitality would help him in the future no matter which class he got, while Strength and Dexterity felt a bit more specialized.

Zac felt that Wisdom and Intelligence were likely the staples of the mage route. Getting an increase in either wouldn't hurt, but he couldn't justify spending points there when there were more tangible improvements that the other stats could provide. He felt the same about Luck. His high Luck had likely helped him survive so far. It was thanks to a lucky roll that he was still standing here today. But Zac did not want to rely on luck to survive. Even if he somehow fell ass-backward into victory nine times out of ten, he'd still die the tenth time due to lack of proper foundations. Luck was intangible, and he couldn't even fathom what benefits he would get from putting points into that stat. It would have to wait until someone explained it to him.

With the points spent, he closed the screen. Suddenly, a surge of warmth far stronger compared to what the amulet provided spread through his body. It felt like his every cell was vibrating with life, greedily absorbing the warmth and improving. He was shocked to see his various wounds were healing at a visible rate, and it felt like he could punch a hole through a mountain. This feeling of strength was quite addicting. Soon the warmth faded, and the feeling of immortality disappeared with it. The wounds stopped healing at an accelerated speed. Still, Zac felt a good deal better, with a good deal of the bruising and smaller cuts completely gone.

There still was some time left of the day, so after a quick meal, he turned his attention to the snake carcass. After a few tries with a kitchen knives, he knew the scaled leather was quite resilient to cuts and would make good protection. He brought a few knives from the camper, and his hatchet, and dragged the carcass some distance away from the camp, and then started skinning it.

He cut along the softer belly, and after twenty minutes, he had cut all along the length of the carcass, ruining a knife on the hard scales while doing so. His forearms were burning with strain after the workout. He had ruined most of the meat along the way, unfortunately, and it didn't seem that there'd be much left over to eat.

After that, he dragged the skin off the carcass and finally scraped as much of the leftover flesh as possible off of the skin with his hatchet. From here, he was not quite sure what to do. He had no idea of methods to cure leather. He had been an office worker before the end of the world, and he was a few generations too young for these types of things to be considered common knowledge. Zac knew he had read somewhere that urine could be used somehow, but he was not about to experiment with that.

He put the skin aside and dug a hole, which he pushed the now mangled carcass into, and filled it with soil. He didn't want anything to head in this direction, even though he was some ways away from the camp.

Zac picked up the skin and made his way back to camp. The skin needed to dry out, so he placed it across the hood of the car, leaving both ends hanging down at the sides. He placed two large rocks down on both ends in order to keep it stretched and stop it from shrinking overnight. He had no idea if he was supposed to do something else, and could only leave it like that overnight and hope that it would work out.

It was starting to get darker, so he decided he was done exploring for the day. He was still feeling beat up, even with the rapid healing. He took thirty minutes to clean up the campsite and take stock of his things. Normally, he wouldn't go through his friends' belongings, but these were desperate times. Unfortunately, there was nothing of value except some extra changes of clothes and some daily necessities.

With the last of the sunlight, Zac found a long fallen branch near the campsite with the thickness of about three to five centimeters and about six meters long. With a few quick swings with his hatchet, he cut off roughly two and a half meters where the branch was the most straight. Then, with his improved strength, he quickly sharpened one edge into a sharp point, turning it into a makeshift spear. It was likely too malleable to be able to stop anything large like the demonling in its tracks without breaking. However, it could hopefully keep some monsters at length if needed. His hatchet was a good weapon, but its length was quite short. It was hard to use while keeping himself out of harm's way.

Zac finally sat down in the trailer for a meal, quietly staring out the window and seeing the ever-present red pillar. Had it not been for the incursion, he might have been able to forget how messed up the world had become for a second.

Life had thrown things at him in the last few days he couldn't even have imagined, and it would only get crazier.

Tomorrow, he would have to go hunting demons.

13

ON THE HUNT

Zac crept through the woods, slowly making his way more inland. He was hefting the hatchet in one hand and his improvised spear in the right. He had found a camouflaged shirt in David's bag, which he had donned. It would hopefully help him blend in a bit. He had planned to make some makeshift bracers and shin guards from some of the snakeskin this morning. Unfortunately, it was still a bit grimy, so he had to leave it for another day at least to properly dry out. He still wore the amulet of the gathering array underneath his shirt, which continuously imbued him with more Cosmic Energy. He had a black backpack on his back filled with a bottle of water and a small batch of medical supplies.

He had actually gained a level from the amulet without noticing while he was asleep. It was still hard for him to know how much the amulet was gathering for him, or how much experience killing other monsters gave. There was no experience bar or notifications of experience gain anywhere in the System that could give him a frame of reference. Hopefully, he would learn more about it from today's excursions. The two free points he had, he had split between Strength and Vitality. When he'd allocated the points, he had felt the energy rushing into his cells again, albeit far weaker when compared to when he'd allocated 30 points.

The goal of today was simple. He needed to kill monsters. Almost a week had passed since the world had been integrated into the Multiverse, and in reality, he had accomplished very little so far.

He didn't dare make a beeline for the incursion just yet. He was afraid that there would be monsters there that he still couldn't handle, such as the heralds themselves. Instead, he was walking around the edges of the island while steadily making his way inland. He had been walking for roughly thirty minutes now and still hadn't seen any monsters. He had seen some animals, though. Most were the same as before the change, but some obviously had evolved from Cosmic Energy. For example, he'd seen a squirrel as large as a golden retriever. Luckily, it seemed very docile, and it immediately escaped into the tree crowns after noticing him.

Finally, he heard a familiar menacing growl from ahead. Zac was afraid he had been spotted, and immediately hunkered down behind a bush. There was no charging demonling heading his way, fortunately, so he crept forward again. While hiding behind a tree, he finally saw the beast thirty meters in the distance. It was the same sort of demon as he had fought before, a six-legged monstrosity of oversized muscle and maw. This one seemed a bit leaner than the first he had fought, but he couldn't be sure. It seemed like it was lazing about in the sun in a small clearing. There was a small animal carcass next to it, so it appeared that it had recently had a meal and was now resting.

Zac had made battle plans based on his first experience fighting these monsters, and now it was time to use them. He inched toward a sturdy tree that was at the end of the clearing, leaving only open field between the tree and the demon. He placed down his spear two meters away from the trunk and picked up a small rock. By now, his heart was racing, his hands almost shaking from a buildup of adrenaline.

"Calm down, calm down…" he whispered under his breath, nerves taut but with a glint of determination in his eyes. He had no choice; he had to push forward, for both his sake and his family's.

With a deep, steadying breath, he walked in front of the tree, standing in full view of the demon. The demonling immediately noticed him and stood up into an aggressive posture. Wasting no time, Zac immediately chucked the stone with full force, and he managed to hit its torso, which elicited a pained yelp.

Clearly the taunt worked well, as the demon roared and barreled toward him like a runaway train. Zac held his position until the last minute before lunging two meters to the side. The demonling zoomed past him, and with tremendous force, head-butted the tree.

This was essentially the same tactic he had used on the first demon. The demons were powerful but seemed quite stupid, so he surmised the same tactic would work again. Now, handy boulders wouldn't be everywhere, but he was in a forest full of thick tree trunks. This time, he had help from being ready and having improved stats. Zac therefore managed to jump out of the way without either taking damage or falling over this time.

Knowing that time was of the essence, Zac wasted no time and immediately was upon the beast. With a fierce overhead swing, he severed the spine at the lower back. With his improved Strength, it felt like cutting through dry wood, and he easily embedded the whole fifteen-centimeter axe-head in the beast. With a tug, he ripped it out of the body, and with it came a spurt of blood. He had planned to also do the same at the neck of the beast, but the demonling was immediately woken up from the intense pain. With a pained roar, it tried to turn and catch Zac with its huge maw. Luckily, its maneuverability was already bad with all working legs. Now it was even slower with the two hind legs listlessly hanging backward.

Zac didn't want to take any chances, as a nasty swipe of the beast could easily make him bleed out in minutes. With a few seconds to spare until the demonling could turn, he slashed a few deep bloody gashes on its side. Both blood and viscera immediately started pooling beneath it. By now, the fight was essentially over, and Zac hurriedly backed off and picked up the spear he had placed down before the fight.

He planned to poke a few holes in the monster to bleed it out faster. However, reality is often disappointing. On the first stab, he only made a flesh wound before the spear started to bend rather than push in further. On the second stab, the demon snapped the spear in two by moving its head with surprising alacrity. The forward momentum of the stab almost made Zac fall right into the eagerly waiting rows of teeth of the beast. Luckily, he barely managed to get out of the way with a push of his left leg, which made him fall to the right of the beast. Still, the beast managed to get in a swipe on his left arm, which left a shallow but long gash.

Ignoring the burning pain, Zac quickly scrambled to his feet and got out of the way. But it seemed that the escape was unnecessary, as the demonling had collapsed after the swipe. The grass beneath it was completely stained red, and a large chunk of intestines was hanging outside its body. It was seemingly completely out of steam, weakly growling between shallow, rapid breaths.

Ideally, Zac would have preferred to wait it out and let it slowly bleed to death, but the monster's roars had been quite loud. He had no interest in sticking around in case there was backup on the way. He had to be calculative at times to avoid unnecessary risks, but sometimes he had to be decisive as well. Gripping the hatchet in a bloody hand, he slowly circled out of sight of the monster. Then, with a few quick steps forward, he swung down with force right behind the middle legs, cutting deep into what he presumed was lungs. The demon tried to rouse a retaliation but was completely out of power, resulting only in a feeble wave of a paw.

Zac repeated an identical slash on the other side, which should mean that both its lungs were punctured, given that the demon's physique was somewhat similar to a normal mammal's, of course. The demon barely responded to the second swing apart from shaking with pain or death throes. Zac wasted no time, and with one final swing, cut right into its neck.

With one final spasm, the monster passed. Zac knew this without having to check, as he suddenly felt the familiar warmth of Cosmic Energy entering his body.

A quick look around the corpse once again showed no sort of loot spawning or dropping. This made Zac more certain of the fact that there was no such thing as a loot system with the System.

With a last look at the surroundings for anything he might have missed, he once again receded into the cover of the forest. The hunt was not over.

14

ZOMBIE HOUND

Zac sat on a rock with a bottle of water in hand. He had just finished bandaging up his arm from the swipe of the demon and was now taking a quick breather. The fight had gone far better than his expectation, but he wouldn't let himself get complacent.

Not wanting to fill his stomach with too much water and later cramping up, he took a few small sips, then put the bottle back. Checking that everything was in order, he once again set out into the jungle, continuing his path of gradually moving inland. He did not bother remaking a spear for now, at least until he found some far stronger wood. Abby had talked about trees taking the properties of metal, and he desperately hoped he could find a tree like that.

It was not long before he ran into another demon dog. This one was slowly moving around, almost looking like a scout or like it was patrolling. He quickly decided on the place for the battle after a quick look around the surroundings. From there, it proceeded much like the last fight. A rock was thrown to taunt the beast, and it almost knocked itself out cold on a boulder. This time, Zac instead swung down his hatchet on the spine between the two sets of frontal legs. He strove to incapacitate two sets of legs and only leave the front-most legs in working order.

This was as close to the head as he dared attack at the moment, though, as he had seen how fast the demonling had swung its head to snap his spear in two. He was somewhat certain that the demon was like a crocodile in that regard; if something entered the maw, it would not leave.

The attack proved far more effective than he could have imagined. The blade fell down right between two vertebrae and continued almost unimpeded into the torso of the beast. Zac saw his opportunity and twisted while he tugged out the axe toward the side. He hoped to wreak as much havoc as possible in the demon's insides, destroying both lungs and heart. The axe was quickly completely ripped out of the chest, and a great gout of blood followed it and sprayed all over Zac.

The forceful tug swept Zac off his feet, and he fell backward into the grass. He quickly got up to his feet, axe at the ready, but soon realized it was unnecessary. The demon was lying on the ground listlessly. Blood was pouring out of the wound like a waterfall. After a shudder, it stopped moving, and Zac felt the now familiar warmth once again enter him.

Zac realized he must have hit the heart of the beast. There seemed to be no other possible explanation for the copious amounts of blood that had streamed out of the wound. Seeing as how he wasn't even out of breath from the fight, he immediately left and continued to look for more prey.

Zac's day continued like this, and by evening, he had killed roughly twenty demonlings with varied amount of success. He still had not leveled up to level 18, but he could somehow sense that he was close. After every kill during the day, some of the Cosmic Energy had entered his body. And if his body could be considered a container, it felt as though the container was starting to get full. Zac guessed that the moment he felt "full" from the Cosmic Energy was the moment he would level up.

Zac stood and overlooked the aftermath of his last victory. He had gained a few new wounds, but nothing threatening. This latest fight had been the most dangerous one so far, simply because he had fought two demonlings at the same time. The second one had burst through the vegetation while he was already fighting the first one.

Luckily, the beasts were truly clumsy, and with dodging around the natural environment, he'd managed to mostly keep out of harm's way until he could bleed them out. Zac hypothesized that the natural environment of these beasts likely had no greenery and very few obstructions. The monsters simply seemed completely unaccustomed to fighting in this type of terrain.

Zac was about to leave, when he suddenly heard a twig snap behind him. Taking no chances, he lunged to his right. He just heard the sound of wind while falling, but suddenly, his left shoulder exploded in pain. Ignoring the pain for now, he got to his feet and finally got a good look at his assailant.

It was a demon, but a different type from the ones he had fought so far. If the demon dogs so far had been depending on brawn, this one clearly leaned toward agility. Measuring up to his navel, the beast somewhat looked like an oversized greyhound dog. If the dog had turned into a zombie. Just like the other demon, it looked almost like it had been skinned. There were some differences with the greyhound, though, such as the head with the oversized maw. The three rows of sharp teeth were clearly showing as the monster silently growled toward him. It had no fur and instead had thin red skin with the wiry muscles clearly showing beneath. This beast also only had the customary four legs, compared with the six legs of the other demons.

Its paws were also larger than a normal dog's, and Zac could clearly see large sinister claws sticking out of them. The sinewy tail seemed overly long, even for a monster of this size, slowly swaying behind it.

Finally, he noticed that one of the front paws was bloodied, dying the grass red. That explained the burning pain on his shoulder. He had no time to come up with any fancy strategies at the moment and could only fall back on his go-to method for dealing with demons. He slowly repositioned himself so that he once again would have his back to a tree. He had immediately discarded the idea to run away. With its lithe build and long legs, it obviously was built for speed, and he had no delusions of being able to shake it off. Hopefully, the high speed would come in handy for him when it slammed into the tree behind him.

Suddenly, the hound shot toward him. Zac knew it would be fast, but it looked like it flew across the ground. The thirty-meter distance between them was erased in seconds, and Zac barely had the time to jump out of the way to let the hound slam into the tree.

Just as the monster was about to slam into the tree trunk, it swung its long tail. This somehow changed the direction of its momentum. Instead of slamming into the tree, it actually used the trunk as purchase with its legs to push itself forward toward Zac's falling figure. Even before he had hit the ground from jumping away, the beast was upon him.

Zac swung the hatchet while in midair, but the beast was too close for the blade to hit its head. He managed to punch the jawline with the haft of the axe, though, stopping the maw from chomping down on his head.

Zac landed with his back on the ground, and the hound fell on him. All the air was knocked out of his lungs, and he could taste the iron of blood in his mouth. He was face-to-face with the beast, its acrid breath filling his nose.

Zac desperately held the head at bay with his left arm, swinging the hatchet with his other. Dismayed, Zac saw that he couldn't generate enough strength to create more than flesh wounds from this awkward position. The beast struggled to reach him with its maw, meanwhile clawing on Zac's chest. Each swipe ripped straight through his shirt and left a bloody gash on his torso.

This stalemate could not last; he would be cut to ribbons if he didn't do something. He swung the beast to the side and slammed it into the ground on his left, giving him a brief moment of respite. He didn't dare hesitate and immediately swung his axe in a broad arc. His body screamed in protest, but he could only grit his teeth.

The axe howled and swung down toward the demon hound.

15

DESPERATION

The axe swung down, and with a thud, sank into the side of the hound. The hound tried to get up, but Zac still had his left hand clamped on its throat, keeping it down. A few more swings in quick succession and the beast was dead. He felt the warm cosmic force enter him again. This time, it felt like he gained almost twice the amount compared to the demonlings. This was also the final amount he needed to gain a level, bringing him to level 18.

Zac was a bit shaky after the encounter, but a day's worth of bloodshed and risking his life had steeled his nerves somewhat. He immediately left the site of the battle, not bothering with the three carcasses lying there. He needed to find somewhere to bandage himself.

While walking, he allocated the two points into Dexterity and Vitality. Zac felt that by now his Strength was enough to seriously hurt the monsters he had encountered with a few swings, and speed would likely help him more than more Strength. He still put a point into Vitality, as he kept getting hurt more and more.

Finally, he found a secluded spot and quickly drank a few mouthfuls of water and patched himself up. Zac was bruised and battered and completely unwilling to fight any more today. He had also run out of gauze after patching up his chest. The demon hound had carved a maze of scratches on his chest. The wounds were not deep, but together they had bled quite a bit. Luckily, his high Vitality seemed particularly effective against these types of smaller wounds. He sensed that the bleeding had already almost stopped, and scabs had started to form over the wounds. It seemed that he would be all fixed up in a day or two.

From the fight, he also realized that the amulet from the gathering array was quite sturdy. The hound had clawed both the little wheel and the string multiple times, and not a scratch could be seen on it. It seemed that a stronger force than some dog claws would be needed to damage it. For a brief moment, he imagined decking himself in hundreds of amulets, making him near-invulnerable.

Of course, that wasn't realistic. But it showed that there were probably many sturdy materials in the Multiverse that could be made into extremely strong defensive gear. He put the stray thoughts out of his head and started his return trek.

On his way back, he walked in an even more surreptitious manner, stealthily making his way back toward the base. He was forced to kill one more demonling, which had accidentally found him while bounding through the forest. He had seen a few more demons but chose to ignore them. It was getting late, and the suns were slowly setting. This made his vision limited, and the forest was gaining a sinister feel to it. Zac decided that even if he wanted the extra Cosmic Energy, he should get back to camp. If another of the demon hounds ambushed him while fighting the demonlings, he might be hard-pressed to fight them off.

He simply was too tired and wounded, and visibility was getting worse. He had accomplished what he set out to do today, and he couldn't get greedy.

As he passed one of the sites of his previous battles, he

suddenly noticed movement by the corpse of the demon. Zac immediately stopped moving and hid behind a tree to scout out the scene.

At first, he thought he saw a child standing by the carcass, but soon discarded that thought. The thing was roughly as large as a six- or seven-year-old child, but it was clearly a new type of demon. The thing looked like an imp from old fairy tales. It was completely naked except for a loincloth. It had purplish skin full of scars and what looked almost like tumors, giving it a sickly look. It almost seemed like it was suffering from radiation poisoning. On its back was a set of bat wings with a span of roughly a meter per wing.

Zac was unsure if the wings were actually serviceable, as the imp had a stocky build with a fat stomach. It had no hair and seemingly no ears. He couldn't make out any facial features, as it was currently looking down and poking the corpse of the demonling. It seemed like it was examining the wounds and trying to figure out what had happened.

That was not good news for Zac. It was one thing if the island was full of deadly but dumb beasts. He could deal with that as long as he went out killing every day, killing some at a time. But if there were smarter enemies who could team up, he might start meeting more and more organized resistance on the island. They might even send out search parties to look for him. The island was quite large, but a concerted effort would sooner or later flush him out of hiding.

He wanted to stay under the radar for a while longer. If the corpses were left alone, hopefully, the local wildlife would eat them. Then it would look like the beasts were killed in fights with other beasts rather from a few swings of an axe. His plans of slowly grinding levels and gaining battle experience would be over if this thing flew back and reported to its superiors.

There was only one solution. He had to kill it.

Luckily, it did not look overly powerful with its small stature and scrawny arms. One good swing with the hatchet and it would be decapitated.

Zac did not want to take any chances, however, and decided on a surprise attack. He slowly circled around and closed in on the imp from behind. He kept a careful watch for its reactions, but it seemed absorbed in examining the corpse.

A snap was heard from beneath Zac's foot when he was only five meters away from the imp. The failing light had caused him to not notice a fallen twig lying in his path. He froze for a millisecond but then immediately charged at the imp with all the speed he could muster.

The imp's preservation skills were impressive. As soon as it heard the sound behind it, it jumped over the carcass of the beast while letting out a high-pitched screech. It managed to turn around in midair with its wings, and Zac saw its face. It had four pitch-black eyes. One set was placed like a human's, and the other set was placed slightly more apart up on its forehead. It had no nose except two holes, and its mouth was a small circle full of sharp teeth. From the few flaps of its wings, it seemed like it was unable to fly, but able to elongate its jump considerably.

Zac desperately tried to catch up, afraid it would be able to get away. The imp did some obscure gestures with its hands while floating away, as Zac was closing in on it and the carcass of the beast. Suddenly, a purplish-black flame erupted on the imp's hand, and it somehow threw it straight toward Zac's head.

Zac barely had time to position his head out of the way, but a part of the sinister flame managed to land on his shoulder. Any plan of killing the imp flew out the window as Zac's mind turned white in a blinding explosion of pain. The black flame was far more dangerous than normal fire, and it seemed that it somehow managed to burn his *soul.* The pain on his singed flesh was nothing compared to that pain.

Zac was completely dazed by the pain and fell over the demonling carcass instead of jumping over it. The imp landed a few meters away, still screeching at him. After a few seconds of observation, it once again started to summon a flame with its mysterious hand gestures.

With a shake of his head, Zac managed to clear his sight. Unbeknownst to him, his eyes were completely red, and tears were streaming down. As soon as he got back up on his feet, he had to immediately jump out of the way from another of those insidious black flame balls. It missed him and fell upon the corpse of the demon instead. The fire caused the corpse to visibly shrink, as though all the moisture was burned instead of the flesh.

He once again charged toward the imp, but it simply kept jumping backwards. Its wings helped it gain momentum, and it was even slightly faster than Zac. It even had time to occasionally turn around to make sure it didn't run into anything.

The imp was essentially kiting him, throwing out a fireball every few seconds. The closer Zac got to it, the harder it was to dodge. After a minute, he had been hit another three times when he got close. The first time, it barely grazed his arm, so it was not too bad, if you could call the pain of getting stabbed a hundred times not too bad. The second hit him in the gut, which almost made him double over and puke his guts out from the agony. The final one hit his leg.

That hit had made him unable to keep chasing the imp. He could barely put any weight on the leg. It felt like it had been paralyzed. The pain was so bad, he almost swung his hatchet to chop it off. He knew that he would not be able to dodge anymore when it threw its next fireball.

In a last desperate attempt to survive, he hurled his hatchet with all the strength he could muster straight at the chest of the flying demon.

16

CHOICES

Zac was on his knees, panting heavily. His clothes were a completely burned and bloodied mess. All around him were signs of the imp's rampage, with pockets completely drained and devoid of life. Zac realized that the fire of the imp did not burn like a normal fire; rather, it burned life-force or Cosmic Energy. His burns looked like all the moisture had been drained from his skin, and it now had a pallid gray color. It was like those parts of his body were that of a desiccated corpse's.

The corpse of the imp was lying against a tree roughly ten meters away from him, the axe still firmly planted in its chest. The constitution of the monster was quite frail, and it had died immediately when the axe hit.

As soon as the monster had died, it seemed as though the source of the fires had been removed. The fires had quickly extinguished, the marks left behind the only proof they had existed at all. Had it not quickly dissipated, then the fire would have completely destroyed him. Maybe not his body, but all his life-force.

Zac was nauseated and on the brink of passing out, but he somehow summoned power he did not know he had and got up on his feet. He shuffled over to the imp and yanked out the axe. He had no energy to search the corpse and simply continued his way back home.

He was almost delirious by this point and was barely able to keep his bearings. Luckily, he was quite close to edge of the island now and almost on the opposite side of the pillar. The monsters were pretty scarce this far out still, and he didn't encounter any more demons that night.

With the last strength in his body, he managed to stumble back into his camp. As soon as he saw the familiar sight of the metallic camper, his legs simply gave out. He fell down onto the ground and let the sweet darkness embrace him.

It was midday the following day when Zac woke up again. His body was stiff, and he sported a splitting headache. It was as if he had been drinking until passing out last night. He spit out some gravel he had got in his mouth and slowly got up.

After a quick checkup, it seemed that most of his wounds were in decent shape. None of the scratches and tears from the demons were still bleeding. Some of the more shallow wounds were just a white line today. A few of the worse wounds would have to stay bandaged for at least another day, though.

The spots where the black fire had burned him yesterday were still a bit gray and shrunken, but had gotten noticeably better. He felt that the headache he had likely came from these wounds. The fire yesterday must have had some magic properties that damaged in other ways than just burning. He shuddered when he remembered the pain from those blasts.

He prepared some breakfast and sat down in a camping chair to go over yesterday's results. He brought up the status window with a thought to go over the gains.

Name: Zachary Atwood
Level: 18

Race: Human
Alignment: [Earth] Human

Titles: Born For Carnage, Ultimate Reaper, Luck of the Draw, Giantsbane, Disciple of David, Overpowered, Slayer of Leviathans, Adventurer, Demon Slayer

Strength: 46
Dexterity: 33
Endurance: 34
Vitality: 43
Intelligence: 29
Wisdom: 29
Luck: 44

Free Points: 0
Nexus Coins: 3,370

He had gained almost three thousand Nexus Coins with just one day of fighting, which seemed quite good. If he based the gains on the amount of Cosmic Energy he got from the different monsters, he could somewhat guess how much each kill gave him. He would say that he had gained roughly one hundred for each demon dog he had killed, and between half as much and double that from the demon hound. The largest amount was rewarded for killing the imp. He still remembered that burst of energy, even though he was almost delirious. If he hadn't gotten that extra energy boost after the fight, he might not have made it home.

Still, the amount gained yesterday was far short of most of the buildings he had seen in the town-building interface. It made sense, as building a whole town was usually not done by the efforts of only one person. If he had a few hundred people who came together and gathered Nexus Coins, the amount gathered would be massive, even if the other people were far weaker than himself. There simply was power in numbers.

The thought gave him a sense of urgency. It was undeniable that he had likely gotten a quite impressive head start compared to most people, even though he was not too happy with his current situation. But if some great leader emerged in a Tutorial village and created a large force, he might lose his head start. Abby had mentioned that the System liked those that stood in the forefront. If someone was going to get titles and other advantages from building a town first, then it should be him.

It might be better for humanity if some country leader or military general got that head start. But it was the apocalypse, and he had his goals. He needed to be a bit selfish in that regard and couldn't just give away opportunities to others and hope they would use them for good.

He also noticed that he had a new title, Demon Slayer. It was from the quest he had received in the beginning, which had told him to kill ten demons. The title gave him 3% to all stats when fighting enemies of demonic alignment. However, he didn't quite understand how the title worked. He should have activated that title somewhere midday, but he had felt nothing different when fighting afterward. Zac guessed that he couldn't sense anything different, as 3% to his attributes was just one or two in each.

He was somewhat disappointed that he hadn't received any sort of follow-up quest, along the lines of "Kill 100 Demons." His other titles proved that there were "higher-level" titles, such as Slayer of Leviathans being stronger than Overpowered. Getting a few more demon-slaying quests might push his advantage against demons a lot higher.

After looking over the status page, he opened the building interface. There were two things that Zac wanted to build, and they cost three thousand Nexus Crystals each.

The first was called an **[F-Grade Nexus Node]** and looked

like a large hovering crystal from the description. Its function was to access certain aspects of the System. Nexus Nodes seemed to have more functions depending on how high grade it was, with F being the lowest. The node was the worst of the bunch, in other words. But it gave access to two functions that Zac was extremely interested in. It gave access to the class system and sold basic skills.

The other was another array, namely the **[F-grade Small-Scale Gravity Array]**. This was an array meant for strengthening oneself, as he saw it. The subject of training was something he had mulled over from the start. Even before allocating the first 30 points he had gotten, he had noticed that his stats were skewed.

When he counted backwards from his titles and the points he had allocated, he had found out that his base stats differed quite a bit. Before the effect of the System, he'd had 7 Strength, 3 Dexterity, 4 Endurance, 5 Vitality, 5 Intelligence, and 6 Wisdom.

He assumed the normal stats were around 1–10 for most humans, as he was somewhat average before the System arrived. He wasn't particularly smart and not extremely athletic. He worked out at a gym three times a week, which would explain the Strength. But he was not limber at all, and he rarely did cardio. Therefore, he had lower Dexterity and Endurance. Vitality and Intelligence seemed harder to train, as they were more of an inborn quality.

Since the stats differed and seemed to be affected by his actions before the System arrived, he assumed that he might be able to improve his base stats from training as well. He probably would not be able to improve infinitely, but every extra stat point counted.

That was where the gravity array would come in. It would affect the gravity in a zone and could increase the gravity up to ten times. At this point, he had 46 Strength and was likely stronger than any human who had ever lived on Earth. Without this kind of array, Zac didn't think he would be able to exhaust himself. He could do push-ups all day without breaking a sweat at the moment.

If he added the array to the camp, he could potentially improve multiple stats, at least Strength and Endurance, as they seemed most linked with the constitution of his physique.

Unfortunately, the descriptions for the buildings were quite short, and both options came with a risk. He had no idea how skills worked and what they would cost. Buying a Nexus Node might be a complete waste of coins at this stage when every advantage was important. On the other hand, he didn't know if his plan for training even worked with the System.

After some hesitation, he finally turned his eyes toward the array.

17

EYE OF DISCERNMENT

Zac sat in front of the campfire, and with a blank, silent stare, he slowly rotated a spit placed above it. The suns were setting over his small outpost, and the surroundings had a subdued silence. On the spit was the leg of a rabbit he had caught earlier today. The rabbit had actually grown to the size of a human, so the meat would last for a while.

Tomorrow would mark the twenty-ninth day since the world had changed. If Hannah or even his family were to see him now, they would likely barely recognize him.

The once neat beard of his was now an uneven mess. There even was one patch almost completely missing after a barghest's claw had cut his face during a particularly intense melee. His hair was even worse, now a mess of uneven cuts. During one of his fights, he had gotten hair in his eyes, and the distraction had caused him to almost get disemboweled. He had fought the gwyllgi half-blinded while using one hand to hold his innards in place. After the fight, he had simply taken his hatchet to his head and cut off as much hair as he could without scalping himself.

He had run out of shirts last week and now used a mix of torn rags to cover himself. Underneath those rags was some makeshift protection he had made from leather he had cured. He had begun by making some bracers for his legs and arms, and a basic heart protector out of the snakeskin he had dried over his car. Over time, he had found another snake and even a crocodile on a shore and had turned those into leather as well.

Now he was decked from feet up to a throat protector in pieces of leather, all tied together with strings or sinew. It was extremely shoddy work, making his whole body looked like a piecemeal patchwork of different animal body parts. It also took almost thirty minutes to take on and off, as there were quite a few knots he had to tie to get it to stay on during a whole day.

Most days, he couldn't be bothered, as he had been out hunting the whole day and simply fell asleep while still wearing the gear. The combination of high Endurance and Vitality seemed to protect him from any chafing or bruises from the coarse leather anyway.

All in all, he looked like a completely insane hobo and would likely be arrested if he arrived in a real city, based on his appearance alone. Zac couldn't be bothered about that, though, as almost a month of living on the edge of death had given him a far more utilitarian mindset.

Zac cracked his neck, nowadays barely being bothered by the constant ten times gravity field that enveloped the whole camp. After his first day of grinding, he had bought the **[F-Grade Small-Scale Gravity Array]** and placed it at a corner of the camp. It had actually proven effective, and he had incorporated a workout in high gravity into his daily schedule. Soon after, he even slept in high gravity, and by now, he always had the array cranked to the max over the whole camp.

Its effect had been above his expectations. He had gained a whole 5 Strength, 2 Dexterity, 6 Endurance, and 2 Vitality from just training his body. His Endurance had increased the quickest, rising up 6 points in just two weeks. He had calculated that he had

4 base Endurance before the System earlier, and now it was 10. However, after it reached 10, it stopped increasing at all. He saw a similar effect on his Strength. He gained 3 points quite quickly, bringing his base Strength to 10. After that, he still had gotten 2 points, but those points took an extreme effort.

He had also gained Dexterity and Vitality, but he guessed that those points actually came from combat rather than the array. Getting hurt over and over had improved his Vitality slowly, and dodging an endless number of beasts had improved his Dexterity.

Zac guessed that the reason for his quick improvements wasn't only the array. There now was a large amount of Cosmic Energy in the air, and it felt like just breathing it in slowly improved his health. He suspected that humans would slowly grow healthier in this atmosphere, provided that they didn't get killed, of course. A quick look at his status showed that his stats had improved quite a bit over the last weeks.

Name: Zachary Atwood
Level: 23
Race: Human
Alignment: [Earth] Human

Titles: Born For Carnage, Ultimate Reaper, Luck of the Draw, Giantsbane, Disciple of David, Overpowered, Slayer of Leviathans, Adventurer, Demon Slayer

Strength: 59
Dexterity: 39
Endurance: 42
Vitality: 48
Intelligence: 29
Wisdom: 29
Luck: 44

Free Points: 0
Nexus Coins: 5,562

Unfortunately, he had not reached his goal even with his gathering array and frenzied carnage across the island. He had hoped to get to level 25 and get a class before the month was over. The advice of the Stargazer still lingered in his head. She had told him to finish the quest of conquering the incursion within a month. He still hadn't found any clues as to what would happen after the month passed, and he hoped he wouldn't have to find out.

Gaining levels had proven harder and harder over time, and he had finally reached level 23 today after four days of relentless killing. He had even used almost all his points and spent a whopping seventy-five thousand Nexus Coins on upgrading his Mother-Daughter Gathering Array to E-grade. This upgrade had substantially increased the amount of Cosmic Energy he absorbed daily through his amulet.

It was clear to Zac, however, that the most effective method of getting stronger was to actually battle and kill enemies. If he would split up the Cosmic Energy he absorbed daily, it would be a 90-10 split, and that was with the E-grade array. If he compared with his old F-grade array, it would be 95-5 or even lower. Grinding monsters and absorbing their energy was simply far more effective, at least with his resources.

It did, however, make him think about the elite of the Multiverse. He had made over a hundred thousand Nexus Coins just by grinding low-level monsters during the first month. Abby had said that the Multiverse was hundreds of millions years old. There were surely some extremely wealthy individuals and organizations. What if they gave every child an A-grade or even S-grade array from birth? They would be higher level than him before even learning to talk.

Those things were too far away from him, though; he needed

to focus on the present. Even though he hadn't reached his goal of getting a class, he still planned to try finishing the quest in the following two days.

Zac carved a chunk of meat from the rabbit leg and stuck it to a fork. He then walked over to the Nexus Node while gnawing the gamey meat. Zac looked at the list of available things on it daily, hoping for something new to pop up every day since the day he bought it. He knew he would be disappointed once again. The skills available were too expensive for him, and the inventory hadn't changed so far.

The only skill that was in his price range was called [**Eye of Discernment**]. And he had already bought it for the price of twenty thousand Nexus Coins. When he had bought it, a stream of energy had entered his head, and new information suddenly formed like an ingrained memory. It was the manual for the skill.

The purchase had taught him a bit about how skills worked with the System. Having a skill did not mean you could simply use it as you wanted. For a skill to work, he needed to actually move the Cosmic Energy built up in his body toward his eyes. From there, he had to imprint the image of a specific fractal on his eyes. The fractal was the same type of pattern that was on the array flags he had bought earlier.

Zac had tried furiously to move the energy around in his body for days. He had felt that his cells were imbued with this extra power, but he had a hard time actually doing anything with it. Finally, after days of trying, he had found a solution.

While sitting in the gravity array, he had imagined a separate set of veins spread all through his body like his circulatory system. In these veins, only Cosmic Energy flowed. He was surprised that it actually worked, and a stream of his Cosmic Energy slowly started traveling along the paths he had imagined.

It took a few days more to learn to keep the circulation going even when not actively focusing on it. Finally, he tried gathering

Cosmic Energy on his eyes to imprint the fractal of the skill. This part went smoother than expected, as he had an extremely precise design in his memory thanks to the Nexus Node.

As soon as he wanted to use the skill, he only needed to focus a small amount of Cosmic Energy to flow into the fractals on his eyes, and it would activate immediately.

Zac was quite glad that the System did not require people to shout out the skill's name like a lunatic.

The **[Eye of Discernment]** was a basic eye skill that essentially worked like an identify or spy skill from a video game. It let Zac glean some basic information about certain things.

It was this skill that had let him know that the stocky six-legged demons he had fought ad nauseam the last month were actually called barghest, and the zombie-looking greyhound monster was a Gwyllgi.

The imps were actually just called Lower Imps, and they had taught him another valuable lesson when using the **[Eye of Discernment]** on them. Even though he had used it from the cover of some bushes, the imp had felt the skill being used on it. It reacted by immediately throwing a fireball at the bush he was hiding in, leading to another desperate fight.

The memory of that fireball still filled him with some trepidation as he stared into the fire, slowly finishing his meal.

18

COSMIC ENERGY

Actually, apart from teaching him the names of his different enemies, the most important thing the skill had taught him was something completely different.

Zac had thought that the stats represented a static change in his prowess, and to a certain degree, he was right. He was far stronger now compared to before thanks to the stats. But there was more to it. Learning to circulate his Cosmic Energy had opened up a whole new world for him.

At first, he had simply focused on learning the skill. But afterwards, he had started experimenting with the Cosmic Energy in his body and had come to some astonishing conclusions. He could actually force more Cosmic Energy into different parts of his body, strengthening them. For example, he could force energy into his arm and back muscles when swinging his hatchet, which resulted in a far more powerful swing.

Forcing energy into his legs would increase his speed, and he had even managed to imbue his skin for a while, making it more durable. There were many different venues to utilize it, and he likely only had figured out a few. The strengthening wasn't limitless, however. It acted as a multiplier on his base stats, but the multiplier was limited. After some experimentation, he had realized he could output almost twice his normal power while circulating his energy into a specific part of his body.

He had gone above this amount once, which had resulted in being incapacitated for days. He had tried increasing the amount of energy in his arms too much in order to perform a particularly mighty swing. His muscles couldn't withstand that much Cosmic Energy forced into them, and ruptured into a fountain of blood. It reminded him of a balloon. If he blew too much air into it, it would pop. Same with his body and Cosmic Energy.

The experiment had left him lying weakly in his base for three days, only being able to train with the amulet and the gravity array for some minor gains.

The second conclusion was that his usage of Cosmic Energy was limited. The more he circulated his energy and empowered himself, the more drained he would feel. When empowering himself to the limit, he only lasted a few minutes before he was completely spent.

The energy used in empowerment was consumed, and he would need to gather more from the environment in order to get back into fighting condition. His amulet helped him recover faster. But when the amulet focused on replenishing consumed Cosmic Energy, it did not actually work toward increasing his level.

In other words, using empowered strikes or skills would slow his leveling speed, as some of the Cosmic Energy gained would be used on replenishment. So it was a trade-off between long-term gains and short-term bursts of power.

The final realization was that his method likely was extremely cost-ineffective. When he used his identification skill, the Cosmic Energy entered the fractals that somehow existed in his eyes. The fractal not only enabled using the specific skill, but also made usage of Cosmic Energy more effectively.

Far less energy was wasted when the energy was focused with the fractal. If Cosmic Energy could be considered a raw material like crude oil, then the fractal refined it into something better and more efficient.

Zac guessed a combat-oriented skill would work in the same way. He would gain new fractals, which he could use to waste less Cosmic Energy while fighting, and also gain a higher power than simply channeling raw Cosmic Energy into his arms. Unfortunately, even the cheapest of the options cost 150,000 Nexus Coins, which was far out of his current price range.

Zac finished his meal and scooped up a glass of water from the pit where he had placed a water-gathering array. The bottled water he and his friends had brought had run out two weeks ago, and the closest fresh water was close to the incursion. Luckily, the System had a cheap solution, namely the **[Small-Scale Water-Gathering Array]**, which slowly gathered moisture from the air to create roughly ten liters of drinking water per day.

For the first time in weeks, he turned off the gravity array when he went to sleep. He needed to be completely rested, as tomorrow he would assail a herald.

Zac had wrestled with himself whether to actually go through with it or not the last few days. At times, he felt it would be safer for him to simply grind for a few more weeks and get a class and skill before going after the big bosses.

He had, however, noticed a very worrying trend over the last few days. The beasts in the forest were getting more powerful. The demon hounds were getting even faster, and the barghest were getting stronger. He had actually seen one charge straight through a tree. The barghest had been completely incapable of such a feat just a week ago.

This made him form a hypothesis. The beasts were slowly getting stronger, and maybe they would gain a power spike once each month. That was what Abby the eye had been indirectly warning him about.

He didn't think that the incursion summoned stronger demons, but rather that they were strong from the start, but were somehow restricted. That was because he didn't actually get more Cosmic Energy or Nexus Coins from killing the empowered beasts compared to the old weaker ones.

It made him once again think about how the System seemed to operate. It rewarded people who dared take risks and strove to improve. That was shown through the title system and also Abby's comments.

Perhaps this was a gift from the System. If someone dared leave the Tutorial village to kill magical monsters at incursions, they'd be rewarded with the Cosmic Energy and Nexus Coins that generally were given out by far stronger beasts. Like an XP boost from an MMORPG game.

Or perhaps the demons simply weren't adapted to Earth's atmosphere. He always imagined in his head that these beasts came from some lava world full of fire and brimstone. He really had no idea which was correct, but his days in solitude allowed him to conjure endless theories.

Furthermore, with risk also comes reward. What Abby meant with her last comment might be related to the quest.

[Off with their heads (Unique): Kill the four heralds and the general of incursion within 3 months. Reward: 10 E-Grade Nexus Crystals, E-Grade equipment, unique building depending on performance. (1/5)]

The last reward was a unique building depending on performance. He guessed that the better the performance, the higher ranked the building he would receive was. He was by now well aware both how powerful some buildings were, but also how extremely expensive they were. He had scoured through the registry for weeks, after all.

Getting a good grade might greatly help him later, provided that he actually survived this ordeal.

So it was with a mix of self-preservation and greed he had gritted his teeth and finally decided to assail the first of the heralds tomorrow, even if he wasn't at the power level he'd like. The last few days he had scouted his target out, and he thought he had a fighting chance after observing it.

He woke up with the dawn of light the next day, and after his preparations, he immediately set out. He had limited time until his self-imposed time limit. Depending on how the fight went, he might try to kill a second herald today as well.

He walked through the forest with practiced ease, avoiding twigs and roots while still keeping a high tempo. The forest had changed considerably during the past weeks. It had grown extremely lush, gaining almost a primordial unsullied air. The trees had grown more robust, and the undergrowth was varied with both bushes, vines and a medley of flowers.

He did not know where they had come from, but it seemed that there were far more critters and other animals as well roaming both the forest floor and up in the crowns. However, it always was quiet around his camp lately, as if the animals instinctively avoided his domain.

Zac made a beeline toward the western central area from the southern edge where his camp was located. During his excursions in the past weeks, he had actually found the second herald, while the last two still eluded him. He guessed that one of them resided in the mountains though, as it seemed that each herald lorded over a cardinal direction of the incursion. He hadn't ventured into the mountains as of yet, as he had his hands full grinding monsters closer to home.

The unlucky herald Zac had obliterated with a lucky roll had been in the southern part of the island. Zac had occupied the domain of the herald in a sense. That had explained why there were relatively fewer demons close to his base, as it was far from the lairs of the three remaining heralds.

19

VUL

Even though Zac moved like a specter through the woods, he couldn't always avoid fights. A barghest was lying hidden behind a few bushes and noticed Zac before he could reroute around it.

It immediately got up and without hesitation charged upon him.

Zac was completely unfazed by the oncoming beast and circulated a small amount of Cosmic Energy through his body down to his legs. With a quick step, he avoided the beast at the last second, giving it no time to adjust. He then followed up with a vicious swing down the throat of the passing beast. The barghest would have been decapitated had it not been for the limited size of Zac's hatchet.

Instead, he tore a huge gash that severed both muscles and jugulars from the top and then continued until exiting down on the bottom, resulting in the head barely staying on.

The demon continued for a few meters before collapsing with a thud. Zac continued on while going over the state of the axe. By now, he had killed hundreds of barghest, and the recent fight barely registered in his mind, even with the power-up of the beast.

Even if the barghest had become stronger, they still were the most common and stupid of the monsters on the island.

The empowered gwyllgi that focused on speed were far more annoying to deal with. He still had a hard time dealing with them without getting a cut somewhere.

When looking over the hatchet, he couldn't help feeling a sour lump in his throat. The axe was in a state of disrepair with scratches all over. The head had become a full two centimeters shorter from repeated sharpening against rocks. Zac knew the only reason the weapon still somewhat held together was that it was made from a solid piece of steel. Still, the shaft had started to bend, showing the strain it had been put under.

The combination of Zac's superhuman strength and the hardness of demon bones had slowly warped the metal. He was quite worried, as he did not know what he'd do when his weapon finally broke. He would be able to buy a shop and hopefully get a weapon that way when he finally upgraded the outpost to a town. But until then, there simply seemed to be no weapons on the island.

Zac sighed and continued on his way.

He barely used any energy during the fight, only enhancing himself for a few seconds. With the help of the gathering array, he would be topped off again within a minute.

Zac kept stalking through the woods like death incarnate. Anything that was foolish enough to attack him was quickly ended with a swing.

He had initially been afraid that his daily excursions would be found out by the demons, but after a few days of observation, he was quite content knowing he was safe as long as he did not hunt too close to the heralds.

Every day, new monsters would appear in the woods, likely summoned through the incursion. More astonishingly, the demons killed each other far more than Zac killed them. He had lost count of the times that he had found a demon hunkered over a corpse of the same race, feasting on its carcass. There seemed to be simply no familiar affection between the demons. That Zac was responsible for a small part of the deaths seemingly went by completely unnoticed.

Finally, he arrived at the area where he had spotted the herald earlier. He immediately became more alert of his surroundings, not wanting to create a stir with his target so close. He soon found the target, and it wasn't hard to notice.

The herald was huge.

[Vul, Level 45]

That was all the information that the **[Eye of Discernment]** gave him. Either his mastery over the skill was too low to show more information, or the skill was simply too basic.

It at least showed that its level was over 20 levels higher than his. He did not know whether Vul was its name or its race. His skill had only showed the race when fighting the random beasts in the forest, but here it also showed a level. The system somehow made a distinction between this herald and the other demons.

He was leaning toward the theory that Vul was a name, because the monster clearly looked a lot like a barghest. If a barghest had been supercharged. Instead of three pairs of legs, it had four, with the additional pair being positioned closer to the hind legs.

Does that mean that it's a spider rather than an insect... Zac mused with a dark sense of humor while looking over the beast.

Vul was also far larger than its barghest brethren. If a normal barghest could reach up to Zac's chest with its head, then this monster was a full head taller than him. It was even larger than a bear and, from its oversized muscles, looked like the bear would rather be prey than a competitor.

Just like the normal demon dogs, it had an oversized head with an abyssal maw, with three rows of sinister fangs lining it. With its size, the monster could easily fit both Zac's head and torso in its mouth for a quick bite. The paws, which looked like talons, had the same three long claws attached, but on Vul, they were as long as small kitchen knives.

It seemed to be the alpha of the barghest pack, although it didn't seem very interested in anything except lazing about and eating.

Zac had observed the monster from a distance a few times in the last week and had also realized that it not only was larger, but it was also a bit smarter. Certainly, it was still a meathead, but he had noticed some burgeoning intelligence from its actions. It luckily didn't seem overly alert, as Zac had used the **[Eye of Discernment]** on it without any reaction.

Perhaps only magically inclined beings such as the imps could actually notice being screened by the skill.

He knew his customary method of killing a demon dog would not work with this monster; it simply was too large a risk. He had gotten swiped almost countless times the last month, each time having a new wound to show for it. A similar swipe from this monstrosity could instantly end him if unlucky, and he was not ready to take that chance.

He slowly eased back into the vegetation after ascertaining the herald's position. Taking down a beast like this would take some strategy.

Zac slowly made his way a few hundred meters away, where his final piece of the puzzle lay hidden. Luckily, Vul mostly stayed in the same area except for when it went on patrols in random directions.

He finally reached his destination, a particularly lush bush that had a thick leafy crown that was roughly the same height as Zac himself. After glancing around, he gingerly made his way into the bush.

Inside, there were four trunks of trees, each roughly three meters long and almost as thick as his thigh. One end of the tree was sharpened into a point. They looked as if they were made to form a palisade, but the real purpose was monster hunting.

The spear he had used the first time he hunted broke on the first demon, so he had learned his lesson.

During his weeks of fighting, he had found a type of tree that had a dark trunk but white-gray veins. He hadn't recognized it and had tried to cut down a branch with a swing of his hatchet, and to his surprise, he found that the tree was extremely dense and hard.

Cutting down the trees to make the four supersized spears had tired him out, even with his superior physique.

He gingerly dug roughly half-a-meter-deep holes with some distance from each other, then placed the wooden stakes into them at a slanted angle. He had placed them so that the spear tips were hidden within the bush at roughly 150-to-180-centimeter height. Finally, he covered the holes and placed down secondary smaller stumps beneath the stakes so that they wouldn't tip over from their own weight before they could be used.

This was the only trap he could figure out that could help in his fight against the huge beast. The only other idea he had come up with was to dig a pitfall. But he did not have the tools for the massive undertaking of digging a pit large enough to trap and kill a monster the size of a large minivan.

He took one more glance at the bush to inspect his work. He would only get one shot at this and didn't want anything to give it away before it was too late.

Satisfied with his work, he finally turned toward the herald and started walking.

20

FIGHTING THE HERALD

Zac had slowly inched his way back toward the herald. It was currently lying on a rock, and it was actually eating a gwyllgi it had caught somewhere.

All eight of its legs except the front pair were lying on the same side, exposing its back toward Zac. He was currently crouching behind a tree only five meters away from the huge barghest. He barely dared to breathe for fear of being exposed too early. He couldn't get any closer without entering an open area and being completely exposed.

Zac's heart was beating furiously, and his hands were nervously shaking. It was one thing to make plans and preparation, but a completely different thing to actually turn those plans into action. Now that he was this close, it was as though he could sense a primal pressure emanating from the beast.

He knew he couldn't wait any longer, as this was a golden opportunity. The beast was feeding and was distracted. If he kept waiting, he would miss his chance and also tire himself out by stressing and fretting.

Zac soundlessly got to his feet and circulated Cosmic Energy through his body. Wasting no time, he pumped his legs full of energy and shot toward the exposed herald like a bullet. His hatchet fell with an empowered swing, striking down at the lower spine of the beast. He was hoping to use the same tactic as he had in the beginning against killer Vul's smaller brethren.

The axe sank into the back of the beast, but it felt like he had tried to chop through reinforced steel when he reached the bone of the spine. His plan had failed, as it ended up as only a flesh wound. His right arm ached from the impact, but he quickly adapted and swung down and created a deep gash down along its side.

He planned to strike its belly as well and hopefully damage some organs, but a thundering roar interrupted him. The herald had finally reacted, and with a jerk, pushed back with all its legs, forcing its whole body toward Zac.

The monster's back slammed into Zac like a truck, and he flew a few meters backwards, spitting out a mouthful of blood.

As he got up, so did the herald. Suddenly, they stood facing each other, and a low growl emitted from the beast's mouth. Its wound was bleeding freely, but that didn't seem to have incapacitated it at all.

Rage was burning in the beast's beady eyes, and it let out another tremendous roar that seemed to cause the very air to vibrate.

Zac wasted no time and immediately ran into the forest. He wanted to make use of the complicated terrain to keep the large, lumbering beast at bay. He kept infusing his body with energy, not daring to let up. The sounds of loud thuds and branches breaking behind him proved that the herald was hot on his heels.

Zac was dismayed to find out that the terrain didn't seem to impair Vul in spite of its huge size and stocky build. It was far more nimble than the barghest, even though it seemed even bulkier than its smaller brethren. Finally, he tried to use another tried and true trick and ran straight toward a thick maple. He could hear that the beast was ever closing in on him and now was only a few meters away from him.

This was a test of sorts of the herald, to see if it would fall for this simple trick. He had his doubts about it after observing it, and didn't want to blow his best shot for killing it. He therefore held off on running straight toward his pikes.

He waited until the last minute until finally jumping to the side and dodging the tree. He turned around in midair, hoping to take advantage of the beast knocking itself out.

Unfortunately for Zac, a herald was appointed a leader for a reason. Zac's suspicions about the herald's superior intellect proved true as he saw the beast's reactions.

Noticing the incoming tree, the herald stopped in his tracks with his front legs while he sidestepped away from Zac's direction with the hind legs. Its front legs carved a deep groove for a few meters before it stopped, while it changed angle to point toward Zac. This resulted in the beast still moving toward the tree, but it instead slammed into it with its shoulders rather than its head.

Due to the braking, the slam seemed to enrage the beast further rather than hurt it. It hadn't lost much time from the slam, and now Zac was in a precarious situation.

The beast immediately jumped toward him, its huge jaws trying to rip him in two from his chest.

Flustered, Zac rolled on the ground down in between the beast's legs, hoping to gain access to the more vulnerable belly. He knew now he needed to thoroughly enrage the beast so that it would blindly charge through the bushes and into his palisade. He was now in an awkward position in between the front legs and could only rely on Cosmic Energy to generate force in his swings.

He slammed the hatchet up into the torso of the beast a few times, hoping to puncture a lung. It was effective, as a stream of blood showered him, and the monster elicited a painful yelp. He only had time for a few swings, though, as he suddenly was slammed on his left side by a kick. Zac flew away once again like a ragdoll, and this time, he felt that he had broken at least a rib, as breathing felt like getting stabbed.

He could only grit his teeth and circulate more Cosmic Energy to keep his injuries in check. He was already starting to run dangerously low, and fatigue was starting to set in.

He kept running toward his trap, but was still afraid to run into it. The beast was enraged, but it hadn't lost its reasoning completely, and Zac was afraid that it would notice the trap. Then he would be well and truly screwed.

He needed at least one more effective assault.

The herald was soon upon him again, this time swiping with its front paw, hoping to catch Zac in its claws. Zac could only frantically dodge and jump out of the way. He tried to get a swing in every now and then to hurt its legs, but it largely proved ineffective. He hit true a few times, but only some flesh wounds were created.

Zac once more tried a riposte after dodging a swing, but this time, its large head closed in with extreme speed. The herald tried to chomp off his arm during his swing.

Zac quickly retracted his arm, and it was almost too late. The maw closed a fraction of a second too late, allowing Zac's arm to disengage. His hatchet wasn't as lucky, however, and the monster chomped down on the head. A crunch was heard, and when Vul opened its maw again to try to take another bite, the axe was released.

The already worn axe was now completely deformed and had essentially turned into a stick with scrap metal on top. The edge was gone, and instead, it more resembled a mace now with some random sharp edges.

A flame of rage ignited in Zac's eyes when he saw his trusty companion being completely ruined by the herald, and he completely forgot about safety. With a roar, he stopped backing away, and instead forced most of his remaining Cosmic Energy into his right arm and legs. With a desperate lunge, he jumped straight for the herald, surprising it for a split second. That was all he needed as Zac plunged the scrap weapon into the left eye of the beast.

The demon forcefully jerked backward from the pain, for a second standing only on its back legs, reaching an impressive three to four meters in height. Pained yelps quickly transitioned into roars of blazing fury, and Vul stomped down toward Zac, trying to flatten him like a pancake.

Zac had no time to care about his beloved hatchet being stuck in the eye of the monster, and started a mad dash away from the beast. He saw that the monster was completely and utterly raving with anger and pain right now, so this was his chance.

He focused the last of his energy on maximizing his speed as he dashed the last distance toward the trap. The herald was hot in pursuit, not caring about anything anymore, completely smashing through any smaller rocks or trees that were in its path.

Finally, he reached the bushes where the poles were hidden, and by now, the huge beast was right on his heels. Zac could even feel the heat from its maw. Zac dove through the bushes headfirst, making sure to keep at a height below that of the placed spears in order to not skewer himself.

It was with great relief Zac could sense that the herald thundered straight into the bushes right behind him, intending to simply rip through them.

As Zac landed on the ground, he felt a huge impact behind him, which caused the ground to tremble.

One of the trees had struck the herald straight in its chest, entering at least a meter and impaling it where it stood.

The beast shuddered and let out a miserable roar, which echoed in the surroundings. Blood was flowing out of its mouth like a waterfall, drenching both Zac and the surroundings. It immediately started wildly thrashing around, heedless of its wounds. The contraption couldn't take the weight and almost immediately collapsed.

Even if it was almost blinded and bleeding out, the herald wouldn't go quietly, as it incessantly wailed and thrashed about. One of the swings hit Zac square on his left arm, punching him down in the ground before he could get out of the way. A loud crack could be heard, and Zac almost passed out from the pain.

It followed up with a few frantic swipes with its claws, which rent long gashes all along his back while he helplessly lay on his stomach beneath the impaled beast.

Luckily for Zac, the thrashing didn't continue for too long, as a huge amount of Cosmic Energy entered him. Some helped replenish a small part of his severely depleted reserves, while most worked toward leveling him up.

The surroundings felt extremely quiet after the sounds of battle had subsided. He lay panting on the ground and couldn't help but smile with bloodied teeth. He'd done it.

But just as Zac felt elated over his victory, a responding roar echoed in the distance. And then another, and suddenly, the forest was filled with a cacophony of bestial roars.

Backup was coming.

21

HURT

Zac only knew pain as he pushed forward through the forest, not even knowing if he went in the right direction. From all directions, he could hear the roars from different beasts closing in. His consciousness was hazy, and he only moved on instinct by now. He had been fleeing for a while since being forced to run from the roars in the forest. He had only had time to yank the mangled hatchet out of the herald's eye socket before using the little Cosmic Energy he had to speed away.

He heard a crash to his left, and a barghest bounded toward him to intercept his flight. He intuitively tried to dodge, but his feet did not listen to his commands, and he fell over. It was lucky too for Zac, as the demon dog flew straight over his fallen form.

Zac numbly got to his feet and continued on. Soon the barghest had managed to run around and came toward him again. The scant Cosmic Energy in Zac's body circulated as he suddenly turned toward the demonling and, with a growl, swung his mangled hatchet down in a mighty overhead arc.

The strike hit clean on the beast's forehead, slamming the maw closed and its head into the ground. The power was so strong that its thick cranium cracked, and both blood and brain matter covered the axe. The beast was stopped right in its tracks and lay on the ground, convulsing.

Zac had no time to finish off the beast, as a movement in his periphery made him instinctively swing outward. The axe-head hit a dark shape and elicited a pained yelp. It was a gwyllgi, which had planned to take advantage of the fight and strike a finishing blow at his head. Unfortunately for the hound, this had happened dozens of times by now, and a response had been engraved in Zac's subconscious.

The gwyllgi fell down, likely with a few broken ribs from the impact of the axe. It had hit the beast with its blunt side, but with Zac's power and Cosmic Energy, such a strike was still lethal if positioned correctly. Zac wasted no time and finished it off with another swing down on its head.

The physical exertion worsened his wounds even more, and he suddenly puked out a mouthful of blood with chunks of something else.

But he didn't stop. Zac trudged on almost like a zombie, felling any foolish oncoming beasts with an eye-for-an-eye type of disregard for his own body.

After either a few minutes or a few hours, the onslaught of demons had ended. A familiar sight jolted his almost dormant consciousness awake. It was a large oak standing solitary in a glade, with an assortment of flowers strewn across the ground. The sight gave almost a spiritual impression, like the oak was a spirit tree of some woodland elves.

And more importantly, this tree actually represented salvation for Zac. He shakily put his axe into his belt and started to slowly climb the tree. His left arm didn't quite respond, and he had to arduously move upwards with his right arm and legs. On a normal day, he could be at the top of the tree in seconds, but now it felt like climbing a mountain.

He had completely run out of Cosmic Energy, and it felt like each cell in his body had been completely wrung out. Every movement was powered by force of will rather than anything else.

Finally, he was roughly five meters above the ground and crawled up on what looked like a plateau. It was three sturdy branches that grew in close proximity in a row, with the middle branch slightly lower. Together they formed almost an enclosure. Along the branches there were vines wired to make walls and flooring, and finally, some cut-off branches full of leafy growth had been placed around to insulate and hide the enclosure.

It was one of the many camps Zac had created over the last few weeks. Every time he found a tree, a cave, or some other natural formation that could be turned into a secluded resting stop, he had stopped and turned it into a camp.

One never knew when one had to hide from beasts or wouldn't be able to get back to camp, so he had prepared these as a precaution.

Zac slumped down on the blanket of leaves that were placed on the middle branch and dragged out a bottle of water placed next to the trunk. It had been placed by him there when building the hideout. He greedily drank half the bottle before the pain in his ribs simply stopped him from continuing. Finally, he could take it no longer and drowsily closed his eyes and passed out.

He spent the next few days stuck in the tree. For the most part, he had slept, as he had problems staying awake when he was so utterly drained of Cosmic Energy. His amulet helped, but it seemed it would take a few days for him to recharge.

Even though he had survived, it did not feel like a victory anymore. The glorious feeling from right after the kill was long gone. He was incapacitated from pain and blood loss, and even with his high Vitality, it would take time to heal. His left arm was broken and possibly a few ribs as well, and the large gashes that crossed his whole back felt inflamed. Every time he moved, different parts of his body screamed in protest, and he could only helplessly stay in the tree.

It was only after three days that he felt strong enough to get ready to head down. He could actually move his arm somewhat, but he wouldn't try putting any force on it yet.

By now, he was ravenously hungry and couldn't wait to get back to his camp. He hadn't left any food in the small tree hideout and had actually resorted to eating leaves and acorns the last two days. He had no idea if they were poisonous, but it felt like he had no options. Since his body had gotten stronger from the System, he also had to eat a lot more compared to before. That was why the food he and his friends had prepared had run out in only one week instead of two.

It was with a tinge of bitterness he prepared to get back. The three-day convalescence unfortunately meant that he had failed in his goal, as the deadline of finishing within a month had passed yesterday.

He still had two more heralds to kill, and also the general, which he still hadn't seen. He could only hope that he had been paranoid, and that nothing bad had happened now that a month had passed. He was, however, quite disappointed that he might have missed out on some extremely powerful building awarded for a quick completion of the quest.

Zac guessed that he would find out during the coming days, and there was no point in ruminating over it now.

He slowly got down from the tree after making sure no beasts were in the vicinity, and started making his way back towards his camp.

Zac tried to glean if anything had changed on the island since the deadline had passed, but he could find no indication of that happening. The two suns still shone in the sky, and the malevolent pillar of energy from the incursion still glared in the distance. It did seem to have intensified somewhat, but Zac wasn't sure if it wasn't just his imagination.

The oak he had stayed in the last few days was close to the edge of the island, in the western direction, and it would take some hours to get back to his camp.

This time, he walked carefully, as he felt he was in no condition to fight any demons, especially not if they had gotten empowered even further.

His axe was for all intents and purposes now simply a blunt weapon after the herald had slammed down on it. Killing monsters now would require a higher energy expenditure than before, as he couldn't simply bleed them out with a quick swing.

So it was with great care Zac made his way through the familiar forests until he suddenly heard rustling in the bushes ahead.

He immediately crouched down and hid behind a tree and some bushes while trying to see what lay ahead. After a quick glance, he almost instinctively got up and shouted out to get attention, as what he saw was three people slowly making their way through the forest.

Luckily, he managed to stop himself in time as he noticed a jarring discrepancy.

The people had horns.

22

SCOUTS

Azzun walked through the forest with his two companions, irritably swatting branches and flies away. It was his first time off-world, and the change in climate was jarring. He missed the soothing monochromatic environment of his clan. Now the only reminder of the familiar red was the incursion in the distance.

Of course, they knew that being able to invade a newly integrated world was a great opportunity. The House of Azh'Rezak had celebrated for ten days and sacrificed ten thousand slaves for luck when they had found out that they had actually managed to get a slot. They were only a medium-sized clan in their sector, but this opportunity meant a chance to grow to a large clan. Maybe they could even gain enough resources to overthrow the regional Lord.

Everyone knew that the Ruthless Heavens mainly opened up the passageways to introduce a challenge to the indigenous inhabitants of the planets. The Ruthless Heavens wanted to test if the original inhabitants were worthy to stay alive, and whether any powerhouses would emerge among them. That was why it let invaders through, but imposed limits on how strong they could be. The challenge needed to be hard, but possible to overcome.

Of course, most powers in the Multiverse were more than happy to be treated as a test by the System. The potential gain of both rare treasures and new domains to own far outweighed the potential sacrifice of some of their young and their untalented. It worked as a great training ground for their young elite, providing opportunities to lead, battle, and gain precious resources.

The elders of the clan were even more ecstatic when they learned that the world had been given a D-rank classification. It was no secret that when the System integrated new worlds, the huge influx of energy could create all sorts of rare and invaluable treasures all over the fresh worlds. The higher grade the new world was, the more treasures would appear. A fresh D-class planet wasn't top tier, but at least it was above average.

It usually wouldn't be the turn of some middling clan to get access to this type of smorgasbord. Normally, some arch-daemon would have nudged the heavens and snatched it from them, but luckily, the Great War was reaching a white-hot intensity. All the real powerhouses had their hands full and couldn't focus on this matter, even though the potential gain was great.

Azzun had grown up hearing stories of how even lowly imps and thralls had managed to turn into arch-daemons after entering a fresh world. They had found some treasure or natural oddity that had helped them shed their lowly heritage and emerge as a powerhouse in their galaxy.

Of course, Azzun knew that even if some treasure was discovered, it wasn't his turn to enjoy it. It would all enter the greedy hands of their general. Even though the general couldn't be considered a top talent of their clan, he had managed to snag this great opportunity. He guessed it helped to have a great daemon as a great-grandfather, who spoiled him rotten.

The old daemon had forcefully elected his only great-grandson, Ogras Azh'Rezak, to lead the incursion. Azzun and the rest had discovered his incompetence even before entering the new world.

Afraid that there would be strong resistance on this world, and that losses of their forces would reflect badly on him, he had simply unleashed beast hordes to kill everything around the incursion for the first month. He had chosen four evolved beasts to lead their packs and simply let them run loose without any supervision from a Beast Master or Tamer.

Even many of the elders had disapproved of such cowardice, but the great daemon quashed any dissension.

He only dared to enter when the first limiter was loosened. Everyone had been shocked to discover that both Ur'Khaz and Vul were dead when they finally arrived.

While neither were particularly strong, both were elites who had been chosen among the thousands of beasts to be leaders of the beast packs they'd sent through to clear the area. They were almost at the limit of what the Ruthless Heavens would allow to pass through the incursion, and it had cost the clan a fortune to send them through. They had been heavily nurtured and given many supplements to increase their physiques. After the restrictions lifted, they would be like kings in a newly initiated world.

Ogras immediately further cemented his erratic leadership upon noticing this fact. He had simply called the heralds trash for dying so easily, and was more focused on the construction of his palace than finding out the reason for their demise.

He had simply sent out a few scout parties, Azzun's group included, in order to gain information about the surroundings. Getting the order felt almost like a death sentence to the unlucky scouts. If something in this forest could kill their alpha beasts, how would they survive? They were only level 30 to 35 with common classes, the weakest of the army that had arrived.

However, they had no choice but to comply with the order.

The hierarchy and rules were extremely strict. Both they and their families would have a miserable ending if that happened. They could only bitterly nod their heads and try to stay alive. He could only hope to garner some type of merit during their invasion, which would allow him and his family to live a bit more comfortably in the clan.

The blast of different colors around him felt stressful and disorienting, and even though they had been briefed on this type of terrain, it was hard to adapt. They were in a constant state of unease, as they had no idea what might jump out from the bushes at any moment.

As if summoned by his thoughts, Azzun heard a subdued rustle, followed by a wet thud and grunt. He immediately drew his weapon and turned around, only to see one of his companions topple over with a crushed skull.

Their assailant was already mid-swing toward his other companion, and she was killed before he managed to even react.

The attacker was a walking horror, completely red and covered in blood. Its body looked like a maze of crudely sewn together body parts, and Azzun's first thought was that the attacker was an abomination or ghoul from the Undead Hordes. If the world they attacked had an empire of the undead, their invasion would be a nightmare. There were few enemy factions in the Multiverse that were more annoying to battle than the undead.

He quickly discarded the idea when he noticed that the patchwork was actually extremely rudimentary armor rather than its actual skin, and he realized he was battling some manner of barbarian warrior.

He didn't have time to analyze the situation further, as the man attacked with a swing of his odd weapon. Azzun quickly lifted his war-axe to intercept the swing, but quickly regretted it when their weapons clashed.

Horrified, he realized the monstrous power that was contained in the swing, and he quickly circulated his Cosmic Energy and activated his defensive skill. An earthen layer quickly covered his arms and torso and stabilized him. Thanks to his quick reaction, he didn't break his arms, but the force still threw him down on the ground, and his defensive skill shattered.

Disoriented and hurting, he threw a wide swing toward his enemy, but only hit air. He tried to get back on his feet and meet his attacker. He didn't get far, however, before he felt a sharp pain in the back of his head, and then everything turned black.

Zac stood panting over the unconscious demon, a sheen of perspiration covering his face. The sweat came from pain rather than exertion, as his charge had opened up some of his wounds. He finally dared to use his skill on the demon, which showed **[Azzun, Level 33]**.

Luckily, these demons didn't seem very strong, even if they were higher leveled. He started to go through their bodies and looted anything that seemed useful. He ended up carrying two sets of gear and had two backpacks slung over his back.

He ignored the protests of his ribs and then dragged the two looted corpses into the bushes and hid them there. He was too tired to bury them, and he didn't want to linger here too long. Hopefully, some beast would sniff them out and eat them before their compatriots found them.

Zac was somewhat surprised at how calm he was with his actions. These three were clearly sentient beings, to the point that Zac had mistaken them for humans for a second. Still, he had butchered them without any mercy or hesitation. He had been slaughtering nonstop for a month, but those had generally been beasts, with the exception of the imps.

He had thought that he still would have some trepidation when dealing with humanoid beings, but it seemed that something deep and primal had changed in him during the last month. He was harder and colder compared to before, and he felt that he likely wouldn't be able to go back to what he was.

Just as the world had changed, so had he.

23

DO YOU UNDERSTAND MY WORDS?

Zac sighed and slung the unconscious Azzun over his shoulder, and the action caused him to whimper in pain. He would have preferred to drag him, but he didn't want to leave a trail straight to his campsite.

He wasn't far away from home now and slowly walked the last bit. When he was a hundred meters away from the camp, he stopped and put his captive down. After making sure that the demon was still unconscious but alive, he got a few vines and tied him up. Then he slowly made a circle around the camp, looking for any sign that there had been foot traffic in the vicinity.

A drawback of the illusion array was that he had no idea if ten demons were waiting inside his camp without him seeing it, so he wanted to make sure that his surroundings were undisturbed. He couldn't find any signs of anyone having walked through here lately, so he quietly skulked toward the camp and took a peek inside the illusion array.

Luckily, the camp was undisturbed, so Zac went back and got his demon and then walked back into the safety of the illusion array.

Finally back, he let out a long sigh that had felt lodged in his chest for the past few days. A growl from his stomach reminded him he had only eaten nuts and leaves in the last few days, and he quickly went over to his car and snatched a handful of dried meat he had hung on a line between the trailer and SUV.

He sat down in his camper chair with a grimace and started to devour the meat while staring at his new captive.

He truly looked exotic, with skin that was tinted a grayish-red. The skin looked coarse and almost like a cross between scales and normal human skin. Red tattoos, which reminded Zac of the fractals from the skills and arrays, adorned his upper arms.

He was wearing formfitting leather armor, which seemed to be made for an agile fighter or scout rather than a fighter. It had vambraces inlaid with a metal plate, which covered his forearms but left the upper arms bare.

The chest plate was formed by a woven mesh of leather strips, which seemed both pliable and durable. He had on a belt, where he had kept his weapons until Zac stole them, and a pair of dark gray leather pants.

It wasn't only the craftsmanship that was far superior in the gear, the materials were as well. When Zac tried to cut through the leather with one of his kitchen knives, he couldn't even make a scratch, even after applying pressure. Zac assumed the leather came from some strong beast on the demon's home planet.

Oddly, neither this demon nor the others wore any shoes, but after an inspection, it made some sense. The demon's feet looked like a slimmer version of the barghest's taloned paws, with three sharp claws in the front.

Finally, the pair of horns that had warned him from approaching them. They were a blood-red color and looked like an artist's rendition of fire. They started in his upper forehead and were bent backwards along his skull. It looked like tongues of fire were reaching upwards along the horn.

It did not seem that they used them for goring enemies; rather, they looked largely ornamental.

The demon was still out cold, so Zac took the opportunity to go over his status window while getting another helping of dried meat.

Name: Zachary Atwood
Level: 25
Race: Human
Alignment: [Earth] Human

Titles: Born For Carnage, Ultimate Reaper, Luck of the Draw, Giantsbane, Disciple of David, Overpowered, Slayer of Leviathans, Adventurer, Demon Slayer

Strength: 59
Dexterity: 39
Endurance: 42
Vitality: 48
Intelligence: 29
Wisdom: 29
Luck: 44

Free Points: 4
Nexus Coins: 14,030

Active Quests:

1. **Unlimited Potential (Normal): Reach level 25. Reward: Unlock class system. (25/25) [COMPLETE]**

Dynamic Quests:

1. **Off with their heads (Unique): Kill the four heralds and the general of incursion within 3 months. Reward: 10 E-Grade Nexus Crystals, E-Grade equipment, unique building depending on performance. (2/5)**
2. **Incursion Master (Unique): Close or conquer incursion and protect base from denizens of other alignments for 3 months. Reward: 5 E-Grade Nexus Crystals, outpost upgraded to town, status upgraded to Lord. (0/3)**

Zac had gained two levels from killing the herald and the other monsters while escaping. From how thick the Cosmic Energy felt, he wasn't far from gaining another level either.

He also noticed that he had gained roughly eight thousand Nexus Coins from his attack on the herald and the subsequent escape. His quests had also been updated, and the quest called Unlimited Potential showed **[COMPLETE]** at the end. His demon slayer quest had just disappeared after completing, but Zac guessed that this quest remained as he still hadn't chosen a class.

Zac immediately placed 4 points into Strength. He had noticed during the last month that each additional point in a stat had a greater effect than the earlier points. It was like the gains were exponential. This had made him feel that specialization was more highly rewarded compared to putting points in every stat.

Besides, with his large number of titles, all his stats were quite high in any case, affording him the opportunity to go deep in a specific attribute.

Since then, he had put all his points from level-ups into Strength unless he felt that some other stat was truly lacking. He thought about placing some more points in Vitality due to his condition, but discarded that idea after a brief hesitation.

He was extremely eager to choose a Class, but barely managed to contain himself. The reason was the unconscious captive in front of him.

Zac had already stumbled along for a long time, using guestimation to guide his choices. He was hoping to use Azzun to get some answers about the System and many other things before he did something irrevocable to himself. He didn't even dare to touch the Nexus Node, as he was afraid some class change process would start that couldn't be stopped.

Zac felt a lot better after having finished his meal. With a grunt, he got back to his feet and filled a bottle with water from the water array.

He walked over to the demon and poured the contents over his face, resulting in the demon sputtering and waking up.

Azzun had a look of shock and horror on his face as he woke up to the sight of Zac, who still hadn't bothered to change or remove the blood that was caked all over him.

"So, uh… I guess I am sorry about your friends. Do you understand my words?" Zac said with a coarse voice. He realized that those were essentially the first words he had spoken in weeks. In the beginning, he had muttered and mumbled things to himself, but soon he had grown accustomed to the silence.

Zac didn't know if it was because of what he said, but the demon snarled and desperately tried to get himself free from the vines. Zac sighed and brandished his hatchet, and with a grunt, he slammed it straight next to the tied-up demon. It produced a loud thud, and a small crater was formed. Had he swung just a decimeter to his right, then one of Azzun's legs would have been mutilated by now.

The demon immediately stilled, as it perhaps remembered the ending of his two companions thanks to the hatchet.

"Do you understand my words?" Zac repeated. He wasn't really expecting the demon to actually speak his language, but rather that the System provided some translation feature. Language would be a pretty large issue if the System connected endless numbers of worlds.

The demon simply stared at him then abruptly closed his eyes.

"Hello?" Zac prodded once again, unsure what the demon was planning. Suddenly, Zac could sense how the Cosmic Energy in the surroundings proceeded to move toward them, and the demon's body started to shake.

Zac got a sinking feeling in his chest and didn't dare hesitate. He immediately swung his hatchet down on the skull of the demon, crushing it like he had done with the other two.

The body slumped down, and blood gushed out of his nose. Zac received a confirmation that the demon was dead from the influx of Cosmic Energy, but the uneasy feeling did not disappear. Suddenly, the body started expanding, and Zac's eyes went wide with alarm.

He barely managed to throw himself away and down on the ground before the corpse exploded with a tremendous bang.

Zac slowly got up on his knees, disoriented and ears ringing. Somehow the demon seemed to have made the energy in his body go haywire, and he had actually exploded like a bomb. The camp was in chaos, with the windows of the car having cracks all over, and the closest had completely shattered. Things were thrown around haphazardly, and there even was an indent on the exterior wall of the camper.

Luckily, he had killed the demon in time, or he might have been able to gather even more energy and created a far more deadly explosion, wiping out both him and the camp.

These demons are going to be a pain, Zac thought with a grimace while looking at the mess.

24

CLASS

Zac slowly moved through the forest. Since the demon blew himself up, Zac had been stealthily roving around the vicinity of the camp. The illusion array blocked sound to a certain degree, but he was afraid that the explosion would have bled through the protection and alerted other demons.

However, he had been moving around the camp in expanding circles for two hours now and had seen no sight of any more of the demons. While he had been scouting, he'd also taken the time to properly bury the two other demons. It wasn't to properly honor the dead, but rather to avoid the bodies getting discovered.

Finally satisfied that he had caught a lucky break and still wasn't found out, he returned to the camp.

He spent some time cleaning up the camp. Some of the loot from the demons had unfortunately been destroyed by the explosion. He hadn't expected his captive to go nuclear as soon as he woke up, so Zac had simply thrown the gear down in a pile not far from him.

The bags seemed to have contained some vials, which Zac supposed were either healing tinctures or poisons. The bags were still whole, but the vials had cracked. Inside was a mess of the different mixtures and glass shards, and Zac certainly didn't want to rummage through it now.

The male's leather armor was ruined, but the female demon's suit underneath seemed intact. But most important was the weapon that Azzun had been carrying.

It was a one-handed battle-axe. It was much longer than his hatchet, reaching roughly eighty centimeters. The head was single-headed, but with a sharp spike sticking out on the other side, perhaps for balance. The edge itself was a half-moon over thirty centimeters long. Zac tried the edge with his thumb and was surprised to see that he immediately started bleeding.

It was hard for a normal kitchen knife to cut his skin now without some effort, which showed just how deadly his new weapon was.

The handle was black, and it appeared that it had some fractals carved into it. However, these fractals somehow seemed far more rudimentary compared to the ones on the array flags. Finally, a strip of some unknown beast hide had been used to create a handle.

This clearly was a weapon for war rather than a tool, as his hatchet was. If he'd had this thing during his fight with the herald, he might even have been able to kill it off with the initial charge.

Zac tried using **[Eye of Discernment]** on the weapon, as the axe seemed to be somewhat related to the System, with the pattern on the handle. However, it gave no response. Either the skill couldn't show information about items, or items didn't work like that. He had a feeling it was a problem with the skill, as it was by far the cheapest skill that Nexus Coins could buy. It would be odd if it was too versatile.

Apart from this, he had scrounged up a hooked sword, a couple of knives, and various bracers and shin guards. There might be something else in the bags, but he would wait until the mess dried out. He didn't really care for the sword and left it to the side, but was delighted with the small knives. They were small and straight with edges on both sides of the blade, giving them excellent balance. He felt they were used for throwing and battle rather than skinning animals and the like.

They would be a great addition to his arsenal, as he was sorely lacking any ranged attack. Every time he wanted to kill an imp, he had to hurl his axe at it or a bunch of rocks. But this would be a deadly alternative that didn't force him to throw away his main weapon. He already practiced throwing rocks and the axe for some time every day, and swapping to daggers shouldn't be too large an adjustment.

After going through the gear, he finally couldn't wait any longer and approached the Nexus Node. It was time for him to get a class, no matter if it was the right choice or not. He pressed his palm against the smooth surface of the crystal and mentally tried to access the class system.

A new box appeared in his vision with multiple rows.

[Top 5 Class choices]

[Warrior – F-Grade, Common. Fledgling combatant. Proficient with melee weaponry. Upgradeable.]

[Acolyte – F-Grade, Common. Fledgling wielder of the elements. Initial proficiency with elemental magic. Upgradeable.]

[Marine – F-Grade, Uncommon. Lowest ranked naval combatant. Proficient with battles at sea. Upgradeable.]

[Demon Hunter – F-Grade, Uncommon. Having dedicated his life to the eradication of the Demonic race, the Demon Hunter

has attained a high proficiency in locating and eradicating anything of demonic nature. Upgradeable.]

[Hatchetman – F-Grade, Rare. Their army is an endless forest, and I'm the lumberjack. Upgradeable.]

[Random F-Grade Class. 92.9% Common. 5.0% Uncommon. 2.0 % Rare. 0.1% Epic. Roll the dice.]

That was all the information Zac could get out of the System. He tried to get a more in-depth explanation with mental commands such as "details" and "info," but the short excerpt was all he could go on.

The first thing he noticed was that classes did not seem equal. All five choices did have the same grade, F-grade, so it seemed everyone started at the same grade. They did, however, have different rarities, ranging from Common to Rare in his case.

He did not know how large a difference there was between the rarities, but he could only assume that a higher rarity class would be stronger than a low rarity one.

The second thing he noticed was that all the classes were upgradeable. That likely meant that he could get stronger classes in the future, but they would be based on the class he chose now. It might be secondary classes or it might be possible to change classes, but he had no information about this. He therefore had to make the choice under the assumption that his choice would influence his future trajectory to a large degree.

The third was that the available choices seemed to be at least partly based on his accomplishments.

The Marine class was likely available because he was situated near an ocean. The Demon Hunter class came from killing demonic creatures nonstop since the System arrived.

He was not sure about the Hatchetman class, but he had used a lumberjack's hatchet for almost all his kills, so he assumed it might be based on that. But it was a combat class, going by the description, rather than a woodworking class.

The last choice was a gamble. Even an Epic class was available, albeit only at a 0.1% chance. His Luck stat might influence those odds, but it was unclear how. If each Luck point increased his chance to get the Epic class by one point, he wouldn't hesitate. He would roll the dice in a heartbeat. But he doubted it would be that easy, so he felt no need to use this option.

He already had a Rare and two Uncommon classes to choose from, so he had no reason to gamble. Besides, there might be classes that didn't help him in combat. What if he got a Rare painter class from gambling? While it might be nice learning a new skill, it would not help him on the island.

He would therefore definitely choose one of the available classes.

First, he eliminated Warrior. It seemed quite basic, and it felt like most other choices were better. Next, he eliminated both Marine and Demon Hunter. He didn't like the prospect of limited boosts. He had no aspirations to live out the rest of his life on the high seas, so a water-centric class did not make sense to him.

He also didn't want to spend his life hunting demons. The Demon Hunter class might very well be the strongest class for him right now, as there still were demons infesting the whole island. However, either he or the demons would be gone in two months, so it didn't make sense to pick this class either.

Abby had told him that the Multiverse consisted of myriad races. This meant that it wasn't like Hell's gates had opened and the universe was being invaded by demons. They were just one of many potential enemies in the vast Multiverse. So even if he survived, he did not know if there were any other demons on Earth apart from in this particular incursion. Wouldn't that mean he essentially crippled himself by choosing a class that could only help him for the first few months?

Finally, it was an Uncommon class. While it was better compared to the Warrior and Acolyte classes, it was worse than the Rare class.

That left Acolyte and Hatchetman. Truth be told, he felt that Acolyte was the most intriguing. He did like the prospect of mastering the elements and firing fireballs and lightning bolts at his surroundings.

However, he felt there were drawbacks as well. For one, he had no idea if he actually was able to learn spells just from getting the class. What if the basic spells normally were something you got in the Tutorial? Also, he had invested most of his stats so far into physical attributes, which might be wasted on this class.

The only reason he could imagine he got this kind of class to choose was that he had gotten quite a bit of Intelligence and Wisdom from his titles. But he almost drooled at the aspect of upgrading the class until he became a Grand Magus, who could burn the sky with a sweep of his hand.

But most importantly it was only a Common class. It felt like it was something that almost anyone could get in the future. Getting a Common class when he had Rare classes to choose from felt like wasting the advantage that the past month had provided him.

The System rewarded the brave and intrepid. The Rare class seemed to be the reward for risking his life every day against the demons.

Of course, Hatchetman sounded a bit stupid, to be honest. The connotation of the word from his professional career was anything but positive, but he felt that it had a somewhat different meaning here.

It seemed that it somehow referred to being a warrior lumberjack from the description. While not exciting, it did, however, check a few of his boxes. The class probably would be very beneficial if he used his newly acquired axe in battle.

Out of all the choices, it also seemed to be the most tailored for his battle style. It also was the only Rare choice. He did not know how much better each rarity was compared to the one before, but perhaps the difference would be even greater compared to the conditional boost the Demon Hunter class would give against his current enemies.

The drawback was that he couldn't quite imagine what the upgrade path would be. Next upgrade was a… stronger lumberjack? A walking sawmill? A corporate shark doing hostile takeovers and selling companies for scraps?

So one of the choices seemed to be able to help him less now. But it might end up with him becoming a great Wizard. He had always played mage classes when playing games, so this was quite enticing. It was, however, only a Common class.

The other choice seemed to be more suited to his stats and direct power, but led into an unknown future.

After a long hesitation, he finally said goodbye to the dream of arcane dominance and chose the box marked **[Hatchetman]**.

25

STRONGER

A strong surge of Cosmic Energy inundated Zac's whole body. It felt like his whole being was purified and reshaped. Instinctively, he felt an enormous fractal imprinting itself and covering his whole being. However, most parts of the fractal were indistinct and blurred.

He also felt the powerful rush into his cells, which indicated the improvement of his stats. Zac was completely oblivious of his surroundings as he was drowning in the sensations. Unfortunately, the feeling didn't last long, and he soon came down from his rush.

From a first look, he didn't feel that different, apart from his condition had improved significantly. It felt like his wounds had largely healed, even his broken arm.

But when he opened his status page, he was shocked. His stats had made a great leap.

Name: Zachary Atwood
Level: 25
Class: [F-Rare] Hatchetman
Race: [F] Human
Alignment: [Earth] Human

Titles: Born for Carnage, Ultimate Reaper, Luck of the Draw, Giantsbane, Disciple of David, Overpowered, Slayer of Leviathans, Adventurer, Demon Slayer, Full of Class, Rarified Being, Trailblazer

Strength: 92
Dexterity: 48
Endurance: 51
Vitality: 57
Intelligence: 38
Wisdom: 38
Luck: 54

Free Points: 0
Nexus Coins: 14,690

All his stats had gained a jump of nine points, except Strength, which had increased a whopping twenty-eight. As he had noticed that every stat point gave a larger increase in improvement compared to the one before, he knew he likely had doubled his actual physical power from the increase in Strength.

He noticed that his class was added in a row, with F denoting the grade of the class. He was surprised to notice that his Race had also gotten graded, as it had been blank before. He was excited at the prospect that he could actually evolve his Race somehow.

Hopefully it meant that his power would rise, rather than growing a tail or a third eye.

He had gained three new titles from getting a class as well. Zac focused on them to get a description

[Full of Class: Reach level 25 and attain a Class. All stats +1]

[Rarified Being: Attain a Class graded as Rare. All stats +1]

[Trailblazer: First to gain a Class in world. All stats +5]

That explained where the all-around improvements to his stats came from. The first two titles were things that anyone could attain. However the Trailblazer title was another title that only he would get on Earth.

Zac felt comforted by what that title represented. He still managed to keep his lead, even over the "chosen" cultivators who got help in the beginner villages. Even if he was deemed trash by the System and left to rot on this island, he had defied fate so far and was still on top.

He had to admit that the feeling of power was somewhat addicting. Finding his family was still his priority, but he also craved the feeling of becoming stronger and stronger. He lived for the moment after every battle when he absorbed the Cosmic Energy and had the pure unadulterated force of life course through his veins.

He had started to think more and more about where the limits of strength lay. By now, he could punch a large rock and it would shatter, and only one month had passed. How powerful would he be in a year? A decade? Just thinking about it made him excited. Of course, he would never let himself forget that to get there in one piece he would have to walk through an ocean of blood.

He didn't linger on the subject, as he was anxious to look through his other changes. He thought, "Class," and a new window appeared.

[Class: Hatchetman, Grade-F, Rare]
Strength +10, +10%.
Level: +3 Strength, +1 Endurance, +1 free point per level.

Skills:
Axe Mastery (LOCKED)
Chop (LOCKED)
Forester's Constitution (LOCKED)

Following that were rows of blocked-out information. At least that showed where the large Strength boost came from. The +3 Strength per level didn't seem to be retroactive; otherwise, he'd have almost twice the Strength by now. But it showed that every level from now would give a much larger boost compared to before.

Zac was annoyed to see that he actually didn't get any skills for free as he had hoped. There were three skills listed that seemed somewhat intuitive. Axe Mastery and Chop seemed offensive, and Forester's Constitution was defensive. At least he hoped Chop was an offensive skill, and not a woodworking skill.

He didn't quite understand how "Chop" would be better than what he had been doing before, but he guessed he would find out. It seemed that he couldn't get any information about the skills until he unlocked them.

The next problem was how to unlock the skills. Soon he found the method in the quest tab. It showed a new category, which was class quests. Each skill needed a quest to be completed.

1. **Axe Mastery (Class): Mastery is born through battle. Fell 1,000 enemies. (0/1,000)**
2. **Chop (Class): First chop wood. Then their bodies. (0/10,000)**
3. **Forester's Constitution (Class): Fight in the forests, be one with nature. (0/30)**

None of the quests seemed very hard to accomplish. The Axe Mastery made no distinction of the strength of the enemies, and with his improved physique, he could grind it out in a week or two if he just focused on slaying barghest.

The Chop quest seemed to take time rather than being hard, but if he changed his daily workout routine to chop wood, it would be done sooner or later. Chopping wood was a great workout anyway.

The last quest seemed either extremely easy or rather hard. Just 30 fights and it would be done. The whole island was a large forest, so finishing it seemed to be the easiest of the three. It depended on what be one with nature meant. If it was just some random words, great.

If he actually had to somehow merge with nature or become a tree-hugger, it felt far more annoying.

Finally, it seemed that he'd found out everything that he could for now. He had entered the outpost shop as well, but it seemed nothing new was added from gaining a class.

There were a few new skills added at the Node, but they were prohibitively expensive, with the cheapest being five hundred thousand Nexus Coins.

All in all, it had been a fruitful day. He was disappointed that the demon had self-destructed rather than answering questions. There were so many things he needed to know. To be fair, Zac would likely have killed him after questioning the demon in any case. That the demon chose making a last-ditch effort to bring Zac with him to hell was a logical choice.

Luckily, the gear he gained and the strengthening made the sting less severe. He still looked positively insane from the blood and broken gear and didn't want to put on the gear while looking like this. He left the camp to patrol the vicinity for a while and then went back.

This would likely be a new addition to the daily routine. The humanoid demons seemed far more organized compared to the dumb beasts that had come through the incursion first.

Satisfied that there were no enemies nearby, he moved water from the water array into the tanker's reservoir. Finally, he ripped the patchwork armor off and took his first good shower in over a week. It was a risky move, but the grime and blood was making even him crazy, and he needed to get it off. He brought his new axe with him into the bathroom in case he was ambushed while in there.

It took half an hour to scrub the layers of dirt and blood off himself before stepping out of the shower.

Even cleaned up, he could barely recognize himself in the mirror. His whole body had undergone a metamorphosis during the last month. Almost all of the fat was gone, leaving only a thin layer covering his muscular frame.

His physique looked *hard*. His muscles were compact and wiry rather than big and swollen like a bodybuilder's. He thought he actually might be smaller now compared to when he worked out at the gym.

Of course, he knew that explosive power was contained in these muscles, and that they were so dense that maybe not even a bullet would penetrate them by now. All over his body were scars of varying size and severity. His tactic of boosting his Vitality and taking blows for landing killing strikes had been effective, but it had left an undeniable mark.

He looked down on his rough and calloused hands. It was hard to believe what these hands had done in the last weeks. Once he had actually ripped the jaws of a gwyllgi straight apart when he had dropped his hatchet.

Zac sighed and put on one of his last whole T-shirts and undergarments. He didn't want to use his rags together with his new gear.

Unfortunately, the chest pieces of both the males' leather armors had been blasted to shreds, so he could only put on the female's armor. He didn't worry about it too much, though, as he had a strong suspicion that there would be many more demons in the woods that could supply new gear.

To get adjusted to his new weapon, he dragged over a thick log. He reactivated his gravity array and started cutting the log into firewood, working out and working on his quest simultaneously. It was already late, and he would not go out hunting anymore today. As he was methodically swinging his axe, a trace of anticipation could be seen on his face.

For the first time since the world changed, he looked forward to going out and testing his might.

26

DEMONS

Zac woke up early the next day. He had slept outside with axe in hand and geared up, just in case of a night raid. He once again set out to scout the vicinity, but nothing seemed to have moved through there during the night.

Zac wasted no time and set out towards the direction of his fight against the herald. He wanted to scout out the situation before proceeding toward the next herald.

He still wanted to complete the quests as quickly as possible, but the new enemies had proved that something had changed on the island. Zac wanted to scout the situation out until he knew what that change meant, and decided to start from where he had fought Vul.

After walking for a while, he ran into a barghest. A creepy smile appeared on Zac's face, and he brandished the axe.

The beast was as aggressive as ever at least, and it mindlessly charged at him. Zac sidestepped to let it run into a tree behind him just to gauge its power.

He was surprised to see that it didn't actually just charge in to the tree as before; instead, it bit into it and ripped a good chunk out of the wood almost impossibly fast. Of course, it still couldn't stop its momentum and hit the tree square with its now closed maw.

Zac wasted no time and, with a swing, completely decapitated the demon. He felt almost no resistance when cutting through the spine of the demonling, and the axe continued down with such ease that he almost cut into his own leg before he could stop the descent. He knew the axe was extraordinarily sharp since yesterday, but he was still shocked how easily it went through.

As he continued, he wouldn't avoid any beasts anymore; rather, he'd go out of his way to kill them if he found them. He looked forward to getting the Axe Mastery skill, and wouldn't miss an opportunity to work on his thousand-kill goal.

He had been annoyed when he had noticed that only the Axe Mastery quest progressed from kills, not the Forester's Constitution quest. He would have to figure out what was missing later. He also confirmed that the Chop quest did not progress from battling, even though it mentioned chopping bodies.

As he was advancing, he noticed that the beasts had indeed improved. They were stronger, faster, and more impressively, they seemed smarter. It was as if a limiter had reduced all stats, including Intelligence. Then it had been lifting gradually during the last week of the month, and as the last day passed, the limit had been ripped off completely.

Overall, he gauged that the beasts' stats had improved by roughly 50% since four days ago. The danger increased more than that, though, as they had started doing feints and use tactics while attacking compared to before. The barghest were, of course, still dumb-dumbs, but not to the point that they'd mindlessly charge into a wall anymore.

The rewards for killing the beasts hadn't been increased with their improved performance. It seemed that Zac truly had gotten a bargain when hunting during the first month. Zac snickered as he imagined the cultivators in the beginner villages hunting rabbits and boars around the edge of the village for a mere two to three Nexus Coins apiece, like in some RPG.

The increase in Strength didn't bother him when it came to the fodder demons that were peppered through the island. They had improved, but so had he. Even the empowered demons were defenseless against his new weapon. It felt like proper gear actually had a greater effect compared to attaining a class.

Of course, the effect of a class would show over time rather than immediately, it seemed. Also the immediate effect on him was not too large, as he already had such high stats from his titles. If someone with only the basic stats got this class with the accompanying titles, it'd likely be a pretty large boost to them.

As he killed another demon with a lazy swing, he felt the familiar burst of Cosmic Energy that came with a level-up. He was delighted to see that he did get his class stat points in addition to his two free points, rather than instead of. So every level, he now got seven points instead of two.

He paused a second to go over how to allocate his points again. He had thought about it a bit yesterday and had come up with a plan. As his class seemed to focus on Strength and Endurance, so Zac would do the same with his free points.

He felt that the skills and class itself might somehow synergize with these stats, so getting them as high as possible would be a good option. Even if he was wrong, it would be okay, as both these stats were strong on him in any case.

If Vitality helped him heal up after getting wounded, then Endurance would protect him from getting wounded. Endurance didn't only help with his stamina, it also toughened his body up. Now that he had a high enough Vitality that he wouldn't die from ordinary wounds, he could focus on Endurance to make him even harder to kill.

The other option he had considered was to put the points in Dexterity, making him quicker. However, for most of the fights so far, speed had not been an issue or limiting factor for him, so he decided to hold off on that for now.

Furthermore, among the skills that had been added to the Nexus Node after he got his class was one that he felt might be able to substitute for the need for Dexterity. It was called **[Steps of Gaia]** and cost 575,000 Nexus Coins. It was a huge amount of coins, far more than he had gathered in total.

But it seemed to fit him perfectly. It was a movement-type skill, which he assumed would help him move quicker. It would both help him charge at enemies faster and also allow him to more easily dodge attacks. It also seemed to be connected to the earth and nature, same as his class, so he felt there might be synergy along the road.

He therefore had decided to start saving up for the skill. He believed that it shouldn't take too long to get the necessary coins, as his speed of killing beasts had improved significantly with his gear and higher stats.

Finally, he decided to put one point in Strength and two in Endurance and kept going. A while later, he reached the area where he'd fought the herald. The aftermath of the battle was evident, with crushed trees and rocks all over. He still hadn't run into any humanoids, and the forest was largely like it was before.

Zac slowly crept toward the spot where the herald had fallen, alert to his surroundings. He was surprised to find that the carcass had been removed from the spot, as had the poles he had planted.

He could only guess that they had been moved back to the base. He wasn't sure, as he hadn't seen it, but he assumed that the base was either right at the incursion or in the mountains. If it was closer to the other sides, he felt that he should have run into more of the humanoids by now.

Unless there only were a scant few of the humanoid demons, of course. But Zac's intuition told him that he wouldn't be that lucky. The System had screwed him over pretty consistently, and he saw no reason that it would stop anytime soon.

He stopped for a while to decide what to do now. He hadn't really accomplished anything so far except for killing some demons. He didn't need to ponder for long, however, as he suddenly heard subdued voices in the distance.

Zac properly hid himself inside a few bushes as the voices drew closer. He was disappointed to find out that he couldn't understand the words. So much for a universal translation system.

It was a surprisingly smooth and melodic language, specked with vowels flowing like a river. He had assumed that the language of demons would be harsh and perhaps even guttural.

Wait, is that racism? A stray thought entered his mind, making him lose focus before setting his sight on the approaching party.

The party looked somewhat similar to the one he had killed earlier, except that this party was comprised of four individuals rather than three.

There were three males and one female. Two of the males looked like a mix of rangers and warriors, dressed in leather armor and wielding a sword each. The female walked in front and seemed to be the lookout, as she was carefully scouting the surroundings and had a bow slung on her back.

The final man was unarmed but seemed to be a leader, or at least of higher status. The quality of his gear seemed to be a notch above the others, such as a chest plate made of the same black metal as his axe handle. It was engraved in the same manner as the handle as well, but more intricate.

Zac had a feeling that these engravings had some sort of effect, like magically imbuing the gear with sharpness or defense. He had found no ways to use the engravings so far, though, and hoped he might get an idea from the unarmed man.

Another reason Zac surmised the well-equipped man was of higher status than the others was that he could sense a formless pressure emanating from him. It felt like he was looking at a dangerous beast rather than an unarmed man.

While Zac was well-hidden, he decided to slowly recede further into the bushes. This party seemed both deadlier and more alert compared to the last one.

His actions were in vain, however, as the female suddenly grabbed her bow and an arrow in a fluid motion and, without hesitation, fired it straight in the direction of Zac.

Zac tried to get out of the way, but there was no time as the arrow slammed straight into his side.

27

ONE AGAINST MANY

Zac almost lost his breakfast as the arrowhead slammed straight into his gut. It punched through the wired leather armor and continued into his body. Luckily, most of the force had been spent going through the armor, and with Zac's high Endurance, it only proceeded two centimeters before stopping.

This kind of wound wouldn't really faze Zac anymore after constantly getting hurt from his fights. However, he still hesitated for a second after ripping the arrow out. Fight or flee? He hadn't prepared to challenge the party like this.

However, he soon discarded any thought of fleeing. He didn't like the prospect of having another arrow slam into him, this time in the back of his head while running for his life. The ranger seemed to have some detection skill, as she could spot and shoot him while he was hidden in bushes a few hundred meters away. He needed to kill the archer at least before fleeing.

He threw the arrow away and pulled out one of his smaller knives from its sheath. Zac wasted no time and threw it straight at the archer, and it flew with at least the same velocity as the arrow that had hit him.

The female demon seemed to have been prepared, and with an

almost impossible nimbleness, jumped out of the way and proceeded up into a tree like a forest elf. She moved like a specter, and in just a few seconds, she was gone from his vision among the leaves.

Zac tsked in annoyance and charged at the party while trying to use trees as cover from the archer. The force of his steps made deep indents in the ground as he charged forth like a runaway bull. The three remaining demons were obviously ready for the fight, as they spread out, intending to encircle him.

Zac could sense that all of them were using some skill, as he could feel the Cosmic Energy react to their bodies. An illusory red gas started floating around one of the combatants, giving him a more sinister feel. The other underling pointed down on the ground, but Zac couldn't see anything happening.

Zac couldn't see anything happening with the leader either, but the sense of danger increased substantially.

As Zac was furiously approaching, he quickly used **[Eye of Discernment]** on the trio and got some basic information about his enemies.

[Metisis, Level 38]
[Gormer, Level 39]

They were roughly 5 levels higher compared to the last party he had attacked. That meant that they should have at least 15 to 20 higher stat points, including the bonus stats from their classes, compared to the last group of demons.

He was also surprised to notice that the third man, the unarmed one, had somehow resisted his skill. There was only a blur above his head. This made Zac even more wary of him. He had even managed to identify the herald Vul, who had been a far higher level compared to himself.

Zac furiously circulated Cosmic Energy in his body and ran

straight toward the weakest enemy, Metisis. When he was just over fifty meters away from them, an arrow came whizzing down from the treetops. This time, Zac was prepared and slammed it away with the broad side of his axe-head.

The force of this arrow was far higher than the hasty one she had shot before. When the axe and arrow collided, he was actually pushed back a bit, his feet making a groove in the ground. Luckily, the axe was apparently made from excellent materials and wasn't damaged one bit.

Zac pushed ahead once again, the last fifty-meter distance gone in just a few seconds.

Just as he was a few meters away from his target, he pushed all the Cosmic Energy he could into his right leg. He instantly kicked off with all the power he could, and shot like a bullet straight at the other demon, Gormer. The force of the push created an explosion in the ground, even leaving a small crater.

They had not expected the speed that a 98-Strength-powered push could give, and Gormer barely managed to lift his hooked sword before Zac chopped horizontally with all the strength he could muster.

The axe moved like lightning, but when it entered the weird gaseous substance, it felt like he was trying to push through water. A good part of the momentum was somehow sapped out of the strike, and his force couldn't properly come to bear.

Zac wouldn't let this opportunity go, though, and with a growl, redoubled his efforts, and the axe continued on and slammed into the demon right under his left arm. The leather armor could afford almost no resistance against the sharp edge of Zac's axe as it embedded itself firmly in his chest. He couldn't push it clean through, though, as the weird strength-sapping effect seemed to be even stronger within the body of the demon.

Zac immediately ripped his axe out, which produced a tremendous spout of blood. He planned to turn around to meet the other two demons head-on next. He didn't believe he'd get a second chance for a surprise attack like this.

But before he could do anything, he suddenly felt something ensnare his feet, and he completely lost his footing. Zac fell head-first on top of the collapsed dying demon. Gormer seemed intent on revenge even with one foot in the grave, as he weakly held on to Zac to keep him from fleeing.

While Zac struggled to get free, he took a quick glance down at his legs. They were ensnared by a handful of purplish wiggling roots, which somehow seemed alive. They seemed to be a skill or magic that came from the other demon underling.

Perhaps they had planned to ensnare him when he got closer, and then attack him from three directions, securing an easy kill. Unfortunately for them, Zac had preceded them with his lightning-fast blitz.

Zac had no time to analyze it any further, as the leader had moved to a position close to him. Shockingly, he no longer was unarmed, but hefted a monstrous great sword that was almost as long as he was and over twenty centimeters wide.

He had mocking eyes and a sneer as he lifted the sword above his head. Zac could once again feel the movement of Cosmic Energy and knew that the leader was using a skill. Dark arcs of power spread from his arms into the large blade.

The dying demon's strength was no match for Zac, and he frantically ripped himself free from his grip. But he only managed to get himself up to his knees when the large blade started falling down on him. It was poised to cleave him in two unless he did something.

Zac pushed his power to the limit and gripped his axe with both hands and swung upward with all his might, hoping to intercept the sword.

With a tremendous clangor that echoed through the vicinity,

the axe and the great sword connected. The force actually created a shock wave that blasted outwards.

Zac was slammed down into the ground again from the force, creating a small crater. Even with his superhuman stats, he couldn't handle the power of the sword. Luckily for him, he at least managed to get the leader demon off-kilter and change the trajectory of the strike. It actually slammed down in the gut of the dying demon. The might was so strong that the torso of the underling veritably exploded, instantly killing him. That wiped the smirk off the leader's face and seemed to enrage him instead.

Meanwhile, the dark lightning from the demon's skill had passed into Zac's axe when they collided, and burrowed into his arm. A blazing pain ran through his whole body, and his muscles spasmed uncontrollably.

That was actually the only reason Zac survived, as a great spasm jerked his head some distance away. Another arrow slammed down right where his head had been before.

This arrow was different than the other, with a jagged arrowhead and being pitch black. It whizzed down with a great force and actually completely embedded itself into the ground, right down to the feathers. The extreme penetrating power was evident from that shot, likely from a skill.

It was only thanks to being bombed with black fireballs by the imps that Zac was able to retain consciousness. He pushed the pain away with all the resilience he could garner, and with a quick swing, cut through the roots that ensnared his feet. The roots were far sturdier than they looked, and it felt like he cut through steel wire rather than wood.

Still, they were no match for his power and the sharpness of his axe, and he was free in no time. He rolled away as quickly as possible, trying to gain some distance before the leader swung down again.

He got to his feet just as another batch of roots closed in on him. This time, they came as a swarm from the ground under the other demon. Zac whirled his axe back and forth in a frenzied manner and cut them down as they came, stopping their advance after a while.

The battle reached a short lull as Zac stood panting while facing the two demons. He tried to survey the treetops but couldn't locate the female archer. Her existence was like an annoying fly in the periphery that made him unable to fully concentrate. Even worse, this fly could kill him with one strike if he wasn't careful.

Fighting one against many truly was a pain in the ass.

28

MELEE

Zac was a bit unsure of how to proceed. He knew that one should maintain the initiative in a battle, but he didn't want to just charge over like a stupid barghest.

His enemies made the choice for him. The leader started advancing on him, anger smoldering in his eyes. Both his hands gripped the great sword, which was angled down toward the ground.

The other man was stationary but mumbling something in their own language.

Zac could only put his game face on. He was still hurting all over from the dark lightning, but he pretended he was fine. With his axe in his hand, he prepared for round two.

Zac really didn't want to meet the great sword straight on. The leader seemed to have roughly the same level of Strength as he did, and even if he managed to parry the strike, he was afraid that he would be shocked again from the skill. He would have to fight around it somehow.

Luckily, a weapon of that size was unwieldy, and the trajectories would hopefully be telegraphed.

Zac took out a second knife, leaving him with only one

remaining. He launched it at the weaker enemy and started to rush forward.

The demon deflected the knife with a couple of roots, even though the force from Zac's throw was immense. The demon obviously was some sort of earth or tree mage, and the roots were far sturdier than something coming from a normal tree.

The demon was interrupted in his chanting, though, which was Zac's main goal. If he actually had managed to hurt him, all the better.

Wasting no time, he rushed toward him, trying to avoid the leader and his great sword. The great sword whizzed in a wide upwards arc, seemingly trying to cut Zac in two.

Zac pushed forward with his legs and jumped headlong into a roll to avoid the swing, but somehow the leader changed trajectory mid-swing and still managed to nick Zac in the side. The cut drew blood but wasn't too deep, and fortunately, the black lightning didn't emerge again. It seemed the leader couldn't continuously use the skill.

Zac ignored the pain and quickly got on his feet and charged at the underling. The leader was right behind him, so he quickly swung his axe downward, hoping for a quick kill.

A thick group of roots shot up in front of the demon and meshed together into a wooden shield to intercept the swing. Zac's stats were overpowering, however, and he slammed through the roots easily. Woodchippings flew everywhere like small projectiles from the strike. Unfortunately for Zac, the brief pause in the swing had allowed the demon to reposition, and he could avoid the swing.

Zac felt an intense danger from behind, and he didn't dare hesitate. He jumped forward and crashed into the underling instead of swinging his axe again, pushing them both a few meters away and bringing both of them to the ground. As he jumped forward, he felt the wind move right above where his head had been, from a swing of the leader.

The demon spit out a mouthful of blood from the impact, but managed to wheeze a few words. A handful of vines shot out of the ground and stabbed into Zac's chest and legs, trying to bore further into him.

The pain was excruciating, but he could only ignore it and hope that his Endurance was enough to protect his innards from the roots. With a roar, he slammed down the axe. With his overbearing power, he completely destroyed the head of the demon and even created a crater where the axe-head hit the ground.

From jumping over until killing him had taken less than a second, giving the leader no time to stop him.

The roots that the demon had summoned didn't disappear, but they seemed to have stopped moving.

As Zac was jumping away from the body, another arrow soundlessly hit his leg, completely punching through it. The sharpness must have been extraordinary, as it didn't seem to slow down at all even with Zac's high defense.

Zac screamed in pain but could only ignore it for now. The leader was upon him with another swing that almost ended him.

Zac was prepared for the swing as they drew huge wide arcs. He lunged forward after dodging in order to get in closer as the swing had passed. It seemed that the demon had ample battle experience, though, and kneed Zac right in the face as he got close. The knee was imbued with the dark lightning, and this time, it zapped Zac straight in the head.

Getting a knee in the face was bad; getting electrocuted in the head by demon lightning was worse. The power of the leader was huge, and Zac was flung away from the strike. The impact nearly broke his neck, and Zac was blinded by the pain.

But he roared and charged in again as he landed. Another arrow whizzed down, but Zac managed to hunker down so it only ripped a flesh wound on his back. He needed to turn the fight into a close-combat brawl, which would render the great sword useless. It would also hopefully stop the intermittent arrows from coming, as the ranger would be hesitant to hit her leader.

He decided to meet the great sword head on in order to get in close. The demon had just used the lightning attack, and hopefully, he needed to wait or charge it up again. The axe and great sword met again in a stupendous clash. The trees in the vicinity were actually moving slightly from the even stronger shock wave, and an incoming arrow was pushed away before even coming close.

When Zac was standing, he could better utilize his strength, and this time, he wasn't pushed away. Shock was evident in the demon's eyes, and he tried to create some distance. But Zac wouldn't let him, so he pushed forward and grabbed the leader's legs, and they both fell over with a thump.

Zac wanted a repeat of his last kill and swung down his axe. However, he was still a bit fuzzy from the shock and in the heat of the moment accidentally hit next to the leader's head.

Zac refocused and started another swing, but the leader was fighting back. He punched Zac straight in the face and tried to push him away. The fist had the force of a wrecking ball, and a loud thud echoed out.

Zac got even groggier, but his constitution was no joke, so he could endure it. He also had been swinging an axe constantly for the last month, and muscle memory helped him. The half-moon edge swooped down toward the demon with superhuman force. As he had been pushed away, he couldn't reach the head and instead aimed for the heart.

Zac noticed a surge of Cosmic Energy entering the armor from the demon mid-swing, and the runes on the chest plate lit up. The wheels were already in motion, so Zac could only bear down and hope for the best.

Just as the edge was about to slam into the armor, a golden sheen enveloped the leader. The axe hit the barrier, and it felt like he had slammed the axe into himself rather than his enemy. The armor had somehow redirected the force back toward him, and he flew up in the air from the rebound.

He slammed down right next to the demon, arms and legs akimbo. The demon quickly whipped out a dagger and tried to plunge it in Zac's lungs just as he landed. He managed to barely edge away in time, but the dagger still drew a nasty gash along his ribs.

The demon kept stabbing down at Zac, trying to turn him into a sieve. The second stab hit straight into his arm, making Zac scream out. He tried to push down the demon again and wrestle the knife out of his hands with his own free hand, but the demon's strength was at least equal to his.

In a last desperate attempt, he could only pray his constitution wouldn't fail him. He let go of the demon's hand holding the dagger, and intercepted the hand that was holding back his axe.

The demon immediately plunged the dagger into his gut, once more unleashing the black lightning. The blazing pain once again erupted in Zac's body, but by now, he had somewhat acclimatized to the attack.

He ignored the spasms in his gut and ripped away the demon's hand and finally managed to swing his weapon down full force at the demon's neck.

A loud bang was heard as the axe slammed into the ground, creating a large crack. A second, smaller impact was heard as the demon's decapitated head fell down onto the ground a few meters away.

Another arrow whizzed down from a nearby tree toward his head. But Zac had expected this and dodged the attack. The ranger had shot a steady stream of arrows at him during the melee, most at least grazing him. Luckily, he had been in such close proximity to the demons during the fight that she had only dared aim at his extremities.

He finally saw where the arrows came from, and as all the other demons were dead, he finally managed to focus and locate the elusive ranger. He spotted her up in a tree not far away from the fight.

With a steely gaze that spoke of death, he got on his feet and started running toward her.

29

INSCRIPTIONS

Zac was kneeling next to the body of the female ranger, panting with exhaustion.

The hunt luckily had ended quite quickly. She had immediately tried to run when Zac started approaching, jumping from one tree to another. Her speed up among the branches had actually been slightly higher compared to his own down on the ground.

She likely was a Dexterity-based class. She even had the time to shoot a few arrows while fleeing. Zac was fully focused on keeping up, so could only manage to deflect the projectiles if they headed straight toward his head or chest. That was because he simply held his axe right in front of his throat, moving it slightly upwards or downwards to intercept the arrows.

Suddenly, as she had tried to jump to a branch on another tree, Zac had used a sneak attack with his last dagger. As she was in midair, he flung it with full force, punching a hole in her back.

She didn't immediately die from the attack, but she did fall down from the treetops. And before she managed to get back on her feet, Zac was upon her. He ended the fight with a swing without any words. He didn't want another suicide-bombing incident on his hands, after all.

It was lucky as well, because if that dagger hadn't hit, he'd likely have been forced to flee instead. He didn't want to try throwing his axe, as it was his most important tool for survival on the island. Then the enemy would have a detailed description of him and his power.

He grabbed her bag and found some cloths he assumed were for bandages. After a quick sniff to make sure that they weren't actually doused in some chemical or the like, he used them to bandage himself up. His whole body had holes punched in it, from everything between arrows and roots, and the bandages were only enough to treat the worst ones.

He was still bleeding, but it seemed that the wounds hadn't hit any major arteries or organs. By now, normal puncture wounds usually stopped bleeding on their own after a few hours. He could still tentatively put weight on the leg, but he wouldn't run a marathon. His whole body felt like he had been used as a punching bag, mainly from the black lightning of the leader.

Unfortunately, the ranger's bow had snapped when she fell down from the tree, so he didn't bother taking it with him as he planned to leave.

He did take the quiver and remaining arrows, though, as they had survived the fall. He also skipped taking the armor, as his axe had destroyed the whole thing.

After dragging the body into some thick bushes, he turned back toward the location of the fight with the others. After slowly walking back for a bit, he was there.

A barghest had found its way to the corpses from somewhere, but surprisingly, it didn't eat them. Zac had seen those demons eat everything, including members of their own race before, so it was interesting that this barghest only dared to sniff and growl anxiously at the corpses.

It reinforced Zac's suspicion that these demons were not wild animals, rather beasts reared by the humanoids. They were a good tool to use as a meat shield to weaken and tire the enemy. Of course, they didn't seem to work too well in the complicated terrain of the island. Zac edged to the beast and killed it with one strike as it was distracted by the bodies.

He didn't bother with it anymore and walked over to the leader. He was most excited about the gear on him, and it was largely intact. The fractals had protected the demon from Zac's strike on the chest, and the finishing blow had been on his head, which kept all the gear in good working order.

Zac, who was getting more and more adroit in undressing corpses, nimbly loosened the clasps and buckles and dragged the chest plate from him. He also gingerly touched the great sword, afraid that he would get zapped again.

Fortunately, there was no charge left, it seemed, and he picked it up. The sword was actually lighter than he expected. Of course, he was a bit unsure of his current Strength, so making exact measurements was hard.

He carefully looked at the weapon for some hidden function. The leader clearly had been unarmed one second, and in the next holding this monstrosity. It must have come from somewhere.

Zac suspected the sword might be able to grow and shrink on command, and it simply had been too small for him to notice before. Or the sword might be able to turn invisible.

After a quick rundown, he couldn't figure it out, and he did not want to delay too long here in case reinforcements arrived. He quickly stripped all the remaining items from the leader, including a pouch, a few runed bracelets, and the large knife.

He put all of it inside a backpack, then proceeded to do the same with the other two fighters. He left their weapons and armor, though, as he simply was overburdened as is. Just bringing back the sword would be arduous with his battered body.

Finally, he dragged the bodies away and looked over the battlefield. A discerning eye would quickly notice that a battle took place here, but Zac couldn't be too bothered anymore. This was the second scouting party he had killed, besides a herald and a throng of demons.

The humanoids would have to be crazy to not know that someone was hunting them by now. They had seen the trap used to kill the herald, so they knew it wasn't a beast either.

He wasn't too sure why they weren't scouring the island for him. He guessed they either had limited resources or were preoccupied with something else. Who knew, maybe there actually was a city with humans hidden in the mountains that waged war on the demons.

He put the axe into his belt, hefted the great sword over his shoulder, and turned back. He had been out for half the day and either had to turn back soon or sleep in one of his hideouts.

He decided to head back, as the fight had given him some insights about the inscribed items that he wanted to try out in a safe environment.

Zac started heading back on a slightly altered path. Even if he was hurt, it wasn't to the point that he couldn't hunt some demon dogs on the way back. The worst part was his leg, and luckily, the demons always came running, so he didn't have to chase them.

He soon ran into one and, with a swing of the great sword, completely split the barghest in two. The sword continued with its momentum and slammed into a tree, cutting clean through it.

The power was great, but it felt too unwieldy for jungle warfare. More importantly, Zac noticed that killing the barghest with the sword didn't improve his quest for Axe Mastery. On second thought, he felt it made sense that the kills had to be made with an axe to complete an Axe Mastery quest.

As he continued on, he had to continuously swap weapons every time he ran into a demon.

Finally, he arrived at his camp as the suns were starting to set. After the customary sweep, he entered the camp. He threw some lumber into the firepit and lit a small fire and got some more dried meat. He was starting to run low, so he'd have to hunt something edible tomorrow as well.

His wounds had actually turned a lot better during his hike back, as he hadn't sustained any new wounds from the lesser demons.

A quick glance at his status screen showed that he had gained roughly ten thousand Nexus Coins in one day. It made sense, as he had more than doubled the speed of killing barghest with his upgrades. Furthermore, the demons seemed to give out roughly a thousand Nexus Coins each.

Zac was somewhat surprised to find out that he actually had gained Nexus Coins and Cosmic Energy from the demon that the leader accidentally killed. He had somewhat felt the rush of energy during the fight, but at the time had been preoccupied with getting zapped by demon lightning.

He also felt that he had gained almost half a level from the intense fights. Risking your life really was the most effective way of getting stronger with the System.

His Axe Mastery had progressed as well, currently showing (69/1,000) progress. Most of the kills had been barghest while traveling, with a few of the more agile gwyllgi peppered in every now and then. Zac felt that if he put his mind to it, then he could kill roughly one hundred lower demons a day, which would allow him to complete the quest in another ten days.

He decided to put the ten days as a deadline. He would also match the quest for **[Chop]**, so he'd chop a thousand times a day. Zac figured it'd take somewhere around two hours per day to get it done. He had no real idea as of yet what to do with the last skill, as it still showed 0/30.

He turned his gaze toward the day's pile of loot after being finished with his meal. He had gained a whole new set of gear and a sundry of miscellaneous items in the backpacks. At the battle site, he hadn't had time to properly go through everything, so he planned to do so now.

The two underlings had had small leather bags that were attached to their belts on their backs. In them was nothing of value. They held some gauze, flint, a whetstone, a small knife that seemed to not be for battle, and a small water bottle. It felt like it was some basic ordnance.

Both the bottles had some very rudimentary inscriptions on them, so Zac wondered if they had some special function. He poured the water out, but was surprised that the small bottle held far more water than it should.

It took almost two minutes for all the water to pour out. Zac was amazed that some inscriptions could do something magical like this. He felt no Cosmic Energy movements around the bottles, and it looked normal when he peered inside.

The magic bottle gave him a new idea about the sudden appearance of the giant sword. If a bottle could somehow store a large amount of water, then it wasn't impossible that the leader had some similar gear that could store items.

30

EXPERIMENTATION

Zac eagerly filtered out all the gear that had belonged to the leader and started to go through it. His first guess was the inscribed bracelets, as they were the only things except the sword and chest plate that had fractals engraved.

He looked over them multiple times and tried pressing different parts of the bracelets, but nothing happened. He tried putting them on and focusing on them, but there still was no response. He could only helplessly put them aside for now and continue to look through the other gear.

Zac picked up the pouch and opened it up. Strangely, the inside was pitch black, and he couldn't see anything. His heart-beat sped up, and he felt that he had found the jackpot.

He first took one of the small knives and plunged it halfway into the darkness, then pulled it out. There was no damage on it at all as far as Zac could tell. He planned to do the same with his finger, but as soon as he barely put it into the darkness, he felt a burning sting.

His fingertip had been singed clean off, and blood dripped down over the pouch. Maybe flesh couldn't enter, he surmised. So he tried the same with a piece of dried meat, but this time, it reacted like the knife.

Maybe it's live things... Zac thought. He had no critter to try this theory out, though, so it would have to wait.

The next task was how to activate the pouch. He had noticed some hints when he had fought earlier. When he had slammed his axe into the chest of the leader, he had felt that Cosmic Energy had entered the armor from the demon.

Zac had always only circulated the energy internally and wasn't sure how he'd push it outside. He tried circulating some energy into his fingers, then tried to push it out from the tip. The only result was that the concentration of energy got too high at the fingertips, and they started rupturing.

He tried many different things for a few hours until he finally gave up. Zac guessed that there was an inherent problem with how he handled the energy. He had followed an image of a circulatory system of his blood when he had started bending Cosmic Energy to his will. Of course, he hadn't imagined it to have outlets where it could flow out.

He started mulling over how to improve his system. He tried imagining a hole at his palm where he could let Cosmic Energy flow out.

But as he changed his energy circulation, a blazing pain erupted in his hand, and it looked like a bloody stigmata had appeared where he had imagined his exit.

A cold sheen of perspiration appeared on Zac's forehead from the pain, and he had a sinking feeling. Just a small change like this and the pain had been this bad. If he wanted to improve the system on his whole body, how bad would it hurt?

He knew that the circulatory system he had devised in no way was an optimal method of using Cosmic Energy; it was just something he had whipped together. He had planned on getting some skill or method for it later when he had the opportunity. But he hadn't imagined that the pain would be this bad.

He was even more dismayed when he noticed that the hole he had created in his hand was continuously leaking Cosmic Energy and draining him of power.

Zac could only reluctantly change his circulation pattern back, bringing forth another wave of torment.

He sat for a full thirty minutes, feeling lost at what to do. He was afraid that he had somehow crippled his future prospects. The more he thought about it, the more he felt that it was extremely important to be able to project energy. The skills the demons had used all had projected energy in different ways. The mysterious mist, the black arcs of lightning, and the root control. They all relied on manipulating Cosmic Energy outside the body.

If he was stuck with this defective system where all the energy was stuck inside his body, would he even be able to use the skills he got in the future?

He needed to find a way to rectify this, even if he had to take the torture of rewriting his pathing. However, the hole he had made didn't work, and even if it did, he was hesitant to use that method anymore. He didn't want to haphazardly get himself deeper and deeper in the hole by making a crappy patchwork circulation method.

He went over to the Nexus Node once more to scour through the skills, in case one of them actually was a circulation skill or something similar. Of course, he subconsciously knew that wasn't the case; he had looked those skills over many times by now and knew there was no such thing there.

The skills available generally could be categorized into offensive, defensive, movement, and support, as far as he could tell. The **[Eye of Discernment]** would fall into the support skill.

But as he moved his hand away from the crystal, he suddenly froze, struck with a realization. All things connected to the

System had one thing in common: the fractals. He still had no idea how to make sense of them, but they were present on the array flags, the weapons, and even the skills used them.

And it just so happened, he knew a pattern that was the exact size of his body. It was the fractal pattern that he had seen when he chose his class. Many details of it had been muddled at the time, but the parts he could make out made a full circuit.

When he got the idea, he couldn't let it go. The more he thought it over, the more it made sense. He could still remember the pattern clearly, and it flowed through every part of his body. It was a far more complicated system compared to the one he had devised himself, but he saw no reason that it wouldn't work.

As for the parts that were hazy and blurred, they might show themselves at a later point when he leveled up or completed quests, at which point Zac could use the new information to improve on the existing pattern.

The only problem was the massive undertaking to change the circulation. Just adding and removing a small hole in his hand had felt like putting the palm in an imp's fire. He wasn't even sure he'd survive such an undertaking.

But at the same time, he didn't dare wait. When he first devised the energy circulation, he'd made some small revisions quickly after. At that time, he hadn't felt any pain whatsoever and assumed that the circulation pattern was just a mental aid for using Cosmic Energy.

Zac was afraid that it might mean that the pattern became harder and harder to change, as though it was fusing with his very being. It was still possible for him to change it, but judging from the pain, it might be impossible soon.

Zac was no stranger to pain by now and wasted no time. Ideally, he would have wanted to wait until all his wounds were healed, but he had a sense of urgency. He started with his left hand to try if it even was viable to reform the patterns.

A blazing pain far worse than when he'd opened the hole engulfed his hand. It felt like his whole arm was dipped in burning acid. His whole body was covered in sweat in just seconds, and his eyes were completely bloodshot. Still, he pushed through and kept imagining the crude system in his hand slowly transforming into the fractal he had been given by the Hatchetman class.

After what felt like an eternity, the transformation was done. His hand was a mess, almost looking as if it had been pushed down into a blender. But where there once was a simple pathway for Cosmic Energy was now a sophisticated pattern that had substituted it.

Zac tried moving his fingers, and while it hurt, it seemed there was no permanent damage. He then tried to circulate Cosmic Energy through his arm and into his rewritten pathways.

It was a weird feeling. He had thought his circulation had been smooth all this while. But after pushing the energy into his hand, it felt like the energy came from cramped pipes in his arms into the open ocean in his hand. The level of smoothness of handling the energy was incomparable.

Zac knew he had guessed correctly by now. The class change had provided him with a complete pattern to utilize his Cosmic Energy. It would likely tie in with his skills as well, he reckoned.

He also knew what that meant and, with a shudder, started converting the rest of his body.

31

INFUSION

The suns were starting to rise over the small campsite.

Zac sat naked except for a pair of ragged underpants, in a cross-legged position by the now died out fire. The ground all around him was red with his blood. There was not one spot on Zac's body that wasn't damaged and bloody.

He had relentlessly continued to improve his circulation pattern the whole night, and he was almost completed by now. It had felt like he had been thrown into hell and had been tortured for an eternity. He had wanted to stop so many times, but had summoned willpower he didn't know he had to keep going.

Of course, that didn't mean that he had stoically endured the pain like some battle-hardened warrior. Luckily, there had been no one around to see him scream himself hoarse, roll around on the ground, and cry until snot ran down his face.

Right now, only the part around his brain remained to be changed. In the class pattern, it was a dense web of fractals that covered his whole head.

Zac hadn't stopped due to changing his mind, but the pain in his head had made him pass out for a few minutes after he tried it the first time. He was currently steadying himself for another try.

He shakily got up and snatched all the remaining dried meat he had left over. He felt severely drained and needed some energy before trying again. He also filled his water bottle from his array and poured it over himself to clean away some of the blood. The sting of cold water over his countless cuts jolted him properly awake.

Finally, he sat down again to complete the fractal. He was afraid if he didn't complete it now, he wouldn't dare to sit down and do it in the future. The pain was to the point of creating a mental scar, and he needed to do it immediately to get it done.

He started changing the pattern a small bit at a time, afraid that he'd pass out again if he improved too large a chunk in one go. Still, the pain was barely within the realm he could tolerate. It felt like a spike was stabbed through his eye right into his head and then started grinding around in there for good measure.

Zac arduously pressed on, tears flowing like a waterfall. Finally, after an hour, the last piece was changed, and the fractal was whole and connected. Zac suddenly puked out a mouthful of blood, but immediately after felt very refreshed.

He still had acute blood loss and was hurting all over, but his body felt lighter and better. He tried circulating some Cosmic Energy and was shocked at the improvement. To compare it with before, it felt like previously he had breathed and blinked manually when pushing Cosmic Energy through his body, and now it was an automatic and natural process.

It was if the energy knew what he wanted to do, and followed his will automatically. It also seemed that he absorbed energy from the surroundings faster, and not by a small margin. It wouldn't help with his level, but it would help him to heal and restore his energy reserves faster.

Finally done with the fractal, he closed his eyes and had a dreamless sleep.

Zac woke up again roughly three hours later. While he felt

drained and still hurting, he wasn't bleeding anymore. With his improved stats, he only needed to sleep a few hours a day to feel rested, and he had no problems skipping sleep entirely for a night or two. The combination of high Endurance and Vitality showed its value once again.

He had initially planned on scouting out the actual incursion today, but decided against it. He wanted to be in optimal condition for whatever waited for him at the end of the rainbow. He needed to find something to eat as well, and it felt safer to grind out some lower beasts while he was incapacitated.

His wounds from yesterday's battle had also improved significantly, with only the leg still smarting.

There was one thing he had to do before setting out, though. An important reason why he had tortured himself during the night was the inscribed gear.

Zac was relieved to notice that he could project energy easily now from his upgrade. He couldn't actually see the Cosmic Energy with his eyes, but he could sense it. It was a weird feeling; it was as though he had gotten a new sense since starting to use Cosmic Energy, and with his upgraded pathways, the sense only seemed stronger. The Cosmic Energy was floating like an invisible mist above his hand that projected it, not showing any signs of dissipating.

His first goal was to check the pouch, as it contained the most mystery for him. He picked up the small pouch and carefully infused some energy into it. He was shocked to notice that the pouch actually suddenly absorbed all the dried blood on his hand.

He didn't have time to think it over, though, as he suddenly saw a large space in his mind. The space was roughly three by three meters and was filled with an assortment of items.

There was another sword inside, also with inscriptions. But this one was a far more normal size compared to its monstrous brother. There were some random tools, a water bottle and a flagon made in silver in one corner. The flagon seemed to have similar fractals as the water bottle, albeit a bit more intricate.

There was also a large reserve of luxurious dishes and fruits in another corner.

More surprisingly, there was an actual table, a parasol, a rug, and two ornate chairs in the space. Zac dumbly stared at the furniture, not knowing how to react. Was the demon invading another world, or was he out on a picnic?

He didn't dare take any of the food, as he had no idea whether the food demons ate was edible for humans. While it looked perfectly normal, who knew if they used cyanide as a spice?

The final items in the corner were a few books and a small pile of crystals. Each crystal was uniform in shape and roughly the size of his palm. He couldn't understand the language in the books at all and could only put them aside for now.

The crystals were more interesting, and he tried to mentally extract one from the pouch. Suddenly, the crystal appeared next to the pouch. Zac grabbed it in the air and started to examine it. It wasn't translucent, but rather a milky white, and cool to the touch. It seemed to emit a faint white light as well.

More interestingly, Zac could feel that the small stone was packed with Cosmic Energy. It was as if his senses were telling him that he wasn't holding a small shiny crystal, but a shining sun of energy.

He remembered that his quests had something called Nexus Crystals as a reward for completing, and guessed he was holding one right now. More impressively, he had roughly one hundred of them in his pouch.

Of course, Zac knew that there was a distinct possibility that this was an F-grade Nexus Crystal rather than an E-grade crystal like the ones that the quests rewarded. It would be odd if he got a hundred crystals from just one enemy if he only received ten for conquering a whole incursion by himself.

He tried absorbing some energy from the crystal, and a pure stream of energy quickly entered his body and energized him. His slightly depleted body was quickly energized, and he was happy to notice that the absorption continued even after his body was "satiated." That meant that absorbing the crystals would work toward gaining levels and not only be a tool for recuperating after a draining battle.

Zac sat and absorbed the crystal for roughly thirty minutes before he stopped. After scrutinizing the crystal, it seemed that he had absorbed roughly a quarter of the stored energy. So completely absorbing it would take roughly two hours. Furthermore, absorbing just one crystal seemed equivalent to killing roughly ten barghest and absorbing their energy.

That meant if he only sat down and used these stones to cultivate, it would actually be more effective compared to running all over the island, killing demon dogs with all his might.

Of course, he wouldn't get any Nexus Coins, but still.

These crystals would be a huge asset for him. There were always times he couldn't be killing beasts. Like when cooking, chopping wood, and even moving between the demons while out hunting. If he could keep absorbing these crystals during all this downtime, he could double his leveling speed.

Next, he walked over to the great sword and tried infusing it with cosmic power as well. However, it was as though the energy was blocked when trying to enter, which stumped Zac. After a brief hesitation, he cut his finger and dripped a few drops of blood on the runes before trying again. He remembered the pouch absorbing his blood, and could only try the same method again.

This time, he felt no resistance as the blood was absorbed into the sword. Information once again entered his mind, this time the usage of the sword. It seemed that the sword could increase and decrease its weight, albeit the effect was quite limited. That might have explained why he slammed into the ground so helplessly in the first clash between him and the leader; he might have maximized the weight for the overhead swing.

Next, he did the same procedure on his axe. Infusing it with energy had no earth-shattering effect. It had a weak auto-repair and sharpen feature. As long as he infused some Cosmic Energy into it, it would gradually fix nicks in the edge and resharpen.

It didn't improve the lethality, but it was convenient for him, who didn't have proper facilities for weapons maintenance.

He finally turned to his last inscribed gear and with the same procedure tried to activate the bracers he had nabbed from the leader. To his surprise, nothing happened when he tried activating them.

32

VANITY

Zac tried everything he could think of to activate the bracers, and by the end, they were completely drenched in his blood. Still, there simply was no response from the items. They might just as well have been normal iron hoops.

Struck with realization, Zac had an odd expression as he turned his eyes toward the almost comically large sword. Then he summoned the furniture out of the pouch. They had an elaborate ostentatious design, and the two chairs almost felt like thrones.

The bracers were fake. That was the most likely answer he could come up with. The demon had wanted to look impressive, bringing luxurious furniture and foods, a heroic great sword, and a dashing breastplate. Perhaps he had wanted to give an even more extravagant impression, so he'd equipped himself with these fake bracers.

The female archer was a beauty... Zac reflected wryly. Had this demon tried to turn the scouting mission into a courtship outing?

That would explain why he'd never used the bracers during the battle, even when they were in a bloody dogfight.

It seemed crazy to Zac that the demon would be so indifferent to the dangers of invading an unknown world, but he also knew he himself was an anomaly. He both had the highest level in the world and a bunch of titles, making him extremely strong for only one month having passed since the integration into the Multiverse.

Had a normal human, or even a group of humans, met the demon, they'd likely have been easily butchered. The demon leader hadn't expected that his life was in jeopardy on this seemingly deserted island.

Zac didn't expect that the demons would underestimate him for long, though. Killing Vul could be explained by him tricking it into killing itself on the poles. But now seven demons had died in a short while, a few of which were pretty strong.

He left the furniture where it was, as they were pretty good-looking after all. He also needed to free up some space in his new pouch in any case.

As half the day had already passed, he hurriedly set out. He was mostly decked in the demon leader's gear now, not including the great sword, of course.

He was starting to get quite hungry and needed to find some prey. Luckily for him, it seemed that the thick energy in the atmosphere was great for the animal population.

The native animals grew much faster, and bigger, compared to before. From what he had seen in his hunts, some were already stronger than the barghest and used them as prey. Most didn't seem to be quite there yet, however.

It was a bit troubling, though, for the world in general. The animals seemed to grow strong faster than humans did. Either they were more suited for absorbing Cosmic Energy, or the System helped them somehow.

Not long ago, he'd killed a human-sized rabbit. Would he have to fight a train-sized snake in the future?

He soon found a small critter while walking, and tried throwing it into his pouch after catching it. He was surprised to see that it didn't work. Nothing happened as he tried to put the struggling squirrel inside.

Zac could only surmise that putting living beings inside didn't work. He was a bit confused why the critter didn't get zapped like the tip of his finger, but it didn't feel like an important distinction.

There was no need to kill the critter, as the demon had stored both beverage and food inside the pouch with no problems.

When he was a good distance away from the camp, he found a hole created by a fallen tree. He threw in all the food and drink the demon had stored, and also the two bracers. He was pretty sure they were fake, but he didn't want to keep them in the camp on the off chance their function was tracking their location, like a revenge-killing tool.

He wasn't worried about running out of food on the island, as it was teeming with wildlife, and many trees were bearing fruit as well. He filled the pit quickly after throwing it all in, and with his strength, he was as efficient as an excavator.

With the unnecessary things in the pouch thrown away, he continued on his journey. He was still hurting from both the fight and the conversion, so he simply killed barghest at the outskirts of the island.

He also managed to find a supersized boar that would last him a good while, even with his enhanced appetite. He was surprised to see that the animal actually gave some Nexus Coins and experience now. However, he only gained a minuscule amount of energy and twenty-one Nexus Coins.

It also gave progress on his Axe Mastery class. It seemed that something had changed lately with the beasts. The boar was quite a bit stronger than a normal human, but it wasn't quite at the level of a barghest. It also didn't seem too much stronger compared to the snake he had killed a month ago, yet the snake had given no currency for the kill. Neither had any other animal he had killed for leather or food.

Perhaps something had changed with the passage of the first month for the animal kingdom, just as it had with the incursion. Zac didn't mind, as it only meant that there were more targets to practice on now.

It was a marvelous feeling fighting with his new and improved circulation pathways. Being able to use magic items and project Cosmic Energy wasn't the only benefit. His powers hadn't really increased, as there still was the limit of how much Cosmic Energy his muscles could take in. But the energy flowed far more smoothly through his body, making it effortless to switch between attack, defense, and movement seamlessly.

He also seemed to use up less energy while fighting, as somehow the new pathways were more efficient. He wasn't too surprised at that, as he had surmised that his usage before had been inefficient since the start. He had noticed how much energy was wasted pushing it into his muscles compared to using his skill **[Eye of Discernment]**.

Higher efficiency meant he'd fare better in a protracted battle. Maybe he wouldn't have been so haggard after killing Vul if he'd had this level of Endurance.

He kept killing demons and animals for the rest of the day, only returning to camp when the suns had practically set. His pouch was full of various large beasts he had killed. He thought he might as well stock up on dried meat in case something happened.

He also wanted to try just leaving some slabs of meat in the pouch, just to see how well they kept.

The fruits that the demon had kept in the pouch before were things he had never seen before, meaning it must have brought them from his home planet. They still looked pristine as though they were just plucked, so Zac hoped that the pouch would also work like a portable freezer.

That would come in handy in case of the weather changing.

The weather had been great since the world changed, with only a smattering of clouds in the sky every now and then.

It seemed the trees didn't suffer from the lack of rain. On the contrary, the forest had kept growing and mutating at an astonishing rate. Zac assumed it had to do with the Cosmic Energy in the atmosphere. It might work as a substitute for both sunshine and water for all he knew.

The island felt tropical by now, like the island was a primordial forgotten vestige at the edge of the world, where dinosaurs and other prehistorical beasts could be found.

That meant that there might come a tropical rain season. Zac really didn't hope that was the case, seeing as everything had gotten bigger and more extreme since the integration into the Multiverse. What would a torrential downpour powered by Cosmic Energy look like?

It took the better part of the night to skin and clean the beasts. He simply threw the skins on top of the car, not really bothered whether they dried properly or not. He didn't really have any use for skins anymore, as the pouch and better armors kept him covered.

He was somewhat disappointed to see that he was unable to absorb Cosmic Energy from a Nexus Crystal while doing other tasks. He first tried putting it in a pocket while he was cleaning a carcass, but he couldn't sense the stone when he did.

Having it in one of his hands was too unwieldy and slowed down his progress on the meat considerably. Finally, he stuffed the crystal in his mouth, hoping the contact with his body would make it possible to absorb the energy without occupying a hand.

The only result from that was that he almost choked himself to death on the energy rock. After a few more experiments, he could conclude that he only could absorb Cosmic Energy from one crystal at a time and that he had to completely focus on the absorption for it to work. As soon as he tried to multitask while absorbing a crystal, the absorption simply would stop.

Disappointed, he could only put aside the crystal and keep it for a later date. He was planning on saving some of them in any case, as he wanted to give them to his father and sister when they met again. They were nifty, but only of limited use for him. But for people of lower levels, they'd be a great tool.

If they could be used to help his family protect themselves better, they were worth saving, even if it meant slowing down his own leveling speed slightly.

33

INFECTION

Zac awoke at the light of dawn, and after preparing an assortment of tools in his pouch, he set out. Today, he would properly gather intelligence. His wounds were largely better now, just a bit red and sore.

He made a beeline for the incursion this time, heading straight toward the center of the island. Large parts would be uncharted territory for him here, as he had stayed somewhat at the outer edge since the start.

He had a theory that there should be a fourth kind of beast somewhere on the island that he still hadn't seen.

There were four heralds, and at least one herald was a pack leader of its race, the barghest. But he had only encountered imps and the gwyllgi apart from the hunkering demonlings.

There should be a fourth type of beast as well somewhere based on this, and Zac guessed that they either were located around the incursion or had moved their territory into the mountains.

Zac kept a rapid pace, moving at a speed that could be considered a sprint for a normal human. Still he made no sound as he passed through the forest, instinctively knowing where to put his feet to soundlessly proceed.

During his travels, he noticed that his third class skill, **[Forester's Constitution]**, had finally had its first progression either during last evening or this morning, now showing 1/30. The problem was that he wasn't quite sure what he did to progress it. The System gave no ping or notification when his quests progressed, leaving him with no information on when it happened.

A log of his actions would have been very convenient, as then he wouldn't have to estimate his Nexus Coin gain from monsters or how much energy they gave all the time.

After he had moved for roughly ten hours, he finally slowed down. He was far closer to the incursion now than he had ever been before. This close, he started to notice some jarring changes. For lack of a better word, the forest was *infected.* The red light of the incursion suffused all the surroundings, and the trees looked different, almost sickly.

Some had weird growths on them; others seemed to have completely lost all their leaves, even though the summer was in full swing. The grass on the forest floor was turning a purplish color. There were also many young sprouts of a pitch-black tree Zac had never seen before, which seemed to thrive in this odd environment. The very air seemed to be different as well, having an almost astringent taste. It didn't seem to be a problem for Zac, luckily, apart from feeling uncomfortable.

It seemed like the red pillar was slowly transforming its surroundings, likely to better suit the invaders. This made Zac even more anxious to complete his quest, as he didn't know if this effect was reversible and whether it would spread outwards. He didn't want to create his town on a desolate island that smelled a bit like farts.

He also was astonished at the number of beasts he saw. It

seemed that all the demons preferred to stay in this environment, and the forest was packed with monsters. He shuddered at the thought of this horde of beasts being unleashed upon a human city. Luckily, they were stranded here on this island.

It also made him realize that it might not have been more beasts spawning during his month of grinding, it was enough that a few strays would leave the central area of the island for the edge of the island to be refilled.

What would've looked like hell for many, Zac saw as a treasure trove. He almost drooled at the prospect of grinding here, but he had a mission today. Most human cultivators would likely have trouble killing one barghest since they had their upgrade, but Zac had no trouble facing multiple at a time by now. He might get a few bites and scratches if there were too many of them, but that wouldn't be anything new for him.

Those plans could only wait, though. He needed to gauge the magnitude of the invasion to make a proper plan. There was a lot to do in the coming month. Of course, he wouldn't hide from the beasts either, so everything that entered his path was met with a swift swing of his axe.

By now, he was only a couple of kilometers away from the incursion, so he started to slow down and focus fully on stealth. He did not want to enter combat again this close to the enemy base. Who knew what kind of forces they had.

The incursion was in a valley, which stretched toward the mountains, and Zac gingerly moved toward the edge to see what was happening inside.

As he was almost at the crest, he saw a solitary demon sitting next to a tree, currently napping. Zac was again shocked at their bad discipline, and it felt like the whole invasion was handled by a group of undisciplined children rather than an army. If he thought that the horde of barghest around the valley would be enough protection and give prior warning of an attack, then he was sorely mistaken.

After slowly looking at the vicinity to ensure there were no more scouts around, he approached the demon soundlessly. He didn't bother to identify him, afraid he would sense the scrying. When he was ten meters away, he switched gears to a sprint, brandishing his axe.

The demon woke in the last moment and made a terrified expression. He didn't have any time to activate any defenses or shout for help, though, as the axe descended and cleanly decapitated him.

Zac quickly grabbed the head and put it on top of the body before hiding again. He had already scrubbed his face with some dirt, giving him a grayish complexion similar to the demons. With his gear already of demonic design, he should probably pass as a demon from a cursory glance from a long distance. Of course, if anyone took a second glance, he'd be found out instantly, so he didn't want to try it out.

He stayed next to the corpse and wormed closer to the edge. This part of the valley ended with a steep cliff, meaning that Zac would have to scale down twenty meters if he wanted to enter. But it also meant that he got a good view of the whole vale.

If the other parts of the wood had started to shift into a demon forest, then the valley looked like it was imported from another world. It was as though even the sky was different up above, feeling washed out and gray.

There should have been a great deal of vegetation just like the rest of the island, but it was sparse and looking sickly. There also was evidence of a large amount of felling, as he saw hundreds of cut-off stumps. The combination made the valley look completely desolate. The ground was partly covered with smatterings of purplish black grass, but most was just black stone.

The demons clearly needed lumber for something. But for

what, Zac couldn't tell so far. His eyes kept going over the valley until finally looking over to the huge red pillar.

Zac could finally see the terminus of the incursion for the first time since he had arrived. It was a huge crystal that reminded Zac of the Nexus Node at his base. However, this crystal was red and at least three meters tall.

The very air around it pulsated from the power the crystal emitted, and Zac could feel the huge energy that it released all the way from his hiding place. It continuously shot out the light that formed the large pillar that had been a constant part of his life for the last month. The glow was so strong that he couldn't see anything of what was happening behind it.

Next to the pillar was a building, and Zac could see a few demons milling about.

Zac planted himself within a bush, and while gnawing on some meat he had brought in his pouch, he started waiting. After waiting for a full three hours, he felt confident that there likely were limitations to the invasion.

He had not seen a single being appear from the crystal, nor disappear into it. Either they only came at certain times per day, or they couldn't go back and forth between the island and their home world. The demons at the small building seemed to be guards left there just to make sure nothing happened to the crystal.

They were mostly milling about or even taking naps in the shade of the house.

Of course, Zac would have to stay for a good while longer if he wanted to confirm that the gate was closed, and he didn't have time for that. However, it made sense that they could only enter at certain intervals, from how the demons had appeared on the island.

The first-wave assault had been the demonic beasts, and they'd arrived as soon as the world was integrated. The second wave was the humanoids, who'd arrived after a month had passed.

At the same time, some limitations had lessened on the beasts, making them stronger.

If the crystal only opened once a month, it would explain why Abby the eye had told him to finish the quest either within one month or within two. It stood to reason that the difficulty would take another noticeable leap within a month.

Zac was not sure if he would be able to handle that, as he was not powering up as quickly anymore as before. He had already gotten his class now, and gaining levels took more time now compared to earlier. The increase in Strength he could gain within thirty days would likely be smaller compared to the one before, meaning that he really should try to end this invasion sooner rather than later.

As nothing was really happening on this side of the valley, he decided to keep venturing further in. He moved along the edge of the valley in a roundabout manner toward the mountains.

The incursion and valley were located between the middle and the north of the island, while the mountains took up almost all of the northern quadrant. So Zac soon had travelled across the whole island, starting from his campsite in the far south.

Daylight was starting to wane, but Zac had already prepared himself to sleep outside today. While he was advancing, he was keeping a lookout for possible temporary places to spend a night unnoticed. He had found some potential spots, but hadn't bothered to prepare them yet.

During his travels, he had killed four more demons. They were quite sparsely placed, making Zac more and more convinced that they were not too concerned about invasion in the immediate vicinity.

Soon he had walked along half the valley, and he could now see what was hidden earlier behind the red glow.

There actually was a town down there.

On a second look, a town would be a slight misnomer. The

buildings were quite large and rectangular, reminding Zac rather of barracks than civilian domiciles. He noticed that the missing trees had been processed into houses and fortifications. There were a few structures that seemed more refined, maybe for the officers and generals of the army. Those buildings did use both stone and lumber in their construction and had a quite elegant atmosphere.

The whole settlement was surrounded by a wall that was a few meters tall and at least thick enough to have watchtowers and a large number of guards patrolling. Zac couldn't fathom how they'd set up such a large wall in only a few days. He could only explain it with magic, as even hundreds of individuals with Zac's strength would have to work for months of gathering stones and setting up the wall.

Finally, in the middle of the town, a grand structure was being erected at a speed visible even from his great distance.

34

CONSPIRACIES

Ogras Azh'Rezak was already starting to tire of this whole enterprise. The humidity of this baby world was far higher compared to what he was used to, and the two blaring suns forced him to keep squinting through the day. The terraforming was helping, but it would still take a long time until the climate got to the point it was comfortable.

He somewhat regretted exhorting his ancestor to let him lead this invasion. With his status in the clan, he still would have been entitled to any good items they could seize on this world, even if he stayed at home.

But he knew this invasion was his opportunity if he wanted to stay alive. If he could find enough goodies for either himself or the clan, he'd be safe until he was strong enough to protect himself.

But who would have thought that the Ruthless Heavens would place them on a godforsaken island? It had rendered his tactic of unleashing his packs through the portal seem like a joke. There had already been voices of disagreement in the clan to such a cowardly tactic, but Ogras had only sneered at their snide remarks.

While most baby worlds were disorganized and paralyzed from the huge changes, some were quite dangerous. There were many anecdotes of new planets resisting and even sometimes completely massacring all the different invaders.

Of course, it was usually the forces behind the other incursions on the planet that were the real enemies, rather than the weak natives.

In any case, he wasn't about to stick his neck through a portal before increasing his odds of survival, even if it was considered cowardly.

His seven elder brothers had been heroic warriors, always charging into the fray, leading any charge in skirmishes. And now they were all food for the maggots. Some had been killed by their enemies, and some had died from machinations of their own clan members.

The path to power was ruthless, and even among kin, benefits preceded loyalty. There had been a large amount of dissatisfaction toward his branch of the clan for a long time. His great-grandfather had originally been a normal soldier who managed to rise to his great power through a few lucky encounters.

His prowess had allowed his progeny to enjoy great benefits and resources, even matching that of the main branch's youth. Ogras suspected that was why his siblings kept dropping dead one after another. He had voiced such concerns to his ancestor, but being a warrior for the clan his whole life, his thought patterns had become rigid. He had bled and fought for the clan for over a thousand years and couldn't imagine that they would backstab him and his kin like that.

That was why only the two of them were left, not counting his great-aunt, who disappeared to become a wandering warrior two hundred years ago. That was also why he kept this ridiculous persona going, pretending to have become a pampered wastrel not interested in cultivation. The fewer of his clan members who believed he was a threat, the lower was the chance he'd wake up with his throat slit.

That was why he walked around in his gaudy outfits and surrounded himself with useless sycophants. It was another type of armor. And if he could further his ambitions while it looked like he was just being spiteful and stupid, then all the better.

He had almost laughed out loud when the news of the death of Kevoran arrived at his desk. That little prick from the main branch was one of his largest contenders for any potential goodies that would be found on this planet.

While Kevoran was afraid of his ancestor, only the youths and unevolved were able to go through the portal. So his attitude had progressively gotten worse with each day since they arrived. Ogras had used a snide remark as a basis for ordering him to go with a scout's squad to canvass the whole island, in order to solidify his position while Kevoran was gone.

Who knew the idiot actually would get himself killed? It was a bit of a shame with Kaela dying as well, as her scouting abilities were top-notch among the youths in the clan. But the death of Kevoran more than made up for it. Ogras could kiss the assailant on the mouth if he found him. Just before decapitating him, of course.

Ogras wasn't overly concerned about the little rats that were hiding on this or some neighboring island. He estimated the number of enemies to be somewhere between ten to twenty, judging from the number of beasts killed. There certainly had to be some elites on this world to be able to kill even his imps and two scouting parties this soon after their world changed, but it didn't matter.

He was well aware of the rules by which the Ruthless Heavens worked. As long as he stayed safe in his palace, then his mission would be a success in roughly two months. The portal would stabilize, and the area would be within his jurisdiction.

The natives' group would have to infiltrate his army base, kill their way through the army, and then kill him in order for their quest to succeed. No matter how strong they were, they still were only weak natives, and such an assault was suicide.

If they had actually been truly strong, they wouldn't have been forced to use trickery to kill his poor Vul. They would simply have slaughtered all his four pack leaders and stopped the invasion before it even started.

Therefore, he would simply stay in the base. Even if everyone thought he was a coward, he didn't care. He had already planned everything out. He didn't plan on staying for too long in this world.

Initially, he had planned to stay here for a long time, protected from his clan by the limitations of the gate. It was an advantage for him that he could finally cultivate in peace here without anyone finding out, as the suppression would keep his real prowess hidden in any case.

But something had changed this. The mountain contained treasure.

More exact, it contained a Nexus Crystal mine. Even Ogras had been shocked when he heard the news. Of course, it was only a small F-grade mine, but still, the wealth it contained was staggering. It could at least rival the whole accumulated fortune of some of the elders in the clan.

With that kind of wealth, he could obtain a Fruit of Ascension. It would save him decades on his cultivation time and would leave his competitors among his generation in the dust. Normally, for a clan of their limited power, using such a luxurious treasure on an F-grade cultivator would be considered far too extravagant. But for him, it was a matter of life and death.

The supreme elders and clan leader usually turned a blind eye to killings within the clan, as they believed it created stronger and more ruthless members among those who survived.

But if someone showed enough promise, they would protect their seedlings from the shadows, as they were potential future powerhouses that could bring their clan to greater heights.

And if he just so happened to pilfer enough crystals for him to cultivate in solitude for a decade or so, he could come back one advancement, maybe even two, stronger. Then he'd be the hunter instead of the hunted.

Ogras was giddy as he looked over the report containing yesterday's haul from the mine. He hesitated a bit and then with a swipe removed a few lines of the report and added back a new tally. This time the extracted number of crystals printed was one thousand lower compared to before.

Unfortunately, he wasn't the only one who had this kind of idea. There had been quite a few children with good heritage that had come with him into the incursion. Everyone was hoping to find the lucky break that would allow them to stand out among the masses.

It was tacitly approved by the elders that the young elite would have a feeding frenzy when they arrived at the new world, as some healthy competition was good for strengthening. As long as enough benefits were lugged back, they did not really care that some didn't make it all the way.

As Ogras was pondering his next steps, the door to his temporary study opened, and a man decked out in extravagant armor entered.

This time, Ogras was angered for real, as such conduct was a blatant disregard for his authority. Still, he wouldn't break character for something minor like this.

"Insolence! How dare you enter my chambers like this! I will have my grandfather flog you when we return!" Ogras roared as soon as the man was inside the door.

"My apologies," the man answered with a face that spoke of

no regret. "I wonder what steps you have taken to capture those responsible for my cousin's death."

The man in front of him was Rydel Azh'Rezak, one of the heirs to the main branch just like the departed Kevoran. Different from him though, Rydel was one of the most heavily nurtured youths in the clan and also one they had spent the most Nexus Crystals to allow to retain as much power as possible when going through the incursion.

The more power you retained in an invasion to a baby world, the better your survival rate would be, and the better your position would be when contending for resources on this new world. But the Ruthless Heavens never just gave anything for free. It charged an exorbitant number of Nexus Crystals if one wanted to keep more of their strength when passing through. And of course there was a limit, or the purpose of the incursions would be lost.

Clan Azh'Rezak wasn't overly wealthy and could only pay up to a point for each daemon going through. Any more and the risk of the invasion turning unprofitable would be too big. The rest would have to come out of their own pockets.

Most of the soldiers couldn't afford it or only got a few levels extra, but the scions of their clan, of course, got some special benefits under the table, either from their elders or even from the clan itself.

Maybe not even Ogras himself was a match for Rydel, though he had a few hidden aces in case they ever came to blows. And it might actually come to that, as Ogras had a strong suspicion that Rydel had been sent through the portal to both keep an eye on things and, if possible, neutralize him. That would eliminate any threat of a branch family becoming too strong in the clan.

"The crystal mine isn't going anywhere, and it would seem a waste to attach such large manpower to quickly excavate it. Also, a large portion of our mages are occupied building your… palace. In my opinion, it would be more pertinent to…"

"It doesn't matter what your opinion is, Rydel. The clan decided I was the most suited for this task, so my orders are what goes. Now leave my study, and remember your manners in the future, or there will be repercussions!" Ogras practically screamed, looking very much the part of a fool enjoying his newfound power.

Rydel only sneered and performed a barely acceptable salute and left the study without another word.

Left silently brooding behind his desk, Ogras prayed that the natives and Rydel would find and kill each other, solving all his problems at once.

35

THE FOURTH BEAST

Zac sat perched on a branch in a large tree, eating an apple he had foraged earlier. The tree was one of the few in the vicinity that still stood tall and unaffected by the corrosive effect of the incursion, and its dense branches provided natural insulation from prying eyes. He had chosen this tree to be his temporary shelter to spend the night yesterday.

He had spent two nights close to the incursion now, trying to gain as much information as possible. Yesterday, he had kept scouting around the demon city and up toward the mountains.

He had made some interesting discoveries. First of all, he had realized how the third skill quest progressed. It was based on time. It seemed that he had to be out in the forests fighting roughly eighteen hours for the quest to progress by one point. That meant that he had to spend most of his time awake fighting every day. He didn't mind, though, as he was planning on doing that anyway.

But it also meant that it would be an extremely close shave to actually manage to complete it before the two-month deadline. He had already decided he didn't dare to wait; he'd kill at least the two remaining heralds as soon as possible. He didn't want to repeat what happened with Vul, being incapacitated and missing his deadline due to waiting until the last moment. He needed time to recuperate in case he got hurt from the fights.

He had also found the fourth type of beasts that the demons had brought through the portal. They were magic monkeys. Or rather, they were called stone monkeys by his **[Eye of Discernment]** and did not look quite as demonic as the other three animals.

They were roughly up to his chest in height but had a bulkier build. They were an anthracite gray and surprisingly had no fur. Instead, it looked like they had plates of rocks covering most parts of their bodies, forming almost a natural armor. The aspect that made them look somewhat demonic was their shining red eyes.

The stone monkeys were the most well-rounded of all the demon beasts so far. The barghest was all brawn and no brain, the gwyllgi high speed but low strength, and the imps were incredibly dangerous but also incredibly frail.

The stone monkeys were strong, agile, and also durable. Even more annoyingly, they seldom moved alone. They seemed to be united in one large group, and Zac suspected that the fourth herald was the pack leader. He hadn't seen it, however, as he didn't dare venture too far into the mountains, as it was crawling with monkeys.

That meant that the final herald apart from the monkey was either a juiced-up gwyllgi or an imp, depending on which of the two he had managed to kill with his lucky roll for survival. He wasn't sure which he preferred to be alive, as both felt like they'd be a pain in the ass to fight.

It seemed that the monkeys stayed in the mountains due to their affinity with rocks. Zac often saw them perched and completely immobile on outcroppings as though they were gargoyle sculptures. Their natural habitat was likely in mountainous regions back on their home planet.

He had been happy to notice that each stone monkey gave a lot of Nexus Coins upon killing them. However, he still would rather farm the less lucrative barghest after his only encounter with the monkeys.

Zac thought he had finally managed to single out a solitary stone monkey. It was far away from any demon activity and seemed to be randomly walking around close to the foot of the mountain. Zac had planned to fight it to test it out.

What followed had truly exceeded his expectations. As soon as the monkey noticed Zac, it didn't try to fight. Instead, it screeched at the top of its lungs and started fleeing back up the mountain. While it was faster than a normal human, it still was no match for Zac.

Within a few seconds, he had caught up to it, and a brief struggle erupted. The monkey's fighting style was a full-on brawl, and it was a whirlwind of punches and kicks in a disorganized and confusing manner. It also had a set of sharp teeth, which it tried using when an opportunity arose.

Zac estimated the Strength of the beast to be somewhere in the 60s, almost on par with Zac's before he got his class. Its other stats were quite good across the board; even its Intelligence seemed higher compared to Earth's normal primates.

Of course, even with its strong stats, it was no match against Zac. He had grabbed an arm with his free hand and threw the monkey down on the ground. A quick swing and it was dead. The stone plating on the monkeys was quite hard but offered little resistance to his weapon.

The problems came after. The screech of the monkey had pulled a swarm of his brethren over, who all had seemed extremely enraged upon seeing their fallen comrade.

Thus Zac had been beset by an avalanche of angry fists and kicks coming in from all directions. Every swing of his axe had maimed or killed a monkey, but they were endless and fearless.

Finally, he had escaped, only because the monkeys seemed loath to leave the mountain and enter the forest. They had stopped right at the foot of the mountain, angrily roaring at Zac.

Zac was completely exhausted by then, both physically and his Cosmic Energy. Even his new and improved pathways had barely managed to sustain him in his escape. He wasn't sure that he'd make it out if that onslaught had started a bit further up the mountain. He'd be drained and then finished off.

The upside from that experience was that it had been the most efficient farming of currency and Cosmic Energy he had ever done, except from when he killed the heralds. In that free-for-all brawl, he had gained a level and over 10,000 Nexus coins. He wasn't sure how many he had actually killed during the escape, but it seemed that the monkeys each awarded around 350 to 400 Nexus Coins.

The individual gain wasn't at the level of the imps, but there was a horde of monkeys and only a scant few imps from what he had seen so far. Of course, there still were many locations on the island he still hadn't ventured to, and there might be a cluster of imps somewhere.

If the monkeys weren't so territorial and had such teamwork, he'd never want to leave the mountain again. He'd gain enough Nexus Coins to buy the movement skill **[Steps of Gaia]** in no time. But he deemed it too large a risk to farm these beasts, at least for now. He would have to venture up the mountain again soon, though, as the herald was probably hidden somewhere in there, maybe in the form of a monkey king.

He'd wait until he had his class skills first until he ventured back to the mountain.

He had also figured out the general composition of the demon forces. He estimated that there were somewhere around five thousand demons on the island in total. Their current activities could generally be divided into three parts.

The first part was the construction of a giant palace in the middle of the town. It still wasn't finished, but Zac was amazed by the design even before seeing the finished product. It looked like medieval Eastern architecture had been fused with nature. The structure was made both from stone and trees.

And by trees, he didn't mean chopped-down lumber, but actual trees. There were dozens of mages who reminded Zac of the root mage he had killed, who grew large black trees out of the ground. They then somehow forced it to grow in shapes that would constitute rooms and walls. It took less than an hour for a few mages to grow one of the house-trees into its final size. There were also mages who summoned rocks out of the ground. Under their care, the rocks seemed like clay, allowing the mages to form them to their will to form a natural feeling to the walls and other stone features.

The palace was only three stories tall at the highest point, but it was expansive, featuring multiple buildings, beautiful gardens, sky wells, and courtyards. The gracefully curved roofs were made with tiles, with their eaves hanging out a few meters from the structures. The most central building in the complex had two layers of eaves, giving it an even grander feeling. Zac supposed that was either the general's living quarters or some type of throne room. Surrounding it all was a black hedge roughly two meters tall. It felt decorative rather than providing any protection, as anyone would easily get through or above it.

The only thing that took away from the grand structure was the dull colors. The palace was mostly in shades of black and gray, giving it a very foreboding feeling. The only flashes of color were splotches of red in some details, the shade reminding him of the shining pillar.

The second group moved back and forth between the town and a cave in the mountain. He wasn't exactly sure what they were doing there, as they held no equipment or the like when moving. They likely had magic pouches just like him, obscuring any hint of what was going on inside. He didn't dare sneak in, as there seemed to be activity inside the cave at all times.

His two guesses were they either were mining or there was some sort of huge area beneath that they explored. He hadn't seen anyone hurt or wounded when walking back from the cave, so it shouldn't be full of subterranean monsters at least.

The last group, and also the smallest, was small parties heading out of the town and in different directions of the island. They looked like small search parties, but not like the ones he had encountered so far.

It seemed that the demons had learned their lessons from their two missing groups and had improved the power of the parties. They all held at least five demons, but that wasn't all. Accompanying them was a varied number of beasts. They all had a few gwyllgi running around to the front and the sides of the party, seemingly acting as scouts. There were also a couple of barghest that moved in the front, filling the role of meat shields. A few parties even had an imp or two subserviently following the demons.

Zac felt like he was no match for a party like this. There were too many variables and things that could damage him at the same time. He hadn't tried fighting those parties, staying far away as possible. Now that he knew what he was up against, he realized he really only had one advantage.

He knew a lot about them, but for them, he was still an enigma.

36

DETERMINATION

After observing the demons for two days, Zac also was certain that they were real living, breathing beings. He had always had a sneaking suspicion that they might be puppets, or NPCs if you will, created by the System to give a challenge to Zac and Earth.

But the last two days, he had watched them go about their day. They had worked; they had joked around and played cards. He had seen a few start a fierce brawl until a leader ran up and broke them apart. In essence, they were alive.

He hadn't really thought about it properly before, but they were just like him. Did they even want to be here, or were they forced by the System just like him? Could he just keep regarding them as the enemy, and killing them simply a means to an end?

But Zac had soon steeled his heart. The world had fallen, and chaos reigned. They were invaders on the island, HIS island. From everything he had seen and hypothesized since the integration in the Multiverse, he knew he couldn't go soft and hope for a peaceful solution.

Even if that somehow was possible before, he already had pulled the trigger and killed a bunch of their kind. Any opportunity for negotiation was already out the window. He would sooner or later have to decide how to act if he ever managed to reunite with humans again, but for now, the only diplomacy he'd deliver would be with the swing of his axe.

He couldn't and wouldn't give up on his goal of finding his family, and he knew that he had to become powerful to accomplish that. He had to become a true Defier, as Abby called it, someone defying fate and breaking through his limits. Just his small island was fraught with danger, and this was only a small corner in this world. He had no idea how the rest of the world looked since the System had merged it with multiple others, but he held no illusions that it had become some sort of paradise.

If he had to sacrifice these demons to reach his goals, then so be it.

Besides, Abby had warned him of not completing quests given by the System. It could have unexpected and horrific consequences, it seemed. It meant that people like Zac were almost like slaves to the System, forced to play its games. Unfortunately, he was incapable of doing anything about it and could only play along.

Zac started heading back to his own camp after his second night at close proximity to the incursion. He had seen what he needed to see and now needed to get back. Being away from his camp for prolonged times filled him with anxiety, especially with the new larger war parties roving through the island for some reason. If a party found his camp while he was gone, he would be forced to hide in the tree crowns and caves until he finished the quest, and he had no desire to do that.

Still, he made himself stop at the demonized part of the forest and farm barghest and gwyllgi for a good ten hours before continuing on. He could never stop fighting and killing in order to progress his skills. Besides, the density of beasts in the central area was so high that he was gaining coins and Cosmic Energy at a furious rate.

The only difficulty was that they were in such close proximity to each other that often one or a few demons would hear the sounds of battle and join the fray. He got a few gashes and cuts from the onslaught, but nothing that would impact him.

Eventually, he left the area and started heading toward the south. Finally, late at night, he started to arrive at more familiar parts of the island. He had seen signs of the demon parties on the way and had made a hasty retreat in order not to get entangled with them.

After a while, he finally arrived back at his camp and kicked off his shoes and sat down on his comfortable, newly acquired throne. In the beginning, he had felt isolated and afraid as he was stuck in his little camp, fretful when hearing roars in the distance. Now it felt like a safe haven, a home.

Even with the dried viscera from the exploding demon, the still somewhat visible aftermath from the first fight with the demonling, and the bloodied indoors of the camper, he felt his heartbeat and breath calm down just from entering through the illusion array. In this little bubble, he didn't need to be a walking slaughterhouse wreaking havoc on the demon population; he could just be.

He sat on his new chair and closed his eyes. He felt the luxurious rug between his toes and the wind caressing his hair. For a second, he could forget the hellish existence he had led lately.

A bestial roar in the distance woke him up from his reverie. Zac sighed and got up on his feet. He still didn't have the luxury to relax; there were things to do.

His scouting excursion had given him most of his answers, but he was struggling with coming up with a plan that might work. From his guesswork, he believed one of the heralds was somewhere up in the mountains, while the other was still unaccounted for.

Finally, he had to kill a general, and Zac guessed he would be the big boss. It likely was one of the fancier-looking demons in their city, but he had no idea as of yet how to actually get to him, or how strong he was.

He held no illusions that he would be able to take the straightforward approach and kick the gate down and charge his way through. He'd be punched full of holes before he knew what happened.

There was the possibility of sneaking in during the dead of night and assassinating the general. But Zac felt that this was unlikely to succeed as well. For one, he didn't know who the general was, but more importantly, he didn't have the skill set to pull off such a caper. He wouldn't have any problem scaling the wall or climbing into a window in the palace.

But doing so soundlessly and without any of the numerous guards noticing was the real challenge. While the scouts at the edge of the valley had been very lackadaisical about their task, the military command seemed far stricter in the actual town.

There were guards in the towers and in the walls around the clock, with changes at intervals Zac couldn't figure out. It seemed almost randomized. He'd seen no chance to sneak in during a guard change. Furthermore, most of the vegetation had been cut down in the vicinity of the town, making a stealthy approach nigh impossible.

Zac had even considered tunneling into the town, but that felt much too risky. If a demon party found his entrance, he'd be stuck inside. Besides, he had seen that the demons had multiple stone mages who built the palace. They might be able to detect him even when underground with some spell.

He had also toyed with the idea of trying to destroy the crystal. But he eventually gave that up as well. For one, it contained such extreme amounts of energy that he was afraid it would explode and obliterate the whole island if he managed to crack it.

But more importantly, it seemed that the demons were not worried in the slightest about the crystal. They just left a few men there and then left to build their town further north. If the crystal was instrumental to their invasion, they'd surely protect it far better, as it seemed to be no effort for them to erect walls quickly.

Zac could only put it aside for now, as he had gotten nowhere the last two days. He would focus on what he could do for now.

He had missed a few days of cutting wood while outside and had some catching up to do. His killing speed on this three-day expedition had been astonishing, mostly due to the sheer number of targets in the center of the island. As he rhythmically swung his axe, he mentally brought up his quest panel.

Active Quests:

Dynamic Quests:

1. **Off With Their Heads (Unique): Kill the four heralds and the general of an incursion within 3 months. Reward: 10 E-Grade Nexus Crystals, E-Grade equipment, unique building depending on performance. (2/5)**
2. **Incursion Master (Unique): Close or conquer incursion and protect town from denizens of other alignments for 3 months. Reward: 5 E-Grade Nexus Crystals, outpost upgraded to town, status upgraded to Lord. (0/3)**

Class Quests:

1. **Axe Mastery (Class): Mastery is born through battle. Fell 1,000 enemies. Reward: (548/1,000)**
2. **Chop (Class): First chop Wood. Then their bodies. Reward: (1,240/10,000)**
3. **Forester's Constitution (Class): Fight in the forests, be one with nature. Reward: (3/30)**

He still hadn't gotten any new active quests since finishing the class quest. He was starting to suspect that the active quests were locked to certain areas and events. He wouldn't get anything like an upgrade-class quest for some while, he suspected, as he had just gotten his class. Meanwhile, maybe the Demon-slaying quest he got was tied to the denizens of the island, and the note said he could only get one such title.

Either that or he was missing something about the quests. Perhaps they simply were quite rare. The one he completed did give him a title, after all, and those were permanent upgrades.

Zac kept cutting wood long into the night before finally sitting down for a few hours of sleep. He still stayed outside, as he didn't want the walls of the camper to dampen any sounds of a potential demon war party heading his way.

The next day, he woke up early and immediately headed out. He had decided to stop killing any demons close to his camp. He was afraid that a complete lack of beasts around a certain area would alert the demons. He headed toward the center, this time toward the eastern part.

He was planning on grinding beasts while looking for clues about the fourth elusive herald. Ur'Khaz had been killed in the south as it occupied the same space as him, and he had killed Vul in the western area. The monkey king was likely somewhere in the mountains to the north, and that left the eastern quadrant. He thought that he would try to gather some more intel while finishing up the class quests.

He went back to camp when the night approached and chopped wood for a few hours. He was lucky that he had found the pouch, as he was starting to accumulate a ridiculous amount of firewood. He had decided to leave most of it in a few dry spots around the island. Just for safety, he'd construct a simple roof with some branches and leaves to protect the lumber from a downpour. The lumber was proof of his effort, and it felt wasteful to just throw it away.

He kept this routine going for a few days. His intense activities left him with less than four hours of sleep, yet he felt refreshed when he woke up. He wondered if he'd get to a point where he didn't have to sleep at all if his Vitality and Endurance got high enough.

Suddenly, as Zac slammed down his axe into the head of a barghest, a huge surge of Cosmic Energy entered his mind, causing him to almost black out.

37

MONSTROUS POWER

While having some difficulty staying conscious, Zac finished off the other three beasts that had arrived due to the noise of the fight. Luckily, the surge of energy soon dissipated.

He quickly retreated after the kills, not wanting to keep battling any more barghest for the moment. After running for a few minutes, he reached one of his hideouts, another construction high up in a tree.

As he sat down on the bedding of leaves, he could finally focus on the new things in his head. Just as he suspected, he had completed the quest for Axe Mastery with his last kill. His speed of killing had far surpassed his expectations. He had given himself a ten-day deadline but had finished it in just below a week's time. It was mostly thanks to the high density of monsters in the central part of the island. The monsters were everywhere, and he didn't have to waste a lot of time traveling looking for his next target.

Zac closed his eyes to go over his new skill and was surprised to suddenly find himself standing on the edge of a cliff. Jolted by the change in scenery, he immediately opened his eyes, only to once again see the familiar sight of his hideout.

It had only been an illusion or something created in his mind, but it had felt so real, he had thought for a second he had been teleported somewhere. Zac calmed his breathing and slowly closed his eyes again.

He once again found himself standing on the desolate cliff. As he looked around, he found that the cliff was part of a seemingly endless canyon. It stretched further than Zac could see, and the bottom was shrouded in a thick mist, giving the impression of being bottomless. The illusory world itself was a dull gray, as though all life had been sucked out of the area.

The most shocking sight wasn't the canyon, however; it was the enormous axe that was embedded in the ground a few hundred meters away from him. It was at least fifty meters tall and gave off a pressure that almost made Zac collapse just from standing in the vicinity.

The axe itself was simple and unadorned, with a straight wooden haft. It was a double axe made in seemingly ordinary steel with curved edges. Even though it looked simple, Zac felt that he was gazing at a supreme treasure just from the towering aura it exuded.

As soon as Zac's eyes landed on the edge of the axe, he stumbled backward, his face turning a ghastly white. It had felt like he was being split in two from just looking at the edge.

After regaining his bearing, he tentatively looked up at the axe again, careful to avoid looking at the edges. But as he did, his vision once more changed.

The bleak dead world changed to one that could best be described as a paradise. Golden clouds hung in the sky, and there were fantastical buildings upon them. A network of translucent bridges connected the sky cities, and flying contraptions could be seen gliding about.

Zac himself was floating far up in the sky, seemingly unencumbered by gravity. Facing him was a vast celestial army. The army shone in a splendor of white and gold, and the generals radiated a terrifying power that Zac wouldn't even be able to begin to grade. A few groups of the army were circling pillars as large as skyscrapers, and it took Zac a moment to realize the huge structures were actually supersized array flags, like the ones he had in his camp.

There were even titans among the ranks of the humanoid army, the shortest standing being at least a hundred meters tall. Their muscular frames looked strong enough to carry mountains.

The army gave Zac a holy feeling, but it also emitted a monstrous killing intent, which largely seemed to be focused on himself. The very air seemed to vibrate with resentment.

Zac was terrified, as he instinctively knew that each and every one of these warriors would be able to end him without breaking a sweat. He tried to turn around and flee, but he couldn't move even his eyes.

A sigh escaped his lips, making him realize he was not just an incorporeal being spectating, but inhabiting a body that was out of his control. It seemed he was viewing the scene through the eyes of someone else.

His eyes suddenly looked down on his body, seeing a muscular frame covered in simple linen clothes. His feet were bare and dusty, looking as though he had walked all day without any shoes. Suddenly, an axe entered his vision. It was hefted in his right hand and looked identical to the enormous one he had seen in the first vision at the canyon.

The hand holding it was extremely rough and calloused as if it had been holding and swinging the axe for an eternity.

His vision went back to the army, who now seemed to be preparing to attack. The air was rife with runaway power, almost to the point that the Cosmic Energy would liquefy.

Thousands of warriors started infusing cosmic power into the towering array flags, which started to shine with a white light that superseded even the pillar on his island.

Suddenly, two enormous gates appeared above the army, summoned by the arrays. As the gates started to open, an even stronger power started to leak out. It felt like a god's punishment was held within those gates, and if they opened, he would be destroyed body and soul.

But even against this force, the being Zac inhabited didn't react. He simply lifted his axe and, with a grunt, swung it down in a vertical arc.

It was as though the world turned white with that swing, and nothing existed except its almighty arc expanding outward. Nothing could withstand it. The celestial soldiers were dismembered without managing to even muster up a defense.

The pillars shattered, and the titans roared and tried to defend against the wave with their superior physiques. It was to no avail as they crumbled when the wave passed through them.

Some of the leaders frantically summoned awe-inspiring amounts of Cosmic Energy to muster up defenses that left Zac in shock. Others ripped open tears in the air itself to escape, shock and horror visible on their faces. But the blade's arc pushed through and crushed the defenses like dry twigs, annihilating the last remnants of the army. Soon after even the void was split apart, and dismembered body parts were thrown out of jagged rifts, and Zac could see it was the leaders who had tried fleeing through the void.

Zac's vision started to blur, but the last thing he saw before everything faded was a hideous scar on the ground that stretched to the horizon. It looked like the world itself was maimed, and vast amounts of Cosmic Energy bled through the gash.

Zac's vision returned to the canyon and the huge axe. Only now he understood it wasn't a canyon, but the rift caused by that endlessly powerful axe swing. The once celestial vision he had seen during the battle was gone, replaced with the empty desolation of a dead world.

Zac's emotions were in turmoil after the battle. He had become steady as a rock after over a thousand battles on the island, but he wasn't prepared for what he had seen. Who was that man, and why was that army trying to fight him?

Was that how a war in the Multiverse looked? If so, then Earth was well and truly screwed. If someone arrived on Earth with only a fraction of the power of the man with the axe, then there was nothing the earthlings could do. It would be like ants trying to stop a tank.

Furthermore, he didn't understand why he was shown this vision. He had just gotten the skill Axe Mastery and suddenly was transported here.

As he was pondering what it all meant, the gigantic axe started emitting a blinding light. When he turned his eyes over to the weapon, the light intensified, and suddenly, the axe was gone.

In its place was a large fractal that shared the same general outline as the axe. It also emitted extreme pressure, making Zac feel as though he could somehow be cleaved in two from this pattern as well.

The fractal didn't stay still for long, and suddenly started to shrink. When it had shrunk to the size of his palm, it suddenly shot toward him like a bullet. Aghast, Zac tried to dodge. It truly felt like the monstrous axe was charging at him.

It was to no avail, however, and it slammed right into his forehead. Zac froze, not daring to move an inch.

Luckily, the release of death didn't arrive, and he found out he was completely fine. The fractal hadn't cut him but somehow entered his head instead. He could now sense its existence in his mind, and it hovered there now, seemingly inert.

Finally, he bit his finger, making a small bleeding wound, and willed himself back to reality. He opened his eyes, still sitting in his small hideout. He was shocked to notice that he was completely soaked in sweat and drained of Cosmic Energy. It also seemed that hours had passed rather than minutes as it had felt like, since the suns had moved quite a distance in the sky. But as he looked down on his finger, it was whole and without any wound.

It seemed that the experience had truly been an illusion. He was already somewhat sure of that but had cut his finger just to be certain. He knew the System was no stranger to teleportation from how it had sent away Hannah and her friends, and needed to know if he was in actual danger if it happened again.

For a final test, he tried to enter the mystic space once more, but nothing happened. It seemed it was a onetime opportunity he had received. He was at least happy to notice that the mysterious axe fractal actually had remained in his mind, as he could still perceive it outside the illusion.

He was quite sure that the new fractal was the **[Axe Mastery]** skill that he had received, but he had no idea how to utilize it as of yet. He had initially planned on heading back to camp to finish his Chop quest as well, but he changed his mind.

He believed he'd seen those scenes for a reason and wanted to go over it while the memories were still fresh. So instead, he rested his back against the tree trunk and once again closed his eyes.

38

INSIGHT

Zac's instincts told him that what he had seen had been important. So he tried to burn every feeling and impression to his memory.

The immense pressure that emanated from the axe and the terrifying sharpness of its edge. The world-ending power of the seemingly casual strike by the barefooted man. He had just swung once, but somehow everything he had wished to cut was cut, and nothing could escape him. Even the people who fled through portals hadn't been spared and were somehow killed in another space.

He tried to figure out why he was shown this vision. He could only assume it came from the System, as he couldn't imagine who else would, and could, show him such a thing.

He did not believe it was something as fantastical as a glimpse into his own future or a prophecy; rather, he felt it was far more likely the System was trying to show him something else. The only thing he could come up with was that it was sort of a training video. The illusion showed him what Axe Mastery at a great, or maybe even the highest, proficiency looked like.

If that was the truth, he wasn't disappointed anymore that he didn't get a Rare or Epic Mage Class. That army had even called upon the gates of heaven to attack, but it couldn't even withstand one chop. That Axe Master had also conquered the disadvantage of being a Melee Class. Everything in his vision was chopped and dismembered, no matter how far or fast they fled.

Of course, Zac knew that even if that was a real event that had happened, it had nothing to do with him. The power levels of those warriors did not seem as simple as having an E-grade or even D-grade class. It felt like a level so far off that it might just as well be a dream.

But still, if he could glean some sort of truth or secret from the vision, he'd likely benefit greatly from it. It also gave him a wake-up call about how formidable the forces out in the Multiverse were. He had known that there would be powerful people out there, but he hadn't imagined it being to this degree. That axe wielder would be able to cleave his whole island in two. That was not something that should be possible for a human being. That was the realm of the gods.

So it seemed actual beings with the powers of gods were out there. If one of them got angered with him or someone else from Earth, there might be irrevocable repercussions. There were already demons on his island, and there might be other forces on the planet as well. It seemed the restrictions were weakening as well, and sooner or later, any old monster might be able to waltz through one of the incursions.

If he wanted to keep himself and his close ones safe, he had to keep pushing forward until he himself was one of those gods.

Of course, he had to survive this island first before starting to fantasize about deifying himself. He refocused and started looking at the new fractal in his mind. He didn't really understand how it worked, but it felt like it was housed in an actual space in his mind rather than it being just a memory.

It was a very weird feeling, as it was akin to noticing your body had secret compartments.

Unfortunately, no matter how he looked at the fractal, he couldn't glean anything from it. He tried driving Cosmic Energy through it, but it had no effect. Since it had entered his mind, its heavy aura was gone, and it seemed dead or deactivated.

Zac sighed, feeling slightly disappointed. He had essentially been shown a pretty cool action scene, and was left with a pattern he couldn't use. He knew he was likely missing something, but could only return to his camp for now.

As he walked back, he kept pondering the vision he had seen. He wondered if he'd ever get to the point of that man in his vision.

He looked down on his axe, and with a half-smile, he swung it down just like the man in the illusion. Of course, no earth-shattering wave of destruction erupted from the swing. Only a slight swooshing sound was the result of the swing.

But after he performed the swing, he stopped. The attack just felt *wrong*. He couldn't put it into words, but it was as though the attack was bland and flat compared to the one in the illusion. And he wasn't talking about the earth-shattering power, but something else.

Even though his swing and the axe-man's had the same trajectory, it felt like the man's swing was real and his the illusion rather than the opposite. Like the man's swing was a forest and Zac's just a picture of one.

His swing was missing something, and it was not form or technique, but something more intrinsic. If he hadn't seen that scene, he never would have figured it out. He would think that a swing was just a swing.

He imagined the intense pressure he had felt when standing in front of the huge axe, and tried to incorporate it into the axe. It was easier said than done, of course, and Zac kept swinging away while walking back. He even used some demon beasts as practice targets to try to get the feel.

He also tried incorporating Cosmic Energy into the fractal while swinging, but it didn't do anything. He was still missing that feeling that would make his swings feel full instead of empty.

He tried to discern what made the axe-man so strong and made him effortlessly defeat the army. It wasn't speed. His swing had been slow to the point of almost feeling lazy. It hadn't been sophisticated or complicated either, but simple and unadorned, just like his axe.

But the swing was sharp. Anything it attacked was cut. It didn't matter if it was the huge titans, the awe-inspiring defenses of the top cultivators in the army, or even the gates of heaven. Everything that the axe waves hit was split in two.

However, what had made the largest impression on Zac was the heaviness the swing had contained. By that, he didn't mean that the axe grew heavy like the great sword, but it felt like the axe had contained an unstoppable force when falling down. It had felt like the weight of a world was contained in that swing, and it had an unbending determination and intractability contained in it. Anything that tried to impede its path would be destroyed.

Zac didn't understand how he could know these things. They should be subjective opinions and personal impressions, but it felt like those impressions were rather inviolable truths. That the man's attack contained these abstruse elements felt as true and real as that the sky was blue.

Zac also somehow knew there was a multitude of other aspects hidden in that seemingly simple swing, but they seemed too far away and elusive for him to grasp on to. He decided to focus on the power and forcefulness for now rather than the sharpness, as he felt the heaviness the most clearly in his mind. He was afraid that trying to study both aspects at the same time would be too hard for him to handle.

Zac tried to bring this sense of force and weight into his swing and started to bring more and more Cosmic Energy into it. His energy started to naturally flow along his pathways, and the whirling sounds from the axe sounded slightly deeper.

Just as he started to feel that he was grasping something, a blue box suddenly popped up by itself.

[Dao Seed gained – Heaviness]

Confused, Zac stopped swinging and brought up his status page.

Name: Zachary Atwood
Level: 28
Class: [F-Rare] Hatchetman
Race: [F] Human
Alignment: [Earth] Human

Titles: Born for Carnage, Ultimate Reaper, Luck of the Draw, Giantsbane, Disciple of David, Overpowered, Slayer of Leviathans, Adventurer, Demon Slayer, Full of Class, Rarified Being, Trailblazer, Child of Dao

Dao: Seed of Heaviness – Early

Strength: 136
Dexterity: 57
Endurance: 77
Vitality: 66
Intelligence: 46
Wisdom: 46
Luck: 64

Free Points: 0
Nexus Coins: 134,780

Zac was shocked when he saw his Strength. He had gained close to 30 points in Strength without gaining any levels.

There were two other changes to his page. The first was that he had a new title, Child of Dao. The second was an entirely new row had been added next to the titles, called Dao.

Zac had heard of the concept of Dao somewhere, but couldn't remember the details. It was a part of Eastern mythology or religion, but he didn't know exactly what it meant. But from context, it felt like it was akin to insight or the like.

He had started to gain insight into the weight behind the man's swing, and he gained a Dao Seed.

He began with checking his new title.

[Child of Dao: Third in world to attain enlightenment and create a Dao Seed. All stats +5, All stats +5%.]

The description gave Zac a start. He was only the third in the world to gain the Dao Seed. Since the integration into the Multiverse, he had constantly been at the forefront, be it with achievements or levels. But he had actually been bested on this aspect.

He didn't know if someone had surpassed him in level since level 25 and gained a seed the same way as him, or whether there were other ways to get them. But it was a reminder that there were billions of people in the world. He had his lucky encounters; why couldn't others have theirs?

Besides, he knew he wasn't a born warrior, and it had taken him an enormous amount of effort to get where he was today. Perhaps there were geniuses who simply were perfectly suited for cultivation and the new world order.

The lost opportunity made him feel a bit depressed, and he

swore at himself for all the time he had wasted. Had he gotten to this point a few days quicker, he might have snagged a better title.

If the third spot got 5 points in all stats and 5% increase, what did the second and first place get? Perhaps as much as 10 points for second spot and a whopping 15 points for the first?

But Zac steadied his mind quickly, as he knew he couldn't get greedy. The number of advantages he had accumulated would probably make anyone on Earth green with envy if they knew.

39

GUIDANCE

Next, Zac wanted to check out the Dao Seed. Soon he managed to open a new screen in the System.

It didn't have a lot of information, just a list in the same manner as the titles.

[Dao Seed of Heaviness – Early. Strength +10, Endurance +5]

While the menu or information wasn't very spectacular, the stat bonuses were quite good. As Zac's main stats were Strength and Endurance, this seed's bonus was a perfect gift. Perhaps a reason why he'd learned the Dao Seed so smoothly was due to this.

It also made him understand the importance of Dao to the System. He'd just gained a seed of the Dao of Heaviness, and it was only an early seed. Both things indicated that he had just taken the first steps to understand this concept, but it already gave a boost worth a few levels.

What would it give if he managed to improve it to a higher level, like the Late stage? And what happened if it stopped being a seed and turned into the real thing? The boost it gave would likely be astonishing.

Zac felt that the seed and the fractal in his mind were somehow connected. He'd gained it while trying to emulate the powerful feeling in that axe swing, after all. He once again turned his sight inward and gazed upon the axe fractal again.

He couldn't tell exactly how, but he sensed that the pattern of the fractal had somehow subtly changed. It also no longer seemed inert as it was before, but emitted an aura that gave Zac the familiar sense of weight and intractability.

It was the same sense of heaviness that he somewhat managed to instill into his swings while trying to emulate the axe-man. Now that he could contrast it to the aura in the illusion, he understood that the Dao of Heaviness was only part of the whole picture, and the suffocating aura of the axe was something far greater.

Still, it was a step in the right direction. His seed was only at the early stage. There surely were ways to improve upon it, and perhaps someday his axe aura, or Dao, might be as mighty as the one he saw.

Now that the fractal felt active again, he once more tried to circulate Cosmic Energy through it. This time, it actually worked, and the fractal lit up.

Suddenly, his vision changed, and fractals started appearing. Some shone up like glowing footprints in the ground, and others were lights forming arcs and trajectories around him. The lights seemed to have no effect on their surroundings, not lighting the ground or trees up in the slightest. Furthermore, when Zac moved his head, the lights moved with him and slightly adjusted, meaning they came from the System in the same manner as his different menus.

It felt like he was wearing augmented-reality goggles, giving him an extra layer of reality that only he could see. At least he assumed only he could see the lights and the menus, as they only seemed to respond and change in reaction to Zac's movements and commands.

He tried to touch the fractals that formed the trajectories, but it was like trying to touch a rainbow. Furthermore, as he moved his hand, the lights adjusted and moved as well. After adjusting to his new vision, he tried stepping on the glowing footprints and moving his body according to the illuminated trajectories. He found himself swinging his axe in a slanted upwards motion. The movement felt smooth and natural, and it felt like he was able to bring the full force of almost his whole body into the swing.

He kept following the glowing instructions and found himself performing a multitude of attacks. There were not only normal swings, but every part of the axe was used. From the butt of the haft to the spike on the back side of the head, everything was used in an array of methods to maim and kill enemies. It even showed how to use the rest of his body, such as grabbing with his off-hand, footwork and tackles.

It couldn't be said that the fractals in the air taught him actual skills, but rather basic guidance on how to properly move and handle an axe.

Every strike had one thing in common: it contained the mass and intractability of his Dao. It made him realize many aspects of his weapon of choice as well. An axe differed from a sword in that it was balanced toward the head, whereas a sword was closer to the handle. This gave an axe a higher forward momentum and higher destructive power.

To master the axe, he should focus on the part where it excelled, meaning this power and forcefulness. Its disadvantage was that it wasn't as flexible as a sword was. The bladed area was also far shorter with an axe, so some precision was needed for a killing strike. At least until he could swing his axe in the fantastical manner of the man in the vision.

Zac kept going through various motions as he moved toward the camp. He was entranced by the beautiful simplicity in the moves and the power they managed to bring out.

Suddenly, he stumbled and fell down, shocked to notice that he was totally and utterly drained. He hadn't completely recovered his energy from his vision earlier, and it seemed like using the axe fractal consumed large amounts of Cosmic Energy.

At least Zac finally felt he had figured out how the **[Axe Mastery]** skill worked. It wasn't what he expected, but he was still very happy with the result.

He initially thought he would get a bonus to stats similar to the Demon Slayer title, like bonus stats while wielding an axe, and perhaps generally get imparted some knowledge about axes. The reality actually trumped his expectations, and the rewards were twofold.

The first part was the vision, which Zac now was certain was shown to him so that he could plant his Dao Seed. The other part was this guidance system that could help him improve his form and fighting abilities. It might have been more convenient if the System crammed his head full of these things, making him master these aspects immediately.

Perhaps that wasn't possible, as it was related to the Dao. Or perhaps the System didn't want to just hand things out willy-nilly. The guidance system was a godsend in any case, as Zac had missed the Tutorial and sorely needed some guidance.

Of the two, he felt the Dao vision was the most valuable. One might be able to gain those seeds by themselves by meditating or being an expert on a subject, but Zac's intuition told him that it wasn't that easy. Otherwise, he wouldn't have been the third but the three-millionth to attain a Dao Seed. The world was full of experts, after all.

He decided on the spot to use the time he earlier spent cutting wood on practicing his axe form in the future. That time would be freed up as soon as he finished the second class quest in any case.

Zac sat down to recuperate and devoured some meat from his pouch before continuing back home. It was dark when he returned to camp, as usual, this time due to his new skill rather than grinding monsters all waking hours.

Still, he couldn't rest, as he was too excited about what his other skill would be like. He started cutting wood at a furious speed, lumber flying left and right. After roughly ninety minutes, he slowed down and caught his breath. He was only ten swings away from finishing the quest for the **[Chop]** skill, and he wanted to be in rested condition just in case.

He drank a mouthful of water and steadied his breath before once again hefting his axe and swinging the ten final strikes.

This time, Cosmic Energy didn't enter his mind, but information. This time, the impartation was akin to when he'd bought **[Eye of Discernment]** from the Nexus Crystal. Zac was a bit disappointed that he wouldn't get another vision that could give him another Dao Seed or the like, but he knew that was a rare opportunity he'd gained.

The skill was another fractal, and the usage was similar to the identification skill. It needed him to circulate Cosmic Energy through his energy pathways in a specific manner, then imagine it entering this fractal. The difference was that while **[Eye of Discernment]** placed the fractals inside his eyes, the new one was on the top of his right hand. It wasn't a physical manifestation; rather, it superimposed itself on his pathways.

This was different from his eye skill, which was isolated fractals in his eyes. The **[Chop]** skill's fractal seemed to actually merge with his class pathways. It didn't look out of place or messy, but it felt as a missing piece of a puzzle was added.

When Zac rewrote his pathways, there were many parts that looked blurry and missing. It seemed from his new skill that they were slots for his skills. Maybe even other skills, like **[Steps of Gaia]** that he was eyeing in the store, could be slotted into his pathway gaps.

He tried doing the same with his ocular skill, but it was a closed-circuit fractal, giving no opportunity to integrate with his pathways. The Axe Mastery fractal was in an enclosed space in his mind, and he had no way to connect it to his pathways either. Unfortunately, he lacked any more skills to experiment with. He actually had enough Nexus Coins to buy the cheapest skills by now, but he didn't want to burn his hard-earned cash for an experiment.

He wasn't sure what benefits there were to slotting it into his pathways compared to simply having them like his identification skill. He would have to test it and find out.

Even though it was late at night, he couldn't wait, too eager to find out the effects of his new skill. Even if he realized it would be nothing like the great spells he saw in the vision, he had already fought against someone with an impressive skill. It was the demon leader with the great sword, whose furniture now adorned his campsite.

The black arcs of lightning had almost gotten him killed a few times. From the simple name of his own skill, he realized that it might not be as extravagant, though. But he did get it from a Rare class, after all, so it shouldn't be useless.

He planned to try out the skill by using it a few times, then find a demon beast to test it on, so he left his camp in search of a decent target.

As he walked some ways from the camp, he made a new discovery. A skill screen had been added to his various prompts. It hadn't been there when he bought the identification skill, which was why it had taken him all day before trying it. He surmised it must've activated when he got his class skills.

Normal Skills:

1. **Eye of Discernment – Proficiency: A glimpse into the unknown. Upgradeable**

Class Skill

1. **Axe Mastery – Proficiency: Early. The seed of Dao is planted. Upgradeable**
2. **Chop – Proficiency: Early. There is greatness in simplicity.**

The screen showed scant information, but it did give Zac a few answers to things he had been wondering about. The class skills seemed to have proficiency, and both were at early stage. His Dao Seed was at early stage as well, and he guessed that if he progressed in **[Axe Mastery]**, the seed might follow.

[Chop] would likely simply get stronger if the proficiency increased. His identification skill had no proficiency, and it seemed that it wouldn't get stronger. He had wondered about whether he could improve his skill and get more information about enemies, or even be able to identify items.

It was, however, upgradeable. He saw no hint of the requirements, but it was good to know that he could improve the skill into a better one. **[Chop]** wasn't upgradeable, which was a bit disappointing. He could only hope the description was true, that there was greatness in simplicity.

If he went by his knowledge from video games, then he'd likely need to raise proficiency to the max before somehow upgrading **[Axe Mastery]** into a higher-tiered skill. As that option wasn't available for **[Eye of Discernment]**, he could only hope to find out some clues at a later date.

Of course, even if he wouldn't be able to upgrade **[Chop]**, he'd still try to max out its proficiency. Who knew if the System would reward a title or new class quests if he did. The System did like it when people put in effort, after all.

40

CHOP

As he walked away from the camp in the dead of night, he was going over his future path of development. He couldn't just focus on training with the new guidance system all day due to the third class skill requiring large amounts of time battling in the forest.

On the way from the camp, he tried using **[Axe Mastery]** in an actual battle with a barghest. He was disappointed to see that the trajectories wouldn't actually assist him in battle and completely shut off right before the battle started. It seemed it was purely a training mechanism.

Finally, he arrived at a small clearing some distance from the camp. He didn't want to accidentally ruin his home in case the skill had any unexpected effects.

He started with using a small amount of energy and channeled it through his new fractal as he swung the axe. The energy transformed as it ventured out through his hand and into the axe. As he swung down, he could see a translucent edge formed by Cosmic Energy.

It was like the axe-head had gotten a bit larger, as the translucent edge ran a few centimeters in front of the actual edge, and its length was roughly ten centimeters longer compared to the actual steel edge. The edge created from Cosmic Energy looked like a copy of his axe's actual edge, with some faint fractals added along its length.

It wasn't spectacular, but he'd used a minuscule amount of energy in the strike. He tried using the skill once more, but this time, he put far more Cosmic Energy into the skill. The translucent blade grew quite a bit larger, now stretching noticeably outward. The blade was now over one meter long, making his once short-ranged axe have almost as long a range as the great sword he had commandeered. Luckily, the edge didn't grow downward along the haft, but rather outward. Otherwise, it would be hard for him to swing it without maiming himself.

It was beyond Zac's expectation it would grow to this size. As he continued putting more power into the skill, it kept growing, but Zac soon felt that he was starting to lose control over the skill. Suddenly, the Cosmic Energy blade simply dissipated, leaving no trace of ever being there.

It seemed there was a limit to how large he could grow the blade without it starting to become unstable. After some experimentation, he knew that he could keep the blade stable at roughly one meter. Any larger, and it would quickly become unstable. The longer he made the blade, the shorter duration he could keep it.

It seemed that this was all there was to the skill. He tried shooting it away like a ranged attack or boomerang, but nothing happened. It was firmly lodged to his axe. Of course, the proficiency was only at early stage, and it might get more functions at higher levels.

Zac was still quite pleased with the skill, even though it wasn't as flashy as the black lightning of the demon leader. It wasn't fancy, but he could immediately imagine a few uses for a skill such as this. For one, he could surprise an enemy. He or she might have thought that they dodged his strike, but instead, they were well within the range of his skill blade.

It was also a brutal instrument when fighting against multiple enemies. If he pushed it past its point of stability, he could wield a huge blade and slash at multiple people at once, at least for a short duration before the skill broke. With his monstrous strength, he believed that he could create a great deal of carnage in that brief window in time.

Of course, that would be a last-resort attack, as cramming that amount of Cosmic Energy into one skill use would greatly drain him.

There was one thing he didn't understand with the skill. He had gained his Dao Seed from managing to incorporate this intangible force of heaviness into his strikes while he was walking back to the camp, but he was utterly incapable of doing the same with the skill.

He tried using a few Dao-empowered strikes, and they did have an air of weight to them. It wasn't as tyrannical as the axeman's, of course, but it felt like these strikes should be harder for someone to block compared to normal strike.

But when he tried incorporating this feeling into **[Chop]**, everything got jumbled, and he didn't even manage to produce the blade. He saw no reason that they shouldn't work together but guessed that he had to practice some more before being able to use it as he wished.

The last thing for him to test out with the new skill was the sharpness. It was somewhat pointless if he got a larger edge if it wasn't sharp. Sure, with his Strength, he'd do damage anyways without a sharp edge, but if the translucent edge was dull, he might as well swing around a tree trunk.

He charged up a meter-long blade and swung down upon a rock almost as tall as him. With a clang, the Cosmic Energy blade cut halfway into the stone. Satisfied, Zac let the blade dissipate.

It seemed that cutting through things would use up the energy faster compared to simply having it summoned, but even while not cutting things, it continuously drained him slowly. Of course, he could likely keep inputting more and more energy and the blade would remain. But it seemed to be a wasteful use of Cosmic Energy.

Zac felt that the skill was best used as either a finisher or surprise attack, not in a long protracted battle. He would only be able to use it continuously for a few minutes at the most before being completely drained.

The sharpness seemed to be roughly the same as his actual axe. It did seem to model itself after his axe's edge, after all, so it made sense that they would share some features. He wondered if the sharpness would improve if he got a higher-grade weapon in the future. He was sure that his weapon was a low F-grade blade, as he had looted it from some random demon, after all. It couldn't be too valuable.

He then brought out a sword from his pouch to test whether he could use **[Chop]** with other weapons, but it at least didn't work with swords.

He was planning on testing some more, but a snap of a twig in the vicinity stopped him in his tracks.

Zac got a sinking feeling, as he had made sure that there were no beasts in the area before trying out the skill. He quickly slunk down into nearby foliage and started to retreat toward his camp, taking great care to not make a sound.

Only the gwyllgi among the demons seemed to be active during the night, but he had never heard those beasts make any sounds while moving through the forest. That meant that the snap of the twig was more likely to be one of the war parties moving about.

He swore at himself for his carelessness. He had been on a high from his new boosts and wasn't as careful as he should have been. Even when grinding beasts, his biggest priority had always been keeping a lookout for these parties. He always kept moving and didn't fight close to his base, as he didn't want to attract attention to that area.

Now he was quite close to his camp, and his swing into the stone had made a sound. He soundlessly passed through the layer and entered his illusion array. He could only hope it was a large critter that was lumbering around in the dark.

Zac held his axe at the ready, vigilantly gazing into the woods. His hopes were soon dashed as he saw one of the roving war parties moving close by. The demons conversed in their language with subdued voices, seemingly arguing about something.

The core of the party consisted of six demons and an imp. They generally seemed to be average soldiers, with none of them wearing expensive-looking gear. There also were a few gwyllgi and barghest surrounding the party.

Zac didn't dare to move, even though he knew that his camp just looked like an empty area with some extra-dense bushes. His illusion array was effective on the eyes, but he had no idea whether there were skills that could sense the array. He had tried it with his **[Eye of Discernment]** without finding anything, but it was also the cheapest skill that the Nexus Node offered.

Suddenly, he saw a gwyllgi was slowly coming extremely close, moving some ways from the group. If it kept moving in the direction it did, it would enter the bushes he had moved to the edge of his camp, and soon after enter his array.

Zac's fears came true as it trotted forward and entered his camp through the dense bushes. Zac was ready, and with lightning speed, he grabbed the hound's neck as soon as it was through the array, and with a twist, broke it. With his strength, he could probably rip its head right off, but he didn't want any blood to spill.

He slowly dragged the corpse into the camp and flung it to the side. Luckily, the array also had sound-dampening, so no one should have heard anything. He resumed his vigil against the rest of the group, and it seemed no one among them had noticed the missing beast. The gwyllgi often moved some distance from the parties, acting as scouts, so it would likely take some while before they noticed their missing beast. Unfortunately, they had stopped just fifty meters away from the camp.

They still seemed to be arguing about something in hushed tones. One of the demons seemed nervous and kept pointing toward where Zac had tested his skill. The others seemed unconvinced and dismissive.

One of the demons rolled his eyes at the nervous one and started to actually walk toward Zac's camp. The nervous demon entreated him, but was just met with a dismissive wave of his hand. He started fiddling with his pants and stopped at a tree just half a meter away from the edge of the illusion array.

The demon was actually relieving himself. He looked around the area while he did so. His eyes stopped a second on the camp. It should look like a normal clearing to him, but the demon slightly furrowed his brows. Soon they smoothed out, and he casually looked away again and continued with his business.

But Zac's heart started beating rapidly after scrutinizing the demon's face.

He knew.

41

APEX PREDATOR

Zac didn't dare hesitate and furiously chopped his axe down through the array while the demon still had his pants down, doing his business.

As Zac suspected, the demon was ready for the strike, and without hesitation, he lifted his sword to meet the oncoming attack. Unfortunately for him, Zac's strength was in another league, and with the addition of the Dao of Heaviness, the force of the swing simply broke the poor demon's arms and continued unimpeded into his head.

It looked like the array didn't hold up to scrutiny when observed at such proximity, or maybe the demon simply used some ocular skill more powerful than his **[Eye of Discernment]**. The demon had noticed something was wrong but didn't want to alert anyone to this fact until he was back at safety in his group. But some discreet facial tics had foiled his plans.

After the swing, Zac quickly grabbed two of his knives from his pouch and hurled them at the war party just as they were shocked by an axe appearing out of thin air and killing their comrade.

One of the knives punched a hole through the imp, instantly

killing it, but the other missed the demon he was aiming for. He'd trained his throwing skills diligently since his embarrassing throw that completely missed the target in his first battle against a barghest. Together with his increased stats in Strength and Dexterity, his aim was quite good by now, but he still couldn't always hit his targets when throwing in rapid succession.

He threw another dagger, but the demon dodged it, and it was ready for the attacks now. The barghest were stupid, however, and a knife instantly slammed into its torso, maiming it badly. He had a decent stock of knives by now since killing the scout demons surrounding the valley with the incursion, and could keep throwing them for a while.

He didn't have any time to kill the other barghest, as he saw one of the demons starting to conjure a fireball. Aghast, he didn't dare to hesitate, and hurled a dagger at the mage. He couldn't have him burn the camp down, or even start a forest fire. Every demon on the island would know a battle was happening here.

A magic shield stopped the dagger in its tracks, so Zac had no choice but to charge out of his array toward the demons. There still were five demons and a couple of demon beasts against him. Fortunately, he'd killed the imp immediately; otherwise, he'd have to worry about those fireballs. They were still extremely deadly, even with his improved constitution.

Suddenly, as he was approaching, spikes shot out of the ground. They looked like thin stalactites, so it seemed one of the demons was a rock mage. Not expecting the attack, one of the spikes managed to stab into his gut before he could react.

His breastplate was high-quality work, but unfortunately, it only covered his upper torso. Therefore, his only protection on the rest of his body was the common leather armor, which barely impeded attacks. He broke off the one impaling him and then destroyed the other with a swing.

An arrow crackling with electricity zoomed toward his head

as he was getting rid of the stone spears. He had to dodge before properly removing the tip of the spike from his stomach, making it do some extra damage while he rolled away.

As he got back to his feet, the fire mage already seemed ready to fire his spell. But to Zac's horror, he wasn't actually aiming at him or the camp, but straight up. The demon intended to use it as a signal flare while the others impeded him.

Zac desperately infused all the Cosmic Energy and heaviness he could into his arm and threw his axe with a grunt. The axe sounded like a propeller as it ripped through the air at the mage. The magic shield that stopped his knife shattered like a mirror, and the axe-head slammed into the mage's chest, instantly killing him.

Luckily for him, the ball of flame snuffed out as soon as the mage died, just like how it did with the imps he had fought. There would be no signal flare or forest fire, this time at least.

But Zac didn't have time to breathe out in relief, as a barghest slammed straight into him. The demonic brutes could charge straight through smaller trees, so the force completely winded him. Had he been prepared, he could have used the inscription on his chest piece, as his chest armor held one charge where it could nullify an attack. But Zac himself had to activate it, and he hadn't been prepared for the body slam.

An arrow shot into his stomach as he was pushed backward as well, piling on to his misery. Luckily, his Endurance was up in the high 70s by now, and it didn't get far into his body before stopping.

However, the arrow released a lightning shock right into his intestines, making him unable to breathe for a second. Zac coughed out a mouthful of blood but didn't dare move the arrow, remembering that leaving the weapon in the wound when stabbed was safer. He could only break it off and ignore it for now.

Instead, he punched the barghest, which caused it to crash hard into the ground.

A flash of pain erupted on his back, and he noticed a gwyllgi had approached soundlessly from behind. Normally, these beasts were of no concern, but he also had to worry about the mage and archer. There also were two more demons who still stayed put. One of them carried a two-handed sword and, with his muscular build, looked very much like a classic warrior.

But the other's gear gave Zac no indication of her means of attack. He assumed she was some sort of mage, as she held a tome in her hands.

Zac growled in annoyance and kept the barghest down on the ground with one hand and grabbed a knife out of his pouch with the other. With a quick stab, he tore its throat out. It was still alive but wouldn't be for long. He just barely dodged another arrow coming at him right after his kill, but simultaneously, an earthen spike tore straight through the dying barghest and headed for his head.

Just as he was about to dodge, a splitting pain in his mind made him completely blank out, and as he tried to dodge the incoming spike, he realized his body didn't respond.

But with a muffled roar, Zac used all his willpower to force himself to move. He succeeded in breaking the odd restriction and managed to move his head somewhat away from the stone spear. It still tore a huge gash in his left cheek, doubling the length of his mouth.

Breaking free from the binding left him with a pounding headache and a bit woozy, and he had to shrug his head to reorient himself.

A quick glance at the enemies showed that one of the demons who earlier had been staying put was puking blood while looking aghast at Zac. It was the one who was holding a tome, looking mysterious. He didn't have time to think about what kind of skill she used, as he was beset from both behind and the back.

A gwyllgi charged at him again, but this time, he was prepared. With a quick stab, blood gushed out of its chest, and it crashed into the ground. He took another arrow, this time to his leg, but it was a worthwhile price for another enemy down.

He grabbed the dying gwyllgi by its neck and used it as a shield while charging toward the group. The distance wasn't far, and he was upon them before they could send another salvo of earthen spears and arrows.

Zac ran toward the downed mage in order to get his axe back, but the warrior demon who had stood rooted until now placed himself in his way. From his bulging muscles, he seemed he focused on the Strength attribute, which actually made Zac relieved rather than anything else. If it was one thing he was confident in, it was his supreme strength.

The warrior roared and swung his sword toward him. Zac didn't dare use his knife to intercept and could only use the beast carcass as a club. He swung it at the warrior, trying to angle it so that he would hit the flat of the blade rather than the edge.

The corpse and the sword clashed, and the corpse exploded in a mangled shower of blood and viscera, drenching both Zac and the demon. But it did its job, and the sword was deflected once. That was all he needed, and he crashed into the demon with all the strength he could muster.

The warrior was flung away like a ragdoll, not being able to muster any resistance in the slightest. He fell down a few meters away, and whether he was alive or dead was unknown. The demons seemingly hadn't expected that outcome of the collision, and he managed to immediately snatch up his axe before they could react.

Zac then made a beeline for the archer. At these close quarters, the archer had actually dropped his bow and instead held a short sword and a blade respectively. Zac would have expected him to gain some distance like the last archer he'd fought. But perhaps he either actually focused on blades, or didn't dare turn his back on Zac while fleeing. Both the blades were crackling with the same lightning as the arrows he had shot at Zac earlier.

Zac ignored an earthen spear stabbing into him and pushed on toward the rogue-looking demon. He wanted to make short work of him and swung a horizontal swing intended to cleave him in two.

However, the demon almost seemed to have no bones in his body and curved his torso to avoid the swing and then retaliated by trying to stab Zac's heart and throat. Zac was out of position with the swing and could only desperately protect himself with his free arm, really wishing he had a buckler right about now.

The knife heading for his heart plunged into his bicep, and the short sword changed trajectory slightly to avoid hitting his arm as well. It at least managed to nick his throat, and a small gout of blood spurted out. But at least it hadn't hit an artery. The electric shocks hurt as well, but with Zac's Endurance he could grit his teeth and simply force his body not to spasm. These arcs of lightning couldn't compare to the black lightning he had tasted earlier as well.

He turned his hand to readjust his edge and tried to swipe the demon on the way back. The demon once again deftly repositioned his body so that he would be able to avoid it, but this time Zac wouldn't be denied. Just as the axe blade was about to miss the demon's throat, a translucent edge grew out a meter and cleanly decapitated the ranger.

Zac didn't really want to show his ace while there still were three demons alive, but he had to kill the ranger. The ranger was the only one he wasn't sure he would be able to catch if they started to flee. And if they were sane, they should. He had decimated half their force in almost no time. His wounds looked grisly but were nothing that would stop him from continuing his onslaught.

With his new skills and power-ups, he truly felt like the apex predator of his island.

42

EXODUS

With only two demons left, not including the knocked-out warrior, Zac charged toward his next targets. The two demons briefly looked each other in the eye, and both launched an attack before fleeing.

The tome-wielding demon's attack was an almost invisible ripple in the air, whereas the earth mage erected a large wall. Zac once again threw his axe just before the wall completely obscured the two fleeing combatants, and then he crashed straight into the wall.

The wall was hastily erected and couldn't withstand Zac's momentum, and he blasted through it like a wrecking ball. Just as he did, the ripple hit him, making him nauseous and disoriented. But the attack wasn't as strong as the earlier one, and he soon managed to dispel the effects.

A quick glance at the demon who used the ripple attacks showed her dead with an exploded chest, with his axe stuck in the ground some distance away from her corpse. But before he could continue on to kill the earth mage, he felt an intense amount of danger as he heard a whistling sound. It was the sword-wielding warrior Zac had punted earlier.

Somehow he had gotten up and snuck right behind Zac without him noticing, and his two-handed sword was bearing down on his throat. Zac had no time to dodge and could only put his hopes on the spell on his chest. The familiar golden sheen of the armor's skill immediately enveloped him, just in time to intercept the large sword.

With a crash, the warrior was flung backward once again, and this time, Zac could hear the sound of bone breaking.

The earth demon was still running, and Zac couldn't let him get away. He barreled after him and threw a knife at the back of the mage. A block of rock rose behind him, intercepting the dagger, but the scare made the mage stumble.

Zac immediately rushed to the fallen demon and ferociously stabbed down at his throat. However, a layer of rock appeared on the mage's skin, creating another layer of defense. The knife simply couldn't cut through it.

Terror was still evident in the demon's eyes, and it stuttered some words in its own language. Zac ignored it and brought out the huge great sword from his pouch. He increased the weight to the max through the inscription on the blade, and slammed it down on the body. It was cruel, but he wouldn't risk letting the mage somehow alert the army to what was going on.

Over 130 Strength and a heavy great sword resulted in a ruptured lump of flesh on the ground, and even a crater was created.

Zac didn't waste any time and immediately ran back toward the last demon. He found him limping away from the scene of the battle, his sword discarded where he fell. He soon noticed Zac approaching, with fear and hatred evident on his face. Suddenly, he completely disappeared, shocking Zac.

He wondered if the demon had used some sort of teleportation skill that would allow it to escape. He furiously ran toward where the demon disappeared and looked around for any clues.

Zac saw a glimmer in the distance and immediately threw a dagger at it. Suddenly, the background looked like it was distorting, and the warrior reappeared, the dagger lodged in his arm. Zac ran over and, with a swing of the great sword, ended the fight.

The last demon had used an illusion skill like his array or something similar. That was also how he'd snuck up and almost decapitated him earlier. Zac was a bit surprised a meathead-looking warrior knew such a skill, as that felt like something that usually belonged to rogue-like classes.

It made him realize he couldn't rely on his gaming experiences for everything. The system was quite omnipotent, and anything was possible.

With the demons killed, there was no hurry anymore, so Zac quickly treated most of his wounds and then gathered up all the corpses and their gear in his pouch. This also made sure none of the demons pulled a ruse on him and played dead, as nothing living could enter the pouch. He also retrieved his daggers and axe, and while doing so, he was attacked by the last barghest and gwyllgi from the roving party.

With their masters dead, they went back to their ordinary hyper-aggressive behavior. Without any demons shooting various things at him, he finished them off easily, officially eradicating the war party.

The fight had gone above his expectation, and he was almost like a fox let loose in a henhouse. His stats were getting increasingly scary for his level. Furthermore, the fight had also made him realize something. Not one of the demons he had fought thus far had used any Dao while fighting. They had used battle tactics and skills, but the indefinable quality of Dao, such as Zac's heaviness and force he could imbue into his strikes, were missing. Perhaps gaining a Dao Seed was something uncommon, or at least hard, making it a rare boost reserved for the elite.

He was also very satisfied with his new skill **[Chop]**. It worked just as he hoped, providing a great method of sneak attacking. He wasn't sure if it was designed to be used this way, but he felt it was the most effective method in this type of combat.

Zac had wanted to use the skill a bit more to test it out in battle, but unfortunately, he'd spent a good deal of the battle without the axe in his hand. He really hoped he would be able to pick up some backup axes or even throwing axes soon. Unfortunately, Azzun had been the only demon so far who fought with an axe.

Even though he'd luckily stopped the signal flare and finished the battle quickly, Zac didn't feel relieved. The fight took place right by his camp, making him realize it was just a matter of time before he was exposed.

He spent the next hour going over the scene of the battle, meticulously removing any traces of battle that he could. He was forced to crush the earthen spikes into rubble, but the wall was crumbling by itself for some reason. Perhaps it was erected so hastily that it couldn't properly stabilize, sort of like his **[Chop]** blade when making it too long.

When finally done, it wasn't readily apparent a battle had taken place outside his camp. There were sections of overturned earth, though, as Zac had to hide the blood and viscera somehow. Hopefully, a day or two in the sun and wind would make it appear more natural.

Finally, Zac returned to the camp and properly stitched himself up. He had already removed the arrowhead, but the ugly gash in his face was still open. He'd prioritized hiding the scene of the battle and had only kept his mouth closed in hopes that it would help the wound close by itself.

After taking a look in the mirror, he saw it was already slowly starting to close. He knew that it would leave an ugly scar, permanently disfiguring his face.

Well, better ugly than dead, I suppose, Zac thought with a sigh. Besides, that scar was only the latest in a litany of wounds on his body accumulated over the last month.

Finally, he closed his eyes to sleep for two hours before getting up. His wounds were getting better. Most of the wounds had been quite shallow thanks to his high Endurance, and he felt healed enough for another day of battle.

While cleaning up the scene during the night, he made a difficult decision about his future. He would abandon camp, at least for now. The risk of returning home after a day of grinding monsters and finding himself in an ambush started to feel too high for comfort. He would only return if absolutely needed.

He started to pack up anything of use to bring with him. Luckily, he'd acquired another magic pouch from the battle, although its space was smaller than his first. It was halfway packed with various rocks and plants. It seemed that the demon parties were roving the island to collect samples of various things. Zac didn't know why, but he felt they didn't do it to compose a botanical encyclopedia.

His guess was that it was for healing remedies or poisons. Even before the world changed, plants with healing properties existed, and if they got crammed chock-full with Cosmic Energy, the effect might be far greater. Maybe the demons had some means to test whether the local flora possessed any value, so they collected it to be tested. That would explain why there were only a few samples of each type in the bag.

He left the rocks and herbs in, as he didn't require a lot of space. The herbs might come in handy in the future, after all. He filled the other half with spare gear and the two luxurious chairs. He kept the table, rug, and parasol in his original pouch. He had grown fond of the furniture and didn't want them seized by the demons if they found his deserted campsite.

He also tried storing the Nexus Node and the array flags, but it didn't work. He wasn't surprised, as he already knew he couldn't move them too far from the camp either. He once tried it earlier, as he had wanted to use the gravity array as a trap device. But when he moved the flags too far away from his designated outpost, the flags started to vibrate ominously.

Apparently, they would self-destruct if they were moved too far. They were bought by the System as an outpost improvement, so the System restricted them somehow. Maybe he could purchase nonrestricted versions in the future in the shops he had seen in the outpost store. He could only leave them where they were and hope that the demons didn't destroy them. Most of the things would be pretty cheap to purchase again, but losing the gathering array would hurt.

Finally, he tried to store his new pouch in his old one, but it didn't work either. Perhaps one couldn't place a magic space inside a magic space, as it would violate some law of space or whatever. He could only carry the two pouches next to each other on his belt.

Having packed all his essentials, he paused as he looked over the camp briefly, some sadness welling up in his heart. He probably wouldn't return here until the demons were dealt with. He now had both brought a demon here for interrogation and also fought a large battle right at the steps of his camp. The risk of staying here was too large.

He could buy defensive arrays, but he held little assurance that something that only cost around a hundred thousand Nexus Coins could keep a whole demon army at bay. Besides, they simply needed to siege him by leaving a hundred men outside, and sooner or later, he would run out of resources and also fail his quests.

With a sour feeling, he set out, moving toward the western part of the island, where he'd fought the herald. After arriving in the vicinity, he dumped the bodies and tried to stage the area to look like it had happened there. He wasn't too optimistic that he'd fool anyone, though, but he didn't want to waste time with burying them. They'd know the party was dead one way or another soon anyway, and he hoped to move their attention to this part of the island.

The corpses were left on the ground without any of their gear and weapons, as it had all been pilfered by Zac.

Done with the task, he set out again, this time heading for the mountain.

43

STONE MONKEYS

Zac moved through the forest with determination. He felt that he couldn't look around for information or clues anymore. He simply couldn't find the last herald, and he was making no headway regarding the general either.

The general was likely holed up in the city, and the last herald either stayed in the cave or in the city as well. He had traversed the whole island while grinding for his quest skills, and hadn't even seen a trace of the alpha beast. The city and the cave were the last two options that he could come up with.

He needed to progress his quests, and the monkey mountain was the only way he could, as he saw it. The other option was entering the cave, but he felt it was too risky for now. There was a lot of foot traffic to and from that cave, and it seemed they placed great importance on it. He had no idea of the topography inside either, meaning he might be stuck in a large cave with no other exits.

The mountain was a safer bet. While it was somewhat close to demon activity, the cave was located at the foot of the mountain towards the southeast. If he kept his activities to the western part and the central area of the mountain, he should be able to act unconstrained without any demons noticing. That was as long as another war party didn't happen upon him, of course.

But the mountain sported complicated terrain with a multitude of outcroppings, caves, and paths, making it convenient to escape even if he was found out.

He soon arrived at the mountain and stealthily started making his way forward, looking for targets. He was planning on thinning the herd for a few days while looking for the monkey king. Since the stone monkeys had a strong sense of camaraderie, he was afraid that the monkey herald would be able to summon hundreds of monkeys with a shout.

But if those animals were already dead, he'd be able to fight the boss without any interruptions. He had already seen that no reinforcements came through the crystal, so every monkey he killed was one less to worry about in the future.

There were a lot of monkeys on the mountain, but nowhere near the seemingly endless number of barghest that were skulking in the forest. He soon found a group of roughly fifty monkeys that sat huddled together and seemed to be sunbathing. They were completely immobile and staring up at the sky. It was a group like this that had almost ended Zac's life just days before.

Zac didn't prepare any tricks or traps for this fight, and after a quick survey to make sure another group was not in the vicinity, he charged into the pack. He charged up **[Chop]** through the fractal in his hand to the limit of what he could control, and with a great arc decimated three monkeys with one swing. Apart from being a good skill for surprise attacks, it also was excellent when fighting large groups of weaker prey.

Between the haft and the elongated blade of his skill, he had a far greater reach compared to a normal axe wielder, and everything within two and a half meters of him was a zone of death. Enraged screams erupted from the pack of monkeys, and they started to frenziedly throw themselves at him.

This time, he wasn't in as dire straits as the last. His Strength and Endurance had increased considerably, and the skills increased his efficiency against large packs of enemies. Last time, he often wasn't able to completely kill a monkey with a swing, only managing to hurt or maim it. But with **[Axe Mastery]**, he'd learned better ways to handle his weapon, and with **[Chop]**, he managed to hit more targets at once.

He was like a harvester cutting down his crops, as with every swing, a few monkeys perished. The rock plating on their bodies offered almost no protection against Zac's inhumanly powerful swings, and rock chips and body parts kept flying in all directions.

The battle only lasted for a minute, but almost every monkey died. Terrified by the onslaught, some of the smarter monkeys had desperately fled when Zac had killed half of the pack. Zac couldn't be bothered with hunting them down, as he was quite exhausted and panting. The fight had been fast, but it also had been furious. Keeping his **[Chop]** skill active at maximum capacity for a whole minute also drained him of a lot of his Cosmic Energy.

Exhausting himself had been worth it, though, as the fight gave him another level. Of course, he had been quite close to leveling up already before the battle. Zac pulled up his status screen to allocate his points while he moved away from the battle.

He quickly allocated two points in Endurance and one in Strength, but as he was about to close the status screen, he noticed that all his stats had improved again after the allocation. He quickly stopped and took another look to see what changed.

Name: Zachary Atwood
Level: 29
Class: [F-Rare] Hatchetman
Race: [F] Human
Alignment: [Earth] Human

Titles: Born for Carnage, Ultimate Reaper, Luck of the Draw, Giantsbane, Disciple of David, Overpowered, Slayer of Leviathans, Adventurer, Demon Slayer, Full of Class, Rarified Being, Trailblazer, Child of Dao, The Big 500

Dao: Seed of Heaviness – Early

Strength: 145
Dexterity: 59
Endurance: 84
Vitality: 69
Intelligence: 49
Wisdom: 49
Luck: 67

Free Points: 0
Nexus Coins: 157,096

He had once more gained another title, this one called The Big 500. He focused on it, and a prompt explaining the title appeared.

[The Big 500: First in world to reach 500 total attributes. All stats +2]

And the strong get stronger, Zac thought wryly. It seemed somewhat unfair that the System rewarded those with the most attributes with even more attributes, but no one said that the System was fair.

Just look at how it sent the talented people to some Tutorial, deeming the rest as trash and leaving them here to fend for themselves.

It wasn't a large boost, but it did cheer Zac up after the Child of Dao title. It also reminded him of his strong points. He might not be as smart and talented as others, and he might not be able to cultivate. But even if the cultivators came back with a bunch of skills and knowledge, he could still beat them up with his pile of attributes if needed.

He found a secluded spot between a mountain wall and some bushes and sat down to recuperate. With the assistance of the mother-daughter array and a Nexus Crystal, it only took him forty-five minutes to restore his Cosmic Energy to its peak. He felt the pinch when using a crystal for recuperation instead of cultivation, but he didn't want to waste any time so close to enemy territory. A crystal lasted for roughly two hours, so his reserve of crystals would be enough to keep a breakneck grinding pace for weeks if needed.

As soon as he was topped off on energy, he kept looking for the next group. He didn't dare look while recuperating, as he never knew when he'd be stuck in an avalanche of monkeys. Soon he found another gathering of the beasts, this one slightly larger than the last. He didn't know if these groupings were families or packs, but he was thankful that they were spaced out a bit in this manner.

After another recon of the surroundings, he once again started a slaughter. There was not much of a difference between this fight and the last, and it soon ended. He was a bit worse for wear, but the blunt hits from their stone fists did not impact his body overly much. He had over 80 Endurance by now, and he gauged the monkeys' Strength to be somewhere in the 60s. They still hurt, but it would take some while for him to take actual damage.

The only real dangers the monkeys could muster up was either from their sharp teeth or from simply tiring him to death with numbers. But with the reach of his weapon infused with **[Chop]**, no monkey maw really managed to get close to him, and he carefully checked the surroundings before every fight for hidden backups.

Zac kept this rotation between fighting and resting going, slowly making his way toward the central area of the mountain. Zac figured the herald should be somewhere on one of the peaks. Unfortunately, the mountain had a number of peaks rather than just one, so he was planning on checking them one by one and killing the monkeys in between.

Zac had already known grinding monkeys would be lucrative, as each monkey gave almost as much Cosmic Energy and Nexus Coins as four barghest. But with his improved stats and skills, his grind speed skyrocketed, shocking even himself. As the suns set, Zac finished up his last battle for the day, which had actually rewarded him a second level, bringing him to level 30.

Done with the fighting for now, he retreated to a small cave he'd found while traversing the mountain paths. It was secluded and seemed to have once housed a bear or some similar animal from the shed fur in the corners. But from the dust gathered, it seemed that no one had been here for weeks.

Zac guessed that this cave had been moved here with its inhabitant from wherever this mountain came from, and that the stone monkeys killed the bear when it ventured out for food.

The cave wasn't huge but provided Zac with sufficient space to practice using the **[Axe Mastery]** guidance system before he finally sat down and rested. He also spent over an hour on trying to gain another Dao Seed. He was trying to actualize the other aspect he had sensed the strongest from his Dao vision, sharpness. If he got another Dao Seed, he would gain another power-up and speed up his farming even more.

But no matter what he did or how, he couldn't take even one step on the path. When he had tried to imagine the one for heaviness, it went very smoothly, and he couldn't quite figure out why the difference in difficulty was so huge. He could only speculate that he either simply had no talent for the Dao of Sharpness, or that the System restricted Dao Seeds somehow.

Perhaps the skill could only reward him with one Dao Seed. If he wanted more, he had to work on it by himself by arduously practicing and meditating on it. He knew that it would likely have taken him years to figure out the feeling for the Dao of Heaviness if it weren't for the vision essentially imprinting the Dao in his mind. He more and more realized the value of that vision as he kept trying to meditate on the Dao by himself.

Finally, he gave up and called it a day. But he would dedicate some time every day for meditation as well, he decided. At least until someone told him it was a waste of time. It had been a long day, and Zac was exhausted. He wiped his sweat and then crept into a small crevice that secluded him even further, and fell into a deep slumber.

44

PEAK

Zac woke up just at dawn and decided to meditate briefly before getting ready. He wasn't sure whether it helped him gain insight and progress his Dao Seed, or helped gain a new one. Even so, he felt it was a worthwhile endeavor. He was starting to get worried about his psyche. He had bathed in blood and battle constantly for weeks, and it had taken its toll. He felt he'd almost shut off all his emotions as a coping mechanism to not go insane, but it wasn't a permanent solution.

He needed to adjust his state of mind to be able to endure. He knew that even if he survived the island, his life wouldn't likely change much. He still had to defend his island from new invaders for three months even if he managed to kick out the demons. At least if he understood his quest Incursion Master correctly.

Incursion Master (Unique): Close or conquer incursion and protect outpost from denizens of other alignments for 3 months. Reward: 5 E-Grade Nexus Crystals, outpost upgraded to town, status upgraded to Lord. (0/3)

Since the quest still hadn't progressed after over a month, he believed it would start up as soon as the demons and the incursion were dealt with. If it meant that he only needed to worry about the critters on the island for three months afterwards, then everything would be well and good. But Zac held no hope that the System would be so nice about it and would likely send some trouble his way.

As he was looking through his quest panel, he also noticed that the Forester's Constitution quest unfortunately hadn't progressed from his day of battling monkeys. There were some solitary trees rooted on the cliffs, but it seemed the System made a clear distinction between a mountain next to a forest and a forest.

He closed the menus and silently stared out over the tranquil view. The mountains were quite a bit calmer compared to the forest, as the stone monkeys didn't have the tendency to incessantly roar like the barghest did. It almost felt like he was just camping again, which made him think about Hannah.

To be honest, he hadn't really been thinking about her and the others a lot lately, as he was focused on surviving and getting stronger. As he was reminiscing about her, he realized he had missed an important clue about the Tutorial. The four of them hadn't returned to his camp after the monthlong Tutorial had ended. He hadn't reflected on it at the time, his mind occupied with the newly arrived demons and his class acquisition.

As he saw it, that could have two reasons. First, they were all dead, and the System didn't bother to teleport back corpses. Second, after finishing the Tutorial, they were not teleported back from where they were snatched up, but somewhere else. Perhaps to human settlements or the like.

He could only pray it was the second reason. He wondered if they were looking for him, or if they just assumed he died. Had Hannah moved on?

Zac sighed and looked out at the sunrise. What obligations did he have to a new girlfriend when the apocalypse came? They had only been together for a few months when the world was integrated into the Multiverse. And even if he managed to find her again, it would likely take a long time. Could they still even be considered a couple? He couldn't find any easy answers and simply tabled the matter.

There were monkeys to kill.

He ate a quick breakfast and headed out. Today, he was planning on scaling one of the peaks to look for the herald. As he traversed the mountain, he made an intriguing discovery. The further up he climbed, the more concentrated the Cosmic Energy felt.

He was clueless if it was related to altitude or if something about the mountains themselves caused the phenomena. But he realized that it might be very valuable in the future. He wasn't a cultivator, but even he felt invigorated by the density of Cosmic Energy in the surroundings.

Perhaps he could rent out the mountains to cultivators in the future at exorbitant rates. He could only assume that cultivating in this kind of environment would be far more effective compared to doing it in a place with a normal density of energy. It could be a great source of income if he got a town up and running in the future. There was something about the thought of becoming a post-apocalyptic slumlord that gave him a comforting sense of normalcy.

Zac spent half the day killing monkey packs and scaling the closest peak, with his efficiency in monkey dismantling starting to reach a sublime level. There were some surprises when unexpected backup that Zac had missed entered the fray, but it generally only resulted in more Nexus Coins for himself. The scariest moment was when a monkey somehow managed to sneak up on him, biting him in his inner loin. Just slightly to the left and the monkey would have eaten his precious jewels.

He reached the peak at midday and, after a brief survey, could conclude that this peak wasn't the home of the herald. The air felt quite fresh up here, and Zac decided to have his dinner with a view. He sat down between some rocks to look more inconspicuous and retrieved some fruit and dried meat from his pouch.

His experiments with food and the pouch was a great success. Everything he put inside kept even better compared to a refrigerator, the fruits and slabs of meat still looking pristine after over a week. He didn't dare start a fire for some barbeque this close to the demon town, though, so he could only stick to his dried rations.

As he ate, he looked over the mountain range. His view from the peak afforded him a unique vantage, and he made some new discoveries.

There were a total of five real peaks, of which he sat on the westernmost. The peak he occupied was slightly off on its own, whereas the other four were a bit more clumped together.

Between the four peaks, there seemed to be a secluded valley that wasn't visible from down below, as it was located a few hundred meters above sea level. The mountain range itself had some sparse vegetation, such as some windswept shrubbery and small trees, but the valley seemed quite lush with an abundance of leafy growth. Zac even thought he could discern a small pond or lake but couldn't be sure, as a large part of the valley was covered in mist.

The valley certainly looked intriguing, like a secret little paradise hidden from sight. If he was on a treasure hunt, he'd bet all his doubloons that any riches the island had to offer were hidden there.

More importantly, it also seemed like a good resting place for a herald.

The only thing making him unsure was the fact that the monkeys seemed to like the rocky outcroppings and cliffs of the mountain. It would be a bit odd if their leader preferred to stay in a forest instead.

The great elevation also allowed him to finally confirm that he was indeed on an island. He hadn't been able to see anything behind the mountain range before, and knew there might have been land on the other side as well. But steep cliffs gave way to the ocean at the end of the mountain range, looking almost as though the mountain had been sliced clean off. Perhaps the System simply had chopped off part of a larger mountain range and slapped it onto the edge of the island. It was quite the sight, with a drop of at least a hundred meters down into the waters below.

Zac finished his meal and made his way back down the mountain slopes again and started trekking eastbound for the other peaks. He kept killing every monkey pack in his way, bringing a storm of carnage to the mountain. He was somewhat surprised that there still wasn't a more concerted effort to catch him by the monkeys by now, as the monkeys seemed to care greatly for each other.

But they stayed in their groups still and made perfect targets for him. He even gradually dared to attack larger packs as his confidence grew. Initially, he skipped the gatherings that were too large, but by now, he felt confident enough to attack most packs.

Zac thought that he would actually gain another level this day, but he was forced to suddenly stop fighting during the evening. It wasn't because he was hurt or lacked targets; the problem was his axe.

His war-axe possessed a self-repairing and sharpening feature through its inscriptions, but it seemed it couldn't properly keep up with Zac's recent activities. During his barghest genocide, it had no problems staying in good shape, but here it was, dull and blemished after only one day.

Zac realized that the tough rock plating on the monkeys' bodies was the problem. His Strength and Endurance provided all the power he needed, but it was his weapon that failed him. He was quite confused about the whole thing, though. When he fought the monkeys, he always used his skill **[Chop]** to create the translucent enlarged edge to cover his actual axe-head. Still, his actual axe was worse for wear.

It seemed that the skill didn't just copy the edge of his weapon, it rather projected it. That was a disadvantage he hadn't expected, but then again, it still was an extremely powerful and diverse skill for being the first attack skill the class offered.

With no other option, he could only find refuge for the night again and instead spend greater time on practicing with **[Axe Mastery]** and meditating. He briefly considered whether to keep going, using one of the large swords in his pouch as a weapon instead. But he eventually decided against it.

For one, he couldn't use his skills with a sword, and there also was another reason he hesitated. He wanted to use other weapons as little as possible in general.

When he picked his class, it generally looked like the options were based on his activities. Since his stats, skills, and experiences all were centered on the axe, he wanted to upgrade in this direction when he got the opportunity to upgrade the Hatchetman class. He was afraid that he might miss out on a good class upgrade if he kept using too many various weapons and not fulfill the prerequisites.

That was why he also really wanted to find more axes, so he wouldn't be forced to use knives as much for throwing or as backups. He even toyed with the idea of stalking the roving gathering parties on the island to find someone with axes and then take them out. But ultimately, it still felt like an unnecessary risk. That he'd managed to kill the party at his camp so smoothly largely could be attributed to the element of surprise. He felt that he could likely wipe out most of the parties by now, but he couldn't guarantee that they wouldn't be able to send out a warning signal like the flame mage had tried.

Zac finally found a decent cave and settled in. As he was practicing his axe technique, he was pondering whether he already had to change his plans. The reason was the huge number of Nexus Coins he was racking up. A day of killing the monkeys resulted in roughly 100,000 Nexus Coins. That amount took him almost a week to gather when desperately hunting barghest.

He currently had 347,000 coins and only needed two days to gather the necessary coins for the movement skill **[Steps of Gaia]**. He felt his current weakness was that his speed was lacking. If he could move faster, he wouldn't have to keep throwing his axe at people, but instead simply run up to them.

Allocating his free points in Dexterity was an option, but he felt it wasn't the correct one. He had already decided to focus on one or two stats and let his titles take care of the rest. He already had 59 Dexterity, which should be considered a lot for anyone not having Dexterity as his or her main attribute.

Besides, after observing the demons he fought, he realized they did the same thing. They were specialized in one or two stats as well. The mages didn't have overbearing Strength or Dexterity and likely focused on Wisdom and Intelligence. Instead, they used things like magic shields and earthen walls to protect themselves from attacks.

Zac felt that this was the way that people powered up in the Multiverse. Focus on the attributes that best empowered him, and have skills shore up the shortcomings.

He knew he likely had survived the mentalist mage's binding during his last bout with the demons due to his high Intelligence and Wisdom. But he assumed that normally a warrior would have a skill to protect their mind instead of wasting their free stat points on those attributes.

The only problem for Zac was that he didn't have a ready source of skills except the Nexus Node. But the choices there seemed quite limited, and he hadn't gotten any new class skill quests yet. If specialization was the way to go, it also meant that he had wasted some stat points in the beginning by putting them into Vitality and Dexterity.

Of course, without the points in Vitality, he might be dead by now, but not being optimized left a bad taste in his mouth.

45

MONKEY CAPTAIN

Finally, Zac reluctantly decided not to get the skill for now. He wanted to find and kill the third herald first.

He really wanted the power-up, but he also realized he was working against the clock here. He was already somewhat surprised there wasn't a monkey army hunting him in the mountains after his activities. It wasn't a small number of stone monkeys he had killed in the last two days, after all.

He was also getting closer and closer to the area where the demons were active, and they could notice his activities at any moment. The mountains were getting filled with sites of desolation, with hundreds of monkey carcasses adorning the hills by now.

He was afraid that if he spent another two days grinding monsters, and then one day to travel to his camp and back to get the skill, his window of opportunity to kill the herald would pass.

After all, the cave where the demons worked all day was quite close to the easternmost peak. It wasn't unreasonable to assume they would wander around the peak as well, looking for more of whatever they wanted in the cave.

He needed to find the herald quickly and kill it. He decided to spend the day moving toward the valley and kill any packs that were in the vicinity of it. Then he'd finally try locating the herald early the next morning.

After he woke up, he briefly meditated and, after confirming his axe was back to tip-top shape, set out toward the cluster of peaks. He gained a level on the first pack he encountered, bringing him to level 31.

He soon arrived at the foot of the westernmost peak of the four clustered mountains. He planned to scale it halfway up, which would lead him to the entrance of the valley. Then he'd make a circle around the peaks to kill off any packs close to the valley.

That would both let him scout out the four peaks for anything out of place and also kill any potential backup that the herald could call for. If the herald was on one of the peaks rather than in the valley, he hoped there would be something different about it to give him some hints.

As soon as he started climbing the first peak, he noticed increased resistance. The packs grew slightly larger, and there were stronger monkeys in the packs. Monkeys in the wild usually had an alpha who led the group of primates, but he hadn't really seen that so far in the groups he had killed. Zac simply assumed that the herald was the big boss of everyone, but it didn't seem that simple.

But now there was a monkey with bulging muscles standing a head taller compared to the others. Zac used **[Eye of Discernment]** on it, but it still was only called a stone monkey. The other heralds both had names, so he could only assume this was not it.

The alpha monkey maybe could be considered a captain, and the herald was the general. Just the fact that the packs were getting stronger felt like a good indication that he was on the correct path. It showed the herald likely was nearby, as he'd hypothesized.

Zac hesitated for a second before doing his customary sweep of the surroundings.

The monkeys in general seemed stronger compared to the outer packs, so he needed to do some preparation. Close to the pack, he found a narrow path up in the mountain, with sheer walls on both sides. It seemed that the rocky formation had cracked in two sometime in the distant past, which had created this path. That would hopefully only let a few monkeys charge in at a time. It would slow down his assault, but he wanted to play it safe until he could gauge the strength of these juiced-up monkeys.

The next part was to lure the monkeys over, and Zac simply picked up a boulder the size of a head. With a grunt, he threw it straight into the clump of monkeys, and with its huge momentum, it smashed a poor monkey's head in.

The monkeys angrily roared and flooded toward him. Zac slowly backed away and placed himself some ways into the crack. He planned to kill a few and then back further in to make room for the corpses.

The battle started as intended, with Zac quickly reaping the lives of a dozen monkeys in quick order. But as he retreated further in, he noticed a very bad sign. The monkeys had no problems climbing the sheer rock walls.

Zac wanted to slap himself in his scarred face. He should have realized that rock monkeys were good at climbing rocks. He had simply forgotten about the nimbleness of their primate brethren, as the stone monkeys always seemed to sit immobile among the rocks rather than climbing them.

Just as he berated himself, he heard a loud roar from the back rows of the group of monkeys. Suddenly, all the monkeys in front of him threw themselves to the ground in perfect harmony, and taking their place was a rock hurtling toward him. It was twice the size of the one he had thrown, and he didn't have time to react before it slammed into him like a truck.

Zac was flung backward from the momentum and spit out a mouthful of blood. It seemed the monkey captain wanted revenge for his earlier throw.

Before he could get up, multiple monkeys hanging on the walls jumped down on him. Rather than trying to pummel him like the monkeys used to, it seemed that they tried to pin him down. They gripped his extremities with all their might and tried to keep him from getting up.

Unfortunately for them, his Strength was 160 by now, and he could lift the monkeys like they were children. He ignored the monkey clinging to his axe arm and furiously swung the axe, killing the monkeys who were gripping his legs.

As he finally was getting up after getting rid of all the monkeys, another projectile was flying in his direction. This time, it was a sharp stalactite, and Zac couldn't understand where the monkey captain had gotten it. He managed to deflect it at the last minute with his axe, but the force made him fall back a few steps.

He immediately jumped into the fray, now fighting both monkeys on the ground and those hanging on the wall. He madly flailed the axe around; the only thing keeping him safe was the great reach of **[Chop]**.

He soon got the answer from where the monkey captain found its stalactite. As he was desperately defending against the deluge of rabid monkeys, he saw the captain grab on to the rock wall. Its fingers actually carved into the wall, and suddenly, he dragged another stalactite straight out of the wall.

It actually looked like the monkey could use a skill, or at least an early prototype of one. It wasn't as fancy as the spikes the earthen mage had used, but he was shocked that a dumb animal could do it. It seemed that skills, and perhaps even exploring the Dao, were not something exclusive to humanoids.

He didn't have time to reflect on it further before another projectile came flying toward him. He saw it coming this time and grabbed a monkey to use as a shield. The monkey absorbed most of the blow, but Zac was still pushed back somewhat.

The monkey captain seemingly was able to keep generating these projectiles, as he once again moved his hand toward the wall. Zac didn't want to keep this status quo going. He wasn't really hurt apart from some bruising so far, but if he didn't do something soon, he might run out of energy or get hit by a lucky projectile.

He stopped his retreat into the crack and instead started to furiously push forward. He was a whirlwind of carnage as he pushed through the horde of monkeys. He wanted to finish off the leader first and then whittle down the others.

Monkeys started to climb around and charge Zac from the back, but with his 90 Endurance, he could shrug off the strikes for now. The only time he stopped his onslaught was when some monkey managed to grab his legs and risked pulling him down on the ground again.

The leader threw another large rock at Zac, seemingly trying to impede his advance.

Zac saw the projectile approaching this time and swung down his axe in a fierce vertical strike to cleave it. He had expected the two pieces to slam to the sides of him but was sorely mistaken. The only result from his strike was that two boulders hit him instead of one, slamming him back once again.

Zac could only redouble his efforts and, ignoring his Cosmic Energy expenditure, kept utilizing **[Chop]** to the max.

Finally, as he was three meters away from the captain, he couldn't be bothered getting in close with it, and overcharged the skill, increasing the length of the blade with a full meter extra. With a roar, he swiped in an upward arc, and the captain was split in two. He could only maintain such a length for a second, but one second was all he needed for one quick kill.

After that, he simply planted his back against the wall and

kept killing until there was no monkey left willing to fight. There were a few monkeys who kept screaming at him from a distance, but Zac hurled another rock at one, instantly crushing its head. Then finally the last remnants of the pack fled.

Zac was truly exhausted and hurting from the fight, but he forced himself to get up and move away from the battle. The sounds carried far in the mountains, and he didn't want to be around if either the herald or some demons heard the noise.

He kept sneaking up the mountain and soon reached the entrance to the hidden valley far up in the air. He didn't dare enter yet, but instead opted to hide between some rocks and recuperate from the battle. The melee reminded him that just because he had gotten the **[Axe Mastery]** skill, he still was by no means a master fighter. His planning had impeded him rather than helped, and he would probably have been better off just charging in as usual.

It felt like he had been fighting for his life on the island for an eternity, but in reality, he had only been on the island for roughly forty days. Before that, he'd just been a desk jockey, completely oblivious to any fighting tactics. He had made a few real beginner mistakes in this fight and could only strive to do better in the future.

46

THE HUNT FOR THE HERALD

As Zac stood at the edge of the valley, he was shocked by the density of Cosmic Energy. The amount in the air was already quite a bit higher in the mountains compared to down on the ground, but in this secluded vale, it was a whole tier higher still.

The density made his suspicion that the herald hid in the valley much stronger. He was sure that the monkey king would prefer the increased amount of Cosmic Energy if even the monkey captains were able to use skills and maybe even cultivate.

The amount of Cosmic Energy made Zac worried that there might actually be demons here as well. While he had observed their activities for a few days, he hadn't really seen any demons enter the mountains further than the cave, but that didn't mean that there weren't cultivator demons stationed here.

He refrained from entering the valley at the moment, as he still wanted to thin the herd of monkeys in the mountains first. A large enough roar from the valley might be able to call for reinforcements from all four peaks, after all.

The fight against the pack with the monkey captain had been a bit shaky, but it was mostly due to his mistakes. The monkeys on the peaks were slightly stronger compared to the ones he had fought earlier, but not to the point that they could stop his onslaught. He only needed to kill the leader and then it was carnage as usual.

There was one more pack he needed to kill on the mountain peak he had climbed. It didn't have any captain, but the monkeys in general were slightly bigger even compared to the last pack.

Zac entered the fray after having restored his energy and made short work of the pack. He made the interesting discovery that none of the monkeys dared to enter the valley, even when they were fleeing for their lives. Perhaps the valley was the private residence of the herald, and they had strict orders not to enter.

Or perhaps something even scarier than Zac lived in the depths of the valley. He supposed he would find out later.

Zac kept his momentum going, moving toward the next peak. He didn't try any fancy tactics anymore; he only tried to knock out the leaders of the following packs by throwing a boulder at them. He didn't even bother with the throwing knives, as they had trouble penetrating their stone armor. No matter whether the throw succeeded or not, he simply charged straight into the throng of stone monkeys, swinging away.

At midday, he reached the third peak, having mostly cleared out the two earlier ones apart from a few who managed to escape. This peak was the easternmost and also the one closest to demon activity. The cave that the demons found so interesting was located not too far away from the foot of the mountain.

Zac was unsure whether he dared to start a battle here, as it might attract the demons below. While the distance was quite great between his location and the cave, he was afraid the sound would carry all the way down. The monkeys got quite loud and agitated during the fights, after all. He decided to find a hiding spot with good vantage before deciding anything further. As he was somewhat ahead of schedule, he decided to wait for roughly an hour to gauge any activity in the area.

Weirdly enough, there was no monkey pack close to the entrance of the valley. Instead, the monkeys were stationed on the outer side of the mountain peak. This differed from the other two peaks so far, and Zac wanted to figure out why. He soon found his answer, as he was surprised to see a monkey captain hurl a large rock at a demon war party that approached the peak of the valley.

It hit one of them, and with a wail, he was flung away from the impact. The demons screamed at the group of monkeys angrily, waving their weapons. But the monkeys were a stoic wall that wouldn't let them pass. After another minute of posturing, the demons could only turn and leave the mountain.

Zac was confused as he slunk back to the inner side of the mountain. Weren't the monkeys the pets of the demons, like the other demon beasts? How did they dare deny the demons access to the mountains?

Zac started to get nervous that the monkeys actually weren't the fourth monster race, but rather, some native beast. The System did say it merged Earth with other planets due for integration, and they might be from another one. That would mean that there actually wasn't a monkey herald, but instead two heralds he couldn't find.

He felt that shouldn't be right, though. Everything pointed toward them being a part of the demonic invasion. Perhaps the monkeys had a higher standing and could actually boot the lower demons from their territory.

He knew he wouldn't get any real answer from just mulling it over, and continued on toward the fourth peak. The weird power dynamic between the monkeys and demons actually helped him out in the end, both removing the threat of demons in the mountains and not having to battle any monkeys that close to the demon activity.

He arrived at the fourth peak and, after an intense melee, finally finished killing all the packs close to the valley. As it was still only evening, he decided to head into the valley after all. Initially, he'd planned to wait until the next morning, but due to the inner side of the third peak being free from monkeys, he saved a few hours of work.

He took his first steps into the valley, vigilant against any hidden monkeys or other beasts. But after a few minutes of walking, it seemed that the forest was deserted. It was odd, as the forest itself felt like a paradise on Earth. The air was fresh enough that his cells felt invigorated just from breathing, and the foliage was lush and healthy. The earthy smell of the area calmed Zac's heart, inviting him to sit down and relax.

However, not even critters were present, making the forest eerily silent except for the occasional rustle from the wind. This stillness felt quite jarring to Zac, as his life had been accompanied by the sounds of the forest constantly since the world changed. From critters in the bushes to the calls of the birds. Even the deep roars of the barghest.

That all these sounds were gone didn't feel natural, and his vigilance only increased instead of it having a soothing effect on him.

As he walked, he noticed that he didn't recognize most of the trees or plants in the valley. Now, he wasn't any botanist; he only knew of the staple flowers and trees. But he felt he should at least recognize some of the vegetation if it was from Earth. There were a few trees he assumed were maples, but the leaves were as large as his torso.

He didn't know if the forest had mutated or evolved from the extremely dense Cosmic Energy in the area, or whether this forest came from another planet, but it felt like the old Earth wasn't able to produce a forest feeling so vibrant.

He was debating whether he should collect samples from the

various flowers and herbs like the demon parties did, but soon decided against it. He had no immediate use for them, and the valley would still be here if he managed to kick out the demons.

He soon arrived close to the small lake he'd glimpsed from the mountain peak. With how pristine the rest of the forest was, he had expected the lake to have clear, beautiful water. While it didn't look or smell stale, it also wasn't clear.

The lake was a mysterious shimmering blue, and he could barely see a decimeter into the water before everything was obscured. The water itself seemed to be packed with Cosmic Energy, as though the lake consisted of liquefied Nexus Crystals.

His body almost instinctively reached down to drink a mouthful of the enticing water before hastily stopping himself. It seemed like such a good natural resource, but still, there were no animals or monsters around, which was very eerie. Perhaps there was something lurking in the depths, preying on anything stupid enough to come too close to the shore.

He couldn't let the water go to waste, though, and he tied a string to one of his magical canteens. He then threw the canteen into the water and waited some time before dragging it out. It now contained the Cosmic Water, but he wouldn't try it before he could feed it to some beasts and see its effects.

Feeling uncomfortable by the mysterious lake, Zac continued onward toward the center of the valley. The mysteries of the azure pond would have to wait until another day.

He was almost at the core of the valley by now and slowed his pace. If the herald was in this valley, then it would stand to reason that he was somewhere in the center. Slightly nervous, he gripped his axe for comfort, as memories of the struggle with the last herald still haunted him.

Not far ahead, it seemed that the forest gave way to open fields, so Zac crouched down and slowly made his way to the edge of the forest. What met his eyes from his hidden vantage point shocked him.

It was a large field filled with shrunken and desiccated fallen trees. There were signs of bushes and flowers having existed as well, but they too looked like they had been baked in an oven. The only thing still standing tall was a solitary tree in the center.

It wasn't very large, only being roughly five meters tall, but it was spectacular. The trunk and branches had a crimson hue and a smooth exterior. The leaves weren't red or green but a pristine white, making it look like crystals adorned the branches.

It was a spectacular sight, and Zac didn't for a second think that this was a normal tree. It was something created with a lot of Cosmic Energy. The tree virtually hummed with power, making Zac wonder if it actually was alive.

Zac guessed that this tree was the reason for the desolation in the vicinity. The tree seemingly had absorbed the life or Cosmic Energy out of everything in its surroundings. Perhaps it even had killed all the animals in the forest as well, explaining why it was so quiet. It was a scary thought that the tree wasn't satisfied with the huge density of energy in the air and needed to drain its surroundings to be satiated.

It took Zac a second to register that something else was next to the tree. A monkey, roughly two meters tall with a build somewhat slimmer compared to its brethren, sat cross-legged with closed eyes under the tree. What made it stand out apart from its build was its color. If the other monkeys in the mountains were made of anthracite rock, then this monkey was made of lava. Red shining streaks ran along every part of the monkey's otherwise black body, emanating a heavy pressure.

It was the monkey king.

47

COLLISION COURSE

The lava monkey didn't look aggressive or violent like the normal monkeys, but rather harmonious. Even if it seemed crazy, it really looked like he or she was meditating under the peculiar tree. It was quite picturesque, the red streaks of the monkey matching well with the crimson trunk.

The good news was that it looked like he found his herald. The bad news was that he had no real idea on how to improve the odds in his favor. He saw no method to sneak up on it, as the dried husks of the vegetation on the field wouldn't provide enough cover.

He didn't dare use **[Eye of Discernment]** to see its level either, afraid it would notice him like the Imps. That it stayed in this forest with higher Cosmic Energy concentration, rather than in its natural habitat of the mountain peaks, was telling Zac that the monkey king possessed some sensibility for Cosmic Energy.

He debated whether he should charge in blind or wait for a better opportunity. Finally, he decided he had to go for it. Finding the herald sitting by itself with no backup in sight could only be considered a perfect opportunity.

He also discarded the idea of creating crude traps as he had for

Vul, the barghest herald. If this monkey could meditate, it likely was too intelligent to run into spikes like an idiot.

The only question was whether this monkey was of roughly the same power as Vul or not. When the limiter had been lifted at the turn of the month, he had concluded that the beasts had improved roughly 50% across the board.

He himself had improved far more than that, though. When he fought Vul, he had only 59 Strength, and now he was at 160. On top of that, his gear had improved considerably, and he'd already gained a class and improved pathways. He felt that even if he met an improved Vul today, he wouldn't have to rely on traps to kill it, and it wouldn't be a desperate struggle either.

But the monkeys were far stronger compared to the barghest. Would the monkey herald be far stronger compared to the barghest herald as well?

There was only one way to find out. He slowly repositioned himself to arrive from the east, which would at least let him approach the back of the herald. It might give him some time to close the distance before it could react.

He steeled his nerves and slowly ventured out of the protective cover of the foliage and entered the dead zone surrounding the magical tree. He took great care not to step on any of the dried twigs or branches that covered the ground, not wanting to alert the monkey of his approach.

But even though he made no sound, it seemed to be to no avail, as the monkey snorted and slowly got up on his feet. Zac held no hope that it was just a coincidence, and immediately pulled two daggers out of his pouch and threw them at the monster in quick succession.

The monkey turned around in a lightning-quick manner and, with two casual swipes, slapped the incoming daggers away into the ground. As the edges collided with its hands, sparks flew, but no wounds could be seen. Zac wasn't surprised, as the daggers were barely any use on the normal monkeys, let alone on this superpowered one.

Afterwards, he gave up any idea of stealth and thundered straight toward the monkey, with his axe at the ready.

While he charged, he used the **[Eye of Discernment]** on the monkey, which gave him a terse line of information.

[Cindermane, Level 58]

That line removed any last doubts whether this monster was a herald or not. A solitary named beast around level 50 fit the bill perfectly. It was a full 13 levels above Vul, who had been level 45 when they battled. He didn't know how levels worked for beasts, but if it was like for himself, it meant it should have almost a hundred more attributes in total. Together with the removed limiters, he realized he might be in for a tough battle.

Cindermane didn't stay put, but charged toward Zac as well. As he did, the red streaks on his body lit up and started to emit a fiery shine like lava. They clashed a few meters away from the red-white tree, with Zac doing an upwards horizontal swipe aimed at its torso.

The monkey actually dared to intercept the strike with its bare paws, which lit up completely to look like magma. A tremendous clash erupted when their attacks collided, the dead plants in the surrounding area being pulverized by the shock wave.

Zac was surprised to see that his strike didn't immediately overpower the herald. With his recent improvements, he'd started to believe there was nothing on the island that could have a comparable level of points in the Strength attribute.

The herald was pushed back from the force; however, Zac didn't emerge unscathed out of the initial collision either. The hands of the monkey did not only look like lava, but they were also as fiery hot as well. The air around them was wobbling due to the heat, looking like a mirage. The axe edge actually showed clear signs of heating up where it had collided with the monkey's palm.

Zac knew he couldn't fight a protracted battle, as the monkey would destroy his weapon if they kept clashing like this. Using **[Chop]** wouldn't help either, as the damage was transferred to the axe anyway.

Angry at being pushed back, Cindermane roared and stomped the ground, causing multiple spikes to erupt beneath Zac. They looked similar to the spikes of the earth mage, with the distinction that they seemed blazing hot and far more numerous.

Zac managed to destroy most of the spikes with a chop, but one managed to stab into his leg. A blinding pain erupted in his thigh, causing him to involuntarily scream. A sickening sizzling sound could be heard, and Zac smelled the fragrance of grilled meat. The spike was actually barbecuing his leg.

Ignoring the pain, he grabbed the burning hot spike with his free hand, ripped it out of his leg, and threw it away. As he did, the herald took the opportunity to grab the ground, dragging out a stone the size of Zac from seemingly nowhere. Its molten fingers penetrated the boulder, and soon the whole rock was glowing a sinister red.

With a roar, it tried to slam the stone down right on Zac, who could only awkwardly dodge. Not daring to hide any of his cards any longer, he infused his strikes with Dao and started swinging away against the herald.

Cindermane possessed either great reflexes or combat experience, as he kept dodging or deflecting the strikes. Zac tried to grab on to the monkey with his free hand in order to throw it down on the ground, but as soon as he got a grip on its arm, the red streaks lit up and the arm became searing hot. Zac instinctively let go with a scream, and the monkey took the opportunity to try to claw out his throat.

Zac saw no choice but to activate his armor, and the golden sheen protected him from getting killed. He wouldn't give up, even with his lifesaving device used up, and wildly kept swinging at the herald, unheeding of any Cosmic Energy expenditure. After a few exchanges, the monkey king managed to get a stab in with one of its hands, pushing a centimeter into Zac's arm. The finger burned even hotter compared to the spike, and Zac couldn't refrain from screaming in pain again.

However, Zac's every strike was overwhelming. He used every trick **[Axe Mastery]** had taught him and weaved a net of destruction with his axe. Marks started to appear on the monkey's hands, and it looked like it wouldn't be able to block his strikes forever. It was lucky, as the edge of the axe was starting to shine with a red sheen from all the collisions. Not much longer and Zac feared that the inscriptions on it would be ruined, which meant that it wouldn't auto-repair any longer.

He also had pushed the herald back toward the tree, and they were currently fighting under the white leaves.

The monkey became more agitated as they approached the trunk, and furiously fought to force Zac away from the tree. There clearly was something special about it, and the herald didn't want to risk it getting damaged. The monkey suddenly emitted a penetrating screech, its whole body lighting up.

It spat out a white-hot ball of magma straight at Zac's chest, forcing him to jump out of the way and away from the tree. As he dodged, he also saw that the lava spit wasn't the only thing that changed from that scream.

Like a scene out of a horror movie, an endless number of bodies rose out of the ground, pushing the dried trees and bushes to the side. It wasn't zombies, but a vast number of stone monkeys, all looking larger and stronger compared to normal ones. With a quick glance, he could make out at least forty monkey captains among the reinforcements.

The monkeys had been lying dormant under the ground, and the roar called them to action to create a trap. He didn't know why it waited so long to unleash them, but he knew that he had run out of time. In just seconds, he would be overrun with stone spears and boulders. He would have problems contending with just the monkey horde, but if he had to watch out for the spells from the herald as well, he'd surely die.

A desperate idea grew in his mind, and he didn't have time to go through pros and cons before trying it out. He was currently two meters away from the tree trunk, and with an exaggerated roar, he swung his axe in a horizontal swipe. As he did, the familiar blade of **[Chop]** rapidly grew, soon longer than he could stably maintain for any longer duration.

Cindermane screeched and hastily jumped to intercept the huge edge from cutting down the tree. Zac's premonition was correct; the tree truly held a great importance to the monkey.

The herald couldn't properly grab the translucent edge with its awkward positioning, and the edge cut into its whole body horizontally across the chest. A deep grisly gash was carved into its body, but its great Endurance prevented it from getting cut in two. It still was badly hurt and bled profusely as it fell down on the ground.

Just as he was about to finish it off with another swing, a boulder slammed into him from the side. He fell over away from the herald, and he barely managed to get to his feet before another hit him again, forcing him even further away from the dying lava monkey.

Unreconciled, he once again charged a great edge and swung it at the prone monkey king. But it still had some energy left and pushed itself out of the way.

He knew his window of opportunity had passed. Boulders and stalactites were approaching from all directions, and the only way to kill the herald was a suicide dive. As he only needed to kill it for a quest, he had no reason to die just to bring it down to hell with him.

Zac didn't hesitate and turned around to run. He could only hope the huge wound he'd inflicted upon it was lethal and that it would bleed to death. The lava monkey wouldn't have it, though, and used its last powers to shoot a few molten spikes in his direction. Zac could only strike away what he could and endure the rest.

Just after a few seconds, he had already gotten hit by another two boulders and was stabbed by three more stalactites. Then the army of monkeys was upon him.

48

SIMIAN HARANGUING

Finishing off the herald was suddenly the last thing on Zac's mind, and he was horrified as he saw an avalanche of monkeys approach him from all directions. He activated **[Chop]** and frenziedly waved it in front of him, decimating any monkeys that would impede his escape.

The assault was slowing him down, and finally, the enemies were upon him, punching and kicking with wild abandon. Every time a punch or kick hit where the lava spears had pierced him earlier, it hurt enough for him to almost pass out.

Zac couldn't care about his Cosmic Energy expenditure anymore and, with a roar, pushed as much Cosmic Energy as he could into the fractal on his hand. An enormous blade over five meters tall blazed into existence, and Zac swung the axe in a mighty horizontal arc.

The edge managed to stay active for less than a second, but the brief window carved out a large pocket in the swarm of monkeys. The swing killed at least twenty monkeys, and he even gained a level. He couldn't bother about that at the moment, as the short respite in attacks allowed him to rush out of the field and into the foliage.

Blood was running freely from Zac's mouth as he was shakily running through the forest, away from the magical tree and herald. The monkeys wouldn't relent and swarmed all around him, jumping between the trees or running on all fours on the ground. Had it not been for his wounded leg, he might have been able to maintain some distance after a mad dash. But now he was stuck in a quick jog, and even that was taxing.

He constantly was pelted with kicks and punches and the occasional mouth trying to bite into him with its sharp canines. A rock whizzed by his head and instead hit a monkey square in its chest. It appeared the monkey captains had problems with keeping the pace and throwing the projectiles simultaneously, at least.

More good news was that the herald was either dead or too wounded to join the pursuit, as there were no molten spears attacking him anymore. But that was about all the positives that Zac could list while he was mindlessly running.

He was already lost and could only run in a straight direction. Since he was in a valley between the peaks, no matter what direction he ran, he would sooner or later arrive at the mountains.

He desperately swung his axe back and forth to maim and kill his attackers. He didn't dare to use **[Chop]** anymore, as he was already running low on Cosmic Energy, and there were still at least a hundred monkeys following him.

He instead infused the attacks with his understanding of the Dao of Heaviness to add some impact to his strikes. It was the first time he was using it so freely and for a prolonged time, and he was starting to feel a headache coming on.

Soon he couldn't even use his Dao in order to empower his strikes, as he was afraid of increasing the pounding in his head.

He kept going, and with every few steps, he killed a monkey, but they seemed endless. Zac's whole body was hurting, but he couldn't stop. Another boulder came hurtling toward him, this one with proper aim. He was already mid-swing against a monkey and couldn't reposition in time, so he could only lift his left arm to block it.

The small boulder slammed into Zac, and a sickening pop could be heard. Zac was pushed back, and his arm hung limply by his side. Something was protruding oddly at his shoulder, and a blazing pain radiated through the arm. After a quick glance, he realized that his shoulder was dislocated.

Zac gritted his teeth and ran straight into the first monkey he saw, slamming his dislocated shoulder straight into the chest of the monkey. A blinding pain almost made him pass out, but it also temporarily dispelled the pulsing headache from overusing his Dao.

While it still hurt, Zac could move his arm again. He had used the monkey as a wall to slam the ball of his arm back into its socket. As a thanks, Zac gave it a quick chop, which decapitated it, and then kicked its headless body into two oncoming stone monkeys.

This couldn't continue for long, as Zac had less than 10% of his Cosmic Energy reserves remaining, while the monkeys showed no desire to relent. Thankfully, the lush forest soon gave way to rocky outcroppings and cliffs, showing that he was approaching one of the peaks.

Due to the haphazard escape, he wasn't sure which one of the peaks it was, but a quick glance outward showed the familiar forest of the island. That meant he wasn't running north, at least, as he'd only be seeing ocean then. He was thankful, as he was afraid he would have been forced to jump down the steep cliff, praying to survive the hundred-meter drop into the ocean.

Zac kept running, and he planned to escape into the forest down on the ground. The first time he fought the monkeys, they had stopped at the foot of the mountain, and he could only hope they'd do the same again.

But almost immediately as he ran, he knew that plan wouldn't work. As he passed a small crest, a larger view of the island came into view, and he could see the incursion and the demon town. The position immediately made him realize he was on the easternmost peak. If he ran right down this peak, he'd be in prime demon territory. Straight out of the frying pan and into the fire.

He stopped for a second, confused as what to do, which allowed a few monkey captains to drag new projectiles out of the ground and hurl them at Zac.

He slammed one of them away, but the other hit him with a deep thud, eliciting a bloody cough. Even with his 90 plus Endurance, it felt like he couldn't take many more of those throws. He couldn't remember how many he'd tanked by now, and it felt like his body was on the brink of collapse.

He sluggishly swung his axe and killed a monkey who was foolish enough to get close, and looked around for options.

In his vision, he saw a cave entrance slightly hidden behind some shrubbery and boulders. After a brief hesitation, he changed course for the cavity. If he continued on along the mountain path, he'd arrive at where he had spotted the demon party earlier, and the risk of running into the monkey packs was great. He couldn't return either, as he wouldn't last running to another peak.

He didn't really want to enter the cave, but he knew that it was his only hope. Right now, he couldn't see any other method to shake off the monkey horde. They seemed truly consumed by rage, which made sense, as he had killed well over a hundred of the assailants by now.

Either the cave was a small dwelling for an animal, or a part of a larger network of tunnels. If it was the former, he'd make a last stand, and at least the enemies would only be able to come from one direction. If it was the latter, he might actually survive by fleeing into the tunnels.

There were roughly ten monkeys in the way, and Zac grimly summoned **[Chop]** for one last charge. His arms and legs felt like they were coated in lead, but he determinedly swung his axe while he advanced.

The monkeys could offer no resistance against Zac's reignited spirit, and he soon was at the mouth of the cave. A rock slammed into his back just as he entered, making him realize he couldn't just stand at the entrance and fight it out. He would be sniped to death. After a quick glance inside, it seemed that the cave actually was just the entrance of a bigger cave system.

The monkeys seemed to have no problem following him into the tunnels, and they charged toward the entrance without hesitation. Zac suddenly was afraid that he would be in even worse straits if he let them enter. They were stone monkeys; who knew what advantages they'd have inside a cave.

Out of options, he could only do something stupid and desperate. He put away his axe and brought out his great sword. With a furious slam, he hit the roof of the cave entrance, causing huge cracks in the roof and making rock-chippings fly in all directions. He didn't stop and slammed twice more with all the strength he could muster, and finally, an ominous rumbling could be heard.

The roof of the cave started to collapse, and Zac desperately ran further into the cave. Falling rock and debris pelted him, and he was forced to leave his sword behind in the chaos. After a minute, the rumblings stopped, and the cave was completely blocked for at least twenty meters with debris. It would take even the strong monkeys a good while to excavate the entrance, if they even wanted to.

His hope was that the monkeys would give up and go back to the valley, but he wouldn't dare put his life on the line for it to be true. So he hesitantly ventured further into the cave to create some distance. His body was hurting all over, but he wouldn't let himself sit down, afraid that he wouldn't be able to get back up in a short while if he did.

The caverns seemed to be a confusing maze of interconnected tunnels and chambers, and Zac saw no change after thirty minutes of slow walking. The caves weren't completely pitch black at least, as there actually was growing moss on many of the walls, which gave off some luminescence. He didn't understand why they would create light, but he assumed that the moss was mutated by Cosmic Energy.

The tunnels were actually full of Cosmic Energy, almost at the level of the valley. The high concentration on the mountain peaks seemed to only be a result of some of the interior energy leaking out. It would be strange if something didn't change with the subterranean flora if they were consistently bathed in Cosmic Energy of this magnitude.

Finally satisfied with the distance from the entrance he had created, he stopped in a quiet chamber, which at least wasn't completely dark due to the glowing moss. He sighed and thumped down on the ground with a grimace. It was pitch black apart from the blue scattered lights from the moss, but he didn't care. He did have a flashlight he had brought from the camper if he needed proper light, but he didn't know how much charge the batteries still had. He instead brought out a Nexus Crystal from the pouch and started absorbing.

It didn't help in healing his battered body, but it did help in recovering his depleted energy. Together with his amulet, he was absorbing energy at a great rate, and after only four hours, he once again was full of Cosmic Energy.

That didn't mean that he was in prime condition, though. His head still hurt from overusing his Dao, and his body screamed in protest as soon as he moved slightly. He could only stay put for a bit longer in order for his Vitality to do its thing. He had nothing in his bag that could help his wounds, which were mainly blunt-force trauma as far as he knew. He did put some ointment on the burns from the herald, even if he wasn't sure whether aloe was effective against burns from magic monkey fire.

Finally done with everything, he rested his back against the wall and sighed despondently. Today did *not* go according to plan.

49

SPELUNKING

Since Zac felt somewhat refreshed from absorbing the Nexus Crystal, he held off on sleeping, and instead decided to take a quick glance at his status screen.

Name: Zachary Atwood
Level: 32
Class: [F-Rare] Hatchetman
Race: [F] Human
Alignment: [Earth] Human

Titles: Born for Carnage, Ultimate Reaper, Luck of the Draw, Giantsbane, Disciple of David, Overpowered, Slayer of Leviathans, Adventurer, Demon Slayer, Full of Class, Rarified Being, Trailblazer, Child of Dao, The Big 500

Dao: Seed of Heaviness – Early

Strength: 164

Dexterity: 59
Endurance: 92
Vitality: 69
Intelligence: 49
Wisdom: 49
Luck: 67

Free Points: 3
Nexus Coins: 485,286

The last few days had actually brought in almost all the coins he needed for the movement skill. Getting his skills and Dao boosts had increased his daily earnings tremendously. Of course, he knew that this was the limit for now. The only targets more lucrative compared to the monkeys on the island were the demons and imps. But he held no illusion that he would be able to charge into fifty of them at a time and start a massacre as he had with the monkeys. He would be blasted to smithereens in no time.

Next, he opened up his quest menu to see the progress of his quest.

Off With Their Heads (Unique): Kill the four heralds and the general of an incursion within 3 months. Reward: 10 E-Grade Nexus Crystals, E-Grade equipment, unique building depending on performance. (2/5)

He was quite disappointed to see that the monkey king apparently survived the slash. Of course, there was the possibility that it wasn't a herald, but he felt the chance of that to be quite slim.

He had gained a level right at the start of the pursuit, and he sensed he wasn't far away from reaching level 33 either. It was a shame that the System didn't provide the same type of service as many games, restoring both health and mana at the level-up. Then he might have actually have had a chance of turning things around and finishing off the monkey king.

The whole experience was quite a letdown and the first real setback except constantly getting hurt. He constantly went over things he could have done differently in order to actually kill the monkey. But soon he threw those depressing thoughts out of his mind, as he knew he had to work with what he had and try to continuously improve.

As he waited for his body to get better, he planned to meditate some on the Dao. He wished to both improve his current Seed of Heaviness, and get another seed, the Seed of Sharpness. These two forces were those he sensed to be strongest in the axe in his vision, and he felt that getting both of them was the first step on the path of true Axe Mastery.

Besides, the Dao of Sharpness might also be of some use for his throwing knives. Since **[Axe Mastery]** came with no manual on how to progress the Dao or his other skills, he could only fumble around in the dark. This time literally.

Unfortunately, he could only focus on the large axe fractal in his mind for a short while before his head started hurting again. It seemed that using Dao was still impossible after his overexertion. Zac wondered if there was something like mental energy or soul power that was used when pondering Dao or using it in battle, but he hadn't been able to sense anything of the sort thus far. He only knew his head hurt and felt swollen like a bad migraine.

Helplessly, he could only go to sleep. He would have preferred to take a look around the area, but his body didn't really listen to his commands anymore. Besides, any sound carried through the tunnels and amplified, and it was completely quiet apart from his breathing. There should be no monsters or creepy-crawlies around at least this part of the subterranean system.

Zac woke up some time later, not being able to tell exactly how long he was out. His watch had broken long ago, and his cell phone had run out of charge. He had learned to tell the time somewhat accurately with the help of the suns, but down in the caverns, this was useless.

Judging from the state of his body, he felt that he had been out somewhere between three and five hours. He was still bruised all over, but at least he could get by. He got up on his feet but stopped before setting out.

He was a bit unsure how to proceed from here on out. After some hesitation, he decided to look around the caves for a while and then find an exit. Nothing had really changed apart from the monkey king being hurt. The general and other herald were still unknowns.

The caverns were the last place apart from the city that remained uncharted on the island. There was a real possibility that the last herald was hiding somewhere in here, as he hadn't even seen the shadow of it before. If he could find something out while he was stuck here anyway, it would be of great assistance to his quest. One of his fears was that he would fail his mission and get punished by the System, not due to a lack of trying, but because he simply couldn't find his targets.

Since the System wanted him to kill these targets, he felt that he should have been provided with some navigation and a targeting method. But if mentally complaining about the System had any effect, he'd long have solved all his problems.

But he also put a time limit on himself. He hadn't given up on killing the monkey king, and would certainly try again. The reason for his failure was the horde of monkeys interrupting. He was quite certain that he would be able to kill him if he got him alone.

That was why he didn't try to rush back. For one, he wasn't sure how to get out, and besides, he believed that the monkey army would be on high alert for his return in the short run. It was a shame, as the monkey king was currently an easy target with its wounds. But he still had half a month until his two-month deadline. He didn't need to risk it all just yet.

Zac took a glance at his axe, confirming that it was almost completely repaired, and continued further into the caves. He still used only the glowing moss as a light source, as he didn't want to alert any enemies. Besides, his eyes were getting accustomed to it by now, and he could somewhat make out his surroundings.

Just before he ventured down, he carved a small Z beneath the glowing moss to mark his passage. He could still track his progress in his mind, but better safe than sorry.

The tunnels he progressed through led steadily downward, and it felt like he was walking toward the foot of the mountain. That also meant that he was closing in on the cave system the demons explored, so he was careful not to make any excessive sounds. He even ripped down some moss from the wall and tied it to the bottoms of his feet to mask his footsteps. It was the nonluminescent kind of moss, of course, as he didn't want his feet to become beacons for the enemy.

As he descended, he sensed that the ambient Cosmic Energy was steadily growing stronger. Not only that, the tunnels started to change as well.

From being dark and dour, apart from the occasional weak blue luminescence from the moss, the caverns were turning into a vibrant fantasy world. Thick vines with purple flowers started to grow out of the ground, large glowing mushrooms lined the tunnels, and the lights from the moss grew stronger and polychromatic.

Zac had never taken any hallucinogenic drugs, but it almost felt like he was high as he walked in these psychedelic tunnels. After walking along dazed for a few seconds, he suddenly started to collect samples of all the various herbs and mushrooms. He was careful not to let anything touch his skin, just in case it was poisonous.

He still had no method to discern if they were of value, but he felt that at least some of the magical plants should be of some use. It seemed quite clear that they had grown due to the high density of the Cosmic Energy, so they might have some magical properties.

Zac started using the vegetation as a basis where to head when he reached crossroads. He simply chose the one with a higher density of subterranean growth, as that passage should have a higher density of Cosmic Energy.

He was starting to get very curious why there was so much energy in the mountain, and he believed that the demons were so interested in the cave for the very same reason. There should be something in the depths that either contained or produced an immense amount of energy, to the point that it leaked out into the whole mountain range and valley.

If the demons removed it and took it with them, then Zac would lose a potential gold mine. He added the task of finding out what created the energy as well before leaving. If it was something small and portable, he would try to steal it. If this much Cosmic Energy could be poured into a couple of arrays, he wouldn't have to worry about the demons ever again.

Zac had walked for almost an hour when a sound made him stop in his tracks and shrink against the wall. It was light hurried steps that echoed through the tunnels not far ahead. They didn't seem to be coming toward him, so Zac slowly ventured forward, careful not to make a single sound.

The steps slowly were becoming a bit more distant, and Zac hurried up until he reached a crossing. He carefully looked around a corner toward where the sounds came from to see what made the steps. And just before it turned another corner, he could briefly spot a small imp trotting along.

Zac's heartbeat sped up, as seeing the imp opened up a possibility. Perhaps the imps' main area of activity was underground, which would explain why he had encountered so few up above ground. And if it was, then their herald was likely down here as well.

50

CRYSTALS

Zac waited for a bit to make sure no other imp or demon was incoming before he ventured down the same path he saw the imp take.

He surreptitiously glanced around any corners or crossroads, but even after a minute, he still hadn't seen any signs of the imp or anything else of interest. Either the imp was a lone explorer in the caverns or it was out of the way for some reason.

A scratching sound stopped his train of thought, and Zac moved to the next intersection to see where the sound came from. He finally found the small imp again, and it was just ten meters away from him, currently digging through some moss. After it removed a top layer, it sneakily put something inside and then carefully put the moss back on top. It got up and turned around, and suddenly found itself staring right at Zac.

Zac didn't hesitate and instantly killed it with a dagger. He walked up to the corpse and put it in one of his pouches before walking over to where it had dug around earlier. Initially, he had wanted to follow it back to wherever it came from, but he had been too careless and immediately got spotted. He'd have to get better at sneaking in these tunnels unless he wanted to get mobbed down.

After removing the moss, he actually found a small stash of Nexus Crystals. They weren't polished and uniform like the ones he had taken from the demon leader, but rather looking like uncut raw gems. Some were as small as a fingernail while the largest was slightly larger than his own crystals.

It seemed like the imp actually was hiding away its wealth in this uninhabited part of the cave system like a cultivating squirrel. So it looked like it wasn't heading to any other imps or demons, but rather away from them. Perhaps daylight robbery was a real problem amongst the imps, so hiding their cultivation resources was imperative.

The imp's actions raised a few questions. First of all, could imps cultivate? They seemed to have some inherent proclivity for magic, as all of them thus far had been able to shoot those nefarious fireballs. But it felt like all of them more or less were of the same Strength, making him believe they couldn't get stronger.

There seemed to be some fundamental differences between the imps and the demons or himself. They didn't have levels when he inspected them with **[Eye of Discernment]**, and it didn't look like they had classes either, as everyone used the same attack. That was why Zac placed them in the same group as the other beasts in his mind.

So what was the use of the crystals? The most likely explanation he could find was evolution. He had seen all kinds of mutations and evolutions in the flora on the island caused by the Cosmic Energy. Who was to say it didn't work with the fauna as well. Perhaps the crystals could help a normal imp evolve into something greater, like the heralds.

It was a bit worrying, as normal imps were deadly enough. If suddenly a throng of them evolved into super-imps, wouldn't they burn down the whole island? He could only hope that evolving wasn't that simple a matter for now.

The second thing on Zac's mind was the crystals themselves. Where had it found them? If there were a bunch of them, it would explain many things, such as why the density of Cosmic Energy was so high in the mountains. It could be due to the proximity of a large number of Nexus Crystals, whose energy bled through into the surroundings.

It would also explain the unceasing flow of demons coming into the mountains. A mountain full of Nexus Crystals should be the equivalent of a Multiverse gold mine.

That, unfortunately, meant that the demons were continuously pilfering the resources that Zac would need to continue to improve and build up a town.

Zac was sorely lacking in Nexus Coins right now. He could barely improve himself, let alone build up a whole town. His gains lately from killing monkeys had been tremendous, but it was nothing compared to the costs of creating and running a town.

For example, there was an array called **[E-Grade Medium-Scale Town Defense Array]** that was a combination of a defensive shield and some attacking functions. It looked like a good all-around addition for a newly established settlement. But that array alone cost five million Nexus Coins, and furthermore, it wasn't free to operate.

There were defensive turrets and anti-siege weapons as well, each costing over a million coins. There was just no way for him to grind that kind of amount of coins. Even if he got twice as strong and murdered monkeys without rest or sleep, it would take years before he got all the basic structures of the town.

But if he had a large number of Nexus Crystals, he might be able to pay all this, and maybe even more. He didn't have any means of selling the Crystals for Nexus Coins at the moment, but there were things such as shops and auction houses in the outpost store. If he purchased one of those, he was sure they'd accept his crystals for some coin.

Of course, it all hinged on him actually getting the crystals. Driven by a renewed sense of purpose, Zac headed back toward where he came from. Since the imp went out of its way to hide the crystals out here, there shouldn't be much activity in the surroundings as well.

Zac made a mental note of the area since he might need a base of operations down here. As he carefully proceeded through the paths, the ambient Cosmic Energy kept increasing, now starting to reach the density that he had felt in the valley with the monkey king.

After continuing on for roughly ten minutes, he heard some shuffling further down the path. Zac immediately stopped, a glint of greed and anticipation on his face. Every demon he found down here would probably make him wealthier. He imagined looting magic pouches packed to the rafters with crystals, a creepy grin slowly starting to emerge on his face.

Unfortunately, it wasn't a walking nest egg he encountered, but a white crocodile.

At a second glance, he realized it wasn't actually a crocodile, but a supersized salamander. It had a thick build and was roughly four meters long. It was mostly white with some purple markings. Zac thought that subterranean species normally possessed no eyes, but this didn't seem to apply to this specimen. It lazily ambled through an underground tunnel, swiping up various mushrooms and herbs with its mouth along the way.

Zac didn't know if it was a guard animal for the demons or just something that lived down here. He shrank into a side corridor to hide, as he didn't want to bother with this huge beast at the moment. The beast seemed oblivious to his existence until it suddenly exploded into motion just as it was next to the side tunnel Zac hid in.

Its maw opened, showing a line of large translucent teeth looking like huge salt crystals. The beast tilted its head and charged straight at Zac's torso, but he was accustomed to this manner of attack from the countless barghest he had fought.

Channeling his Cosmic Energy, he grunted and punched the lizard in its head, slamming it into the wall of the tunnel, creating large cracks on the stone surface. That type of attack was usually enough to kill barghest by now, but it only seemed to enrage the salamander. He didn't want a prolonged fight, though, and swung vertically with a maxed-out **[Chop]**, cleanly decapitating it.

A surge of energy entered his body, and he saw that he'd gained roughly eight hundred Nexus Coins. That was even more compared to some of the weaker demons, surprising Zac somewhat. It had been pretty quick for its large size, but it felt like less of a challenge compared to a demon.

As he was mulling it over, a sizzling sound interrupted his train of thought, and he turned his head toward the sound.

Smoke rose from the ground next to the chopped-off head, and it almost sounded like something was being fried. He went closer to take a look and was appalled to see that its saliva was highly corrosive. The sounds came from its tongue touching the ground, and it had already corroded a small hole where its saliva dripped down. Zac realized even a flesh wound from a bite might cost him a limb when fighting these salamanders.

It was a shame he couldn't use his eye skill on it, as it was already dead, but it didn't matter much what the System called the animal. He went over to the headless carcass and observed the body. At least the blood wasn't corrosive; otherwise, the huge pool of blood forming beneath the body would have carved out a new path among the tunnels.

Zac barely managed to cram the beast inside his smaller pouch after chopping off the tail, and then moved on. He didn't want to leave a carcass out in the open that was clearly killed with something sharp. He still didn't know what the relation between the demons and this animal was, and he'd just have to lug it along until he did. Or found somewhere to dump it where it wouldn't be found.

Zac continued on, diligently marking crossroads with a Z. By now, he was starting to fully acclimatize to the cold light of the moss and various other plants and had no problem discerning his surroundings.

After a while, the tunnels started to change once again, and he saw spots glimmering between the pieces of moss on the walls and ground. He walked over to the closest spot that shone and saw that it was a crystal.

His heartbeat quickened, and he quickly pried it out with a knife. The stone was far harder than he expected, and the extraction taxed even him with his huge Strength. But he only increased his pace with a widening smile adorning his face, and soon he held his prize in his hand. The crystal he pried out truly was a Nexus Crystal, roughly half the size of the ones in his bag.

As he looked around the walls, he saw glimmering crystals embedded all over the walls.

He was *rich!*

51

STENCH

After a bout of excitement, Zac suppressed his giddiness and refocused. As much as he wanted to, he couldn't start a mining operation at the moment. He had things to do.

Besides, it likely was more effective to let the demons mine the crystals, and then commandeer it when it was all extracted and gathered. They shouldn't have sent their most powerful warriors to mine, so an assault wouldn't prove to be too difficult. He longingly took another look at the glistening walls and then kept going.

This obsession with wealth was something new he had started to develop. He hadn't really cared too much when the world was still normal and he was just a white-collar worker. He was happy as long as he had enough to live a comfortable life.

But lately, he was running toward corpses like it was Christmas morning and the bodies contained presents. It was a weird type of callousness that translated corpses into loot. He had always enjoyed the grind in video games, waiting for that rush of seeing some glimmering unique or valuable item drop. He was starting to get the same feeling in real life as well. Just the thought of finding a magic pouch full of crystals made him want to forget about the heralds and go on a treasure hunt instead.

But he knew he couldn't, at least not for now. As he walked, he started to gradually hear rhythmic sounds of metal hitting rock. It was still far in the distance, but Zac presumed he was hearing mining operations.

He hesitated for a bit, but then reluctantly decided to go in another direction. There was no real need to see the miners at the moment, and he wouldn't risk getting exposed this early just to steal a peek. What he currently wanted to explore was whether the thrifty imp was a loner who had snuck into the caves, or whether it was part of a larger group.

As he crept along the paths, the sounds of pickaxes hitting rock didn't diminish; rather, it was a constant drone in this part of the cave system. This made Zac realize that the mining operations were on a larger scale than he had expected. After walking for thirty minutes, the sounds finally started to diminish, letting him know he was moving away from the mining operations.

Suddenly, he heard another sound, and he stopped in his tracks. It was the familiar sound of light scuffling on the ground that the imp had made, but this time, it sounded like it came from multiple sources. It was accompanied by some clanking and subdued inane chatter that didn't quite sound like a language.

He gingerly crept forward, careful not to make a sound. He wasn't sure how sharp their senses were, and he didn't want to find out. Zac took a quick peek around a corner and saw that the tunnel led into a cavern that was roughly ten by ten meters. The roof was also higher compared to the usual two to three meters of the tunnels.

The first thing he noticed was that he didn't have to be careful of the imps smelling him out, as a wall of overbearing stench hit him as soon as he looked around the corner. It seemed that sanitation and hygiene were alien concepts to the small humanoids, as that level of smell could only come from a buildup of waste and excrement.

What entered Zac's vision could tenuously be called a camp. Moss had been ripped from the walls and placed on the ground to make simple bedding, and in the middle of the room was a handful of lumber together with vines making a fire, whose black smoke polluted the cave. Luckily for the imps, there seemed to be some cracks in the roof, which kept the cave ventilated; otherwise, they might have killed themselves accidentally by inhaling all that smoke. Piles of food waste and other unmentionables were strewn randomly about the camp, and in a corner, there was a large rotting carcass of a smaller version of the salamander Zac had fought earlier.

There were roughly twenty imps that inhabited the disgusting campsite, and it looked like they were turning in for the night. Zac was a little fuzzy about the exact time but felt that it should be somewhere around 4 to 6 a.m. He had assaulted the herald in the evening, and after his escape spent a few hours on absorbing energy, then a few hours of sleep.

From what he'd seen from his travels across the island, the imps weren't nocturnal, and he guessed that their sleep schedule had gotten messed up from living in this subterranean cave.

Most of the imps were already lying on the ground, snoring away, while a few lazily milled about. Two had a small scuffle over a moss bed, and after a short while, the victor lay down while the loser skulked away. It seemed the beddings closest to the fire in the middle were the most desirable, and the losers had to pick some spot further out.

Zac waited, and only fifteen minutes later, the whole group was fast asleep, and they didn't bother with sentries or the like. Perhaps that was what the bedding arrangement was for. If they were attacked, the weaklings in the outer rim would be attacked first, and their death wails would be the warning alarm for the others.

Zac deliberated whether to attack or to go around the camp. He felt that such a large group of imps indicated that the caves might very well be the main area of the imps. The imps he'd encountered in the forests had been mostly solitary, but here, he immediately saw two dozen of them.

That meant the likelihood of the herald being down here had gone up by quite a few points. He didn't want a repeat of the battle of the monkey herald, where it summoned a throng of subordinates to wear him down. And being attacked by hundreds of imps seemed far more deadly compared to the monkeys. He'd be blasted to smithereens in no time.

But he also was still quite unclear about things down in the tunnels. He only possessed a shaky grasp of the layout down here so far. But soon he came to a decision and brought out some rags from his pouch. They had once been a shirt of his but had been ripped up for bandages long ago. He wrapped the rag around his mouth and nose and then brought out a large dagger he had taken from the last fight with the demons.

The rags were a small defense against the smell. He was already getting nauseated just smelling it from a distance, and he did not look forward to experiencing the stench point-blank. He crept forward, with his dagger at the ready.

He soon arrived at the mouth of the cave, and the overwhelming stench almost made his eyes tear. He forced himself to ignore it and moved over to the closest imp. He bent over and with quick movements, put his padded hand over its mouth, and simultaneously cut a huge gash in its throat, almost completely decapitating it.

The imp had no time to scream or struggle, and after a few shudders, it was dead. Zac stopped for a second to survey the surroundings, but they were all still fast asleep. He kept going and moved to the second one, repeating his actions.

In short order, he'd killed eight of the imps without alerting anyone, and he moved to the ninth. He was approaching the innermost circle of beddings now and was quite close to the fire. As he did, he reflected that the only thing that smelled worse than imp excrement was hot imp excrement.

Zac was starting to wonder if a stench could physically hurt someone, as his eyes were tearing up from the stink. If he was forced to sleep in a camp like this, he'd rather sleep on the edge of the cave at risk of getting eaten by a salamander, compared to sleeping next to this putrid flame.

The smell was so bad that he couldn't properly focus, and he accidentally hit the sleeping imp with his foot as he approached. He quickly bent down and finished it off, but not before it managed to release a high-pitched screech.

Zac knew he wouldn't be able to sneak around anymore and immediately swapped out the dagger for his axe. He activated **[Chop]**, and with three quick swings, another five imps were dead before they managed to properly wake up.

By now, the surviving imps were up, and all of them charged up a purplish-black fireball without hesitation. Zac managed to kill another two before they were done charging, but afterwards, four fireballs slammed into him. The cave was simply too small, and he had no time to dodge them. Normally, he would have used his chest piece here, but he wanted to save it unless it was a true life-and-death scenario. He might meet a herald soon, so he needed all his tools at the ready.

Zac could only grit his teeth as the nefarious flames hit him, sticking to him like glue. He knew that the fires would die out when their owners did, so he wasted no time and charged at the remaining four imps. They screeched and started to flee toward a tunnel opposite where Zac came from, but Zac wouldn't give up.

Ignoring the impractically large consumption of energy, he elongated the **[Chop]** edge and managed to hit two of the fleeing imps, bisecting them in an instant. Their two compatriots didn't care and only started flapping their wings more fervently in order to escape.

Zac fished a throwing dagger out of his pouch, and as he followed, he threw it into the back of one of the two imps. He took out another dagger, intending to quickly end the fight. But as he prepared the throw, a huge white maw suddenly emerged out of a side tunnel, snapping shut over the imp in a lightning-quick manner.

It was another salamander that emerged from the tunnel, contentedly chewing on the small demon. It lumbered forward toward the other imp that Zac had downed and gobbled up it as well, knife and all.

Zac wasn't in a mood to fight against the salamander unless needed, as he liked the idea of these huge lizards walking around in the tunnels and helping him out by whittling down his enemies. Therefore, he quickly receded into a side tunnel in order to avoid its approach. The huge monster soon came to the entrance, looking toward Zac's direction, and seemed to be hesitating for a few seconds. Zac didn't understand how they kept sensing him, as this time he had fled even further back, but he could only get ready to kill this white giant as well.

Finally, it turned around and ambled away, toward the now deathly silent imp camp.

52

ODOR

Zac let out a breath of relief as he saw the beast lumber off. Not that he was afraid of fighting it, but the enemy of his enemy was his friend, even if the monster itself didn't know it.

Zac moved some distance away and applied some more aloe cream on his burns. His skin looked gray and sickly, but not like a desiccated corpse's like it had the first time he fought an imp. His Endurance was quite a bit higher by now, and while the fireballs still hurt like hell, it took them longer to drain his body.

Zac felt he was at the cusp of leveling up, and continued onward through the tunnels. It didn't take long until he found another cave with sleeping imps. This time, it was a bit smaller, with only fifteen imps. This group also seemed to be a bit more vigilant, with one imp standing guard. It seemed to barely understand the concept of being a lookout, though, as it was leaning against a wall, half-asleep. Occasionally, it would rouse itself, but only to scratch its butt, then go back to dozing off.

Zac saw no way to get next to it without being spotted, even if it wasn't too vigilant. He really wished he could get the skill the crafty swordsman had used, and turn invisible for the approach.

Even the lackadaisical imp would notice his approach and warn the others if he tried to sneak up on it.

Seeing no alternative, he took out another throwing knife and threw it at the guard. It hit straight in the middle of its torso, almost instantly killing it. It slumped down onto the ground with a small whimper and then stopped moving. Zac froze, waiting for any reaction from the rest of the group.

However, they snored away contently, oblivious to their impending doom. Satisfied, Zac ventured in and repeated his grisly assassinations. This time, he managed to keep going unnoticed until only three were left before they were alerted, but Zac finished off the last stragglers with a few quick chops.

The kills in the second cave gave Zac another level-up, bringing him to level 33. He put one point in Strength and two points into Endurance, bringing the attributes to 171 and 99 respectively.

Zac soon trudged on, continuously looking through the seemingly endless tunnel system. He found a few more imp camps on the way. Not all the camps were sleeping, though, and he skipped the ones who were awake for now. He had been forced to eat four fireballs earlier, which hurt quite bad, and didn't want to imagine how getting bombarded by twenty of those infernal balls would feel.

After traveling for an hour, he felt that he should be below sea level by how much he had descended. Of course, it was hard to get an exact feeling when everything felt the same. But it opened up a new avenue of escape for him. He had been pondering whether he should build a raft to leave the island if the demon quest didn't pan out.

But the thought of being stuck at sea on a crudely built raft, with no knowledge of how far he was from land, soon squelched that idea. Besides, who knew what kind of monstrous things lurked in the depths after the integration into the Multiverse.

The caves felt like a safer option. Even if he found no way out, he could always backtrack to the island. The only downside was the claustrophobic feeling of these tunnels. The tunnels were quite beautiful right where he was, but he guessed it was due to the high amount of Cosmic Energy in the surroundings. If he left this area, the tunnels would likely be far more dour and oppressive.

As he continued his exploration, he started to smell a very acrid odor, differing greatly from the earthy scent of the vegetation or the putrid stench of the imp camps. Intrigued, he decided to find the source and started to slowly follow the smell.

After a few twists and turns, he finally managed to find the right direction. It seemed that none of the stats really improved his senses overly much, so his plethora of titles hadn't given him eagle eyes or a super sniffer. He, therefore, made some wrong turns before being able to tell what direction the smell came from.

As the smell got stronger and stronger, he saw that the tunnel was starting to change. There were signs of mining activity in the area, with holes in the walls peppered about. Most of the greenery had also been ripped out, leaving only some of the luminescent moss for some lighting. It looked like the source of the smell was man-made rather than something natural.

He started to take greater care for any potential enemy or trap cropping up, but still decided to continue toward the source of the smell. As he peeked around a corner, he saw a few imps milling about near the mouth of a large cave. He couldn't properly see what was going on inside the cave due to the distance, but it was well lit up, and he could see purplish smoke wafting about inside.

It would be impossible to approach without alerting whoever was in the cave, so Zac retreated to find another entrance. After twenty minutes of looking around, following his nose, he found another cave mouth, but this one was guarded as well.

He turned toward the last path he found that had a stronger

smell compared to the others and tried his luck one last time. This time, he was led to a dead end, the path simply stopping after a while. The acidic smell was extremely strong, though, almost to the point of making Zac light-headed. After looking around for a while, he found a small crack in the wall behind some luminescent moss.

He ripped down the moss, and another light shone from the wall, but this time, it was light bleeding through a small crack. It appeared he was right next to the cave, but with a thin layer of rock in between.

He tried to look through the crack, but it was too small for him to see anything, so he brought out one of his thin throwing knives from his pouch and started to carefully carve out the crack. It was a slow process, as he didn't want the sounds to alert anyone inside, and it took almost half an hour until the hole was large enough for him to be able to see through.

He eagerly glanced inside, and what met his eye made his heartbeat speed up. The cave was one of the largest ones he had seen so far, being a full thirty meters across. The first thing he noticed was the large cauldron in the middle of the room, and it was the source of the smell and the purple smoke he had seen. It was almost as tall as Zac was, and was held in the air by a crude rock and lumber contraption.

The source of the fire confused Zac, as it didn't produce any smoke. He only saw a handful of the raw Nexus Crystals placed seemingly haphazardly on the ground, and above them, a blue-white flame was steadily emitted, heating the bottom of the cauldron. Zac made a mental note, because if he could burn crystals without creating smoke, he would be able to provide warmth and cook food without having to worry about demons finding out.

Next to the cauldron were various mounds of resources. Zac recognized almost all of them as the various herbs and plants he had seen while walking the tunnels. There were mushrooms, vines, and purplish grass neatly separated into their own piles. He also identified a few plants that he had seen above ground in the transformed area close to the incursion.

On a stool stood an imp slowly stirring the contents of the cauldron with a large wooden ladle. At least he thought it was an imp, but he couldn't be sure because it was almost as large as an adult human. But it shared many features with the imps, such as its purplish skin and bat wings.

In contrast, its skin wasn't mottled and irradiated like it seemed with most imps, but rather smooth and clear. It also wore a proper, albeit simple, robe. The most advanced clothing he had seen on an imp thus far was a dirty rag used as a loincloth, while most of them were simply naked.

It lacked any horns or ears, and as it turned its head to grab a mushroom to throw into the pot, he could also see its face, making him sure he was dealing with an imp and not a demon. It had the extra set of eyes placed in its forehead, just as the normal imps.

He had found his fourth herald. He couldn't see any other explanation than that. It looked far too different compared to its brethren, and its intelligence seemed to be on another level if it cared about things such as clothing.

Zac didn't dare to use **[Eye of Discernment]** to make sure, though, as even the normal imps could sense it when he used the skill on them.

The herald wasn't alone, unfortunately. There currently was a group of roughly ten imps milling about in the cave. They were sorting a pile of resources and moved them to their respective mounds close to the cauldron. When an imp made a mistake, it was ruthlessly slapped in the head with the boss' ladle, eliciting a scared whimper.

Zac decided to wait for a while in order to let them finish their task and then hopefully leave. Between this group and the ones just outside, there simply were too many imps for comfort. But before they were even halfway done with the task, a few imps entered the cave and dumped an armful each of various plants.

Meanwhile, the herald kept throwing some plant or mushroom into the pot every now and then, constantly stirring. Zac started to feel that the cauldron had to be a magic item like his pouch, as it never seemed to flow over, even after Zac had watched the herald throw things into it for an hour by now.

It looked like the imps wouldn't leave the cave in the end. Zac deliberated whether he should wait some more or fight. By now, he was more or less completely restored from his escape from the monkey herald, apart from being covered in tender bruises. Finally, he opened up his quest page to make sure of the progress of his dynamic quest, slowly reading through it.

With all preparations done, he threw his worries and doubts out of his mind and hefted his axe.

53

BLITZ

The wall separating Zac and the cavern was less than a decimeter thick and wouldn't be able to hold against him kicking it down. Luckily, there were no crystals embedded that strengthened its integrity. He moved his axe to his left hand and gripped a throwing knife in his other.

After a few deep breaths, he put all his weight on his left leg and kicked forward with all the power he could muster. A deep thud echoed out, and a large part of the wall completely crumbled. Zac shouldered his way through the newly created crevice, not caring about the few cuts he got from the sharp rocks.

He immediately threw his dagger with full force at the herald, hoping for a quick conclusion. Unfortunately, it didn't work, as the blade seemingly combusted by itself and turned to ashes as it approached the large imp.

Zac wasn't surprised, and without hesitation, pushed forward. He managed to kill two of the smaller imps with daggers on his approach, and then he was instantly within ten meters of the herald.

The boss roared angrily and lifted the ladle, using it as a staff.

A huge wave of pitch-black flames rolled outward toward Zac. Anything it touched turned to ashes immediately, even a few unfortunate imps that were incinerated since they stood in the wrong position in the cave.

A golden sheen enveloped Zac completely, and he jumped through the wall of flames. He could hear a peal of eerie laughter and a snap; then he was through the flames. He didn't hesitate and pushed all the Cosmic Energy he was able to gather into the fractal on his hand, creating a five-meter blade, which whooshed toward the herald.

The blade slammed into an invisible barrier and started sizzling, causing extraordinary pain somehow transmitting into Zac's mind. But Zac's power wasn't for show, and after a brief struggle, the blade pressed on, slamming into the herald's body.

Zac expected the herald to be bisected, but with a shocked expression saw its seemingly simple robe light up and protect its body. The robe couldn't remove the huge momentum from the swing, though, and the monster was shot into a close wall like a rocket.

Zac rushed after it and was almost upon it to end the fight.

The herald spat out a mouthful of purple blood from the impact and screeched angrily at Zac. Its four eyes started blazing ominously, and once again, it summoned flames. This time, nothing in the cave was safe, as black insidious waves billowed in all directions from floor to ceiling. The herald was like a demonic sun that radiated nefarious flames that wanted to consume the world. The mounds of resources instantly turned to ashes, and the few leftover imps perished as well. The only thing that could stand the onslaught was the cauldron, which seemed completely unaffected by the flames.

Zac had already used his armor's onetime defense inscription and could only grit his teeth and force his way through the sea of fire. The fires would extinguish as soon as the herald died, so he placed a bet that the fight wouldn't last long.

The scorching pain that enveloped him was far worse compared to the normal hellfire of the smaller imps, and it caused him to scream and stumble. The swing that was supposed to cleave the herald in two lost much of its power, and his aim went off-kilter. But he at least managed to slice one of the herald's arms clean off, spraying blood everywhere.

He shakily prepared to swing his axe once more, but the herald had had enough. With a few flaps of its wings, it desperately tried to flee, leaving a trail of burning blood in its wake as it escaped through the flames. Every flap of its wings caused the flames to erupt in the air, creating a natural barrier from chasing it.

Zac couldn't afford to let yet another herald flee his pursuit, and charged most of his remaining energy into **[Chop]** once again, then furiously swung a five-meter edge after the fleeing imp. But the imp was quick, and he saw that his edge wouldn't reach even when maxed out.

That was extremely bad news, as the whole cave was still covered in the black flames, and they were quickly consuming him whole. If he didn't kill the herald, he would likely perish before getting out of there. Anger and desperation filled Zac's mind as he maniacally tried to increase the reach of the blade.

"REACH!" he roared as the edge was moving horizontally in the imp's direction.

Suddenly, the blade detached from his axe and continued outward like a wave. It moved as fast as his swing did, and soon reached the back of the fleeing herald. It proceeded and penetrated the imp without any resistance from the magic robe, splitting its torso and wings in two.

The various body parts of the herald fell to the ground, and Zac thankfully saw the flames covering the cavern quickly snuff out. He didn't have time to go over the battle scene, as a gang of screeching imps entered through the entrances. Now that the hellscape had subdued, the backup could finally enter without being incinerated.

Zac was in no mood to fight these little demons and threw out the huge salamander carcass to block the incoming fireballs. With the newfound room, he placed the herald's cauldron in his magic pouch and dashed out the same way as he came.

He kept running through the tunnels to create some distance from the area controlled by the imps, elated with the result of the fight. His bet had been successful.

He had planned to avoid a drawn-out fight with the herald and had thrown everything he had at it from the start. With how dangerous the small imps were, he knew that the herald would be a true terror if allowed to fire off its attacks. He hadn't even taken time to use his **[Eye of Discernment]** on the boss, afraid it would slow him down a fraction of a second.

He had also learned his lesson from the fight with the monkey king, ending the battle before reinforcements could arrive. Certainly, last time he had been tricked into thinking he'd killed all the backup until they sprang out of the ground like mushrooms. But that only showed that anything could happen in a fight, and the longer it dragged on, the more variables could crop up.

With his blazing speed, the imp boss had only managed to shoot two attacks before he was killed, and only one of them had managed to hit him.

Zac touched his scalp as he ran and grimaced as he felt that all the hair on his head had been singed clean off. After a quick confirmation, the same held true for his eyebrows and beard. He didn't have a mirror with him, but he could only assume he looked like a beggar monk by now.

His body felt drained and burned, and he stopped as soon as

he felt the distance was enough. He had consumed almost all his Cosmic Energy during the fight, and the hell flames the imp had spewed out burned his Vitality or soul as well, making him feel truly wrung out.

He sat down on some moss, brought out a bottle of water, and opened up his status page.

Name: Zachary Atwood
Level: 34
Class: [F-Rare] Hatchetman
Race: [F] Human
Alignment: [Earth] Human

Titles: Born for Carnage, Ultimate Reaper, Luck of the Draw, Giantsbane, Disciple of David, Overpowered, Slayer of Leviathans, Adventurer, Demon Slayer, Full of Class, Rarified Being, Trailblazer, Child of Dao, The Big 500

Dao: Seed of Heaviness – Early

Strength: 175
Dexterity: 59
Endurance: 100
Vitality: 69
Intelligence: 49
Wisdom: 49
Luck: 67

Free Points: 3
Nexus Coins: 545,716

The battle had only given him one level, compared to the almost three from the last herald he killed. He currently felt he was roughly halfway to level 35. That showed just how much harder it was getting to level up the higher his level became. The only reason he kept leveling so quickly was that his killing speed had improved faster compared to the increasing level requirements.

Before doing anything else, he quickly opened his quest page to make sure whether what he'd killed was actually a herald or not.

Off With Their Heads (Unique): Kill the four heralds and the general of an incursion within 3 months. Reward: 10 E-Grade Nexus Crystals, E-Grade equipment, unique building depending on performance. (3/5)

It was indeed the third herald he'd killed. He sighed in relief, elated with finally having moved his quest forward. He had been looking for this boss for weeks and had started to worry whether he would find it in time to complete the quest. But this part was finally solved.

He already knew where the last herald was located, and it was badly wounded to boot. The last missing piece of the puzzle was the general. Zac still had no idea how to locate and eradicate him or her, but one step at a time.

However, the good news didn't continue.

Zac closed down his quest page in order to allocate his points into Strength and Endurance as usual. This time, something went wrong, however, and he was unable to put his free point into Strength. He put two points into Endurance without a problem, bringing his total to 103. But no matter how many times he tried, he simply couldn't allocate his last free point into Strength. Zac started getting a sinking feeling in his stomach, worried he might have screwed up quite badly.

It looked like he had reached his cap for Strength. This was extremely bad news, as his main stat was Strength, and he automatically got three points allocated every time he leveled up. Would he be able to level up at all? Would he just lose those three points if he gained a level? What if his Dao Seed improved or he gained a new title?

He didn't believe that 175 Strength was the limit of what was possible in the Multiverse. Those titans he'd seen in the vision should have had thousands in Strength from the aura they emitted. Therefore, the problem came down to how to increase his limit.

Zac pondered for a few minutes and came up with a few ways that might work. The simplest method, and the one he desperately hoped was true, was that the cap would increase with a set number of points every time he went up a level. Then his problem would be taken care of. If the increase per level was low, he could simply allocate his free points into more Endurance or a third stat.

But if this wasn't the case, his problem got a lot thornier, because the only other method he could think of currently was getting an upgrade. Both his Race and Class were currently F-grade. If he upgraded one of them, his limits might get increased as well.

The problem was that he had no idea how to do that. Usually in games, you got a class upgrade when you reached a set level. Unfortunately, Zac didn't know whether this was at level 35, 50, or even 100.

As for Race, he was even more clueless. He had seen no indication anywhere what to do about race, and the only hint he had gotten that it was actually upgradeable was that the grade got added when he'd attained a class.

It might take a long time until he found a solution to this problem. The thought of losing tens of levels' worth of attributes while he waited for an upgrade made Zac truly sick to his stomach.

Zac's vision started to close in on him, and his thoughts were getting scattered. Suddenly, he puked out a large mouthful of blood and bile before falling down on the ground.

Something else is making me sick as well, Zac realized just before passing out.

54

LUCK

Zac woke up woozy and disoriented, and his innards felt like they were on fire. A sheen of sour perspiration covered his whole body, and he was weakly shaking.

If he didn't know better, he'd think that he had caught a bad case of the flu. However, he felt that he should be immune to things like the flu or a common cold since his constitution improved.

His next guess was poison, and it felt far more likely. He had somehow been poisoned during his fight, and it started taking effect on him after he left and settled down. His first guess would be the cauldron. He'd just barely touched it when he put it in his pouch, but he did breathe its fumes for a good while.

And it felt far more likely that a creepy imp was concocting poisons down in a subterranean cave rather than a healing potion. If so, he felt that he'd scored an amazing weapon by chance. If just the runoff fumes were this poisonous, he didn't even dare imagine what the liquid inside would do.

It didn't help him with his current predicament, of course. The most advanced healing tinctures in his possession were some aspirin and aloe cream meant for sunburn, neither likely to be effective against demon poison. He did have the mysterious azure water from the pond, but he didn't dare drink it in case it only made things worse. He could only hope to slowly flush it out by drinking lots of normal water.

He had no real appetite at the moment but forced himself to drink a large amount of water. He tried eating some rations as well, but his stomach started churning threateningly at the mere smell of food. He arduously moved some distance in the tunnel, as the pool of his puke had turned the area quite putrid.

Zac took out a Nexus Crystal and started absorbing it after he found a new resting place. Being full of Cosmic Energy couldn't hurt in case something happened. He actually felt that his body was getting slightly better as he was absorbing the energy, but it could be his mind playing tricks on him.

After a few hours, he had absorbed all the energy he could. If he continued, it would turn from restoration to cultivation, and he didn't want to gain any experience before he made sense of his situation.

The poison had interrupted his train of thought, but he was still met with the same problem: his capped Strength. If he returned to the mountain, it would only take a day or so of furious monkey slaying to reach level 35, something he was loath to do before he knew his options.

He decided to slow down his leveling speed for now, and even stop pondering on the Dao. He even took off his gathering-array amulet and put it into his bag in order to not even passively move toward the next level.

He'd focus on his axe technique instead, as that was the only safe option left. Lost over what to do, he opened up his status screen again, staring at the free attribute point. He knew he likely would have to gain a level to see what would happen, risking throwing away his Strength points. But for now, he wanted to look for another method at least for a while.

His conviction of focusing on only one stat had taken a hit from reaching the Strength cap. For now, it was only Strength, but Endurance would be there sooner or later as well if he threw all his points into it now that he couldn't put anything into Strength.

His eyes lingered on the other attributes, hesitating over what to do. Finally, his eyes landed on Luck.

It was an attribute he had completely put aside since the beginning, as he didn't want to hinge his survival on something as unreliable as luck. But by now, he was a walking juggernaut. The last fight had been risky, but he had completely overpowered the herald. The monkey king wasn't his match either and only survived due to his reinforcements.

By now, he could put some points into Luck, as his basic survivability was taken care of. He might not be exactly sure how it would help him, as he couldn't quantify it. But since he desperately needed a solution to both his Strength-related predicament and finding the general, getting some more Luck couldn't hurt.

Satisfied with his plan, he placed his remaining free point into Luck, but once again was stopped from actually allocating it.

"Goddamn it…" he muttered under his breath. "System, could you explain what's going on?" he entreated while looking up.

It was the first time in a month he had tried to communicate with the System, but he was still ignored like the last times. Maybe the System had lost interest in the world soon after the integration and left everything on autopilot before leaving.

He felt that the situation with Luck wasn't the same as with Strength. He only had 67 points in Luck at the moment, a far cry from the 175-point cap. All his Luck came from titles, and he'd never allocated any points into it so far, and Zac realized that might be the only way to increase his Luck.

Luck had a major difference from the other attributes. All the other stats could be improved even before the integration into the Multiverse. Strength and Endurance were the most obvious, but even things like Intelligence could be slightly improved with active training and a good diet. But there was no way to train up your luck.

If this was true, then getting the titles gave an even greater advantage than he thought, as they improved an attribute that should be static. He still didn't understand how the Luck stat worked, but it might help him win a battle against someone equally strong but less lucky.

He suddenly wished that Charisma existed as an attribute as well, as getting that stat to over sixty points might have turned him into a handsome hero instead of his current look of a bald creeper.

With a sigh, he allocated the last free point into Vitality, hoping it would speed up his recovery a bit. There was one last thing left that he needed to check out. He brought up his skill window to take a look.

Normal Skills:

1. **Eye of Discernment – Proficiency: A glimpse into the unknown. Upgradeable**

Class Skill:

1. **Axe Mastery – Proficiency: Early. The seed of Dao is planted. Upgradeable**
2. **Chop – Proficiency: Middle. There is greatness in simplicity.**

[Chop] had improved, as he suspected. In his fight with the herald, he'd actually shot out the edge like a projectile, something he hadn't been able to do before. The desperation in the fight had helped him break through from early to middle stage of the skill.

He truly hoped he didn't need to be on the verge of death to improve his skills in the future, but it seemed that pushing oneself to the limit was effective in improving not only levels and titles, but even skills as well.

As he was done with everything he could do for now, he closed his windows and helplessly closed his eyes.

It took a whole day before he could move about again, and another until he felt strong enough that he dared resume exploring.

He set course for the area where he had heard sounds of mining a few days earlier. As he approached, he heard some shuffling ahead. He hid in an unlit side tunnel, getting ready for a battle in case the imps discovered him.

To his surprise, the two imps weren't alone but accompanied by three demons. They did not seem like miners, as they all were holding weapons and carefully looked around. They all seemed to be warrior classes, as none of them held staffs or tomes or the like, and Zac's eyes lit up when he saw one of the demons actually held an axe of exactly the same make as his own.

He'd originally planned on avoiding the fight, as he didn't want to rack up a body count, but now he charged at them as soon as they were within a few meters. With a **[Chop],** two of the demons instantly died, not even having a chance to react. Zac grabbed the remaining one with his free hand and threw the terrified demon down on the ground. With a mighty swing, he ended him as well, leaving only the imps standing. The imps barely managed to start summoning their fireballs before one was decapitated and the other was kicked into the wall, the force breaking most of its bones and killing it.

Zac looted the corpses, then threw them into his pouch. He didn't love the idea of carrying around a bunch of corpses, but he also didn't want to just leave them lying there to be discovered. As if answering his prayer, a salamander lumbered into view a few minutes later, and Zac tried throwing one of the demons at it.

It quickly snapped up the body and with a few disgusting chews had eaten him whole, the saliva creating a sickening sizzling sound as its acidic nature quickly melted parts of the body before even swallowing it.

Zac continued to throw bodies at it, and it actually managed to eat the whole party except one of the demons. But it grabbed him with its mouth and, after a glance at Zac, turned around and returned to wherever it came from. It looked like the salamanders truly weren't a part of the demons' forces.

Zac continued forward, now holding an axe in each hand. He was delighted to see that the **[Axe Mastery]** skill still worked while dual-wielding the axes. But after trying it out for a bit, he felt it was very hard and unwieldy to use. He preferred using only one axe, and having a free hand seemed more convenient for him. Even using a dagger in his off-hand felt more natural.

He reluctantly put his second axe in his pouch and continued on. He might just be lacking experience, and he would have a lot of time to train his axe-work if he couldn't level up for a while. As he walked through the shimmering tunnels, he finally started hearing the droning sounds of tools hitting the hard walls.

Zac knew by now the effort it took to mine the Nexus Crystals. It had taken him quite some effort to dig out only one crystal from a wall, and that was with maxed-out Strength. It seemed as though the dense Cosmic Energy empowered the rock that encased the crystals, making it far harder than it normally was. It was no wonder that new demons kept streaming down into the tunnels from the demon town.

55

HEY THERE, BUDDY

Zac wished he had a mirror to more sneakily look around the corners, but could only work with what he had. He rubbed some dirt on his face and singed scalp to cover his skin, and then wrapped some of the vines around his neck and head. Somewhat satisfied with his camouflage, he carefully peeked around a corner, mostly hidden behind a huge mushroom.

The tunnel Zac peered into contained five miners, and he was surprised to see that most of them used different means to extract the crystals.

Two were using basic pickaxes to gradually chip away at the walls. But each swing only made some tiny chippings fall, proving that their strength was nowhere near Zac's. If he used one of those pickaxes, he would likely be able to slam a decent hole in the wall, even if the rock was strengthened.

Another two of the miners were actually mages, and they simply held their hands to the wall. It took some time to see what they were doing, but he saw that a Nexus Crystal slowly was emerging out of the wall after a while. Apparently, the rock was even resistant to spells, as the earth mages Zac had encountered so far usually had a far easier time manipulating stone.

The last miner was slamming away at the wall with a mace, and his Strength was overbearing. Every slam created a reverberating thud that made stone chippings fly.

The miners were all demons who looked well fed and cared for and didn't really look weaker compared to the scouts he'd encountered. He had hoped that the demons placed their weakest in the mines, which would make Zac's next actions more convenient. But the Strength of the mace wielder seemed to be even higher compared to the demon with the great sword and black arcs of lightning.

Next to their feet, they each had a sack of extracted Nexus Crystals. The mace-wielder's sack was filled the most, and the mages were second. It was all these sacks that were the goal of Zac. He had decided to scout out the demon activity in the cave for a bit and steal as many Nexus Crystals as he could. He wanted to see if the crystals could help him in evolving his race or class before biting the bullet and gaining a level to see what happened. He knew he was grasping at straws, but he was really out of options.

Zac based his guess on two things. First the monkey packs. The higher density of energy the packs stayed in, the larger they became. The packs closest to the valley sported the largest monkeys, and a few even evolved to the point of using skills. The second clue came from the imp that was hiding crystals in a stash. He guessed that it maybe wanted to use the crystals for evolving as well.

If the beasts could use Cosmic Energy to evolve, then why couldn't he? So he wanted to steal a large amount in order to experiment. Perhaps there was a method of usage that would evolve his body, but not improve his level.

Zac slunk back into his tunnel, moving further on. His target wasn't these half-filled sacks. Moving onward, he spotted quite a few tunnels with miners, and rhythmic thumping on the walls filled the tunnels. He soon found a deserted tunnel whose crystals all had been extracted. He picked this tunnel and started moving through it, ascending slightly as he did. He wanted to get closer to the center of demon activities.

All these miners had sacks, but Zac never saw anyone carrying them back to the demon city. That meant that either they were collected and put in a pouch or were left here in the caves. In either case, they should be collected somewhere.

The tunnels that had been mined looked truly bleak compared to the magical feeling of the untouched ones. Not only were the crystals in the walls removed, but most of the vegetation had also been ripped out of the tunnel. The only thing left was a smattering of moss to somewhat illuminate the area. Luckily for Zac, these exploited tunnels were completely deserted, as anything of value had been taken. It made it easy for him to move around the active excavations and into the inner area closer to where he expected the cave mouth to be.

He really felt thankful that his titles had improved his mental stats quite a bit. Normally, he would be completely turned around after days in the tunnels. But while he couldn't exactly pinpoint where he should be in relation to the mountain, he generally knew the layout of the tunnels he had traversed and the direction he was moving. This was completely different from the old Zac, who could almost get lost in his own neighborhood, and could only be attributed to either Intelligence or Wisdom.

Perhaps putting points in these stats wouldn't be a waste for a warrior, and not because it would help with his lacking sense of direction. He had been pondering on attributes a lot while healing up from the poison. If he was to throw his one-stat-strategy out the window, he needed a new direction. One alternative was to focus on all his physical stats, including Dexterity and Vitality. Find a good balance between the stats that still had Strength as the main focus, but not as lopsided as now.

But a new alternative he hadn't thought about was to start focusing on Wisdom and Intelligence. When he let go of his chosen path, he started to think more deeply about what the various attributes could help him with, and he believed the mental attributes might help him with the Dao and skill advancement.

If putting his free points in Intelligence allowed him to improve his Dao Seed faster and acquire new ones, it might be more effective compared to putting them into more physical stats. If putting ten points in Wisdom helped him get another Dao Seed that gave fifteen bonus attribute points, it was a worthwhile investment.

It might also be possible that even physical attacks needed those stats. His **[Chop]** skill was approaching the realm of magic, as it could be turned into a projectile now. Perhaps Wisdom and Intelligence would help it fly faster or further, rather than Strength.

He could only put aside those things for now, and for the hundredth time sighed that he had no one to ask about these things.

The sounds of battle in the distance interrupted his thoughts. Who would be fighting down in the tunnels? Intrigued, Zac moved toward the clangor. He soon arrived at the mouth of a cave and saw four huge salamanders in a pitched battle against twice the number of demons.

Earthen spikes were shooting at the monsters while warriors were keeping the lizards at bay. A pyromancer conjured a huge fireball that shot into the open maw of a salamander, burning it alive from the inside. It started to furiously thrash about, slamming one of the warriors into the wall, at least breaking a few bones.

It was clear that apart from the fireball, the salamanders held the advantage. Had the demons met only one or two of the monsters, they'd likely have been able to defeat them, but four were too many.

The warriors didn't have the power to keep the monsters occupied, and the earth mages' attacks were largely ineffective. After their kill, one of the warriors, sporting a large hammer and a shield, shouted something in demonic, and their party started to move backward.

Zac was happy to let this play out and hid behind a boulder, but the development put him in a predicament. The demons were moving in his direction.

After some deliberation, he picked up a few rocks and started pelting the demons. With his Strength, he could likely throw them hard enough to blast through their bodies like bullets, but he controlled his power output. The first stones hit one of the warriors in the neck and in the back of the head of another.

It didn't knock them out but contained enough force to daze them. In a pitched battle like this, a brief mistake could be deadly, and the salamanders unhesitantly pounced. They bit onto the two demons and, after a few furious shakes, threw their mangled corpses away.

A small stream of Cosmic Energy entered Zac, and he was delighted to see that the System only awarded a small part of the full amount to him. It looked like the System did use some sort of distribution method that somehow gauged contribution or damage dealt.

He managed to throw another stone that actually knocked one of the mages out cold before he was discovered. One of the mages screamed angrily and shot a few earth spikes toward him. But a few hastily summoned spikes posed no danger to Zac, and he broke them off with a wave of his axe.

Zac moved forward, quick as lightning, and grabbed the scruff of the mage. Then, with a grunt, he threw her like a doll right at the warrior who ordered the retreat. She slammed into him with enough force that they both helplessly went sprawling on the ground.

The salamanders were quick on the uptake and started helping out with the pincer attack. The two downed demons were quickly dealt with, and suddenly, it was four demons left versus three salamanders and Zac.

With the front line down, the remaining mages were in dire straits. They desperately erected defenses against the hulking monsters and then tried to force their way through Zac. But Zac was well-versed in anti-mage tactics by now and quickly threw the pyromancer over the hastily erected wall. The mage wailed and then went quiet forever.

The salamanders weren't standing idle either, and with a roar, the largest one slammed straight through the defenses and snapped up one of the demons. Another one followed and started biting one of the earth mages. The stone skin the mage used was completely ineffective against the lizard's saliva and strong jaws, and he screamed as he was being eaten alive.

Only one solitary demon remained, and with a desperate roar, he started gathering Cosmic Energy from the surroundings. With the large density in the air, it felt like a whirlpool of energy was forming. Zac recognized that sign and immediately cleaved the demon in two from head to crotch, just before jumping for cover.

He held his hands over his head for a few seconds, but the expected explosion didn't come. Perhaps Zac had managed to kill him before the energy managed to reach a critical mass. Somewhat embarrassedly, he got to his feet and found himself facing three salamanders silently staring at him.

"Hey there, buddy, let's be friends," Zac croaked toward the largest salamander, hoping to sound friendly.

56

ILL-GOTTEN GAINS

Zac spoke to the salamanders with the same voice he used to chat with his old neighbor's dog. While he felt that fighting three salamanders wouldn't be an impossible feat, he didn't want to move closer to another level unless he needed to. Besides, who knew if they would remember him as an ally if he kept feeding them demons and imps. Having an army of giant lizards to help out against the demon city would be very handy.

One of the salamanders ignored his request for friendship and started lumbering toward Zac, who helplessly backed away with his hands held up in response. Thankfully, the leader's maw opened, and a surprisingly childish squeak emerged from its mouth. The squeak stopped the advancing salamander in its tracks, and it lumbered back toward one of the demon corpses.

Zac surveyed all the corpses for anything of value. He quickly noted that none of them carried a magic pouch, and the only other gear he found interesting was the shield one of the warriors had carried. It lay flung to the side by the corner of the cave. In case he spotted anything of real value or a magic pouch, he would probably have initiated a fight, but he now saw no need to.

He briefly wondered what would happen if a monster ate one

of the pouches, while he moved away from the cave. Would it explode like a magic piñata, spewing its contents all over the place? Or would the items simply be lost? Would a tear in space occur, sucking anything in the vicinity into some unknown void?

He waited some distance from the cave for fifteen minutes until the sickening sounds of feasting were gone, and sneaked back to the site of the battle. The salamanders were gone, apart from the dead one lying in a corner. All the bodies of the demons were gone as well.

Everything that the demons had worn seemed to have been ingested together with the bodies, but the things they had dropped were left where they lay. Zac went and picked up the shield from the corner and examined it. It was slightly dented and corroded from the battle, but overall in serviceable condition. He threw it into his pouch and left again, not bothering with the damaged swords on the ground.

He was happy to see that the salamanders were actively hunting the demons, as that would provide an explanation for why some demons went missing when Zac started his activities.

With gusto, he returned into the tunnels, looking for some stash house or clues where the mined crystals were gathered. But after looking around in vain for some time, he changed his strategy. He found another group of miners and made sure he could get to both sides of their tunnel through side paths.

After making sure he had a good grasp on the surrounding topography, he simply sat down in a tunnel close by, waiting to see what happened with the sacks. Luckily, he didn't have to wait long, as the group of miners had been going at it for some time judging by the bulging sacks. Zac heard footsteps and hid his face deeper among the vegetation, hiding the rest of his body around the corner.

Five demons arrived at the tunnel, with the one in the middle wearing a fancy dress and having an air of haughtiness. The four others accompanying her were clearly bodyguards judging from their attire and how they encircled her. When she arrived, the miners immediately stopped their activities and saluted the lady.

With a few words, she brought out a clipboard from a pouch, and one by one, the miners brought their crystal sacks over to her. She lifted the first one up with her free hand, and after a comment, wrote something down on the clipboard. She then put the whole sack into one of the pouches in her belt.

One of the guards brought out an empty sack from a backpack and handed it out with an expressionless face. The miner bowed and went back to his position. This process went on for two more miners without anything of note happening. But when the lady commented on the fourth miner's sack, he couldn't help but grimace and hesitantly say a few words in demonic.

The bodyguards immediately perked up and started radiating a dangerous aura, but the lady waved them down. She simply pointed to the bag and said a few words with a smiling face. The miner looked horrified and went down on his knees, looking like he was begging for his life.

The exchange continued for some time until, finally, the lady put the sack into another magic pouch, and the miner could only return to his position with a devastated expression. The other miners simply stared down at the ground, not wanting to be implicated by their mouthy associate.

After the lady was done, she simply turned and left, with her four bodyguards in tow. The miners sighed and sat down to eat, conversing with subdued voices. Zac didn't linger and instead crept behind the party of five.

Don't worry, buddy, I'll mete out justice for you soon. Zac gave a silent prayer for the unlucky miner as he skulked away. He kept a healthy distance from the group, afraid that any sound would alert the group and the walking treasure trove would slip out of his fingers.

The group soon arrived at another tunnel with a group of miners, and the process repeated itself. Zac kept following the group for an hour and watched them collect sack after sack of crystals. He wasn't sure whether the group he first spied on was among the first the lady visited, but just going by what he had observed, the pouches on her belt contained an astonishing number of crystals by now and could only be counted by the thousands.

Zac felt he couldn't wait any longer and got himself ready. He steadied his breathing and placed himself at a side tunnel that the party should be passing after finishing their collection. It was some distance from the mining group, so Zac had no vision of his target anymore. However, they were moving in a very systematic pattern through the tunnel system so far, and Zac could only assume they would continue.

Sure enough, soon the telltale echoes of the steps of the party were approaching. Zac held his breath, not wanting to give any indication of his presence. The first two guards came into view, but Zac didn't react.

As if sensing something was wrong, one of the guards started to turn around, but it was too late. Zac entered the tunnel right behind the two and, without hesitation, swung a Dao-empowered strike at the lady in the middle. She looked shocked, but a golden sheen immediately enveloped her as an inscription pattern lit up on her dress.

Zac knew that inscription very well by now and forcefully stopped his swing. It hurt his muscles to do so, but it was better than getting the whole force of the strike redirected at himself. Instead, he lightly punched the golden barrier, and the recoil traveled through his arm, bringing some discomfort.

Having fulfilled its purpose, the golden layer shattered, leaving the lady once more exposed. Black lightning arcs flittered all over her body, but Zac swiftly decapitated her with a grunt.

The black arcs traveled all over his body, making it feel like he was being electrocuted, and he actually blanked out from the pain for a second.

During the brief pause from the shock, a sword stabbed into his side, drawing a small gout of blood. The pain shook him awake, and he immediately pounced on the two guards who had stood behind the lady. They were alarmed, but still warriors. One had produced a spiked mace, whereas the other's hands started glowing with lightning. From his muscles, he didn't seem like a mage, but rather, a pugilist.

They tried to pincer Zac, with the mace-wielder swinging at him from the left and the pugilist attacking him from the right with a clawed hand. Zac ignored the martial artist and instead swung his axe to meet the mace.

The collision was completely one-sided, as the force from Zac's swing slapped the mace out of his hand and made the demon lose his balance. Simultaneously, the clawed hand slammed into Zac's back, easily destroying the leather protection and trying to tear into his flesh. Unfortunately for him, Zac's skin was all the armor he needed, and the demon only managed to create a small flesh wound. The lightning entered Zac's body, but by now, this level of power had scant effect on him.

He grabbed the mace-wielder's neck with his free left hand and slammed him down on the martial artist. The sounds of bones breaking could be heard, but Zac was interrupted as he planned to finish the two. A blade was flying right toward his throat, and Zac activated his armor to block it.

But he was shocked, as no golden sheen enveloped him, and he could only desperately lift his arm to block the strike. The blade cut into his lower arm, only stopping after carving into bone. The pain was blinding but only served to enrage Zac. With a furious **[Chop]**, the blade-wielder was bisected, and then the two demons on the ground followed him into death.

He turned toward the last bodyguard, only to see him desperately fleeing, heedlessly throwing away his weapon. Zac started running after him, throwing a few daggers his way. But the bodyguard was surprisingly nimble, managing to dodge most of them while running. One hit him in his back, but he only staggered slightly but kept moving.

Suddenly, he started shouting at the top of his lungs, horrifying Zac. He threw one more dagger at him, but the demon turned a corner and disappeared from his vision. He could still hear the screams, though, as they echoed through the tunnel system.

Zac hesitated a second, but then ran back toward the killed demons. With furious speed, he grabbed the pouches on the lady's belt, then threw her headless body into one of them. He then ran away in the opposite direction from where the screaming bodyguard was fleeing toward.

After a minute, he stopped and quickly bandaged his wounded arm. It was bleeding freely and was currently creating a trail to his location. After making sure the blood didn't get through the bandages and rags, he started running again. After he had run for an hour and completely left the area with mining activities or imps, he finally slowed down and found a good resting spot.

The fight wasn't very taxing, but he was worried about the results. First, he dragged his chest piece off his torso and inspected it. The armor itself looked whole, but the inscribed fractal on the front had multiple cracks in it. That should explain why the shield hadn't materialized earlier and he got maimed instead. But a smile crept on his face as he glanced down at his belt. He knew he would be able to afford to buy a new one with his ill-gotten gains.

57

DRESSING UP

Zac suddenly remembered hearing a snapping sound when he'd used the shield against the imp herald. He had no idea how to fix the inscriptions and could only reluctantly put the armor into his bag. He didn't want to risk damaging it further until he could fix it, as it had been a great life-saving tool so far.

He then brought out the headless body from his pouch. After a great deal of hesitation, he stripped the bloody dress from the body, leaving the corpse only in its undergarments. He then put the dress on himself with a sour face before putting the body back into the pouch.

It wasn't ideal, but the dress had the same inscription as his armor, and it could be the difference between life and death. The dress he'd put on was a neutral beige and reached down to his knees. The design was luckily armless and somewhat nondescript, making it almost look like an overly long tank top. He put his belt over the dress, then turned his eyes to the pouches.

A creepy grin was slowly surfacing once again as he grabbed the closest one of the three he'd looted and took a peek inside.

If this had been an old-school cartoon, then Zac's eyes would have turned into dollar signs by now. The bag was almost filled to the brim with sack after sack of raw Nexus Crystals. If he had to guess, he'd have to say there was at least an equivalent of ten thousand crystals in the pouch. The shapes and sizes were completely random as well, ranging from the size of a finger to almost a whole hand. Most of the crystals were encased in some stone and needed one last processing before being pure.

The second bag was unfortunately empty except for a few solitary sacks, likely a spare in case the first one was filled up. The third one was the personal pouch belonging to the noble lady herself. It held various personal effects such as daily necessities, clothes, and jewelry. It also had a nasty-looking claw weapon with fractal inscriptions. Zac brought it out and tried to put it on his hand, but it seemed to have been custom made for the demoness, or at least made for ladies, as his hand didn't fit.

Most noticeably in the pouch there was a sizable mound of raw crystals. There even were a few sacks as well. It looked like the lady foreman was skimming off the top after all, as crystals worth a couple of hundred standard-sized ones could be found in the pouch.

Satisfied with his haul, he took out some food and water from his pouch to have his dinner. As he did, he started to plan his next step. He had planned on stalking the tunnels for a while longer, but unfortunately, he had already been exposed. He didn't doubt that the fleeing demon soon would warn all his superiors about Zac. The demon had seen the whole fight, where Zac showed many of his cards as well.

After half a month of living with the demons, he had finally been exposed. It was better than he expected, to be honest, as he wasn't really the stealthy type. It seemed he could only begrudgingly give up on finding any more mining foremen, and instead refocus on the monkey king. It was time to head back the way he came from and search for an alternative exit.

But suddenly, Zac felt an acute sense of danger and instinctively dove to the side. A soundless black arrow flew past where his head had just been, and a throng of earth spikes followed right after. Zac scrambled to his feet and found himself face-to-face with over twenty demons swarming into his cave from all exits.

This clearly was an ambush that they had prepared for some time, as they'd entered from both exits simultaneously. Feeling like a caged animal, Zac growled and immediately ran toward one of the groups, trying to avoid a pincer attack.

As if practiced beforehand, the group started to back away from him, with all the mages erecting barriers to keep him at bay. There were translucent magical barriers accompanied by earth walls and earthen spikes. There was even a tree mage who manipulated the subterranean vines to ensnare his feet.

Meanwhile, Zac got pelted by the other group of demons with an array of ranged attacks. He could only give up his charge in order to avoid most of it. As he dodged, he turned around toward the attackers who harassed him from behind and swung his axe in a mighty horizontal arc.

A translucent blade grew to four meters long in an instant and then shot toward the surprised group. Only a few in the back managed to dodge in time, and the others could only hastily erect defenses.

With Zac's power, the defenses of the average demon were simply insufficient, and it tore through them one by one. The blade wasn't perfectly stable, though, and after slicing through six demons, it flickered out of existence.

Two daggers came whooshing straight behind the huge blade, one slamming into an eye and the other into the gut of another demon. Satisfied, Zac turned back and started pressing forward through the defenses of the group.

He summoned his large edge but kept it at maximum stable capacity for now. As the attacks from behind had paused from his strike, he could once again focus fully on the group he had initially charged at.

He slammed the axe down on one of the translucent barriers, and it cracked like fragile glass. Two spears stabbed into him as he advanced, one lodging itself in his side, and the other got stuck on the bone of his pelvis.

It was two warriors who used their long weapons, trying to keep him at a distance. Zac ripped one of the spears out of the hands of the demon, making him stumble forward, and slammed the butt of the spear at the other warrior. The spear broke in two and made the demon fly into the wall with a thud.

Immediately after, he actually threw his axe straight in the chest of one of the mages. He didn't know which kind he was, but he died instantly from the strike. He brought out his identical axe from his pouch and continued to press forward.

A few arrows slammed into his back, but only elicited a grunt in response as he pressed forward. He once again got the prickling sensation of danger and sidestepped without hesitation. An arrow flew straight past him and once again missed his head. Unfortunately, the archer who shot the superpowered black arrows was still alive.

He kept pushing forward, and with a great leap, he was within the group of demons. He ate a spear strike and two stalactite attacks by the earth mages due to his reckless charge, but now he was within striking distance of the demons. Zac started madly swinging his axe, with **[Chop]** charged to its limit.

He kept taking various hits, but for every strike he received, he returned one in kind. And with Zac's far superior stats, he whittled down the group to only three combatants from nine in under ten seconds. The survivors from the other group joined their brethren in the fight, and Zac found himself encircled by the last six surviving demons.

Zac was completely drenched in blood by now, both his own

and the demons', and filled with small wounds from head to toe. Almost ten arrows were sticking out of his body at various spots, making him look like a demonic porcupine. He was panting, and it looked like it was a chore to keep his axe raised, but he was still standing. Fighting twenty demons at once was a bit more than he could confidently handle, even in an enclosed space like this.

None of the demons were keen on being the first to attack, as over fifteen demons already had made the ultimate sacrifice, and they didn't want to be next in line. They seemed to be content to simply watch as Zac slowly bled out.

They all kept a healthy distance from him, making him unable to reach them even with **[Chop]**, and he currently didn't dare use his ranged attack due to the huge consumption of energy.

Zac knew he couldn't keep stalling and threw a dagger at one of the mages, who quickly summoned a barrier. The translucent wall shook when the dagger hit it, but it held true, and the dagger dropped to the ground. Zac didn't want to throw his axe, as his other one still was lodged in the mage some distance away.

Needing to break the status quo, he moved his hand down to his belt and, with an underhand throw, hurled a large crystal sack at another demon. The demon slightly froze from seeing a small mountain of wealth flying in his direction, and even instinctually reached out his hand to catch it.

But how could a heavy sack thrown by Zac be so easy to catch? It hit the demon, who crashed into the wall behind with a wet thud. He slumped down on the ground and didn't move. The other five demons all charged at him as if by command, throwing desperate attacks at him.

With only five demons left, Zac finally threw his axe at a mage keeping his distance. He hastily erected an earth wall, but the axe had the momentum of a meteor and passed the rising wall and blasted a hole through the mage before he could also activate his stone skin.

He took one of his large swords out of his pouch and with a sweep slapped away two incoming spears. He then charged straight at the closest warrior. The warrior tried to keep Zac at bay with his spear, but Zac simply swung his sword at it with enough force that it broke the fingers of the warrior, and continued into melee range.

With a growl, he stabbed the great sword into the demon's gut and, with a ferocious upwards tug, ripped him in two, drenching the surroundings in a storm of blood. A second spear stabbed into his side, but it only added yet another shallow wound to the tally. The three remaining demons seemed to understand that they didn't have the power to contend with him, and simultaneously started absorbing inordinate amounts of Cosmic Energy.

Zac didn't want to see what a triple suicide explosion looked like, and desperately ran toward the closest target and decapitated him. He continued toward the next immediately, but as he approached, a resounding explosion threw him ten meters away and straight into a wall.

Zac puked out a mouthful of blood, and his wounds only got worse. Just as he shakily got up to his knees, his vision filled with a bloated demon falling down in front of him. It was the last living demoness, chock-full of Cosmic Energy. The demoness stared into Zac's eyes as she shed one solitary tear before she blew up with a tremendous explosion.

58

QUEST

The world was shaking nauseatingly, and an incessant ringing filled Zac's ears. He shakily got to his feet but immediately fell down again. His state was already pretty bad, but the last blast completely messed him up. His new dress had used the golden protection just a few hours ago, making it unusable for another day.

Luckily, he'd managed to drag a corpse over at the last second to use as a shield from the blast; otherwise, he might have bit the bullet, 103 Endurance or not. And now he was covered in blood mush from the demon shield to boot. However, the last minute protection was far from enough, and it felt like everything in his body was broken.

But he knew he couldn't stay where he was. The demons somehow knew his position, and he had no other recourse but to flee. He shakily got to his feet and collected his two axes, and only swiped up a few knives if convenient. Zac didn't dare to properly loot the bodies, as he needed to put distance from the cave.

His movements were extremely slow, even if he mentally screamed at his legs to move faster. He desperately wished he had some health and stamina potions right now like in a game, but the only thing he had was a cauldron full of poison.

After hesitating for a few seconds, he took out his canteen with the azure water from the pond. The water was crammed full of Cosmic Energy and might help him recover enough for him to properly flee from the area. The problem was that he had no idea whether it also contained something else, like poison or deadly super bacteria.

Zac knew he couldn't be picky at a moment like this and had to risk it. With a few chugs, he downed a couple of mouthfuls of the azure water. It tasted sweet and cooling in his mouth and hands down was the best-tasting beverage he'd ever had. But as soon as the water entered his throat, it started burning worse than the strongest spirits he knew, making him feel like he'd swallowed a sun rather than some water.

The burning feeling didn't abate in his stomach, but rather kept intensifying. He felt his body was turning into a pressure cooker that was ready to burst. Veins popped out all over his body, and he was forced to stop walking from the intense pain. Sweat was pouring down his face like a waterfall, and even his eardrums popped from the pressure.

Zac was starting to worry for real that he might explode like the demons any time now. But soon the intense pressure abated, and the scorching heat in his belly turned into comforting rays of warmth that spread all through his body.

Zac felt his Cosmic Energy reserves rapidly filling up, but his wounds were barely reacting to the water. He thought he might be seeing some improvement but couldn't be sure. It rather felt like he had taken a dozen shots of adrenaline and simply couldn't feel the pain any longer.

It was better than nothing, Zac thought as he continued onward at a brisker pace. As he walked, he dumped everything from the lady foreman's pouch onto the ground, leaving only the

Nexus Crystals. He still didn't feel secure, however, and started to meticulously scan through the bag containing most of the crystals.

He went through them one by one to see if anything was amiss, trying to find out how the demons were able to track him. Perhaps there were bugs planted in one of the sacks he had stolen from the lady foreman, as that was when the trouble started. Soon his scanning stopped at an inconspicuous rock that was placed in one of the sacks. Most of the sacks had some rock-chippings mixed in with the crystals, but this was the first time he'd seen a rock of that size. He brought out the sack and groped around inside until he found the stone.

As he glanced at it, it did not seem overly suspicious, but he could see some slightly odd veins on the stone. He brought out his flashlight for the first time and shone it on the rock. In brighter lighting, he could see that the veins actually were fractals. Zac grimly stared at it for a second before he crushed it under his foot.

He immediately backtracked a bit and changed direction. As he walked, he kept checking each and every bag, and eventually found two more similar stones. Finally sure that was the last of them, he sped off, ignoring any protesting wounds.

As he walked, he multitasked by checking his status page. The fight with the demons had pushed him over the limit and gotten him to level 35. He had already been somewhat close to leveling again after killing the herald, and the melee was all that was needed.

His fears were unfortunately realized, and he saw his Strength was still stuck at 175 instead of increasing from the class bonus. It looked like he really had to try to evolve somehow. He helplessly allocated his three free points into Vitality, as he didn't dare put any more in Endurance for now either.

Hoping for a class advancement quest activating from reaching a "big" level, Zac opened up his quest window next.

Things weren't that convenient, as no advancement quests popped up.

He did, however, receive a new class quest.

Loamwalker (Class): Walk a thousand kilometers touching the earth. Reward: Loamwalker Skill (0/1,000)

He suddenly was pretty happy that he didn't spend a few days to grind in order to buy **[Steps of Gaia]** from the shop. He only lacked five thousand coins for the skill by now and could now use them to improve other things instead. **[Loamwalker]** was clearly some type of movement skill, just like **[Steps of Gaia]**.

Honestly, his class skill sounded quite a bit blander compared to the one in the shop, but he had learned not to underestimate the dull-sounding skills he received from his class. It was also very convenient to complete, as he only needed to walk around.

A slight scuffling interrupted his thoughts, and he could only bring out his axe again with a grimace. He placed himself at a corner in wait, and soon a demon came into view. This one was highly alert and immediately noticed Zac's presence.

But Zac was ready, and the axe was falling down on the demon's head just as he appeared, instantly killing him. He immediately entered the tunnel and unleashed a maximized **[Chop]** edge that flew outward before he could even register what was in the tunnel.

A few screams and groans were heard, and the demons were almost all dead before they knew what hit them. There were two that were badly hurt but alive, but Zac made short work of them as well.

There was one final demon who for some reason had been doubled over when the edge passed through the party and was completely unharmed. Horrified, he started running, but Zac wouldn't let yet another straggler escape. With a grunt, he threw his axe at the demon and then started his pursuit.

Luckily, this time, he hit, and the party was no more. He stopped by the fallen body and ripped out the embedded axe while glancing at the bloodied tunnel. He didn't know who had made the sound while walking, but that mistake had cost the whole group their lives.

It looked like the demons hadn't given up the chase. They had finally identified him and seemed determined to remove the problem. He quickly threw all the bodies and gear into his empty pouch and continued on until he found a secluded cave, where he dumped them all, including their things. He actually wanted to bring them with him to hide his pathing, but who knew what else the demons could detect.

His speed slowed down somewhat due to taking even greater care to be completely silent and thoroughly checking side tunnels. But as he moved, he was steadily moving upward. Zac figured the demons might be impeded by the monkeys if he managed to exit into the mountains again. It was easier for him to hide as a solitary person, compared to their large groups.

He saw a party again as he checked a tunnel, but this time, they were moving away. Zac kept completely still until they moved far away before skulking forward. At least it was clear that they couldn't locate him anymore. It had just been a guess, but it truly seemed that those stones were some sort of tracking device.

He kept skulking forward and avoided any demons that he came across. He was lucky that the tunnels amplified sounds, and it was almost impossible for a group of ten people to be completely silent at all times.

He was forced into one more fight but ended it quickly before moving further up. After another hour, he hadn't seen any demons for thirty minutes and finally sat down and brought out a crystal. He should be some ways up the mountain by now and could happen upon an exit at any time. Even if he didn't want to stop, he needed to recuperate before reentering the mountains.

The tunnels were endless, and even if the demons sent hundreds into them, it was still somewhat unlikely for them to happen upon him, as there was so much ground to cover. Meanwhile, he was afraid that the herald had prepared an ambush for him the moment he reemerged.

So he finally allowed himself a break, eating some dried meat, and then quietly waited for his wounds to get better. After two hours of quiet rest, a loud ding entered his ears and forced him to his feet, warily looking around. But the area around him was completely deserted, with not a demon in sight.

[Special Dynamic Quest activated. Emerge victorious and seize the Fruit of Ascension. Struggle for supremacy.]

It was the familiar emotionless voice of the System entering his ears, but Zac barely had time to reflect on its words before his vision changed.

He suddenly was up amongst the clouds and stared down toward the familiar sight of his island. He could clearly see the whole topography, but the sea around it was blurred somehow. The vision moved, and he closed in on the island with terrifying speed, hurtling toward the mountains.

Soon he arrived at the valley where he'd fought the monkey king earlier, but it looked different from how it did when he visited. The zone of death around the red and white tree had expanded to stretch across almost half the valley, and even the azure pond was shrunken down to half its size.

After having almost exploded from the energy contained in just a few mouthfuls, he was shocked at the amount the tree had absorbed.

The vision kept moving, and in seconds, he was next to the

tree. Zac would have thought it would be even lusher after absorbing the surroundings and the lake, but it actually looked a bit dried out. A couple of leaves had even fallen to the ground.

Neither the herald nor any other monkeys were anywhere to be seen, but Zac didn't ponder it overly much, as his eyes were glued to a pair of fruits that had grown on the tree. They were similar to a cantaloupe apart from their color. Instead, they were a glistening red mixed with white lines that almost looked like fractals.

The fruits were beautiful, but more importantly, they had some magical effect on him, even though it was just an illusion. It felt like every cell in his body was screaming in desire, wanting nothing more than to consume the fruits. He hated the fact that he was just there in a vision and not in reality.

As quickly as the vision appeared, it suddenly ended, leaving Zac in the cave with a mixture of greed and hesitation.

59

NOW OR NEVER

"That fucking monkey!" Ogras roared, this time enraged for real. No wonder it sent its underlings to keep his search parties out of the peaks. He thought it was just posturing that he'd allow for some time before setting the monkeys straight. But Cindermane had likely found the Tree of Ascension long ago and just waited for its fruits to ripen. Somehow the monkey must have broken free of the clan's mental restrictions; otherwise, it would have been compelled to report such a find.

"But if you think that breaking free from my grasp is that easy, you're in for a rude awakening…" he muttered and then turned to his aide. "Assemble the regiments. We're heading toward the mountain."

"Yes, sir. What about the search parties in the mines?" the aide asked.

"Leave them. Hopefully, they will keep that human busy while we deal with this."

He had been shocked to learn that the group of natives he'd discounted earlier actually was only one human. At least he hoped there was only one of them, as his power seemed high enough to give even him a headache. Of course, the human wouldn't be a threat to him if all the limitations on him were removed.

Worse yet, the human had killed Qugo and stolen the poison that was supposed to be one of his aces in case everything went south. Ogras had actually decided to hide the news of the third herald's demise, afraid that his clan members would chain him up "for his own protection" while gleefully stealing all the loot Ogras had rightfully pilfered.

As if summoned by his thoughts, Rydel walked in through the door, as always unheeding or dismissive of proper protocol. He wore resplendent silver battle armor that matched his long white hair well. Strapped to his back were two swords with intricately carved hilts.

"Cousin, I assume you have seen the proclamation by the Ruthless Heavens?" he said with a smile.

"I'm not blind, Rydel. Of course I've seen it. The army is setting out immediately. And here on the baby planet, I'm General, not cousin," Ogras spat out in annoyance.

"It is ironic, wouldn't you say, cousin? It was you who championed sending the beast hordes through the gate first. But it seems they have only turned into lucrative target practice for the humans instead of paving our way, and now one of the hordes is even revolting. I wonder how the elders will react when they hear of this." Rydel smilingly continued, seemingly unperturbed by the troubling developments.

"That's not for you to worry about, Rydel. Know your place. I'm leading the armies myself to fix the monkey problem, and that human hiding in the tunnels will soon be caught." Ogras couldn't stand being in the same room as this thorn in his side any longer and prepared to set out.

Ogras didn't actually want to lead the army, but faced with the emergence of a D-ranked treasure such as a Fruit of Ascension, he couldn't sit still. He needed to secure it by himself, and if that failed, destroy it so that Cindermane or some crony of Rydel didn't get it.

If someone from the main branch managed to get the Fruit of Ascension, he might as well lie down and kill himself, as the family assassins would find him as soon as the incursion stabilized anyway. His plan was to turn the wealth of the crystal mine into acquiring a treasure like the Fruit of Ascension and use that as a springboard to become the future hope of the clan. But if suddenly Rydel had the fruit as well, then he knew who the clan would favor.

"I'm sorry, cousin, but I need to correct you on a few accounts," Rydel said while holding up a hand to stop Ogras' exit, his smile slightly widening. "The human has escaped the ambush, leaving at least thirty corpses behind by now. He also seems to have figured out the tracking stones, and now we can't locate him. Furthermore, the one who will lead the army to fix your mistakes is me, not you."

"Are you revolting against the clan precepts, Rydel? You know the elders appointed me at least until the incursion stabilized. Are you sure you want to face the wrath of my grandfather?" Ogras spat out, a dangerous glint entering his eyes.

"Your grandfather is well aware. As you were untested when appointed general, the elders came to an accord with your ancestor," Rydel retorted as he retrieved a parchment from his bag. "In certain events that are deemed to be critical to clan Azh'Rezak's future developments, the military command is temporarily transferred to me. Just to make sure nothing goes wrong due to inexperience."

The bright smile looked like a death sentence to Ogras as he snatched the parchment with a snarl. After reading through it, he saw it was true. He immediately sensed his grandfather's magic sigil on the decree, telling him that this was real. The parchment detailed certain events that would result in a transfer of leadership to Rydel, and the emergence of a D-class treasure or higher was one of them. It looked like his grandfather had been forced to make some concessions in order to snatch the leadership position for him.

"But not to worry, cousin. As soon as this matter is dealt with, I will return the command to you as per the instructions. I suggest you stay in your beautiful castle for now, as your safety is paramount to the clan. I have allocated a few of my guards to protect you. We have to make sure that the humans don't assault you while we're up at the mountain." A cold ray flashed through Rydel's eyes as he retrieved the parchment from the now mute Ogras. "Well then, I have a fruit to retrieve. I will be seeing you later, cousin," he said as he exited Ogras' study, the last sentence rife with hidden implications.

Ogras briefly considered having it out with Rydel then and there, but soon gave up the thought. Rydel likely was ready for him, and he could also see multiple main branch members standing outside, sneering at him.

Should he call upon those four? No, that would just expose their true identities prematurely. The real issue was that Rydel had the precepts on his side this time. If Ogras wanted to do something, he needed to be smarter about it.

Ogras glared after Rydel, looking like a volcano ready to erupt. The aide sensed the atmosphere and made a quick excuse and fled the room, closing the door behind him.

Soon the energy left Ogras' body, and he slumped down in his chair.

"Shit."

Zac's heart was still beating quickly after having seen the vision. He wanted to immediately rush toward the valley but first checked his quest tab.

As he suspected, a new quest had arrived.

Dynamic Quests:

1. **Ascension (Limited – Open): Seize the Fruit of Ascension upon ripening. Reward: Fruit of Ascension. [Time until ripening: 11:58:23]**

The classification of the quest was new, Limited – Open. His other two dynamic quests were classified as Unique. If he guessed correctly, limited meant it was a short-duration quest. And he hoped he was wrong, but he believed open meant that everyone within a certain area got it.

The System said to emerge victorious and to struggle for supremacy. Then it conveniently showed the location of the treasure a full twelve hours before it ripened. It wanted a bloodbath.

Zac slowly sat down again and took a small sip of the azure water. He wasn't in the mood to wait any longer and needed to heal quickly. The burning sensation spread through his body again, but this time, the amount was manageable. Once again, he felt his wounds slightly improve and the throbbing pain he had felt come back once again was gone.

As the heat spread through his body, he pondered on what to do. He was hesitating if he should actually compete for the fruit, as going against both the monkey horde and maybe even the demons sounded like a suicide mission. He also felt he had no choice.

He didn't know what a Fruit of Ascension did, but from how it managed to create a quest, it couldn't be a small matter. If his enemies got it and received a huge power-up, he might be screwed. The most likely recipient would be the monkey herald, as he was the owner of the tree. It was a pretty even fight before; what would happen if it evolved once more?

Besides, it also presented an opportunity for him. The fruit would help someone ascend, judging by its name. It sounded awfully similar to evolve, and he guessed it might help him get a better class or evolve his race.

He also almost knew for certain he would find the herald by the fruit in twelve hours, hopefully still hurt from his slash. Zac knew the monkey possessed high values in Strength, Dexterity, and Endurance from their fight, and could only hope that it also didn't have a strong Vitality. It also felt reasonable that the general would be there to commandeer one of the fruits. That would mean that both his targets would be gathered at one place in roughly twelve hours.

In a sense, the quest represented an all-or-nothing gambit. If he succeeded, all his problems might be solved, including his incursion quest. But the danger would likely be off the charts. If he failed, his mission would turn harder, no matter who got the fruit. If he even survived.

But he felt it was do or die. Time was running out, and he needed to take some risks. With steely determination, he decided to participate in the fight.

Of course, there was no reason to rush there. He only needed to travel for less than two hours to get to the crimson tree. And getting there early would make him a sitting duck. He was only one man in what might be a huge free-for-all battle, and he needed to avoid attention as much as possible.

His goal should be to sneak in at the last minute, kill the monkey king, and steal the fruit. If possible, he should kill the general as well, or at least identify him. Then run for his life and see what the fallout was.

He sat down again on the ground and, while keeping a lookout for more demon parties, only focused on getting back to prime condition. He waited a full six hours before he felt well enough rested to be able to give it his all.

The wounds from the ambush were somewhat healed by now, but a few wounds would likely reopen if he exerted too much force. But there was still a couple of hours before he should see any action, and hopefully, he would be in even better condition by then.

He set out again and, after some trial and error, found a way out of the mountain. It wasn't the same path as the one he had entered through. He didn't want to dig through meters of fallen rocks, and besides, it might be marked by the monkeys.

Instead, he found a tunnel that should end somewhere on the inner side of the peak, close to the entrance of the valley. It didn't actually have a cave entrance, but a few holes in the rock let sunlight through. The wall was quite thin here, and with a few minutes of effort, he would be out.

The outside was completely quiet, so Zac decided to wait some more before emerging. As he waited, he started chipping at the wall with a dagger, not completely breaking through but making a quick exit easier. Finally done, he sat down and continued to recuperate. When the timer showed roughly two hours until the fruits ripened, a cacophony of roars broke the silence.

Zac's heartbeat fretfully hammered in his chest as he opened his eyes and stood up. It was now or never.

60

ENTERING THE FRAY

Zac immediately got ready, even though his wounds hadn't completely healed. But between his high Vitality and the numbing effects of the azure water, he was in an almost perfect fighting condition. With no more time to lose, he finally pushed down the rock wall that blocked the entrance while hefting an axe in his hand. It made quite a crash, but it was nothing compared to the roars of thousands of monkeys, with demon screams peppered in.

As soon as he got out, he was stunned by the mayhem.

Zac had emerged from a secluded spot on top of an outcropping, giving him decent vantage over the peak and down toward the valley. Everywhere he looked, he saw throngs of monkeys duking it out with legions of demons.

The air sparked with energy as fireballs and lightning bolts filled the sky. The ground rippled from a multitude of spears and other projectiles shooting out. Even nature itself had entered the fray as trees slowly reached down to grab unsuspecting monkeys before ripping them apart.

The other beast types were here as well, as a thick wall of barghest stopped the monkeys from getting into melee range of the demons. They mindlessly charged toward the monkey groupings, completely heedless of their survival.

Groups of gwyllgi roamed the battlefield with far more finesse compared to the hulking demonlings. They roved in packs and struck weak spots or lone stragglers almost with surgical precision and then quickly got out of harm's way.

There also was a smattering of imps placed together with the mage demons, but to Zac, it seemed that most of them still were in their underground dwellings, as their numbers were quite sparse. Perhaps Zac recently killing their boss had caused some sort of chaos in their ranks, making it hard for the demons to control them.

The monkeys wouldn't be outdone, though, and the air was filled with flying debris, from the stalactites from the monkey captains to anything that the normal monkeys could get their hands on. Zac even saw corpses being used as projectiles, flung at the magical barriers erected by the demon mages. The barghest that came close to the monkeys were largely helpless after their first impact and were pelted and bitten to death by the angry monkeys.

The magical shields held for the most part, but every now and then, they got overtaxed and shattered. The monkey captains were quick on the uptake and focused their energies on those areas. The focused fire turned the unlucky few behind the broken shield into crushed meat paste beneath a mountain of boulders.

However, most of the projectiles didn't reach the demons but rather slammed into the demon beasts, who fulfilled their purpose of being meat shields.

Overall, the demons clearly held the advantage, and they steadily pushed forward. For every demon the monkey horde killed, at least five monkeys died. It still was early in the battle, though, and from experience, Zac felt that the demons would run out of juice sooner or later. Those spells cost Cosmic Energy, while the monkeys likely could keep hurling debris for a good while. As long as the monkeys could withstand their furious onslaught long enough, they might have a chance to turn the situation around.

Besides, the terrain was not ideal for the organized warfare that the demons were trying for. He saw that the orderly lines were starting to splinter, and the legions were forced to split up as they advanced.

Zac didn't know why it had come to a full-scale war, but he didn't complain. This kind of chaos was the best news for him. He wondered if the monkeys' disadvantage was because of him. He had thinned out their horde quite a bit, after all.

Some movement in the distance grabbed his attention. It was a solitary group that emanated a pressure a notch above the other demons. They were steadily pushing forward and were entering the valley at a furious pace. None of the magic shields were breaking, and the monkeys could offer no resistance to their advance.

In the front, a few demons in resplendent gear were personally reaping the lives of monkeys like they were harvesting wheat. Especially attention-grabbing was one male demon with shining white hair that was dancing in the wind. He held a sword in his hand and had another strapped to his back, and as he moved forward, it almost looked like dancing rather than being engaged in battle. The sword moved in graceful curves and moved around him in a mesmerizing pattern. But Zac knew it was no performance art, as that demon's speed of reaping monkeys seemed to eclipse even his own.

It looked like he had located the general.

Satisfied with what he had found, he started to make his way down from the cliff. He had wrapped his head in rags to hide his features and covered as much skin as possible. Zac hoped that the demons would be too preoccupied with the monkeys to realize he lacked horns and wore shoes instead of having taloned paws.

He skirted around the main army and aimed to enter the valley from a slightly different direction. There were a few clumps of demons along the path, but none, thankfully, reacted to him. It was lucky that the demon armies all used individual clothing and gear, making their composition look very chaotic.

As he walked around a bend, he almost ran straight into a party of six demons. The one in the front snapped something in demonic as Zac passed, but Zac only waved his axe in response. His heartbeat quickened as he kept running, waiting for the demons to go their own way.

It seemed the proximity was too close, as an arrow came whizzing at his back. Sensing danger, Zac whirled around and blocked the arrow with his axe-head. Sighing, he made a 180 and rushed into the demon group while he summoned **[Chop]**. The man in the front held a sword, which by itself started burning as he swung it to intercept Zac's chop. The demon hadn't imagined the power contained in the axe, and the edge hit him like a truck, breaking most of his fingers as the sword was forced away. The swing continued onward as it chopped off his upper body and continued to decapitate the unlucky demon who stood next to him with a short sword and shield.

Zac pushed on and made quick work of the last four demons, whose feeble attempts to stop him couldn't even slow him down. After the blitz, he was bleeding a bit from two small wounds, but it was nothing serious. A few of his old wounds had opened as well, but there was nothing to do about that for now. He was also drenched in demon blood and could only hope that the smell wouldn't attract any beasts.

He slowly kept moving forward, and after half an hour, he reached the forest at the edge of the valley, taking twice the time compared to if he had rushed straight in.

As he moved forward, he saw that the orderly war at the slopes of the mountain had turned into a chaotic melee in the valley by now. There were clumps of demons fighting monkeys scattered all over the place. In most places, the demons still held an advantage, but at a few others, they got overrun by sheer numbers.

He saw an unlucky group of ten demons getting ripped to pieces by an angry horde of monkeys. They put up a valiant defense, but two fists couldn't defend against ten, and in just moments, they were mangled corpses strewn on the ground. A few of the monkeys had even ripped off limbs and contentedly chewed on them as they moved toward the next pack.

Zac tried to avoid battle as much as he could, not wanting to get any more experience until he seized a Fruit of Ascension. He stayed clear of any larger battles, zigzagging forward in a careful manner. Of course, every now and then, he got accosted by either a group of demons that figured out his identity or a group of enraged monkeys happy to target any humanoid.

The clashes resulted in furious melees, as Zac wanted to finish the battles as quickly as possible. Unheeding of energy expenditure, he ravaged any party that got close with great chops using his skills. When he ran low on Cosmic Energy, he took a sip from the lake water and let the burn quickly restore his deficit. He did avoid using the Dao of Heaviness, though, as he didn't have any means to restore his mental energy apart from sleeping.

Soon he arrived at the field of desolation, his body covered in a multitude of shallow wounds by now. Due to the consumption of the water, he didn't feel any pain, though, and still felt he was in peak condition.

The vision the System had shown him earlier was accurate, and a huge area was now covered in dried-out and dead trees. The once lush forest was gone and replaced with a dead space.

After a quick look, he saw that it was only fifty minutes until the fruits ripened. Even if he had blazed through all the resistance in the forest, it took some time to traverse the distance. He figured that if he ran, it would take him twenty minutes or so to reach the crimson tree. He was hesitant whether he should leave the cover of the forest to enter the field, as he would be completely exposed if he did.

After some deliberation, he ran along the forest edge toward the opposite side of the field. The demons should be concentrated on the eastern side, as they'd entered the valley from there. The army might have spread to encircle the tree by now, but it should at least be thinner at the opposite side.

When he was a bit more than halfway to the other side, he veered into the dead zone and headed for the tree. He was running out of time and needed to get to the fruits. The area was largely devoid of combatants, either monkey or demon, and soon he saw why.

As he approached the tree, he saw a scene of utter chaos. The magical tree still stood tall as it had before, with the addition of the two ripening fruits. Covering it was a glimmering shell covered in dense fractals. Zac felt that the shield should be the work of the System, as the fractals felt perfect and in harmony with the universe, just like the ones on his array flags. The inscriptions on the demons' weapons were far more simplistic in comparison.

Packed around the shield was a confusing and bloody carnage between monkeys and demons. There were no lines of demarcation, no strategy, and no order. There were just hundreds upon hundreds of bodies crammed together, desperately trying to kill anything on the opposing side. They all tried to claw their way closer to the shield and the tree, to be as close as possible when the shield dropped.

Right by the edge of the shield, a few areas almost devoid of people could be seen, and in one of them, Zac saw the white-haired demon fighting against the monkey king. The herald had a few supersized monkeys by his side, and they furiously did everything they could to support their leader. It looked like the herald was mostly healed up, but a huge scar adorned its chest now.

Every strike between the herald and the general created rippling shock waves in the area, keeping all the grunts at bay. The ground looked blazing hot with fire and molten rock, likely a result of the herald's onslaught.

But the general clearly held the advantage, and with dizzying swordplay was whittling down Cindermane's defenses. The large scar on his chest had started to open up, and new wounds over his arms accompanied it. Zac realized the lethality of the general, as even Zac's own mighty swings had only left a white mark on the herald's sturdy hands. The hulking monkey captains were covered in wounds from head to toe as well. One of them even had a whole arm missing.

Meanwhile, the general still looked pristine apart from some soot marks, as though the carnage and fire in the surroundings were isolated from himself. The monkey captains were doing what they could to ease the pressure, but it seemed that they wouldn't be able to hang on for long unless something changed. Since Zac didn't want the general to kill the herald, at least not yet, he was determined to be the change that would turn the tide.

61

PITCHED BATTLE

The ground was barely visible beneath the forces, as blood and broken bodies covered most of it by now. Even fires were starting to erupt at various spots around the battlefield, likely from the attacks of pyromancers and the herald. With the dried-out tree husks on the ground, the whole valley would likely be an inferno of flames in a short while.

Zac could see that more combatants from both camps were steadily streaming in from the surroundings and immediately joined in on the mayhem when they arrived. He checked his quest and saw that the timer showed **[00:10:03]**.

Zac once more glanced at the mouthwatering fruits glistening on the tree, and after a few steadying breaths, he charged into the frenzy. He steadily moved forward, wielding an axe in one hand and a dagger in the other. He refrained from using **[Chop]** in this crammed melee, afraid to draw attention to himself.

He mainly used the axe to deflect or hook incoming swings, and finished off the enemy with a quick stab in their throat or heart before moving forward. It was a quick and dirty method that didn't announce his monstrous Strength.

He steadily moved forward, forced to kill a combatant almost with every step. His disguise was still assisting him immensely, as it often took the demons a second to register that they weren't facing an ally. And a second was all that Zac needed to quickly and discreetly kill them.

Soon he was just thirty meters from the edge of the shield, and the area actually was getting less cramped compared to more. Every single monkey at the core was a captain, and they were furiously fighting with various well-equipped demons. The monkeys had to fight a few captains per demon, not being able to match their might.

Each battle had its own space, as the swings and shock waves could kill or at least disrupt anyone coming too close. Getting hit and distracted in an intense situation like this could be a death sentence, so everyone kept their backs clear.

It was obvious that the demons steadily were gaining the upper hand, as almost all the bodies on the ground were monkeys. That couldn't go on, as Zac needed the fight to keep going to a point where they whittled each other down. Zac took out a dagger and discreetly threw it straight into the back of a well-geared demon. The make of his armor was the same as Zac's old chest piece, only covering the upper torso, so Zac's dagger slammed straight into his back without giving the demon time to react.

The hit destroyed the demon's spine, and he helplessly fell on the ground. The monkey captains immediately pounced and punched his head into the ground until it was a bloody pulp, before moving on to assist its brethren. Satisfied with his work, he continued on and acted as a hidden reaper.

He was still forced to kill monkeys and demons coming too close to him, but he kept moving around to avoid being exposed. He also kept a healthy distance from the battle between the herald and the general, who were still going at it with extreme prejudice. Every chance he got, he threw a dagger at one of the stronger-looking demons. Sometimes he got a perfect hit and actually managed to kill them himself, and at other times, he managed to at least maim and distract them, allowing the monkeys to finish the job.

Soon he ran out of knives and was forced to start throwing Nexus Crystals at the demons. They weren't as effective as the knives, but with Zac's strength, anything he threw could be considered a weapon. Soon the war at the center of the battlefield was starting to sway in favor of the monkeys.

After Zac helped kill so many of the demons, there currently were far more monkey captains fighting every single demon, and the extra help was often enough to turn the tide.

But the demons quickly figured out something was wrong, and a mountain of a man angrily shouted something with a piercing voice that carried over the sounds of battle, pointing a huge battle hammer straight at Zac. Many of the demons immediately spotted him, and it looked like his ruse was over.

However, he had already mostly accomplished his plan, and a great number of demons were killed due to his machinations. Also, the general and herald's battle was reaching a white-hot intensity, and they couldn't be bothered with the scream. The herald was quite ragged by now, and the old monkey captains had been replaced with new ones. Zac had a feeling that the only reason the monkey king was still alive was that the demons knew he was of importance to the incursion. Otherwise, Zac couldn't imagine that the general didn't have some ace to kill him after all this time.

He tried sneaking back into the chaos of the battle, but a few of the demon leaders wouldn't have it, and they charged straight at him. A rock wall was erected in front of Zac, halting his escape. He tried shouldering through it, but it was far sturdier compared to the walls he had encountered earlier. It held together against Zac's slam, although it sustained some cracks from the impact.

Suddenly, he sank down into the ground and couldn't move

his feet. The ground had first liquefied, then solidified in quick succession, making it seem like he was wearing cement shoes.

Zac didn't have time to rip himself free, as a huge mallet was falling down upon him. Through some means, the mallet was getting larger as it fell down toward his head and soon was large enough to completely smash him into a pulp.

Zac saw no choice but to infuse his hatchet with his Dao, and brought his axe in a two-handed swing, holding nothing back. Zac had severely overestimated the demon from his size and choice of weapon, and when his axe collided with the huge mallet with a terrifying clash, it flew out of the hand of the demon like a rocket. It sailed over the crimson tree and landed somewhere on the other side of the battlefield.

Zac was startled, but not as startled as the demon. He wasted no time and slammed the axe haft down on the demon's shoulder, and then used the spike on the back of the axe-head as a hook to pull him to melee distance. As Zac dragged him close, he ended the demon with a quick stab in his throat with his dagger and then used the body to intercept a few ranged attacks.

The force from the weapons colliding had actually cracked the ground he was standing on, freeing him from the binding. He located the earth mage some distance away and grabbed a monkey captain by its arm.

The monkey captain furiously slammed his fist in Zac's chest, but Zac only took it with a grunt before he lifted the huge monkey up in the air and threw him like a boulder at the demon mage. The earth mage hastily erected another wall to intercept the monkey projectile, but the force behind the beast powered through it.

Zac was not far behind as he entered the wall through the breach, and with a quick chop, decapitated the demon, who didn't even manage to activate his stone skin skill in time.

Zac moved on toward the next demon, who had tried to gang up on him, but a blinding light interrupted his plans. It was the large shield covering the tree that started to shine many times brighter compared to before.

Zac glanced around, and when he saw no one was attacking him at the moment, he brought up the quest skill again and saw the timer go down from two seconds to zero. With a bright flash, the shield immediately winked out of existence, exposing the tree to hundreds of greedy eyes.

No one moved for a split second before all hell broke loose. Everyone started rushing toward the tree, holding nothing back. Even demons were hitting other demons in a struggle to reach the fruits.

Zac wasn't any different, and taking full advantage of his close proximity to the tree, he pushed forward, driving massive amounts of Cosmic Energy into his legs. The ground cracked with every step he took, and it would be more accurate to say Zac pushed himself forward by slamming into the ground with his feet rather than running. He summoned **[Chop]** and killed any monkey or demon getting too close, and soon he was almost underneath the tree's branches.

Zac was among the first, but he was still behind two individuals, Cindermane and the dazzling general. Both had already moved toward the fruits, their arms reaching to grab them first. The monkey king had actually created large lava pillars that lifted it up toward the branches, and the general somehow stepped on black arcs of lightning as he moved upwards through the air.

Zac knew he was out of time, and with a roar, he created a huge edge with **[Chop]** and unleashed it at the two. It seemed that no one of the other camps dared intervene with the two in the forefront, perhaps afraid that they would inadvertently ruin their leader's plans. The edge shot up at the two, cutting a few of the crimson branches on the way.

The herald screeched and looked horrified as he stared at the incoming edge, and actually missed his steps and fell down from the pillars it had created. It appeared that Zac's last chop had left a shadow in the herald's mind.

The general looked surprised to be ambushed at this moment but still managed to smoothly dodge it. He was far up in the air by now and only needed one more step on the black lightning steps to reach the fruits. Desperate, Zac infused his axe with the Dao of Heaviness and hurled it at the demon. The fruits were five meters up in the air, so Zac and the general were extremely close. With Zac's power, it almost looked as though the axe teleported as it slammed into the general.

The general had skillfully blocked the strike with his sword, but between Zac's huge strength and the Dao of Heaviness, the momentum of the throw wouldn't be denied. The demon was forcefully pushed away from the tree, and the shock wave destroyed most of the branches of the tree.

Even the branch that held the two Fruits of Ascension was broken off, and they were falling straight toward Zac. Not wanting to waste such a God-given opportunity, he jumped up in the air and snatched the fruits and immediately stashed them into his pouch.

He couldn't believe how easily he had acquired the fruits. It looked like 67 Luck wasn't just for show. But the elation of getting the treasure quickly dissipated as hundreds of murderous glares focused their suddenly undivided attention on him.

62

CRESCENDO

Zac brought out his second axe from his pouch, nervously glancing around. His plan had been to kill the herald as well, but being stared at by hundreds of hungry eyes quickly extinguished any desire to remain. For a second, he thought about throwing out the cauldron but soon discarded the idea.

The runoff fumes from when the imp herald was concocting the poison had been enough to do a number on him, and he didn't dare imagine what the finished product would be like. Unfortunately, he had no method to control the dissemination of the poison, and best scenario, he managed to kill some of the demons. But that would still leave him to fight his way out against the survivors, now with one less ace in the hole. Worst-case scenario, the poison took too long to activate, or he poisoned himself as well, dying in a bout of friendly fire. The poison would have to be for when he truly was out of options as the last Hail Mary.

Zac instead shot back away from the tree and started cutting his way out of the packed masses. But how could leaving with the treasure be so easy? Combatants from both camps furiously impeded his path, and he was immediately beset by attacks from all directions. New wounds joined a litany of old ones, and even with Zac's great constitution, he was starting to feel the pressure.

With a furious roar, he overcharged **[Chop]** and created a wide circle of death with a radius of six meters with one fluid motion before he pressed forward. But he only managed to take one step before an intense hair-raising danger made him turn around.

A silver sword was aimed straight at his throat from behind, and Zac barely had time to block it with the enlarged edge of **[Chop]**. The power of the strike was enormous, and Zac was flung back from the force. He didn't even have time to land before a molten spear struck him in his back, the searing pain eliciting a howl.

Neither the herald nor the general were ready to give up the fruits, and for a second put their differences aside in order to hunt down Zac. The same couldn't be said of their underlings, of course, as their furious melee quickly resumed after the fruits were snatched. The monkey horde was once again starting to lose control of the situation, but this time, Zac was too occupied to do anything about it. The fires started to grow, and soon the whole valley would likely be consumed in a conflagration.

Zac was in no position to worry about his island burning down, as he currently had two formidable foes to contend with. With steely eyes, he activated chop to the limit he could sustain it and charged at the duo. With a roar, he swung the axe in an upward curve, rending a huge gash in the ground as he did. The edge flew toward the general, who Zac estimated to be the most formidable foe.

With a slanted blade, the demon managed to nullify most of the force and redirected the swing upward. He then immediately followed up with a quick forward stab aimed straight at Zac's heart. Zac barely managed to inch his chest to the side in order to avoid the blade, but it still tore a bloody gash along his chest. The sword had to be of superior make, as it actually ruined the inscribed dress he wore over his armor. If Zac had known this would happen, he would have immediately used its charge instead of holding out for a more threatening situation.

The herald wouldn't miss the opportunity either and spat some magma in Zac's direction. Most luckily missed, but some splattered on Zac's arm, and some nauseating sizzling could be heard. Zac could only press forward, hoping to end things quickly.

He used every trick he had learned from **[Axe Mastery],** trying to get past the sword of the general in order to do some damage. Each swing was imbued with all the strength he could exert, and the wailing sounds of his axe filled the air. He even swapped between using his Dao and using **[Chop],** trying to disrupt the general's rhythm.

But it seemed that nothing worked against the demon. He smoothly deflected or dodged every strike that Zac put out, not even looking strained. His Strength clearly wasn't at the same level as Zac's, but he made up for it with skill with the blade. Still, Zac judged his Strength to be far above one hundred, though, as every strike with the blades created terrifying collisions, the shock waves keeping any fire out of their way. The ground beneath their feet kept cracking and getting destroyed as well.

Even more dangerously, it looked like the demon also possessed a Dao Seed, or at least was beginning to comprehend one. His strikes contained a sense of sharpness, and the shock waves from his strikes actually cut small wounds on Zac's body when the air hit him.

The herald had gone somewhat passive, content in letting the two duke it out for a bit as he recuperated. By now, it likely knew that it was not the match of either one of the two combatants and probably hoped they would kill each other. Although it threw the occasional spear or boulder at Zac, it mostly focused on helping out his brethren against the demon army. A few demons had tried to join the general in his battle against Zac, but the herald luckily killed them as they came. Unfortunately, the general was in no need of backup and was doing just fine on his own.

Zac was steadily accruing wounds from his fight with the demon, as he wasn't able to dodge his lightning-quick stabs. The best he could do was to avoid the sword hitting fatal spots by adjusting his body. Even worse, the general was one of the demons who used the black lightning attacks.

He used it far more freely compared to the first demon he had met. Every strike contained the biting sting of the arcs, and the lightning was actually slowly accumulating inside Zac's body. His arm suddenly jerked from the shock, completely exposing his chest. The demon was prepared, and with a lunge, stabbed his sword straight in Zac's chest.

Lightning poured freely into his body, and Zac coughed up a mouthful of blood from the damage. He normally might have passed out from the pain, but the lightning kept him awake. To make matters worse, lava spikes erupted from the ground between Zac's legs from a stomp of the herald.

Surprisingly, the spikes shot toward the general, with the largest one aiming straight toward his exposed heart. It looked like the herald had been waiting for an opportunity for a double knock-out. However, the general simply snorted, and from nowhere, all the spikes were cut into pieces. Hovering next to him was the sword that the demon had kept on his back throughout the battle.

It crackled with black lightning and seemed to have no problem with defying the laws of gravity. It hovered a few rounds around the general before it returned into the scabbard on his back on its own.

Abruptly, the spike on the back of Zac's axe-head slammed into the temple of the herald, instantly killing it. Zac had taken advantage of the brief pause of the herald after its attack and used it to mount a surprise attack. Zac had consistently focused all his energy on attacking the general thus far, and the herald had grown lax. He hadn't actually planned on killing the herald before the general, but he saw an opportunity and took it.

A huge surge of Cosmic Energy entered Zac's body, and he felt himself gain another level. There was no time to go over it, though, as the general renewed his attacks on him. Zac once again found himself at an impasse, steadily losing ground. The chest wound was creating trouble for him to breathe and move freely as well, and the fight turned even more one-sided. He wanted to somehow create an opportunity to flee, as he had accomplished all he needed for now. But the general would barely let him breathe, let alone leave the scene.

A tremendous amount of roaring erupted in the surroundings as well. The monkeys lost their minds upon seeing their leader fall and started madly swinging at everything around them. In their madness, they completely gave up on defense and started dropping with even faster speed compared to before. One after another, the monkeys died, becoming food for the expanding fires. The flames hadn't died out due to the death of the herald, instead truly becoming a force of their own as they spread over the dried leaves and husks.

Zac desperately tried to swing faster and with more power to turn the tide, but the general felt like an impenetrable wall of deft blades. As he kept fighting and swapping back and forth between **[Chop]** and the Dao, something suddenly clicked in his mind, and he once again summoned the fractal blade.

This time, it was different, as it held a darker hue and emanated the aura of a lofty mountain. Even the fractals on the edge had grown denser, weaving another line of inscriptions along the edge. He'd finally managed to integrate his Dao with his skill, and the result wasn't as simple as one plus one equals two. Something new was born out of the fusion.

With renewed vigor, Zac roared and furiously swung his axe at the general, aiming to end it all with one strike. It was a huge overhead swing aimed at the demon's head, and it carried the aura of a falling meteor.

The demon immediately sensed something was wrong but didn't have time to dodge. Looking serious for the first time, the demon roared as the sword on his back flashed into his free hand, and he held up both his swords in the air in order to block the strike.

Just another sword wasn't enough, and the force slammed him down to his knees, the impact blowing any debris or bodies in the surroundings far away. The general tried to deflect the force, but the Chop of Heaviness was intractable as it pushed his blades down. A golden sheen flashed into existence around the demon, but it only held for a second before it cracked. The force in the strike contained everything Zac had learned and gained so far, and a flimsy armor inscription wouldn't stop it.

An amulet around the neck of the demon started shining with a blinding light, and a silver shield winked into existence next. It looked like the shield of a celestial, as it shone with brilliant fractals as it met the oncoming axe.

The collision didn't create a huge impact as Zac expected, but it rather seemed the shield somehow absorbed the momentum. After the strike, the shield started to crack, and the general groaned miserably as a crack could also be heard in his right arm. It looked like using that amulet didn't come without its price. But it was sufficient to stop Zac's monstrous swing.

The general didn't seem lax as before, and with an angry roar and his hair in disarray, he got to his feet. With a couple of furious slashes, he created some distance from Zac, then pointed his sword toward the sky. His second blade crackled with an extreme amount of lightning and rapidly flew over ten meters up in the sky. The lightning kept expanding around it, creating a wide field of a lightning hellscape.

The black arcs changed and actually turned into sword silhouettes covered in fractals. It reminded Zac of his own Cosmic Energy edge, but the danger he felt from the roughly hundred swords sinisterly hanging above was above anything he had felt thus far. The general didn't pull any punches anymore and wanted to completely eradicate him.

The lightning blades started falling toward Zac like a heavenly punishment. Any one of the blades could kill Zac if it hit, and there were over a hundred of them incoming. Knowing there was nowhere to hide from the strike, Zac could only fight it head-on. Cramming all his remaining Cosmic Energy into the fractal on his hand, he created his largest edge thus far, sporting an almost eight-meter-long blade. It was imbued with the Dao of Heaviness, and with a roar of defiance, he launched it like a projectile up against the sword rain.

For a second, it felt like a colossal mountain rose from the ground to intercept the heavenly thunder above, in a struggle between the Heavens and Earth. The collision was earth-shattering, and the chaotic energies temporarily blotted out the sky. Errant lightning blades fell all over the area, killing and maiming monkeys and demons alike.

Zac had managed to avert most of the attack with his colossal edge, but he was completely drained, and his head hurt. Furthermore, his swing wasn't able to destroy all of the falling blades, and he found himself impaled by multiple lightning swords. The general was panting as he walked over to Zac, one arm hanging limply to his side. He didn't look like he had much fight left in him either, but it was enough to finish Zac off.

His second sword floated above his head, looking like a sinister scorpion's stinger. Its crackling lightning had dimmed considerably, but it still held a strong killing intent within. Their eyes met for a brief second, and the sword shot down toward Zac's head. He tried to muster up a response, but he could only feebly lift his axe in an attempt to avert the incoming sword.

A spear of complete darkness suddenly emerged out of the general's chest and lifted him up in the air, forcing him to puke out a huge amount of blood as his body started spasming. The sinister-looking weapon had truly impaled him and likely completely obliterated his heart.

Behind the general, a hooded demon in average gear was standing, with a determined glint in his eyes as he looked upon his dying leader. The general arduously turned his head, and when he saw his assailant, his eyes shrank to pinpoints.

With his last breath, he let out a ragged roar that covered the whole battlefield, garnering the attention of all the combatants.

"OGRAS!"

63

PURPLE HAZE

The sinister blade that was supposed to end Zac's life powerlessly fell to the ground as the general died. Zac mutely stared at the impaled demon, unable to comprehend what was going on. The same seemed to be true for the hundreds of demons who watched the betrayal. They stared blankly at the scene until they were awoken by an angry roar from one of the well-dressed leaders.

Suddenly, a murderous din filled the air as multiple demons were screaming and pointing their weapons at Zac's unexpected ally. The demon stood up from his hunkered position as he looked around at its supposed allies with a sneer. He threw away the corpse of the demon leader like it was trash with a whip of his lance after looting his pouch, and then turned toward Zac with a half-smile.

Suddenly, the killer took something out of his pouch and popped it into his mouth. Unsure of what was going on, Zac shakily got ready for another round of battle as he finally scrambled to his feet. The wounds where he was impaled by the lightning blades screamed in protest, but he forced himself to stay upright. He looked at the demon in front of him with a dubious expression, wondering why this man had saved his life. Zac's eyes widened as the demon unexpectedly puked out a huge amount of blackened blood and fell over to the ground. With a few spasms, he lay dead next to the general.

"WHAT?" Zac exclaimed, completely unable to follow the quick turn of events. Was the man an assassin or a member of a death squad that some rival demon group had sent after the general? But why would they want to ruin their own invasion? From what Zac understood, the incursion would close the moment the four heralds and the general were dead.

But he could only put aside his doubts for now, as he was completely wrung out but still surrounded by hundreds of demons. At least they looked shell-shocked by the turn of events as well, as they hesitantly stared at the two corpses on the ground. Zac used this brief respite to quickly take a swig of the azure pond water, the familiar burning sensation quickly spreading through his veins, temporarily muting the blazing pain in his various wounds. He knew he had to treat himself real soon, though, as he was starting to feel woozy from blood loss, even with the water strengthening him.

Just as he put away the bottle, the assassin suddenly spasmed again, and with a few wretched coughs, he rose from the dead. Zac didn't want to take any chances and started to advance on the zombie demon.

"Wait, human, we are on the same side," the demon croaked as he weakly scrambled to his feet.

Shocked at hearing something other than demonic for the first time since he'd met Abby, Zac paused and hesitantly stared at the demon. The surrounding demons suddenly woke up from their stupor and started angrily screaming at the assassin again, which was completely ignored by him.

"We don't have time for a chat, human. You should have a

cauldron of poison from the imps. Throw the contents into a fire if you want us to survive," he continued.

"Why should I believe you? Why did you kill that man?" Zac questioned, loath to just follow some stranger's instructions. He glanced around and saw that most of the demons were closing in, except for a few who were taking care of the leftover monkeys.

"It doesn't matter. Unless you do something, we're dead. Even if you drink the whole bottle of the Cosmic Water, your wounds will kill you before you're out of this valley if you keep fighting," the demon interjected, having seen through Zac's original plan of trying to slash himself out with the help of the azure water. An arrow whizzed past Zac's head as a reminder he was strapped for time, and he needed to act fast.

After hesitating for a while, he decided to comply with the suggestion. He subconsciously knew he wouldn't make it out, as the only thing keeping him on his feet was the temporary boost from the water. He had held off until now, but it was Hail Mary time.

He brought out the large cauldron and, with a grunt, threw it into one of the fiercest fires created by the herald. The contents spilled out over the fire, and instantly, a huge purple cloud, far more sinister compared to what he had seen in the imp herald's cave, swelled out. The poison vapors created in the caves had only been from the small fires underneath the cauldron heating the concoction, but this time, the poison was actually burned instead of heated up. It looked like it fused with the smoke of the raging fires, and quickly spread outward.

"What now?" he asked as he turned to the mysterious demon.

"Now I wish you the best of luck, human," the demon answered with a slight smile as he popped another pill into his mouth. It was a different type of pill from the one that temporarily killed him, giving out a refreshing herbal scent. He then took one step and disappeared into thin air.

Zac got a sinking feeling as he turned back to the cauldron. The fire was spewing out purple gasses in a terrifying volume, and they quickly expanded outward. Judging from the horrified faces of the demons, he realized he might have made a big mistake. Not wasting any more time on the enigmatic demon, he madly ran for his life back toward the forest. He stumbled and couldn't keep a very high speed even powered with the water, and his wounds kept bleeding as he ran for his life. With the mountain winds helping, the poison cloud would likely soon envelop the whole valley, judging from its rapid expansion.

Only a few of the demons bothered with Zac after seeing the expanding purple haze, and instead fearfully dashed away from the battlefield, unheeding of any wounded comrades screaming for assistance.

A few of the wounded demons went for Zac with madness in their eyes, bent on taking him with them to hell. However, most of those who had given up fleeing were even more wounded than Zac and could only helplessly glare at him as he stumbled away, fueled by the azure water. An errant arrow hit his back, but Zac only grunted and continued on.

But the cloud moved too fast, and soon it was right at Zac's heels. As he ran, he took out a rag from his pouch and put it over his mouth, hoping it would at least provide some protection against the approaching cloud.

Just before the cloud overtook him, he took one last deep breath of fresh air. Soon after the world turned purple, and a stinging sensation made his eyes tear. He couldn't see very far ahead anymore but could only keep moving forward as long as the air in his lungs let him. He madly dashed as quickly as his broken body allowed toward where he remembered the closest peak to be. Still, he knew it would take over thirty minutes at his speed to get there, and even then, he might not be safe.

The wounds of his body seemed to be entrances for the poison as he started to get nauseous, even though he kept his breath so far. After a while, he couldn't hold on any longer and was forced to inhale a lungful of poison. He immediately started getting extremely woozy, his power quickly leaving his legs. The strength of the poison truly was on another level compared to the fumes down in the herald's cave.

As he started despairing over what to do, the familiar sight of the magical pond entered his vision. He lacked the luxury of having time to think things through, and immediately jumped into the azure water. He would have to risk meeting a pond monster, as even a few more breaths of that poison would kill him.

He planned to swim down to the bottom of the lake and hopefully find a passage down into the mountain. Since the water was crammed full of Cosmic Energy, Zac guessed it was connected to the crystal mine somehow. But he only managed to swim for ten seconds deeper into the pond before his whole body felt like it was on fire. It was the water, as it seeped into his body through his wounds and perhaps even his pores.

The heat quickly became unbearable, but it only kept building up. Meanwhile, his insides were churning from the poison, only adding to his misery. Zac's whole body started to swell up, and in seconds, looked completely bloated. His whole skin was red, and if he weren't underwater, he'd likely be steaming from the heat.

Zac felt hopeless and desperate. It was heartbreaking to think that he actually managed to defy all odds and beat the incursion, only to end up in this situation. He had killed the four heralds personally and even helped set the stage for the general's death by destroying all his protective treasures and forcing him to expend all his energy in the fight. Almost two months of ceaseless life-and-death struggles, only to explode from over-ingesting super-water.

Completely unreconciled, Zac made one desperate attempt to survive. He grabbed one of the fruits from his pouch and tore into it with his teeth. An unimaginably sweet taste exploded in his mouth and made him almost forget that he was dying. It was by far the tastiest thing he had ever eaten, and it felt like he was munching on something that gods feasted on in ancient stories. As he swallowed it, a fresh cooling sensation entered his body, immediately sweeping the poison away.

He devoured the fruit completely, apart from some juices that leaked into the water, completely frenzied from the taste. He even accidentally swallowed some water with the fruit as he forgot himself from the otherworldly deliciousness. The cooling sensation spread throughout his extremities as he feasted, and actually started combating the burning sensation from the magical water.

Zac was relieved, as it looked like his gambit had been successful. But the relief didn't last for long, as his body quickly started to go from blazing hot to freezing cold, over and over again in quick succession. Two forces were fighting for supremacy, and the ravaged battlefield was Zac's body.

Even though he was underwater, he couldn't stop himself from desperately screaming in pain, with even more water filling his lungs. He couldn't even register it, as the pain was all-consuming, far worse than getting burned or stabbed in his chest. With every change in his body, it felt like his cells were melted down into a puddle, then frozen solid again by the freezing cold of the fruit.

Zac sensed that his spirit could collapse at any moment, and every second felt like an eternity for him. Soon he couldn't take it anymore and brought out a dagger from his pouch. With his last energy, he stabbed it toward his throat, hoping to quickly end the suffering.

The dagger tore into his throat and then sank to the bottom of the lake as Zac let go with relief. He felt a sting of shame when thinking of his family that he never was able to save, but he felt they would understand if they knew what he was going through.

But the sweet release of death didn't arrive. The wound closed with visible speed, and soon his neck was as good as new. Zac despaired, not knowing what to do. His body wouldn't listen to his commands anymore, and his brain was overtaxed by the pain signals bombarding his synapses.

The continuous changes in his body kept on going, uncaring about Zac's plight. Finally, his eyes rolled up into his head as he passed out into blissful darkness, and as he fainted, his body slowly kept descending into the depths.

64

TAKING STOCK

With a scream, Zac woke up from his head hitting a sharp rock formation. Groggily, he tried to orient himself and found that he was bobbing about in the azure water in a cave. Afraid that the burning pain would start again, he quickly scrambled up on a piece of dry land.

His body felt surprisingly good after all it had gone through. The mental scar from remembering the excruciating pain was far worse compared to anything his body was actually experiencing right now. Just thinking about it caused his hands to shake and almost made him cry. That had been too harrowing, far worse than risking his life in any of the fights or the pain from getting wounded.

It took some time for him to regather his wits before he finally looked at his surroundings. He was currently in a decently large cave that was ten by twenty meters. Almost half of it was submerged in the azure water, and the other half was crammed full of subterranean plants. It made sense, as Zac had never encountered any tunnel or cave with a density of Cosmic Energy that could compare to where he was.

It was as though the boost from the crystal mines below had

fused with the boost of the lake and created something even more intense in the enclosed space of the cavern. Zac was unsure of how he had gotten here. After snatching the fruits, he had fled the purple cloud of death and jumped into the mysterious pond. After that, everything had turned fuzzy, apart from the very real memory of the pain.

He could only guess that some stream had brought him down into the depths of the mountain while the Fruit of Ascension kept him alive. Even though he felt generally restored, he wasn't ready to set out, as there were many things he needed to check out after the cataclysmic final battle.

Name: Zachary Atwood
Level: 36
Class: [F-Rare] Hatchetman
Race: [E] Human
Alignment: [Earth] Human

Titles: Born for Carnage, Ultimate Reaper, Luck of the Draw, Giantsbane, Disciple of David, Overpowered, Slayer of Leviathans, Adventurer, Demon Slayer, Full of Class, Rarified Being, Trailblazer, Child of Dao, The Big 500, Planetary Aegis, One Against Many

Dao: Seed of Heaviness – Early

Strength: 189
Dexterity: 69
Endurance: 130
Vitality: 84
Intelligence: 57
Wisdom: 57
Luck: 77

Free Points: 3
Nexus Coins: 746,317

The first thing he noticed was that his Strength now was at a full 189 points, having increased by 14 points since he last checked. He had actually broken past his limit of 175 points and could only attribute it to the fact that he'd luckily evolved to an E-ranked human according to his status page, whatever that meant. He did a quick check all over his body and was relieved to find there were no wings or other new appendages that suddenly grew on him. He even checked between his legs and was half disappointed and half relieved that no evolutions had taken place there as well.

He didn't really feel any different, but he guessed that he would find out sooner or later what it meant to get a higher race class. He at least knew it helped him increase the limit of his attributes, which was one of his most important goals.

He had also gained two new titles, and he brought up the title menu to check them out.

[One Against Many: Fight against 500 warriors of the same tier and survive. Endurance +10]

[Planetary Aegis: First to stop an incursion in world. All stats +5, All stats +5%]

The first one was not bad, a nifty reward for staying alive through those odds. He guessed that there were tiers to that title, and he'd have gotten a better one if he'd actually defeated them rather than fleeing after throwing out a bunch of poison.

The second was even better and was the fifth one he possessed that gave a percent boost to all stats. The title didn't mention anything about solo kill like some of his other titles, and he wondered if it was because he wasn't the one who actually killed the general.

He couldn't be bothered about that mysterious demon right now, even if he could speak the human language and seemingly had helped him. Zac was sure the demon had survived from how he had acted before disappearing. Since there only were so many places to go on the island, Zac figured he'd find him sooner or later and get his answers then.

After having checked the titles, he closed the panel and did some mental calculations. He realized that he actually had missed out on another three points of Strength when he turned level 36. He still received the stats from the new title, though, which confused him a bit, as he should have received the title before he evolved and broke his attribute cap.

He was also a bit surprised with the number of Nexus Coins he amassed from the battle. He had gained roughly 150,000 from his whole day on the battlefield. While it was not a small amount by any means, it still didn't feel like it added up. That poison cloud should have killed hundreds, if not thousands, in the valley. Only the strongest combatants had been right by the tree, while the rest were spread out through the valley. Perhaps a few of the speedier ones had managed to escape; there couldn't be too many survivors with how rapidly the purple cloud had expanded.

Zac shuddered at the thought of having poisoned hundreds of beings to death but forcibly threw the thought into the back of his mind. Either all those kills didn't actually improve his level or give him coins, or they all were still alive.

Zac was convinced that they'd died from the poison. Just one breath of the poison cloud made him, who had over 100 Endurance, keel over, and he couldn't imagine normal demons or monkeys surviving that. Furthermore, he had seen the horrified looks on their faces when they saw the billowing purple clouds.

Zac briefly considered trying to swim through the pond to get back into the valley, but soon perished the thought. Even if he managed to actually swim through the water now, the poison might still be up there.

Suddenly, a thought popped up into his mind, and he opened the quest screen.

Active Quests:

Dynamic Quests:

1. **Off With Their Heads (Unique): Kill the four heralds and the general of an incursion within 3 months. Reward: 10 E-Grade Nexus Crystals, E-Grade equipment, unique building depending on performance. (5/5) [COMPLETE]**
2. **Incursion Master (Unique): Close or conquer incursion and protect outpost from denizens of other alignments for 3 months. Reward: 5 E-Grade Nexus Crystals, outpost upgraded to town, status upgraded to Lord. (0/3) [43:12:32:11]**

Class Quests:

1. **Forester's Constitution (Class): Fight in the forests, be one with nature. Reward: Forester's Constitution Skill. (8/30)**
2. **Loamwalker (Class): Walk a thousand kilometers touching the earth. Reward: Loamwalker Skill. (0/1,000)**

Zac sighed in relief, as the first incursion quest finally could be confirmed as complete. This had been his goal since Abby's warning, and it was thankfully done with after almost two horrible months. He already had been pretty sure he completed it the moment the general got impaled, but it was nice to finally see it set in stone.

He was also relieved to see that the quest said **[COMPLETE]** instead of just disappearing, as that meant the System hadn't spit out the reward somewhere while he was unconscious. As one of the rewards was related to his outpost, he assumed he would have to get back to his camp to collect them.

The next quest had gotten a timer just like the limited quest. If he read it correctly, he either had to finish it within forty-three days or something would happen in forty-three days.

Finally, he was surprised to see that the Loamwalker hadn't progressed at all since he got it. He wasn't exactly sure how far he ran yesterday, but he had been pushing it pretty hard with his inhuman stats for a few hours, so he felt that he should at least have run a marathon on the mountain slopes. And walking on a mountain should constitute touching earth in any sense of the word.

After a brief hesitation, he took off his shoes and threw them into his bag. He was reminded of the man in the vision and could only try copying him. Perhaps his soles had to actually physically touch the earth for it to count, and if true, he wondered what that meant when using the skill in the future. Would he become a barefoot warrior in the future just like the axe-man? At least his Endurance was high enough that his soles wouldn't get cut or damaged, even if walking around on glass shards.

Satisfied that he had gone through everything for now, he brought out some food and water. He was generally happy with the progression, but also a bit pissed off that that harrowing experience in the water hadn't done anything except boost his Race a level.

From how precious the Fruit of Ascension appeared, he thought that the fruit alone would be enough to ascend a stage, but with the harrowing molding his body had gone through, he figured he should at least have been awarded some bonus attributes or a title. He wondered if the System had a complaint department he could contact, as its rewards weren't balanced.

Internally grumbling, he tore into a piece of dried meat, and he was surprised to see that his appetite was simply monstrous, and he ate a couple of kilos of meat before he felt satiated. Looking at his slightly protruding belly, he wondered if evolving his race meant that he got a separate dimension tucked into his stomach.

Finally all set, he stood up and ventured out. He had, after some deliberation, chosen to head into the tunnels instead, as he simply refused to enter that water again. He refilled his canteen, though, just for emergencies.

The cave he was in was connected to the larger tunnel system, he found out after some traveling. Only a small hole was open, though, and Zac was forced to cut his way out with a sword. As he worked with the sword, he felt that his body was more coordinated than ever, as every muscle was working in perfect harmony. He wasn't really stronger or more agile, but rather had greater control of his body. Normally, he would think that it was due to increased Dexterity, but the change was too large that just a few extra points from his new title couldn't cover it. He guessed instead that it was another advantage of being an evolved human.

After some hesitation, he carved out a couple of boulders from a nearby wall and covered up the path again. That secret cave would be an excellent cultivation cave in the future, and he didn't want a salamander or wandering demon to ruin it.

Perhaps it wouldn't be useful for himself, but maybe for his sister or Hannah if he managed to bring them back to the island. Now that the demon threat was taken care of, he needed to actually start preparing for the future.

At least he hoped that the demon threat was over, but he couldn't be sure. He never got any indication of what would happen when he finally killed the heralds and the general. There should be quite a few demons still around even after the huge battle. There had been at least a thousand demons in the mountains, but even if all of them died, there should be hundreds in the tunnels. Add to that the demon town and the roving parties, and most demons should still be around.

Putting the matter aside, Zac pushed forward in the tunnels. Soon he found a familiar cave, whose tunnels led to the demon mining operation. After a brief hesitation, he headed over there to check things out. As he walked, he heard absolutely no sound of activity, which could only be considered a good sign.

The mining tunnels were completely deserted, as he'd hoped, with not a single demon in sight. As he continued on, he soon exited the cave entrance he had seen the demons use daily. Still, he didn't see a single demon anywhere. A few sacks and tools were thrown here and there, hinting at a hasty escape.

More importantly, for the first time since he woke up on this hellish island, there was no huge red glaring pillar shooting into the sky. The incursion was simply gone.

But that didn't mean his work was over.

65

FIRST CONTACT

With a spring in his steps he hadn't felt for a long time, Zac moved along the road toward the location of the now-gone incursion. He was planning on heading back to his campsite to complete his quest, but first, he wanted to check things out and make sure that the demons were truly gone.

He moved along the path leading to the fortified city, meeting no resistance on the way. Soon he reached the forest edge close to the town; any further, and he would be exposed due to all the vegetation having been cut down to supply the construction.

He hunkered down and stared at the town for a good while, trying to see any signs of demons. The good news was that the previously well-manned walls were completely deserted. Not a single guard was patrolling along the wall walk, and the towers were empty. The bad news was that he saw a few lines of smoke rising from the inner parts of the town.

After some hesitation, he decided to take a closer look. The lines of smoke might just be left-behind fires, and if there actually were demons here, they must be disorganized for some reason. He briskly jogged over to the fortifications, and with a few tugs, pulled himself up along the wall. He didn't encounter any arrays impeding his path either, making him wonder if demons couldn't use them for some reason. He hadn't seen them use a single one so far, after all, unless inscriptions on tools could be called arrays.

He looked out over the demon town and found it more or less deserted. He was disappointed to see that there actually were a few demons milling about, but they looked listless and without direction.

He also noticed that the town had grown considerably since he had seen it the first time a few weeks ago. Most of the military-looking rectangular buildings were gone, replaced with structures of various sizes and designs. It almost looked like a medieval town by now rather than a military base. But the craftsmanship and cleanliness were far greater compared to some old city, and no garbage or excrement lined the sidewalks. Perhaps the large barracks were only temporary housing they used while they constructed the real city.

Zac soon spotted a solitary demon, who walked toward a house right next to the wall. There were no other demons close to him, and the small building would provide perfect cover, making him a perfect target.

Zac crept along the wall and, with one swift motion, jumped down right in front of him. Quick as lightning, he grabbed the startled demon by his tunic and dragged him behind the house. Without any pause, Zac slammed him against the building's wall with one hand and brought out his axe with the other.

"Scream and you die. Do you understand what I'm saying?" Zac asked with a steely glint as he held the axe at his throat, ready to decapitate the demon at a moment's notice.

The demon looked truly horrified after he saw Zac's face. Tears started falling like rain, and even a snot bubble started to grow. He incoherently started whispering something in the demonic language, regularly interrupting himself with large sobs.

Zac was stumped, not expecting such an exaggerated

response. Perhaps his deeds on the mountain had spread, and the demon was afraid he'd poison the town to death. But then again, this demon differed from the ones he had encountered so far. He didn't look at all like a hardened warrior. Rather, he looked like a civilian. He didn't wear any weapon, and while his arms looked sturdy, he also had a pretty large gut. Furthermore, he was middle-aged, whereas most of the warriors he had encountered seemed quite young.

Just as he was considering whether he should kill the demon and find a new interrogation target, a shaky voice behind him interrupted his thoughts.

"Um… P-Please let my dad go. He can't understand your words."

Zac instantly whirled around, holding the stocky demon as a barrier against this new voice. He found himself face-to-face with a small bespectacled demoness. She was the shortest one he had seen, just about reaching up to his chest, and had her silver hair in a neat bun. She didn't carry any weapons and shook with fright as she faced Zac's murderous glare.

"Move over to behind the house. If you scream, you both die," Zac instructed the scared demon with a low but harsh voice. Seeing her pallid face and remembering his words, he was starting to feel like a villain, even though the demons were his enemies. "I just want some answers. Help me out, and I'll leave," he added in a softer tone.

The demon didn't seem very comforted by his words and still shook like a leaf. Still, she complied with his words, much to the dismay of the middle-aged demon. He started wheezing something out and soon even tried to scream. He likely wanted his daughter to run away from them and get to safety. While Zac could appreciate the sentiment, he couldn't let her go, as he finally had someone he could question. With a quick thud, he hit the pudgy demon in the back of his head, instantly knocking him out and shutting him up.

"Sorry about that, but he is alive. I can't have him scream and warn the whole town." Zac sighed as he placed the unconscious demon next to the demoness.

"Why is it that I can speak with some of you, but most only speak gibberish?" Zac questioned, eager to finally get some answers.

"Gibberish?" The small demon seemed a bit offended but quickly readjusted to a timid face. "You… You need a skill to speak with other races. But it is expensive, so most people don't have it. I am a merchant, so the clan provided it for me." She seemed somewhat proud of the fact, as it was quite a glorious job to have.

"Your class is Merchant?" Zac asked with a renewed relief that he hadn't gambled for the Epic class when choosing a class.

"No, I'm a Scribe, a Common-rarity class. But I am following, I mean I was following, the upgrade path towards a real mercantile class in the future," the demon answered, looking somewhat deflated.

What she said about upgrade path was something he was interested in finding out more about, but he had more pressing matters.

"Why are you people still on my island? Your invasion should have failed when the incursion ended. Why haven't you gone back to wherever you came from?" This was the most crucial question on Zac's mind right now.

"Going back… Some of us can't," she answered with a melancholic smile. "We embarrassed the clan and cost it a lot of money when the invasion failed. If we went back, bad things would happen. Some chose to stay on this planet instead."

Zac felt a headache coming on when he realized he suddenly had a bunch of demon refugees on the island.

"How many of you are still left?"

"I don't know..." she answered with a low voice and hastily explained when she saw Zac's eyes narrow dangerously. "I truly don't know. I usually just file documents. Ogras should know. He is, was, the leader of the expedition. But most of the warriors left. Their status is better in the clan."

"That's impossible. I saw your leader die right in front of me," Zac growled, taking a step toward the demoness.

The Scribe seemed to have been reminded that the person was a dangerous enemy warrior and once again started shaking.

"I swear he is alive. I saw Ogras exit his palace before. He didn't go to the mountains, I think?" she managed to stutter out through clattering teeth.

It didn't seem like she was lying, which confused Zac greatly. His mission was completed, and he had seen the general die from the huge black spear. Besides, she'd called the leader Ogras, which was the last thing the leader roared before he perished.

"Does this Ogras have white hair, silver armor, and fights with two swords. Oh, and he can make the sword fly?" he tentatively asked, a guess forming in his mind.

"No... That is Rydel. He was second-in-command maybe? His grandfather is the clan chief, after all," she answered, happy that Zac's murderous air receded somewhat.

The answer only made Zac more confused. If the one who died wasn't the general, why had he led the forces? If this Ogras was the real general instead, why had his quest been completed if he was still alive and kicking? Because he briefly killed himself? Why would he do that? He was certain that the mysterious demon was Ogras, but he didn't understand why he would kill his own ally and even suggest poisoning the whole army. This girl said Ogras hadn't participated in the battle, so it sounded like he had snuck out of the town behind his own army without their knowledge.

"Where is Ogras now?" he asked. It seemed this demoness held a low rank in the clan, and her knowledge was limited. It would be better to simply ask the source. Besides, he had a bone to pick with this Ogras, as he almost got him killed with his poison idea. Of course, Ogras saved his life by killing this Rydel character, but he still had a sour feeling when thinking about the torment he'd been forced to endure when he jumped into the pond.

"Dad said he heard Ogras question many demons; then he left the town toward the south," she answered, seemingly excited at the prospect of sending Zac on his way to become someone else's problem.

Zac mulled things over for a few seconds before determining his next action. There were many more things he wanted to know, but he had a sneaking suspicion Ogras was heading toward his outpost. It was the only thing of interest to the south; the rest was just forest. And nothing good could come from the insidious demon fiddling around with his stuff, so he decided to briskly head back home.

As Zac had come to his decision, he asked one final question. "Oh, by the way, what is your name?"

"I'm Zakarith. My dad calls me Zak," she quickly introduced herself.

Zac's mouth tugged a bit, trying to avoid smiling. "Well, Zakarith, welcome to Earth," he said and immediately slammed the butt of his axe in between her horns, instantly knocking her out. He felt a bit bad about it, as she reminded him a bit of his little sister, but he couldn't have her running around right now. He felt no need to kill both of them, as it seemed the demon threat was largely gone. And even if they came to blows again, he didn't feel a little Scribe and her pudgy father would be able to turn the tide.

He quickly tied up both the unconscious demons and left them hidden between the house and the outer wall before quickly leaving the town the same way he had gotten in. Same as with Ogras, his course was south. He was going home.

INTERLUDE – MY DINNER WITH ZAC

Ogras swatted some flies out of his face as he walked through the alien landscape. His decisions were born out of desperation, but it was just now the fact that he was stranded on this foreign planet truly hit home.

The two suns in the sky were even more glaring now that the soothing canopy of the incursion disappeared, and the bombardment of colors was unsettling. Everywhere he could only see forests, and no civilization was in sight. He missed the bars, the pruned hunting grounds, and the whores. Gods, the *whores!* Why hadn't he insisted on bringing along a brothel instead of a few of the farmers?

Even though he had cultivated a horrible reputation in his clan, he wasn't the type of man who would force himself upon an unwilling woman. Unfortunately, the very same reputation was what now kept the town's women at arm's length. Well, there was Namys, who was more than willing, but she had the face of a netherbeast. He spat in annoyance and decided to stop daydreaming and refocus on the task at hand.

Still, though he lost many things, he had gained perhaps something even greater. Freedom. He brought up his heavenly screen and took a look.

Name: Ogras Azh'Rezak
Level: 53 (73)
Class: [F-Rare] Shadowblade
Race: [E] Demon
Alignment–

Titles: Demon Slayer, Adventurer, Giantsbane, Disciple of David, Overpowered, Tower of Eternity – 3rd floor, Astral Pond – 20m, Full of Class, Rarified Being, Betrayer

Dao: Seed of Shadows – Early

Strength: 112 (Weakened)
Dexterity: 134 (Weakened)
Endurance: 63 (Weakened)
Vitality: 63 (Weakened)
Intelligence: 38 (Weakened)
Wisdom: 35 (Weakened)
Luck: 23 (Weakened)

Free Points: 0
Nexus Coins: 300

Gone was the alignment to his old clan, leaving the space a liberating blank. Gone was also the constant need for machinations and pretension. Gone was constantly looking over his shoulder, afraid that he would be the eighth and last sibling to be killed by jealous clan members.

The surviving demons would soon understand the true Ogras. There already were some murmurs of discontent from the search parties who were stuck in the tunnels when the countdown began.

It was on his orders that they'd entered the mines, and now they couldn't leave this baby world. Many of the warriors didn't wish to stay here, as their status would have kept them somewhat safe, even in the case of a return in defeat.

But soon they would understand that even without his ancestor, his title as leader was unshakable.

Ogras inwardly groaned at the fact that the Ruthless Heavens actually confiscated the Nexus Coins of everyone when they stayed behind. He'd never read about this and swore at the information missive he'd bought at the Pavilion of Myriad Eyes. It had been exorbitantly expensive and should have covered everything one needed to know about venturing into a baby world.

He was approaching the level limits as well, bringing him one step closer to evolving. He had been furiously leveling up from his unimpressive level since he arrived at the island. With the limitations in place, he could quickly gain levels without anyone finding out. He had done so in secrecy by absorbing the high-quality Leveling Pills his grandfather had helped him bring along, allowing him to shoot up a few levels per day.

He ran out at level 73, falling just short of his goal of hitting the limit, but it had still felt amazing to move away from his self-imposed image as a wastrel. He had kept himself at a low level on purpose earlier in order to not let anyone realize his high stat growth.

He was one of the few in the clan with a Rare class. Combined with his, admittedly bought, achievements in the Tower of Eternity, his progress would outpace almost everyone in the clan. Normally, it would have been a cause for celebration, but for his branch, it was a death sentence. But now, he could finally grow into the limit and focus on his constitution. He grimaced at the fact that the human who snatched both the fruits was now gone.

Ogras could only hope that he could find the body and the Cosmos Sack as soon as the poison cleared out in the mountains. If the fruits were lost, he would have to slowly cultivate his body until it evolved, and that would waste a lot of time while others around him were becoming more powerful. And that would be the smallest of the losses from not getting the fruit.

He cursed himself for not simply snatching the bags when he had the chance up on the mountain. He had already been stressed out from killing Rydel and subsequently killing himself, and he might have made an error in judgment. Ogras felt something dangerous in the human's eyes and instead had opted to cajole the human into using the poison. Besides, if any straggler lived to tell the tale, it would be clear that it wasn't Ogras who did the deed, but the wretched human.

Soon he arrived at the area where the scouts had found the human's small camp. He activated **[Omniscient Eyes],** and after walking around for a few hours, he finally found the bubble of the illusion array. After testing it out, he found it was a simple one-layer array, with no defensive or offensive options.

He entered, and his eyes fell upon the base of operations of Clan Azh'Rezak's nemesis. Even though things had turned out somewhat okay for him, Ogras couldn't help but become pissed off at the sight. This human lived like some kind of animal in a dirty metal hovel and still had managed to bring about the downfall of their invasion?

There were scraps of items and rags strewn about the campsite, and the domicile the native lived in was actually a large can. The can was dented and in disrepair, and there were even splotches of blood on it. As he walked inside it, Ogras immediately was too depressed to continue the search and quickly left the cage. To live like this and not go crazy must have required certain mental fortitude, as Ogras was getting stressed out just thinking about spending the night in there.

There was another metal contraption in the camp, and after going over it for some time, Ogras realized that it was not another odd domicile, but rather a transportation device. It seemed like it was an extremely rudimentary version of the contraptions the Technocrats use to traverse the Multiverse.

He knew that some baby planets had gone to impressive depths into what the Technocrats called the Dao of Technology. But of course, the Ruthless Heavens didn't acknowledge that Dao, so most newly integrated worlds soon discarded it for the pursuit of the true Dao and to wield Cosmic Energy.

But this wasn't why he was here. He quickly walked up to the large crystal, which looked just like the ones back home. Of course, this was a proper one meant for City Lords, whereas the ones he had used were basic subordinate Nodes with just the basic features.

The missive stated that when the mission failed, he and the other demons would be barred from attaining System-sanctioned properties and towns for roughly a decade, but he needed to make sure. If he could gain ownership of the crystal, he would gain the tools to not only survive, but to thrive in this new world.

While they were on a desolate island, he knew he wasn't safe. The Ruthless Heavens wouldn't allow the peace to continue forever, and would force some events into being. It thrived and existed for conflict, after all.

He touched the Nexus Node, infusing it with his Cosmic Energy. But it was as though it hit a wall and couldn't enter the crystal. He bit his finger and dropped some blood on it, but it wasn't absorbed and only ran along its smooth surface. Ogras even brought up a small vial of blood and poured it on the crystal, but it didn't have any effect either. The vial contained blood from the human that scouts had collected in the mines, and Ogras thought it might be the key to gaining access to the Town Shop system.

Ogras sighed in disappointment. It seemed that he couldn't integrate his town after all. They would have to do everything themselves. At least there were quite a few demons who stayed behind who would be useful in building up a sphere of influence, sanctioned or not by the Ruthless Heavens.

A movement in the distance immediately grabbed Ogras' attention, and he whirled around. His eyes widened as he saw the very same human he'd met in the mountain valley. How the hell had he survived? Was he a walking behemoth who just couldn't be killed?

Ogras watched this grimy-looking man look at the footsteps of the search parties and lumber around, trying to act sneaky, and he couldn't stop himself from grimacing. This was the man who caused the downfall of Clan Azh'Rezak? He looked like a thoroughbred lunatic, without any hair at all on his face, and was dressed in rags and a ripped-up lady's gown.

Sometime since the mountains, he appeared to have lost his ratty shoes as well, walking along with his impractically soft bare feet. Was he intentionally looking like an idiot in order to lower his enemies' guard? Genius. He also looked like he had been living as a battle slave for a decade, with scars covering all parts of his exposed skin.

But the scars were far less pronounced compared to when he'd seen the human up in the mountains. Before, they were grisly jagged lines along his body and face, making him look mutilated, and now they were simply thin white lines.

The human had eaten a Fruit of Ascension. Ogras' teeth immediately started to itch when he saw that this human had gobbled up a supreme treasure, probably without knowing its value. His eyes soon moved to the pouches on the human's belt, and his eyes lit up with greed. His Fruit of Ascension had delivered itself to him. At least he hoped the stupid brute hadn't eaten both of them.

He retrieved his spear from his pouch. It was made from a rare metal that could only be found thousands of meters down in the depths of the Black Sea and weighed over two hundred kilograms, which gave it a nice feeling compared to normal ungraded metals. Most importantly, it could absorb shadows and help him unleash his attacks in a far more deadly manner.

This was a great opportunity for him to break through his limits and truly become someone with great prospects, eclipsing even those of Clan Azh'Rezak. But as he watched the human fumble around, his eyes moved to the Nexus Node in hesitation. After a brief pause, he placed his weapon back into his pouch and quickly wiped off any traces of blood from the large crystal.

He instead brought out a large table and a comfortable chair and sat down. Soon a tray of fruits was placed on top of the table. Ogras knew that these fruits from his home world were of limited quantity now that the Nexus Hub was closed, but one needed to make strong first impressions.

Of course, he also charged up tens of shadow blades in the shadows below the table, just in case it came to blows.

Soon the human seemed to have come to a decision to enter the illusion array. He brought out one of the standard regiment axes he likely had taken from some scout, and then a mottled shield. For Ogras, the whole thing looked like a play, as he could watch the whole thing unnoticed behind the array.

But he knew that this was no joke. This human seemed to be close to the limits in at least Strength, and maybe Endurance as well. He was a monstrously strong cockroach that was prohibitively difficult to kill. He mentally controlled his shadow blades to be ready to strike at a moment's notice, but donned a lackadaisical face.

Soon the human charged in through the array, weapons at the ready.

"You natives truly are barbarians, so aggressive," Ogras said with a theatrical sigh as the almost unnoticeable blades inched closer. It was time to get creative.

66

MY DINNER WITH OGRAS

Zac quickly jogged due south and soon arrived at the part of the valley where the incursion was located. The crystal was still there, but it now looked inert. It had lost its colors and no longer radiated any power.

The area seemed deserted, so Zac snuck up to the small house, finding it empty as well. Knowing no demons were around, he walked up to the huge crystal. Fractals completely covered the whole thing, barely leaving an inch free. It reminded him of an evolved version of his Nexus Node in camp, and after a brief hesitation, he touched it. No menu or prompt arrived, and he could only feel the cold and smooth surface of the crystal.

Zac thought about infusing the crystal with some Cosmic Energy, but soon decided against it. He had too little information about the thing and was afraid that he'd accidentally teleport himself somewhere. He was in no mood to suddenly arrive at a demon planet after having been stuck on a demon island for so long.

Zac could only leave it be for now and add it to the list of things he would squeeze out of Ogras if he found him. After a final check, he left southbound. As he walked, he noticed that the foliage in the surroundings unfortunately hadn't turned back into normal trees and bushes. They were still sickly-looking from the influence of the red pillar. He could only hope that the area would gradually heal now that the incursion was turned off.

He kept going through the valley, and after some trial and error, he found an ascent leading up to the forest. Soon he was walking familiar paths south he had walked many times before. There still were quite a few barghest in the forests, but it seemed that the war had thinned them out somewhat at least. Or perhaps they'd left together with the surviving demon army.

More surprisingly, he found out that the reward had lessened substantially when he killed one. The remaining ones still were hyper-aggressive, and he was forced to kill one that came rushing toward him with a kick. After killing it, he actually gained less than 30 Nexus Coins. It was disappointing, as he had actually considered rounding them all up somehow and then killing hundreds of them with his **[Chop]** skill. That would have netted him quite a decent income while simultaneously cleaning up for his town.

He saw two possible reasons for the decrease. Either the reward for killing demons lessened now that the incursion was over, or the reward lessened as his level increased. He had gained quite a few levels in the mountains and tunnels, and now the System maybe didn't want to award as many resources for killing weaklings.

Zac actually hoped it was the second. Then he could at least save a lucrative grinding area for other people. If the barghest could actually breed on the island, he could have a perpetual farming ground going. But if it was the first, he simply had a nuisance on his hands.

After half a day of jogging, he finally was in close proximity of his camp. He started his usual sweep of the area and actually found some worrying signs. There were footprints in the ground around where he'd battled the demon party, and even though he was no expert tracker, it looked like multiple sources.

At the same time, the illusion array was untouched, and he quickly equipped his amulet as well. He had actually removed it earlier in order to avoid getting any experience, and forgot to put it back on. The familiar warmth from the amulet told him that the mother-daughter array was still working.

With a heavy heart, he retrieved his axe and got ready for battle, and he also took out the shield he had found in the caverns. He held the shield in front of his head and madly dashed through the illusion barrier. Zac even charged up his **[Chop]**, ready to swing at everything in the camp, even if he had to cut his beloved camper in two.

"You natives truly are barbarians, so aggressive." A familiar voice could be heard from the vicinity, followed by a helpless sigh.

Even though it wasn't completely unexpected, the voice gave Zac pause. He quickly glanced around the camp, his axe still at the ready. What entered his vision made Zac visibly groan and lower his shield.

It was the mysterious demon comfortably sitting in an opulent chair, lazily eating fruits that were placed on a golden tray in front of him. The tray was placed on a large table even more intricately designed than Zac's own ostentatious table he had stolen. Did all demon noblemen walk around with obnoxiously over-the-top furniture just to be able to posture at any given time?

Thinking about the annoying smile of the demon right before escaping the poison inferno, Zac couldn't stop himself and cleaved the table in two with a swing. The brows of the demon rose a bit in alarm, but he quickly regained his composure when he saw Zac didn't continue.

Zac removed a chair from his own pouch and sat down as well with a grunt and retrieved some dried meat.

"Ogras?" he questioned, still finding it a bit hard to find the words after months of silence.

The demon looked slightly surprised; then it seemed he realized something.

"The very same. I guess you visited Camp Rezak on your way back. Ehm… Are my subordinates still alive?" Ogras asked, looking a bit troubled, but not to the point he was ready to come to blows.

"They are alive. I just caught a few to ask some questions. Why are you here, and how did you find the outpost?" Zac asked, still with a guarded expression against this unpredictable demon.

"You're using an F-grade illusion array for protection. Any decent skill can detect it. We actually found your home a few days ago after investigating your… activities," Ogras answered with a dismissive wave of his hand.

"I can't believe you live in a cramped and bloodied tin can. Don't the humans of this planet know how to build decent structures? In any case, we found you in the tunnels before we could use the knowledge of this place to our advantage." Ogras gave Zac a pitying glance as he looked around at the small campsite, with the dented camper and ruined car.

Irritation once again started to build up in Zac, and he was unsure whether he should defend his camp or Earth's architectural ingenuity. But he once again calmed down quickly. This demon seemed like the crafty type, and Zac didn't want to give out any undue information by mistake because he was goaded into anger.

"You still haven't explained why you're here. And why you and the others are still on my island." Zac felt it was important to make it clear that they were refugees while he was the landowner. This was his planet, and he had completed the quest to gain control of the area.

Ogras seemed to understand the implication of his words but only smiled in response. "Well, I came here to meet with you, of course. I figured you would return here after the battle. The incursion is over, and so is our need to be enemies. I think it's time to discuss an alliance between our group and yours."

Zac was about to say it was only him but quickly stopped himself. If the demons thought he was just the spearhead of a larger group, his position was only strengthened.

"You should know that this world was only integrated into the Multiverse less than two months ago. There are things we do not know. Explain to me why we shouldn't keep hunting your kind," Zac said, happy to keep the fib going.

"When you finished your quest, the incursion ended. We were given twelve hours to return through the Nexus Hub before it closed down. Some of us couldn't get there in time, and others simply chose to stay behind for various reasons. After the Ruthless Heavens has closed the hub, it won't open again for a long time, and never to our home planet," Ogras answered, seemingly prepared for the question.

"In other words, we made the choice to cut ties with our clan and our home, and it is unlikely we will ever be able to return. Even if we wanted to, it would be almost impossible due to the cost of traveling such a distance. We also won't get any backup in the future. Therefore, it makes no sense to keep a war going against you natives."

"That's a pretty flippant attitude after so many of your kind has died. Why did you even come to our planet? And what's the ruthless heavens?" Zac asked after mulling over Ogras' answer. He couldn't find any lies in what the demon told him from what he had observed and what the demoness had said. But he wasn't so naïve to believe everything he said either. Someone who could kill his ally with a stab in the back could only be a duplicitous character.

"The Ruthless Heavens, the Endless Heavens, the Cosmic Warden, the System. It has many names, but you should know what I'm talking about," Ogras explained with an expansive gesture. "And why should I care if some clansmen died? Life and death mean nothing in the Multiverse. Long before I came here, all my siblings had already been killed in battle and assassinations by my very own clan members," he continued, as though such a tragic life had nothing to do with him. He then leaned forward and stared at Zac with a glint.

"As for why we came here? Resources, of course. The Ruthless Heavens thrives on conflict, and war is expensive. Baby worlds like yours are usually a treasure trove of wealth that can help a clan or country ascend. There are likely multiple forces across your planet that are gobbling everything up like locusts at this very moment. Clan Azh'Rezak was just unlucky being stuck on this island with a humanoid monster."

Zac chose to ignore the last sentence and focused on the other information. There were many points of interest in the demon's answer, but one more than the others. But before he could ask, he realized something.

"Wait, why hasn't the System punished you? I was told the System might kill me if I failed the missions. Why are you demons fine after failing yours?" Abby had clearly warned him to properly complete the quest, at the risk of death and mutilation. Meanwhile, Ogras was just fine and dandy, even though he should hold the main responsibility for the demons' invasion.

"Urh… What?" Ogras seemed truly confused, so after a brief hesitation, Zac told him about parts of his conversation with Abby the eye.

Ogras looked stunned at Zac for a good while before he started laughing self-depreciatingly.

"All our plans ruined because of a lying Stargazer… The Ruthless Heavens truly have a wicked sense of humor," Ogras said and sighed.

"Lying? What do you mean?" Zac asked skeptically. So far,

everything Abby said had been true, and he instinctively trusted her far more compared to this demon.

"The Ruthless Heavens doesn't punish. At worst, it loses interest in you. What did you think, a lightning bolt would zap you if you left the island on a raft? Don't be silly. The only result would be that you no longer qualified to become a Lord and missed out on the rewards from the quests," Ogras said with a snicker after having regained his composure.

"Just think about the quest for those fruits you picked up. Would the System just kill off everyone who didn't rush to the mountain? That's crazy." He continued, "By the way, are you interested in selling those fruits to me?"

Zac ignored the business proposal and pondered what the demon said. He didn't know what to believe. It did make sense what Ogras said, but Zac didn't understand why Abby would lie to him like that.

"What would she have to gain for telling me to fight you guys? Are Stargazers and demons enemies?" he inquired.

"Bah, Stargazers don't have any enemies. Pretty much all of them work for the Ruthless Heavens. Who would dare mess with them? I guess she wanted a promotion. If you become a Lord, you get a permanent administrator to help you out. Then she could get appointed to a baby world to one of its leaders and get access to both many good resources and opportunities for advancement."

Zac was stumped by the answer but refused to believe that the floating eye would send him against a whole demon army just to get a chance to get a promotion if he actually survived.

"You need to toughen up, human. The Multiverse is a cold place where the honest and brave get butchered while the calculating and shrewd survive. Everything else is irrelevant in the face of benefits," the demon said, with stone-cold eyes that spoke of a deep-rooted cynicism toward the world.

67

DIPLOMACY

Zac sighed and tabled the whole matter, as there was no way for him to know who told the truth at the moment. The thought that he had almost died numerous times due to a lie was almost too depressing to handle. Of course, it was thanks to that lie that he'd pushed himself forward and now confidently stood at the forefront of humanity.

"You said your incursion is only one of many? Do they all contain demons like you?" Zac quickly asked, eager to change the subject. Besides, this was something he had wondered about since day one. He was thinking of his family and was worried that another incursion could pop up next to them at any moment. It had worked out for him, but he had been given a huge advantage from his many titles. For normal people to contend against a demon army, he knew how that story would end.

"As far as I know, us demons only got one for this world, unless a higher-tier clan got one as well. I'm not privy to their activities. The others are from various forces in the Multiverse. That's why we need each other, human. Because if you think that our little clan was bad, you haven't seen anything yet."

Zac got a really bad feeling when he heard that the other

incursions could be even worse compared to the demons on this island. It didn't seem like the demon was lying, and his desire to get back home to his family only got stronger.

"Need each other how?" he asked, curious to hear what benefits the demon could provide.

Ogras grinned, obviously pleased that Zac tentatively opened diplomatic relations.

"We both have things the other party needs. My side has manpower. Many of those who stayed behind are noncombat classes who would be very helpful for someone who wishes to build up a base. We have builders, farmers, blacksmiths, and traders, for example. I can also provide information about many things that could help you in the future." Ogras rattled on, sounding like a salesman trying to secure some business.

"And what would you want from me in return?" Zac asked, as he knew there was no such thing as a free lunch.

"Sanctuary. You may not know this, but the Ruthless Heavens limits the powers of foreign entities in a baby world," Ogras explained, to which Zac only tersely nodded. "Well, after the incursion failed, the limiter remains, and we will have some… problems… getting stronger. Even if we gain a few levels, we might only actually be able to use the additional power of one level. But the Nexus Coins and energy we give out when killed is the full amount. We essentially become walking treasure troves the longer we reside on a baby planet."

"Why do you need me for that? If you just stay holed up here, won't you be fine? We're on an island, after all," Zac interjected, as he didn't see how he fit into the picture. If Zac was expendable for the demons' survival, then he could be killed at any moment.

"Breaking the restrictions will take a very long time. Sooner or later, some force is going to find the island, and what would happen when they found an island full of monsters and inhabitants that gave ten times the reward upon killing them?" Ogras explained, but Zac looked far from convinced.

"More importantly, you have become a Lord so you can provide the sanctuary of a System-sanctioned city. That's not something we can do by ourselves now that the incursion failed. We failed our quest and are barred from seizing a system town," the demon continued as he glanced at the Nexus Node.

"What's the difference between a System-sanctioned city and a normal one? And besides, I'm not a Lord. I still need to complete a quest for that," Zac corrected him, feeling that particular information was no problem to share. In case they would actually form an alliance, the demons would have to help out defending his outpost against the denizens of other alignments, after all.

Ogras looked slightly surprised by this information, but quickly recovered. It seemed that even these invaders didn't have all the answers after all, which was comforting.

"The biggest difference is that you can buy structures from the Ruthless Heavens in a sanctioned city. In a normal city, you have to build everything yourself. A sanctioned city is much safer as long as the Lord has coins to spare. Only an idiot would invade a sanctioned city unless they held an overwhelming advantage. The Lord could simply spend a few generations' worth of Nexus Coins and blast the attackers to pieces with a new defensive structure."

Zac felt that it made a lot of sense. He hadn't thought about it before, but if he was really put against the wall, he could instantly buy the strongest array he could afford and immediately improve his outpost by a few grades. It was essentially the time-tested strategy of throwing money at the problem until it went away. That kind of strategy was impossible unless you had access to the outpost shop.

"Can you explain what you need to accomplish to become a

Lord, human? And you have me at a disadvantage, as I still don't know your name," Ogras continued.

"I'm Zac. It says I need to protect the outpost. I have a timer that counts down toward the three-month mark after Earth entered the Multiverse as well," Zac explained, and Ogras visibly relaxed.

"I think I know what that means, but could you share the quest just to be sure?"

Zac's eyes immediately thinned at that, rife with suspicion. If he shared a quest, wouldn't Ogras become a Lord as well? Could he usurp him if that was the case?

"You misunderstand, hu… Zac. Sharing the quest just means showing me the quest prompt from the Heavenly Screen. Just focus on that particular quest and make it visible with your will," Ogras quickly explained when he saw Zac's distrustful face. "I'm sure you and your allies have shared various prompts with each other," he added with a slight smile.

Zac had a distinct feeling the jig was up, and the demon knew he was alone. But he chose to keep the charade going in any case, not wanting to give out any confirmation to the demon's suspicions.

Deciding there was no harm, he decided to try it out. He singled out that particular quest, and it appeared alone in a blue window. He then focused on making that particular window visible. And soon it got "fixed" in the air instead of following his vision. He even managed to adjust what was shown so that the reward wasn't visible to the demon.

Incursion Master (Unique): Close or conquer incursion and protect outpost from denizens of other alignments for 3 months. (0/3) [43:01:17:47)

Ogras' eyes lit up, and he looked through the quest. But soon his face went from interested to grimacing.

"It's actually a monster horde quest…" Ogras said with a frown.

"What does that mean, and how can you tell?" Zac asked, eager to know more about how the quest system worked.

"It says denizens and not forces or factions, which means it will send beasts rather than intelligent forces such as us demons or other factions in the Multiverse. It is one of the more annoying quests the Ruthless Heavens can throw at a Lord," Ogras explained with a dour face. "A few thousand years ago, a city on my home planet was overrun by millions of Blight Rats. When the quest ended, the whole city was just a huge crater with everything from its structures to citizens eaten."

Zac didn't know if it was true, but if millions of anything attacked him, it would be a quick game over unless he learned how to make his **[Chop]**-edge a kilometer long. He could only hope the System adjusted the difficulty for his power level.

"When will it start?" Zac probed.

"After the timer. It seems like a normal monster horde quest, so the Ruthless Heavens will likely send one horde a month for three months. The faster you kill the monsters, the more time you will have to prepare in between. Too slow and you will be facing multiple waves at the same time."

If the demon could be trusted, it meant that he had one and a half months to strengthen himself and the town as much as possible. He grimaced at the thought of having to fight a horde of beasts constantly for a month, only for it to be topped up with another horde. Besides, he was sorely lacking Nexus Coins to get anything worthwhile for his outpost.

"Where are the crystals your faction has mined? If we are going to work together, then your kind needs to contribute to the town construction." Zac immediately went into fundraising mode now that he knew he had to fend off hordes of beasts.

"I'm afraid they all got taken with them by our clansmen

when they left through the Nexus Hub," Ogras answered without hesitation with a completely straight face.

"..."

"..."

The two only silently stared at each other for a full minute until the demon finally coughed and added a sentence.

"Well, maybe they didn't find them all, and I can go back and see if they forgot to look in some places?"

"I'm *sure* you can find some," Zac answered with an equally straight face. "If a foreman could steal hundreds of crystals in only one day, I'm sure there are quite a few crystals hidden through the town."

"Ah, yes, Azra. Can I ask why you are wearing her dress? And why the sudden interest in raw crystals? They're not very efficient for leveling up," Ogras asked, seemingly eager to change the subject of how many crystals he had stashed away.

"I'm planning on buying a store in the shop and selling them for Nexus Coins. That way, I can buy defensive structures to survive the quest," Zac answered, completely ignoring the part about wearing a dress.

"Usually, I'd say that it's a waste to use crystals to get some Nexus Coins, but it's our best bet right now, I suppose. But I'd suggest that we buy a smelting furnace as well to turn the raw crystals into proper graded ones first," Ogras agreed.

"Our? We?" Zac said skeptically, still not having decided what to do with the demons.

"Yes, we. You should understand how useful it is to have us around after our short talk. Even for your own plan, we're integral. After all, are you planning on mining the whole mountain range for the crystals by yourself?" Ogras said with a smile.

"Maybe the two of us can work together since I've seen you kill that Rydel person. And you helped me kill half your army, so you seem to hate your kind far more than I do. But would the others even work with me?" Zac was highly doubtful that he could get a successful partnership going after what he had done to the demon ranks over the past weeks.

"Most of those left behind have some grudges with our previous clan in any case, so they aren't too upset with the armies dying. There are a few who might be troublesome. But I am sure we can handle that."

"Like you handled Rydel?" Zac asked, to which Ogras only smiled slightly.

"Well, regarding that, let's keep that little detail between us, shall we? I won't go into it, but it was either him or me. Everyone who witnessed that is dead by now, so only the two of us know. But if the citizens of Camp Azh'Rezak find out that I was up in the mountains helping your rampage, and not staying in my castle, they might lose trust in me. And our partnership would suffer in turn."

Zac mulled it over for a long time. He'd rather not work with a snake like this man, to be honest, as he would have to constantly watch his back. But he had made a few good points. Zac desperately needed assistance, both in the form of information and manpower, if he wanted to create a successful town and a sanctuary for his family. Since there was no one else to turn to, he could only enter this dubious alliance.

Besides, just having someone to talk to, even if it was a sneaky demon, felt extremely good.

"Okay, I'll keep quiet about it. So, what else can you tell me that's useful for our short-term goals?" Zac asked, hoping for some simple tips that would save him some coins or increase his chances of beating the quest.

"Well, now that you asked, are you aware that you have been drinking poison?"

68

PROGENITOR'S ADVANTAGE

"WHAT?!" Zac immediately jumped to his feet, with his axe at the ready, afraid he had fallen into some trap of the demon's making. He charged up **[Chop]** to a meter-long edge and advanced on Ogras.

"Calm down, calm down!" Ogras screamed and scrambled out of the chair. "The Cosmic Water you have been drinking!"

"You poisoned the pond as well? Why?" Zac glared angrily at the demon, ready to start a war.

"What poisoned? It was poison from the start. Only lunatics drink that stuff raw. It burns your pathways from inside. Haven't you noticed?" Ogras spat back and waved his hands.

The trees rustled in the wind, and shadows were flickering all over the ground as Zac glared at the demon, but he eventually stopped his advance.

"Explain," Zac growled through gritted teeth, extremely pissed off that the demon hadn't mentioned anything about this for the whole duration of their conversation.

"That kind of water can be born in areas where there is extremely dense Cosmic Energy. It was probably created when the Ruthless Heavens crammed a Nexus Vein into the mountain range," Ogras grumpily explained. "It is pretty rare and somewhat expensive. Normally, it's used as an ingredient in alchemy, but some forces give their death squads some of it to use just in case. It restores your Cosmic Energy in seconds, but it damages your body and can even kill you."

"But I feel fine?" Zac said doubtfully.

"You just used some Cosmic Energy; try restoring it naturally without using any tools," Ogras said as he sighed and sat down in his chair again while he muttered something under his breath.

Too stressed out to care about any glib remark from the demon, Zac unsummoned his enlarged blade and tried to sense the Cosmic Energy entering his body. He wasn't a cultivator, but even mortals could naturally restore their Cosmic Energy as the ambient energy slowly entered their bodies. It was normally a slow but steady stream that entered his body, but now it could barely be called a trickle.

Zac's face went white, and he stared at the demon. He was still suspicious but somewhat believed the demon told the truth. It took him hours to restore his Cosmic Energy even with a crystal, but it almost happened instantly with the azure water. He hadn't reflected on it before, but how could there be such a good thing with no side effect?

He simply didn't notice the effect since he'd used crystals or more water every time he needed to restore after chugging the Cosmic Water the first time. He had been strapped for time and didn't have time to wait for his energy to naturally restore itself. He had been angry that he wasn't given a power boost from bathing in the stuff earlier, but now he was just happy to still be alive.

"How do I fix this?" Zac asked.

"I've heard that there are pills for it, but I don't know where to get them. It's extremely rare, because idio… individuals who drink it almost always die within a day, you know?" Ogras said. "I think I've heard that spending time in energy-rich areas can help your body slowly heal various types of damage to your pathways. So that might work, but I'm not sure how much time it would take. And that is if you still can absorb some energy. If it's a full stop, it's over for you, I'm afraid."

"What happens if I keep using it? Can't I just refill my energy with crystals if I can't naturally absorb energy anymore?" Zac asked. He had enough for a lifetime or two in the pond, and while not being able to naturally restore was regrettable, it wouldn't be the end of the world.

"You need to heal up your ruined pathways. If you keep cramming energy into your body in your current state, even if it's from crystals, you will keep getting worse. First it's natural energy that stops; then it's Nexus Crystals. Soon not even the Cosmic Water can restore your energy, and you truly become a cripple until you die of energy starvation. Then what good are you?"

Zac was horrified at that outcome and quickly unequipped his amulet. The good news was that at least his situation wasn't completely irreversible, and it almost seemed a miracle that he was still alive from how Ogras described it. Death Squad members died after chugging that stuff just once, but he'd used it multiple times in the duration of a day. The first time was after the ambush in the tunnels, but after that, he'd used it multiple times during battle. It sounded crazy, but it almost felt like taking the bath actually saved him. His body was unceasingly refined after he ate the Fruit of Ascension, and perhaps it did something to increase his resistance or heal up irreversible damage.

But the predicament was extremely troublesome since there was a monster horde coming. If he wasn't healed by the time the monsters arrived, he would have to fight without using any Cosmic Energy. If he kept using **[Chop]** like with the monkeys, he'd soon have to use crystals to restore himself. It would be a vicious circle that would end up with him in the same situation as now.

He swore to do everything that he could to get healed in time, and he needed to go to the mines anyway to prospect as many crystals as possible to get Nexus Coins. Zac asked a few more questions about how to improve his recuperation, but Ogras either didn't know much more or was holding back on him. Zac could only sigh and move to the next subject he needed to know about.

"What are the attribute limits when you're an E-grade Race?" He really wanted to know where the limits lay now that he was E-grade. He didn't want to lose any more points than he already had. With his Title boosts, he'd already lost over 10 Strength, which by no means was a small amount.

"Attribute cap? Why do you…" Ogras stopped himself and stared blankly at Zac for a few seconds. "You goddamn progenitors just make my teeth itch. And you even got a Fruit of Ascension to save your ass! Just disgusting. Well, don't worry, attribute caps are not something you will need to worry about for a long time now."

"Progenitors? What are you talking about?" Zac wondered. Abby had called him a Defier, not a progenitor.

"You first-generation cultivators of a baby planet," Ogras spat out, looking loath to even think about the subject. Zac didn't feel the need to correct him that he wasn't a cultivator at the moment, as the demon was starting to work himself up in a huff.

"Haven't you realized? You have many advantages that your descendants won't get. The Ruthless Heavens gives you a running start. There are many unique titles, the System crams the planet full of unique treasures, and you even get the Tutorial. It's even easier to gain Dao Seeds for some reason. It just makes us normal cultivators want to lie down and die of jealousy."

Ogras looked about ready to explode with greed and jealousy as he talked about it. Zac felt he had found his match in his quest for wealth, and he also vowed to never show the demon his Title page. The demon might just fall into an apoplectic rage and start swinging that scary spear at him.

The demon soon found his bearing again and, with a cough continued, "Cough… In any case, those who manage to grasp a decent number of the limited advantages a new world provides will have a lifelong advantage compared to most people in the Multiverse. These individuals are called their planet's progenitors, as they usually end up creating influential clans or sects on their home planets. On the off chance they don't get killed, that is."

Zac thought that made a lot of sense. So far, he had only compared himself with the cultivators and tried to keep his head start going. He hadn't even thought about the following generations and how they would grow up in this environment. But it was true, many of the titles he snatched would probably never appear again on this planet, closing that door for an advantage forever.

As time progressed, most limited titles would be taken, leaving only maybe the most obscure and well-hidden ones for future generations. Otherwise, they would have to settle for the mediocre unlimited ones, such as the Adventurer title.

Ogras was a veritable treasure trove of answers after having fumbled about blindly for so long. For example, it was very interesting to know that normal cultivators in the Multiverse didn't get access to the Tutorial, making it an even more rare opportunity. Zac kept coming up with various questions that had hounded him and threw them at the demon randomly as he thought of them. The smiling façade of Ogras soon cracked, and his answers got shorter and terser until he slammed his hand on the armrest of his chair.

"Goddamn it! Do I look like a Tutorial fairy to you? I'll be back tomorrow," he spat out and threw a crystal at Zac, who deftly snapped it out of the air. "Read that instead of pestering me."

"Read? How?" Zac looked at the crystal in his hand, confused. It looked similar to a Nexus Crystal, but the color was green like a watered-down emerald. It was also covered in intricate golden fractals.

"Just imbue some energy in it." The demon sighed, obviously still annoyed, and walked toward the edge of the camp. "I'm done answering your inane questions, human. Put your energy toward survival instead."

Ogras soon left the camp and afterward disappeared like he had up on the mountaintop. There were many questions that were still unanswered, but he had gotten many of the more pressing issues cleared up. He looked at the crystal in his hand and, after a long hesitation, poured a minuscule amount of Cosmic Energy into it. The demon was very helpful so far, and it felt unlikely he would give him a bomb after all this. Still, he was ready to hurl the crystal far away if needed.

A screen similar to the ones the System provided suddenly popped up as the crystal lit up. The design of the window was a bit more intricate, though, and covering it was an image of a grand pavilion with a Stargazer floating on top of it. It clearly was a man-made item, and the intricacy made Zac marvel. It was something on a whole other level compared to the cruder enchantments on the demon's gear pieces.

Soon the image changed, and it turned into what could best be described as a web page. There were menus with various categories and images. Luckily, Zac could understand the content just fine and was amazed at what was written. The crystal contained a thorough guide of what happened when a world was integrated into the Multiverse.

Granted, it seemed to be written for the invading forces, but still, most of the information was very helpful to Zac. But the more he read through, the more troubled he became. It became very apparent that the natives were largely discounted, and that the web page considered the other incursion forces the only challenge for a successful invasion.

It did mention that there was a small chance of encountering extremely strong forces on an integrated planet, but most civilizations couldn't even be considered F-grade. From how the text described it, Zac knew that Earth's civilization wasn't considered anything much and was not what it meant when it mentioned strong forces.

For normal civilizations like Earth's humans, the missive simply stated that enslavement usually was most convenient. It would increase the resources that could be gained on a new planet, as manpower usually was limited.

It also listed the most common tactics of various forces in the Multiverse, and Zac was shocked to find out that the demons truly were some of the more decent forces. They usually created a country and entered trade negotiations with surrounding forces, native or foreign, to amass wealth. They did enslave the native populations on their lands, though.

But there were many forces that simply eradicated everything and ceaselessly strove to increase its influence until the whole planet was theirs. There was even a force that entered incursions just in order to annihilate the natives and didn't care about the resources at all. It was a cult that called itself the Church of Everlasting Dao.

Unfortunately, the missive gave no information about the forces themselves, so Zac couldn't find out more about them. But it was clear that almost none of the forces cared an iota about the natives and only considered newly integrated worlds treasure troves of wealth.

All in all, the crystal was just what Zac needed, and he swore that he'd pester the demon until he handed out more goodies. The crystal said it was the first crystal of two, so hopefully, he could annoy another out of the paws of the demon tomorrow.

69

REWARDS

Even if the demon was gone, Zac stayed put for some time, going over the conversation he'd just had. Everything that came out of the mouth of the demon seemed to be the truth, but he didn't feel it was that easy. He guessed that many of the things he learned today weren't any hard-to-gain secrets, maybe with the exception of the things in the crystal he received.

How things like quests, races, and classes worked should be the most basic of things and not something that the System would keep hidden. Still, he would work under the creed "Trust but verify." He believed that he would get access to a secondary source of information soon now that various buildings were unlocked in the Town Shop. It would be easy to compare and contrast the words from the demon with what he learned in other places. From there, he might actually be able to learn the demon's agenda, from finding out what he lied about through omission, for example.

Satisfied, he turned his attention to the Nexus Node. It was time to do what he'd initially returned to the camp for. He had some rewards to cash in on.

Off With Their Heads (Unique): Kill the four heralds and the

general of an incursion within 3 months. Reward: 10 E-Grade Nexus Crystals, E-Grade equipment, unique building depending on performance. (5/5) [COMPLETE]

Not wanting to wait any longer, he walked over to the crystal. Zac knew Ogras might actually be spying on him from the shadows, but he didn't have any means to locate him at the moment and could only let him be.

As he placed his hand on the crystal, it started pulsating for a few seconds until the familiar voice of the System appeared.

[Incursion subjugation complete. Calculating personal contribution. Contribution 88%. Time taken: 47 days. Support: 1. Completion Grade: A. Distributing rewards.]

Two boxes appeared on the ground, and Zac picked up the smaller one first. Zac still felt it was unsettling that the System could just make things appear out of nowhere. There was no sound, no ripples of power, nothing. One second emptiness, the next the boxes just were there.

As he opened the lid of the smaller box, a blinding light radiated out from its contents. They were the E-grade Nexus Crystals from the reward. Zac could easily discern that anything he had seen so far was F-grade at best, as these crystals were on a completely different level.

Each crystal contained a terrifying amount of energy inside, perhaps as much as a thousand crystals in his bags. But it was condensed into the small space of his hand. Zac felt that one single crystal might hold enough power for him to gain more than a level, and if these crystals could be absorbed as quickly as an F-graded one, he would instantly skyrocket in power.

But unfortunately, he didn't dare try them at the moment, not while his predicament with his energy poisoning still remained.

He could only reluctantly close the lid of the box and place it into his pouch with a sigh. Next he picked up the larger box, which should contain a set of equipment from the reward.

But before he had time to check it out, a large rumbling interrupted him. The ground was ominously shaking, and a deafening noise could be heard from somewhere close by. Zac instantly got a bad feeling from the sound. Had Ogras lied, and the demon horde was already upon him? He quickly threw the box into his pouch and summoned his axe instead.

He quickly looked around but saw no change. The noise clearly came from the south, so he ran there after a brief hesitation. The only thing to the south was the ocean, and Zac was afraid an aquatic beast horde had started if it wasn't the demons making trouble. As he ran, he opened up his Town Shop, ready to buy a defensive array at a moment's notice.

He soon arrived at the edge of the island and immediately spotted a familiar figure. Ogras was staring out over the cliff with his mouth ajar.

"What did you do?" Zac angrily huffed at the demon as he ran up to him, axe at the ready.

"What did *I* do? Nothing. I heard the noise and thought you had done something crazy. And it seems that I was right," Ogras snappishly retorted and gestured at the odd scene in front of them.

The cliffs were magically rearranging themselves in a baffling manner. It was as though an earth mage untold times more powerful than the demon mages was reconstructing the whole shoreline to his liking. The previously natural cliffs flattened out into orderly land.

Huge rectangular breakwaters grew out from the land and created a sheltered basin hundreds of meters across, and two piers emerged out of the sea, displacing all the water into mighty waves. Furthermore, fractals appeared on the emerging rock formations as all the various changes took place, glimmering in a mysterious golden hue. They expansively covered the whole shoreline, the piers, and the breakwaters. The script itself differed from both the System's fractals and the simpler demonic inscriptions, and it actually reminded Zac of the squarish text in very old computer environments.

The changes didn't only happen on land, though, and the duo was forced to scramble to safety as the ground gave out and created a wet dock where they stood. Next, various buildings flashed into existence. The largest was an enormous warehouse-looking building that was at least three hundred meters long and a hundred meters wide, where one of the short sides ended close to the sea-line. It was probably the largest building Zac had ever seen, and he thought few structures on Earth would be able to match it.

Soon the rumbling subsided, and Zac looked out over the majestic harbor that had cropped up in under a minute. The design was cubic and looked extremely robust, and Zac felt that not even the worst storm would be able to do any damage to the structures. The cubic fractals covered all the structures as well, and Zac started to believe that they were some sort of protective inscription.

[E-Grade Medium-Scale Iliex Shipyard Awarded]

The System blared in his ears, but Zac had no time to react before he was interrupted.

"What the FUCK!" Ogras screamed as he agitatedly grabbed on to Zac's arm. "Is it upgradeable, IS IT UPGRADEABLE?" Gone was the wiseass know-it-all, replaced with a spluttering madman who seemed to have fire in his eyes as he glared at Zac.

"Goddamn, calm down," Zac said and freed his arm from the crazed demon. "What are you talking about?"

"Inspect the building from your town menu and share the

information," Ogras hastily said, almost dancing on the spot in excitement.

Zac didn't know what Ogras was talking about. But from his face, it looked like he would explode from impatience at any moment, so he tried various mental commands instead of asking anymore. As he used the command "Town," a new menu opened up. He knew he had tried that command a long time ago with no result, and guessed it had been activated when he'd completed the incursion quest. His camp should still be classified as an outpost, though, as it was only promoted to city upon completing the next quest.

The new menu was a list of all the structures he had bought or gotten from the System. Everything between the water-gathering array to this huge construction in front of him was there. However, his camper or the car was not listed, so only System-structures were included, it seemed. He focused on the shipyard but stopped himself from sharing the prompt.

[E-Grade Medium-Scale Iliex Shipyard. Upgradeable.]

"Maybe it is, maybe it isn't," Zac defensively said, feeling that this might be important information from the demon's reaction.

"Just how high is your Luck, human? A Creators' shipyard. This changes everything," Ogras said, ignoring Zac's attitude.

"It says it's an Iliex shipyard, though? And why are you getting so excited?" Zac couldn't understand his reaction. It was a nice-looking shipyard, but that was it. He was likely going to build or buy one like this sooner or later since he was on an island, so it was nice being able to save on that expenditure. But he'd much rather have a town protection array or some turrets as a reward since there were monster hordes incoming.

"Truly pearls before swine. The Iliex are a race of living golems who are among the greatest builders in the Multiverse.

Most just call them Creators, since that's pretty much all they do. A shipyard that's manned by the Creators will create faster, stronger, and more durable ships compared to normal ones. But more importantly, the shipyard is upgradeable."

Zac was starting to get excited as well since it seemed the System had actually given him something pretty good. But still, Ogras' reaction seemed exaggerated if that was it.

"So what else?" he asked the excited demon.

"Well… Creators can also make some of the most sought after cosmic ships and sky fortresses. Owning a shipyard means you can sell those in the future. It can net the Lord hundreds of times more income compared to the crystal mines in the mountains," he explained after a brief hesitation. "I haven't heard of a single faction that actually has access to the Creators."

"Cosmic ships? Like spaceships?" Zac asked, now starting to get excited as well.

"Something like that. Ships that can traverse the endless distances of the Multiverse. They can travel to any points on a planet in seconds as well, very convenient. But they are not 'spaceships.' They are Spiritual Ships that travel using the Dao of Space and Cosmic Energy rather than relying on technology."

Now Zac was on board the hype train as well. Travel anywhere on the planet in seconds? This was exactly what he needed in order to search for his friends and family.

"How much do you think it costs to buy one of those cosmic ships?" Zac asked eagerly.

"Slow down. An E-grade shipyard can't create things like that. I think it must be D-grade, maybe even C-grade before you can create those kinds of things." Ogras immediately doused the burning desire Zac was building up. "We need to upgrade the shipyard first before we can start reaping the benefits. And before that we need to keep it safe and hidden."

"How do I upgrade it? And why hidden?" Zac asked,

confused, but the next second froze, knowing that he had exposed himself.

"Yes, hidden. This shipyard is a treasure, and any force would drool after it. If the word spreads that you control a Creator shipyard, you will have endless troubles coming your way," Ogras said after a smug smile at Zac's mistake. "As for upgrading it? No idea; try asking the Creators."

"I mean, I get that this is a good thing, but why would even you foreign forces go crazy for it? Can't you just buy your own?" Zac asked, starting to feel he was sitting on a hot potato.

"You can't just buy a shipyard from the Creators when you wish. There are so many requirements that have to be met. They are extremely picky whom they work with and where they work. You'd never be able to build such a thing on this planet if it weren't a reward from the System. This applies for most of the good things. Just check your Town Shop," Ogras impatiently explained. Clearly he knew it wasn't a purchase of Zac, rather a reward, just from how rare this thing was.

Zac opened up the Town Shop, and the screen displayed the various shops. He had looked it over briefly as he trekked back toward his camp, as he'd needed to buy a shop to sell his crystals. But now the screen was changed. The shops were now actually purchasable, but almost all of them shone with a red light on the screen. Confused, Zac focused on one of the red ones called **[Parlaz Consortium – General Store]**.

A new window with deeper information about the shop opened, something he hadn't been able to do before. A list of what type of services it provided was listed on one side, and it truly seemed comprehensive. It sold everything from seeds for farming to construction materials to weapons and armor. It also dealt in basic information, having stocks of crystals explaining most things, from plants to blacksmithing to even town-building.

On another row, a number of requirements were listed. Zac's

outpost didn't actually fulfill a single one, except having enough space. There were requirements for minimum town size, population, town daily turnover, and security. Since Zac's town was just an outpost and a shipyard with no inhabitants, it wasn't possible to fulfill those demands.

As he flipped through various buildings, he saw that most of them had varying severity of requirements. Some even demanded a town population of a hundred million, or that it was the planet capital. There were myriad choices, but the ones he could actually choose were a scant few. It seemed that the merchant conglomerates of the Multiverse were quite picky.

70

TOWN SHOP

Frustrated, Zac focused on the shop he actually could buy. It was actually just called **[F-Grade General Store]** with no mention of a faction or company behind it. Confused, he turned to Ogras.

"I can't buy almost anything in the store. Most things are restricted. But there is a shop called F-grade General Store that has no requirements. Why's that?"

"That's the Ruthless Heavens' store," Ogras answered.

"Wait, the System runs stores as well?"

"The Ruthless Heavens is the largest employer in existence, though it's not a very hands-on boss. Running a Multiverse takes many hands, after all," the demon explained with a roll of his eyes.

"So why should I get any other store if I can just get the one from the System?" Zac knew he was straying from the subject of the shipyard, but he felt another opportunity to drag information out of the contrary demon had appeared.

"Because the Ruthless Heavens is goddamn greed… ehm, economical. It provides basic facilities in almost all fields that have no requirements, but its prices are between 50 to 500%

higher compared to the average." Ogras looked like he would be sick as he talked about the daylight robbery of the System-run stores.

The image of the almighty system being an intergalactic price-gouging bodega owner gave Zac's image of the System somewhat of a thorn, but he guessed running a universe, or multiple universes, wasn't cheap.

"The corporations have far better rates on almost everything and can also procure things for you if you're in need of a specific item. For a fee, of course. But they operate for profit and would never open up a branch if they weren't sure if they'd be able to turn a profit in the location. The corporations have to foot most of the bill of coming here themselves, and it's not cheap, from what I understand. Therefore, they'd never open a branch without some assurance," Ogras continued.

"Some factions have even more requirements. The Creators, for example, I think they normally only open a branch in B-graded worlds or higher. You also need to have a referral from an actual Creator to even get the application process going. And getting that from one of those living machines is almost impossible. Well, I'm not sure about the details since that is so far above my pay grade. Even my grandfather has no qualifications to know about what goes on in B-ranked worlds. So you see why this shipyard is so valuable."

Excitement and unease were building up simultaneously in Zac once again. He might actually have gotten a curse rather than a treasure. The shipyard was extremely valuable, but one needed to be alive to reap its benefits.

"So what do you suggest we do?" Zac hoped for some input from the demon. He was crafty, and he knew how the various forces worked.

"Two options. Either hide it completely, buy a huge illusion array to start. An E-graded one at least, as many can see through an F-graded one. As soon as you can, upgrade it to a D-graded one. Then we build walls around the whole area and say it's the Lord's residence, only giving you access. Later, you can add on slaughter arrays to the illusion array, killing any trespasser. Then you build your town far away." The demon clearly had a meticulous mind, already having formulated strategies.

"Second is to hide in plain sight. Ask the creators to redesign their shipyard and hide their characteristics. Make it look like a normal shipyard. Don't make a big deal out of it; just make it look like a decently important place with some defensive arrays protecting it."

Zac mulled it over and preferred the second option if it was possible. He didn't believe an illusion array was the answer. Sooner or later, something similar to the peeing demon would happen, and he would be exposed. Then everyone would know he was hiding something and would get even more curious.

Besides, his goal was to build a town, and that had to happen around the Nexus Node. He couldn't move the crystal very far, and the area where he could place town structures from the outpost shop was limited as well. As soon as he walked too far from his camp or the crystal, the shop turned to a browse-only mode. The area would probably grow along with the population, but for now, it was only a few kilometers in every direction, far too short to create a town on other sides of the island.

"I will do a mix. I'll wall off the area from my camp to this shipyard to make it my private property, and then build a town outside. Inside the inner wall will be my residence, the shipyard, and other critical structures I might build in the future. It should look like I'm just protecting the important parts of the town and not raise too much suspicion," Zac decided.

Ogras mulled it over a bit, then nodded. Zac glanced in the demon's direction, and his thoughts started to turn in another direction. The demon seemed very helpful right now, but he clearly was ambitious and ruthless. Now that Zac was sitting on an even greater pile of treasure, how would the demon act? Should he nip the problem in the bud and kill him?

But Zac soon gave up that idea. Ogras was still needed to control the demons, and he didn't want to fight against the former general unless absolutely necessary with his current condition. Such a battle would take all the Cosmic Energy he had, and if he was forced to drink the azure water just to defeat him, it would truly be a pyrrhic victory.

Maybe just as important, he didn't want to become the kind of person who started to preemptively murder people in cold blood to protect his wealth against possible perceived threats. He didn't want to devolve into a crazed paranoid dictator. Certainly the number he had killed by now would horrify anyone in a civilized world, but it had been done out of necessity. And it wasn't like he would adapt to some naïve no-kill policy in this ruthless new world. His hands were already bloodied, and he knew that this was only the start. But there needed to be balance.

Ogras seemed to measure his choices by how many benefits they would bring, and Zac was convinced that he was more valuable alive than dead after reading the contents of the crystal. He knew Ogras was unable to forcefully seize the town for roughly a decade due to being locked out of that system. If he were Ogras and were planning long term, he'd do everything to make the town as successful as possible for now and then forcefully seize it in the future.

But a lot could happen in ten years, and Zac planned to keep utilizing his advantages to get stronger to the point that betrayal would be more foolish than staying on as a confidant.

Ten years sounded like a long time, but Zac knew it might not be too long in this new reality they lived in. He had been surprised by Ogras telling him that longevity actually increased as people got stronger. As he increased his Race-ranking to E-grade, his life expectancy had actually increased to a full five hundred years.

It was crazy to think that he already had the life-span like some elf, and that was just after one upgrade. Furthermore, Ogras told him that the life-span of a D-ranker was counted in the thousands rather than hundreds of years, and the grandfather he'd mentioned was over 1,600 years old. Above that, he seemed unclear, as apparently that was the highest official rank on his home planet apart from some mysterious emperor.

Zac had initially thought that, in the Multiverse, there would be no limit to the powers of the factions. As long as one had time, they could keep killing monsters and level up. But apparently, it got harder and harder to increase Strength, and many bottlenecks kept peoples' power in check.

Generally, the powerhouses of a planet held the same Class-rank as the planet itself, meaning that the general limit of Earth was D-ranked classes. If someone wanted to break through their limits, they were forced to venture out into the Multiverse and look for enlightenment or lucky opportunities. Eager to find out more, Zac had pestered Ogras about the details of getting stronger and ranking up, but it was around this time he flipped out and left the camp.

"I will keep any demons away from this area for now. Though I don't think anyone has the guts to seek you out anyway. Between your actions and your… fashion sense… you have cultivated a rather strong image among my people," Ogras said and woke Zac up from his thoughts. He realized he'd have to stay out of his own head a bit more now that there were actually others around. He couldn't just be blankly staring out into the distance like an idiot.

After exhorting Zac some more about the importance of secrecy, Ogras once again left toward the center of the island.

Still curious, Zac wanted to enter the shipyard to look around, but first, he wanted to check out the gear. He looked insane at the moment, and from how Ogras had explained it, there should be the very famous Creators inside. He didn't know if they were peculiar about propriety, but first impressions were important.

The larger box was brought out of the purse, and Zac opened it eagerly. Inside was actually a full set of clothing neatly packed. As he lifted it up, he was initially confused, as it seemed the System had gifted him another dress. Did the System have a sense of humor?

But soon he realized that wasn't the case, but the item was rather a robe that felt distinctly Eastern in its make. It was of excellent quality and had a deep green color. He wanted to try it on but once again was reminded how grimy he was. Being bathed in the poison water had at least cleansed him somewhat, but he was still pretty disgusting.

After hesitating a bit, he ran back to camp and threw himself into the shower. After furiously scrubbing himself for a few minutes, he finally was clean again for the first time in a long time. He stepped out of the shower and took a look at himself in the mirror.

Zac was shocked to see what was looking back at him. It was him, but *better*. Most noticeably, most of his scars were gone. Only the worst ones were still there, such as the nasty wound on his cheek. But even those had faded considerably and turned into thin white lines.

Not only that, his body looked like perfectly sculpted marble, and even his face seemed to have improved somehow. He couldn't put his finger on it, but it felt like small adjustments had been made to enhance imperfect features. If some old friend saw him, they'd probably think that he had gotten some plastic surgery done. Of course, he didn't look like a movie star or something, but he had gone from average to above average at least.

Of course, the fact that he still was completely hairless since the fight with the imp herald detracted from the image somewhat. At least it looked like some stubble was coming along, and he wouldn't look like a monk much longer.

He guessed that it was a result of evolving his race. New benefits kept cropping up, it seemed. When he reached D-rank, all the scars might be gone, and he would become a real hunk, he thought with some eagerness.

Finally clean, he quickly donned all the new items the System had gifted him. After checking himself out in the mirror, he could only say he looked pretty dashing.

71

FIRST IMPRESSIONS

The clothing consisted of two layers. The inner layer was essentially a long-armed shirt, with the exception that it didn't have any buttons. Instead, one side was wrapped above the other, and both sides were fastened with a clasp to stay snugly on his chest. The arms and shoulders had a slightly looser fit and didn't restrict his movements at all. It fit perfectly, and Zac felt it must have been custom-made for his frame.

His pants were made in some smooth cloth as well, and were a darker brown compared to the beige of the shirt. They were slightly baggy at the thighs but snugly fit around his calves, and they reminded Zac of some jester's pants. But at least they weren't tapered in bright colors or had bells attached.

The outer layer was a green robe that was put on in the same manner as the inner shirt, with one side placed over the other. But instead of being kept in place with clasps, it stayed fastened with a wide leather girdle. It was sleeveless and went down to his knees just like the dress he'd used earlier, which was why he got turned around earlier. Adorning the hem of the robe was intricate fractals in the same style as the array flags, meaning they likely were put there by the System, or its own craftsmen at least.

No shoes were provided, though, by the System, which was fine by him since he couldn't wear them at the moment in any case. All in all, it seemed the System tailored the rewards to his needs, which he guessed was due to getting such high marks on his completion.

A stream of information entered his mind as he touched a fractal, and he was delighted to know that the gear had quite a few features. It was self-cleaning and self-mending, which translated into Zac not looking like a murder-hobo again in a few weeks. It even had two forms of protection.

One was that it displaced force over his whole body instead of only at the point of impact. Quite some force was needed to break through that passive defense, and Zac wouldn't keep getting the small flesh wounds from bites and arrows. That should come in quite handy when fighting the hordes of beasts in the future.

It also carried a similar protection such as the one on the demons' armors, except that it didn't provide any recoil force. Instead, it could be used twice in a day and could stop a much stronger attack, which was far more valuable, as Zac saw it. His strongest Dao-empowered strike had been able to break through the golden shield in his fight with Rydel, so he knew roughly where its limit lay.

Looking fresh and presentable, except for his bare feet, Zac once again headed back to the shipyard. It still seemed deserted, as there were no sounds of activity breaking the silence. Still, Zac entered a building next to the huge warehouse that seemed to be either an office or rec house.

The inside was made of stone, cut and polished to perfection. All the furniture and details were created in heavy stone as well, and Zac couldn't see one curved line. Everything was squared, and the whole lobby gave Zac a truly brutalist impression.

The room clearly was a lobby. Apart from some stone furniture, a huge counter was placed in the middle, and behind it stood a statue of a humanoid. It had no facial features, and its face was instead covered in a large fractal in the computer font. It was dressed in a simple silver-colored robe and looked somewhat human apart from the fact that it had a few extra fingers on each of its hands. All in all, it looked like a robot statue carved out of soapstone or onyx.

It was completely still, and Zac wasn't sure whether this was one of the so-called Creators or just an elaborate decoration. Ogras had called them living golems, and this kind of fit the bill.

"Hello? I'm Zac Atwood. Am I disturbing you?" He tentatively tried to call on the statue.

"Greetings, Mr. Atwood. I am Rahm, liaison of Iliex Precosmic Shipyard Nr. 65,238 now located at your planet. Future inquiries are preferably directed at me, and I will endeavor to resolve any issues and complaints in an expedient and equitable manner."

The statue came to life and answered in a perfunctory and slightly lifeless voice. It then even followed up with an aristocratic bow in Zac's direction. It seemed that the Iliex conversed in the same manner as Abby had, using some magic instead of a mouth. Zac quickly bowed back with far less grace, flustered at the cordiality.

"Ha ha, don't mind Rahm, that rigid old goat. We're not some dour robots like he would have you believe," boomed a similar, but far rowdier voice from the interior of the building as deep thuds approached the lobby. Soon the speaker entered through a passage, and Zac had to stop himself from taking a step back.

It was a three-meter-tall amalgamation between spider and robot. It had five huge legs that bent at the middle, each over three meters long. If they stretched upward, the weird-looking Creator would stand at over four meters. The torso itself was largely humanoid, with the face sharing the characteristic fractal. It did, however, have four arms instead of two, and it actually looked like the body was full of either tools or weapons.

Zac could only stare at the monstrosity with mouth slightly ajar, which seemed to please the spider robot immensely.

"Pretty impressive, isn't it, brat? Took me the better part of three hundred years to fuse form and function into the great body before you. Even had to steal some C-graded nebulous copper to finish it. Well, I guess that's why I was demoted to the foreman of this shithole. No offense," he shouted as he slapped one of the metallic legs, creating an echoing clangor throughout the building.

The more normal-looking Creator didn't react at all to the entrance and tirade of this fantastical being, seeming used to its antics.

"So, kid, what do you wanna build? Terrornaughts? Modified destroyers? If you can get some D-graded crystals, we can make some nasty cosmic bombs, blow one of the neighboring islands off the face of the earth! Attack is the best defense; who knows what kind of assholes live there!"

The man's legs started tap excitedly at the floor as he started to list what could only be terrible weapons, each tap actually punching a hole in the ground. Zac was unable to react for a second, his mind working overtime to grasp the new information. Luckily, the liaison saved the day with a timely interjection.

"D-grade battleships such as terrornaughts and destroyers are not within the accord with the Great Shaper. Please review the preapproved designs."

Two crystals appeared in its hands, of which Zac graciously accepted one. The metal spider-being waved his copy away, though, and Rahm could only put it back.

"May I present Karunthel, foreman and foremost expert of this shipyard. And he was relocated here after a few… unfortunate…

experiments, not some minor item acquisition infraction," the liaison, who started to feel like a long-suffering butler, said as he gestured toward the spider.

"Bah, I know, I know, no blowing up any islands or continents of the baby world," Karunthel said as he rolled his shoulders.

"Actually, I'm not here regarding any ships at the moment. I was wondering if it was possible to, uh, camouflage the fact that this is a Iliex shipyard, make it look like it's a normal one?" Zac asked tentatively, gauging the reactions of the two golems.

"Ha ha, afraid of a little heat, brat? Any greedy forces nearby? You should just carpet bomb anything that looks at your stuff, far more effective," the foreman said with a booming laugh.

"Well, I guess we could make it look like a human dock, hide the inscriptions and such. But such changes are not included in the standard package," Karunthel continued, seemingly entering into business mode.

"What do you mean?" Zac asked with a sinking feeling.

"Money! We don't work for free, and restructuring the whole thing to make it look uglier is gonna cost you."

"How much?" Zac asked, determined to just grit his teeth and bear the cost, almost no matter how large.

"Eight millio–"

"Five hundred and twenty-five thousand Nexus Coins," the liaison quickly interjected, only to be lightly kicked with one of the spider legs as the foreman muttered something Zac couldn't discern.

Zac was starting to get a headache, as it seemed everyone entering his life lately was filled with greed. Luckily, Rahm had come to his rescue, and he helplessly accepted the reconstruction, leaving him with a huge hole in his pocket. A window looking like a purchase confirmation appeared in front of him, and he accepted.

"Remuneration confirmed. Expected duration for project, four hours. May this be the start of a long and mutually beneficial cooperation," Rahm said and once again bowed toward Zac.

More impressively, his whole body started flickering, and he changed into an actual human. Of course, there was a tinge of lifelessness in the Creator's eyes, belying his real identity to Zac. Though that might just be the personality of this particular individual rather than a failure in the camouflage. But after watching its movements and mannerisms for a few seconds, he saw some imperfections in the disguise. But from a distance or for a short while, no one should be able to tell at all.

"Bah, how boring. Call me when you want to create things that go boom. And don't expect me to turn into a stupid bipedal after getting these shiny legs. But don't worry, no brat on a baby world will be able to expose me, native or foreign," the foreman said and started to walk away with a wave.

"Um, are you able to build anything that can help against a monster horde?" Zac asked, as this was the most pressing issue now that the reconstruction was dealt with.

Karunthel stopped in his tracks as he was leaving and eagerly turned toward Zac once again. But after a few seconds of hesitation, he answered.

"I'm sorry, kiddo, but most of what I'm allowed to create right now is meant for naval exploration with limited functions for naval battle. It's cheaper if you buy the fortifications and arrays from the shop. It's not Creator quality, but it's more effective against beast hordes. And don't expect us to help you kill any critters. We're only here to build things."

Having nothing else to do at the shipyard, Zac thanked the two golems and left. As he left, he saw quite a few humans efficiently scurrying about as they remodeled the whole area. But he knew that it wasn't actual humans, rather more camouflaged Creators.

He was very pleased with the result of the visit, apart from having been forced to spend most of his hard-earned coin. But since there might arrive more people or demons at any moment, he didn't hesitate to spend it. If what Ogras said was true, then not even a whisper of any rumors could be allowed to grow.

He was a bit disappointed that they wouldn't provide any assistance in case of an attack. But he had a feeling the System put various restrictions on those who worked for it. Abby wasn't allowed to explain certain things, and Rahm had told him they were only allowed to build preapproved ships. It meant that the golems likely weren't even allowed to provide assistance outside doing their jobs. Otherwise, Zac believed that the crazy foreman wouldn't pass up the opportunity to blow up hordes of monsters, even if it was just for fun.

He arrived back at the camper and once again opened up the Town Shop. It was time to start the improvements. First, he bought an **[F-Grade Middle-Scale Cosmic Smelting Furnace]** for two hundred thousand Nexus Coins, leaving him with a scant twenty thousand Nexus Coins. Luckily, the shops only cost a symbolic sum, as they made their money through trade.

The purpose of the furnace was to refine various F-graded metals and minerals, and Nexus Crystals were one of the things it could refine. It was an expensive purchase, but Ogras had promised it would be far more profitable to refine the materials by himself before he sold them, as every shop would try to scam him on rates when he sold raw crystals.

It was a large black box roughly two meters tall and three meters wide. On one side, it had a chute for throwing in the raw materials, and on the other, it had a hole leading out to a large tray. He immediately summoned a sack of crystals and threw the contents into the chute and contentedly watched his wealth grow. It took roughly ten minutes for the whole sack to be processed into crystals, and when they came out, they looked identical to the ones he had stolen long ago. Gone were any defects or rock remains, leaving only unblemished uniform crystals.

Next, he needed someone to buy his products.

72

THAYER CONSORTIUM

Calrin despondently surveyed the various reports strewn about his table. Twenty thousand years of heritage teetered on the brink of destruction, all under his watch. He knew that he was partly to blame for the situation, but others were far more culpable.

'Greed is the fuel which pushes us forward. Honor is the compass which keeps the course.'

That was the creed inlaid under the painting of his ancestor, hung behind him in an ornate frame. He didn't need to turn around to know the words, or to remember every single detail of his ancestor's face. The slight upward tug of his mouth, the ever-present Ancient Empire coin in his hand, ceaselessly whirling between his fingers. The mischievous light in his eyes that seemed to see through all lies and posturing.

Almarillo Thayer was born a beggar in a lowly E-graded world on decline. He had no family, no education, and no prospects, but through his intellect and drive, he managed to become an assistant to a shop clerk. From there, he gained the Assistant class, the first step that ended with him founding the

[Thayer Consortium], a System-sanctioned mercantile corporation with branches in hundreds of worlds, and its headquarters located on a bustling C-ranked continent.

Those awe-inspiring offices were long pawned off, even before Calrin Thayer was born. For the last five hundred years, the company had been in a steady decline. Calrin, with his quick wits and solid business acumen, was chosen to steer the company back on course and was given the chairman position at the young age of eighty. But all he'd accomplished was the reduction of branches from twenty-six to one last struggling location.

He knew the cause wasn't only himself. His family remembered the first half of their founder's creed perfectly well, but the second half had gotten blurred over the years. Shady and short-sighted business practices made them lose a few branches and simultaneously made them quite a few enemies. A few family members even betrayed the Thayer name for personal wealth, and even if they were eventually found out, the damage was already done.

But the downfall started for real roughly twenty-five years ago. The great Tsarun Clan had turned their avaricious gazes toward the Thayer Consortium. Or rather, at the Mercantile License their founder had gained all those years ago. The license was something awarded by the System and not something that could be forced away or stolen. Even eradicating the whole Thayer family wouldn't do any good and would even result in a punishment by the System.

But a business license could be seized through business. Normally, it should be almost impossible to snatch a license from a sanctioned corporation, and it would be far easier to try to gain one through normal means. But between the Thayer Consortium being in tatters and the Tsarun Clan's vast connections and wealth, they'd actually managed to incrementally bring down their corporation, one world at a time.

If they lost their last branch as well, the System would void the Thayer Consortium's license and revoke access to the Multi-verse Mercantile System, rendering them completely and utterly powerless. The merchant's protection they currently enjoyed would disappear as well, and Tsarun clan would begin a wholesale slaughter of the remaining family members. No need to risk a comeback, after all.

Calrin desperately tried to open up new branches to keep the situation afloat. He had tried every means, such as lowering the requirements or offering great rates on various common resources. He even tried bribing various fledgling city lords, but nothing worked. Between the machinations of the Tsarun's elders and the awful reputation his consortia had amassed due to multiple scandals, no one would place their branches in their cities. And if they did, it would soon be closed after a visit from a Tsarun clan emissary.

His intellect strained to find some way out, but the numbers in the reports were clear. In three days, their last branch would be declared defunct, and he would have to flee for his life.

It was time for one last desperate gambit.

Zac skipped sleep that night in favor of watching his pile of wealth grow. He unceasingly kept throwing sack after sack of crystals into the chute and then ran over to the other side to gleefully gather the refined crystals. A completely filled bag took roughly ten minutes to completely process, and it resulted in around two hundred finished crystals.

That meant that the machine could refine almost 30,000 crystals every single day, which should be enough for the mining operations for now. Instead of the numerous sacks, he now carried exactly 11,328 crystals, including the first ones he had stolen.

In the downtime, he kept training his axe-work. He only dared to use half of his Cosmic Energy to activate the **[Axe Mastery]** guidance system, leaving the rest as a backup. Then he let his body slowly recharge the energy instead of using any aids.

The beast hordes were coming, and it was a real possibility he might have to face the sea of monsters without the aid of his skills. He needed to get faster, stronger, and better at using his axe. He remembered how all his moves were in vain against the demon leader. The difference between them hadn't been skills or attribute points; it was the huge difference in technique.

Around midnight, the sounds of activity from the shipyard ebbed out, and Zac guessed the transformations were done. He kept going for about another five hours until all the refinement was done. Luckily, the furnace seemed to need neither rest nor maintenance and unceasingly spit out crystals as long as it had something to process.

The next step was to get a shop to sell the crystals in order to start shoring up the defenses of the town. Since the transformation was complete for the shipyard, he didn't really need to worry about gossipy shop clerks leaking the secret, but as he opened the Town Shop, he paused after a few seconds.

Initially, his idea had been to buy the only store that he was able to purchase at the moment, which was the System-run one.

He was, of course, loath to buy it after hearing about the ridiculous prices since he believed that the System would give equally abysmal rates on crystals as well. Unfortunately, none of the privately run businesses in the Multiverse deemed his island good enough to open up a branch at the moment. However, that had changed since he last checked the store.

In a sea of red, a green-marked shop had silently appeared, called **[Thayer Consortium, Headquarters]**. For some reason, this shop was not only ready to open a branch at his island, but it actually wanted to move its headquarters here. When he opened the store, he realized that it wasn't luck that he somehow managed to fill all its criteria. The Thayer Consortium had removed every single normal restriction such as population and security and only demanded two things. First, they required a far larger space compared to the other shops. Secondly, they required the world to be within three years of integration to the Multiverse.

At first glance, it looked like a God-given gift, but he wanted to wait for Ogras before he did anything. If something seemed too good to be true, it usually was. Zac felt that it was fishy that a large corporation would move their headquarters to a place like Earth. Any newly integrated planet should be quite chaotic and poor and should be a bad place to move your business to.

Perhaps they weren't actually traders, but rather bandits who wanted to gain access to a new world through the outpost and then start a massacre when they arrived. Even if it was an opportunity, he'd forgo it rather than potentially making a fatal mistake. As it was still quite early, Zac decided to get a few hours of sleep while he waited for Ogras. He simply sat down with his back to the furnace and went to sleep with his axe in hand.

After who knew how long, Zac was awakened by a loud sound. Immediately alert, he jumped to his feet, axe at the ready. Soon he relaxed as he saw the now familiar face of the demon outside his array. Ogras seemed content to just stand there and idle about, so Zac ventured outside to meet up with him.

"What are you doing?"

"Basic etiquette not to enter someone's array without permission. It's an easy way to get your head cut off," the demon answered off-handedly. "By the way, impressive work with the little demoness. She's growing a third horn now in her forehead," he added with a snicker.

"Well, tell her I'm sorry about that. Couldn't have her scream after I left. Anyway, I need to ask you something," Zac answered with a shrug, and proceeded to share the window of the Thayer Consortium while explaining his concerns.

"Hmm… Very interesting. You don't have to worry about them being raiders, as the Ruthless Heavens places extremely strict restrictions on those who use the Mercantile System. Even if a shop clerk turned out to be an A-ranker hegemon in disguise, he wouldn't be able to do anything to you," Ogras explained.

"So isn't this a great opportunity, then? They demand quite a bit of space, but that shouldn't be a problem," Zac eagerly asked.

"Well, they are merchants for certain, but there is something wrong with them wanting to come here. They likely are escaping something. It's almost impossible to find a baby world except by going through an incursion, so they are excellent places to hide out in. So if you accept them, you'll likely have a bunch of refugees rather than well-stocked merchants," Ogras explained.

"So kind of like you demons, then?" Zac retorted gruffly, annoyed that the golden opportunity didn't turn out so golden after all.

"Cough… well, something like that. The thing is that if they are forced to flee here, they will likely be barely stocked at all with items and crystals and will have an abysmal support system for acquiring treasures in the Multiverse. Only moving their headquarters here might completely clean them out. So even if you wanted to task them with finding some specific item, they'd probably not be able to help you out."

"So which should I buy? The system-run store or this Thayer Consortium?" Zac didn't understand how the so-called Mercantile System worked, and could only ask for directions for now.

"You should get the headquarters. They are likely desperate for sanctuary and will be extremely weak in negotiations," Ogras said with a ruthless grin. "After all, since you will pretty much be their only customer for a while, you can single-handedly run them out of business if they don't comply."

Zac felt a bit of sympathy for this Thayer company that was forced to escape some unknown hardship, only to be exploited here on demon island. Well, he didn't really have a good time being stuck here, so why should anyone else?

73

FOUNDATIONS OF A CAPITAL

Zac and Ogras walked northbound away from the campsite. If they were going to get a compound full of merchant refugees, they couldn't be too close to the future core of operations of the town. As they walked, Ogras asked about the shipyard, and when he heard that they had somehow transformed to look like humans, he whistled, looking very impressed.

"You didn't know they could do that?" Zac asked, confused.

"Clan Azh'Rezak is a middling family in a D-grade world. The Creators wouldn't normally even step on C-grade worlds, and all the information about them we have is hearsay. Buying a missive on them from one of the information merchants would have bankrupted us from the expense," the demon said defensively, looking unhappy that his image of an omniscient veteran of the Multiverse was crackling.

"Well, now that they are already hidden, wait here a second. Don't mention anything about Creators," Ogras said and rushed into the forest without waiting for a response.

Zac stopped, confused, at his current location, hesitantly looking around. It wasn't a very good spot for an ambush, so he didn't feel too worried about waiting there. But he did bring out his axe just in case.

After a couple of minutes, sounds of footsteps alerted Zac to someone approaching. What made him wary was that it didn't sound like just one person, but a group. Angered at the betrayal, he got ready for a battle as he looked around for a path of escape if needed.

He quickly scaled a tree in order to be able to mount an ambush. His pathways were still a problem, so he would have to finish the battle quickly. Ogras should be the strongest demon still alive, and if he managed to quickly execute him, then the rest shouldn't prove too large a problem.

Soon he saw a group of ten demons walking behind Ogras as they approached his location. They were almost beneath him, and Zac wordlessly jumped down as he infused his axe with the Dao of Heaviness. With a grunt, he swung down toward Ogras' head, aiming to quickly cleave him in two.

"WHAT THE F–" Ogras screamed as he desperately brought out a spear from his pouch. Shadows from all around him gathered into it as he swung it upward to block the incoming axe. The collision of the weapons created a huge shock wave at the level of his battle against the other demon leader, and the group of demons were flung away from the shock wave.

Ogras was slammed into the ground from the impact, but Zac was thrown away as well. The demon had actually managed to defend against his Dao-empowered strike, although not effortlessly, which showed that his title as leader of the demons was not just for show.

Suddenly, the demon melded into the ground and appeared twenty meters further away from Zac. He stood up and angrily pointed his spear at him.

"What the fuck are you doing? Goddamn lunatic!" the demon screamed as he spat out dirt from his mouth.

"It's better to get the first strike when getting ambushed," Zac retorted tersely as he approached the demon.

"Ambush? With these fucking civilians?" Ogras shouted as he waved his spear at the other demons. They had managed to scramble to their feet and looked completely shell-shocked.

Zac stopped his approach, and for the first time, he took a good look at the group. Quickly, he realized that he might have made a mistake. They truly looked like a bunch of weaklings. None of them carried a weapon, and two were actually pretty fat. Every single demon he'd fought so far had been in tip-top shape, even the mages. Even more importantly, the little demoness he'd interrogated yesterday was in the group.

She looked like a deer in headlights, ready to bolt into the woods, but her legs not listening. As Ogras had mentioned, she had a pretty comical bulge in her forehead between her horns from where he'd thwacked her with his axe.

"What's going on? Why did you bring a bunch of people here?" Zac asked, a bit embarrassed, but he still didn't lower his axe. He realized that the last two months had made him too primed for battle, but those were also the habits that had kept him alive.

"Damn it, almost shat my pants…" Ogras muttered as he put the black spear back into his pouch. "Crazy natives. These people are representatives of the various departments needed to properly run a city," he continued as he waved at the group, obviously still quite annoyed. "If you just start throwing out buildings randomly, it's going to look like shit, and problems with things such as infrastructure and sustainable growth will start cropping up as the town grows. These people will help you make a proper town that can be grown all the way into a world capital if needed."

Zac stared mutely at the demons for a second. They looked back with horror at him, no one daring to move an inch, afraid that he would swing his axe at them as well. Zac inwardly groaned, as he had hoped to create a better rapport with the demons now that they were going to work together. But this first impression might have set him back quite a bit in his quest for diplomacy.

"Well, sorry about that; thought you were here to kill me. I'm Zac," he awkwardly greeted the group, wondering where his social skills had gone. Had focusing on Strength turned some of his brain cells into more muscles? His greeting received no response as the group mutely stared at him.

"Uh…" Zac glanced at Ogras, who rolled his eyes.

"Don't stare like some country bumpkins! We have work to do," Ogras snapped, and in the next second, he started taking out a wealth of items.

First, it was a large mat that covered most of the clearing they were in. Next, he placed a rounded oblong table, large enough to fit everyone present, on it. Next followed chairs, and finally, a red canopy covering the whole area from the glaring suns. Clearly the bag in Ogras' possession was far better compared to those Zac had stolen so far.

Zac hesitantly put his axe back into his pouch and sat down on a solitary chair at one of the short sides. Ogras sat down on one of the two chairs that were the closest to him, and what followed was a discreet but energetic melee for the chairs as far as possible from him.

The small demoness was the loser, who could only grit her teeth and take the other chair next to Zac after having been physically bodied away from a more distant chair by one of the fat men. Zac tried to improve the relations by nodding at her, but she stared straight ahead without moving, like a zombie.

After everyone sat down, Ogras summoned glasses and a few jugs of what smelled like liquor and poured himself a drink. The others poured themselves some as well, but were clearly not as comfortable as their leader. Zac declined the offer and instead took out one of his canteens of normal water.

"So, now that everyone is settled, we can discuss the construction of… uh… what name have you chosen for the town?" Ogras asked as he turned toward Zac.

Zac was completely stumped, as he'd never bothered about such a detail while struggling for the last month. Now that the incursion was gone, his temporary outpost was turning into a town. He called this place "demon island" in his mind, but he couldn't name his town that. Maybe something with his name? In case his town got famous and his family heard of it, they might come here. Zachary Town? No. Atwood sounded better for a town. Atwoodtown? Atwoodville? Camp Atwood?

"Port Atwood," he finally said after some hesitation. It had his name, and "Port" was a pretty normal addition to coastal cities, so he felt it sounded pretty neat.

"Hm… Okay. The construction of Port Atwood. You have seen the general area already. Remember, it needs to be defensible within forty days," Ogras said as he rolled out a parchment. It was a surprisingly detailed map of the general area. It had his camp and the harbor marked, and even the large warehouse was drawn out. After scanning it for a few seconds, he knew that it was completely accurate when comparing it to his memories of the area. Of course, the only error was that the details of the harbor were quite indistinct, and nothing was mentioned except the line "shipyard."

Zac wondered how he could have produced such an accurate map in such short order, but he didn't want to make a fool of himself in front of so many people, and could only ask later. The conversation was a bit stilted at the beginning, where Ogras had to drag the words out of the craftsmen's mouths. Zac himself was content to just listen for now, as he realized he had no idea how to build a city.

He had thought that it would be like a strategy game since he possessed the Town Shop. He just bought the buildings, and they produced or did whatever they were designed to do. But as the group started discussing everything from plumbing, to district allocation, to traffic flows and congestion points, he started to zone out.

Between the hard liquor and the fact that Zac kept mostly quiet, the demons started to get more and more animated as they discussed and debated various points, each individual clearly convinced that their specific field was the most important for a burgeoning town's success. Soon an early blueprint for Port Atwood was starting to take shape, with Ogras pushing things forward.

The general idea for the beginning was to create four zones. The inner zone was to be a walled-off area belonging to Zac alone. It would also encircle the shipyard, with walls going down to the water a few hundred meters to both sides of it. Another wall would be erected between Zac's camp and the shipyard. Ogras explained it was to protect the Lord's manor against naval attacks, but Zac knew it mainly was to keep the Creators separated.

Outside the core area, three zones would be established. The first was on the southwest side of the core, expanding alongside the wall all the way down to the water. It would be the trade zone where merchants and craftsmen had their headquarters.

On the other side of the core zone would be the military encampment. Zac was confused, as he didn't have an army, but let them go ahead with the plans anyway. Having an army would be convenient, as that meant he wouldn't have to spend as much on defensive arrays. And if he became a real Lord, there actually might be a time when he had a proper army.

The central area would be residential, with some businesses such as bars and bathhouses peppered in, and it would be connected with the mercantile zone with a large square. Most space around the square was earmarked for various key institutions, such as an auction house and a bank, which Zac didn't qualify to own yet.

They even allocated a large space for an academy. After asking, he realized it wasn't like a school on the old Earth, but rather to help the students to get a class they wished for and guide them with their cultivation. This was something very interesting to Zac, who had just fumbled around when he got his class choices.

He was already getting bored with the discussion about the town construction and set his eye on the demon who appeared to represent the field of education.

74

CLASSES, CULTIVATION, AND OLD HEGEMONS

It turned out that actions truly influenced the available Class choices. After some hesitation, a slender demoness in charge of education started explaining the mechanics behind classes, quickly finding her confidence after entering lecturing mode.

"The Ruthless Heavens allow you to start progressing on the path of cultivation starting at the age of sixteen for both humans and demons, but it varies between species. Many forces are able to bring up the levels of their young to 25 in a day with various pills and Nexus Crystals, so preparation before they officially enter the path of cultivation is necessary. An academy prepares the young generation and helps them attain the Class they wish for, or at least have the most aptitude for," the schoolmistress started to explain.

"If they want to become a Sword Master, they will have to arduously train with their sword, and physically train their natural attributes to the peak. If they wish to become a magic user, it's a bit more complicated, but essentially they have to study the elements and learn all they can about Cosmic Energy. Craftsmen classes are best gained by apprenticing themselves to someone," she said.

It was as Zac had assumed. His classes were largely based on his actions, and it was possible to influence the options the System gave. But it seemed unlikely that too good a class could be attained from just swinging a sword around within the safety of the school.

"What rarity of the classes do the students get this way?"

"It depends on the grade of the school. Normally, only Common classes can be attained at an academy, with one or two lucky students out of a thousand getting an Uncommon one. Out in the Multiverse, there are far greater academies that have curriculums that can guarantee Uncommon classes, and even give a decent chance for a Rare one," she said as her eyes glistened, obviously yearning to visit such a place.

"Besides, if the youth accomplishes great things after becoming sixteen years old, instead of rushing to level 25, they can improve their chances to get a better class."

"Still, being stuck with a Common class doesn't seem too great, no? Won't it negatively influence their future?"

"Getting Common classes is by far the most common starting choice in C-graded to E-graded worlds. Classes like Warrior or Swordman have a multitude of well-documented advancements paths. For example, it is well known that a Warrior can advance to an E-graded Uncommon Champion. They can also advance to E-graded Uncommon Captain, then D-graded Uncommon General" she explained, getting more and more animated as she started looking at Zac less as an axe-wielding lunatic and more like a student.

"They won't get as many attribute points or as good skills as someone who gets a Rare or even Epic class in the start. But the requirements for each advancement is well-documented, giving cultivators a clear and unimpeded path of progression. The Multiverse has an endless amount of classes, and only a small part of them is public knowledge. Many promising youths have had their path of progression cut short since they got an unknown Rare class and weren't able to progress it."

Zac found all of this very illuminating and decided to have this teacher accompany him into the mines to keep his education going while he tried to get his pathways repaired.

"If the Multiverse contains endless classes, why did so many of your kind seem to have the same class?" Zac probed, his memories slightly clashing with the teacher's explanation of the class system. For example, there had generally been three types of mages: earth, lightning, and fire. But no demon mage seemed to use wind, ice, gravity or any other types.

The demoness slightly hesitated and looked at Ogras for instructions. He shrugged and continued the explanation himself.

"It's called Heritage," he said. "The progression paths are public knowledge, but the details are fiercely guarded secrets. Those classes that Alyn mentioned are public knowledge, but the exact method to advance past E-grade is not. Clan Azh'Rezak has bought guides that explain the progression to E-grade Uncommon for over a dozen classes, but only had two clear paths to reach D-rank."

"Buying a full progression path from F to D with all required attributes, Dao requirements, and hidden requirements is costly enough to set back a D-ranked force quite a bit. So most only have one or two, and they are the foundation of the clan. Clan Azh'Rezak has the progression path of Lightning Warrior, which evolves into Tempest Warrior, and finally, Stormblade. It's a mix of lightning magic and bladed weapons. Rydel followed this path, for example, and only the main branch of our clan is allowed to progress on this class path," the demon continued, and Zac immediately remembered the three demons he had killed whose skills contained the dreadful black lightning.

"The stronger the Heritage of a clan, the greater its prospects. The more and better progression paths, cultivation techniques, hidden titles, access to hidden pocket-worlds, and unique cultivation resources a force has, the better the Heritage is.

"Of course, the stronger Heritage you have, the more attractive a target you become, and wars are constantly fought across the Multiverse to snatch Heritages," Ogras said. "The greatest forces in the Multiverse are said to have progression paths all the way to at least B-rank, making their Heritage an unimaginable treasure," he finished, with yearning in his eyes talking about those lofty clans.

"And how does cultivation fit into all of this?" Zac continued. This was one of the most confusing things for him so far. From Abby, it seemed that cultivation was extremely important, but so far, he had progressed just fine without being able to cultivate.

"Cultivation has various benefits. First, it improves your advancement speed in levels. At a certain point, one can forego sleep completely and instead cultivate, making it possible to ceaselessly progress levels. At low levels, it doesn't make a large difference, but at high levels, a single level can take a year or more, and at this point, the difference starts to show."

The schoolmistress Alyn picked up again. "Secondly, cultivation doesn't only improve levels; it also improves our very foundations. It can improve our very beings over time. Essentially, it can help evolve our races, which is the biggest difference between a cultivator and a mortal," she said.

"Most mortals are forever stuck at F-grade Classes, since they can't afford the means to evolve into an E-rank Race. Advancing the Race is the most basic requirement for any class advancement, and no matter the Dao enlightenment or titles, without an advanced Race, you simply will not progress. And as mortals progress, it becomes unimaginably hard to find the treasures to keep their advancement going."

"Finally, cultivators can increase their combat power compared to a mortal if they have a suitable cultivation method.

Say the cultivator is a Pyromancer Class. If she has a fire-attributed cultivation technique, her attacks will get even fiercer. Conversely, if she use a water-based cultivation technique, she might get weaker or even hurt herself over time."

Zac finally understood how classes worked in the Multiverse and was a bit troubled that he seemed to have gone down a harder path. His Rare class was a boon in the form of giving good skills and extra stats, but it seemed it was far harder to progress compared to the normal classes.

Even worse, it seemed that getting stronger truly was easier for cultivators. It would become harder and harder to keep his lead, it seemed, as time went on. At least he had caught a lucky break snatching up a Fruit of Ascension, solving the issue of his race for now. Still, he would have to find new treasures to keep advancing, whereas the cultivators could just, well, cultivate.

"Can a mortal become a cultivator?" Zac asked, as that would solve his issues easily. Besides, Abby had said only 10% of the population of Earth was able to become cultivators, so most earthlings could benefit from turning into cultivators. Alyn seemed to hesitate a bit before answering.

"Perhaps. It is said that mortals will automatically become able to cultivate when they reach a certain power level. But I am not sure whether it is true. Some say it is at C-rank, others at B-rank. Some say it's just a hoax to give mortals false hope. I only know it's not possible at D-rank or lower," she said. "There are a few treasures able to turn a mortal into a cultivator, though, but they are so rare, they might as well be rumors as well," Alyn then added after some thought.

"Those treasures are real but unfathomably rare. One was put up for auction on one of the core planets of our horde fifty thousand years ago and hasn't been seen since. When it arrived, it created a bloody storm that impacted the whole world. Besides, getting one of them can be a death trap. There are so many old monsters in the Multiverse that have a grandson or granddaughter who can't cultivate for some reason. They are fine with slaughtering a whole country to snatch the treasure for their kin, making it extremely dangerous to own it," Ogras added.

"There even was an old hegemon who went to war with a ruling family of a B-ranked planet just to get a supreme treasure that would allow his beloved pet to become a sentient god-beast. Billions of lives were lost because of that stupid mutt," the demon then said, his mouth curving slightly upward.

"What happened?" Zac asked, intrigued.

"The hegemon essentially destroyed the world and took the treasure. The mutt became a god-beast, and over tens of thousands of years, started to rival even its old master in power. Soon the beast could transform into humanoid form, and it had the appearance of a stunning woman. The old master actually fell in love and wanted to marry his old pet, but the god-beast didn't reciprocate his feelings.

"Mad with rage that he was rebuffed after all he had done for her, he immediately tried to kill her. It backfired spectacularly, and the beast was victorious after an earth-shaking battle. Now she is a hegemon herself and the leader of a grand beast world. It is one of the most famous stories about the dangers of owning too valuable treasures," Ogras narrated with a sneer, obviously considering the old master a true idiot.

Zac almost laughed out loud when he heard the story, and said a silent prayer for the old master. More importantly, it seemed it was possible for him to become a cultivator in the future. Of course, it seemed impossibly hard, but he had time and a huge amount of Luck. Not wanting to hold up the meeting any longer with this tangent, he changed the subject.

"What about the defenses of the town? The monster hordes are coming soon."

This was what mattered the most to Zac right now. The town

needed to be standing at least until he could buy a teleporter or a cosmic ship so he could finally start his search for his family. And if possible, he wanted to defend Port Atwood from the incoming animals in order to turn his island both into a sanctuary and bastion.

75

GAMING THE SYSTEM

The demons were aware of Zac's quest and started discussing various means of defense. They soon came to an agreement that it wouldn't be possible to complete an outer wall in the duration that remained until the first horde arrived, and they would have to focus on the inner wall instead.

Zac was a bit skeptical, as he knew the whole wall around their own town had been erected in just a few days' time. Were they holding back on him? However, it was soon explained that the whole force had come together and immediately fortified their position when they arrived at the island. Now they were left with only a tenth of their force, and almost all the earth mages who had been instrumental to the construction were either dead or back in their home world.

"What is the point of the wall anyhow? I could easily scale your wall in seconds. I can just buy a defensive array instead," Zac probed, wondering if all the work of erecting walls was even worth it.

"Defensive arrays need power to run. If no one or just a few assailants are attacking, the ambient energy is enough. But as soon as it comes under attack, either cultivators or crystals are needed to provide energy to keep the shield active. Imagine ten thousand beasts simultaneously clawing and ramming their bodies into the shield. The energy consumption would be terrifying, and you'd become broke after a few weeks of maintaining it," Ogras replied. "Walls are cheap and effective below E-rank. They are the first line of defense that is easily replaceable and provide a vantage where we can grind down the enemy forces before even wasting a single crystal on maintaining an array. Only if they break through the walls will we need to spend resources on maintaining the arrays."

"What about the merchant headquarters? According to the blueprint, the compound will be placed outside the inner wall." While Zac was no angel, he didn't want to summon the poor traders just to be eaten by monsters in a month. He wasn't that cruel.

"Many structures provided by the Ruthless Heavens have certain protections in place. It will automatically be protected like the Tree of Ascension was," Ogras explained, which reminded Zac about the impenetrable shield that had covered the tree while the fruits were ripening.

"Can't we just hide inside there, then?" Zac asked. Having a safe spot where nothing could harm him would be extremely convenient while assaulted by a sea of monsters.

"We can enter and leave, but only during business hours if we're not members. And no, we can't just become temporary members during the beast horde attacks." Ogras ruthlessly crushed Zac's hopes. "Also, that protection only applies to buildings connected to the Mercantile System, so nothing else you build will be safe. The horde's main targets will be you and the Nexus Node, and everything impeding its path will be destroyed. Trying to exploit various loopholes such as surrounding your camp with protected merchant shops won't work either. Everything has been tested over time, and the loopholes have been fixed by the Ruthless Heavens billions of years ago. "

In the end, they decided to focus on erecting a wall around Zac's camp. The radius of the wall was to be five hundred meters, giving Zac a huge personal area to build a proper home in the future. Medium-scale arrays would also fit properly inside a fortification of that size.

Parts of the wall were only temporary, since the main plan was for the walls to go all the way down to the water in the future. For specific arrays, they held off for the moment, since they didn't know the amount of Nexus coins they'd be able to scrounge together before the first wave appeared.

Content with the results, Ogras dismissed the others to speak to Zac privately. They decided that Ogras would travel between demon town and Port Atwood to keep both the mining efforts going and oversee the construction of the wall. Zac would head to the mines to try to restore his pathways and excavate as many crystals as possible.

Before they left, Zac showed Ogras the screen for the Forester's Constitution skill after some hesitation. It was still stuck on (8/30), and Zac explained the situation.

Forester's Constitution (Class): Fight in the forests, be one with nature. Reward: Forester's Constitution Skill. (8/30).

Yesterday, Ogras had told him how he'd managed to speak to Zac on the mountaintop. He also explained how Zac had finished the quest, even though Ogras as the general was still alive. Before the completion of the incursion quest, Ogras wouldn't be able to speak to Zac, even if he had the translation skill. The System wouldn't let communication happen between natives and invaders until one side was defeated, as it didn't want to see any peaceful solution. Therefore, the completion of the quest was necessary.

It was the first pill the demon had swallowed right after killing Rydel that made it happen. The pill was actually called **[The**

Coward's Escape] and truly killed the user for a short duration. It was a tool for escaping various situations that would only end with either death or success, such as inheritance sites or being the target of a quest.

It would complete any quests that demanded his death and often even teleport him, the "corpse," out of the inheritance site. The downside of the pill was that all active quests were considered forfeited upon death, so using it could be extremely detrimental if you had an important quest active. It was also the reason Zac didn't get 100% contribution upon finishing his quest, as the last target had killed himself.

Obviously, Ogras had some experience in exploiting the rigid system, and Zac needed some of that ingenuity. He was strapped for time but wanted to complete his constitution quest before the beast horde arrived. But he also needed to stay in the mines with its high concentration of energy in order to heal his body broken by the Cosmic Water.

He would have used the mountain valley for both purposes if it hadn't been turned into a poisoned hellhole after the forest fires and poison clouds made it uninhabitable. Ogras had explained with some embarrassment that it could take months before it was possible to get back up there.

"From the description, it is either a Seed-quest that gives you a vision for a Dao Seed, or it requires a Dao Seed connected to nature. Perhaps Seed of Grass or Seed of Trees."

"Not Seed of Nature or Seed of Earth?" Zac asked skeptically. Seed of Trees did not seem very impressive.

"The Dao of Nature and Earth are high-tiered Daos, and not something you can touch," Ogras sneered derisively. "I've never heard of this skill. What class did you say you had?"

Zac ignored him and waited for the demon to provide some solution instead.

Seeing that Zac didn't intend to answer, Ogras could only

mutter something and continue. "Fight in the forest is very vague, and you can probably exploit it. What constitutes a forest, and what constitutes a fight? If you want to complete it without wasting too much time, we need to do two things. First, find the spot closest to the mines that the Ruthless Heavens considers forest. Second, find out how often you need to kill something to be considered in battle," he said as he was tapping the table with his hand.

"You said you were steadily gaining progression when you fought the barghest even though you instantly killed them, so there is an allowed downtime. Find out how long it is, and if it is long enough, you can easily exploit it. Simply have someone drag a barghest to the forest spot and run out of the mine and kill it. Then run back in and continue mining. If you're lucky, you will only need something like five to ten minutes of travel time per kill and can spend the rest on mining and focusing on recuperation."

Zac was stunned. He would never have thought of that method and was glad he'd confided in the demon. He was a shady character but could also be very useful. And Ogras didn't know it, but his solution would also help him progress his other class skill for **[Loamwalker]** through all the running.

There was only one thing more to do before he headed toward the caves, and that was to buy the **[Thayer Consortium Headquarters]** and have them start buying his crystals. It was obvious that they were desperate to be bought, as they cost a fraction compared to most others for buying the building in the Town Shop, and Zac didn't want anyone else snatching the building up before he did.

Zac and Ogras moved toward where the large merchant compound was to be located. It was quite far from both his camp and the shipyard, with only trees and stones around. After a double-check, Zac opened up the Town Shop and bought the headquarters.

Soon changes to the area started appearing just as with the creation of the shipyard. Trees and rocks disappeared, and replacing them were gravel and cobblestones. Soon structures appeared as well, one by one sprouting up like mushrooms out of the ground. But that was where the similarities with the shipyard ended.

The Creator structures were crafted with meticulous care, looking pristine with mighty fractals covering every inch. But what appeared in front of the duo could almost be called a ghetto. The buildings were a mix of stone and wood structures that once might have been proper structures. But the houses looked like they had been abandoned and then put through decades of harsh weather.

There were broken windows, mold, tiles missing, and they could even spot a few buildings where a wall had simply collapsed. No fractals covered anything, and Zac was actually loath to enter most of the buildings from safety concerns. The only building that looked to be in decent order was also the largest one. It was a three-story building where each floor should have an area of roughly a thousand square meters, and if Zac had to guess, it was the actual store for the Thayer Consortium. The other structures should be warehouses, support buildings, and homes for the employees.

"What is this shantytown?" Ogras asked in shock. "You may just have enlisted the worst merchants in the Multiverse. I can't believe how poor they look."

Zac was very much inclined to agree. The goal of merchants was to amass wealth, just like the goal of a cultivator was to get stronger. Judging by the state of disrepair of the structures, he could only assume the Thayer Consortium was really incompetent at their job.

But there was nothing to do, there was no refund button in the Town Shop, and they could only suppress their misgivings and enter the shop. The inside was slightly better than the outside, and at least everything was spotlessly clean. It was the store as Zac expected, but it reminded him of a struggling convenience store with mostly empty shelves.

There were a few pieces of equipment in various racks, but they looked worse compared to the ones the demons used. There also were a few information crystals behind glass displays, but the displays weren't even a quarter full. In some corners, various materials were sold, and there also were some herbs and plants, though they all looked a bit dried out.

Manning the desk were a few humanoids that somewhat reminded Zac of gnomes. They were less than a meter tall but didn't have the stockiness, or beardiness, of dwarves. Their skin was also light blue and they had deep sapphire-colored eyes, with pointed ears like elves. Perhaps they were genies?

Before Zac and Ogras could approach the clerks, another genie came running toward the two. He looked much like the others, with the blue skin and no hair. He wore what looked like an old-fashioned suit and had an ascot tied around his neck.

"Greetings, honored customers, I am Calrin Thayer, chairman of the Thayer Consortium. Excuse the slight disarray; we are currently setting everything up. Can I presume one of you is the distinguished Lord?"

76

BUSINESS TACTICS

Calrin looked over the reports and agreements strewn on his table, his feelings not much better compared to when he was holed up waiting for the Tsarun Clan to hunt him down. He had cried in relief when someone finally purchased their headquarters, the window with the teleportation prompt looking like a writ of amnesty.

He had thought that the Thayer Consortium would be able to slowly regroup and recover on this new world. The newly integrated planets and continents were filled with valuables that needed a buyer, and the natives seldom knew the worth of what they held in their hands. A single trade could result in a profit that would cover expenses for months.

But who would've expected that they got placed on a deserted island instead of some burgeoning town? Apart from a shipyard, there wasn't a single building, and the Merchant's Window showed that Port Atwood, as the presumptive town was called, only housed one solitary citizen, its Lord.

Worse yet was the Lord's companion, the System-blasted demon. For a second, Calrin was ecstatic when he heard that the

Lord controlled an actual Nexus Crystal mine. That meant there was a Nexus Vein on the island, and sooner or later, things like farms with valuable plants would pop up. Even cultivators would relocate here for the high density of energy, which would only help business further.

Until then, he would be able to turn a tidy profit buying the crystals and reselling them through the Mercantile System. A native had no idea of the value of things, and if they added a larger margin, who would know?

But that demon wasn't actually a native, but a defected invader. He ruthlessly started to pressure down the profit margins to a razor's edge, even threatening them with a trade embargo. He obviously had a general idea of the Thayer Consortium's situation and knew that if they didn't produce some profit and turnover, the System would rescind their business license.

Gone were the dreams of a mighty comeback, replaced with a nightmare of toiling under a demonic taskmaster for little to no profits.

Zac was quite happy with the result of the negotiations as he moved through the forest. Ogras kept proving his worth as a teammate. The little genie, whose race was actually called Sky Gnomes, made a big production of support and mutual cooperation after he heard about the Nexus Crystal mine. After almost wiping away a tear of self-sacrifice, he offered the most generous price of 35 Nexus Coins per crystal.

The price seemed to have awoken a dragon in Ogras, and he started making a scene. It turned out that the value of a crystal was actually closer to 50 Nexus Coins, and after subtracting transaction costs for using the Mercantile System and some profit for the merchant, the crystals were generally bought for 44 to 46 coins at most merchant shops. The price-gouging System-run stores only gave 35 coins, though, and it seemed that the gnome had planned on offering the same price and pocketing the difference.

What followed was an almost surreal exchange between the gnome and the demon, where the demon initially wanted to get 54 coins per crystal, forcing the trading firm to eat a loss for each trade.

The gnome tried every trick in the book to keep the prices reasonable in order to make some profit. At one point, he had even tearfully ordered one of the clerks to fetch a noose, as he said he would "rather hang himself than keep suffering this kind of injustice." Not long after, the noose was long forgotten, and instead, the chairman paraded two little gnome children in front of Zac and the Ogras.

They were some of the cutest things Zac had ever seen, but they were wearing frayed clothing and looked hungry with large puppy-dog eyes. Zac was tempted to stop the demon at this point, but Ogras waved him away and ruthlessly pushed forward. Zac did, however, spot the demon surreptitiously place candies in each of the kids' hands, without pausing in his screaming contest with Calrin.

Ogras' trade tactic was simpler, as it was just a long stream of threats, insults, and angry gestures. He tried everything from threatening to fill the area with competing businesses to enacting trade embargoes on the Sky Gnomes.

Finally, the price they agreed upon was 47 Nexus Coins per refined crystal, a rate that obviously was one of the best one could get without selling them directly to a customer who needed them. Both Ogras and Calrin were heaving and sweating at this point, looking like they had just finished an arduous battle. Zac quickly handed over 11,000 crystals and immediately received 517,000 Nexus Coins in return.

Next, Zac asked about a pill that could help with his situation with his pathways, but as expected, the little gnome had nothing of that quality in the store. He did, however, promise to acquire one through his channels, but it didn't look like he even believed himself.

Content, Zac and Ogras left, as there wasn't much else of value to buy in the shop. Besides, both of them were suffering from a lack of funds at the moment. Ogras told him that the System had confiscated all the demons' Nexus Coins when they stayed on Earth, but Zac wasn't convinced. After watching the previous display, he was more inclined to believe that he simply refused to expose any hidden wealth.

Not long after they were done at the consortium, they parted ways, with Ogras heading to the camp to start converting more raw crystals he had "found" in the town. Meanwhile, Zac headed toward the mines to start mining himself while staying in the energy-rich atmosphere of the tunnels. Ogras estimated the daily turnover from the mine to be roughly 5,000 crystals now that most of the demons were gone and they were short on manpower.

That meant that together with whatever Zac managed to excavate, the daily Nexus Coin gain would be roughly 250,000. It didn't seem like too much compared to the prices of some of the structures in the Town Shop, but it was a steady source of wealth that could be increased as soon as more citizens arrived. And judging from the tunnels he had walked through before, the crystals would last for years.

That meant that before the horde arrived, he would be able to afford the **[E-Grade Medium-Scale Town Defense Array]** he had spotted earlier for 5 million Nexus Coins, and even add in some more fortifications.

After walking for half a day and killing a barghest every now and then, Zac finally reached the mines once again. Less than two days had actually passed since he last was here, but it felt like much longer for some reason.

After walking some distance into the tunnels, he felt the air had filled up to the density of Cosmic Energy that suffused the depths, and going any further wouldn't make the environment any better. Unless he went to that cave he woke up in, but it was too far into the mountain for convenience.

Thus began Zac's monotonous days down in the mines. On the first day, he only focused on recuperation and seeing whether staying here actually helped with his situation. He expended some Cosmic Energy by using the guidance system, and was ecstatic to notice that he actually recovered quicker here when compared to at his camp. It looked like the demon had told the truth. The difference was small, though, but it gave Zac some hope.

The following day, he retrieved Alyn, enlisting her as a private teacher to go through various subjects about the System, cultivation, and the Multiverse. Every time he paused after having furiously whacked at the mines for a few hours, they would go over some subject. Alyn also helped him recruit a few ranger demons who would lead a barghest to a patch of grass next to the mine entrance. It was the closest spot that the System considered a forest, and killing a beast there did advance his quest.

After two days of trials, he learned that he only needed to kill a monster every hour, and then that whole hour would be considered as "fighting in the forest." After that, his daily life took on a very structured schedule.

He'd mine for roughly forty-five minutes, then run out of the caves to kill a barghest. After running back to his mine shaft, he'd have a mini-lecture of five minutes with Alyn while he had a small break before starting mining again. He felt a bit bad for the demoness having to just fiddle around for fifty-five minutes an hour, but she seemed perfectly content taking out a book and reading on a comfortable couch. And Zac guessed it beat toiling to erect a wall.

On the fourth day, Zac got ten axes identical to the two he had from a scared-looking demon. It looked like it would take some time until they warmed up to him. He didn't want to use other weapons even while mining, and instead used his weapon of choice. His mining wasn't only for gaining wealth, but also to improve his proficiency with his axes.

Every time he hit the wall, no matter if it was with the edge, the spike, or the butt, he tried to remember the trajectories and methods that he'd learned from the guidance system. He had realized that while blindly following the paths had made him stronger, there was a limit. If he wanted to truly improve, he needed to internalize the teachings and understand *why* he swung like he did.

He realized that just some small differences in how he applied force, or a slight change in angle on impact, could have a huge difference in how much rock he managed to cut. As Zac progressed through the days, more and more rock started to gather at his feet. His furious assault on the mountain walls kept damaging the axes, and he was forced to keep circulating them and let the old ones rest.

As time passed, he felt that his pathways were truly slowly healing, as every day he could sense his recovery speed had increased a bit. Still, the improvement was very limited, and he wasn't sure if he'd make it in time for the beast horde.

If he had to point out one negative about his current lifestyle, it was the complete and utter lack of progression in levels. He'd unequipped his amulet long ago, and the few barghest he killed per day could barely move his level forward.

Zac had simply run out of targets on the island. The demons and their beast hordes were some sort of allies by now, leaving only the small critters in the forest. There also were the salamanders, but those huge lumbering beasts were too few and far between to actually be an effective target for improving further.

He knew that he would likely get more targets than he could wish for as soon as the beast hordes arrived, but it clearly showed the long-term problem that he had outgrown the island. If he wanted to improve further, he needed to venture out into the world.

77

WHAT IS THE SYSTEM?

Zac was wiping off some sweat as he sat down on a small stool. He had been mining and running back and forth between the tunnels and the plot of forest for over six hours and needed a break. This was the ninth day in the mines, and his speed of accruing crystals had progressed greatly as his mastery with his axes improved. He brought out a canteen of water and some food as he looked over to his companion in the tunnel.

Alyn was sitting in a comfortable chair, reading a book at the moment, seemingly unaware of the clangor in the tunnels. She had been extremely uncomfortable being left alone with him in the beginning but was starting to warm up to him a bit, it seemed. Zac unceasingly peppered her with questions about various aspects of the System during every break he took, and instead of being annoyed like Ogras, she seemed to be very much in favor of his thirst for knowledge.

"So you've explained so many things about the System to me. But you haven't explained what the System itself is. Does anyone know?" Zac probed.

The demoness put down her book and looked over to Zac.

"I was wondering when you were going to ask. In fact, almost everyone knows what the System, as you call it, is and how it came to be. It is no secret. But to explain that, you first need to know about the Ancient Empire," she said, quickly going into lecturing mode. "It is also commonly referred to as the Limitless Empire.

"Billions of years ago, the System did not exist. Instead, cultivators strove for immortality by cultivating the Dao without any guidance, windows, attributes, or prompts. They used their cultivation techniques to gather the spiritual energy in the cosmos, and improved by reaching higher and higher cultivation stages.

"In this ancient era, there existed an endlessly powerful empire, which stood on top of the cultivation world for hundreds of millions of years. It spread over myriad worlds in the universe and unceasingly kept expanding. Leading this great nation was a man called Emperor Limitless. He was said to have reached the peak of cultivation, and many still consider him the strongest being to have ever existed. Of course, many also believe that the System has allowed the powerhouses of the Multiverse to reach further heights compared to the ancient cultivators.

"Emperor Limitless had already reached the peak of cultivation long ago and instead set his boundless ambition upon his empire. His goal was to turn all creation into his empire, to control all life in existence.

"Therefore, he waged wars, fighting for millions of years, the empire ever expanding. The battlefields grew more numerous, and the empire actually started to run out of soldiers. Trillions of lives were lost in the battle across millions of worlds, and the empire had problems producing new powerful warriors. Almost all cultivators were forced into the battle, leaving few competent teachers behind to train the next generation.

"Emperor Limitless and a few of his closest generals and magistrates came up with a daring solution. They wished to create a synthetic being that would connect with every single cultivator in the empire and train them into strong warriors. A cosmic teacher that would lead the empire to further heights, as no potential genius would go unnoticed, and no cultivator would train inefficiently due to bad teachings.

"The creation of this entity took an astounding time, and everyone who worked on the project died, generation after generation, from old age, except Emperor Limitless with his almost infinite longevity. The resources that were poured into the project can't even be calculated, and just a small fraction of it would cause a bloody storm to erupt, even on an A-ranked continent.

"But finally, they were done. The last step was to activate it and attach it to the Heavenly Dao itself, allowing it to spread to all space. Billions and billions of the strongest of the Ancient Empire gathered at their main continent, and together infused this construct larger than a sun with energy.

"The activation was a success, and the cosmic being spoke its first words to the world."

"What words did it say?" Zac interjected, entranced by the story.

"'Insufficient energy.' Those were the first two words of the System, and every cultivator in existence heard it. What followed were the Dark Ages.

"Something had gone horribly wrong with the being, and it forcefully started absorbing energy. First the cultivators who were part of the activation were absorbed until they died. Even the emperor was almost killed. He escaped after paying a terrible price, but the System wasn't done and started absorbing the ambient energy from the universe.

"The absorption continued, and soon once glorious cultivation havens were turned into wastelands due to lack of spiritual energy. Even worse, the Dao of the Heavens had somehow become clouded, and progression on the path of cultivation became impossibly hard. All the powerhouses in the Multiverse were furious, as Emperor Limitless' experiment essentially cut off their path of progression.

"With the empire being weakened and all forces banding together, the Ancient Empire crumbled. Emperor Limitless was slain as well, as the System had stolen most of his power already. The chaotic times continued for a million years, and the sparse energy and obscured Dao became the new norm. Emperor Limitless was remembered as the sinner of the world of cultivation.

"But one day, it all changed. Energy came flooding back into the universe, and all cultivators once more heard the voice. This time, it said, 'Initiation complete.' After over a million years, the System had completed all the preparations, and then it started to actually diligently fulfill its purpose. It opened the path of progression again and started to train warriors and powerhouses. All cultivators who resided on planets that once were part of the Ancient Empire got integrated with the System, just like you and me.

"It soon became clear that many things had changed, as the System had constrained and categorized the myriad Dao itself. Gone were the cultivation levels and cultivation through meridians, and instead empowering through levels was introduced.

"The fact that the Dao was usurped is why a few factions in the Multiverse, such as the Technocrats, call the System 'the Cosmic Warden.' They believe that by constraining the Dao, it has cut off the avenue for new Daos, such as the Dao of Technology or the Dao of Guns, to emerge. Their goal is to destroy the System, and, in their words, 'free the Dao.' Other factions consider the System the liberator of the Multiverse, though, and are stuck in a perpetual war with the Technocrats," Alyn animatedly explained.

The fact that the System was an ancient training system gone haywire seemed like a huge cosmic joke to Zac. An almost endless number of beings had been affected because this Ancient

Empire wanted to streamline their war efforts. But at least it explained why it wanted people to struggle and take risks. Its very purpose was to create strong warriors and even powerhouses, and those could only be born through battle and hardship.

"So why did the System integrate Earth? If the System is only supposed to be a training system for this Ancient Empire, why bring us into the mix? Was Earth part of the Ancient Empire?" Zac asked.

"No. Earth isn't even in the same universe as the Ancient Empire was located. The System not only fulfilled its purpose by training warriors, it also somehow inherited the goal of Emperor Limitless. Since the System's birth all that time ago, it has kept expanding. After a while, it spread to the whole universe it resided in, and soon after, it started finding new ones to spread its influence into. Since then, it has kept ceaselessly expanding.

"Of course, this is just the most generally accepted theory of the System's origin. The reason that it's taken as the truth is that it is the history that is taught by System's pixies in the Tutorial of all newly integrated worlds. There are some who believe that the System hides its true origins for some sinister purpose, but such things are far beyond us small F-rank individuals.

"The exact details can't be confirmed for certain, as it happened in another universe an impossibly long time ago. We do, however, know that the Ancient Empire was real, and that it was ruled by an Emperor Limitless. There are multiple historic remains from the empire, and there are many collectors of relics from that long-lost time."

Zac was truly in awe of the power of this synthetic being spreading through whole universes with nothing being able to stop it. At least if what Alyn said was true, Zac didn't feel that the System was either good or evil. It was just an impossibly powerful AI let loose, eternally fulfilling its purpose. Unfortunately for Earth, that meant that it would throw the planet into struggle, heedless of the cost in lives. As long as strong warriors were created out of the turmoil, the System was happy.

He briefly thought about the Technocrats. They had to be truly brave or true lunatics to want to fight against the System. It was like going to war against the basic rules of the universe by this point, like trying to fight Death or Time.

It seemed that there were some parts missing from Alyn's explanation, though. From her description, it seemed that the System was designed to train and strengthen cultivators for the Ancient Empire. But the System did much more than that. It also helped mortals become stronger, and it also seemed to work with beasts somehow.

It even had side features such as the Town Shop and the Mercantile System, which enabled trade over the vast distances of the Multiverse. And that was just what Zac had discovered so far in the scant two months since being introduced to it. Perhaps there were even more functions that waited to be discovered.

"How come the System affects all beings, then, like mortals and even beasts? Didn't you say it was designed to train cultivators?" Zac probed.

"Good question. It is as you said: the System initially only trained cultivators, and only those able to cultivate were connected to the System. But the System has changed a few times throughout history, each change disrupting the way of life in the Multiverse. To understand these changes, we must talk about the Apostates. Those scant few who managed to throw the laws of the universe out the window and bend reality to their wills.

"The number of Apostates who have emerged since the System was created can be counted on two hands. Each was a being of unlimited power who actually managed to change the way the System operates. Very little is known about the first Apostate, not even his name. He is simply known as 'the First Defier.'"

78

THE APOSTATES

The subject of the origin of the System was very interesting to Zac. He had a hard time imagining an empire strong enough that it dared to wage war against a whole universe, and an individual powerful enough to change the basic rules of the universe by creating the System. Just a glance of someone like Emperor Limitless was probably enough to blast him into molecules.

The subject of Apostates also piqued his interest to the point that he actually put down his axe and decided to keep listening instead of resuming his mining operations.

"So you mean that these so-called Apostates managed to actually change how the System worked?" he asked, intrigued.

"The actual reasons are quite unclear. Some believe that the System rewards the Apostates for reaching the peak of their path by letting them design or change aspects of how it operates. Other say that they reached such a height that their ideals and convictions shape reality itself, and the System was forced to comply. None of the Apostate has actually broached the subject to tell us what the truth is," Alyn answered.

"Are they still alive?" Zac probed.

"It's not clear, at least not to us in lowly D-ranked worlds. From what has been passed down through the Multiverse, the last Apostate and change happened roughly 880 million years ago. Even with the enormous longevity of such supreme beings, they shouldn't be alive unless immortality is real. Besides, the Apostates reportedly disappeared roughly at the same time the change they brought to the System appeared. That's why a third theory for the change is that the Apostates actually merged with the System."

Zac felt it was reasonable that even the schoolmistress didn't have all the answers. These were the top characters in the Multiverse, and there should be many hidden things behind the curtains that the general population wasn't qualified to know.

"So what changes did they bring?"

"Well, we can begin with the latest Apostate. He is called the Apostate of Greed, but his real name was Orlan Stillsun. His contribution was the Mercantile System that Calrin and all other merchant organizations use. He was a progenitor of a planet, just like you, and rose to the peak in only a few dozens of millennia.

"But his class wasn't combat-oriented, and there are very few mentions of him ever battling. The peak he rose to was through business, and his company is still around today, even though he is not. Being able to get a Stillsun Family shop in your lordship is one of the greatest signs of your status in the Multiverse. Of course, they would never open a branch on a D-ranked world, as they still are one of the most powerful entities in the Multiverse.

"His accomplishments were only possible because of the Apostate of Mercy. I have no real knowledge of her, and I don't even know if there is a family line that can trace to her like the Apostate of Greed. She reportedly felt sorry for the myriad people in the Multiverse being forced into conflict. In her era, all classes were combat-oriented, and the only method to get stronger was to fight and kill.

"She enabled the noncombat class system, also known as the craftsman class system. Thanks to her, it is possible to gain levels and improve classes without having to risk your life in constant battle. Of course, the craftsmen need to still arduously improve and practice their craft to gain Cosmic Energy and levels."

"What about you?" Zac asked.

"It is generally a bit rude to ask someone about their class, but it doesn't matter in this case. My class is simply Teacher, an F-ranked Common class. My skills pertain to knowledge retention and dissemination. I also get ocular skills that can help me see Cosmic Energy circulation in others so I can guide students' cultivation practice. I even get some defensive spells to protect myself and my students, but no offensive ones. And I am actually gaining Cosmic Energy as I am explaining these things to you, as I am fulfilling the purpose of my class."

"Are there upgrade paths for the Teacher class as well?"

"Any class has the potential to reach the peak of power, noncombat classes included. There are some restrictions in general when it comes to class upgrades. We explained some of it when we discussed Heritages earlier, but this is a good point to go over class upgrades," Alyn said, swiftly jumping in between subjects.

"The first class upgrade is at level 75. There are generally three things that are needed to upgrade to E-grade: Race, Dao, and achievements. Your Race needs to be E-grade, you need to have grasped at least one Dao Seed, and your actions must enable the class. Some classes have even more restrictions, such as status restrictions or Title requirements, but those are exceptions rather than the rule. Classes with higher rarity almost always have more stringent requirements in Dao and achievements.

"If you don't fulfill all three requirements, you will not be able to upgrade your class and progress from level 75. It is therefore known as the first bottleneck. Furthermore, many are able to upgrade their class but still choose to stay down there, even until the day they die."

"Why would they not upgrade if they are able to?" Zac asked, confused. There seemed to be only upsides to upgrading and becoming stronger.

"There are a few reasons people stay on at F-class, at least for a bit. First, there are certain trials and titles that are only accessible before advancing. The Tower of Eternity is one such example. The second and more important reason is that people desperately try to gain access to a better class," Alyn said.

"What do you mean?" Zac already felt pretty happy getting a Rare class, but if it could increase the rarity even further when upgrading to the next tier, that would obviously be better. The tower thing sounded interesting as well, but one thing at a time.

"Achievements is the third requirement, and the most diffuse. Only with a full Heritage can you know exactly what you need to do to be able to gain a class. But examples are to fight in wars, to have killed enough enemies, to have seen and explored certain areas. Generally to have grown as a being and have accomplished things above the norm.

"Warriors do not only wait to get a better class in order to gain better skills and attribute points, they do it since they do not want to cut off their path of cultivation. There is another minimum requirement for class advancement that is related to class rarity. An F-ranked class can be any rarity and still gain an upgrade. But an E-ranked class needs to be at least Uncommon rank to be able to advance further. So if you pick an E-ranked Common class, then your path of cultivation will end at E-rank, no matter how deep your insight of the Dao is or how grand your achievements are.

"And with every stage, the requirement increases one step. A

D-ranker needs to have at least a Rare class, a C-ranker at least an Epic one, and so on. There is an endless number of individuals with greater ambition than talent who throw themselves into perilous situations to gain achievements in hope of gaining a better option for a class. Most die, but some succeed. Of course, the Fruit of Ascension you ate is a shortcut in a sense," Alyn stated with some obvious desire in her eyes as she mentioned the fruit.

"What do the fruits I ate have to do with class options?" Zac asked, confused. He thought they were only good for upgrading his Race, and that was why they were named Ascension.

"Ogras didn't tell you?" Alyn asked, surprised. She hesitated a long while before she seemed to have come to a decision. "Well, this part you didn't hear from me, then. The main goal of a Fruit of Ascension isn't improving your Race, although it is a good time-saving effect for most people, cultivators included. It is the effect it has on your class upgrades. It's not a true D-grade treasure based on the low energy it contains, but it's ranked like that because of its usefulness. Its effect is limited, but essentially, it improves your choices when you upgrade your class.

"Even if a warrior normally only qualified for Common classes when upgrading to E-rank, after eating a Fruit of Ascension, they would be guaranteed to only have Uncommon classes to choose from. If you could already get Uncommon ones, it is not too unlikely you will get Rare options as long as you have some other achievements to help you along. It can even help push you toward getting an Epic class if you were close to qualifying but falling just a bit short. The fruit is a cheat, or a shortcut, that immensely improves a warrior's future prospects. That is why it's one of the most sought-after natural treasures for young cultivators," she finished with a longing sigh. "At least on D-grade worlds."

Zac's heart started to beat rapidly, finally understanding the gravity of what he had eaten. No wonder everyone had scrambled to get those fruits on the mountains. He had already heard that most warriors in the Multiverse, even on established D-rank planets, started out as a Common class. This fruit would enable them to qualify for D-rank in the future. Of course, there were probably more requirements to take that next step in cultivation.

In his case, the use was still great, as it might be what pushed him into getting an Epic class when upgrading. From what he understood, an Epic class was extremely rare, and it would be a huge event if an Epic class emerged on a D-ranked world. He didn't wish to stay on this topic, though, as he still had another fruit sitting in his pouch like a hot potato.

"So what did the other Apostates change?" he asked, changing the subject.

"The one before Lady Mercy was called the Apostate of Order. He was a great scholar who strove to understand all Dao under the heavens. The change he brought was the codifying of the Dao. You should know it as the patterns or fractals you see from everything from our weapons, to skills, even to your pathways," Alyn answered, jumping back to the original topic without any hiccup.

"It is thanks to him we can gain Dao Seeds and further our understanding of the Dao through study of the fractals," she continued.

"What do you mean?" Zac asked, once again getting derailed by an interesting topic. He still hadn't found a way to upgrade his Dao Seed and had tried various tricks.

"The fractals contain a hint of the Dao. It is most clear in the fractals awarded from the so-called Seed-quests, as they emanate the Dao itself. But it is possible to gain insight from almost anything, from the inscriptions on a piece of gear to continuous usage of a skill. It is generally more effective to study fractals than to sit in silent meditation, though many consider a combination of the two the best.

"In any case, the two first Apostates do not actually have any Apostate designations but are rather called the Beast Progenitor and the First Defier, and they are strong contenders for the title of the most powerful beings since the inception of cultivation."

79

THE LIFEBRINGER

Zac was walking back through the forest toward the camp. He had spent the last sixteen days in the mines and felt the need to check up on the battle preparations. He wanted to be done with everything in something like ten days before the first horde arrived in case something went wrong, and he was now halfway to his deadline. While Ogras had proven himself quite useful, he wasn't too comfortable leaving the demon to his own devices in his camp. Besides, who knew how many crystals he was stashing away while Zac was preoccupied.

Zac sighed, as he knew there was nothing much he could do about that for now, as long as it was kept within reasonable limits. He would just have to see it as a salary for the demon. As he walked, he activated the **[Axe Mastery]** guidance system, once more following its intrepid pathways.

Two days ago, as he was swinging away at the tunnel wall, he actually evolved the skill. It seemed that the method to level up Axe Mastery was to learn and internalize everything the trajectories had to offer, and he had arduously kept trying to improve his form over the last two weeks. It was now at Middle mastery, just like **[Chop]**. The changes weren't as obvious as with his other skill, though, only adding some techniques and strikes.

It did, however, also incorporate both his Dao of Heaviness and his skill **[Chop]** into the mix. Just as it before had fluidly changed between various techniques and attacks, it now also incorporated those two elements in the ever-changing barrage of strikes. He had quickly realized some new usage methods for the skills, such as using **[Chop]** like a retractable lance, almost instantly impaling enemies as the energy edge expanded when he held the axe at the right angle. For that attack, he didn't even have to move his arm, just charge the skill as he held it stationary, making it a great surprise strike.

He also found out he had been using the Dao empowerment inefficiently, since he only really needed to empower the strike in the last second as it approached the enemy. Until now, he'd charged his strike up as he did with Cosmic Energy, starting to infuse the Dao even before the swing started. That both gave the defender a warning and wasted too much mental energy.

Unfortunately, the improved **[Axe Mastery]** didn't show any strikes where the Dao and his skill were combined, like with his final furious strikes in the battle between him and Rydel. It also didn't provide him with a new vision like it did when he first received the skill. He had hoped that the skill would give him a new vision that would help him finally understand the Dao of Sharpness.

He felt he was actually progressing there, though, and might grasp it on his own soon. He was diligently trying to improve the sense of sharpness of his strikes, cutting increasingly large gashes in the tunnel walls.

There was another reason for Zac leaving the tunnels this day. He was very close to completing the quests for both his **[Loamwalker]** skill and **[Forester's Constitution]**, and he felt it would be better to complete those skills when he was alone.

Since Alyn had explained to Zac how Luck worked, he was far more ready to listen to his gut. It turned out that the attribute wasn't only good for things such as winning in card games or getting good rewards from quests. Luck was an extremely convenient attribute that greatly improved a warrior's survivability, and cultivators across the Multiverse desperately looked for means to improve their Luck. There were actually fruits like the Fruit of Ascension that could permanently improve an attribute, and those that improved Luck were hundreds to thousands of times more expensive compared to the other ones.

It could be said that Luck gave a person a sixth sense, and the higher the Luck, the more pronounced it would become. At lower levels, they could vaguely sense that something was wrong, causing a general sense of discomfort. As Luck improved, it would give the person an acute sense of danger in case their life was in peril, allowing them to survive where an unlucky person would die.

Zac thought back to some of his fights, especially the ambush in the caves. He had suddenly felt an extreme sense of danger just before an arrow slammed into his head, and it was that feeling that saved his life. Only now did he understand that it came from his extremely high Luck.

Alyn had also told him that it didn't only work against bad things, but also for fortuitous encounters as the attribute kept increasing. She mentioned how a person with extremely high Luck could sometimes get an almost irresistible urge to walk in some random direction, and as long as he followed his gut, there would be a treasure waiting at the end. But to get lucky to that point, one needed hundreds of points in the attribute.

Therefore, since Zac's gut told him he should be alone when completing the quest, he didn't hesitate to head out, using the fact he wanted to check out the camp as a convenient excuse. He once again checked the class skills.

1. **Forester's Constitution (Class): Fight in the forests, be one with nature. Reward: Forester's Constitution Skill. (29/30)**
2. **Loamwalker (Class): Walk a thousand kilometers touching the earth. Reward: Loamwalker Skill. (983/1,000)**

After confirming the status, he kept moving through the forest, westward rather than going south. He wanted to get out of the way, as there was some foot traffic through the forest that could interrupt him. Or rather jungle, as it started to feel like. The path between Port Atwood and Azh'Rodum, which was the new name for the demon town, was getting to the point that an actual trail was being created.

Ogras had decided to rename it since it didn't make sense for the town to be named after the clan they abandoned. From Alyn's explanation, Rodum simply meant "capital" in their native language, and the Azh prefix was a reminder of their origin.

Apparently, there had been sort of an uprising in Azh'Rodum while Zac diligently trained in the mines. Zac learned that Ogras' influence came from his extremely powerful grandfather, but his own reputation was less than stellar. Some demons felt that they would do a better job at running the town now that they didn't have to fear repercussions from the clan or Ogras' ancestor, and sought to seize control.

It was a group of demons who had been stuck in the mines looking for Zac when the incursion ended, and who were still disgruntled that they couldn't get home. Different from most of the town, the demons who were in the mines had had no choice whether to go home or not and had been involuntarily stranded on Earth.

The rebellion had been short-lived and extremely bloody.

Ogras unleashed a level of power that dumbfounded the town, and Alyn was still shocked as she retold the events. Just as interestingly, Ogras had been aided by multiple powerful demons who had been thought to be noncombat-class individuals until that moment. They sprang up from nowhere and suppressed the town with their power as well. They captured the dissidents in quick order and with overwhelming power.

The rebellion did not just end with the rebels being caught. What followed caused even the stoic Alyn to be shaken. Ogras ruthlessly tortured the group of demons in front of the rest of the town, their screams echoing through Azh'Rodum for hours before they finally were allowed to die. After that Ogras had once again become an unquestioned leader. Zac didn't believe that those methods were sustainable; ruling with fear could only take one so far. But they were strapped for time, and Zac needed the demons to work as if their lives depended on it, because in a sense, they did.

During the past two weeks, Zac had learned a few words and sentences so that he could at least greet the demons who didn't possess the language skill **[Book of Babel]**. The name greatly confused Zac when he heard its name since it was clearly based on the biblical origin myth. But Alyn explained that the skill also translated many things into something that made sense for the listener. For example, the skill was named after an ancient devil with a million mouths in demonic, which was based on their own mythology.

Soon he was close to the edge on the west part of the island, far away from any demon activity. Zac marveled at the surroundings, as the forest had changed so much after only two weeks in the cave. Some trees were starting to grow impossibly large, and all sorts of plants and flowers peppered the forest floor. Many of the flowers were things that he'd never seen before, and he wondered whether they were mutations or something that had drifted over from a neighboring island.

As he walked along, he killed a barghest every now and then in order to keep his quest progressing. He hadn't been too surprised when he'd learned that the demons had sent through hundreds of thousands of the beasts, as they were literally everywhere on the island.

When he asked why they didn't send more demons instead, Alyn explained that going through an incursion had a cost, and the more powerful a warrior, the more expensive it would be. Noncombat classes like Alyn were somewhat affordable to send through, but individuals like Ogras and Rydel alone cost almost as much as the whole barghest hordes.

Suddenly, Zac felt the familiar gathering of energy in his mind, and his heartbeat sped up. Ogras had told him that the skill might be a seed quest that was designed to award a Dao Seed, but Zac didn't dare to hope for it after he'd already gotten a vision for the Dao of Axes.

Alyn had explained that a Rare class could get two Dao Seed quests at the most, and an Epic class was needed to be able to get a third. Even getting two was considered great luck, and generally an indication that the Rare class was top tier amongst its kind.

Zac quickly ran to a close by tree and nimbly climbed its branches. After a thorough check for any inhabitants, he sat down on one of the wider branches and closed his eyes.

He was a small pod in the darkness. Nothing existed apart from the warmth of the surroundings and the refreshing pearls of water that sometimes ran along his surface. Time was irrelevant, and the only thing that mattered was to keep reaching upward. Zac had no idea how long he stayed in the darkness, until one day, a burst of light, or rather of life, inundated him as he struggled upward.

He had broken through the earth, a small sapling being greeted by the endless sky. The blast of light woke up Zac for a second, and he realized he was in another vision. This one was different, though, as it seemed endless. Days quickly became years as Zac slowly forgot about his quest, his town, even himself. The only thing on his mind was to keep absorbing life and growing.

Seasons came and went and beset him with an ever-changing trial by nature itself. Winds whipped his branches, trying to rip his leaves away from him. Rain pelted him relentlessly, quickly turning from a refreshing shower to a deluge threatening to drown him. The water froze and became a layer of snow and ice, freezing him and forcing him dormant, dreaming of the sun. But the trials always ended and were sooner or later replaced with the warm kiss of the sun.

Zac started to realize he was different from his brethren around him, as while their growth stopped after a few centuries, he kept growing. Soon he was towering in the sky, his kin only small dots hidden among his roots. He kept growing for millions of years, unceasingly absorbing the warmth of the sun and the sweet life in the atmosphere. Every inch of his being vibrated with vitality, every leaf glistening with life.

Small beings started to live around him, treating him with great reverence. Some even started to move up to his branches, forever denouncing the ground. Zac let them stay on, as some company was welcome in this eternity.

He kept growing upward, eventually breaking through the vault of the heavens. Sparkling dots glimmered in the darkness as Zac started floating in the vast expanse. His old friend the sun stayed behind, but the whole cosmos provided him with sustenance instead. He once again went dormant as he floated through the void, ever growing. Every place he passed as he slept was changed, desolate worlds rousing themselves, suddenly teeming with vitality.

He was the Lifebringer.

80

LOAMWALKER

Zac woke up, disoriented for quite some time before he found his bearings. This vision was even more impactful compared to the last in a sense. Living millions and millions of years was a completely surreal experience for someone who hadn't even turned thirty in reality. Luckily, the passage of time was made fuzzy somehow for him; otherwise, he might have turned mad.

The vision showed him the peak of power just like the one with the axe-man, but in a completely different sense. That tree he had grown into was truly gargantuan and reminded him of the old tale of Yggdrasil, the world tree. It was larger than a star by the end, but more importantly, it contained an endless source of life.

Zac closed his eyes again and started to imprint the feelings he felt in his mind. He knew this time was critical and wouldn't waste it. It was only hours later he once again opened his eyes and checked out his new skill.

[Forester's Constitution – Proficiency: Early. Man and Nature One Entity. Endurance +5%, Vitality +5%. Effects doubled while in a forest. Upgradeable.]

Next, he quickly checked his monster horde quest and

breathed out in relief as he saw the timer. Only one day had passed in the real world, even though it felt like eons in his vision. He was once more happy he hadn't finished this quest in the caves. While everything looked fine on the surface, he didn't relish the thought of going into a trance for a whole day right in front of a bunch of demons. Who knew which one of them held a secret grudge for a friend or family member killed, just waiting for an opportunity to strike? Relaxed, he once more refocused on the skill.

He had initially thought the Forester's Constitution would be some sort of defensive skill like the stone skin he saw the earth mages use, but he was only partly correct. It was rather a passive buff skill that worked like a title that improved his survivability. The bonus was quite good, especially considering it would give double the bonus at most parts of the island.

Zac wondered if he could carry around a patch of forest in a pouch, and throw it out whenever he was entering a battle. That way, he'd always have the improved bonus. He was curious if there were any other functions of the skill, as **[Axe Mastery]** had given him the training system, so he tried finding another pocket space in his body.

As he suspected, when he turned his gaze inward, he found another area in his body, this time in his chest. The last fractal he'd gained in this manner looked like a large axe, exuding the Dao of Heaviness. This fractal rather looked like the Tree of Life he'd seen in the vision, but inert.

Next, he checked his status page to see what other changes might have occurred.

Name: Zachary Atwood
Level: 36
Class: [F-Rare] Hatchetman
Race: [E] Human

Alignment: [Earth] Human

Titles: Born for Carnage, Ultimate Reaper, Luck of the Draw, Giantsbane, Disciple of David, Overpowered, Slayer of Leviathans, Adventurer, Demon Slayer, Full of Class, Rarified Being, Trailblazer, Child of Dao, The Big 500, Planetary Aegis

Dao: Seed of Heaviness – Early, Seed of Trees – Early

Strength: 189
Dexterity: 69
Endurance: 147
Vitality: 105
Intelligence: 57
Wisdom: 57
Luck: 77

Free Points: 3
Nexus Coins: 538,317

He'd actually already acquired another Dao Seed during his meditation without even noticing it. It was called the Dao Seed of Trees, and a prompt showed its properties.

[Dao Seed of Trees – Early. Vitality +10, Endurance +5]

The properties of the Dao indicated that it wasn't a Dao meant for battle, but he was fine with that. He already had the Dao of Heaviness for battle, and he was making inroads on the Dao of Sharpness from his activities in the mines. Having a defensive Dao to accompany the offensive ones seemed quite good. And if he was going to fight in a sea of beasts, having an improved Endurance and Vitality would come in quite handy.

He was a bit disappointed that the seed he gained felt pretty distant from the supreme entity that was the Tree of Life. Then again, the vision of the axe-man was quite distant from the Seed of Heaviness as well. Besides, Ogras had already warned him against hoping he would gain some high-tiered concept as a Dao.

Zac knew what to do now that he knew he had a new Dao Seed, and started channeling the Dao of Trees into the fractal, and it lit up with a green luster.

The once dead tree started to emanate an aura, but it wasn't oppressive like the one from his axe. Instead, it gave a refreshing feeling, but also spoke of unyielding perseverance. Of course, the aura was like a firefly against the towering sun that was the Tree of Life in his vision.

If the endpoint of his first vision was the Dao of Axe or Dao of Destruction, then this one rather led toward the Dao of Life or Dao of Nature. The duality of his vastly different seeds reminded Zac of yin and yang, and he felt that it was an extremely well-balanced foundation to build his future upon.

No prompts lit up his surroundings like with the last skill when he'd infused the tree made from fractals, and the only discernible difference was that he felt it start to emanate a warmth that spread out throughout his body. It felt a bit like when he drank the azure water, but he instinctively knew that this warmth wasn't hurting him.

He tried swinging his axe a bit while he was infused with the Dao of Trees, but he felt no improvement in his speed or strength. He was even having trouble keeping the Dao active as he moved around, the warm feeling noticeably subsiding. It made sense since trees weren't really mobile unless Ents were a thing in the Multiverse. Besides, Zac had already surmised that the new Dao wasn't meant for battle from the attributes it awarded, and this somewhat confirmed it.

Having an idea, he cut a wound on his left arm and once again sat down. As he started to infuse the Dao and some Cosmic Energy into the tree again, he felt the warmth properly spread out once more. The wound on his arm started itching within seconds, and Zac felt how the warmth moved toward his wound and started healing it. It wasn't to the point that he could see the improvements with his naked eye, but he knew it was improving his recovery rate. Unfortunately, it didn't seem to work on his damaged pathways, at least not with Early mastery.

Satisfied, he once again focused on the status screen. He noticed that there was no new title this time for attaining a second Dao. He felt it should be due to the fact that there was no award for a second Dao, rather than multiple people having beaten him to it. There shouldn't be too many who already had a second Dao, it wasn't like one could just stare at a fire for a few days and suddenly know the Dao of Fire.

He realized he still had three free points from his level when the herald died. After some hesitation, he allocated them into Dexterity, bringing the stat to 73. Alyn had told him earlier that the general view on the connection between Dexterity and Strength in the Multiverse was that one of the stats shouldn't be more than 100% larger than the other. After that, the effectiveness started to wear off.

For example, with great Dexterity but no Strength, one would be able to hit the enemies in a dizzying blur, but each strike would be too weak to do proper damage. Conversely, Zac's case was that he possessed monstrous Strength, but very low Dexterity. His strikes would be strong, but they would be slow and clumsy, making it easy to deflect or dodge them.

It had only really been a problem when he'd faced Rydel so far, but in the future, he would meet more and more enemies with stats that could match his, so he needed to get his attributes balanced as soon as possible.

It felt a bit weird to forgo his min-max strategy that always had been his method when playing games, but he needed to get used to the fact that video game knowledge could only take him so far in this reality. Of course, there were exceptions to the general guidelines of stat allocation, but you really needed to know what you were doing.

Zac felt that he should stick to the most-accepted route for now at least, and only change it up in the future if he was absolutely certain. Besides, his Strength would keep increasing through his Dao and his class bonuses, even if he didn't specifically allocate any more stats there for a while.

Finally done with everything, he set out toward Port Atwood, but after only an hour of walking, he was once again interrupted. This time, it was his **[Loamwalker]** quest that was completed. Eagerly, he checked the skill out, and as he expected, this time, it was a fractal that went on his legs. More specifically, it was two identical fractals that were placed on the soles of his feet, directly touching the ground below.

Zac didn't hesitate and immediately infused the new fractals with energy. As he stood still, he noticed no difference, but when he took a step, the world turned blurry for an instant. Afterward, he found himself standing two meters away from his original position. The skill actually increased the distance he traversed somehow.

Zac kept trying to figure the skill out by repeatedly moving around, but he had a hard time grasping what the skill actually did. Initially, he thought that it teleported him small distances, but he noticed that the movement wasn't instantaneous. Next, he guessed that he got super speed while he moved, but he felt that wasn't quite right either. He tried swinging an axe while he moved, but the movement was far quicker compared to his swing.

It was as though the earth moved around him rather than him moving on the earth.

Did the skill somehow disconnect him from Earth's rotation? That couldn't be correct either, as he had no problems moving in any direction. After a while, he gave up trying to explain it with logic, and could only conclude he magically moved quickly somehow. As long as he was touching the earth, that is. He also tried jumping and running, but as soon as he stopped touching the ground with at least one foot, the effect disappeared.

He kept using **[Loamwalker]** as he walked toward his camp in order to get used to the skill. It was an odd feeling to move faster when he leisurely walked compared to when he ran. After a while, he was forced to stop using the skill, as the consumption of Cosmic Energy was quite high. It wasn't made for long-distance movement, but all in all, he was quite happy with the skill.

He wouldn't be able to do magical feats such as strolling in the air as Rydel did, but the skill would be quite convenient in battle. He could keep moving between targets deceptively fast, and use the skill for both ambush and retreat. Of course, it would take some practice until he was proficient in combining the movement skill with battle skills.

His grasp over how far he walked right now was terrible, and he slammed into trees like a barghest four times in a short duration due to his lack of control. He could only put it aside for now and keep walking until he arrived at Port Atwood.

The wall was coming along nicely, and it was even taller compared to the one in Azh'Rodum. The demons knew a beast horde was coming and didn't dare slack off. If the town fell, their settlement would be next, and they wouldn't have the defenses of strong arrays or System-bought fortifications helping them out there. Saving Port Atwood was essential, even from a selfish standpoint.

He entered through a gate and started to look for Ogras. He

couldn't find him anywhere, and he wasn't able to ask the resting demons either, as none of those present seemed to possess **[Book of Babel]**. He first went to the merchant compound to check whether the demon was there. Calrin met up with him and, after a few pleasantries, explained that the demon hadn't been there today.

Zac also asked for a status update regarding his order, but Calrin explained he still hadn't been able to acquire a pill that could heal pathways, looking a bit embarrassed. Zac sighed in disappointment but thanked him and left, heading for the shipyard.

Ogras shouldn't have any reason to approach the Creators, but he couldn't be sure. As he closed in on the shipyard, he actually heard some subdued voices. Suspicious, he brought out his axe and closed in on the source of the sounds. Soon he saw Ogras, and together with him were two other male demons Zac hadn't seen before.

"Ah, you're here. That makes things easier," Ogras said as two spears wrought from shadows impaled the chests of the demons, instantly killing them.

81

SUBJECTS

"What the fuck are you doing?" Zac loudly exclaimed, shocked as the two demons fell lifelessly to the ground.

"These two were snooping around the shipyard on their breaks. I'm not sure what their goal was, but we couldn't have them walking around as they wished. These two will also set an example for any other curious individuals," the demon tartly explained as he brought out an axe identical to those Zac used from his pouch.

With two swift swings, he decapitated the lifeless bodies before he slammed the axe into the thin wounds on their chests, effectively masking their true cause of death. Zac mutely looked on, having some problems processing what was happening. Was the demon framing him right in front of his eyes? Ogras felt Zac's stare and glanced in his direction, giving a slight shrug.

"It's better if you killed them. It will remind the others that you are not to be provoked, and you don't take kindly to people looking into your business. If it was found out that I killed them just because they were looking at some humans at the shipyard, I will start losing my grasp on the other demons."

Zac silently stared at the two demons on the ground, a cold feeling gripping his heart. He felt he had grown a bit lax against the demons, particularly the one in front of him. While Zac believed it was in Ogras' interest to keep Port Atwood and Zac protected for at least a decade until he could try to usurp it, he couldn't be sure of the demon's plans.

This was a person who had no problems betraying those close to him without batting an eye as long as it benefitted him. Besides, he couldn't be sure whether Ogras' story was true. For all Zac knew, he'd happened upon a clandestine meeting, and Ogras killed his allies rather than let his plans be exposed.

But Zac also realized that might just be how the Multiverse worked. Might makes right, and benefits trump friendships. He knew that he had grown callous as well, as he wasn't about to clamor for justice for these two or start some sort of investigation. There was no benefit to it, and he'd rather just bear the blame so that people would keep away from his shipyard. Getting tired of the whole situation, he could only move on. It was a bit annoying to be framed for the murders, but he had already killed hundreds of demons. What was two more to the tally?

"How are the fortifications coming along? And where are the crystals?" Zac asked as he put away his axe, not bothering with the two fallen demons any longer.

Ogras, looking pleased that Zac wasn't making a big deal of the situation, swiftly took out a few Cosmos Sacks from a pocket and threw them over.

"The wall will be done with a few days to spare, and the mining operations are proceeding splendidly. Now that there aren't a dozen main branch assholes embezzling a part of the cake, the daily output is above expectations. We have mined and refined a total of 109,344 crystals so far, meaning slightly more than five million Nexus Coins. A few issues have cropped up, though."

"What now?" Zac asked with a grimace. He should have known it was impossible to only get good news.

"First of all, the lizards down in the tunnel are getting more aggressive, and we don't possess as much manpower as we did, making it hard to keep them at bay. Secondly, I have run into a snag with the gnomes, but we may be able to turn it into an opportunity. But most importantly, I've run out of moving pictures," he said.

"Moving pictures?" Zac asked, confused, to which Ogras fished out Izzy's portable video player from a sack, waving it at Zac. Zac had completely forgotten she had brought it with her when the group went camping, but it seemed that the demon had found it while idling in his camp.

"I have watched everything inside this device, and I must say that this planet is pretty interesting, making all these things. I bet we can make some money if we figure out how to turn the moving pictures into crystals and sell them. Is there any more than what's contained in this device?"

Zac was stumped, his mouth curving a bit upward. He knew that the demons didn't use much technology, as it was frowned upon on their home world just like large parts of the Multiverse. The demons were very much in favor of the System, which put them against the so-called Technocrats, and they disdained to use devices that weren't created with fractals and inscriptions.

"There's enough for you to watch until you die, even if your longevity gets a few upgrades. I don't have any more with me, though."

"Then we need to quickly beat the beast hordes and find human settlements."

"Uh, yeah. How are you charging the player anyway? It should have run out of power long ago. And what about the merchants?"

"Any decent lightning mage can charge up the energy

containers on this type of device. Even normal cultivators can do it when their fine control of Cosmic Energy gets high enough." Ogras waved dismissively. "And it seems we might have pushed the Sky Gnomes a bit too hard. I've had a talk with Calrin, and they might actually go under if we keep forcing these prices."

"*We* pushed them?" Zac asked pointedly as he stored the little information nugget that one could use Cosmic Energy to charge devices. Perhaps he could even resurrect the car with some training.

"I didn't see you stop me. In any case, from what I understand, the merchants have made some truly troublesome enemies, and they have managed to put pressure on the Thayer Consortium, even through the Mercantile System. Calrin is unable to make a profit as it stands, and the Ruthless Heavens might actually revoke their license." Ogras sighed.

"So we need to lower our asking price? Are you sure it's not a business tactic? That little guy seemed to be pretty thick-skinned," Zac asked, not relishing the thought of lowering the price. A difference of only a few coins per crystal would turn into a huge amount when put to the perspective of the whole mine.

"It doesn't look like he's lying. He truly fears for his life from the look of his eyes lately. But that doesn't mean we need to just throw away money. We're not a charity. I've worked out a deal that I think will benefit you in the long run instead," Ogras answered, the greedy face once more showing.

"We only demand 42 Nexus Coins per crystal. In return, Calrin hands over 25% of the consortium to us."

"That's a lot of profit to give away for a run-down shop where I'm the only customer. And what do you mean to *us*?" Zac said, unconvinced.

"What we're investing in is not the shop itself, but their Mercantile License. They are notoriously hard to acquire and very sought after since they give access to the Mercantile System, allowing you to trade with the whole Multiverse. In a normal situation, you'd have to pawn off a whole continent to get the license, but now we're in a position to snatch up a stake for just a few million Nexus Coins.

"If we help them get back on their feet and help them grow, more and more coins will enter our pockets. Imagine your whole planet full of branches selling all the essentials to billions of people, and all that profit will find its way back to us. Then we can even expand to other planets, the income only becoming larger. Progressing and becoming stronger gets insanely expensive as you get to higher ranks, and this can help out a lot." Ogras became more and more animated as he launched into his business plan, and Zac was starting to get excited as well. If it was as he explained, this was a great opportunity to make some money.

"What about their enemy? Won't they become our enemy as well? What do you know about them?" Zac still hesitated, as he had enough things on his plate. Adding some formidable foe into the mix wasn't an option, even if it meant giving up potential profit.

"It's a powerful family on some faraway C-rank world. We should be somewhere at the edge of the universe, and I don't think they will start a search for your planet, even if it's for a Mercantile License. Besides, the Ruthless Heavens obscured your planet for a hundred years, making it almost impossible to find.

"Therefore, I wouldn't worry too much about it, but if they do come knocking, we can just throw our shares to them as a greeting gift, feigning ignorance of the conflict, and then sell the gnomes out," Ogras said dismissively.

Zac hesitated a while over what to do. The enemy of the Thayer family sounded troublesome, and he didn't want to bring that kind of headache to Earth. But they were protected for a hundred years through the System. Even after that, it was not like they could easily find Earth even if they wanted to, and transportation costs would likely be huge. They might deem it not worth the trouble and get the license from someone else. There must be more struggling corporations to exploit in the Multiverse, after all.

After some time, Zac agreed, and Ogras veritably dragged him to the storefront to sign the documents at the consortium without pause. It appeared that Ogras' initial plan was an even split of 12.5% stake each between the two, but after a glare, the split was changed to 20-5.

Zac still let the demon get some stock in the corporation. He figured it would tie the demon to Zac's wagon, and hopefully, it would make him work more diligently if he had some stake in its success. Besides, it wasn't bad to give something valuable to the demon, as he could threaten to take it away if needed.

Zac was in dire need of some talented people working for him, after all, and Ogras was by far the best option for now. Zac already knew he wouldn't be an active ruler, sitting on his throne and making decrees. He wanted to leave the island as soon as possible to find his family. After that perhaps even explore the Multiverse. And he needed to get stronger, which he couldn't do from a throne room. Therefore, he needed subjects, or at least employees, who could look after his little island kingdom while he was gone.

The sky gnome looked ready to vomit as he signed the documents after a great deal of hemming and hawing. He only looked a bit better after a promise that Zac would help give the consortium a strong position on Earth. Of course, it was Ogras who was promising things far and wide, and Zac only looked on helplessly. He had no idea how to do that, and he didn't even know if there were any towns left.

Next, he ordered some demons to collect a large amount of meat for the salamanders. They had obviously warmed up to Zac when he had fed them various corpses, and perhaps it was possible to bribe them on a larger scale. If not, it would at least keep the monsters satiated so the mining operations could go on unimpeded.

Finally done with everything he wanted to do, Zac once again returned to the caves. The next time he emerged would be to meet the hordes of beasts.

82

THE HORDES

Only wind and creaking from leather armors interrupted the silence as Zac stared out from his fortified position, a steely glint in his eyes. He was trying to gain any hint of what was to come when the timer went to zero in ten minutes. Everything that could be done to prepare had already been finished during the past month, and the only thing remaining was to actually fight the hordes.

The once lush forest next to his camp was gone, replaced instead with a forest of jagged spears jutting out of the ground. Thousands of poles, which reminded him of his first fight with the herald, were embedded in the earth, and moats ran along the wall at various distances. Apparently, no one would get any Nexus Coins if an enemy impaled itself or fell down a trap while they stood up on the wall, but from what Ogras had told him about beast hordes, it wouldn't matter. What made the beast horde a horde was the seemingly endless number of beasts, more than anyone could possibly finish by himself. No one would have to worry about not finding targets, even after the traps did their job.

He wasn't alone on the battlements, as roughly two hundred demons stood on the wall with him. Most had eager expressions in their eyes, while some looked quite pale. Down on the ground, the rest of the demons were at the ready, preparing to serve as various types of support. Zac was at first confused why the demons happily agreed to man the walls without any persuasion needed, but Ogras explained it with only one word: money.

A beast horde was extremely dangerous, but it could also be considered an endless stream of Cosmic Energy and Nexus Coins. The demons who stayed on had lost most of their wealth and needed to refill their pockets. Many of them were mortals just like Zac and needed millions and millions of Nexus Coins to be able to advance past their bottleneck.

The cheapest method to become an E-rank Race was a medicinal bath that you took over and over that incrementally improved the constitution. But this method took years and cost tens of thousands of coins for each bath, making the monster horde a prime chance to be able to afford some more ingredients.

The method Zac had used with the Fruit of Ascension could be considered an extreme luxury, as the fruits were prohibitively expensive if you could even find a seller. The baths did, however, incrementally improve the attribute limits, meaning that none of them would ever be in the same awkward position as Zac had been earlier.

"Are you ready to make some money?" Zac heard a voice from his left and saw Ogras approaching. With him he had his four underlings, each with enough power to contend with the top-tier warriors of the invasion. Zac had sparred a bit against them the last few days as he waited for the monsters to arrive, and had been surprised to see that none of them used classes from Clan Azh'Rezak's Heritage.

They were Ogras' hidden ace that he'd recruited and trained using his grandfather's wealth in order to have some backup against the main branch forces in case it came to blows. He had smuggled them in after killing a few of his clan-mates without any strong connections or close friends, having these four take their places. In fact, none of the four were actually real members of Clan Azh'Rezak.

Ilvere was a burly man who had masqueraded as a farmer when he entered through the incursion. He fought with a flail whose chain could extend to over ten meters according to his will. He was actually trying to gain insight into the Dao of Heaviness in order to combine it with the Dao of Lightness. That would apparently create the Dao of Momentum, which could imbue the spiked ball with a terrifying force as he swung the weapon. When the demon heard that Zac actually possessed the Seed of Heaviness, he'd plastered himself next to Zac, to the point that Ogras finally had to kick him away due to the annoyance. His class was only an Uncommon class called Strongman, and it didn't give him any class skill that helped him with the Dao, and he desperately wanted to observe and feel Zac's Dao in order to gain some insights.

Janos was a thin, dignified-looking man who compulsively adjusted his spectacles as he looked around. He was quite terse in his communication and seemed to enjoy solitude over any company. That made it a bit surprising for Zac to learn that the demon actually was a support mage who couldn't really fight on his own, making him require teammates to grind levels. He walked the path of illusions, and used skills that confused and weakened his enemies. It wasn't enough to kill them, but it would completely disrupt their rhythm, making it hard to fight properly.

Namys was whirling her blades as she looked provokingly at Zac. She was one of the few in the camp who was a truly willing follower of Ogras. She even had a class that looked similar to his, as it utilized darkness and shadows to create an assassin-type combat style. She was extremely unhappy that Ogras was placed as a sort of second-in-command behind Zac, and his spars with her were the most dangerous. More times than one, Zac felt that she had truly tried to hurt him with her large daggers.

Alea was his largest headache, though. The beautiful demoness looked at him with a slight smile as she winked her large eyes at him. She wore what looked like an old-fashioned dress from the 60s. Apparently, she had asked Ogras what humans from Earth wore, and Ogras had explained in detail, armed with outdated information from old-timey movies on Izzie's device.

Alea liked the strong and ruthless, and Zac fit the bill nicely, as being able to single-handedly thwart an incursion made him quite the dashing figure, in her words. Furthermore, she possessed a class related to poison, and the fact that Zac essentially poisoned two armies to death was a cosmic sign that they were compatible in her eyes. The fact that one of the poisoned armies was her own people seemed to be completely irrelevant to her. Zac wasn't sure if her interest was real or whether Ogras was trying to plant a honeypot by his side, but in either case, Alea was a continuous source of exasperation.

Ogras didn't kick her away as he did with Ilvere, leaving Zac to fend for himself. In private, Ogras told him that he didn't want to poison test every swig of water or bite of food he took due to angering Alea, as she was slightly crazy like most poison masters were. Something about breathing poison fumes for years made their wiring a bit off. That nugget of information only served to increase his discomfort.

Even the schoolmistress, Alyn, would make a measured but immediate retreat when Alea found him in the mines, and the poison master sometimes took over the role of lecturer. It was from Alea he found out the general rules of grinding beasts. He had asked why she chose a poison class when poisoning enemies to death didn't seem to reward Nexus Coins or Cosmic Energy. If it did, he would be quite a few levels higher after throwing out the cauldron up on the mountain. But he was surprised to hear that she actually got rewards from poisoning enemies.

She explained the distinction the System made was whether effort or skill was involved in the kill. In her case, she generated the poisons herself and disseminated them using her class skills. The System awarded her Cosmic Energy for that. Zac had just snatched a bunch of poison and threw it out, and the System didn't consider it enough effort. For the same reason, getting a machine gun or even an atomic bomb couldn't help you gain levels at all.

The System considered those types of tools not to require skill. It did consider using a bow and arrow requiring of skill, though, and would award everyone, not just archer classes, Cosmic Energy from that type of kill. From her words, the System generally didn't award energy or coins from kills when technology was involved. It was something about the System not liking tools not made with Cosmic Energy.

Zac felt that many armies in the world would be in for a rude awakening after hearing that. He believed that many would have a hard time letting go of their weapons and instead fight monsters hand-to-hand in order to gain levels. That would mean that the beasts would get continuously stronger due to the System pumping them full of Cosmic Energy, whereas the armies stayed stagnant. Sooner or later, it would reach a tipping point, where conventional weapons were useless. Zac was pretty sure that he was mostly bulletproof by now, for example. It might hurt, but a bullet should barely be able to penetrate his skin. Especially if it hit his E-graded clothing.

"You all seem to be in a chipper mood," Zac said dourly. He didn't relish the thought that he would have to spend the next three months continuously fighting for his life. He felt he was on the cusp of finally being able to leave the island and look for his family, but first, he was stuck in an endless battle.

"Birds die for food; men die for money," Ogras answered with a shrug. "If worse comes to worst, we can just jump ship and sail for kinder shores."

Ogras was referring to a small Creator vessel that Zac had bought for one million Nexus Coins. It was powered with Nexus Crystals and could comfortably house ten people, or thirty if people covered every inch of the deck as well. It was one of the cheapest creations available for sale at the shipyard, and Zac planned on using it for exploration, or fleeing if necessary.

Now that he knew the System wouldn't punish him for failing a quest or fleeing for his life, he wasn't as ready to risk everything just to finish the quest and become a Lord. He had confirmed that what Ogras said was true from a few sources, and that Abby had in fact lied. The largest punishment for failing quests was that he couldn't get them again.

However, if he failed too many quests, he risked not getting awarded new ones for a while. For example, Ogras would likely not get any quests for a couple of years due to eating the **[Coward's Escape]** Pill. But for a cultivator whose life could be counted in the thousands, it was a small price to pay for escaping with his life.

That didn't mean that he wouldn't diligently try to complete the quest and rebuff the three monster waves. The more he learned about cultivation and the Multiverse, he knew he was sitting on a rare chance. The island was likely one of the safest places on Earth right now. There were no dangerous beasts skulking around apart from the salamanders, and they kept to their caves. The reason for this was simple: it was the hordes of barghest. They had hunted everything that started to evolve since they arrived, stopping any species from gaining Strength.

That made this island a haven and an amazing source of wealth, for himself and his family. As he was the Lord, that wealth would turn into further safety, as he could keep buying defenses if some force meant him harm. To give this up would mean he would turn from a so-called progenitor to another refugee without a place to call home.

Alea walked over and greeted him with a smile and a light touch on his arm, and Zac could only bear it for now with a grimace. He knew from experience that telling her off or pushing her away wouldn't work, and if he got too insistent, she might poison him in a rage. Nothing lethal, of course, but something strong enough for him to be puking his guts out for a few hours.

So they stood at the top of the wall, surveying the battlefield, looking like an old couple until finally the timer went to zero.

[Ladder activated. Struggle for supremacy.] The emotionless voice of the System entered his ears just as the third month ended and the timer went to zero.

"Huh, what's this ladder that the System mentioned?" Zac said as he turned to Ogras. But immediately afterward, he turned back toward the forest as he saw tens of gray pillars flash into existence roughly a kilometer away. They looked just like the incursion, just in a different color and a lot smaller.

"The Ruthless Heavens spoke to you? Ladder? Must be some function it is using on this baby planet. It has all types of modes that it can activate that change how–" Ogras explained but was interrupted by the System itself, this time speaking so everyone heard it.

[Special Dynamic Quest activated. Defend what's yours, and vanquish the hordes. The strong will be rewarded.]

83

WOLVES

"It actually handed out a town-protection quest," Ogras exclaimed gleefully, as most demons around him looked like they had eaten stimulants.

"What's going on?" Zac asked as he looked over at the gray pillars. Nothing had emerged from them yet, but he knew it wouldn't be long now.

"It's a bonus quest. Everything you kill will award contribution points apart from the usual Nexus Coins and Cosmic Energy. You can trade these points for all kinds of goodies at a temporary Nexus Node that should pop up somewhere close. Those who rack up the most points usually are awarded some bonus prize as well," Ogras answered hurriedly as he took out his spear from his sack. It looked like he wanted to simply jump down from the wall and run to the pillars, not able to wait for the enemies to come to them.

Zac started to get excited as well, but was very annoyed that he still wasn't completely healed. He was a lot better by now, but not to the point that he dared use crystals or his amulet to quickly regain his energy. He wouldn't be able to heedlessly use his **[Chop]** skill to quickly gain contribution points. In other words, his two Daos weren't helpful in fighting large groups of monsters. He still hadn't gained the Seed of Sharpness, which he guessed would be convenient when fighting against packs.

He didn't have time to ruminate over his condition any longer as gray silhouettes started to pour out of the portals and immediately flooded toward the wall.

"No offense, my friend, but I'm aiming for the top spot. It's a shame we can't have a completely fair competition with your condition," Ogras lamented with mirth and greed in his eyes. It looked like he already considered the prize for the most contribution points his.

Zac decided to ignore him, as the horde was closing in on the battlements, and he could finally see their visages. It was an enormous wolf pack that charged as one. Each had mottled gray fur and the rough size of a gwyllgi, reaching almost up to Zac's chest.

He could also spot larger versions at various areas in the sea of wolves, and he guessed that they were the equivalents of the monkey captains. A piercing howl arose from the pillars as Zac surveyed the horde, and Zac spotted a far larger wolf skulking around in the back. All in all, it looked like there were a few thousand wolves, almost all of them the normal-sized ones.

Zac didn't feel that this looked too threatening, and he cast a questioning glance at Ogras.

"This is just the first wave of the first horde. It will get more… exciting… soon enough," he said as if he understood Zac's unspoken question.

The wolves streamed toward the walls, and Zac saw that the erected poles didn't have much effect on the nimble monsters, as they simply dodged them without any effort. A few unlucky wolves were accidentally pushed into the pitfalls by the wolves behind and skewered there, but generally, the horde was unimpeded.

However, the erected wall was where their charge ended, and

the monsters simply had no method to scale it. They clawed some scratches at the foundation, but at that speed, it would take days for them to tear down the wall.

In the demons' eyes, this meant that the wolves turned into target practice, where each hit awarded some money. Arrows started flying out in rapid succession, and the wolves dropped one by one.

Some were even more efficient, such as the mages who managed to skewer multiple wolves with each earth spear attack or create multiple fried carcasses with a large fireball. But the most efficient was clearly Ogras. Any shadow on the ground created by the wall or a wolf was a weapon for him, and shadowy needles kept poking up from the ground, hitting the throat or heart of the wolves. Wolves kept keeling over wherever Ogras turned his outstretched hand, and he was creating patches of utter death down on the ground.

Zac tried to keep up by throwing rocks he had prepared in a few pouches. Each rock he threw slammed into a wolf, the force almost always enough for an instant kill. Still, he couldn't keep up with some of the stronger demons, let alone the sneaky spears of Ogras, and knew his contribution ranking wouldn't be too great if things kept going this way.

He paused after killing a few and checked his status screen. It looked like each of the normal mottled wolves awarded around a hundred Nexus Coins, which seemed very generous for helpless targets. The feeling of seeing an endless stream of money slipping out of his fingers was extremely uncomfortable, and he knew he needed to switch up his tactics.

Alea looked annoyed as well as she stood next to Zac.

"They keep dying before my poison kills them. I only get a small part of the money. You're supposed to be the Lord; do something, and I'll give you a reward," she whined as she looked entreatingly at Zac.

Zac ignored her with a roll of his eyes, but he agreed that something needed to be done. After a few seconds of hesitation, he took out one of his axes and simply jumped out from the safety of the wall.

As he fell, he imbued himself with the Dao of Heaviness, and he slammed into the ground like a meteor. A huge shock wave spread out as Zac punched into the ground ten meters away from the wall. Any wolf in the vicinity was killed or at least badly maimed from the impact. Zac stood up from the crater, and he summoned **[Chop]**.

His plan was simple. Even though his pathways weren't completely healed, they were in far better condition compared to a month ago. Together with his improved attributes, his recovery might even be higher than before he'd ruined his body with the Cosmic Water. He planned on going on a rampage as long as his energy allowed, reaping as many wolves as possible before swapping back to killing without using any energy. With his stats, he wasn't afraid that some of these weak wolves would threaten him, even if they came in droves.

He started to weave a net of carnage around him as he moved full speed ahead. His energy would only last for a short duration at full power, but that should hopefully be enough to thin out most of this wave and perhaps a few more. He headed straight toward where he had seen the huge wolf, hoping that killing the boss would offset his slow start.

No demon dared to shoot their attacks in his vicinity, with the exception of Ogras, who kept summoning spears at some wolves around him. Zac glared angrily in the demon's direction, but Ogras simply looked back innocently and waved.

Zac wasn't the only one who jumped down from the wall, as some of the stronger melee fighters followed suit. They generally stayed close to the wall to keep their backs free, not daring to wade into the thick of it like Zac.

Zac was soon drenched, as every wave of his axe created a fountain of blood and a few bisected corpses strewn around. He realized he had actually missed this feeling, and relished letting loose after over a month of being stuck in the mines, mindlessly chipping away at the walls.

He steadily progressed toward the portals, and soon not even Ogras could kill steal his wolves due to the distance. Each swing created a swath of death in front of him, but it was quickly filled with new wolves. He truly felt like the description of the Hatchetman class; *Their army is an endless forest, and I'm the lumberjack* was an apt description at this moment, as he methodically cut everything down like lumber as he waded forward.

The wolves desperately tried to bite him, but the few that managed to get close couldn't even puncture his skin. A few tried to rip open his robe, but the clothing was even more durable than Zac himself, and not even a scratch could be seen on the green overcoat. Even so, the animals pushed forward toward their death, heedless of anything else. Zac started to suspect that the System had done something to these animals, as they were completely frenzied. Wolves should be smarter than this, especially evolved ones like these guys were.

After a few minutes of swinging away, he was in close proximity to the portals. It should have been even faster, but he took some detours to kill the even larger wolves that were peppered around the horde. They only gave two to three hundred Nexus Coins each, but Zac thought they might be more valuable in terms of contribution points, as the System might consider them mini-bosses.

Wolves had stopped pouring out of the multiple portals a minute ago, and the area was getting a bit thin, as most wolves headed straight for the wall. There were some exceptions, though, most notably the hill with the leader. It looked almost identical to the smaller versions, apart from the fact that its eyes had a silver glisten compared to the duller brown of the others.

Zac approached the hill and started to kill the larger alpha wolves that surrounded their leader, but a movement in his periphery made him infuse his axe with his Dao of Heaviness and launch it at the wolf leader in a surprise attack.

The wolf's reactions were quick, but not quick enough, and the axe ripped a hole in its throat, instantly killing it. Immediately after, two large spears of shadows rose from the ground and impaled the corpse. However, Ogras was too late, as the energy entered Zac's body as the spears rose, confirming his kill credit.

Zac grinned at the demon, who emerged from the shadows with a tsk as he took out another axe from his bag. This one was different from the ones he had used lately and looked like a misshapen monstrosity.

Its handle was roughly a meter long and the edge itself was almost two meters, formed in a rudimentary facsimile of his axe when he used **[Chop]**. It was something Zac had ordered a blacksmith of the demon town to create for him, meant to be used to retain some kill speed while he restored his energy.

It was ugly and completely unbalanced, but it got the job done. Unfortunately, none of those remaining had the skills to add the self-repair inscription on a weapon, and instead this one had an inscription that slightly increased its durability. Still, someone would need to fix it up every now and then after Zac's onslaught.

"I'm starting to see why you guys were so excited," Zac remarked at Ogras as he started to swing at the remaining alpha dogs, heading to pick up the boss carcass and his axe.

"Don't get complacent. This is just the warm-up. If some mangy dogs were all that the Ruthless Heavens threw at you when creating a monster horde, then it would be a reward, not a quest. It's going to get much worse than this," Ogras retorted, obviously a bit irritated that his kill steal hadn't worked out. As if to confirm this, the remaining wolves in his surroundings died by being impaled by multiple shadow blades rather than the usual one per monster.

As if they responded to the demon's words, the portals pulsed and started to spew out another wave of wolves, but these ones looked quite different.

84

SUPER BROTHER-MAN

Zac turned toward Ogras, a bit confused.

"Why are there already more monsters pouring out? How does the System decide?" he asked hesitantly. He felt that it was too big a coincidence that new monsters just started spawning after Zac and Ogras arrived here and killed the boss.

"You ask me, but who am I going to ask?" Ogras responded. "I think there might be certain triggers that push out new waves. Perhaps killing the boss immediately sends the next one through. There may be a limit of how long you can stall, even if you keep the leader alive. The Ruthless Heavens has its name for a reason, and it won't let you breathe too easily by finding a loophole."

If what Ogras said was true, the System really created a conflict of interest. Killing the boss would spawn more monsters, but it also probably awarded a good number of contribution points. Greedy warriors would hunt it for the points, not caring about the results. Soon the whole camp would be overrun by waves upon waves of wolves.

"We need to set some ground rules," Zac immediately said as he turned to Ogras. He didn't mind the demon killing the odd wolf around him, as that was only playing around. There were almost an endless number of targets, and Zac didn't worry that he wouldn't be able to hunt his fill. But running for the bosses in greed for contribution points couldn't be allowed.

"The boss is off-limits until only a quarter of the wave remains," he said as he stared at Ogras, who only grimaced but nodded after some deliberation.

He didn't have time to keep thinking up plans, as the new wave was upon them. Zac first thought it was large rats when he saw them exit the portals. They were a lot smaller compared to their brethren, the normal ones only reaching his knees in height. They also looked completely wretched, with their mangy fur fallen off on large patches of their bodies. Their eyes were a sinister red, and the feeling he got from them was that they were putrid cursed creatures.

Ogras seemed to agree, as he started backing away as he kept throwing out shadow blades at anything approaching. He even seemed loath to use his real spear, afraid it would get dirtied by the new beasts.

"These things look pretty disgusting. Try not to get bitten. I am willing to bet an arm these things carry some weird diseases in their bodies," the demon said with a wrinkled brow. "If you capture a few live ones and gift them to Alea, I'm sure she will be delighted. I bet she can create some sinister concoctions from these things after some experimentation. Anyway, I'm off. Good luck."

With that, the demon was gone, using his escape skill to move through the shadows. Zac was left alone, pondering whether to stay here right by the portals or to head back. The gnarly wolves didn't wait for him to make a decision, and they stormed him with speed belying their small shriveled frames.

As they scurried close to him, they launched themselves in the air toward his face in order to rip into more vulnerable areas. Zac turned his huge axe and, with a horizontal swing, smashed multiple wolves into broken pieces of flesh with the broad side of the edge. Even their blood smelled rancid, and Zac didn't want to get any of that on his face. He rapidly backed away and quickly put a handkerchief over his nose and mouth.

Next, he swapped out his huge unwieldy axe for two normal ones. The new foes were too small, so he couldn't easily kill them with the giga-axe. A wide swing would simply fly past above their heads, and he felt that using two normal axes would be more effective. He kept swinging away, decimating anything that moved close as he gradually retreated toward the walls. His kill speed wasn't as great as when he used **[Chop]**, but it was respectable.

Since he'd upgraded his Race, he found that his body's coordination improved noticeably, and it had made him resume his training with two axes. The first time he'd tried it out, he felt it was too unwieldy, but by now, his arms moved independently from each other, each creating gouts of putrid blood wherever they hit.

Soon enough, he was closing in on the wall and saw that most of the first wave was dead by now. A perimeter of melee fighters had been erected, and Zac saw some scared noncombat demons scurrying about the battlefield. They were throwing the wolf carcasses into Cosmos Sacks, to be dumped and burned further away from the camp after anything of value was stripped from the bodies.

It was to avoid pestilence spreading, but also to not allow bodies to accumulate to the point that they started to form a ramp up the wall. Their work was extremely efficient as they rapidly moved along, barely stopping as they threw the carcasses into the Cosmos Sacks. Obviously, the melee fighters had done a do-over of the corpses first with quick stabs, ensuring that everything was dead.

When they saw Zac and the putrid wolves approaching, they

all scurried through a gate to safety. The gate wasn't some thick wooden door like in a medieval castle, but a section of the wall itself even thicker than most other sections. It was created in conjunction between some craftsmen and earth mages and required ten Nexus Crystals to power every time it opened and closed. It was a bit slow, but it didn't present a point of entry or weakness like classic castle gates did.

One exception to the escape through the gate was Alea, who gleefully charged straight toward Zac.

"I heard you're bringing me gifts?" she exclaimed, looking absolutely delighted. She heedlessly ran straight into the frenzied pack of the mangy wolves, and Zac's eyes widened in alarm. It was one thing for him with his huge Endurance to be running around in the midst of the beasts, as these small ones couldn't hurt him either.

But even he was wary of their blood, as it looked positively unclean, with a grayish murky color instead of red. Luckily, his clothes had a self-cleaning feature, and the blood just slid off after a short while. But for the slender demoness to do the same approach seemed suicidal. He wasn't sure on what stats a poison master focused, but it didn't feel like it was Endurance at least. He quickly changed direction and ran to help her out.

Soon he realized he was worried about nothing, as the beasts that got too close to her simply melted into pools of goop. Zac immediately stopped in his tracks, afraid to get caught in whatever poison the demoness had surrounded herself with.

Next, she quickly threw out a small needle at one of the beasts that looked extra wretched, and it powerlessly fell down on the ground immediately after the needle embedded itself in its throat. She walked over to it and picked it up, and for some reason, it didn't melt like the others around her. Zac first thought the beast was dead from the needle, but the frantically whirling eyes of the beast told another story.

"It seems its condition is due to living in a weird environment. The Ruthless Heavens calls its race Blackswamp Wolf, so it probably lives in a miasmic swamp. Something in the waters is corroding these wolves, and over time, they have transformed into these cute little things. Perhaps it's possible to extract whatever's the cause and add it into a concoction," she started to mutter mostly to herself, seeming eager to try to weaponize the wolves' affliction.

"People with less than 80 or so Vitality shouldn't come in contact with their blood, or they will probably get sick," she added with a louder voice up toward the walls before she started to continue to examine the beast. She quickly broke all its limbs with a deftness that hinted that this wasn't the first time she had done experimentation on animals, and started to retreat to the wall while she flipped it over to look at every detail of the poor creature.

Zac simply moved away without a word and kept killing wolves with his two axes. These small wolves were a bit more annoying to kill since they were so small, but he wouldn't stop. Each one gave around 110 Nexus Coins, even better than the last wave, and he was accumulating wealth and Cosmic Energy at a terrifying speed. It was barely more than a barghest, but they were everywhere. If the density of barghest was this crazy, he would have finished grinding for his first class quests in less than a day instead of a week. Of course, with his stats at that time he might just have died from being swarmed rather than just having more targets to kill.

Less than thirty minutes had passed since the start of the quest, but he'd already managed to accumulate something like 30,000 Nexus Coins. He had only used less than a quarter of his Cosmic Energy so far and could keep going for a long time. The attacks from the wall had reduced somewhat, though, as some of the demons were sitting down and absorbing energy from Nexus Crystals that Zac provided.

Some of the other demons kept blasting away, greedily farming some money, and a few burly-looking demons even dared to jump down from the wall as well, apparently trusting Alea's judgment. This wave was starting to thin out as well after the furious melee continued, and it gave Zac a brief chance to catch his breath.

He had been busy with the monsters, so he'd ignored the prompt from the System that had entered his ears just before the monsters arrived. It said that a Ladder was activated, and he was curious to see what that meant. He kept killing any beasts who approached with a quick swing of his axes, but it was mostly by instinct as he focused on the new screen that popped up.

[Ladder System initialized. Enter pseudonym or real name?]

That gave Zac a start. He started to feel that the Ladder System was akin to a ranking that he could see in many games, where his level was listed against others. It sounded like something the System would do. It wanted to force people to get stronger, and a Ladder would generate competition amongst the elite.

Entering his real name would let his friends or family know he was alive and fine, but it might also cause them trouble. He was pretty sure he should be up there in the rankings if the Ladder was only for Earth, even after his month of not gaining levels. Someone might want to exploit his family, or even kidnap them to threaten him if such a connection was made public. He already had created a beacon with the name Port Atwood, which should hopefully be enough when the town gained some fame in the future.

After coming to a decision, he chose a pseudonym, and a new problem presented itself. What should he call himself? At first, he thought of just using his class name, but he didn't know if people learning of the name Hatchetman would have some implications. Suddenly, he had an idea, and he chose "Super Brother-Man" with a nostalgic look in his eyes. He could only pray that MacKenzie, his little sister, would remember.

She was only five when he played pretend-superheroes with her, using the name Super Brother-Man. He hadn't thought about it for over a decade, and no one but her should know about it. As soon as he chose it, a large window popped up, and he quickly realized that he was right; it was a ranking Ladder containing various names and their accomplishments.

As he went through the list, his mouth started to widen into a grin.

85

FOUR FATES

Kenzie blew an errant wisp of frizzy auburn hair out of her face as she once again opened the Ladder system. It had almost become a compulsion over the last two weeks since the new function was enabled.

"Browsing for a husband again?" a teasing voice came from behind her as another girl moved up to the fire and sat down. It was Lyla, who came back with some dinner in her hands. It was a few cans of various vegetables and fruits, and somehow she had even scored some canned beef.

"Whatever," Mackenzie answered with a roll of her eyes. She stared at the familiar alias for a few more seconds before she reluctantly closed the window and turned to her friend.

Lyla had been by Kenzie's side since everything had turned crazy. Kenzie was just sitting at home, playing with her phone, when she suddenly found herself in a square in a medieval town with hundreds of others. When reality set in that this was not a dream, she soon realized she didn't recognize a single person. Zac or Dad wasn't there with her, leaving her vulnerable and scared.

It was shortly after she met Lyla, another scared and confused nineteen-year-old. It was by sticking together they survived that hell that the System and fairies called a Tutorial, and in a sense, they were returned as reborn people like the fairies promised.

But they soon realized that just because they had been returned in one piece, all wasn't well. They were placed in a town called Kingsbury, which actually was a chaotic hodgepodge of four different cities mixed together into a cauldron of conflicting interests and goals.

During the month of their absence, all order collapsed, and chaos reigned supreme. Roving gangs of thugs terrorized their blocks, and rape and murder were just commonplace events. It didn't even take an hour after returning before a group of men accosted her.

Luckily, the Tutorial had truly reforged her. A scenario that would have petrified her in the old world was only a small annoyance now. With a few quick attacks, the group of thugs lay on the ground with her not even taking damage. The thugs of Kingsbury just stayed in the safety of the town, preying on other people, and likely weren't even level 5.

After the returnees appeared, it only took a few days for a new order to be enforced on the town. A few of the stronger cultivators allied and started a bloody cleansing, and soon held the population in an iron grip. There was no government, no vote; only forced obedience. The leaders named themselves the Kingsbury Council and set themselves up as kings.

Mackenzie and Lyla followed Ruth, a forty-eight-year-old lady whom they got to know a bit in the Tutorial. She had been a cleaning lady before the integration, but now she held command over a large district, subduing any discontent with surprising brutality. Ruth was harsh, but she was the best of the bunch. None of those who stood out were saints, as they had all bathed in blood during the Tutorial to get their current strength.

It was actually due to one of the other councilors that Mackenzie and Lyla decided to volunteer to scout out the undead problem that was spreading. They needed to get away from the town and hopefully gain some Strength while away. Harold was an insatiable old goat, and he already considered himself an emperor and had started amassing women for his harem. Some of them were willing to get the protection of a powerhouse, as food was running scarce and monsters were roaming the outskirts of the town, but most reportedly were unwilling captives. There was a lot of discontent about his conduct, but Harold was possibly the most powerful cultivator in Kingsbury, and even Ruth didn't dare to confront him outright.

Of course, Harold was a joke compared to the people on the Ladder, like a fly compared to giants. Especially her brother, Super Brother-Man…

With a thundering swing, Billy crushed the skull of the rat-like monster, gray smelly goop splashing all around. It was one of the last of their kind, and he could finally catch his breath with deep guffaws. The whole field around him was filled with big holes from his mighty thwonking.

The new world was good. Before, everything had been confusing and complicated. People had given Billy stinky eye all the time for no reason. But no one looked down on Billy now. Not even Papa, not after the thwonk on his head set him straight.

Billy didn't understand why so many didn't like the new world. It was so simple. Hit things on the head and they gave you money and made you stronger. But people hid behind the walls and cried instead of going out thwonking. People were the idiots, not Billy.

"Good work, great chief! You are so strong. The name Billy is surely known around the world by now!" a voice came from up on the wall.

It was Nigel. Nigel was smart but dumb. He was smart because he understood Billy was a good chief. He was dumb because he didn't thwonk monsters with Billy and instead stayed on the wall.

"I bet not even Super Brother-Man is a match for you and your club, Billy! See how those large rats got destroyed!" Nigel continued, even waving the flag of the town, Billyville.

When Billy heard the compliment, his back straightened a bit further, and the bulging muscles on his huge frame swelled, but he soon shrank back a bit.

"Super Brother-Man is probably super-strong. He has thwonked a lot more than Billy. But Billy is going to catch up. There are still many rats to bash," he said with the type of modesty that Mama always said a gentleman should have. He really missed Mama, but she had been gone when Billy came back from the funny town with the mini-people. Nigel said that she had died, but Billy knew no monster would dare hurt such an angel.

Billy really wondered who Super Brother-Man was. It was a great name and caused Billy to regret the one he chose, Thwonkin' Billy. He really wanted to see who could swing a club the best. Having another smart friend to bash rats with would be great.

Billy was right about the rats. There were so many of them, and some help would be nice. He had tried counting them, but he got a headache from it. They all came from that gray weird shining light in the distance. Nigel called it an incursion, but Billy preferred to call it a ratlight, since it created rats and was a light.

Nigel always told him that the thing needed to be closed for some quest, but Billy didn't care about any of that. He needed no reason for thwonking rats. It felt good; it gave money and made Billy stronger.

Billy was truly in heaven.

She moved through the forest, a flittering shadow between the trees. Any unsuspecting beast that came within a few meters was bisected into pieces by a quick flash.

Thea was days from any backup or civilization, but it was out here in the wilderness that she felt most at home. No politics and intrigue, only survival. She had hoped that the integration would make the world simpler, but it was anything but the truth.

The Marshall clan went into overdrive the moment Earth was integrated, ever hungry for empowering the family. She was tired of it and had essentially become a nomad, fiercely battling in the wilderness nonstop since she came back. The pixies had called her a once-in-a-millennium genius, but she didn't care about any of that. She relished the feeling of balancing on the edge of life and death, pushing the limits of her power even further.

Still, she was shocked when she saw the Ladder. Her tireless effort and fortuitous encounters seemed almost like a joke in front of that man. She thought herself the true elite of Earth, as no one in her Tutorial town even came close to her accomplishments. It only took her a week of grinding after the Tutorial was over before she attained her class, and it was of the Rare-rarity, something that was almost impossible to get.

Yet she barely maintained the third spot on the Ladder. She had even pushed herself beyond what she thought was possible in order to catch up, refusing to lose to someone with such a stupid moniker. But no matter what she did, he steadily increased the distance between them. Who the hell was Super Brother-Man?

She sighed and opened up her quest panel and stared at her newly acquired mission. Completing it might be her only option to pass that monster, but was it worth it?

Order was crumbling. Thomas Fischer sat on the short side of the large table and quietly stared at the troubled faces in the meeting room.

"What about recruitment?" Thomas said with a sigh.

"Eighty returnees, or cultivators as they call themselves, have signed up to the special government task force in the last week," a bespectacled middle-aged lady answered. "Unfortunately, most of them are in the lower tier who barely came out of the so-called Tutorial in one piece. The stronger ones have largely stayed ambivalent, adopting a wait-and-see response."

"We need to get tougher! People are running around playing superheroes. Or even worse, super-villains. We need to round them up. If they don't want to join and register, they need to be locked up!" a robust scarred man shouted while thumping emphatically on the table. It was Hank, the representative of the army.

Thomas was somewhat inclined to agree with him, but not really due to safety. The more powerful of these cultivators were setting themselves up as local Lords, completely ignoring the government. If this was allowed to continue, then Earth's countries would just become a memory.

"What about the Rankers? Have we located any of them?" Thomas probed. Getting the support of a few of the Rankers would hopefully once again legitimize the government in the eyes of the population, and rebuilding work could begin in earnest.

"Why bother with them? The training program for the elite forces of the army is coming along well, and there are cultivator servicemen who have reported for duty leading them. Soon we will have an army adapted to this so-called System. It is better to rely on patriotic soldiers than some warlords who can betray us at moment's notice," Hank interjected.

"What's the average level so far among the trainees?" Julia asked, breaking her hour-long silence. She was the newly appointed liaison with the unaffiliated cultivators, and one of the four cultivators herself in the meeting.

"The average level is 19, and we already have two people who have gained their classes," Hank answered proudly.

"How can you compare some fodder to the Rankers? Any one of them is probably able to decimate your army in a minute," Julia said dismissively and turned back to Thomas.

"We have located five of the Rankers so far. Rank 34, 58, 63, and 94 on the Level Ladder. We have also located rank 87 and 99 on the Wealth Ladder. Rank 87 is, as you know, the same individual as rank 34 on the Power Ladder.

"There are also about a dozen individuals who used their real name that we have identified with some certainty. Most notable is Thea Marshall of the Marshall family, who is ranked third on the level ranking. Unfortunately, we do not know where these people are located at the moment, with the effects of the reshuffling still being mapped out."

"Any word on Super Brother-Man or Salvation?" Thomas asked. Thea Marshall would be a good get for the government, but the Marshall clan likely had their own plans in this new world order. And he didn't want to wage war against that ancient family when there were both the incursions and the new natives to worry about, so he could only turn his eyes toward the other two top Rankers. Of course, neither of them seemed to be quite sane from their choice of pseudonyms, but one couldn't be picky after the apocalypse.

The hesitant look in Julia's eye was all the answer Thomas needed as he sighed.

"Next on the docket is the situation with our new… neighbors… to the west."

86

LADDERS

Zac opened up his eyes after an hour of meditation. Alea sat next to him like an ever-present shadow, but even she lacked the energy to banter lately. Even Zac felt exhausted after the last three weeks of wholesale slaughter, and the demons were even in worse shape. He had killed thousands upon thousands of wolves in all shapes and sizes, as the waves unceasingly kept coming once every hour from the start of the quest. In the beginning, the wolves were just free money for the defenders, and each wave took between fifteen minutes to half an hour to complete.

But their Strength incrementally increased with every wave, and after hundreds of waves, they barely managed to finish the last one before the next one arrived. Zac and Ogras had been forced to create rotating groups of the stronger demons, as there had been a wave that actually caused a crack in the wall since almost everyone was resting.

There were some good signs, though. If he and Ogras were correct, they only needed to hold out for another three days before the first part of the quest was completed. A new wave arrived at the hour unceasingly, and they needed to defeat 720 waves in a month. They had already cleared 641 waves in three weeks due to quickly finishing the early waves, and hoped that would mean that they got the rest of the month off until the next part of the quest started.

More good news was that Zac hadn't been forced to use any of his aces so far, with the walls and demons having been enough for now. Perhaps they would be able to finish the whole first part without any tools, which would save a lot of Nexus Coins for the next parts of the quest. Since it was getting incrementally harder, he assumed that things would only get worse with the second and third hordes.

It was his turn to man the walls in just ten minutes, so he started to get ready. He opened his status screen to check his progress before heading out.

Name: Zachary Atwood
Level: 48
Class: [F-Rare] Hatchetman
Race: [E] Human
Alignment: [Earth] Human

Titles: Born for Carnage, Ultimate Reaper, Luck of the Draw, Giantsbane, Disciple of David, Overpowered, Slayer of Leviathans, Adventurer, Demon Slayer, Full of Class, Rarified Being, Trailblazer, Child of Dao, The Big 500, Planetary Aegis, One Against Many, Butcher

Dao: Seed of Heaviness – Early, Seed of Trees – Early

Strength: 248
Dexterity: 125
Endurance: 165
Vitality: 108
Intelligence: 62

Wisdom: 57
Luck: 77

Free Points: 0
Nexus Coins: 21,281,353

He had gained a whole twelve levels from the last weeks of desperate struggle, which averaged to roughly a level every other day. He'd put all free points into Dexterity until he reached a two-to-one ratio of Strength to Dexterity, and after that started putting points in Vitality. By now, his build was far more balanced compared to before, and he wasn't a lopsided one-trick pony anymore. That didn't only go for attributes. He had battled every imaginable kind of wolf as of late and gained tremendous battle experience in a very short time.

Zac gained most of his levels in the first week of the monster horde, and it started to slow down considerably after that. The last four days had gone by without a single level. When he complained about it to Ogras, the demon got so agitated he started to spit after him. Apparently, his leveling speed was out of this world. It had taken Ogras five whole years to reach the same level as Zac. Of course, Ogras wasn't pushing toward getting levels, but rather focused on the Dao and his body grade. Otherwise it would have been a lot quicker.

But if a cultivator didn't level through battle like he did, and instead only relied on their cultivation techniques, it would take years and years to get to this point. A few days ago, he'd gained a new title, which was quite telling about his life on the island so far.

[Butcher: Kill 100,000 beings in solo battle. Reward: Strength, Dexterity, Intelligence +3.]

The absolute majority of those kills were the wolves from the last weeks, but he had been steeped in blood and gore constantly since the world changed.

Next he opened the Ladder to see if any changes had happened in the last few days.

Ladder – Level

Rank | Name | Level

1. Super Brother-Man | 48
2. Salvation | 39
3. Thea Marshall | 38
4. Joker | 35
5. Enigma | 34
6. Dahlia | 34
7. Dillinger | 33
8. Thwonkin' Billy | 33
9. Abbot Everlasting Peace | 33
10. The Gravemaker | 32

…

100. Santiago30

Ladder – Wealth

Rank | Name

1. Super Brother-Man
2. Smaug
3. Joker
4. Enigma
5. Thwonkin' Billy
6. Salvation
7. Greed
8. Little Treasure
9. Thea Marshall
10. The Eternal Eye

Ladder – Dao

Rank | Name

1. Abbot Everlasting Peace
2. Guru Anaad Phakiwar
3. Thea Marshall
4. The Eternal Eye
5. Silverfox
6. Abbot Boundless Truth
7. Super Brother-Man
8. Father Thomas
9. John Doe
10. Daoist Chosui

He had mostly memorized the Ladders by now, and the top ten spots didn't really change in the last few days. The ranking boards only showed the top hundred, and it was clear that a few front-runners were solidifying their positions as future progenitors, as Ogras called them. Beneath the true powerhouses were the elites, and it seemed the elites in the world should have gotten their class a few weeks ago, and now were around level 30.

When the Ladder was introduced, the hundredth spot on the leveling ranking had been level 27, which meant it took them roughly a week per level-up until now. Beneath the top twenty, the list was a lot more volatile, with people changing positions every day. He had also seen over a dozen names just suddenly disappear, which he assumed meant that they died.

When he first checked the Ladder, he'd found himself only two levels ahead of Salvation, which shocked him quite a bit. Certainly, he hadn't improved his level for over forty days while in the mines, but he'd started out at level 16 with extremely boosted stats due to the lottery he had been forced into. Furthermore, he had almost only killed incursion monsters who awarded an increased experience. Yet this Salvation, and to a lesser degree Thea Marshall, were right behind him in progress.

That changed over the last few weeks, though, as his level kept steadily increasing while they could only helplessly fall behind. Still, their speed was respectable, and Zac assumed they'd found great grinding spots as well, likely incursions with their improved experience rewards.

The wealth ranking thankfully didn't broadcast the exact wealth people possessed, but it did show he was number one in that ranking as well. Surprisingly, the second spot belonged to someone who wasn't in either the Level or the Dao rankings. He had named himself after the dragon in *Lord of the Rings*, so Zac assumed he alluded to the fact that he was sitting on a pile of treasure.

Otherwise, there was some correlation between the level ranking and the wealth ranking, as everyone on the list must've killed an enormous number of beasts and farmed Nexus Coins. But the level Rankers only accounted for roughly half the names on the wealth rankings.

Ogras believed that it was due to dumb luck. Some individuals had found some great treasures and sold them in the System shops that should have cropped up at various places by now. Some might have scored millions of Nexus Coins just from one herb or rare metal. Neither Zac nor Ogras was sure how the System calculated wealth. Nexus Coins were a given, but what about his other treasures, such as his remaining Fruit of Ascension? What about the Creators' shipyard? Either of those were worth a fortune, far more than every coin he had gained so far. Calrin might know, but they hadn't visited lately due to constantly being in battle.

But even without those two treasures, he wasn't too surprised about his number one spot. He'd gained over 10 million Nexus Coins from the crystal mine and another 20 million from the last three weeks of carnage. He had a hard time imagining anyone gaining coins at his speed.

Last was the Dao ranking. He was only ranked seventh on that Ladder, even though he'd already acquired two Dao Seeds. He wasn't sure whether the ones above him had somehow gained even more seeds, or if they'd managed to upgrade the ones they had. More interestingly, a large part of the Rankers seemed to be spiritual people from the old world. There were priests, gurus, monks, and even a shaman represented on the list.

He learned from Alyn that a combination of meditation and study of fractals were the best combination to improve the Dao, so it seemed that these individuals hit the ground running when it came to pondering the Dao. They were already quite used to meditation, and maybe even entered the System with certain useful insights.

The Dao list was also the only list that wasn't filled, with only sixty-eight spots occupied so far. There were a few that got added every day, though, so Zac expected this list to be filled within the month. This list was also the one that moved the least. He had only seen one movement, where Thea Marshall instantly went from the twenty-third spot all the way to the third. Ogras said she must have had an epiphany or a fortuitous encounter that gave her Dao a level-up.

Actually, the Dao ranking was the one that shocked Ogras the most. There were only three demons currently on Earth who actually possessed a Dao, according to him. And two of them only gained their seeds after arduously meditating for years. Ogras believed that it was the Tutorial giving a huge hand in some way; otherwise, only those who got Dao Seeds from quests like Zac should have touched the Dao this early.

Zac was surprised to see that many of the top ten individuals of the level ranking actually hadn't gained a Dao Seed so far, not even the second-place individual named Salvation. Zac didn't know whether that made him more or less scary, having reached that level without any Dao to assist and empower his or her skills. Actually, he and Thea were the only two people represented on all three lists, with his rankings slightly better.

Finally, Zac closed down the windows and got ready for work. Alea roused herself as well and mutely followed behind him as he proceeded up to the wall walk. Ogras approached not long after Zac arrived at the top of the wall, the usual lackadaisical attitude missing. He had a grim visage as he nodded toward Zac before once more looking out toward the battlefield. His hand didn't stop moving, and the large bristled wolves beneath died one by one.

"Third casualty this wave," he curtly said, worry evident in his eyes. The demon forces were limited, and every death hurt them in the long run. Over the course of the whole monster horde quest, it meant thousands of additional monsters the others would have to kill. Three deaths in three weeks might sound good, but only roughly two hundred of the demons were combat classes. Three deaths were noticeable; besides, the quest wasn't even one-third completed, and Zac could only assume it would keep getting worse.

It wasn't that the wolves were extremely strong. The large wolves beneath the wall could roughly be considered as strong as the monkeys in the mountains by now. But their numbers were endless, and the demons were tired. And tired people made mistakes.

The wolves of this wave apparently were able to shoot out the bristles on their backs in a wide-range attack that targeted both friends and foe. One demon had been unlucky and actually got skewered up on the wall from an errant flying bristle. Normally, he should have been able to erect a defense or dodge in time, but he'd spaced out due to extreme fatigue.

Zac only grunted in affirmation as he looked out over the battlefield. Most of the wolves were dead, with just a few large packs remaining. He could already see the next wave's approach from the distance, so he didn't hesitate as he jumped down right among the bristled beasts. The impact killed eight of them, not giving them any chance to shoot out their projectiles.

With a large **[Chop],** he immediately created a circle of death, and then he methodically started killing the beasts with a blank look on his face. A few bristles flew in his direction, but they were no threat to him. The ones hitting his body he simply ignored since his clothes nullified the impact, and those flying for his head he blocked with his axe-head.

Just as he killed last of the Bristleback Wolves, as they apparently were called, the next wave was only a hundred meters away. These wolves were of average size and build and had a grayish-black color. What made them stand out was that they actually looked a bit translucent as he saw them approach.

Hesitant, he brought out a rock from a pouch and launched it like a rocket at one of the front-runners. It was his standard move lately whenever a new wave of wolves approached. He'd started using it after wave 372, which had consisted of "Wolves of Kar'Ka'Venum."

He still had no idea what Kar'Ka'Venum was, but when he charged into the group of wolves and swung his axe in a large **[Chop]**, every single monster exploded in a huge shock wave upon death. The blast from his swing almost killed him then and there, and after that, he swore to be more careful.

To his surprise, the stone whizzed straight through the monster like it was a ghost. Zac got a sinking feeling as he saw the approaching horde, and without hesitation, he turned around and roared, "ACTIVATE THE ARRAY!"

87

SPECTRAL WOLVES

Ogras was quick on the uptake, and he immediately shouted down the other side of the wall, where Janos stood next to a large crystal. The illusionist immediately activated the array with the help of a pile of Nexus Crystals, and with a deep hum, a shimmering dome grew out of the ground, covering the whole inner area of Port Atwood. It reminded Zac of a large soap bubble, with prismatic colors covering the whole shield, slowly swirling about. But the observant watchers could see that the swirls weren't really random, but rather followed some pattern, and that the stripes of colors were reminiscent of fractals.

It was the **[E-Grade Medium-Scale Town Defense Array]**, Zac's first purchase with his wealth gained from the crystal mine. The town planners had gone over various other solutions, such as purchasing defensive and offensive arrays separately, but the Town Defense Array simply gave an unparalleled bang for the buck for these low-tier battles. In the future, an established force would likely have tens of arrays available, each designed for a specific defense or attack, but with their limited resources, they went with the generalist approach.

The only downside was that it cost quite a lot of crystals to operate. But with a crystal mine in his possession, Zac wasn't too worried about consumption. Initially, its radius was roughly fifty meters shorter compared to the wall, creating an inner death zone between the wall and the barrier. But after some adjustments, it grew to stop ten meters outside the walls, not allowing the spectral wolves access to the fortifications.

Zac took a few quick steps backward with **[Loamwalker]**, allowing him to cross over a hundred meters almost in an instant. He smoothly passed through the barrier without creating a ripple. The shield wasn't intelligent enough to distinguish friend from foe, but as the owner of the array, he had some perks.

Normally, he would have preferred to keep the array at its original size and test whether the wolves could actually run through the wall, but there were too many tired demons up on the battlements at the moment. They were changing shifts with this wave, and everyone hadn't left their posts yet. Instead, he had to expend some money in order to ensure the group of demons heading further in to rest wouldn't be assaulted by these ghost wolves. They were wrung out and didn't have the energy to resist anymore.

Soon the beasts heedlessly slammed into the shield, some even dying from the impact. The shield was a product of the System itself and didn't even flicker from the impact. The wolves weren't disheartened and started to claw frenziedly at the translucent barrier, but it had no effect at all. After a few seconds, it was obvious that these beasts' only strong point was their incorporeal state.

Zac didn't want to waste even more crystals by activating the offensive component of the array as well, and instead took out his axe and headed out through the array once more. Attacks from the wall also started to fall down at the wolves through the barrier, as it only stopped things from going inside and not the other way.

It immediately became clear what worked and didn't work

with these things. The arrowheads helplessly embedded themselves into the ground after passing through the transparent bodies of the wolves, with a few exceptions. Any arrow that was imbued with some skill, such as lightning or darkness, had no problem killing the beasts. Meanwhile, the mages had no problems at all and gleefully peppered the wolves full of holes.

Zac saw the same results. His axe just passed through the wolf it targeted, and it responded by trying to bite his free arm. Zac actually let it in order to see the result, and surprisingly, it managed to grab hold of the small of his arm. Its bite had no effect on Zac, and he felt that its power was only equivalent to the beasts on the two-hundredth wave or somewhere around there.

He charged a minimal amount of Cosmic Energy into the fractal on his hand, and a small edge from **[Chop]** appeared. It was barely as long as the normal edge, but it cost almost no Cosmic Energy. Normally, there would be little benefit to using it like this, but with these particular wolves, it was very effective.

The wolves were like normal beasts to the edge created from Cosmic Energy, and its head was split in two. However, no blood spurted out, and the beast simply broke down into motes of darkness before it was completely gone. Next he tried using only the Dao with his axe, and it worked as well in letting him kill the monsters. Obviously, the beasts would be extremely dangerous to normal humans, but against skills, they were pretty weak.

Still, the speed of whittling down their numbers was quite slow, as not all the demons possessed ranged skills. Those who were melee classes usually helped out by throwing rocks or shooting arrows from the wall when the battlefield was too dangerous, but now, they could only helplessly stare on.

Very few demons dared to pass through the barrier to fight head-on. It wasn't like the wall that had the gates or ropes hanging from it that would allow the demons to quickly retreat if needed. If they passed through, they would be stuck on the battlefield until the barrier was lowered, as they couldn't come and go as they pleased like Zac.

The longer the barrier stayed active, the more crystals would be consumed, and Zac felt the need to end this battle quickly. He started to charge up his **[Chop]** skill until it was five meters long, then with a mental command, the edge multiplied into five identical parallel edges. They were right next to each other with less than a centimeter between them, making the edge look like a thick block of fractals.

Zac rapidly swung his axe horizontally five times, and with every swing, one of the edges flew out in a different direction. Each blade created a huge path of death, and Zac felt a constant torrent of Cosmic Energy enter his body as a large part of the battlefield turned into black motes of light.

The new attack was the result of constantly being in pitched battles for weeks. Both his **[Axe Mastery]** and **[Chop]** had improved once again, reaching Late Mastery. According to Alea, the mastery stages of skills were Early-Mid-Late-Peak before they reached their limits and needed to be upgraded, meaning the skills were close to completion.

The improved **[Chop]** currently held stable at five meters instead of one, and now allowed multiple blades to be created. Initially, he had only managed to create two, but as his control over Cosmic Energy improved from constant battle, the number of blades he could maintain stably increased. The extra blades had no purpose when they were attached, but greatly improved his area damage when he shot them away.

[Chop] was more and more turning into an area skill, but it didn't really improve the power of his strikes. He would have to imbue his Dao into the blades in order to improve the lethality compared to a normal swing. Luckily, area damage was just the thing he needed with the monster hordes, so he was quite happy with the improvements.

Initially, he wasn't sure what the point was of creating five blades in this new manner since he could just create them one by one and shoot them out in succession instead. But he realized that the Cosmic Energy consumption was a lot lower for copying an existing blade rather than creating it from scratch for some reason. Creating five blades the new way only required half the Cosmic Energy compared to creating them one by one. Each blast he shot out usually killed a good number of beasts, so being able to launch twice as many was a huge improvement.

He hadn't really explored the effect of **[Axe Mastery]** yet, as he didn't have the luxury of spending Cosmic Energy on the training system with the hordes constantly requiring attention. He hoped he'd get some days off where he could try it for a bit after the first horde was finished with.

Zac spent a decent chunk of Cosmic Energy in quickly reaping the lives of a large part of the wave, which allowed the melee warriors to head out and help out with the remainder. Soon only a few stragglers remained, and Zac could deactivate the shield. The shield had only been active for roughly thirty minutes, but Zac knew that it had cost him over a 100,000 Nexus Coins. Even with his large number of kills from using his area attacks, he knew he took a loss from this wave.

That was why he had refused to use the shield thus far, even though it cost the lives of a couple of demons. It might seem callous, but no one was stepping up to share the cost of maintenance, with everyone trying to amass as much wealth as possible from the waves.

He could force them to hand over some of the earnings, in a manual shakedown of sorts. But he didn't feel the need for that as of yet, and saw their gains as a salary. But if it came down to it, he wasn't above commandeering everything they had in order to protect his base. The demons were aware of this fact, and many even braved the dangers of the wolf hordes in order to burn all their cash at the Thayer Consortium when their pockets became heavy.

Apparently, Calrin was well aware of the situation and had hiked up the cost of the herbs needed for medicine baths to twice its normal prices, citing the troubles of restocking during wartime. Zac suspected this was all baloney, as the gnome had access to the Mercantile System, which allowed him to easily restock the supplies at any time.

The demons could only grit their teeth and cough up their hard-earned Nexus Coins. Zac really looked forward to the shareholders' meeting of Thayer Consortium in two months when he would get his quarterly dividends from the proceedings. He had a feeling that the little gnome should have squeezed out an extraordinary amount of coins from the poor demons by then.

Since the ghost wolf wave was largely dead, the System quickly pumped out the next one, and the army went back to business as usual. This time, it was large lumbering things that looked made out of rocks, and some even had moss growing on their wide backs. The wolves were easily the largest kind so far, each reaching over three meters tall, with the leader towering over five meters. It was a bit troublesome, as the walls only stood at eight meters, meaning that the huge thing might be able to reach the top if it stood on its hind legs.

The saving grace was that there only was a little over a hundred of them, but each felt like a walking siege machine, and Zac started to wonder whether he should erect the barrier again before these hulking things started to break down the fortifications. Imagining the cost of maintaining the barrier with these monstrosities charging at it quickly helped Zac arrive at a decision, and he charged toward the wolves after the customary rock throw, which only elicited an angry growl this time.

88

A DAY IN THE WOLF HORDE

Zac intercepted the group of wolves some distance in front of the walls, not wanting to give them a chance to ruin his fortifications. These hulking things really looked like they could cause a dent in the wall. Zac really wished that the walls were inscribed with protective inscriptions like the whole shipyard, since then he wouldn't have to worry about this. Unfortunately, there was no one with the skill set to inscribe the wall among the demons.

It was a recurring problem with the noncombat class demons in Azh'Rodum. Only a handful possessed great proficiency or promise in their field, with the rest generally being assistants or simply untalented. Most of the more talented ones enjoyed almost the same level of reputation in the demon clan as the warriors and had decided to head back, as their punishment would be bearable. That left a large number of people fumbling around, kind of like Zac. Ogras had obviously oversold the competence of his people the first time they met.

A huge rocky maw approaching woke him from his thoughts, and he sidestepped a few meters with his movement skill. His normal axes were much too small to do any real damage to these massive things, so he swapped it out for his huge elongated axe. He didn't want to use too much energy this wave, as he'd spent more than usual the last one.

Fighting the monster waves was a marathon rather than a sprint, and conservation was key. He jumped up a few meters and, with a grunt, decapitated the huge monster. Rock-chippings flew all about as the head fell down, and Zac felt that the cut barely was enough. The axe took noticeable damage as well from cutting into the hard monster, even though it had strengthening inscriptions.

Suddenly, his Luck stat warned him of something approaching from behind, and he immediately pushed to the side. It surprisingly was the head of the fallen beast. Or rather, it was a few smaller versions of the large rocky wolf that somehow were born out of the decapitated head. Zac was surprised but quickly killed them with a few swings.

He looked over to the main part of the body and saw that it was starting to squirm. Soon over ten wolves were born through its various parts, the transformation creating jarring sounds of rock scratching against rock. These wolves were apparently like some type of matryoshka dolls, containing more monsters inside. Even worse, he saw the smaller version he'd just bisected once more turn into even smaller wolves, these ones the size of medium-sized dogs.

After some deliberation, he chose to ignore these new smaller beasts and instead ran toward the next huge wolf. With a large jump, he approached the next wolf from above, and at the last second, he infused his large axe with the Dao of Heaviness. The swing contained the momentum and weight of a falling meteor, and not only was the beast cut in two, but cracks ran all along its body.

A large surge of Cosmic Energy entering his body told Zac that the swing had destroyed a lot more than just a few beasts like his last swing did. It seemed he needed to do large-scale damage to the rocks if he wanted to destroy the smaller versions along with the main body. Since most of the beasts in this one were dead, he proceeded to the next one. The large ones were the real trouble, as they might be able to threaten his walls. After they split into multiple smaller targets, their threat lessened greatly, and the demon army could handle that.

Zac went from beast to beast and, with large swing, destroyed one towering beast after another. Every time he infused the swings with the Dao, almost half the monsters inside died due to cracks forming all over from the impact. After roughly a dozen wolves, his large axe was starting to distort from the force, and he could only helplessly tuck it away, instead bringing out a large mallet. It was reminiscent of the large hammer a demon had used on top of the mountain, and Zac found it pretty interesting when he'd raided the demons' armory.

He still preferred using axes, but sometimes other weapons were simply more convenient. Blunt force was clearly the best tool against these beasts, and that wasn't something axes excelled at. Unfortunately, Zac had problems using his Dao of Heaviness with the large mallet, but with his enormous Strength, he only needed his body against these wolves.

One by one, the large wolves were decimated by Zac's approach, and he actually managed to destroy eighty of them before they reached the wall. Left behind in his wake were broken rocks and smaller wolves, who resumed the approach.

The demons on the wall had a lot of trouble destroying these large beasts, as it took them an inordinate amount of effort to destroy another ten of them. Helplessly, they could only focus on the smaller ones, as they began a methodical dismantling. The number of wolves was staggering by now, as most of the wolves survived after Zac switched to the mallet.

The last surviving whole wolves heedlessly ran into the wall, creating huge impacts that could be felt to the bone. Worst was the area where the boss rammed the wall, as large cracks ran all the way to the foundation. The earth mages on top of the wall quickly stopped their attacks and instead focused on mending the cracks before they spread any further. A few unlucky demons were even flung off the wall to the ground by the shock wave.

After the initial impact, the normal wolves couldn't do too much damage. They scratched and bit the walls, and with every attack, deep gouges were created. Still, it would take some time before they got through the thick walls, so Zac wasn't too worried about that. The boss was another matter.

With surprising nimbleness, it backed away a bit and stood up on its hind legs. The monster was huge, reaching a fair bit over ten meters in height when it stood like this. It looked like bad news to Zac, forcing him to action, even though he usually tried to ignore the boss as long as possible. He even swapped out the mallet for his usual axe, and charged up a **[Chop]** as he approached. With one quick motion, he cut off one of the hind legs, but it was too late. The monster was already falling down toward the wall, and with a tremendous crash, it slammed into it. Rocks from both the boss and the wall flew everywhere, and the shock wave forced even Zac back some distance.

Luckily, the wall was sturdy enough that a single body-slam wasn't enough to destroy it. A section of the top wall was crushed, however. Even worse, the boss created a sort of ramp up toward the other side, and it looked like most of the wolves were ready. They stopped their assault at the wall and charged toward the now unmoving boss.

The fact that Zac had gained almost no Cosmic Energy when he lopped off the leg told him that the boss was still alive and simply kept still in order to let its minions over the wall. This put Zac in a predicament, as he didn't know whether to kill the boss or try to stop the invasion on its back. If he destroyed the boss, the security breach would be fixed, but the next wave would spawn prematurely. Conversely, if he left it alive, some demons risked dying from the onslaught.

After some hesitation, he started chopping off parts of the large boss, making the walkway along its back a bit thinner. He quickly stopped after the walkway was only three meters wide at most parts, though, as he was afraid the System would count it as a kill if he continued on.

After that, he placed himself on the back of the wolf to meet the oncoming onslaught. Hundreds of stone wolves were converging on his location, and Zac destroyed them one by one as they approached. He once again took out a second small axe to dual-wield against the incoming sea of wolves. He was like a grinder where wolves entered and small chunks of rocks exited. Every now and then, some of the smaller wolves slipped through the cracks and ran past Zac up toward the wall. A second line of defense consisting of a few melee warriors had already formed behind Zac, though, and they were quickly dealt with.

The other demons weren't idle either, and they bombarded the wolves below. Zac's actions created a chokepoint, and the wolves trying to get up their leader's back were packed tightly along the wall. Any attack was having great efficiency, as it was essentially impossible to miss by now. A group of warriors also scaled the wall down to ambush the wolves from behind as they all tried to move toward Zac.

The number of wolves was steadily decreasing, and the battlefield was starting to fill with rocky debris. It was worst around Zac, as most of the action was centered around there. It was actually starting to create a problem, as every death added onto their boss, and the wolf ramp was growing wider and sturdier as the battle went on.

It was getting increasingly hard for Zac to kill everything that tried to get up without expending any Cosmic Energy, as he simply had trouble reaching both sides of the widening ramp. Every now and then, he stomped the ground with a Dao-empowered foot, creating a small landslide of rocks and gravel. It helped to somewhat allay the problem, but it was only delaying the inevitable.

"Stash the rocks into Cosmos Sacks!" Zac shouted behind him, and a few demons moved forward to comply. He had actually attained the **[Book of Babel]** some time ago by using contribution points.

The skill wasn't available in his Nexus Node, so he was quite excited to see the skill in the temporary contribution shop. The shop was actually another crystal that spawned close to his camp, along with a huge monitor that listed the rankings of contribution. It only showed the top ten, though.

The skill cost a week's worth of Zac's contribution points, but he felt it was worth it. Communication was getting more important as the waves got harder and some teamwork was needed. Besides, he would need the skill soon anyway when he set out from the island. He had no idea who he'd meet when he left since the world had gotten randomized, and it would be quite frustrating if he finally met humans but couldn't communicate with them.

The wave was finally starting to thin out, but the battle on top of the boss had continuously caused damage and cracks to the hulking beast they stood on. Finally, some threshold was passed, as Zac saw the portals start pulsating in the distance. Since there was no reason to be careful anymore, Zac ordered the demons to back up to the wall again.

Next he charged up a huge fractal blade on each of his axes, and even empowered them with the Dao of Heaviness, turning the blades darker and giving them a palpable pressure. With a roar, he swung down on the boss below, and the power from his swings completely decimated the beast and everything along with it.

The landing that had accumulated over time from the kills was completely destroyed as the strikes made debris fly in all directions, and even the closest wolves were thrown away. He immediately removed the Dao empowerment from the blades but kept them up for a few seconds as he completely destroyed any remainders of the siege. It would be impossible for the noncombat classes to pick up all these small pieces of gravel, so he had to spread them out as much as possible.

Tens of the stone wolves were caught up in Zac's wide swings, and along with the efforts of the demons, less than 10% remained. Finally content, Zac let the fractal edges dissipate as he turned toward the next wave that was already approaching. These wolves had a washed-out cyan coloring, and the ground actually froze to ice where their feet touched as they ran. Zac sighed as he picked up one of the larger rocks from the ground and moved toward the incoming wave.

The day was far from over.

89

THE FINAL FOUR

As the days passed, the fights got increasingly desperate. Zac had improved quite a bit over the last weeks, enabling him to pick up some of the slack. But the same thing couldn't be said about the demons. He was surprised to hear that most of the demons who entered the incursion were actually level 75 already, stuck in the first bottleneck. Their current power was around a level 50, or a level 30 elite. This made Zac realize that levels were only a half-decent indicator for actual power.

The continuous battling was a crucible that let a few warriors push through their limits and improve their skills. There had even been a few warriors who gained a Dao Seed in their desperation. A nondescript demoness gained the Seed of Tinder, and her fireballs suddenly created waves of death as the flames quickly spread into their surroundings. But it wasn't enough.

Ogras was truly impressive, both in the number of his kills and his leadership. Over the weeks, his role as the leader of the demons went from something born out of fear into willing submission. Unfortunately, Ogras didn't have the inhuman Endurance and Vitality of Zac, and as the fights got more intense, the shorter amount of time he was able to keep going.

Initially, the two split the fighting fifty-fifty, giving both sufficient rest, but now Zac fought in 75% of the waves. In some waves, he simply acted as a backup to the tired Ogras, but the other waves, he was forced to almost single-handedly carry.

Just in the last day, Zac had been forced to activate the shield on eight of the waves, rapidly draining his crystal reserves. One of the waves he actually decimated with the offensive component after letting everyone rest for a full fifty-nine minutes.

In a perfect world, he would have done that in every single wave for half a day, but it, unfortunately, was impossible. The offensive attack took twelve hours to recharge and cost 2,500 crystals to use. Even though he had a crystal mine to his name, the actual number of crystals he had on him wasn't too large, so he had to use the attack sparingly.

Zac was running quite low on crystals, even though Ogras had reluctantly fished out a surprising number of them a week ago. They were his private hoard he'd kept as long as possible. Zac regretted that he'd traded so many of them for Nexus Coins prematurely. He was afraid the whole wave would come in one go instead of the incremental way the wolves had, and splurged on the array and a few offensive options to be able to meet a storm of beasts.

Only afterward did he know that he was wrong, and Ogras was as surprised as he was. It was easy for him to sometimes see the demons as some omniscient beings, but Ogras was only a youth from a D-ranked world just like him. There were an endless number of things he didn't know the specifics of either.

Zac had even gone to buy back some of what he sold to Calrin, prepared to eat a loss. He was dismayed to learn that Calrin's reasons for hiking up the prices of herbs weren't actually purely a business tactic. There apparently were restrictions put in place the moment the waves started and the protective shields of the shop were erected. The System stopped the trade of certain items, and crystals were one such thing.

Crystals were used in powering most powerful arrays and war machines, and Calrin said he believed the reason for the embargo was that the System didn't want people to finish hard quests with money alone. It made sense, as the beast horde quest would become a joke if Zac had unlimited funds. He could just sit on top of the wall and watch as powerful arrays ripped the wolves to shreds. He had seen the terrible power of the arrays the one time he'd activated the offensive functions. The blasts had left nothing alive of that wave.

He already had an advantage from possessing the mine and the knowledge of the demons. Without either, the quest would be far harder, but still manageable. Unfortunately, the restrictions on trade meant that Zac couldn't just keep the array active for the last four hordes. His remaining crystals simply wouldn't be enough.

"Just four more waves," a voice said next to him as Zac stood on the wall. It was Ogras, who looked uncommonly rested. Both he and Zac had taken it somewhat easy the last day, even though the waves were getting quite extreme, which was partly why he had been forced to use the shield so much. The two could only assume the finale would be pretty bad from the escalation of difficulty.

Zac grunted in affirmation as he threw rocks at the stragglers of the wave below. These wolves were extremely thin and excelled in speed, so Zac only managed to hit them every ten throws or so. He could have gone down, but these wolves were actually quite dangerous. Their claws were razor sharp, and together with their speed, one of them had actually managed to cut a wound on Zac's throat before he managed to react. He had quickly climbed up the walls again after the scare.

If the wolves were a bit faster, the wave would have been really calamitous. With their amazing speed and light frame, they actually managed to run up most of the wall before being impeded by gravity. A few actually made it all the way, but they were quickly ganged up on before they could orient themselves and do any damage.

The rest had slowly been dealt with using quantity over quality. The monsters were too deft to target, so the demons simply focus-fired in certain congested areas, pelting it with spells and arrows. A whole area with a radius of fifty meters quickly became a zone of death, and even these quick wolves couldn't escape.

Still, the elusive wolves took time to kill, and some still were running about below the wall even as the summoning of the next wave approached, every so often trying to scale the fortifications. The portals in the distance pulsated, which signaled the next wave's arrival.

Soon the 717th wave was approaching. These wolves looked quite normal apart from the fact that they were completely white, making them look albino. But instead of the red eyes that usually accompanied that condition, even their eyes were without any color, making them look blind. The only exception to the monochromatic color scheme was a perfect black circle in their foreheads.

They trotted toward the wall at a uniform speed, not heedlessly charging like most of the waves did. When they were a few hundred meters away, they suddenly stopped and let out a synchronized howl toward the defenders.

The sound pierced Zac's ears, and he immediately became woozy. He forcefully refocused his mind and looked at the surroundings and saw most of the demons hunkered over. Many bled from their eyes or ears as well, a testament to the penetrating power of the howl.

"Mental attack," Ogras hoarsely said, his eyes a bit red from the impact. He glanced at Zac, who seemed completely unperturbed by the assault. "Jeez, just how high is your Intelligence? Such a synchronized attack didn't even affect you."

Zac ignored the comment as usual. Ogras tried to dig out some information about Zac's class and attributes every so often through innocuous comments. Zac didn't trust himself to weave a believable net of lies and then keep track of it, and could only stoically ignore the remarks. He instead focused on the psychic wolves in the distance, and suddenly, his eyes turned into pinpoints.

"DOWN!" Zac roared at the top of his lungs, and most demons immediately threw themselves at the ground. Over the past weeks, most had learned to trust Zac's nose for danger and wouldn't hesitate to follow his commands. However, a few were still dazed by the mental attack, and they paid dearly for it.

Another earth-shattering howl somehow created an enormous shock wave that pushed toward the fortifications with lightning-quick speed. In just over a second, it closed the distance to the wall, ripping the straggler wolves from the last wave to shreds on the way. The wave slammed into the wall with a tremendous impact, and the only thing stopping the demons from falling off was the protruding wall on the inner side of the wall walk. Multiple cracks ran along the fortifications, and some parts even completely crumbled.

The few demons who hadn't reacted in time met miserable ends as well. Some at least managed to activate one type of defense or another, such as stone skin or a magic shield. But the defenses quickly shattered as the demons were thrown off the wall into the distance, their life and death unknown. The demons who hadn't even erected defenses immediately turned to mangled pieces of flesh and bones that splattered their teammates.

"Fucking imbeciles," Ogras muttered as he shook off a piece of brain matter that had fallen on his legs. He had been the first to throw himself to the floor, his survival skills simply impeccable as always.

"We can't let them shoot off another blast like that. The wall will completely crumble," he continued as he turned toward Zac.

The shaking from the impact quickly subsided, and Zac hesitantly looked up over the wall. The wolves simply stood rooted in the same position as before, their white eyes staring at him. Not one of them took a single step forward, and they seemed to be waiting for something.

Zac guessed that it took some time to charge a blast of that power, but he didn't want to find out how long. This race of wolves clearly preferred ranged attacks, and if they were left alone, they would quickly turn the whole wall into rubble.

He didn't dare erect the shield, as he wasn't sure that it could even withstand such a concentrated attack. It was one thing for it to defend against a multitude of claws and bites, but to withstand the concentrated power of hundreds of fused attacks at once? Zac felt doubtful. Even if it held, it would take a massive number of crystals just to defend against an attack of that magnitude, and Zac might find himself without the use of the fortifications against the next three waves.

"We need to go," Zac simply said and got ready to jump over the wall.

"What the fuck? Are you crazy?" Ogras immediately said, clearly unwilling to brave such an army.

Zac only ignored him and jumped down, creating a thud as he landed. At least there were no wolves of the last wave remaining standing after the blast wave. He unhesitantly charged straight for the ranks of the psychic wolves. As he started running, he heard an exasperated, "Goddamnit," and a lighter thud behind him.

With a wry smile, he kept running and took out a huge boulder from his pouch. It weighed a few hundred kilos and looked like something a catapult should throw rather than a human. Zac launched it straight into the middle of the pack with a resounding roar, wanting to disrupt their rhythm.

A shimmering shield actually winked into existence in front of the group, and the boulder slammed into it with terrifying force. The shield wobbled and flickered from the impact, but it barely held true. But just as the stone helplessly fell to the ground, a black javelin slammed into the very same spot, cracking the shield with a snap. As the large shield broke, many wolves let out a pained yelp.

The wolves' magical defenses were down, and an opening was created. One human and a demon rushed inside, each creating a storm of blood.

90

WORSENING CONDITIONS

The psychic wolves weren't as deadly in close quarters, but Zac still was constantly pelted with waves of mental attacks, which strained his mind. Fortunately, his stats made him able to barely hold on, but he was worried about his partner. A quick glance showed him that he was worried about nothing.

Ogras was creating corpses all around him with his deadly spear. Zac also saw that the demon wore a circlet he had never seen him use before. It was a simple metal band with engravings, and on the forehead between his horns, a large milky white gem was inlaid. The gem flashed with power every now and then, giving out a hazy light. It looked like the demon had a tool that protected him from psychic attacks.

Zac didn't have that kind of luxury and could only painfully withstand the attacks as he wildly swung his axe around. The two were quickly decimating the wolves, but the wolves weren't just sitting around doing nothing. The flanks of the wolf wave split off from the rest while the main group kept the two powerhouses busy, and instead headed closer to the wall.

Zac tried to move to stop them but was overwhelmed with shock waves and mental attacks from all directions, and couldn't get out in time. The offshoots started to bombard the wall with attacks, mainly targeting the damaged area.

The demons on the wall, led by Alea and Namys, tried to handle the wolves as quickly as possible, but most of the attacks were ineffective against the wolves' newly erected shields. Besides, many warriors on the walls still weren't back to fighting condition after the initial psychic blast.

Hearing the ominous sounds of rock cracking, Zac could only grit his teeth and summon **[Chop]**. He hadn't wanted to use any Cosmic Energy in this wave in order to save it all for the last three, but he saw no option. He expanded the blades to five meters and, in conjunction with **[Loamwalker]**, created huge swathes of death in the main group of wolves.

Every step moved him a few meters into a new group of wolves, who immediately were bisected by a swing of the enormous edge, before he disappeared to the next cluster. It looked like large blood explosions erupted amongst the wolves in quick succession, as he wasted almost no time on movement between the swings.

Over the countless battles during the month, he had mostly mastered his movement skill and could freely move within a few meters of his position with a speed that almost looked like teleportation. It had a huge effect on his kill speed in conjunction with his enlarged edge, but it also cost a substantial amount of Cosmic Energy.

When he felt he had pruned the group of wolves to the point that Ogras could take care of it himself within the remaining time of the wave, he charged toward the offshoot groups. Ogras seemed to be incensed from seeing Zac rack up a huge number of contribution points in short order, and his spear turned into a blur as he moved through the wolves. He used some odd skill that caused holes to erupt in the throats and heads of wolves even when the spear was meters away, making it look like there was a sniper in the distance assisting him.

The flanks that assaulted the wall had splintered into even more groups in order to avoid the attacks from the demons, and small shock waves were constantly flying up at the cracks on the wall. The wall looked ready to fall down, with spiderwebs of cracks running along large stretches. A few earth mages frantically infused the wall with energy in order to patch it up, but it would take some time to restore its structural integrity.

In some areas, large chunks of the wall were even lying down by the foundation, having been blasted clean off. Fixing those large breaches would take time and require a lot of manpower to lift the pieces back, which there obviously was no time for.

The battle started calming down over time, as Zac eased the pressure for the demons by charging at the wolf packs one by one and decimating them. He was starting to get a pounding headache from all the mental assaults, but he couldn't do anything but grit his teeth and continue. Another fifteen minutes later, Ogras came running over, a sheen of perspiration covering his head. He stopped and took a few deep breaths before he turned.

"Lunatic! Leaving me alone with all those beasts," the demon spat out between deep breaths, looking miffed but obviously not too angry.

"Well, it worked out fine, didn't it? Do you have some solution for the wall?" Zac answered with a shrug as he waved at the crumbling battlements.

The two had taken stock of the available crystals right before the last four waves, and there were enough Nexus Crystals left to power one widespread attack and to use the shield for roughly an hour unless the attacks were too powerful. With three waves remaining, he didn't wish to start using the shield already, potentially leaving them undefended against the last two waves.

As if reading Zac's thoughts, a deep rumbling could be heard from the wall, and a whole section crumbled, leaving a three-meter-wide opening through the wall.

"FUCK!" Zac screamed and didn't wait for Ogras' answer, immediately running toward the breach.

The last stragglers of the psychic wolves were already converging at the hole as well, seemingly wanting to cause some damage before they were wiped out. To make matters worse, the pillars started pulsing again at this very moment, the 718th wave starting to pour out from the shining lights.

"REPAIR THE WALLS!" Ogras roared as he ran after Zac, shooting out shadow spears at the charging psychic wolves.

With Zac and Ogras holding up the wolves, a few dozen burly demons frantically started moving large pieces of rubble back into the wall, where earth mages melded the pieces back into the main structure. The earth mages had been tapped hard lately, and they looked like walking corpses by now, completely pale and with sunken eyes.

But they were the only ones who could fix these types of things in short order and simply had to keep going even if they overtaxed themselves. They knew that if the wall fell, most demons would die. If they were overrun, the two leaders in the front might be able to escape, and perhaps the generals like Alea and Ilvere as well. But the earth mages didn't specialize in escape techniques, and the wolves would hunt them down sooner or later. So they kept infusing the wall with Cosmic Energy, to the point of harming their bodies.

Ilvere and Namys appeared next to Ogras, who started to give out orders.

"Ilvere, help with the repair of the walls; only you and Zac can hold the largest blocks of stone while they get reattached. Namys, help me control the remaining psychic wolves. Zac, can you go ahead and try to stall the next wave?"

Zac looked around for a second and judged the situation was

under control, so with a nod, he sped off toward the next wave. He held roughly the same pace as the new wolves, so he met them right between the wall and the mini-incursions and frowned when he saw the new adversaries.

The new wave consisted of metallic wolves full of jutting edges and sharp blades, looking like some steampunk tool of war. Just from a glance, he couldn't tell whether they actually were machines or living beings. Of course, that line apparently was a bit blurred in the Multiverse, with the Creators being a prime example of that. He guessed that destroying one should give him the answer, as he would see whether parts or metallic blood would spew out.

He took out another rock and threw it with full force at one of the wolves in the front. It moved its head to not take the stone right in its snout, so it slammed into its shoulder with a tremendous crash. The wolf was thrown away a few meters from the impact, but Zac saw the beast shake its body and get back on its feet right away. Where the stone hit, only a small dent could be seen, and it didn't seem damaged at all apart from that.

Zac possessed over 250 Strength by now and had the power to lift a small car. That a full-powered throw from him only caused some superficial damage to the beast told a troubling story about this wave. How were they going to destroy these wolves in time? There would only be a scant few that could deal with these things apart from himself and Ogras.

But he had a job to do, so he could only grit his teeth. He charged up a five-meter **[Chop]** and unhesitantly imbued it with his Dao of Heaviness. The blade turned darker and more intricate as he swung at the incoming stampede.

He felt a shock travel up his arm as he mowed through the metallic beings with his axe, their sturdiness being far and above anything he had fought so far. Even the rock wolves from earlier weren't any problem for him with his overpowered stats.

Luckily, the wolves didn't fare any better, as they were destroyed into metallic pieces over the ground. Zac did everything he could to impede the charge, expending both Mental and Cosmic Energy in wreaking havoc. Many of the wolves headed straight for Zac in order to avenge their brethren, but some still ignored him and continued onward toward the wall.

Some packs kept trickling past him as the main force kept trying to mob him to death, and after fifteen minutes, he was pretty wrung out and needed a break. His arm was actually starting to feel sore, and he had been forced to swap axes six times in the short duration, as they simply were getting destroyed on the tough bodies.

He started to push back toward the wall, and he could only hope that it was somewhat fixed at least. Unfortunately, he saw that it was still an open entrance, and the metallic wolves were trying to get in. At least the hole was mostly shored up, the opening being quite a bit more shallow.

Zac soon arrived at the breach and met a tired-looking Ogras accompanied by Namys and Ilvere. A quick glance showed Janos and Alea at a walkway that was built above the crack, giving the demons above a spot to throw down large boulders of debris at the monsters. The boulders were too heavy to be carried, but they simply used Cosmos Sacks for them, summoning them up above and letting gravity do the rest.

"These fuckers are so hard to kill, there's no way we will be able to take down all of them," Ogras grunted, clearly starting to fade from his high Cosmic Energy expenditure. The two demons looked ready to keel over, but they coordinated their attacks to take down wolves one by one in a stoic manner.

Zac planted himself in the crack and helped arduously destroy one wolf after another. Eventually, they ran out of time, even as quite a few wolves remained. The pillars started to light up as usual, but this time, it looked different. The glow looked almost blinding, and soon Zac saw why.

The 719th wave was an endless sea of wolves, tens of thousands of them. And even as they approached the wall, the pillars kept spewing more out.

91

LIGHTNING PUNISHMENT

"RETREAT!" Zac roared as he saw the insane number of wolves approaching. If he had to guess, he would say that the System had crammed twenty to thirty waves' worth of wolves into one.

The demons immediately complied and moved down from the wall to a far lower one roughly fifty meters further in. It could barely be called a wall, not even reaching three meters in height, and was rather a purchase to gain a bit better vantage when fighting. The wall wasn't made to physically rebuff enemies, but rather it was there as a line of demarcation, showing where the Town Defense Array would cover.

Soon only Zac, Ogras, and his two confidants were holding off the remaining metallic beasts, as the rest had moved back to safety.

Ogras looked a bit hesitant as he turned to Zac. "Are you sure about this?"

In response, Zac only nodded and took a blue glass ball out of his pouch, not stopping his attacks with his other hand. The glass ball crackled with lightning, as though a thunderstorm had been caught and crammed inside the bauble.

"Alright. See you on the other side, friend," Ogras said with a solemn expression as he nodded to the other two demons. They rapidly moved backward, leaving Zac alone in the crack, facing a sea of wolves.

Soon after the last three demons were inside, the defensive array flickered into being, covering the inner area of Port Atwood. Zac instead moved out toward the incoming waves. Some of the metallic beasts charged after him, while some tried to claw their way into the array.

As Zac pushed forward, he started to infuse the glass ball with Cosmic Energy, making the thunder inside flit about more and more erratically. After roughly two minutes, a large part of Zac's remaining Cosmic Energy was consumed, but finally, a change happened in the ball. It was as though it had reached critical mass, and it started to absorb a huge amount of Cosmic Energy from the environment itself.

The ball started to flow in the air on its own, and both Zac's hands were freed to protect the device. It would take a few more minutes before it was ready. He stayed put and mindlessly killed any wolf that came close, and he was surprised to see that he recognized many of the wolf types from things he had fought during the past weeks.

It was like the System had summoned an all-star combination of the wolf waves for the 719th assault. Zac was pelted by all types of attacks, but luckily, his E-grade robe protected him from most of it. As he fought, the sky started to darken, and ominous rumblings echoed out through the island. A huge bolt of lightning flashed, and suddenly, the hovering ball next to Zac was gone. He knew his mission was completed and started to bolt toward the protective array with full speed, not caring about the wolves anymore.

As he ran, the battlefield turned almost pitch black from huge dark clouds that amassed with impossible speed, and then all hell broke loose. Huge pillars of lightning slammed into the ground all around the area, frying any unlucky wolf that was too close. But that was only the start, as the chaos kept intensifying.

The area was blasted with such a number of lightning bolts that the whole southern tip of the island was brightly lit up. The ground crackled and exploded at every place the bolts landed, completely destroying any wolf corpses or fortifications strewn about. In some areas, the lightning was so intense that they started to spread along the ground, creating what looked like lakes made out of lightning. These lakes kept expanding, creating a field of death for anything caught inside.

Zac desperately ran toward safety, shocked at the efficacy of the device. It had sounded mighty from the description when he'd bought it for 3 million Nexus Coins, but he hadn't expected it to be of this scale. Of course, something like this would only work on dumb beasts who refused to flee. The area of attack even spread toward the array, and lightning bolts slammed into the shield every now and then, making it light up.

The ball Zac used was actually a purely offensive array called **[E-Grade Medium-Scale Lightning Punishment Array]** that he'd bought as preparation for the monster wave. Different from the offensive capabilities of the town array, it was a onetime usage attack. It was an array that consumed itself to summon the monstrous cloud in the sky that would rain death and destruction over the area.

It was Zac's ace in the hole that he had hoped to keep until the last wave and finish it off with a bang. But he immediately knew there was no way for them to manually kill the endless number of wolves that spawned out of the wave, especially not with the wall in shambles. They would have been tired out, then overrun from the numbers.

An acute sense of danger warned Zac, who immediately used **[Loamwalker]** to move away as far as possible. Soon after, he heard the ground explode behind him from a lightning bolt, but he didn't bother turning around. He was closing in on the safety of the array.

The lightning actually kept increasing, and Zac was forced to keep dodging the bolts. But even with his movement skill, he didn't come out unscathed, as the lightning ran along the ground between two nearby bolts, shocking Zac on the way.

His world turned white for a second, and he stumbled, but he shook himself awake and continued. It felt like he was cooked from inside, and the pain was even worse than the black lightning arcs that the main branch demons used. He was forced to eat a few more secondary blasts of lightning before he finally threw himself through the array and fell down panting.

Smoke was rising from his body, and the short hair that had grown out lately was singed clean off, once again turning him into a bald monk. After a few steadying breaths, he got up and turned toward the battlefield. Now that he wasn't running for his life, he could actually properly inspect the lightning storm, and the sight was truly exceptional.

He felt it was a joke he'd considered Rydel's final attack to be a punishment from heaven. This was what real heavenly thunder looked like. It was as though the god of thunder himself wanted to smite this whole part of the island out of existence as huge bolts unceasingly slammed into the ground.

He looked up and saw that the cloud was spread a bit further than he had hoped, and errant bolts kept slamming into the shield. He winced with every blast, as he knew that each time lightning struck the shield, it cost him Nexus Crystals.

"Good hustle, human," Ogras said as he approached with his trademark half-smile. "I didn't expect the lightning punishment to be this intense. It might be because there's a Nexus Vein beneath the island."

Zac nodded and brought out a canteen of water that he poured over himself, the water cooling his singed body.

"I'm not sure the crystals will last," the demon then added with a low voice, his face turning somber. "The amount of lightning striking the shield is more than we expected."

"Are the rods ready?" Zac asked in response.

The demon nodded and waved toward the small wall that now was adorned with five-meter-tall metal spears jutting out at some intervals, leading down into the ground. It was lightning rods they had asked the blacksmith to create in case the lightning got out of control.

"Lower the power to the shield, and it might last longer." Zac sighed.

Ogras nodded and waved toward Janos, who still was managing the shield. He touched the large crystal ball, and soon the shield dimmed somewhat.

"Move away from the wall!" Ogras shouted, and people spread out some distance from the wall.

Even with weakened energy output, the shield defended against most of the lightning bolts. Every now and then, a crack was blasted open, letting a few slip through. Luckily, they harmlessly entered the rods, which pushed the lightning down into the ground, until the shield repaired itself again. However, it was clear that each rod would only be able to take one or two of these magical bolts of lightning, as they partly melted from a strike.

They didn't have to worry about the metallic wolves outside either, as they had been the focus of the lightning since the start due to their composition. They were quickly reduced to molten pools of metal on the ground outside.

Finally, the lightning bolts started to subside, and the skies cleared up with noticeable speed. Zac and Ogras finally dared to exit the shield to look at the result. They quickly moved up to the mostly ruined wall and surveyed the battlefield. Even Ogras looked shocked by what they saw. The scene was like something taken out of a horror story. Thousands upon thousands of mangled and burned carcasses covered the ground, which by itself was burnt and pocked.

Zac was surprised to see that only one pillar of light remained in the distance. Had the Lightning Punishment even destroyed the portals? As if sensing that the offensive array's onslaught had ended, the last incursion started pulsing, and out walked a humongous beast. It was the 720th beast wave, and it was the complete opposite of the last one. As soon as the monstrous wolf walked out of the portal, it winked out of existence.

The wolf looked abyssal with six pitch-black eyes and a much too large maw. It actually gave Zac the same vibes as the demonic beasts he had fought so far on the island, and he turned toward Ogras and found him looking pale.

"E-grade Fiend Wolf," Ogras exclaimed with some fear evident on his face.

"From your home world?" Zac asked, as Ogras clearly recognized the monster.

"No, but it lives within demon territory. They are extremely dangerous. Luckily, there's only one. Usually, they rove in large packs of thousands. Still, it's going to be a tough fight. It's evolved to E-rank and possesses at least one Dao Seed."

The wolf started approaching and let out a demonic roar that echoed through the battlefield. The howl felt like a physical blow to Zac, and he saw that some bloody gashes actually appeared on Ogras, who lost his balance.

The wolf swiped its claws toward the two, and even though there were two hundred meters between them, Zac felt a terrifying sense of danger. He immediately grabbed the falling Ogras and unhesitantly jumped down from the wall.

As he landed, he heard a swishing sound from above, and the next second, the wall was simply blown away, cut into multiple pieces. A terrifying wave continued on and slammed into the shield, instantly destroying it.

"Dao of Sharpness…" Zac muttered, convinced that it should be the Dao Seed he had been trying to gain for so long. He realized the wave of destruction from the sharp claws felt very familiar, and he was sure that it had the added feeling of the Dao of Sharpness he once sensed in his first vision.

"It's too strong. E-rankers are simply different from us unevolved. We should give this one up, human," Ogras muttered as he spat out some gravel from his mouth.

But Zac paid him no heed as he stood up and glared at the last wolf who stood between him and his goals.

92

FIEND WOLF

The wolf obviously was able to do great damage from such a distance, so there was no point in hiding behind the wreckage of the walls. Zac didn't have any more tools or arrays to take care of it, so he would have to finish this last wave by hand. He took out an axe and charged toward the beast with determination in his eyes.

The Fiend Wolf spotted him and, with a mighty roar, set off against him as well. As they approached each other, the boss once more swiped with its claw, making three edges rend a path toward him. In response, Zac charged up five **[Chop]** edges and launched them to meet the blades one by one.

The wolf's attack demolished the first blade without being impeded in the slightest, and the following four blades didn't fare much better. The five blades somewhat slowed down the attack and weakened it, but it was nowhere enough to stop it. It forced Zac to use his movement skill to dodge it, happy that at least his axe didn't take damage from using the Cosmic Energy blades after they detached from the axe.

The attacks of the wolf were on a higher tier compared to his own, and he didn't know whether it was due to the Dao of Sharpness or the power of the beast itself. He knew that evolving into an E-grade class was supposed to give a huge power boost, but he still felt he should be able to contend with his enormous stat boosts from his titles. Luckily, his movement skill was great for dodging attacks, and he sidestepped the incoming strike.

Soon he was upon the beast, and it felt even more threatening this close. It was even larger compared to the huge rock wolves he'd fought some time ago, reaching over six meters in height. But that clearly wasn't its only difference. The very air around it hummed with power, and he actually felt himself getting cut by innumerable air blades. Some small cuts even appeared on his body with his huge Endurance, so Zac knew that an unevolved human would be cut into ribbons by simply walking close to this monster.

It was the beast's Dao Field. Ogras and Alyn had explained the magical effects of Dao in battle. For example, when a warrior's insight got deeper, he could actually spread his Dao out into the vicinity, creating a field that empowered himself or hurt his enemy. An early-stage seed was too weak for that, though, meaning this wolf not only possessed the Seed of Sharpness, it was also an evolved version.

He moved underneath the monster, careful to avoid its long serrated claws that looked like they could bisect him in a second. He quickly summoned **[Chop]** and swung at one of its hind legs in an effort to chop it off. He had no wish to stay in this field too long, as he'd be slowly whittled down to just bones.

The five-meter edge slammed into the leg some ways above the knee and penetrated into the thick sinewy muscles. But the axe didn't get far before it was stopped. Even with Zac's monstrous power, he couldn't lop off its leg. The swing pushed the leg back, but soon the axe in his hands started to bend.

The standard-issue axe simply wasn't good enough to cut through the monster, at least not without the aid of his Dao Seed or a stronger skill. Even odder, it was as though some force rebounded his energy, annihilating the Cosmic Energy he used in the swing, which nullified much of the effectiveness of the strike.

He threw away the ruined axe and brought out a new one, but the wolf wasn't content just to let Zac scurry about underneath its stomach. It pushed away with extreme speed and repositioned itself so that it could bite or claw after him. It started to furiously swipe at Zac, who could only once again rely on his movement skill to move away.

It destroyed the ground all around him as the waves from the claws rent gashes as deep as Zac was tall, which stretched tens of meters away. The beast wasn't using any skills, only the power of its body empowered with its Dao, and still the effect was even greater compared to when Zac used **[Chop]**. Gravel and charred body parts of wolves were flying all over the area from the Fiend Wolf's assault.

Zac tried to move closer to the beast, but it held him at bay with its claws and huge maw, making it impossible to get around. He soon gave up and infused a **[Chop]** with the Dao of Heaviness and furiously swung it at the claw to intercept it. The collision was enormous, and Zac was pushed twenty meters away, the axe in his hand completely destroyed.

The wolf wasn't unscathed, though, as it yelped and backed away a bit. Nothing was cut off, unfortunately, but the empowered strike at least broke some bones in its paws and perhaps destroyed some muscles. The Fiend Wolf obviously didn't want to put any weight on the damaged paw, even though it didn't actually bleed.

The wolf only seemed to get even more enraged, and the air distorted around it. It furiously howled up in the air, then exploded into action. With a frenzied charge, it ignored its hurt paw in order to close in on Zac, who once again was forced on the defensive. Zac's Cosmic Energy was over halfway depleted even before starting the battle, and he knew he couldn't just keep dodging. **[Loamwalker]** had an amazing effect, but it was his most draining skill.

Without seeing any alternative, he pushed forward right after dodging a swing, moving straight toward the beast's head. The maw of the monster was immediately upon him, rows of jagged teeth closing in. But just as the mouth was about to slam shut, a green shimmering sheen enveloped Zac.

It was the defensive option of his clothing, something he hadn't used apart from some experiments during the past month. As top-tier E-grade equipment, the shield from his robe stopped the teeth in their tracks, even causing many of them to crack or break off.

The pain must have been blinding for the monster, as it howled in pain while its head jerked away by reflex. Zac saw his opportunity and charged up his **[Chop]** with the Dao of Heaviness, and ruthlessly chopped at its exposed throat. The power of his swing was enormous, and he could actually hear some things in its throat breaking. He also managed to cut some ways into its throat, making a great deal of almost pitch-black blood spurt out.

The power of the swing together with the Dao of Heaviness actually threw the huge monster over ten meters away, where it landed with a deep thud. The ground beneath Zac's feet caved from the pressure, chips flying in all directions.

Unfortunately, the swing wasn't enough, as the monster had no trouble getting back on its feet. It was frothing at its mouth in anger, and a deep growl incessantly escaped its mouth. But just as it got to its feet, nine large spikes materialized around it from clouds of green shimmering gases. Zac's sense for danger started tingling from just looking at the meter-long spikes, and he glanced around.

He saw Alea standing some distance away with a pale face, ready to keel over. Just as he saw her, she closed her fist, and a penetrating screech erupted from the wolf. Zac quickly turned back and saw that the large spikes had penetrated deep into various parts of the beast's body.

The wolf let out an enraged roar and furiously shook to remove the poisoned spikes from its body. However, they were firmly lodged into its body, and even with its thrashing, they stayed inside. The wolf howled in anger and ignored Zac to swipe its front claw toward the demoness, who desperately scrambled away. The movements of the wolf were weird and twitchy after being impaled, but it still was able to send those sharp edges out.

The nail attack had clearly used up all of her power as she stumbled around while she tried to avoid the incoming blades. Zac knew that should have been Alea's ace in the hole, as he could barely draw blood with his huge swings, yet all nine of her spikes had penetrated the tough hide.

The onslaught quickly became too much, and the edge of a swipe hit her shoulder, drawing a great spurt of blood. She had actually used some defensive option at the last minute, but the attack immediately destroyed the cloud that formed in front of her. She yelled in pain but kept moving away from the wolf, but it wouldn't have it.

Zac tried everything in his arsenal to stop the assault of the enraged wolf, wildly swinging his axe at it, but it seemed intent on bringing the poison master down. Apparently, those spikes had hurt far more than anything else it had felt during the battle. It furiously gathered a great deal of Cosmic Energy in its claw and swung a huge arc after her when it saw that she was moving further away.

Zac saw that she wouldn't be able to dodge it and moved in front of her with a few quick strides of **[Loamwalker]**. He activated the second charge of his shield, once more enveloping him in the protective layer as he positioned himself in front of the demoness. The enormous wave of destruction approached, and

Zac was punched back from the impact. But luckily, the shield held even against this huge attack.

He managed to soak up most of the damage that appeared, but the wave was simply too large. Some parts passed by him, and an errant streak of power swiped Alea, making her scream and topple over. A huge gash appeared on her clothes, and blood immediately started to pool beneath her. It looked like the strike almost completely bisected her.

As he saw his companion, who received such a terrifying wound because she wanted to help him out, a blazing fury erupted in his mind, and he charged toward the hurt wolf. The only thing in his rage-addled brain was the need to destroy the Fiend Wolf. Zac didn't even notice that Cosmic Energy was gathering toward his head as he furiously charged toward the boss.

The wolf was in quite bad condition from Zac's swings and the poison, but it roused itself to intercept his strike. Just as it did, tens of black spears rose up from the ground, striking various weak spots. A large spear whistled through the air and impaled its undamaged front leg, making it fall down again with a yelp. Zac didn't care about any of that and, with a roar, pushed off the ground, sailing through the air toward the monster.

While he jumped, he gripped his axe with both hands and lifted it over his head. As he did, an enormous edge over ten meters formed, thrumming with sharp power. The edge was neither the pale blue as usual nor the darker shade from imbuing it with the Dao of Heaviness. It glistened with a silvery luster, and it looked like the very air itself was cut apart as Zac moved forward.

With a bestial roar, he swung down the axe, infusing all his anger and Cosmic Energy into the strike. He completely cut the beast in two, instantly killing it. It didn't end there, though, as the strike slammed into the ground, tearing a fifty-meter gash into the ground with a thundering sound. It was like a miniature version of the huge canyon created by the axe-man in Zac's first vision.

Seeing the beast dead, it was as though all power left Zac, and he unceremoniously fell down after the strike. The last furious charge completely overtaxed him, and he was almost completely out of Cosmic Energy. As he lay panting on the ground, the shadows next to him flickered, and Ogras appeared through his movement skill.

A flash of fear filled his heart as he saw the ruthless demon stare down at him, but he only bent down to give him a hand.

"Good hustle."

"I thought you were going to retreat." Zac sighed tiredly with a glance at the demon.

"I was just waiting for the right opportunity to tip the scales. My normal attacks wouldn't be able to hurt it, so you needed to do the heavy lifting," the demon answered with a half-smile.

Zac knew the demon probably only hid in the shadows until he saw an opportunity to kill the Fiend Wolf. If it didn't appear, he would have receded into the darkness and left without so much as a goodbye. Still, he knew the demon was under no obligation to risk his life for him, so he wouldn't comment on the flakiness.

Normally, this would be the time to celebrate with the first horde defeated, but he quickly remembered himself and ran toward the demoness, who was still bleeding out.

93

VERUN'S BITE

Zac was overlooking the reconstruction and cleanup taking place around the battlefield. There weren't many demons working, but they were efficient. Ogras had already taken most back to the mines to refill the stocks of Crystals for the next horde. The demon only gave his underlings one day of rest before work resumed.

There were only twelve days before the next stage of the quest started, and they needed to get ready. Luckily, Zac wasn't needed for any heavy lifting, as people didn't need any strength to throw boulders into Cosmos Sacks.

Satisfied with the progress, he turned around and headed toward the crystal that contained the temporary Contribution Shop. It stood roughly halfway between his camper and the battlefield, and when he arrived, multiple demons were milling about, likely looking over their options in the store. Everyone had accrued a decent number of contribution points over the past weeks, and there were quite a few products inside that could help them in various ways.

When they saw Zac arrive, they made some room for him and nodded with respect. The demons respected the strong, and Zac's feats over the past weeks left a deep impression on them, especially the last battle with the Fiend Wolf. There had been a few who held strong grudges against him, mostly because of Zac having killed a family member or friend when the two camps were still at war.

But Zac knew that Ogras and Namys secretly made these malcontents have "accidents" during the wolf horde to quell any unrest or disharmony. He felt it was a bit overkill, but he wasn't about to complain to Ogras about such a detail. He knew he'd likely have failed the quest unless he had the demon's help.

It was clear to Zac after having gone through the quest that it wasn't meant for a lone warrior like him. A Lord was expected to have subjects and perhaps even an army to assist in this type of battle. He felt extremely lucky that things had worked out somewhat with the demons so far; otherwise, he'd be forced to give up on his island after all this struggle. Zac realized that his alliance with the demons was only a fragile cooperation based on benefits, but it was better than nothing.

When he came within a few meters of the crystal, a screen automatically popped up, containing both a ranking list and a shop. A quick glance showed he possessed roughly 45 million contribution points. It seemed he'd received a full 5 million of those for killing the Fiend Wolf, as he had just below 40 million before that fight. Generally, the contribution points awarded were on a one-to-one ratio to the Nexus Coins he'd gained, with the exceptions of the wave leaders giving a substantial bonus above that.

The 45 million points placed him in the comfortable lead of the Ladder, but the others were no slouches either. Ogras held a stable second spot with 24 million points. The former general had held the lead until halfway through the waves, at which point Zac eclipsed him. It was a combination of his pathways slowly healing, allowing him to use his area skills more, and that Zac's power leveling started to give an advantage.

Ogras grumbled quite a bit about it, but he could only helplessly watch himself get overtaken. He had tried to buy the Fruit of Ascension in order to get a power-up, but immediately got shut down by Zac. Ogras wasn't too disappointed about it, though, as there actually was one for sale in the shop for only 50 million contribution points.

While gaining contribution points was roughly the same as Nexus Coins, the prices were far cheaper. He'd never be able to buy a Fruit of Ascension with 50 million Nexus Coins, not even ten times that. Since he already got 24 million in the first wave, he shouldn't have any problems getting the last bit before the quest was over.

Zac was looking at something else entirely, **[Verun's Bite]**. It was an axe that cost a whopping 40 million contribution points. It was called an **[F-Grade Spirit Tool]**, and Zac wasn't sure whether it was worth it at first. But after asking around, he found out that Spirit Tools were not the same thing as F-grade equipment or weapons; it was a far more valuable thing.

Spirit Tools possessed an actual soul and could almost be considered a living being. Only the most talented blacksmiths could create them, and only using the best materials. They held a power level far above a normal weapon and even had their own skills. They also had the basic functions such as sharpening and repair as well, making them a great long-term companion.

What made them an even better investment was that they could be evolved if you gathered the right materials for it, making it a great weapon to use even after ranking up. Even Ogras' grandfather still used an E-grade Spirit Tool he had nurtured for almost a thousand years, according to Ogras. It was one of the only three E-grade Spirit Tools in the whole clan, as far as Ogras knew at least, showing how precious they were.

A great weapon was something Zac really wanted, as it was one of his current shortcomings. Very few demons used axes as a weapon of choice, as it was generally considered a brute's tool. Only a few of the lower-tier soldiers used it, so there were no better axes than the military standard issue on the island.

With Zac's current power, his weapons couldn't really keep up. He was forced to cycle various weapons, as they couldn't withstand the force he utilized nowadays, and it hampered his efficiency. There were a few other interesting things in the shop, such as skills and other gear, but the axe was the most interesting for him. He initially considered taking the fruit so he had one for both his father and sister, but he reluctantly gave up that idea.

First of all, he needed to focus on strengthening himself at the moment, and he didn't want to create any new reasons for Ogras to conspire against him. He felt that the two of them had forged somewhat of a friendship over the past month, and he didn't want to mess things up with two more waves on the way. He wouldn't lower his guard against the demon, however, as it was far too soon for that.

Besides, he knew that he didn't have to worry about the demon suddenly evolving and becoming too strong to control, as there were still the restrictions on the invaders that would stay on for some time.

He also considered buying some of the skills to power up, but also decided to hold off on that. The analysis by the demons was that the skills were actually of high quality, differing from those in the Nexus Node. Those were actually "overpriced garbage," as Ogras put it, and Zac could only agree after hearing the difference between his **[Eye of Discernment]** and the skill Ogras used. In the end, he felt a real weapon would be a better immediate power-up.

Besides, there was another reason he didn't feel the need to buy a new skill right now. He once again brought up his status window before making the purchase.

Name: Zachary Atwood
Level: 50
Class: [F-Rare] Hatchetman
Race: [E] Human
Alignment: [Earth] Human

Titles: Born for Carnage, Ultimate Reaper, Luck of the Draw, Giantsbane, Disciple of David, Overpowered, Slayer of Leviathans, Adventurer, Demon Slayer, Full of Class, Rarified Being, Trailblazer, Child of Dao, The Big 500, Planetary Aegis, One Against Many, Butcher

Dao: Seed of Heaviness – Early, Seed of Trees – Early, Seed of Sharpness – Early

Strength: 257
Dexterity: 139
Endurance: 173
Vitality: 113
Intelligence: 69
Wisdom: 57
Luck: 77

Free Points: 0
Nexus Coins: 21,510,103

His stats were becoming more and more monstrous, with even Endurance getting close to his original attribute cap. His Dexterity was getting up there as well, partly thanks to his third Dao Seed.

[Seed of Sharpness – +10 Dexterity, +5 Intelligence]

The seed also pushed him up to the fourth spot on the Dao ranking, and he was still surprised that he still wasn't first with a full three seeds.

He opened up the quest screen next and looked at the reason for not feeling the need to buy any skills at the moment.

Active Quests:

Dynamic Quests:

1. **Incursion Master (Unique): Close or conquer incursion and protect town from denizens of other alignments for 3 months. Reward: 5 E-Grade Nexus Crystals, outpost upgraded to town, status upgraded to Lord. (1/3) [12:17:45:16]**

Class Quests:

1. **Nature's Many Faces (Class): Decapitate 10,000 enemies – OR – Plant 10,000 trees. Reward: Nature's Punishment – OR – Nature's Nurturing Skill. (0/10,000) – (0/10,000)**

It was the first time he saw a branching quest. He immediately decided to go for Nature's Punishment rather than Nature's Nurturing as soon as he saw the options, even though he only could finish Nature's Nurturing right now. The choice reminded him of his musings about his Dao Seeds. He currently trod both the path of destruction through his offensive seeds, and the path of life or nature with his Tree seed.

The choices in the quest did the same. He currently was like a walking cockroach with his monstrous attributes, so he'd go with the offensive skill Nature's Punishment. From the sound of the other name, he guessed that it was a healing skill, or something that had something to do with plants.

Neither of those options sounded like something he needed right now, while a stronger offensive skill than **[Chop]** was something he would really benefit from. **[Chop]** was still great against hordes of monsters, but against strong singular enemies, its effect was limited.

He closed the screen and, hesitating no further, bought **[Verun's Bite]**. An elaborate large box appeared next to him, and he immediately put it into his Cosmos Sack without opening it. He knew these demons would eventually find out what he bought in battle, but for now, he felt no need to spread rumors.

With a nod, he left the demons to their business and walked toward the hastily erected town close by. The settlement consisted of mostly tents with a few rudimentary buildings peppered in, and was the temporary living space for the demons during the quest.

He entered one of the larger structures and looked around. It was the infirmary, and it was thankfully only half-filled. The effect of Vitality was generally that something either killed you, or you bounced back in a week or two at most. Apparently, it was different at higher levels, though, where the skills could contain weird energies and Daos that impeded recovery.

Alea was lying at a bed in the corner, pale but breathing steadily. Zac felt some sourness as he watched the red bandages that wrapped around her. She had become a comforting presence to him over the weeks, although he wouldn't call it love. To see her lying here because of her desire to help him against the Fiend Wolf caused some guilt in his heart, and his desire to get powerful only got stronger.

"How is she?" Zac asked the physician making rounds between the beds.

"She's stable. Due to her… interests, she has focused on Vitality, which is now helping her immensely," the young man answered with some disgust on his face. Clearly, he didn't approve of her dabbling with poison, which in a sense was the opposite of his occupation.

Zac only nodded and fished out a small vial from his Cosmos Sack.

"Will this improve her condition?" he said as he opened the stopper, letting an earthy scent waft out. It was a healing pill he'd bought at Calrin's for a full 2,500,000 Nexus Coins before coming here. Normally, warriors kept it as a last-resort type of thing, as it was too expensive to use as one pleased. But Zac hadn't hesitated to cough up the coins.

The man looked at the pill inside with some greed in his eyes but, quickly remembering himself, nodded his head. Zac handed it over and watch him gingerly feed it to her, using some skill to make her swallow and absorb it in her sleep. The effect was immediate and obvious, as some color appeared on her face, and her breaths became deeper.

"It's helping, but she will stay asleep for some time," the physician noted.

Zac nodded and left after observing her for some more time. Next, he found Ogras and told him that he didn't want to be disturbed for the next few days unless it was something important. He headed back to his camper and sat down with a grunt.

First, he took out the large box and dripped a drop of his blood on his new axe to establish a connection. He would normally try it out a bit, but there was something he was even more eager to do at this moment, so he put the axe back into his pouch.

Next, he took out another vial out of his pouch and looked at the pill inside. It was a deep blue with some shimmering white spots, glistening very beautifully. The pill was actually called **[Rivers of Cosmos]** and was something Zac had commissioned from Calrin the first time they met. The price tag was far more expensive than he expected, reaching 7,500,000 Nexus Coins, but its effect was also amazing. Not only would it help heal his pathways, but it would also somewhat stabilize them and make them more resilient.

His pathways were mostly healed by now, and even if he left it alone, he might get better soon. But he refused to spend any more time mindlessly staying in the mines. He had things to do. He immediately swallowed the pill and just sat down cross-legged and let the medicine do its thing. A soothing sensation soon spread through his body, like his veins were filled with clear spring water.

The healing process took a full day, and after he inspected the result, he was more than happy. The Cosmic Energy that he naturally absorbed for restoration flooded his body at a pace that was far and above anything he'd ever felt before. He wasn't sure whether it was because of the experience in the pond or just from evolving to E-rank Race, but it was at least three to four times the speed from before.

After almost two months of holding himself back, he finally felt confident enough to start using tools and crystals to restore himself. He thought he might have been able to do it sometime earlier, as his pathways had been in pretty decent condition lately, but neither Ogras nor the physician really knew too much about his condition. He'd decided not to do anything rash and wait until he was completely sure.

Next, he took out his small box of E-grade Nexus Crystals and immediately started to absorb one. A huge surge of pristine energy entered his body. It was on a completely other level compared to the F-grade Crystals. If the F-grade crystals were a water faucet, then this was a waterfall of energy that poured into his body. Still, he didn't feel any discomfort from the deluge of power coursing through his pathways.

The energy was completely tame and quickly added itself to him, and he felt how he steadily climbed toward level 51. The amount of energy required for a level was immense by now, but it only took twelve hours for him to reach it. He kept absorbing throughout the day, but was interrupted by the sound of a bell on the morning of the second day. He opened his eyes and with a frown looked toward the source of the sound. But as soon as he saw his guests, his eyebrows rose in surprise.

As Zac suspected, he saw Ogras, but with him was Rahm, the Creator liaison. Zac quickly invited them through the array and asked what was going on.

"A boat of humans arrived at our docks twenty minutes ago, and they are at present being detained."

94

HUMANS

Megan glared at their captors as she was stomping around in fury. Something was clearly wrong in the head with these people, as they silently stood like zombies with a blank stare in their eyes. The only time they moved was when she or someone else tried to leave the pier they stood on. They even blocked access to the ship, stopping them from leaving.

The only reason things hadn't come to blows was the polite man from earlier who said that he would fetch the so-called lord of the island. Megan already disliked this mysterious person; what kind of jack-ass named himself a Lord? She decided that he would get a proper lesson in manners when he arrived.

Of course, she knew that her anger was simply a coping mechanism. The last months had been like something out of a horror story. She and her friends were in Vietnam on vacation when the apocalypse came, just as they were visiting a fishermen's village. Suddenly, they found themselves stuck on some island with a group of fishermen who barely spoke any English. Two of her friends had also simply vanished into thin air, and she still didn't know what had happened to them.

The shocking changes were only the first trouble that

appeared. The animals on the island slowly turned insane, and they grew way too large. In the beginning, they could fight them off, which was how they learned about levels. But the monsters grew too strong too fast. Hundreds of rats as large as Labradors charging their small village was what broke the camel's back, forcing them to set out to sea on one of the dingy fishermen's vessels.

It was a risk, as two boats had already set out without coming back, their situation still unknown. But those rats simply tore through anything, and they were extremely aggressive. Mr. Trang had saved their lives by fending them off while they started the boat, and he still wasn't recovered from his wounds as he sat down nervously on the pier.

Finally, she saw movement in the distance as three men were walking toward them. One was the polite man from earlier, but he walked back to his house after bowing to the other two. One was a completely bald man who looked like a monk, while the last one looked extremely weird, with grayish skin and almost white hair. He even wore some odd crown on his head with horns jutting out. Megan was feeling pretty confident that he was the so-called Lord.

She was getting ready to blast off a salvo of vitriol at the two, but as the duo closed in, her flame of rage snuffed out like a weak candle in a storm. Something about the monk forced her attention on him. It was as though she were facing a mountain as he approached. Every step he took was like a sledgehammer hitting her, and she felt suffocated from just being in his presence.

Most of the other castaways were faring even worse, as they backed away with pale faces. Some even knelt down on the floor, unable to stand in front of the monk's towering aura. The pressure was so all-consuming that Megan only noticed that the gray man wasn't actually wearing a crown when he was right in front of her.

She was looking on a bona fide demon from mythology, and her terror only intensified.

What kinds of monsters inhabited this island?

———

"Control your aura, human. You will kill these weaklings," Ogras said with a subdued voice.

Zac drew a sharp breath in realization before quickly taking control of the energy naturally coursing through his body, making sure that nothing leaked. He had forgotten about that lesson from Alyn after spending time with the demons for so long. As a warrior became stronger, their presence intensified as well, and if the discrepancy in power was too large, it could even be considered a weapon. It wasn't something like the Dao Field, rather just an effect of beings in different stages of existence. There wasn't any point in controlling his presence among the demons, as most of them were actually higher level than himself and immune to its effects. But against low-level individuals with weak willpower, he might actually be harmful.

The fact that these humans were ready to keel over was quite telling about their power. Zac quickly used his **[Eye of Discernment]** on the twelve people, and to his surprise, the highest leveled person was only level 21.

"Pathetic," was the only comment from Ogras, who'd obviously performed the same type of scan, and Zac had to agree. How could people survive with such low power? If these humans were representative of the average population, then Earth was well and truly doomed. His image of the outside world was maybe skewed from looking at the Ladder, which only showed the powerhouses. Maybe the average humans were as weak as these people, who probably couldn't even kill a barghest.

"Ahem… Welcome to Port Atwood. I'm Zac. What brings

you here?" Zac tentatively asked, unsure how to proceed from here.

The group only stared fearfully at the two, no one daring to step forward. Zac was starting to think that his language skill wasn't working with the humans until a thought struck him, and he turned to his companion.

"You're scaring them. Go away," Zac said, making a shooing motion.

"Yeah, I'm the problem. Why don't you blast off your Daos as well while you're at it?" Ogras retorted with a roll of his eyes, but he walked some distance away and picked out a chair from his pouch. Next he took out a piece of fruit and started eating while pointedly ignoring the humans. The Creators also took this as a signal their work was done and wordlessly headed toward the huge warehouse.

It seemed to calm the people down somewhat to be left alone, but they still looked very warily at Zac. Finally, a woman who was the second strongest in the group stepped forward. The strongest person was actually an old Asian man sitting down, clearly still nursing some old wounds. That revelation only lowered Zac's opinion of the youths in the group, letting an old man stand on the front line while they cowered behind.

"I'm Megan. We're from an island two days' sailing from here. Um… what's going on with your friend?" she said as she fearfully glanced at the demon loitering in the distance.

"That's Ogras. He lives on my island."

That answer seemed to only make the group more fearful, but Zac couldn't be bothered to explain any further. Going into the demon's origins would be too troublesome, and Zac and Ogras had long ago decided that they were going to pretend the demons were natives who were brought here during the integration. That little lie should hide the fact that there had been an incursion here, and that the demons were actually invaders. At least for a while.

"Young man, how come I can understand you? I don't believe you are speaking Vietnamese," the old man sitting on the pier said with a weak voice.

Zac willed the screen for the language skill into being, making it hover in front of the group.

"It is a skill I have that allows me to understand and be understood when speaking with anyone," he answered.

"Skills, what's that?" the girl called Megan asked as she looked at the screen in wonder.

That question made Zac realize that these people were even worse off than him during his first months on the island. They obviously had no idea about many aspects of the System, not even knowing about skills. He realized he only knew about skills because of Abby and the Nexus Node, where he'd bought **[Eye of Discernment]**.

He was lucky in a sense that an incursion had spawned on top of him. If he hadn't gotten to build an outpost, he would have been as ignorant as these people, fumbling around in the dark. The first time they came in contact with skills would be at level 25 when they got their class. If they could even attain a class on a deserted island.

"You still haven't explained why you people are here," Zac said as he ignored the question.

"The animals became crazy on our island. They kept growing, and even the rats were as dangerous as wolves in the end! We couldn't stay anymore, so we left to find a safer place. After two days at sea, we saw your harbor and thought that there might be a town here," the girl explained.

"We're from Chicago. Is there an airport close? Have you had any contact with the government? Why hasn't there been any rescue operations?"

The girl kept peppering Zac with questions, giving him a headache.

"The governments have likely fallen. You should have heard the voice in the beginning. The world has been integrated into the Multiverse, Earth got fused with a few other planets, and everything got mixed together." Zac sighed.

The castaways looked ready to explode from that declaration, but a voice cut through the mounting chaos.

"Can we stay here, young man? There is safety in numbers."

It was the old fisherman. The three other Asian men looked at Zac with some hope, whereas the Caucasians looked confused, prompting Zac to translate the question.

"Mr. Trang is right, there's safety in numbers! We have become quite strong over the past months and were only forced to leave the island due to the huge number of rats!" one of the young men said.

The proclamation elicited a derisive guffaw from Ogras in the distance. He obviously was listening in on the conversation using some skill, and he looked very entertained.

Zac pondered what to do about the small group. It wasn't really any problem to let them onto the island, as they didn't lack food or water. But there were also many secrets on the island, things that he didn't want to make public to the world. Besides, he wasn't sure that letting them stay was doing them any favors, with the next beast wave coming in less than two weeks.

"You can't let them leave. This place can't be discovered yet, there are too many treasures here, so you need to solidify your position as Lord first. You either need to kill them or let them stay on the island." Ogras' voice could be heard from the shadows.

"What if they leave and they tell the story of the island with demons and superpowered humans? People will rightly think that there's some secrets on this island and set sail in search of treasure," the demon continued. He used some sort of skill that projected his voice from a distance, and it didn't seem that the other people could hear him at all.

Zac sighed, as he knew that putting them back on the ship was out of the question now. Ogras would likely sink it with a shadow spear the moment it left the pier in order to protect his interests. Besides, he agreed with his points. He wanted to turn this island into a true sanctuary for those close to him and didn't want random people to come here for some sort of treasure hunt.

"You can stay here. But you should know that this island is likely far more dangerous than your old home," Zac said after some deliberation. "We don't need freeloaders. You will have to work to earn your keep. There are some areas that are off-limits on the island, and this shipyard is one of them. I'll show you the way to the town."

When told that this place wasn't safe as well, the group started to hesitate. But the old fisherman got to his feet with a grunt and without hesitation, followed Zac, who turned to leave. The other fishermen followed suit, and soon the Caucasian youths followed as well.

Zac saw Ogras flash over and put the boat in his pouch, which caused some alarm and shock to the refugees, but he only said a few comforting words and continued on. As they walked some way, the people started to find their courage and pelted Zac with various questions. They asked about everything from what amenities the island had, to how the System worked, and the situation of humanity.

These people were thirsting to know what was going on, just like Zac had been before he finally got things explained by Alyn and Abby. He tried to answer as much as possible, but by the time they arrived at the tent town, he was thoroughly tired of answering questions.

The refugees were dismayed to see that the whole population was demons, and two actually tried to run away in panic. Zac could only sigh and flash over with **[Loamwalker]** and carry the struggling people back. It took some time to settle the refugees, and Zac couldn't be bothered with them anymore afterward. He pawned them off to Alyn and Zakarith, who both had the language skills that could help them acclimatize. He also had a few warriors keep an eye on them just in case they tried something stupid.

Zac held mixed emotions as he walked away from the inquisitive group. It almost felt like he had been robbed of something from the encounter. One of his largest wishes over the past months was to reunite with humanity, but he didn't expect it to be like this. A group of listless people who'd barely scraped by the past months. Obviously, none of them had left the safety of their village overly much. Otherwise, they'd be at a higher level by now.

His own countrymen were the worst. They clearly were mainly concerned about their own well-being, focusing on questions such as food and lodging for themselves. None of them asked how they could help or listed things they could do for a town. The fishermen mostly kept quiet after a few questions about humanity. Zac had hoped that his first encounter with humans would finally allow him to get some news about the state of the world, but it looked like he needed to switch back to his original plan.

He informed Ogras of what he was about to do, and the demon seemed to think that it was truly foolish. Zac didn't care. Almost four months had already passed since the world changed, and it felt like ants were crawling all over his body by now.

He opened up the Town Shop interface as soon as he arrived at the spot designated by the city planners and bought an **[E-Grade Teleportation Array]** for ten million Nexus Coins. A new interface opened up, and his heart sped up when he saw that there actually was a destination available.

[Winterleaf Village. Public. Fee: 0 Nexus Coins]

After making sure he had everything he needed in his Cosmos

Sack, he took out a hooded cape that covered his elaborate clothing and a pair of leather shoes that one of the craftsmen had made for him. Ogras told him that it was easy to see that his gear was valuable and something provided by the System, and since he didn't want trouble, he simply covered it up. Next he set his own teleportation array to private in order to make sure only he could use it. He didn't want anyone using it either to teleport in or out while he was gone.

Finally done, he gazed around at the island that had been his home, and prison, for four months. With a sense of trepidation and excitement, he stepped on the engravings on the floor with determination in his eyes.

With a flash of light, he was gone.

95

WINTERLEAF VILLAGE

Selas sighed as he stood in front of the teleporter, waiting alongside the rest of the village leaders. His nerves were fraying, as he didn't know what would step through the magical inscriptions. As Leader of the Hunt, he had always been in charge of protection of the village, even before the Great Fall, but it was different now.

Everything kept changing, and as an old huntsman, it was getting increasingly difficult to keep up. Gone were the paths that he and his ancestors had walked through the mountains, the songs detailing the hunting grounds all but irrelevant by now. In just a few years, he should have retired to teaching the art of the hunt to the next generation, but now he was stuck as some castellan of the town.

When the fall arrived, he'd found himself transported to a fantastical world with some of his village members. Determined to keep the youths safe against the twisted challenges of the System, he pushed himself beyond what he knew was possible, and for his struggle, he was rewarded with a Nexus Node. But even with all his effort, he couldn't keep everyone safe, as many of his villagers perished, one of them his son Winterleaf.

Not even allowed to properly mourn the death of his progeny, he was instantly pushed into one desperate situation after another since he was returned to his village. Even now, the village was teetering on the brink of ruin despite everyone's efforts.

It was their tree whisperer who came up with their current gambit after using his Soothsayer class' limited skill. He said that salvation would come through the light, and urged the town to pool their Nexus Coins to build this teleporter. But as the days passed and nothing happened, anger and unrest started to build against the elder.

There were even rumblings about putting the elder in house arrest for the time being. Ten million Nexus Coins was a huge amount and could have bought weapons, armor, and precious herbs at the store. Many felt that they should have made a last stand before the beast, using everything at their disposal instead.

That all changed when the teleporter blazed into life, its inscriptions lighting up by themselves. Selas had barely managed to gather the elders when he got the notification that a new teleportation point was added before it blazed to life, indicating that someone was already coming over.

Selas stood with his spear at the ready, staring at the light that shone with increasing intensity. Behind him stood his hunting party at the ready to protect the villagers against whatever came through that gate.

Whether it would be salvation or damnation was still to be determined.

Zac only felt darkness for a little over a minute before he once again gained his sight back. The first thing he noticed was that the climate was clearly different, with an autumn chill in the air. Next he glanced around and found himself placed in the middle of a village square. The buildings were foreign to him, though, being medieval but not of some style that he recognized.

Soon he understood why, as a group of people approached. Zac's heartbeat sped up in alarm when he saw that it wasn't actually humans that greeted him. Did he teleport himself into an incursion? Ogras and the crystal both said that invading forces couldn't build teleporters since the System wanted to limit their expansion, but perhaps they were wrong.

The humanoids who closed in on him made him think that they were a mix of humans and animals. They seemed to have normal hands and feet, but they also possessed clear animalistic features.

They wore simple but seemingly high-quality gear and carried various weapons, mostly spears and bows. Most of their exposed skin was covered in brown or white fur, sometimes mottled with spots. They had large black eyes and a normal face and a mouth. Their ears somewhat resembled those of an elf's, though. His assessment was that these beings were a seventy-thirty mix of a human and a fawn.

They didn't look frail, though, as even the fur couldn't hide their sturdy frames and muscles. They also carried themselves with the grace of warriors, and these people were clearly different from the hapless humans he'd encountered earlier. The group stopped some distance from him, and they simply stood staring at each other for a few seconds.

"It's one of the hairless monkeys. What do we do?" Zac heard one of the fawnmen mutter.

"Onyx, you learned some of their words in the Tutorial, right? Greet him," another one said as he prodded one of the females in the group.

That made Zac relax somewhat. If these people had been in the Tutorial together with humans, then they shouldn't be invaders. It looked like when Earth got mashed together with other planets, new civilizations were added after all.

The female hesitantly looked at the leader of the group, a middle-aged man holding an intricately carved spear with a long line of leather bands attached, and took a step forward after an encouraging nod from him.

"H-Hello, human," she stuttered, but before she continued, Zac smiled and spoke back. At least he thought he smiled since it almost felt like he had forgotten how to do it by now.

"Hello. No need for a translator. I understand your words," he said.

The group looked a bit surprised, but not overly so.

"Welcome to Winterleaf Village, human. I am Selas, castellan of this town," the middle-aged warrior said. "May I ask what brings you here?"

"Our town is located in an extremely isolated area, and we couldn't find a single person nearby. So we bought a teleportation array in hopes of finding other humans," Zac answered.

It wasn't exactly his reason, as he'd bought the teleporter in order to start looking for his hometown during the downtime of the quest. He finally had the resources and the time to put his plan into motion, and even though the expense was high, he felt it worth it. If he ran out of Nexus Coins, he would simply extort some of the demons, as they'd all made a fortune from his monster horde quest.

"I am sorry, but what… are you people?" Zac tentatively followed up, unsure how to properly frame such a question.

"You must really have been isolated if you haven't met any of the Ishiate so far. We may be the most populous species apart from you humans on this new world of ours," Selas answered with some surprise. "Please join us in our town hall. Meeting of new friends is always a joyous occasion. I can fill you in on the area as we walk."

Zac nodded after some hesitation and followed them. His guard was up, though, ready to bring out **[Verun's Bite]** at a moment's notice. These people were real cultivators who had done the so-called Tutorial. Even Ogras didn't know exactly what benefits you could get in there, but from all accounts, they were substantial. He knew his level likely was far above everyone here, but that didn't mean that they couldn't pose a threat. They might have received bonus attributes, titles or extraordinary skills in the Tutorial, things that could even out the odds.

"Winterleaf Village is built upon the remnants of our ancestral home before the fall. We were lucky at least to retain most of our structures. Many towns in the area were pushed together into a confusing mess by the System, which severely harmed their cooperation. It's thanks to our unity that so many of our clan members are still alive, even with the changes constantly testing us."

Zac's heartbeat sped up as he finally was starting to get some information about the world. His words painted a somber picture, but he was mentally prepared that there would be widespread death and tragedy. Even if no incursion was nearby, he knew that just the wildlife would create problems.

"Are there any human settlements in the area?" Zac asked. That was the priority. He still didn't have a picture of just how the reshuffling of the world worked, but perhaps humans had already started to map the locations of their old towns. They still should have technology such as aircrafts that they could use to scout, even though such tools didn't provide experience when killing monsters.

"The closest one is a four-day journey from here. We don't have any contact with them, though, as that place is chaotic and dangerous. No offense," the hunter answered.

"What do you mean?" Zac asked with a sinking feeling.

"The settlement is run by a man named Roger. He has set himself up as a warlord and rules with an iron fist. Mutilated corpses adorn his walls at all times, and he is known to have kidnapped many women. He even tried to kidnap a few female Ishiate, but stopped after furious revenge from us.

"Still, he is very strong with a few powerful followers, so no one in the area dares to escalate the conflict with them. We keep our distance and put patrols to make sure that they don't approach, and luckily, they keep to themselves mostly," the beastkin answered solemnly.

Zac was disappointed when he heard the news. He would have to check things out himself to make sure, but he leaned toward believing the humanoid. Since the beginning of the apocalypse, he knew that some people would use the fall of order as an excuse to live out their twisted fantasies. That someone wanted to play emperor sounded not only believable, but expected.

He asked a few more questions as he walked alongside the beastmen toward a large structure. As he looked around, he didn't see many structures that stood out. The only building he recognized was the **[F-Grade General Store]** that the System provided. He didn't sense any arrays gathering energy in the area either, and the ambient Cosmic Energy was actually far lower here compared to how it was on his island.

He hadn't realized how large the difference was from living on top of a so-called Nexus Vein, but his island must seem like a paradise to cultivators. Even better were the mountains, which finally were starting to become habitable again, as the poison was mostly cleared out. He reaffirmed his decision to keep his portal closed until at least his beast horde quest was completed and his position as Lord was solidified.

As he walked, he became more and more confused as to how they could afford the huge expense of the Teleportation Array. Zac only was able to afford it due to the Nexus Crystal mine, and the monster horde gave him an absurd number of Nexus Coins.

But from what he had seen so far, nothing really made these

people stand out. Certainly, the village was decent-sized, and quite a few of these fawn-people looked like adept warriors. But unless they'd recently found some extremely valuable treasure, they must have collected much of their wealth to construct it.

It didn't take long after they sat down at a round table that he found out the reason behind its construction.

"I am not used to small talk, so I will immediately get to the point, Zac. The reason we spent most of our resources on the Teleportation Array was that we're in desperate need of assistance."

96

TERROR OF THE MOUNTAINS

"Assistance?" Zac asked skeptically.

"As you know, wildlife is quickly changing. A beast has appeared in the mountains, and we fear it will evolve soon if left alone. It has started hunting citizens of Winterleaf Village and the neighboring settlements. In the beginning, it was just for food, but lately, it seems it hunts us for Cosmic Energy judging by the numbers it's killed. The people are unable or unwilling to join us in fighting it.

"Most of the other citizens in neighboring settlements feel they can simply leave the forests if it gets too dangerous. But this is our ancestral home. We can't just abandon it. That's why we pooled our resources in order to find new allies through the teleportation array," Selas said, with multiple eyes staring hopefully at Zac.

"If the monster is causing trouble for your town, why don't you buy protective arrays?" Zac questioned. A beast evolving seemed troublesome, but they could just trap it with an array and then throw something like a Thunder Punishment at it. Zac doubted even the Fiend Wolf would survive if it got stuck in the middle of that crazy lightning barrage. For the money they'd spent on a teleportation array, they could have blasted even Zac to Kingdom Come.

The townspeople glanced, confused, at their leader, who only looked a bit depressed.

"Unfortunately, my achievements in the Tutorial weren't enough to unlock those items. I have a quest to unlock it, but it is far outside the scope of what Winterleaf Village can handle at the moment, much more difficult than simply killing the beast," he explained.

Zac was surprised but careful not to let anything show on his face. He had no idea that different Nexus Nodes possessed a different collection of options. It wasn't anything Ogras or the others had mentioned either. He thought that the System was uncharacteristically generous by allowing him to buy things such as the Thunder Punishment and the arrays. But perhaps it was because of his achievements. It was either that or the fact that he'd gained his town by defeating an incursion instead of getting it in the Tutorial.

He sighed and looked around the table. He could sympathize with these people, but he was not some savior who had time to go around and save the villages. His goal was simple: find his hometown and his family. It was already a daunting enough task without making detours all the time. He was about to reject their request for assistance, but a window popping up stopped him in his tracks.

[New Active Quest: Monster hunt (Normal): Slay the beast in the mountains. No assistance allowed. Reward: [F-Grade Automatic Map] (0/1)]

This development surprised him. Was anyone simply able to give out quests? But it didn't look like it was something the people around the table did, as they were simply looking at him hopefully. He guessed that it likely was the System that wanted to force him to fight the beast.

"The beast is not only a threat to us, but to all the settlements in the area. Both Ishiate and human lives are at stake," another person added, taking Zac's silence as hesitation.

"Have you heard about something called an Automatic Map?" Zac suddenly asked, confusing the people at the table, who looked at each other.

"I know!" one of the younger people suddenly piped up. "I heard about it in the Tutorial. It's a spiritual map that shows the area around you almost no matter where you are. It marks any settlements and towns on itself. The better the grade, the more detailed it is, and the larger area it covers."

Zac started to get eager, as this was something that would be really useful for him in his travels. He felt a bit helpless that the System once again dangled something he needed in front of his nose, but was starting to feel that was simply how it operated. Unless the rewards were tempting enough, many wouldn't risk their lives.

"What type of animal is it?" Zac probed.

"It is a mutated mink. It is around three meters long and extremely aggressive. We have tried to kill it, but it's extremely nimble. It sneaks into the towns at night and kills until it is discovered, and is gone before we can mount an effective counter," Selas answered with a sigh.

"And its level?"

"Last time it was spotted, it was level 68. That was five days ago. It might have gained a level or two since, as it levels up quite quickly."

Zac mulled over what to do. The animal sounded strong, but not overly so. He possessed his new weapon and the Seed of Sharpness, which increased his lethality quite a bit against solo enemies. The monster wasn't evolved either, and wouldn't be anywhere as strong as the Fiend Wolf he'd fought recently. But it wasn't some weakling if multiple villages couldn't kill it, and he needed to solo kill it to receive the map.

The deer-people thought Zac's silence was an expression of hesitance, and Selas added some incentives.

"Of course, we don't expect you to do this for free. I gained two spots to the worldwide treasure hunt in three months during the Tutorial. I am willing to cede one of those spots to your town if you decide to help us," the leader added with a serious face.

"Treasure hunt?" Zac asked, confused.

"It is a limited event the System arranges seven months after the fall, where participants will be teleported to some unknown area like with the Tutorial. It was possible to gain entrance tokens to the event during the Tutorial, but it was notoriously hard," the leader explained, and couldn't help but straighten his back as he did. "It contains various valuables, from gear to herbs. There's even limited titles available inside, from what the pixies said."

"Can anyone go?" Zac asked, interested, as it sounded like a pretty amazing opportunity. He was ahead of the curve in terms of power, and there likely weren't many places on Earth where he could keep his empowerment going. This event sounded like a good opportunity that normally wouldn't have anything to do with him since he wasn't a cultivator.

"Anyone can go as long as one is a native of this planet and has an entrance token. I believe it will be the first gathering of the elites of all the races."

The slot was something he would definitely want. He should be able to sell it for a great sum even if he didn't end up using it. The map itself was reason enough for him to fight the super-mink, and this was a great bonus. Still, he wouldn't jump into it blindly and asked some more questions about the monster. Finally satisfied, he was ready to set out, not wanting to waste any more time.

"Okay, deal. Lead me to its den," Zac said as he stood up.

However, none of the beastmen stood up, and instead glanced at each other doubtfully.

"We… um… appreciate your enthusiasm, but killing this beast will take the cooperation and planning of a few villages. We are not ready to challenge it from our end," the old huntsman said with some hesitation.

"I need to observe its habitat and hopefully its power personally to report back home; otherwise, they will not send manpower here through the portal." Zac decided to lie. It felt like too much of a bother to convince the group that he was powerful enough to do this alone.

Still, no one seemed ready to set out and just looked down with troubled faces. Finally, Selas sighed and stood up.

"I will lead you to its habitat. But beware, it is extremely fast. If it targets us, I will only be able to protect myself, if even that," he said. It looked like many of the other beastmen in the meeting were about to protest, but he silenced them with a wave of his hands.

"Give me ten minutes, and we will set out."

Soon the two walked along a path in the forest, heading toward one of the mountains in the vicinity. It was believed the mink lived by a river that ran through the mountain, claiming the area as its habitat.

As they walked, Zac learned various things of interest. The history of the Ishiate was quite interesting. Apparently, their society had been on the cusp of industrialization when they got integrated into the Multiverse along with Earth. However, their society held nature in high regard and even saw the forests and mountains as their gods.

It caused a schism between those who chose to live as one with nature and those who embraced technological progress. Conflict was common lately between the two camps, one trying to stop the desecration of their gods, the other trying to move their race forward. Winterleaf Village was part of the former group, consisting mainly of simple hunters and foragers. Zac believed that this lifestyle likely helped them survive far better in this new reality than the average people of Earth.

He also learned that apart from humans and the beastmen, there was at least one more race that got thrown into the mix. However, Selas didn't know much about them, as he had never seen them himself. From the description, they sounded like humanoid insects, and they kept to themselves. They made no contact with the other two races, from what the hunter knew, and they were extremely territorial. Anything that came close to their hives was met with furious and unrelenting violence.

There also wasn't any incursion in the vicinity, and Selas had only heard about their existence from the lessons in the Tutorial. That gave Zac some hope that they weren't peppered across the globe, so his hometown could very well be in a more peaceful area as well. If he had to choose between the wildlife and the organized forces of the incursions as an enemy, he'd pick the stupid beasts every time.

He also tried asking some questions about the Tutorial, but Selas clearly grew suspicious from the questions. Zac didn't want to broadcast the fact that he, or his "faction," didn't know anything about the Tutorial, and could only put those questions aside for the moment. Soon they arrived at the foot of the mountains and could see the river cutting a path through it.

"We really shouldn't venture further in than this, my friend. There have been multiple reports about the beast in this area, and it could pop up at any moment as long as we walk along the river."

Zac nodded and took out **[Verun's Bite]** from his pouch. This was the second time he properly glanced at it.

The axe was slightly larger compared to the military axes of the demons, and the adjective that would best describe it was primal. It had a large, almost straight edge that ran roughly forty centimeters long, moving some ways alongside the handle. The metal of the head looked worn, with multiple scratches and imperfections. However, Zac knew that the edge was razor sharp after testing it out a bit before.

On top of the head, there were grisly teeth of some unknown beast embedded that were blackened and serrated. The same type of teeth were fastened at the bottom of the slightly uneven handle. The handle itself was made of some wood and almost fully wrapped in coarse leather. All in all, it looked like something Zac imagined an orc war-chief would use, and it even emitted an air of danger.

Selas backed away warily as he saw Zac arm himself.

"What are you doing, human? You can't possibly be…"

"I am heading in. Please do not follow me. Anyone that approaches me during battle will be considered an enemy, and I will attack," Zac said as he unleashed his presence.

The hunter was clearly shocked by the terrifying force that suddenly was gushing out of Zac, as he further backed away. After making sure that the Ishiate wasn't following, he simply nodded and headed toward the river, each step moving him over five meters away.

Soon he was walking alongside the water, carefully on the lookout for any type of domicile like a cavern. The beast was quite large, and it shouldn't be too hard to find as long as it stayed somewhere close to the river.

A tingling of danger made him instinctually swing his left hand back as he moved his head sideways. The punch resulted in a deep thud, and Zac was actually pushed forward a bit as he heard a pained yelp. He quickly turned around and saw that his target had found him instead.

The huge mink stood a few meters away from him, a bit hesitant now that its ambush had failed. Zac wouldn't give up this opportunity and quickly charged up **[Chop]** while swinging down his weapon. The teeth fastened on the axe possessed a magical effect, making it almost sound like the axe growled as it ripped through the air.

The mink was elusive, and it felt like it didn't contain a single bone in its body as it dodged the swing, jumping between outcroppings along the rock wall. Zac grunted and copied five large edges to his axe. The new Cosmic Energy blades looked a bit different now that they copied **[Verun's Bite]** instead of the old blade.

In an almost impossibly quick manner, he threw out the five blades, both trying to hit the animal and any places where it could try to dodge. Their distance wasn't too large, and five blades each five meters long covered a huge area, cutting off all paths of retreat for the beast. It managed to dodge four of the blades, but the fifth slammed into its front leg, cutting a deep gash.

With a pained screech, it fell down toward the ground, and Zac immediately used **[Loamwalker]**. As the beast was falling, an axe imbued with the Dao of Sharpness rose to meet it. And just like that, the terror of the area was slain.

97

FREEDOM

Zac looked down at the slain beast, very satisfied with his new axe. The swing had almost fully decapitated the monster, and he swiftly cut the last pieces off with another swing, bringing the progress in his class quest to one. He realized that he didn't really need to use Dao of Sharpness on an enemy of this level; his new axe alone was sharp enough on its own.

Since it was only an F-grade item, he had been afraid it wouldn't be too strong in the beginning, even though it was a Spirit Tool. But he quickly realized that he was worried about nothing. Its edge was far sharper compared to his old axes, and it had no problem accommodating his power.

As Zac looked down on the weapon, he was surprised to see that the mink's blood wasn't dripping off the weapon, but rather got absorbed. He already knew from before that Spirit Tools needed to absorb various materials to evolve, but he didn't expect one of them to be blood. Unfortunately, the axe didn't come with an instruction manual of what it wanted, and Zac could only try various things.

He already knew that it didn't want Nexus Crystals, which was sort of a relief. After some hesitation, he broke off an incisor from the animal and pushed it toward the teeth on the axe, but nothing happened. It looked like he wouldn't have to go around ripping teeth out of his foes like some demented dentist to feed the Spirit Tool.

Next, Zac started looking around the area for anything that looked valuable since Ogras said that strong beasts sometimes built their nests close to some natural treasures, as living in its vicinity would help the beast grow faster. Since the beast was clearly stronger compared to other monsters in the area, there should be something of value here.

As he looked around, he was once again astounded by the amount of Cosmic Energy his body naturally absorbed now. It almost felt like a torrent entered his body to restore his missing energy. He would have to ask around later about whether that was due to reaching E-rank Race, or if it was due to something else.

Even after looking for an hour, he couldn't find any treasure, and he could only return with a frown. It appeared that his high Luck couldn't help him out in every scenario. Zac was soon back at where he'd left the deer-human and found him still fretfully walking about, seemingly unable to decide whether he should follow or go back. As he saw Zac approach, he sighed in relief and approached.

"My friend! It is good that you are okay. Luckily, it seems the beast was awa–" he said, but his words got stuck in his throat as Zac took the carcass of the beast out of his pouch and let it fall down on the ground with a deep thud. Next, he took out the decapitated head and placed it to the side of the body.

"This should be the mink you were talking about," Zac simply said.

The Ishiate hunter blankly stared at the carcass lying in front of him.

"You can take the head as evidence if you wish. Can you help me skin it?" The fur of the monster was extremely soft and luxurious, and it'd be a waste to leave it. But with his self-taught skills, he was afraid he'd ruin it. Normally, he'd want to take the meat as well, as the stronger the beast was, the more delicious its meat would often be. However, it seemed that this monster had eaten quite a few humans and beastmen, so it felt pretty disgusting to eat its meat by now.

"Ah? Yes, certainly!" the hunter said and quickly got to work after grabbing a skinning knife from a pouch on his back. "May I ask… Is that a Cosmos Sack you're using?" he tentatively asked as he glanced at Zac.

"Yes, why?" Zac asked. Selas shouldn't have actually seen the pouch, as it was fastened to his girdle beneath his cloak, but there obviously weren't many ways that one could make a huge corpse appear from nowhere.

"Do you have any more? Winterleaf Village would love to buy one. We'd offer a competitive price."

"I only have one with me at the moment. But I'll see what I can do next time I pass by," Zac answered, not wanting to commit. He did have a couple of them lying around at his camp since looting them from the demons, and there were quite a few of them waiting up on the mountaintops. But he wasn't sure whether selling them was a good idea or not.

"What about the entrance token to the event?" Zac asked. He'd already received the map immediately after killing the beast, but there were still rewards to reap.

Selas once again reached into the sack on his back and took out a smaller pouch. He opened it, and inside were two tokens. They appeared to be made out of stone and were almost as large as a palm. Zac immediately saw that these things were something made by the System, as the telltale fractals completely covered them.

Zac fiddled with his token a bit before he imbued it with Cosmic Energy, and a stream of energy entered his mind. He could quickly discern that this was the real deal, and the only thing needed to enter this so-called treasure hunt was this badge. As long as it was in your possession when the event started, you would be teleported there. There was no ownership or restrictions at all, making the item a hot potato.

He wasn't worried for himself, as he felt that there were very few people who were able to snatch something out of his hands. But his eyes turned to Selas, who tensed up from the glare. But soon he resumed working his knife on the carcass.

"Please keep it a secret you got it from me. Very few people know it's in my possession, and it needs to stay that way for the safety of Winterleaf Village."

Zac simply nodded and said no more. Soon the beast was skinned, and Selas held up the large pelt.

"It's done, but it needs to be properly treated," the hunter said.

"Could you help me with that too? I need to visit the human settlement before I head back to my hometown. I will be back to your village in a few days."

"Of course. Their town is that way," Selas answered and pointed east. "I would say be careful, but I feel that it is not you who's in danger," he added as he glanced at the large head next to him.

Zac wryly smiled and turned to leave.

"Oh, and, Zac? Thank you," he heard from behind, and only answered with a wave. There were obviously multiple meanings to those two words.

As Zac walked, he sighed slightly and shook his head. The hunter was clearly afraid that Zac would kill him to take the second token as well. And Zac knew that many might have done just that. Zac didn't even consider it, as he had no real use for another token. Even if he quickly found his sister, it wasn't something that he would want her to possess.

Just owning it meant having a bullseye on one's back. And

even if you survived and went there, the competition would likely be extreme. The most powerful and ruthless people gathered at one spot, competing for great treasures? It would likely make the battle at the monkey mountain seem like a day at the spa.

He wasn't too keen on going himself and certainly wouldn't send someone he loved there. Of course, he also knew that going there might be the best opportunity to get a real sense of the situation in the world and get some power-ups. If people from all over the world gathered, someone might even be from his hometown.

Becoming the strongest or whatever wasn't really his goal, and he'd simply fought to survive so far. He hoped that his visit to the human settlement would give him some answers to what was going on. If not, he would try again next month. He only had a few days to spare, after all, and needed to get back to Port Atwood sooner or later.

As he walked, he took in a fresh breath of air. It finally felt like he had some control over his actions after months battling. He constantly found himself pushed into one situation after another, putting him in a constant reactive state. But now he had full freedom, at least for a few days. The fact that he would have to get back soon ruined the mood a bit for him, but at least for now, he relished the feeling of just adventuring.

He took out a crystal from his pouch as he walked and imbued it with some energy. A window opened up with a rough map inside. It was black and white and didn't contain a lot of detail, but it did cover a large area and marked the towns. He saw Winterleaf Village was the closest, and he currently was heading toward Fort Roger.

Both of the towns had crystals next to the name, and after some confusion, he realized it meant that they probably possessed Nexus Nodes or Lesser Nexus Nodes. Lesser Nexus Nodes gave access to the class system, but needed quests to unlock the town management systems.

Apparently, there were differences between the nodes with access to buildings as well, where he got a throng of options, whereas most of the towns only got the bare essentials. Nexus Nodes were extremely common, though, from what Alyn told him, which made sense, as people needed to get their classes somehow. Alyn didn't explain how they appeared, as they generally had been around for thousands upon thousands of years on their home planet.

That Winterleaf Village possessed a proper Nexus Node with a Town Shop was clear to Zac, but he doubted that anyone in the surrounding towns knew that. At least not for now. From his impression of the small village, he felt that they weren't careful enough. They really lucked out that Zac, and not someone else, had walked through that portal.

Zac hadn't inspected anyone out of politeness, but he never felt any sense of danger from any one of them, meaning that they shouldn't have been too strong. Of course, they were strong enough to both get a Nexus Node and gather enough money for a Teleportation Array, so they were no slouches either.

They were even open about possessing the entrance tokens before they even knew him, which seemed crazy to Zac. He had a feeling that unless they wised up, they'd end up in dire straits. Possessing too many valuables was a crime in troubled times, after all. If it were the old him, Zac wouldn't have felt anything was wrong, but Ogras had started to rub off on him.

Zac kept walking and, out of habit, started using **[Axe Mastery]**. It felt like the trajectories were slightly changed to accommodate his new weapon, making Zac once again marvel over the skill. It was also the first time he properly used the skill since it reached Late mastery, and as he expected, it better incorporated his Dao Seeds into the mix.

What surprised him was that it actually even incorporated the Dao of Trees. Until now, that Dao Seed had remained unused in battle, but the guidance system showed him its usage. Every now and then, it told him to imbue his free hand with it as he used it for grabs or blocks. Zac wasn't sure what the exact use was, perhaps except that it improved the resilience of his arm, enabling him almost to use it as a shield. However, he still felt that a low mastery seed was too weak for that kind of usage at the moment.

Zac kept moving throughout the day and the next, unceasingly using his skill. It was almost addicting to be able to once again use Nexus Crystals to restore his missing energy, especially now that it apparently only took a fifth of the time to absorb the energy contained in an F-grade Crystal.

The hunter said that the town was four days away, but with Zac's huge attributes and speed, it went far quicker. Finally, he reached his destination, Fort Roger. And as he looked upon the ramshackle town with its weak fortifications, he felt that the description of Selas didn't do the town justice.

It was much worse.

98

FORT ROGER

It would be more appropriate to call the wall that ran around the small town a large fence. It consisted of trees with their ends sharpened, and was between three and five meters tall, as the length of the poles weren't uniform. There even were some holes in the wall due to uneven placement, giving enough room for a person to sneak through.

The town was located right on the edge of the forest, with large trees giving way to expansive fields. The fields might actually have been farmland before, as they were flat, and Zac thought he spotted a tractor. But the fields were in complete disrepair, overgrown with weeds and unmanned.

With the new energy in the atmosphere, anything would grow faster compared to before, and Zac felt it was very telling about the town that they didn't utilize such a prime source of food. They would only have to clean up the fields and throw some seeds in there, and they would have grain in no time. But he saw no one even try it.

There was a path leading to an actual gate that Zac stepped out on as he walked the last distance. He didn't plan on sneaking into the town and didn't want to alarm them. He also slowed down his speed to normal walking from his attribute-empowered movement.

As he closed in on the wall, he saw there were two corpses hanging from the wall, one on each side of the gate. It was a man and a woman, both in their thirties or forties. It was hard to tell since they had obviously been tortured before they were killed. Attached to their feet were plaques that simply said "TRAITOR."

Zac was starting to hesitate whether to actually enter this place, but he knew there weren't many alternatives. There was another town on the Automatic Map, but it would take at least another two days to get there. With his return to the portal, he would barely make it in time for the next wave, and that was barring any unexpected incidents on the way. After making sure his odd clothing wasn't visible through his worn cloak, he started walking. As he approached the gates, two guards perked up and warily glared at him.

"Stop! Why are you here?" one of them gruffly asked.

"I'm traveling to find my hometown," Zac simply answered. There should be lots of people like him who weren't at home when the world got integrated, forcing them to travel to find their way back home.

"Pfft, another idiot looking to be eaten by the beasts," the guard said, and the other one snickered in derision.

"Five Nexus Crystals to enter. If you don't have it, you can fuck right off."

Zac was a bit surprised they used Nexus Crystals rather than Nexus Coins as a currency. Then again, Nexus Coins were only usable in System-affiliated stores, whereas Nexus Crystals were not only used for currency, they could also make you stronger.

Zac pretended to look troubled, but reached inside his cape and pretended to grope around while he took out five crystals from his Cosmos Sack. He handed them over to the guard, who quickly put them in a backpack.

"Is there somewhere to get a drink?" Zac asked.

The guards were a bit more amenable now that they'd gotten paid, and Zac didn't care whether the entrance fee was real or not.

"There's a bar down the main road, the Royal Oak," the guard answered with a wave.

Zac nodded and headed into the town. He only took a few steps before he stopped, as a wall of stench slammed into him. It wasn't to the level of the imp camps in the tunnels, but it was bad. The town was obviously human, likely from America or the UK, as the worn signs were in English.

But four months into the apocalypse, the whole town looked ready to collapse under the weight of its own filth. Piles of dirt were thrown into the alleys, and disgusting streams of mystery liquid ran along the pavement. He even saw a corpse lying in an alley, halfway buried under the filth. Zac was infinitely happy that he had decided to put his shoes on, as he'd almost puked at the prospect of stepping on the ground here.

Clearly there was no such thing as sanitation in Fort Roger. People just threw garbage wherever. There were a few people on the streets, and they looked worn and malnourished. Zac decided to use **[Eye of Discernment]** on a few of the stragglers and was shocked to see that many were below level 5. There even were a few that still puttered around at level 1. He wasn't sure exactly how much experience was needed to gain levels in the beginning, as he'd essentially started at level 16, but he couldn't imagine it was a lot.

These people were likely mortals just like him. But different from Zac, they had simply stayed within this disgusting town since the integration, afraid to venture out. Zac couldn't imagine that these people would have a happy ending in a world of cultivators and local tyrants. The rule of law was gone, replaced by the creed "might makes right."

He didn't know why, but he actually felt some disdain for

these hapless people. He knew that it would be weird to expect people to rush out into the forests to risk their lives fighting animals. But for people to just give up, like these people clearly had, felt like a joke.

They could work together to kill some weaker beasts and slowly but gradually gain the power that would allow them to feed and protect themselves. They would also get Nexus Coins for the kills, which could be turned into Nexus Crystals at any System-run shop. They could even just do some work for Nexus Coins and use that to purchase crystals.

Zac resisted the urge to grab these people and shake some sense into them and instead kept going. He was planning on heading straight for the bar, but something caught his eye. It was a large electronics store, now used by a few people to loiter around. There was no electricity, so none of the TVs were turned on, but Zac simply ignored the people and headed into the warehouse in the back.

He found the box containing one of the larger flat-screens and simply threw it into his pouch after making sure no one was in sight. Next, he took a video player and boxes and boxes of movies. It was mainly for Alea, who liked watching movies just like Ogras. But Zac was interested in whether they could actually make some money from these things like Ogras hinted, so he took some technology with him back home.

Finally, most of his pouch was stocked up with electronics and movies, and he headed on toward the bar. He wasn't looking for a drink, but simply to sit down and ask some questions. Soon he arrived at the Royal Oak and saw it was an old Irish pub. It actually looked like it was in decent shape, with a clean storefront and no garbage piling up around the structure. Clearly, there was a proprietor who still had some sense of pride.

He walked inside and saw that the interior was just as he expected. The only difference between this and all other classical pubs he had visited through the years was that, instead of normal lights, there were candles burning on the tables. Zac already expected it, but it looked like there was no electricity in the town.

He had guessed that things like power, internet, and water supply would be essentially gone with the integration, as the randomization of the world would ruin the network of tubes and cables that had been built over the years. Perhaps there would be some lucky areas that were right next to a water power plant or a farm of windmills or solar panels that might be okay, but most would likely have to do without electricity.

The bar was largely empty apart from a few tables. Everyone kept to themselves, and the conversations were kept at a low volume.

"A new face, I see," Zac heard and turned toward a portly middle-aged man who likely was the proprietor.

He stood behind the bar, which he was cleaning with a rag, looking very much the part. The man was British from the sound of it, and it looked like this town was truly from somewhere in England, as it was the same with the guards.

Zac walked over and sat down on a barstool in front of him.

"What can I get for you?" the man asked, looking neither excited or bored.

"Information," Zac simply said as he placed a few crystals on the counter in front of the bartender.

The barkeep's eyes slightly widened, and he quickly swiped up the crystals with the rag, quickly hiding them from view.

"You'd better be careful of flaunting your wealth, young man," the bartender said with a serious face. "You're obviously new to town, so I'll warn you to not stick out. Safety isn't one of the strong points of Fort Roger."

"I understand. I have been traveling looking for my hometown, and need some information. I need to know if a pattern of how the world was reshuffled has been found." Zac spoke with a low voice.

"Have you been hiding under a rock all this time? Well, in any case, it's all random, from what I've heard. I'm from northern England, but the next town over is mainly American. No one knows what's going on. From what I understand, a few governments are working together trying to get order back, but I'll believe it when I see it," the man said with a scoff. "How are they going to enforce order when people suddenly are able to shoot fireballs and run around like supermen? Never thought Armageddon would look like this."

Zac sighed at the answer. He at least hoped there was some discernible pattern to the randomization, but it seemed it was too much to ask for. At least the governments were trying to get things under control. He somewhat agreed with the bartender's assessment, but the information also provided some hope.

Perhaps the government had some means to map out the world. Maybe there were satellites still in orbit, or at least they could communicate by radio. There were many emergency contingencies in place in case of war or the like. Obviously, nothing could have prepared the countries for the System arriving, but they might have figured some things out by now.

"Is this town under the British government?" he asked, hoping to get in touch with an official.

"Pah, what government? This town is run by Roger, a cultivator. Most towns don't have any affiliation to any government; they are just run by whoever has the biggest fist," the barkeep said with a low voice. "However, a town called Fairfield is a week's journey from here. I haven't gone myself due to the danger, but I hear that it's quite a large town. And supposedly, there are some government people from the United States there. They might know more.

"You were quite generous, so I'll warn you. You should probably leave here sooner than later. Travelers usually have a tough time here," he said as he made an almost indiscernible nod with his head toward a few of the tables.

"Why are people still here? This place looks a bit…" Zac said as he hesitated how to finish the sentence, but the bartender understood what he meant and sighed.

"The road to Fairfield has large packs of monsters above level 20. Very few dare to go that way without pushing through with a car. There's also talk of even stronger pack leaders roving about. But Roger has most of the cars and all the petrol, so it's better to stay here and eke out a living."

Zac was about to ask something else, but a loud ruckus outside interrupted him. A loud crash and a few angry roars bled into the bar, whose customers slightly perked up. A young girl's scream came next, and the bartender sighed again with sadness in his eyes.

"It looks like they found her."

"Found who?" Zac asked curiously.

"You should have seen the two bodies out on the gate? The scream probably came from their daughter," the bartender answered with some disgust on his face as he continued with a low voice. "Roger took a liking to the young girl, but the parents tried to sneak her out of town. Truly a miserable family."

Zac's eyebrows scrunched together, somewhat unsure of what to do. He wasn't some hero saving the damsel in distress. But could he just watch these things happen with a clean conscience, knowing he could help?

It didn't take long for him to decide. He couldn't save the world, but at least he could save this girl, and only pray someone would do the same for his family in case it came to that. He got to his feet and turned toward the door. The bartender tried to signal him to stop, but he only answered with a wave as he walked toward the ruckus.

99

EMILY

As Zac stepped out of the bar, he saw that there was already a small crowd gathering. After a quick glance, it was clear that no one was there to help, but rather to watch a show. All the noise came from three grimy-looking men who'd cornered a kid.

The men all had somewhat matching clothes, with a large uneven R patch sewn to their chest. It looked like the leader of the town truly wanted to set himself up as a medieval lord, already making his underlings wear a crest. Zac shook his head and looked toward the inner part of the town, where another wall was erected. That should be the residence of this Roger and his cronies.

One of the men was bleeding freely from his head, and the glass shards on the ground around him explained what had happened.

"You little BITCH! After Roger gets tired of you, I'll fucking feed you to the dogs!" the bleeding man roared at their cornered prey.

It took Zac a few seconds to realize that the kid was actually a small girl somewhere in her teens. She wore wretched-looking rags for clothes, and her face was caked in dirt apart from a few tear streaks drawing clear lines along her cheeks. Even her hair was a mess, and it looked like she or someone else had randomly cut most of it off with a knife.

The teenager was holding the remains of a bottle as a weapon and ferociously stared at the three men. The outlook didn't look good, as two of them took out daggers as they approached her while the last man stood at the ready. Zac sighed and used **[Eye of Discernment]** on the group, and saw that the girl was named Emily.

She didn't even have a level yet, which meant that she was too young to start using the System. The other three were around level 15 to 17, weaklings in Zac's eyes but perhaps strong according to the level of this town. Certainly, for a young girl without any powers, it was a futile struggle.

"WHO IS SPYING ON US?" the third man without a knife roared as he glared in Zac's direction.

Zac rolled his eyes as he stepped out from the group of people. He really needed to get a better inspection skill. Anyone with Intelligence above 15 points would be able to sense his scan, above 30 and they'd know it was him. Apparently, the homeless-looking man actually focused on Intelligence, which was a bit surprising.

"Wanting to play the hero? Or maybe you just want her for yourself, eh? In either case, you'd better fuck right off," the bleeding man said.

Zac shook his head as he wondered how people could devolve to this stage after just a few months. Were the laws and fear of punishment the only things that held some people back before the integration?

"You'd better turn back right now–" one of the men said, but threw his dagger at Zac's head mid-sentence in an attempt to ambush him.

Zac couldn't even be bothered to respond, and he simply

caught the dagger in midair as he released his aura. Screams of panic immediately erupted as the onlookers frenetically tried to back away. He held the knife in his hand, still unsure of how to act.

"Don't move, or I'll kill the brat!" one of the men said as he grabbed the girl, who had lost focus due to Zac's aura. He was deathly pale, and his whole body was shaking in horror as he maniacally stared at Zac.

Zac frowned and threw the dagger with a quick motion. It tore through the air and punched into the head of the man holding the girl hostage. The force of the throw was so great that his head burst like a watermelon, instantly killing him.

Next, Zac took out one of his regular axes from his pouch and charged up a **[Chop]**. The other two ruffians didn't even have time to react or scream before two headless corpses fell down on the ground. A large tear was rent through a house as well from Zac's lightning-quick swings, and it looked like it would collapse at any second.

Zac walked over to the girl, who now was drenched in the man's blood. She still had the bottle in her hand, and though she looked scared of Zac, she didn't flinch. Zac's impression of this girl was far better compared to the castaways on his island.

"Let's go," was the only thing he said to her as he controlled his aura and turned toward the central area of Fort Roger. But he only had time to take three steps before the bartender stopped him.

"Wait, young man! I understand you're angry, but please don't do anything drastic. If you kill Roger and his henchmen, then most of the people in this town will perish from the animals."

That made Zac stop in his tracks, and after some hesitation, he turned around and started walking toward the gate instead with some sadness in his eyes.

There wasn't anything left to do here. Information in a hovel like this was limited, and he'd have to travel to Fairfield in order to find out more. This Roger fellow might know more, but he had a feeling that going to visit him would only result in battle and more death.

He wasn't sure how to deal with people like Roger. Obviously, they were scum, but they were also the ones who kept civilians safe, just as the bartender said. There were even level 1 wastrels still surviving to this date in Fort Roger, and that was mostly thanks to Roger.

In his anger, he hadn't thought about the consequences, but he wasn't ready to support this whole town. He just had no way to migrate a whole town through the forest and through the teleporter in time before the next wave started. And it wasn't like he could afford it in any case, since each activation cost a bunch of Nexus Crystals.

It wouldn't help to build his own teleporter here for the same reason, not that he was ready to waste that many crystals on these people even if he could. The wolf waves had tapped almost all his remaining crystals, and he wasn't about to spend another 10 million Nexus Coins on a teleporter. He needed that money to ready himself for the second wave.

He'd learned from Selas during their walk that villages regularly were beset by beasts. It wasn't to the point of his own beast waves, but there could be hundreds of frenzied animals who heedlessly charged at the villages. Selas believed it was the work of the System, and Zac agreed.

But still, leaving like this gave a bad taste in his mouth, and his monstrous aura once again flared out. He turned back around and supercharged another Cosmic Energy edge, bringing it to over ten meters. With an echoing roar, he unleashed the edge right toward the inner wall in the distance.

As it traveled, it destroyed the paved road, creating a huge scar that ran right through the village. It smashed through the rudimentary gate, leaving only wood chippings in its wake. Finally, when the blade was only twenty meters away from the mansion, the blade winked out of existence.

"Deliver this message to Roger. I will return through this area shortly, and if I find him still acting like some wannabe warlord, I will judge him and all his henchmen. Let my strike be the reminder," Zac said with a loud voice empowered with Cosmic Energy. His huge aura was still billowing out, forcing people to back away or go down on their knees, and the visage of his swing would likely follow these townspeople for the rest of their lives.

All the villagers of Fort Roger quickly got out of the way as he once again retracted his aura and walked away. Their faces were white with terror, and they didn't even dare to look up. Some shuffling from behind told him that the girl had decided to follow him.

Soon they were at the gate with Emily's parents hung up. And for the first time, he heard the girl speak up.

"Please… please help me take them down," a weak voice came from behind him, and he turned around to see tears pooling in her eyes.

Zac wordlessly started to charge **[Chop]** again, preparing to cut down the two.

"HEY, WHAT ARE YOU DOING?!" one of the guards shouted and ran toward Zac.

With the bartender's words echoing in his mind, Zac felt no need to keep killing, and only lightly slapped the man to knock him unconscious. The other guards only fearfully stared in the distance, not daring to approach.

He charged up **[Chop]** to a five-meter edge, and with two lightning-quick swings, the whole part of the wall that held the two bodies was cut down. Zac freed the two corpses, simply ripping apart the chains that held them. Then with a nod toward the girl, he walked toward the forest with the two bodies under his arms.

The remaining guards mutely stared at Zac's back and the ruined gate, unsure what to do. Soon one of them ran toward the large mansion on the other side of the town.

After a few minutes of walking, Zac felt confident that no one was planning on following them, so he placed the two bodies down on the ground then put them into his Cosmos Sack.

"What did you do?!" the girl asked, aghast, seeing the bodies of her parents simply vanish.

She pointed the shattered glass bottle she still carried at him.

"I placed them in a magic bag," Zac answered as he started to take off his shoes.

She hesitated a bit, then put down her makeshift weapon.

"Why didn't you kill Roger as well? He is much worse than the ones you killed," she asked in an almost accusatory tone.

"I am not sure more good than evil would come from me doing that," Zac said as he glanced at her. He held the shoes, which were now caked in all kinds of things from walking through Fort Roger, and simply chucked them into the woods with some disgust. He'd rather get new ones than put these defiled ones back on.

Emily hesitated a bit before she gritted her teeth and started to undress.

"As long as you kill him, you can do whatever you want with me," she said with her eyes reddening.

Zac's eyebrows rose, and using **[Loamwalker]**, he almost teleported in front of her and flicked her forehead.

"Don't be stupid. Keep your clothes on," he said with a roll of his eyes. "I'm not interested in little kids."

"I'm fifteen," she said defensively, but she still started to put on her clothes while blushing a bit.

"That Roger isn't very strong. If you want him killed, just

work hard and kill him yourself," Zac said. "I am not some mercenary who goes around killing people. I have my own problems to deal with."

"Then help me get strong! I've never heard of anyone being as powerful as you, and I've been to multiple cities," Emily asked, a burning desire in her eyes.

Zac had initially planned on dumping the girl in Winterleaf Village before heading back, but something in her eyes made Zac change his mind. He guessed that Alyn had her first student for the Academy.

"Why have you been to multiple cities? Traveling is pretty dangerous," he said.

"I have a big brother and a big sister. Both are cultivators. They disappeared right from our home. We looked around but couldn't find them. After a little over a month, we heard about the Tutorial, but the cultivators didn't return to our city. We guessed that they were dropped off somewhere else," she explained. "We decided to look for them, so we have traveled looking for them for a few months and arrived at Fort Roger a week ago."

She didn't continue from there, but Zac could guess the rest of the story from her eyes once again reddening. He sighed and wondered how many people had died trying to find their family members or trying to get back home. The world was fraught with danger, and the incursions and monsters might not even be the worst ones. Humanity had always been its own worst enemy.

"I can take you with me to my town. However, that place is extremely far away, and you will not be able to look for your siblings if you do. Where I live is very dangerous, but you can get stronger there. It's up to you to choose your path," Zac said as he looked at the teenager.

Emily only hesitated a few seconds before she looked at him with determination. "I'll go with you."

"Okay. Then jump up on my back," Zac said as he turned his back to her.

"What?" she asked with a flabbergasted face.

Zac had already decided to head back to Port Atwood after this small excursion. There were five days left until the next part of the beast waves, and he wasn't sure he'd make it to Fairfield and back within that timeframe. He felt it was more worthwhile to go back and increase his power with his remaining E-grade Crystals.

Besides, Emily seemed to have visited multiple towns, and she might have even more answers compared to the barkeep or Roger. All in all, he was happy with the result of this expedition. He even got a nifty map and, more importantly, the magical token.

"Come on, jump up," Zac repeated as he hunched down a bit. Walking with an unevolved human in tow would waste far too much time, so he would have to carry her. Since he wanted his arms free in case of an attack, she'd have to climb up on his back.

She hesitated a bit before she climbed up with a slight blush on her face. As soon as she put her arms around his neck, he walked off with his usual speed.

A shriek echoed through the forest as Zac strolled through with the speed of a runaway train.

100

TRAVEL COMPANIONS

Zac stopped for the night at a small clearing and let Emily down from his back. Even the fading light couldn't hide the fact that her face was deathly pale. Moving almost at the speed of a car through dense forest on the back of another human was apparently quite jarring, and Zac had been forced to stop a few times to let the girl take a breather.

There were many things he wanted to ask the teenager about the Tutorial and society after the fall, but he didn't want to push her either. They'd buried her parents in a beautiful glade just a few hours ago, and she hadn't said anything since then. There wasn't any ceremony, with Zac simply using a broadsword to rip open a hole in the ground where he placed the two together. Since the bodies were naked, he first placed a cover over them before he refilled the grave.

Meanwhile, Emily carved the words *Remembered by E+J+O* in a tree with a dagger she got from Zac. They simply stood staring at the grave for a few minutes before she silently climbed up on Zac's back, and they wordlessly left the glade. Zac had offered to bury them on the Island, but Emily wanted to bury them closer to their home.

Zac prepared a small fire in silence as Emily was looking at the dagger Zac gave her earlier.

"What level are you?" she suddenly asked as she looked up at Zac, who froze a bit.

"Um…" he said, unsure how to respond. He wasn't sure whether exposing the fact he was over level 50 was such a good idea.

"Well, are you on the Ladder?" Emily changed her question when she saw Zac's troubled face.

"Yes. Can you see the Ladder?" Zac asked, a bit surprised.

"I knew it. You are way too strong to not be a Ranker," she said, looking a bit excited. "Everyone can see the Ladder. I guess that you are considered role models by the System? So it wants to display you for us as well."

"Do you know if there are any other Rankers close by?" Zac probed, a bit curious.

"No idea. I know that the government is looking for you people," she answered as she started cutting the air with her dagger. However, her movements and technique were horrendous.

Zac took out a spit and large chunk of meat from his sack and placed it on the spit close to the fire. He had grown tired of the tough dried meat long ago and now preferred to barbecue. Now that he was forced to stop for Emily, he had the time to spare.

He sprinkled some salt over the slab and left it to slowly be grilled. He mentally kicked himself for not looking for some spices at Fort Roger, as the ones from the camper had been used up long ago. Then again, he felt that any foodstuffs should have been pilfered long ago in a wretched town like that.

"Why are they looking for us? No, not like that; move like this," Zac asked as he showed how to properly distribute her weight.

"I dunno. They are trying to get all the cultivators to register and become like an army or something? Maybe they want the

Rankers to lead the cultivators?" she answered as she mimicked Zac's movement.

"Hmm…" Zac only answered as he kept moving. He felt that it wasn't that simple. The world was collapsing, and from his brief visit to Fort Roger, he knew that the government's control was tenuous at best. Perhaps they needed Rankers to keep people in check. "Are many cultivators complying?"

"I don't think so. We tried going to the government when we looked for Johanna and Oscar, but from what we heard, most people haven't joined yet. But new people join every day, and the government offers pretty good things," she distractedly answered without stopping her stabs.

"Like what? Now shift your weight like this. It gives more reach to your stab," Zac asked as he kept moving.

"Access to system-exclusive things like training facilities. Good salary. Oh, and they have claimed good areas that have a lot of monsters. Anyone who wants to train there has to be a part of the government; otherwise, they are attacked," she explained.

"Aren't there monsters everywhere? Why would that matter?"

"That forest is good because it doesn't have any very strong monsters, it seems. It's a pretty safe spot to level up. Most places have a random mix of animals, and it's super dangerous to fight there. Some super-strong monster can pop out anytime and kill you. So finding good spots is very important."

Zac nodded, as it made a lot of sense. His situation was the same. His whole island had turned into a farmer's paradise in a sense, as the demonic beast hordes killed off any normal animals that could have become a real threat. There was no supercharged mink on demon island, only barghest and gwyllgi. They were dangerous compared to most animals, but there would never be any surprise beast or boss jumping out of the bushes.

They kept going for some time before they sat down to eat.

Zac was by no means a knife-master, but some things he'd learned from his guidance system were universal.

"Do you know why so many towns have Nexus Nodes?" Zac suddenly asked.

He knew that he wouldn't be the only one with a Town Shop system, but after seeing Fort Roger, he was a bit surprised to see just how low the bar was set.

"Um, because people like to live together?" she answered, looking a bit confused.

"What?"

"Well, those crystals appear when enough people live together in a town, right?" Emily answered.

"Hmm..." Zac only answered.

"Then everyone gets a quest to fight for ownership. It can get pretty crazy. My parents got such a quest once, but we immediately left town and hid out until it settled down. But I heard those crystals are always the worst ones and only give classes," she continued after looking at Zac. "Only those who get their crystals from the Tutorial can actually build things with it, and it is different there as well. Like if they impressed the System in the Tutorial, they get to buy more things. I'm not sure."

It looked like Lesser Nexus Nodes could pop up just from population density, and a quest like the one for the Fruit of Ascension would start. These nodes gave almost no options, but he was sure that the one who claimed ownership would get some quest to evolve the crystal.

He was a bit irritated earlier that others already had towns when he created his, since he might have missed out on some good titles. It took him a few days to figure out how to create an outpost, after all. But it seemed their progression was limited. After all, he doubted the people of Winterleaf Village had single-handedly closed a freaking incursion in order to establish theirs.

Emily soon fell asleep, since she was tired from today's

events, but Zac only needed a few hours of rest. He sat down with his back against the wall and started pondering the Dao. There was no fourth Dao Seed he felt close to attaining, and instead, he needed to focus on upgrading the ones he had.

He turned his eyes inward toward the axe fractal in his mind. Since he'd gained the Seed of Sharpness, the axe had two colors, with one side being dark blue with some brown, and the other a steely gray. The colors represented the two seeds he possessed, Sharpness and Heaviness. There was a clear line of demarcation between the two Daos, and the auras didn't mix in the slightest.

He knew that one of the things he needed to do in the future was to fuse these two, but it was very far off. Alyn explained that there were two ways to improve the Dao. The first was fusion, and it was the path he had been walking since the start. Since the day he saw the vision, he knew that the Seed of Heaviness he'd gained was only part of the terrifying aura in the axe-man's swing. He would have to fuse more concepts into it to create a true Dao of Axe.

The path of fusion often walked from simplicity to complexity. It combined simple concepts into something greater than the sum of the parts. The other path was generally referred to as evolution. It meant pushing a Dao Seed to its limit, and from there letting it evolve into a higher Dao of the same category.

That was his plan with his Dao of Trees. There might be a possibility to fuse it into his Dao of Axes as well, but Zac felt it would weaken it rather than strengthen it. Instead, he'd work toward evolving it by itself. Unless he suddenly gained a fourth seed somewhere and tried his hands on fusing that as well.

Neither fusion nor evolution was better than the other, according to Alyn; they were just different. However, she told him that most focused on evolution since fewer Daos were necessary to progress with that path. With fusion, he'd always need to gain enlightenment on at least two Daos.

Dao was generally considered the true watershed in the path to power. Over time, most people were able to hit their level cap, and money could solve the issue of Race evolution. But Dao was something you needed to figure out yourself. There were some tools and treasures that could help out, but it mostly depended on personal aptitude and insight.

Zac felt he probably wasn't some genius since all three of his seeds essentially came from his visions. He did gain the Seed of Sharpness a few months later, but the foundation for learning it came from the same vision as the Seed of Heaviness. He was afraid that evolving all three at the same time would be more than he could chew.

He still was hesitating whether to put aside two of the seeds and only focus on one, or to focus on both the offensive ones. The Dao of Trees was the lowest priority for now, as its use simply didn't feel as readily apparent.

Finally, he made a decision in his mind. He would focus on the Dao of Sharpness, at least for now. It was the seed he'd had for the shortest time, but it felt like the most useful one. He stared at the axe in his mind, trying to glean anything out of the silver fractals.

He also played the vision of the axe-man in his mind, feeling the terrifying force of the strike. Finally, he revisited the fight with the Fiend Wolf. He remembered the feeling of standing in the Dao Field, where even the air turned sharp from the Dao. He remembered how the casual swings of the beast rent long lines into the earth without any Cosmic Energy needed.

He also pondered upon what sharpness actually meant. It wasn't as simple as the thinner the edge, the more damage he could do. Sharpness needed control and technique to be properly applied as well. He remembered seeing clips before the fall where people tried using razor-sharp swords and barely were able to cut anything since their technique was bad.

He kept going for a few hours before the mental strain became too much, and he fell asleep. He woke up a few hours later, only to find Emily intently staring at him.

"Are you Abbot Everlasting Peace?" she asked curiously.

"Urh… what?"

"Well, you look like a monk, and when I woke up during the night, I saw you meditating. You already told me you are on the Ladder. So are you Abbot Everlasting Peace? Or Boundless Truth? Is that why you weren't interested in me? Is there nothing down there?" she peppered off, almost overtaxing Zac's exhausted brain.

"Boundless? Wait, what? I'm no monk. My hair only got singed off in battle recently. And I'm not missing any goddamn parts, okay?"

101

FIRST IMPRESSIONS

After another day of travel, they finally reached Winterleaf Village. Zac slowed down before entering the town though, not wanting to make it look like he charged at them.

"Careful. This is a beastman village! They are usually very strong," Emily hastily said as she pulled at his cloak.

"I know. I am friends with them," Zac offhandedly answered as he entered the town. He slightly frowned as he saw that the village was almost completely deserted, with no one in sight. Had something happened?

He quickly calmed down, though, as he soon saw Selas run toward him.

"Greetings, Zac. We didn't expect to see you for a few more days."

"My trip was cut short, so I'm heading back, I hope you don't mind. Is everything okay here? It looks a bit… empty?"

"Stupid, they can't understand English," the girl softly said by his side, but Zac only rolled his eyes in response. It was a bit cumbersome when only one party had the language skill in these situations.

"Not a problem. I'll lead you to the teleporter. Most people are just out working for now," the Ishiate answered with a cough as he ushered them toward the array.

Zac felt that the beastman was lying but couldn't be bothered to untangle that. They simply walked back toward the teleportation array, making some small talk, while Emily looked on, confused. Next to the array, a large package was placed.

"The package contains the fur and a few tokens of thanks by the villagers for the help you provided us. Good luck with your endeavors, my friend. I hope to see you again in the treasure hunt," Selas said with an awkward smile.

Zac nodded and, after placing the crystals needed to teleport the two of them, stepped on the array with Emily in tow. He initially had wanted to discuss some matters of trade, such as keeping a channel open for goods between the two. However, it seemed pretty clear that they were worried he'd go berserk, to the point they'd even evacuated the town to avoid him.

With a flash followed by some darkness, he once again materialized. To his surprise, he only saw walls and quickly looked around. With a sigh of relief, he headed through a door, and the familiar sight of Port Atwood came into view.

It seemed that someone had erected a small house to shield the teleportation array while he was gone. Initially, he thought that Ogras had planned some trap for him, but that clearly wasn't the case.

"Wow, that was so cool. Were we teleported?" Emily exclaimed next to him.

"Yeah, it's a teleportation array. It can take us almost anywhere on the planet, as long as there's another array there," Zac answered. The way Selas acted was quite suspect, so he brought up the teleportation interface just to make sure of his suspicions.

Just as he opened the window, he saw the line with Winterleaf

Village wink out of existence, no longer available to choose. Zac only sighed and closed the interface. It looked like the beastmen were careful after all. His plan to visit Fairfield after the next wave would have to be canceled.

"Let's go," he said as he headed toward the temporary town.

Zac noticed that the progress was coming along well as they walked toward the center of Port Atwood. The wall was almost completely fixed, and new poles had been erected on the outside. Their use had been limited the last time, but it was better to have something than nothing. There was, however, an extremely unsettling smell in the air, and Zac furrowed his brows.

"Wow, your town smells like poop," Emily exclaimed, and Zac was forced to agree with some embarrassment.

As they closed in on the town, the shadows flickered, and the familiar demon appeared in front of them. Emily shrieked in surprise and jumped back a few steps, her dagger immediately in her hand.

"This one seems a bit better than the last ones, even if she looks a bit feral. I didn't know you liked them this… young. If that's your taste, you can always pursue Zakarith. Your names match and everything," Ogras said with a half-smile.

"She was in trouble, so I picked her up along the way," Zac answered with a roll of his eyes. "How are the preparations going, and what the hell is this smell?"

"WAIT! Why is there a demon here, and why is it speaking English?" Emily shrilly interjected as she started tracing large crosses in the air to ward off evil.

"What is she doing? Is she brain-damaged?" Ogras skeptically asked as he gave a glance of mock pity.

Zac only half-grinned and briefly told him about the demons in Christianity and other folklore.

"Hmm, very interesting. It might be a coincidence, or perhaps your planet had visitors from the Multiverse a few thousand years ago, and the details got jumbled over the years," Ogras mused.

"Wait, people could come from the Multiverse even before the integration?" Zac asked.

"Well, yeah, but it would be like finding a needle in a galaxy, so to speak. Your planet would be almost impossible to locate, but nothing is stopping you," Ogras answered with a shrug.

"This is Ogras. He's living here along with a few hundred more of his kind. Actually, the town mostly consists of demons. They're like the beastmen," Zac explained to the frazzled girl.

That seemed to calm her down somewhat as she curiously glanced at the demon.

"I know I'm handsome, but don't go falling in love with me. I prefer mature ladies," Ogras said as he struck a pose.

She only blushed a bit and moved a bit further away.

"Are there no other humans here except you?" she curiously asked Zac.

"Well, there are a few more, but they arrived just recently," Zac answered.

"Pah, don't remind me of those wastrels," Ogras spat. "Pain in the ass every single one of them. Well, the old guy is okay, I guess."

"What's going on? And the smell?" Zac reminded the demon.

"Entitled little shits. They keep complaining and don't want to work. They just hide in their house after seeing one little barghest, crying and demanding to see you. When they found out you weren't here anymore, they flipped out," Ogras said with disdain. "As for the wretched odor? You try tanning tens of thousands of wolf hides at once without making the area smell like a Devourer's asshole."

"How did they come in contact with a barghest? There shouldn't be any alive this close to town, right?" Zac asked.

He knew that they would treat the hides, as the noncombat

classes had arduously skinned and salvaged anything of value from the monster hordes. He hadn't expected this level of stench, though. Most of the parts of the beasts were useless since the grade was too low to trade with the Mercantile System, but some things might become useful, and with the volumes they were handling, they would make a decent profit.

The hides of the more sturdy ones could be made into F-grade leather armors, which would sell for a decent penny, especially on a newly integrated world like Earth. With their almost infinite stock of leather, they planned on using it as a selling point for visiting the town when they opened the gates for the public in the future.

"They said they wanted to get stronger, and since none of them are cultivators, Ilvere took them to hunt a few barghest," Ogras answered in response to the question about the humans. "If they worked together, they shouldn't have any problems killing such a dumb beast. But apparently it was chaos, people fleeing for their lives, even pushing each other down to escape. Ilvere had to kill the beast before a fight even started." He snickered.

Zac could only sigh, feeling a bit embarrassed on their behalf.

"What's a barghest?" Emily asked curiously.

"It's a large demon dog that looks like it has been turned inside out," Zac answered. Ogras looked like he was about to correct Zac but, after some thought, nodded his head.

Zac turned to Emily after some thought.

"How do most human towns handle people who can't fight?"

"Eh… Some get jobs doing various things, I guess? There are still people needed for all kinds of things. The people who have simply given up are usually ignored or kicked out of town. I heard the most ruthless leaders have even used them as human shields against monster waves," the girl answered after some thought.

"There's an idea," Ogras muttered.

"Where are they now?" Zac asked with a sigh.

"We put them in the infirmary since it's empty by now."

"How's Alea?" Zac quickly asked, reminded of the demoness.

"She's up now, but still not completely restored. She's been asking about you," the demon answered with a devilish grin.

"Who's Alea?" Emily perked up.

"Why do you care, little brat?" Ogras grinned at her.

"Whatever," she answered with a pout.

Already regretting coming back this early, Zac sighed as he started walking toward the infirmary.

"More importantly, did you find any?" Ogras asked.

"Any what? Humans? Yeah, I visited a human settlement," Zac distractedly answered.

"Who cares about that? Movies, human? Did you find any movies?"

Zac stopped and glanced at the demon.

"Are you really that free right now?"

"The wall is essentially rebuilt, and I still can't buy anything with contribution points. I'm just waiting around," he answered impatiently.

Zac shook his head but took out the large box containing the TV, and the small mountain of videos. Ogras inspected the things with glee, but he looked a bit confused.

"What are these things?"

"The large box contains a much larger screen to watch the movies. The small packages each contain one movie or a series. That box over there contains the device to play them. Both the large screen and the player need a steady stream of electricity through a cable. You can plug them into the camper, but you need to figure out how to keep the battery charged yourself."

Ogras nodded excitedly and put all the things into his pouch.

"I'm sure you have many things to do. I'll help this kid get used to the area," he said, and as he grabbed the shoulder of

Emily, both of them disappeared, leaving only a startled shriek in the air.

Zac smiled a bit and continued on toward the infirmary. He wasn't afraid that he'd hurt the teenager, but rather knew he'd need some tech support. Actually, it even looked like he approved of her ferocity. Soon he arrived outside the infirmary and, to his surprise, saw Janos sitting outside the door.

"What's going on?"

"Kept escaping. Put them in illusion," the demon tersely answered.

"Uh, okay. You can turn it off. I'm going in," Zac said with some annoyance. He didn't know if these people really were a handful, or whether the demons were too heavy-handed, but something needed to be done. He didn't have the resources to baby these people all the time.

With a sigh, he entered the infirmary. As he entered, the humans saw it was Zac and rushed toward him with a litany of complaints. Zac simply released some of his aura to silence the group, then stared at them until they had calmed down.

"I hear you have been asking for me?" Zac said.

"You lied to us! We want off this hellhole of an island. Those demons said you have a method to leave the island. We want to go home," Megan angrily huffed.

"You're safe, clean, and fed. That's better compared to most of humanity right now. You have access to a Multiverse Town Shop that has the herbs needed to evolve your race. You have a forest full of prey that gives a huge amount of Nexus Coins and Cosmic Energy. And you sit here complaining," Zac retorted as a twinge of anger flared up at these people. Their situation would likely cause envy from most people, even cultivators, yet they only sat here thinking life was unfair.

"You want off this island with your powers? You'd die within a day. And even if you somehow survived and got to a settlement, you'd be made slaves or worse, since you're powerless."

The castaways hesitantly looked at each other before the girl once again gathered her courage.

"Those hellhounds in the forest? We saw it bite clean through a thick tree. You want us to fight that? We aren't suicidal. And do you think we'll just believe you when you say that the world outside is dangerous?" she angrily said, and from the looks of the faces of the others, they agreed.

"I am sorry we haven't been able to help out very much, young man. Us old folks have some trouble adjusting to this new reality," the old fisherman suddenly interjected.

"I currently have 46,000 Nexus Coins from fighting animals on our old island. If possible, I would like to borrow 36,000 Nexus Coins in order to buy the **[Water Spear]** skill from your Nexus Node for 70,000 coins. The remaining coins I would like to use to buy some of your crystals at 50 coins per Nexus Crystal," the old fisherman said.

"Your name is Trang, right?"

"My name is Sap Trang. What do you think of my proposal? I know it is a lot of coins, but with it, I hope to be able to kill the demons you call barghest, and from there, slowly get stronger. The crystals are mainly for my fellow villagers, who plan to become what your… friends… call noncombat classes. They have slowly gotten levels from fishing, but the crystals would speed it up substantially. It looks to me that you are founding an island kingdom, and us old folk have lived on the sea for all our lives. We believe we can be helpful even in this new world."

Zac was a bit surprised. This old man clearly was no fool like the brats. Sap Trang had learned everything he could from Alyn and Zakarith and formulated a path for himself and his villagers. He also didn't mention Megan and her clique, so he guessed he wasn't too fond of them either.

And it was true, having a couple of seasoned seamen would be convenient. A goal of his was to explore the neighboring islands when time permitted. Who knew what treasures the System had put there.

Besides, what Sap Trang said was true. He did want to create a sphere of influence, and since he was situated on an island, it would pretty much have to be an island kingdom.

102

THE DAY BEFORE THE STORM

"I'll give you 100,000 Nexus Coins as an investment to get you and your fellow villagers on the right track. You should know that the number of crystals I can sell is limited at the moment, as we need them for the war preparations. But enough to last you for a few weeks of cultivation shouldn't be a problem," Zac said after mulling it over for a few seconds.

There were only six villagers, with four elderly men and two old ladies, and their expenditure shouldn't really impact their daily production. He didn't mention anything about paying it back, as he might as well consider it a gift in case they proved useful. If not, he could always come to collect at a later date.

The Vietnamese villagers looked excited and quickly got to their feet and bowed toward Zac, who lightly nodded back. However, frowns appeared on the other group of people, who also started to glare at the fishermen.

"Why are you only giving them all those resources? What about us?" one of the men angrily asked.

"They seem like they can be useful to my town. You do not. Why should I spend Nexus Coins on you?" Zac said with a dismissive glance, which only made the former tourists angrier.

"There are various tasks that need to be completed on this island. Go earn your keep if you want coins but don't want to fight. Mr. Trang, take your villagers and come with me," Zac continued and started to head out.

The fishermen quickly followed in tow, but when the tourists tried to follow, a glare from Zac stopped them in their tracks. As he left the infirmary, he briefly updated Janos, who sighed and reactivated his illusion, keeping the humans inside.

Next, he walked over to Adran's canopy. Adran was a stocky demon who was in charge of the logistics of the temporary town, and one of the people who had been present at the meeting discussing the town design some time ago. He was a Common noncombat class called Administrator, Zac had learned earlier, which was an important reason for his current position.

It was apparently quite similar to the Scribe class that Zakarith possessed, but their differences lay in their upgrade paths. The Scribe class had upgrade paths that veered toward the Mercantile class. It could actually also be upgraded into Inscriber, a Craftsman class that focused on inscribing fractals onto gear.

Administrator focused more on the management of towns and countries. It could be upgraded to things like Magistrate in the future, where the individuals almost became like supercomputers, keeping track of innumerable things in their heads. It apparently also could be upgraded into certain Mentalist classes.

There actually wasn't a too rigid system that split up the types of classes, but it was rather fluid. Some classes were mixes of various things, and the type of class could change when evolving it. Of course, planning out your path from the start often was preferable in order to not allocate attribute points in the wrong direction.

Zac had Adran make arrangements for the humans. He simply provided the Nexus Coins and different lodging for the fishermen. For anything else, they first would have to prove themselves. As for the tourists, he set some ground rules to whip them into shape. If they didn't volunteer to do some tasks around the camp, then work would be handed out. If they didn't complete it, then no food or lodging that day.

He didn't want groups of people who just drifted about like in Fort Roger. And if they wouldn't pick themselves up like the fishermen, then Zac would drag them forward no matter their opinion. Besides, he had a feeling that incoming second monster horde would help them realize their new reality. If thousands of monsters charging at them didn't wake them up, nothing would.

After dealing with his latest citizens, he left to look for Alea. After asking around, he found she was meditating on top of the repaired wall. He soon found her sitting down with the sun at her back, illuminating her horns to truly look as though they were licks of fire.

Zac did not want to interrupt her meditation and simply sat down close to her and gazed out over the mostly prepared battlefield.

"You're back," Zac suddenly heard Alea say after some time and looked over at the demoness.

"I am glad to see you're better," Zac said after some hesitant silence.

"Your pill was very effective," Alea answered as she looked calmly at his face.

The intent stare was starting to make Zac a bit uncomfortable, and he tried to come up with something to discuss. Finally, he detailed his excursion through the teleportation. The Ishiate, the mink, and Fort Roger. Alea calmly listened through the story, seemingly content to let Zac blabber on, until he got to Emily.

"This human, is she cute?" she asked with a light voice.

"She's just a kid," Zac answered with a roll of his eyes. Then he caught himself, as it felt like he was defending himself to a girlfriend.

"Hmm…" was the only answer from the demoness as she slowly closed her eyes to keep meditating. Zac felt that he was approaching a weird territory and, with a grunt, got up to his feet. Before he jumped down off the wall, he looked down on the meditating demoness a few seconds.

"Thank you," he said before he left. That was the real thing he wanted to convey. Alea had risked her life to help him in the battle against the Fiend Wolf and was still recuperating from its attack. She was under no obligation to do that, but she still did it, and Zac was truly grateful.

With that, he was done with everything he needed to do for now. The demons knew what they needed to do, and Zac's only goal now was to get stronger. He didn't want to get mired down in weeks of battle again. The few days of freedom as he explored the new planet made him feel alive, and he was anxious to get back to it.

The fact that the beastmen had closed their portal was a bit troubling, as it threw a wrench in his plans, but since that small village had managed to buy a teleportation array already, then many other towns would likely follow suit soon. Perhaps even a government-run one that wanted to gather people.

He went back to his camp, and to his surprise, saw Ogras and Emily sitting under a red canopy in a comfortable chair each, contentedly watching a movie. They obviously were successful in setting up the new television, as it currently was showing a rom-com movie with an extension cable running through the illusion array, presumably toward the camper.

He wanted to kick the demon and make him do something more productive, but he also felt that it might be good for Emily to have some company. The apocalypse obviously had toughened her up, but both her parents had been killed just a week ago, and no one could simply shake that off.

"I am going to absorb some crystals before the next horde

arrives. Don't disturb me unless it is something important," Zac said as he looked over at the demon.

"No problem; I can charge up the energy storage of your tin can through that wire, so we won't need to disturb you," Ogras answered without taking his eyes off the TV.

Zac blanked out a second before he understood the demon meant the camper's battery and the extension cord.

"What are you doing?" Emily perked up as she looked over at him.

"I need to train and get stronger," Zac answered.

"Can I do it too?" she eagerly asked. Zac had noticed her hunger for power since they started traveling together, and was very much in favor of it.

"Not until you turn sixteen. Find Alyn later. She'll help you prepare. If you follow her instructions, you will have better prospects in the future," Zac answered with a shake of his head.

"Oh, the disgraced teacher will finally have a student again," Ogras said with a pitying glance at Emily.

"Wait, what do you mean?" Zac asked with a start.

"She got fired because of her, uh, unusually strict training methods in our clan. She was mainly brought over here because she already had the language skill, and people figured she would make a good slave driver," Ogras said with a widening smile. "Otherwise, what use would a teacher be during an invasion? Did you think we would go around opening a bunch of schools for you humans?"

The eyes of both Zac and Emily widened at this, and Zac's image of the calm and proper lady clashed with the image of Alyn screaming at the top of her lungs while whipping a bunch of slaves.

"Well… don't let her overdo it. Emily, stay strong," he said as he entered his camp.

"Wai–" the teenager tried to interject, but another shield

superimposed over the illusion array. It was an **[F-Grade Small-Scale Defensive Array]**, the cheapest and weakest defensive option in the Town Shop.

It wasn't something Zac bought to protect himself, but rather a means to show the surroundings he didn't want to be disturbed. It only cost 75,000 Nexus Coins, and a random punch by him or Ogras would break it. It was, however, effective against a girl who still hadn't started on the path of cultivation.

For the next four days, he simply sat down and absorbed his **[E-Grade Nexus Crystals]**. He was able to absorb roughly two a day, and he'd already consumed two of them before. He left his tenth and last crystal for emergencies, though. During the whole time, he barely slept or ate; he just sat down and let the huge power wash over him.

He stood up, and after a quick shower and dinner, he opened up his quest panel.

Incursion Master (Unique): Close or conquer incursion and protect town from denizens of other alignments for 3 months. Reward: 5 E-Grade Nexus Crystals, town upgraded to City, status upgraded to Lord. (1/3) [1:03:22:34]

A little over a day remained until the next wave started, and only the finishing touches were needed now. He removed his defensive array and walked out to the makeshift movie canopy. During the four days, it had gotten some upgrades, with walls that kept the glare off the TV, and a rug and coffee table. It was, however, empty, so he headed toward the town.

After asking around, he learned Ogras was with Adran, and walked over. As the two saw Zac approach, they nodded toward him.

"How are the preparations?"

"Everything is finished. This time, we had time left over to create a few siege weapons. They may be useful, and they can even be manned by the noncombat classes or your new citizens after some training. The only thing remaining is purchasing the aces with Nexus Coins," Ogras answered. "I have taken the liberty of collecting 3 million Nexus Coins for the war effort. I mean, 5 million," he continued, correcting himself after a glare by Zac.

Zac nodded and, after some discussion, purchased a few defensive measures.

"How are the humans?" Zac asked Adran after that was done.

"The old people are working hard cultivating with Nexus Crystals. Their leader has even gained a decent speed at killing barghest by now. He has been getting assistance, though, of course," the administrator answered.

"The youth are a bit more troublesome, but they're getting there. Nothing is as effective in getting people in line as a few days of filling old latrines and digging new ones," Adran continued with a small smile while Ogras openly snickered. "Oh, and speaking of the last little human, here she comes."

Zac turned around and saw Emily approach like a small thundercloud. Next to her a visibly irate Alea and Alyn were walking along. Zac sighed and stood up and unhesitantly started to power-walk away.

103

THE SECOND HORDE

"Zac!" a few voices shouted after him. And he could only sigh and turn around.

Since he saw her last, Emily had undergone a drastic transformation. She was properly cleaned and wore new clothes. Zac noted with some interest she had chosen the men's style with the pants and leather armor rather than the dress robes that the two demons by her side wore. Her messy hair also was turned into a pixie cut instead of the uneven mess of a crazy person.

All three, especially the teenager, carried an angry energy as they approached him, and he could only helplessly shake his head.

"Hello, the three of you look lovely today," he said, preemptively trying to avoid whatever trouble was coming his way. It was a trick that had usually worked on Kenzie back in the day. Unfortunately, it seemed to have quite limited effect, as there was barely any change in expression on their faces.

"These two are crazy! I want to learn cultivation from you instead," Emily angrily huffed.

"This child has a great talent for the elements and would become a great mage, healer, or poison mistress," Alyn interjected. "But she is very rambunctious and keeps demanding to learn how to use axes. It would be a waste of her talent."

"And also very unladylike," Alea added on.

"So we have been trying to correct her ways, but she is very stubborn," Alyn said with a frown.

"So what do you want me to do?" Zac asked.

"Punish the child. Hanging naked in the town square for a few days should make her temper milder," Alea said.

"Don't be absurd. She needs to get married in the future. Just a public whipping would do," Alyn retorted with a slight frown.

"I told you, they are crazy! They have tortured me constantly since you left me with them. Let me train with you instead. You saw I learned quickly," she said while glaring angrily at the two demons.

"How do you know what talent she has?" Zac curiously asked, ignoring the teenager for now.

"I had a few warriors contribute some of their Nexus Coins to buy a simple testing device from Calrin," Alyn simply answered.

Zac was starting to understand why Ogras thought Alyn would make a good slave driver. He felt it wasn't as easy as the warriors simply willingly gave away their money after risking their lives. He could only nod and focus on Emily.

"Why do you want to fight with axes? You should be happy that you have the option to become a mage. You can just blast the enemies from a distance," Zac exhorted. "Poison isn't a bad idea either. Have you heard about our contribution quest? Alea is on the third spot there with her poison attacks."

When Alea heard the comment, she smiled proudly and looked down at the teenager with a triumphant face, but she only rolled her eyes.

"But you are number one, right? Much better than that stupid old hag. And you can blast enemies from the distance as well," Emily said grumpily, drawing an angry glare from Alea.

"I've bled over every inch of my body the past months. There's almost not a single part of my body that hasn't been wounded and scarred from my battles. Fighting in melee range is to constantly put yourself in harm's way. A single mistake and you're dead. You should think long and hard before you decide to follow in my footsteps. There are innumerable paths to power, and mine is just one. Try to focus on yourself, and think about what would suit you," Zac said with a sigh.

"Why are you here, anyway? I thought only Alyn was in charge of Emily's education?" Zac asked of the poison mistress.

"When I heard about her talent, I wanted to check her out. I noticed she's also a bit ruthless and crazy, so I think she would make a good disciple of mine," she said with a slight smile.

"Who'd be a disciple to you?" Emily shot back with a scathing glare.

"I can't help you train at the moment. Listen to Alyn. She is far more knowledgeable about these things than I am. And think long and hard about your future path before deciding. The choices you make for your class and attributes in the future will impact your whole life," Zac said as he started to walk away. He didn't want to comment about the discipleship, as that was something between the two of them, and he didn't want to butt in.

"Oh, and no hanging or whipping. She's a student, not a slave," he added as he moved away.

All three of them looked like they weren't finished, but Zac used **[Loamwalker]** to move away. The rest of the day, Zac simply relaxed and adjusted his state of mind. He watched a few movies and took a walk along the shore. Finally, when the counter reached one hour left, he walked over to the wall. Not long after, Ogras and his four generals joined him.

As time passed, more and more of the warriors arrived, and thirty minutes before the next horde arrived, every combatant was at the ready. Adran was also there along with the humans, who nervously looked around. It was on Zac's command they were brought here. They needed to see the reality of this new universe.

They thought they'd escaped calamity when they fled their island, and hoped to get back to normalcy now. But that was impossible, as their experience with the frenzied rats was only a small greeting gift from the System, and it would only get worse. Unless they started to take things seriously, the world would move forward without them.

Alyn and Emily also joined them on the wall. Emily wanted to walk over to Zac, but Alyn kept her close to the stairs leading down, together with the other noncombatants. They didn't know what would come from the next wave, and they needed to be able to quickly get down to safety if it was needed.

The time slowly crept forward, and everyone gazed upon the battlefield with a solemn expression. Some tried to spark a conversation to lighten the tension, but any talk quickly died out under the heavy atmosphere. The moment his counter went down to zero, a huge blinding light appeared in the distance. The next second, a large construct appeared, most closely resembling a hive or anthill.

It looked to be almost a hundred meters tall and was somewhat shaped like a pyramid. The whole construct was a dark gray, almost turning black. There were also green lights covering the hive, almost making it seem like they were windows wrought out of emeralds. On the ground, a few large entrances were visible.

The structure gave an oppressive feeling, like the whole thing was a large lumbering beast.

"What do you think?" Zac asked Ogras, who was standing next to him.

"Some sort of nest. It looks like this second horde is a bit different compared to the first. There are no pillars unless they are inside that thing. I'm not sure where we go from here. I get nothing when trying to use my identification skill on it," Ogras answered with slightly furrowed brows before he increased his volume. "Anyone recognize it?"

Only frowns and shakes of heads and a few short answers followed. None of the demons knew what they were facing. The minutes passed, and the unsettling feeling only grew larger as nothing happened.

"Should we go in? It doesn't feel like a good idea to just leave that thing alone. Who knows what's going on inside there," Zac asked with a frown.

"I sense something!" a voice suddenly shouted. It was one of the earth mages among the demons. He jumped down from the wall and placed his hands on the ground. "There are subtle vibrations in the ground. I think the things inside the nest are digging downward," he said with a serious expression.

A few more demons jumped down, and they confirmed the suspicion. Something was going on inside that hive, but it was happening beneath the ground.

"We can't let this go on. We need to head in," Zac said as he jumped down from the wall as well. "First group, follow me!"

Twenty-five demons quickly jumped down behind Zac. They were a mixed group of both ranged, support, and melee classes. They'd shared the same shift as Zac during the fights with the wolf horde and were the demons Zac was most acquainted with apart from Ogras and Alea. They also had two earth mages in the mix, who would be able to help with the scouting.

They carefully approached the huge hive. It was quite far from the wall, and Zac noticed with a frown that it was outside the range of all his offensive arrays or fortifications. If they wanted to destroy this thing, they would have to do it by hand. Perhaps they could construct siege engines that were more designed for structures compared to hordes of enemies.

When they were a few hundred meters away from the black

nest, one of the earth mages shuddered and put his hands on the ground. Zac immediately stopped and glanced around carefully.

"They've stopped whatever they were doing underground," the mage said.

In response, the group immediately took out their weapons, unsure what would happen. Zac's eyebrows suddenly rose in alarm as he stared at the large holes on the ground floor of the nest.

"Get ready!" he shouted as he took out a large rock from his pouch.

A huge stream of insectoid monsters was pouring out of the nest, heedlessly charging toward the group. Their colors matched the hive, a mix of black and green. They had large chitinous shells that covered their bodies; both their appendages and mandibles looked like sinister weapons.

There seemed to be three types of insects in the army. The most populous looked like a mix between an ant and a mantis. They had three pairs of legs with three joints much like normal ants, but they were as large as a pony. The front set of legs were sharp hooks, and it looked like they were made for digging or fighting rather than running. They could be regarded as the normal soldiers of the insect army.

If the first group could be considered 80% ant with some mantis peppered in, then the second group could be seen as mostly mantis. They were at least 50% larger compared to the normal insects, reaching over two meters in height with their bodies, with their torso stretching upward. Their two front legs were huge sinister blades, looking extremely dangerous.

The last group of insects was very different compared to the rest. Their legs were shorter and their bodies were fat, almost bulbous. The other creepy crawlies were mostly black with some green details, but these ones were mostly green. They also had huge heads with oversized circular maws.

Zac immediately threw out three rocks, each targeting a different type of insect. He still preferred this type of test on new enemies.

The first rock slammed into the foot soldier, crushing its head and instantly killing it. The larger mantis-like being actually managed to react and tried cutting the incoming rock. However, the force in the throw was too strong, and the insect missed as the stone slammed into its chest. The shell of the insect actually didn't break as the stone cracked from the impact. The insect was thrown away and fell down twitching on the ground. If it wasn't dead, it at least was dying from the impact.

The last insect exploded into a large pool of green goop that instantly started scorching the ground. Zac realized, with some shock, the last things actually were large walking vats of acid or poison. He didn't even have time to digest the information before the green acid monsters spit out large balls of the green liquid at the demons.

"ACID! Target the green ones!" Zac shouted and moved out of the way from the incoming projectiles. A few defensive spells were erected as well to protect the group.

Feeling he had a good enough grasp of the beasts, Zac charged up his skill and set out to decapitate some enemies.

104

THE WAR COUNCIL

"It looks like they are expanding their nest underground, moving downward. We believe they are digging toward the Nexus Vein," one of the earth mages reported to the group who was sitting around a table.

Twelve hours had passed since the hive appeared, and they had made some discoveries. The ants were called **[Ayn Hive-beasts]** and the three types they encountered so far were called Ayn worker, Ayn guard, and the green acid shooters were actually called Ayn vomiters.

After the initial clash, they quickly learned that there was an enormous number of beasts inside the large structure, as they kept pouring out as they fought. But the moment they retreated, so did the ants. But just a few minutes after Zac and the demons stopped their assault, the digging was resumed, according to the earth mages.

They were currently holding a war council while two regiments led by Ogras' four generals were keeping the ants busy. They needed to figure out a strategy for this new horde, as their old one wouldn't work. Most of their preparations were in vain, as the new monsters didn't seem interested in attacking the town. The wall stood unassaulted, and the arrays couldn't reach the hive due to the distance.

Zac almost felt that the System specifically chose this type of challenge since the last wave almost felt like a gift of experience and money rather than a challenge. Certainly, the last waves were tough, but never to the point of true desperation.

"That's it, then? We'll head in and destroy it today," Zac said with a frown.

The Nexus Vein was the lifeblood of his island. It created the crystals in the mine and the high concentration of Cosmic Energy in the atmosphere. Anything from cultivation to crafting to even farming would be far more efficient in this area. If he bought an island-wide gathering array in the future, it would truly become a paradise. He couldn't risk his city's foundations just for the opportunity to farm some insects.

"Wait a bit," Ogras hastily interjected. "We also have concluded that during our attacks, they are stopping their excavation work to meet our attacks. We can simply farm them without risking the vein as long as we keep the attacks going, letting you keep your lead against the other humans," he added.

It was a fair point, but Zac had a feeling that it was more about the contribution points for the Fruit of Ascension than letting him gain levels. Besides, he held a commanding lead over the others as it was, and didn't really need to gain levels at the moment. He was fast approaching the first bottleneck at level 75.

Zac mainly needed to improve his Dao insights at the moment. He already possessed a Rare class, and his goal was to upgrade it into an E-rank Epic class. His only options at the moment were Rare or Epic, as the rarity couldn't downgrade when reaching the next tiers. He already knew that his situation was pretty bad since the Multiverse was full of examples of geniuses whose cultivation journey got cut short since they couldn't upgrade their special classes.

Still, he didn't want to give up his advantages. Upgrading to a Rare class wasn't the best option. He treaded the path of the elite, spearheading the powerhouses of Earth. Since he was already locked into this path, he would go all the way and keep upgrading the rarity of the class. He knew that Early stage seeds were not enough for an Epic class, so it was time to upgrade his Daos. If that was at the expense of his lead in levels, so be it. He wouldn't limit his future achievements just to become the first person to reach E-rank Class.

"Constantly attacking out in the open is different from defending on top of a wall. We will not be able to last as we did during the wolf hordes. Besides, we do not know whether the insects will grow stronger over time like the wolves did, and it is safe to nip the problem in the bud," Zac said.

To be honest, safety concerns weren't the only reason he wanted to end this horde quickly. He'd just had a taste of freedom and adventure as he'd explored in search of his hometown. He was loath to spend the next four weeks slaughtering insects. He knew that the gain of Nexus Coins would be huge, but he would still net good income if he sent people down into the mines instead.

He was also even more anxious to get home after seeing the life of civilians in Fort Roger. Emily would have met a miserable fate unless he had been there, and worry over his friends and family was starting to keep him up at night. He even had trouble focusing during meditation, as the intrusive "what-ifs" kept popping up in his head.

"Three weeks. Let us fight and farm for three weeks, and after that, we will invade the hive," Ogras entreated.

"It's too long. You can have ten days. After that, I'm heading in," Zac flatly refused. That would leave him three weeks to travel the world before the final wave, twice what he had last time.

"Bah, you're throwing away a great opportunity," Ogras muttered in discontent.

Zac only rolled his eyes at the demon. What they gained from the quest was already great, and they shouldn't get greedy. The longer they waited, the more weird things could crop up.

"Did Calrin find any information about the beasts?" Zac asked as he changed the subject.

"He did manage to buy a short missive about the **[Ayn Hive-beasts]**. They are an extremely prolific species led by hive queens. As long as they have enough Cosmic Energy, the queens can almost indefinitely spawn soldiers. The stronger the queen, the mightier warriors it can birth, and more types as well," Adran answered. Since he wasn't part of the fighting force, he tried to help the war efforts by gathering information.

"There are examples of the beasts' insatiable expansion, completely infesting a planet if left alone. We believe that the threat will be over when we manage to kill the queen. After that no more beasts will spawn, and we can simply slowly exterminate the survivors. Killing the queen will likely mark this horde as completed as well," he continued.

"How strong is the queen?" Zac asked.

"It should be E-grade Class equivalent. It might also have a few bodyguards close to that in power for protection," Adran answered.

"Okay, what does it look like? What are its powers?" Zac probed further.

"Actually, the large construct we see is not a structure, but the queen herself. The Ayr Hivebeasts live inside their queen's body for the most part, and the queen slowly grows to accommodate a larger population. The digging we hear is the insects making room for her body expanding down into the ground," Adran answered with a grimace.

Everyone's eyebrows rose in surprise at this.

"How the hell do we kill something that large?" Ogras asked with a frown.

"Apparently, it has a core somewhere inside. You need to get inside to its core room and destroy it, and it will die. The exact details were unclear in the missive we obtained, though," Adran said with a sigh.

"Good job. See if you can find out anything else, as long as the information doesn't become too expensive," Zac said.

That the huge construct was an actual being didn't change much, in Zac's opinion. They'd still farm for ten days, after which Zac would enter, and drag Ogras with him no matter if he was willing or not. Inside, they would find the boss and kill or destroy it.

With that, everything was settled, and Ogras immediately set out with a company of soldiers, loath to miss even a single contribution point. Zac stayed put since he would be needed to relieve Ogras when he ran out of steam so that they could put continuous pressure on the insects. He really didn't want that huge queen beast to get her hands on his Nexus Vein, so no expansion could be allowed. And who knew if the hive queen would have some strange mutation from getting too close to the vein.

As the days passed, an advance wall was erected. It was nowhere near the size of the regular wall, but it would allow some protection while retreating. The craftsmen also refitted a few of the siege machines so that they would be able to attack the hive queen. However, the large boulders and bolts only bounced off the black structure without so much as leaving a mark.

Zac tried as well and ran up to the structure with his movement skill and slammed into it with a Dao-empowered **[Chop]**. It was effective, creating a large scar, but the response was horrifying. It was like the ants turned crazy and surged against the demons in a frenzy.

The mantis things actually started throwing the vomiters in retaliation, and as they sailed through the air, they overcharged themselves much in the same way as the suicide attack the demons possessed. Zac was forced to expend most of his Cosmic Energy in a short time, furiously throwing out projectiles in order to clear the rabid waves. But he still got a few acid burns on his face and hands that would take time to heal, as most of the vomiters were hurled in his direction.

Seeing that Zac's swing only made a small crack on the gigantic structure, they knew that a siege wasn't really possible against this thing, and they'd have to enter the tunnels if they wanted to kill the queen.

On the seventh day, Zac's fears were realized, as a new foe started emerging out of the hive along with its three siblings. It was called an Ayn titan and was a hulking insect at over three meters tall. Its shell was at least twice as thick as on the others, and it was impossible to penetrate for most of the demons.

They were forced to slowly whittle it down by first disabling its legs by attacking the joints, all while avoiding its terrifying smashes with its claw-like front arms. Since the thing was so heavy, its mobility was quite bad, and if they fell down with broken legs, they stayed down. After it was downed, it seemed the simplest method to kill it was to just boil its head in a fireball.

If Zac or Ogras were present, they could penetrate or crush their skulls instead. However, the time it took to kill the titans increased the pressure, as the ants unceasingly kept pouring out of the hive. There were no breaks, no lulls; just constant, unrelenting battle. The only reason they weren't overrun in just a day or two was the fact that the monsters were quite weak, and even the siege machines they'd brought had no trouble killing the foot soldiers.

The only thing strong about them was their carapaces' sturdiness, but that wouldn't impede the skilled warriors overly much. In the few cases when they were starting to get overrun, Zac or Ogras would unleash their most powerful area attacks. Zac simply threw out his huge edges that created large swathes of death and destruction.

As for Ogras, he created a sea of shadows that moved across the battlefield, where dozens of spears unceasingly sprang up to kill everything around. It wasn't an attack that Zac had seen before, and he suspected that the demon had made a breakthrough with either a skill or his Dao some time recently.

With his new skill, the demon's killing speed was terrifying and almost eclipsed Zac's own speed, which was doubly impressive since he no longer suffered from an energy shortage. Zac was shocked by the display of power, as he knew that the power of the demons was still limited by the System.

There were a few more who excelled at area battle such as Alea and Rivea, the pyromancer who'd learned the Seed of Tinder during the wolf waves. Her fire kept spreading among the ants and was particularly deadly to them. It simply stuck to their carapaces and slowly cooked the beasts, and from there, spread to their brethren.

The windfall was so great that Zac relented and actually prolonged the farm-fest another day, much to the delight of the demons. Ogras was like a storm, grinding his contribution points at a furious pace.

Zac had thought that this kind of situation was something unique, but he was surprised to find out that most large forces in the Multiverse kept zones and forests that were a bit like this, teeming with monsters. It provided their young and their soldiers with ample training and outlet for growth, and the clan didn't need to provide any salary, as access to the farming zones was benefit enough to join the army. The elders of the clan took care of the evolved monsters and immediately rooted out any beast that got too strong.

But all good things must end. The eleventh day approached, and the core warriors started to rest up and prepare their aces. Tomorrow, they would assault the hive.

105

INTO THE HIVE

"Is everyone ready?" Zac asked as he glanced back at the group. It was time to find the queen, and a strike force was assembled. It would be led by Ogras, with Zac second-in-command. Zac didn't mind not being the leader, as he didn't have any experience leading an operation like this. He didn't want to risk his teammates getting killed due to his inexperience. Besides, he could always overrule him if he felt it warranted.

The group consisted of only six people. Apart from Zac and Ogras, Janos and Alea also joined the group. Ilvere and Namys were left behind, leaving them in charge of the main army, whose job was to keep the fight going outside while they entered the hive. Janos was a support mage who hopefully could turn the odds in their favor, while Alea's attack had proven itself effective even against the Fiend Wolf.

The last two were Rivea and Herod. Rivea was the Pyromancer with the Seed of Tinder. Herod was the earth mage who first spoke up about the digging on top of the wall. It turned out he possessed the Seed of Tremor, making him extremely perceptive to even small tremors in the ground. His job was to act as a scout in the tunnels, whereas Rivea was just additional firepower.

They didn't bring any more people, as quantity didn't really work against E-grade evolved beings. Most of the soldiers would only be a hindrance rather than an asset inside the hive. Even Rivea was mostly brought so that she could defend their backs while the rest fought the queen and the bodyguards.

"Human, why not just wait a few more days?"

"You're pretty close to affording the Fruit, huh? Remember, if I die, the mission is failed, and the contribution crystal is gone," Zac answered with a small smile.

It was true. Since Ogras had started using the wide-scale shadow attack, his contribution points skyrocketed. In only ten days, he almost got as many as he did during the three weeks of the first wolf horde, and he possessed over 40 million points by now.

Ogras muttered something under his breath but didn't seem overly worried. There was a whole third wave, after all, and there still were a lot of contribution points to be gained inside the hive. Zac had gotten over 5 million points for killing the Fiend Wolf, and he heard afterward that both Ogras and Alea received quite a few points for helping out. Killing E-ranked beings at this stage seemed truly profitable.

They were currently at the back of the fight against the insects and started to move forward. As they did, both Ogras and Janos cast a skill, shrouding them both in shadows and illusions, making them almost invisible. They easily slipped past the ant army and headed into one of the large tunnels.

The inside looked just like outside, with black walls and green crystals. The crystals thankfully emanated some light, though it was a lot darker compared to the tunnels in the mines. They could light up their path with the help of Rivea, but held off on that for the moment, wanting to maintain their cover. They didn't expect to be able to sneak all the way to the core room, but the faster they proceeded without being bogged down in fights, the less pressure on the fighters outside.

Groups of ants kept coming through the tunnel to join the battle outside, and most simply ran right by. With Herod's timely warnings, they usually had time to press themselves against the wall while their skills hid them. However, they were still discovered every now and then and were forced into a furious battle. It was mainly Zac and Ogras who slaughtered the ants without using up too much Cosmic Energy, and then threw the bodies into Cosmos Sacks.

They quickly realized something was wrong as they walked. The inside of the hive actually seemed larger compared to the outside. The hive was shaped almost like a pyramid, reaching about a hundred meters in height, and was a few hundred meters wide at the base. But they had walked over ten minutes in an almost straight tunnel without reaching an end. They were frequently forced to stop as they walked, due to the incoming packs, but they should long ago have crossed the whole structure.

"The hive is likely a spatial being, containing something like a hidden realm," Ogras said with a low volume when no ants were nearby.

"Not illusion. Unless extremely strong," Janos added with a nod.

"Does this change anything?" Zac asked.

"Not really; the mission is still the same. But it will be much harder to find the queen. We don't know just how large the inside of the hive is anymore," Ogras answered with a sigh.

As they proceeded further into the hive, they ran into fewer and fewer packs of ants. Soon the group found themselves at a crossroads. The path split into three, and it looked like the left descended while the right ascended. The middle path stayed the course.

"The core room should be in the depths since that place would be safest from external attacks," Ogras said, and the group veered off to the left path. There was no talk about splitting up since perhaps only Zac and Ogras would be able to survive if they ventured out alone.

As they moved further down, the rocky walls started to transform, looking more and more like flesh. It reminded them that they weren't actually inside a mountain, but rather inside a huge being.

"Trap!" the earth mage suddenly exclaimed, and soon after, the ground opened up beneath them. They barely had time to jump forward, and as they turned back, they looked at a pool of acid seething where the floor once was.

"Does it know we're here?" Zac asked.

"Who knows? The information missive never explained how aware the hive queen is. It might just have been an automatic reflex from us stepping on this path. The ants might know which spots to avoid," Ogras answered with a frown.

It did not take long for the group to find the answer to the question, as a group of huge ant warriors streamed toward them. They were almost as large as the titans but far more nimble. Their name was **[Ayn Elite Guard]**, and their front legs looked very specialized. One of the arms had the same sort of long blade like the mantis-like captains, whereas the other was extremely thick almost like a crab's arm. It almost looked like a shield, Zac thought as he watched them approach.

As usual, Janos erected a mirage around them, making it seem they were part of the wall as they pushed against it. The guards looked a bit confused as they slowed down as they looked around. As if in response, the green gems in the wall behind Zac and the others started shining more brightly. The guards immediately perked up and resumed their charge.

Seeing that the illusion wasn't effective anymore, Zac threw a rock toward one of them. The stone hurtled toward the front elite guard, which lifted its thick arm in response. A deep clang resounded as the ant was slightly pushed back, but not a mark could be seen on its arm. Clearly, the thicker arm was extremely reinforced.

The ants approached, and Zac moved to the front and, with a grunt, swung his axe against the shield to test its might. A massive shock wave pushed both his target and a few of the other guards back, but the thick shell even held against his new weapon. There was a small crack, though, and a few more swings would probably do the trick.

Zac was surprised at the sturdiness of these things, as there weren't many things below E-grade that could survive a swing of his anymore. If they could take the shells of these things, they would likely be able to create some pretty damn durable armor. With some treatment and inscriptions engraved onto them, they might even become E-graded gear.

"Don't ruin their shields," Zac said with some greed in his eyes. Of course, perhaps only he was actually able to damage them in any case.

In the end, it fell to Zac, Ogras, and Rivea to kill the group of guards. Zac was actually forced to use the Seed of Sharpness to kill the ants while Ogras used his black spear to penetrate into the joints of the guards. As soon as the tip of the spear breached their armor, spikes made from shadows poured out of the tip and wreaked havoc on their insides. Rivea lobbed a few fireballs that stuck to their heads and quickly boiled their brains.

Herod tried to help with a few earth spears as well, but his power wasn't enough against these warriors. He could only help out by erecting earth walls to protect the noncombatants. It was a strain on him, as they weren't in an actual cave, but a living being. The earth mages drew power from the ground, which enabled them to do more with less expenditure, but it wasn't possible in here. Alea was simply staying put. Her poison spikes would be able to kill these things, but they consumed a huge amount of Cosmic Energy, so it was better for her to wait for more formidable targets.

They threw the most well-preserved carapaces in Cosmos Sacks and pushed further down, not bothering as much about stealth anymore. They had clearly been spotted somehow, and it would be better to just rush through.

Soon they came to a large circular room, and after a brief hesitation, they ran toward the door that seemed to be leading downward. But just as they approached it, the pathway simply closed up by the walls moving together.

"If it's only the entrance that's closed, I can break it down in less than a minute, but if the whole tunnel is collapsed, we need to find another way," Zac muttered as he touched the closed doorway.

"No, let's retreat befo–" Ogras quickly interjected but was interrupted by the pathway they came from opening as well. "Shit, break the door we came from!" the demon shouted.

Zac didn't hesitate and used **[Loamwalker]** to appear next to the door and furiously slammed into it with a Sharpness-imbued **[Chop]**. A large crack appeared in the door, but before Zac had time to swing again, the floor beneath them opened up.

It was as though the ground was a huge maw that opened up, and the group helplessly fell down into the large hole.

"Grab on to each other!" Ogras shouted, and luckily, the demons were quite close to each other.

However, Zac, who'd used his movement skill earlier, was over twenty meters away from the others, and he had no way to cross the distance while falling. A rope was flung toward him, but the winds in the hole pushed it out of his reach.

Suddenly, the seemingly endless hole split up, separating the groups, and Zac was suddenly utterly alone while falling into the abyss.

106

THE DESCENT

Zac picked up speed as his descent continued through the black hole. He desperately tried to grab on to the wall as he fell, but the surface was almost completely smooth. Seeing no alternative, he grabbed **[Verun's Bite]** with both hands and stabbed forward while summoning a sharpness-imbued **[Chop]** at the maximum length he could maintain.

The Cosmic Energy edge cut into the wall, and Zac removed the Dao empowerment as soon as it did. Luckily, the walls inside the hive queen were quite a bit softer compared to the hard-shell exterior. The harsh deceleration almost ripped the axe out of his hands, and he barely managed to hold on as he ripped a large scar along the wall while moving downward. Soon he stopped just as he saw some green light below.

Since his momentum was gone, he took out one of his backup axes from his pouch and stabbed it into the wall with another cosmic edge. Like this, he climbed downward toward the exit. He initially thought about climbing up to find the others, but he soon discarded that thought. They should be down here somewhere as well, and going downward might be a better bet to find them.

Besides, their goal was to go further down to find the core

room in any case. So Zac started using the fractal edges of his axes as ice picks as he slowly climbed down toward the exit. And as he saw what created the green glowing light, his eyebrows rose.

It was a large pond of acid. If Zac hadn't stopped his descent, he would have fallen right in, and even with his armor and Endurance, he wasn't sure he'd survive the bath. As he hung close to the edge, Zac was pondering what to do. He could see that there was dry ground roughly ten meters away from the hole, but he doubted he could climb the ceiling all the way over there, as his axes would just slide right out.

He took out his huge elongated axe from his pouch. It had accompanied him during many of the wolf waves when he wasn't able to freely use his skills, and by now, it was mostly warped and dull. It wasn't really as useful lately since he didn't have to be as stingy with his Cosmic Energy anymore. Its total length was a bit over two meters, and it would make a decent measuring tool for the pond. Careful to hold it completely vertical, he simply dropped it straight down.

The axe fell down, and just as it was about to be completely submerged, it stopped with a thud for a few seconds before it fell down into the pool completely. It looked like the depth was only roughly two meters. Even if it was shallower than he had dared hope, it was still enough to completely submerge him if he dropped down.

He didn't have any more time to ponder, as the edge he hung from with his axes suddenly cracked, and he fell down together with a large chunk of wall. He quickly threw out a bunch of nonessential tools and items from a pouch, such as his large table and chairs, and a few boulders he used for ranged battle. They smacked into the pond with a large splash, and Zac felt a burning sensation on his feet from the splashing acid.

He landed on a boulder that was rapidly sinking, and without hesitation, used two of his standard axes as stilts with the help of **[Chop]** as he pushed down with elongated edges. He hoped that he would be able to jump over the pool like a pole vaulter, but the fractal energy edges broke almost immediately, dashing that hope.

Instead, he kept throwing out rocks on the ground, gritting his teeth as the splashes hit his hands and face. Luckily, the distance wasn't very long, and after a few more boulders, he was close to the edge of the acid ponds, so he leaped through the air. He sailed toward dry land as the boulders he stood on earlier quickly disintegrated.

He landed in a pile with a grunt and quickly took out a rag to wipe the acid off his blistering feet with a grimace. After smearing some healing ointment on them, he got up and looked around, a bit stumped. He couldn't believe things turned out that well. The blisters hurt but wouldn't leave any lasting damage, and he only lost some furniture and two axes in the escape.

As he surveyed the area, he found himself in a cave that was roughly thirty by thirty meters. There was no other hole in the roof, meaning that the others couldn't have ended up here. Most of the room was the large pool of acid, and as Zac looked around, it almost felt like a digestive system rather than some sort of trap. Perhaps the ant workers normally filled the room they'd entered earlier with whatever a hive queen ate, and it dropped down into what was essentially its stomachs.

There, unfortunately, were no visible exits in the room, and Zac was afraid that the acid could rise at any time, judging by the markings on the walls. There was a clear line on the walls at roughly the height of his waist that indicated that the liquid at one point reached all the way there. He quickly walked to the wall and started tapping it.

After tapping for a while, he heard a hollow sound roughly at the height of his head and started to carve the cave wall using his axe. Even though the walls weren't as hard as the exterior, he was still forced to use the Dao of Sharpness once again. He briefly wondered if a beast as large as the hive queen could feel him ripping a hole in what might just be its stomach, but he guessed that this couldn't even be considered a wound for something this size. In just a few minutes, he carved a hole large enough to crawl through and found himself in a large tunnel.

The deserted tunnel looked completely organic, which was an unsettling change from the mostly rocky or chitinous appearance from earlier. The walls even looked like they were slowly pulsating to a heartbeat. He could only hope that the increasingly biological makeup of the wall meant he was getting closer to the core. He started walking along, ignoring the stinging pain from his burned feet, and since the tunnel was completely deserted, he dared take out an F-grade Nexus Crystal to recuperate his energy as he moved.

He was completely lost by this point and wasn't sure whether to try to complete his quest or try to look for his teammates. Then again, he had no structured method to do either, so he chose to simply move forward and take things as they came. If he found Ogras and the others, great. If he found a core-looking room, he'd try to destroy it.

The power of the queen and her guards sounded daunting, but he'd made significant improvements since he fought the Fiend Wolf. He both had his new axe and the Seed of Sharpness, pushing his lethality to a completely new level. He also possessed another ace in the hole, he remembered, as he touched his right forearm with some anticipation.

After walking through the deserted tunnels for a bit, he came to a fork. One of the paths was pretty much the same as the one he was currently walking. The other had a surprisingly low amount of Cosmic Energy. He unhesitantly walked toward the pathway with a higher amount of energy but, after a hundred meters, stopped himself and backtracked.

Something was absorbing the Cosmic Energy in the other tunnel, and it might just be the queen. It should take huge amounts of energy to keep spewing out all these ants, even to just survive when you were this big. He couldn't even imagine the energy requirements for a humongous hive queen if Zac's own caloric intake had increased by a few times since he evolved. That kind of requirement should be impossible to satiate unless it was through Cosmic Energy.

He held his axe at the ready as he silently crept into the tunnel. As he moved further, the energy kept getting sparser, to the point that there almost was none left in the air. The feeling was extremely uncomfortable, almost like there was no air to breathe. It was the first time he'd felt the atmosphere to be like this since the integration, and he was surprised to see how reliant he'd become on Cosmic Energy.

Finally, he entered a huge cavern, and what he saw made him stop in place and just gawk. It felt like a scene out of a horror movie, with an uncountable number of monster pods. The whole cavern was filled to the brim with receptacles that shone with the same green light as the crystals embedded in the hive walls. They stood up on the floor, leaving only thin pathways, and were even affixed to the walls and the roof. Zac couldn't be sure, but it felt like there were tens of thousands of pods in the cavern.

Zac quickly entered a path and inspected the closest pods. Inside was an embryonic version of one of the worker ants that made up most of the armies. After walking through the path, he quickly saw that all the pods were mostly the same; the only difference was the stage of growth of the ants. That meant that this likely was only one of many pod rooms, and the more powerful types were created somewhere else.

He thought a second about destroying the whole cave, but that would take a crazy amount of effort going by how large the place was. It wouldn't make sense for him to completely expose himself when there likely were many more caverns just like this. His goal was to kill the queen, and if he did, most of these pods should likely die out on their own.

He stealthily made his way forward toward the other end, but a sudden movement made him freeze. It was a shadow that flickered oddly beneath a pod. Zac frowned and moved toward it, which caused the shadow to actually move away. Zac realized what was going on and started following the flickering shadow until he reached a small path hidden behind a few pods.

Inside, he saw Ogras, Alea, Janos, and Herod hiding at the entrance of a tunnel. They'd obviously met a similar situation as himself earlier, as their clothes were full of burned holes. Zac couldn't help but sneak a peek at Alea, and was rewarded with a pout and a teasing wink.

Herod was even worse off compared to the others, with his whole arm singed to the point of pieces of flesh being missing. He was completely white with beads of sweat covering his face, and he was shivering as though in shock. His eyes were alert, though, fearfully darting back and forth.

With a furrowed brow, Zac noticed that Rivea wasn't with them, but just as he was about to ask what was going on, Ogras quickly signaled him to be quiet. The demon pointed to the walls, and for the first time, he noticed something was different about the tunnels compared to those they'd walked through earlier.

It wasn't the usual biotic walls anymore, but it rather looked like there were a multitude of cables, or veins, running along the surface. The veins split up as they entered the large cavern, and Zac could see a thin line was attached to every pod.

Zac's heartbeat increased as he started to realize what was going on. He took out a piece of paper and wrote "Queen?" as he pointed toward the other end of the small tunnel they hid in.

With a serious face, Ogras nodded.

107

ASSAULT

Ogras picked out a crystal from his pouch and closed his eyes for a few seconds as he held it tightly. Next, he handed it over to Zac and indicated for him to pour some Cosmic Energy into it. As he did, he suddenly heard Ogras' voice in his head.

"This is a communication crystal. The other end of the tunnel is a hundred meters in. We believe it's the core room of the queen. There are four more things walking around in the room, according to Herod. The smallest of them is almost as heavy as the titans judging by the vibrations caused when it's walking. These things seem very vigilant. They started running around when we spoke earlier. We believe that they are the royal guards.

"Rivea is dead. We fell into a vat of acid, and she didn't make it. We found this place through Herod, and he also sensed your footsteps approaching. Everyone apparently has a unique vibration, and he recognized yours. I was planning on heading further into the tunnel to scout it out before we found you. Stay here, and I'll check things out."

Zac opened his eyes and, after mulling the information over a bit, nodded his head toward Ogras, who melded into the shadows.

As he waited for the demon to come back, he properly looked over his teammates. Apart from Herod, the other two looked mostly okay, though they both sported somber expressions.

Zac couldn't help but agree the situation wasn't ideal. When they'd made their plans before the assault, they had escape as an option. That was pretty much the only reason they'd managed to get Rivea and Herod to join, as they both were clearly unwilling to enter the belly of the beast.

They'd thought that while the structure was large, in a panicked rush where Zac and Ogras didn't hold back, they could be out in a minute or two, even if they were forced to mow through an army of ants. They didn't expect the inside to be this gigantic. Now that they also had fallen who knew how far down, he wasn't even sure how to get out. Their backs really were against the wall.

Soon Ogras came back and took out another crystal. This one actually displayed a window, but different from the one he'd borrowed long ago with the information; this window was actually visible for everyone. Zac started looking at the pouch of the demon, wondering what other goodies he kept for himself in there. He already knew that the space inside should be huge since he could throw a whole fishing vessel into it without any problem.

Zac quickly refocused and studied the screen. It was a still image of a large cavern. The whole surface was riddled with tubes that emerged from various tunnels much like the one they were in. They covered the ground and the roof, leaving almost no space free. The tubes converged in the middle of the cave and were latched to a huge green crystal.

Zac had never seen a core of a monster before, but if that wasn't it, then he'd be extremely surprised. The core was guarded by four monstrous ants, as Ogras had already explained, and they each covered a direction. Interestingly enough, they all looked somewhat different from each other.

Two of them looked like supercharged versions of the mantis and titan respectively. The titan was the closest to their tunnel and was a huge hulking thing much larger than an elephant. One of its arms was a gigantic shield, and the other looked like a large mallet. Distinctively from the normal ants, this thing actually had at least ten pairs of short legs. Perhaps only three pairs wouldn't be able to carry its weight.

The mantis-looking ant had long serrated blades for front arms, and its long and graceful build seemed built for speed. It was nowhere as large as the hulking centipede-ant, but still larger than the normal titans.

The other two royal guards were a bit different from any ants they'd seen so far. One of them seemed barely mobile, as it almost exclusively consisted of a head. It did have a body, but it looked small and almost shriveled, and Zac didn't understand how the small frame could keep the head floating, as the head alone was as large as the mantis guard.

The size wasn't the only odd thing about the head, as it also had a great number of eyes. The one in its forehead was enormous, and Zac guessed that it was at least as large as himself. The other eyes were generally placed along the main eye, but some seemed to be looking in different directions. He felt it was lucky that Ogras had been the one doing recon, as this thing would probably have noticed him even if he made no sound.

The last guard was mostly hidden behind the crystal, but Zac felt that it almost looked like a spider rather than an ant. It was comprised of a large bulbous torso, with long legs sticking out from it. He couldn't see any head, though, and had no real idea of how it looked.

Ogras made a motion toward Zac, and with a start, he handed over the communication crystal. Ogras once again closed his eyes for a few seconds and then handed it over to Zac.

"The green crystal obviously is the core. I say we try an

ambush where we destroy the crystal before the guards can react. Zac and I both blast it with the strongest strike we can instantly summon. Me from the left, and Zac from the right. We'll bypass that huge bugger by both sides. Alea and Janos, try to delay the guards' reaction time as much as possible. Herod, stay in the tunnels; try to sense whether reinforcements arrive.

"We stay silent until the first attack is finished, and depending on the outcome, we take it from there. Hopefully, the attack will destroy the core, and we can choose whether to kill the guards as well or flee. Each of them should net quite a bit of contribution points, so we should kill them if possible.

"We only have one shot at this. Nod if you agree and are ready; then hand the crystal to the next person," Ogras' voice echoed inside Zac's head.

Zac thought it over as he looked at the still-displaying image of the core room for a few seconds. The huge tank-ant was the one closest to their tunnel. The plan meant that Zac would go to the right of it, which would place him between the tank and the large-headed one, whereas Ogras would rush in next to the sword-wielding ant. He mulled it over and felt that it was a decent proposal.

Ogras was more suited to dodging quick swings from a sword than Zac was with the help of his Dao and class. Zac himself was pretty nimble nowadays with the help of **[Loamwalker]**, but it was nothing compared to the demon and his shadow dancing. The large head was likely some sort of mage, if he had to guess, and between his huge endurance and defensive option on his armor, he should be able to withstand at least one blast without a problem before he reached the crystal.

All four of those things looked quite dangerous, but he was already mentally prepared for a tough fight. He nodded and passed the crystal to Alea. After a while, everyone had listened to the instructions and agreed with the plan. They slowly made their way forward until they were just ten meters away from the exit into the core room.

Everyone steadied their breaths for a few seconds before Zac and Ogras nodded at each other. Ogras already held his black spear, and Zac was tightly gripping **[Verun's Bite]**. Ogras started blending into the shadows as he speedily moved forward, and Zac activated his movement skill and moved toward the exit as well.

Footsteps behind them told that the others were following in tow, but Zac had no time to think about that.

The tunnel exit was two meters above the ground, and Zac immediately dropped to the floor and started rapidly moving forward. The royal guards were obviously alert, as a deep penetrating screech erupted from the large one that was the closest. The huge armored centi-ant felt even larger as Zac saw it in person, towering even higher than the Fiend Wolf.

The royal guard immediately started moving its throng of small chubby legs as it rushed toward him, as it seemed it didn't notice Ogras in his shadows. Zac kept infusing Cosmic Energy into his feet, and luckily, his skill worked inside the hive queen as well, even though he was technically standing on a body part of a supersized insect rather than the ground. He quickly moved forward through the huge cave, and as he did, a blazing cacophony of colors and sounds erupted above him, pushing like a wave toward the guard.

It was Janos who clearly held nothing back as he pushed out a blanket of distraction. A sweet smell in the air that almost made Zac giddy was a sign that Alea had released something that added to the confusion air as well. Suddenly, a huge pressure slammed into Zac as he ran, and he almost stumbled and fell. A quick glance showed that all the numerous eyes of the gigantic head ant were glaring at him.

The pressure wasn't physical, but rather a mental pressure. Only the stare made him feel like he was carrying a mountain, but he could also see that the eyes were starting to shine with a green luster. Luckily, the crystal was close, and he pushed an extreme amount of Cosmic Energy into his legs. He pushed away and shot like a cannon toward the core. From the moment he exited the tunnel until now, only a bit more than a second had passed, and the huge guards barely had time to start their attacks.

Zac charged up a five-meter edge with **[Chop]** and flooded the fractal edge with the Dao of Heaviness since he wanted the crystal to crack. Ideally, he'd have wanted to use both his offensive Daos, but he still couldn't infuse both of them into a single strike yet.

The large edge slammed into the crystal with the force of a runaway train, as the growls from the teeth on his axe menacingly echoed in the cave. Ogras materialized at the other side almost at the same time, and with a furious stab, slammed the spear straight into the other side of the crystal. As he did, a beam of darkness erupted from the spear and also hit the target like a laser.

A crackling sound was heard, but Zac's eyebrows rose when he saw that the crystal was completely undamaged. The crackling sound came from the huge tank, who had gotten two wounds on its torso as it stumbled and almost fell.

"SHIT! Life-bound protection! The core is shielded with the life-force of the guards; we need to kill at least the large fucker before we can damage it," Ogras screamed as he quickly distanced himself from the crystal as the mantis guard was rapidly approaching.

Zac was about to do the same, but a terrifying force slammed into his back and shot him forward, straight toward the descending scythe of the mantis guard.

108

FIGHTING THE ROYALS

Zac frantically lifted his axe to meet the incoming swing, and with tremendous power, the two weapons clashed. Since Zac was airborne, he had no real force behind the swing and was ruthlessly slammed into the ground, creating a small crater and ruining any tubing that covered the area.

Zac spat out some blood but quickly scrambled to his feet, even though he felt like every bone in his body broke from the impact. Another swing was already upon him, but this time, he dodged with his movement skill and moved under the large guard. He didn't hold back and infused a **[Chop]** with the seed of Sharpness, aiming to tear a large gash all along its belly.

The mantis' speed wasn't a joke, though, as it almost teleported away from the swing. But the velocity of Zac's swing wasn't anything to scoff at either, and with a roar, one of the insect's legs was lopped off, causing a torrent of green blood to pour out from the guard. It screeched in anger and backed away a few steps, using one of its sword arms as a crutch to keep itself stable.

The brief respite let Zac take a glance around. The huge tank-looking thing was still occupied by the combined distraction of

Alea and Janos, and Ogras was fighting the fourth herald that truly looked a bit like a spider, apart from its head, which reminded him of a vomiter.

But instead of acid, small pitch-black ants were pouring out of its mouth, looking absolutely horrifying. Tens of lances were erupting out from the shadows between the tubes on the ground to stab the spider-looking guard and its spawn, but the small things seemed almost endless.

The guard was also conjuring netting toward Ogras, but the nimble demon was deftly dodging any attempt to catch him. Zac felt that Ogras could handle himself for now, which left two of the guards for him. Before he could decide which one to attack next, he realized that they were trapped inside.

The tunnels with the tubes were all closed, not even providing enough space for a hand to push through. Blood was streaming out of the exit they'd used earlier, and Zac realized that Herod had been crushed to death. The only upside to the situation was that it hopefully meant that they wouldn't have to handle a horde of small ants as well.

Two elite warriors of his demon army were dead in under an hour, and Zac was reminded of the harsh reality of this new world. Not even powerhouses were safe. A quick glance at the mantis showed that it still was a bit distracted from its missing leg, and its lethality was likely impacted. It clearly was focused on speed and offense, but missing a leg would take away much of the danger.

Zac's eyes turned to the final guard and saw that its eyes were glowing again. He didn't know what kind of skill it used to hit him last time, but it hurt quite badly, and he was in no mood to take another one of those shock waves. Besides, if it hit Alea or Janos, he wasn't sure whether they'd be able to keep fighting.

He quickly charged up a **[Chop]** and infused it with the Dao of Sharpness as well, giving the fractal blade a silver sheen.

Without any break, he sent the five-meter edge right toward the main eye of the large-headed royal guard. But as the edged ripped through the air, it suddenly changed color and turned into the normal pale blue.

At the same time, Zac felt a heavy atmosphere descend upon the cave, like another type of mental pressure. It was as though he had lost one of his senses, but not one of the normal five. The fractal blade kept moving toward the large eye, though, but the eyes blazed into light for an instant, and the attack was smashed into smithereens.

Zac planned on sending a stream of blades toward the eye, but to his shock, noticed that he wasn't able to infuse the skill with his Dao anymore. The mental pressure was persistent, and it somehow blocked him from empowering his skills. He quickly looked around and saw that the core of the hive queen was shining in a brighter light compared to before, emitting a huge amount of energy. It appeared the queen was somewhat sentient and helped her guards from the sidelines.

"My Dao is blocked!" Alea shouted, telling Zac that he wasn't the only one affected.

He gritted his teeth and used **[Loamwalker]** toward the large-headed mage. He might not be able to use his Dao, but skills were still possible to use. He ran around the huge tank-monster, which was wildly flailing its thick arms around, trying to hit whatever was blocking its sight. But Janos and Alea simply kept a safe distance and mainly kept their eyes on the mantis and the eye-monster.

With his speed, he was upon the large-headed guard in no time and felt that he was almost physically punched by just the eye's glare. He didn't understand whether it was some sort of mental pressure or actual air pressure, but no matter how he struggled, he couldn't move the last meter to reach it. As all the eyes stared at him, he was even starting to get pushed away, no matter how much he strained his muscles.

Two huge spears slammed into the side of the large-headed guard, eliciting an enraged screech, even though they barely seemed to penetrate the hard shell. Many eyes quickly swiveled toward Ogras, and Zac temporarily felt the pressure disappear. He didn't hesitate and, with a roar, pushed himself right onto the head of the beast, wildly swinging **[Verun's Bite]** into the large central eye.

A quick glance toward Ogras showed that he was currently beset by both the mantis and the spider, and the attack on the large-headed one put him in dire straits. The mantis was swinging down one of its swords on him, and he was receding into the shadows to dodge. However, the blade somehow pulled him out from safety and tore a large gash over his chest, blood freely pouring in all directions.

Zac wanted to help out, but he first needed to finish off this one. He took a deep breath and actually pushed himself into the large eye, frenziedly swinging his axe around. The ant spasmed and pushed all around, waves of energy flying in all directions. Zac didn't let up, however, and kept hacking further into the head until a huge surge of Cosmic Energy told him his work was done.

He was completely covered in brain and eye goop by now but had no time to clean up. He rushed toward Ogras, who was in big trouble at the moment. He was desperately dodging the nets from the spider and the sword swings from the mantis. There were also three small pitch-black ants latched onto his body, and he seemed to be trying to get them off.

Zac rushed toward the mantis and was about to commence an attack, when a deluge of small spiders started skittering toward him.

"Don't let them touch you!" Ogras wheezed out, but it was too late.

Two of them instantly latched on to Zac's legs, and it felt like he suddenly was in a gravity array. The spiders were emanating a gravity field in some way, and their effect seemed to be stacking. He tried to rip them off while dodging the other small spiders who ran toward him, but it was to no avail. It was as though they were fused to his leg, and he was unable to remove them with force.

"They are stuck. I think we need to kill the spider to get them off!" Ogras shouted as another sword swing was descending on him.

The demon gritted his teeth, and a blue sheen enveloped him from a necklace. The sword smashed into the shield, and Zac almost tumbled away from the shock wave the strike created. Luckily, it cleared most of the small spiders from the area, as they were blown away from the force. The blue force field was the type of shield that returned the force back to the attacker, as cracks appeared on the arm of the guard, and it stumbled back from the recoil.

"Now!" Ogras shouted as shadows were starting to gather around him.

Zac activated his movement skill and sped toward the mantis. With the two spiders attached to his legs, it felt like he was slogging through waist-deep water, but he could only endure and push through. He appeared next to the hurt mantis and started swinging toward the insect's side with a **[Chop]**.

The first swing was intercepted by the sword arm of the mantis, but the huge force of Zac actually destroyed it. It was already cracked by the recoil of the shield, and Zac's power did the rest. Now the mantis only had four legs remaining, and it was forced to choose whether to stand up or attack, as it needed to use its second sword to maintain balance.

It quickly made its choice as it swung its sword toward Zac while it was tipping over. The air was rippling with power from the swing, as it clearly pushed all its remaining energy into it.

Shadow spears rose up to meet the falling body and pushed into its torso using the momentum to its advantage. It screeched frenziedly but completed the swing.

Initially, Zac was intending to dodge it, but unknown to him, another two spiders had attached themselves to him, making him almost keel over. The Dao was also still blocked, and he couldn't use Seed of Trees to increase his resilience. He could only activate his armor, and a green shield enveloped him. The sword of the mantis slammed into the shield, and Zac was launched like a rocket into the wall.

However, just as he was readying himself for a follow-up, he felt another stream of Cosmic Energy, this one quite a bit smaller compared to the last. It looked like Ogras had taken the main contribution from the kill. That left just the tank and the spider alive. Unfortunately, Janos and Alea were clearly struggling by this point, even though less than a minute had passed since the start of the fight. Alea was carrying a deathly pale Janos on her back as she dodged the huge monstrosity.

"Janos is out of Cosmic Energy. Hurry!" the demoness shouted as she scrambled away from the ant.

Each slam from its huge arms created tremors in the ground as it tried to crush the two into meat-paste. It looked truly irate from being confused for a minute from illusions and hallucinogenic poison, only to wake up to two of the royal guards dead.

"We need to take out the spider first. If Alea gets a gravity ant on her, both of them will die," Ogras said, and Zac could only grit his teeth and agree.

The spider was clearly focusing on entrapment, spawning both the gravity-minions and shooting out waves and waves of thread that were starting to turn a large part of the cavern into a sticky trap. However, both of the offensive guards were dead, and its own lethality wasn't too high unless it managed to stack enough spiders onto someone, simply crushing them from the weight.

When there were no more interruptions from the other guards, Ogras had no trouble avoiding both the spiders and the sticky webs, and gracefully moved toward the large body of the guard. It screeched in alarm, but the huge armored guard actually ignored it, intent on killing the two pests next to it.

Zac didn't have the nimbleness of the demon and could only do a more simple approach. He launched a large blade that flew toward the head of the spider, ripping any webs or spiders into pieces that were in the way. The attack essentially created a path for him, and he quickly moved through the passage with his movement skill. It took less than ten seconds for the two to finish off the third royal guard.

Zac and Ogras were breathing heavily, but they couldn't stop yet. Ogras was still bleeding from his wounds, but he somehow was reducing the blood loss with the help of shadows that tightly twisted around his torso. Zac's whole body was hurting from being slammed by various attacks and shock waves, but he got on his feet with a sigh and started charging toward the fourth royal guard.

There was still one to go.

109

THE FINAL PUSH

Alea was in dire straits—dodging and movement weren't her strong suits—and she was further impeded by carrying Janos around. The mage was weakly trying to confuse the last royal guard with illusions after having absorbed enough energy from a Nexus Crystal, but it was as though the huge armored ant was locked on to them.

Zac saw with some surprise that the cracks that appeared when both he and Ogras assaulted the crystal were already closed up, making the chitinous armor look as good as new.

"He has regenerated the damage already," Zac said, and Ogras only nodded in response.

Zac sighed and readied his axe, but Ogras held up his hand.

"What?" Zac asked, anxious to help Alea and Janos out.

"When we kill this big guy, all the royal guards will be dead, and we'll be able to attack the queen's core. But we don't know if the hive queen will be able to unleash some sort of last desperate attack when the guards are down and the shield is removed. The queen is a true E-ranked being, while the guards only seem to be elite F-grade beings on the cusp of evolving," Ogras said while looking over his wound.

"We should instantly destroy the crystal the second the last guard dies to avoid any unexpected things. If I kill this big fucker, do you have a finisher to use against the crystal?" the demon continued.

Zac thought it sounded like a good idea and, after some hesitation, nodded.

"I need ten seconds of time to charge the attack," Zac said. Actually, he barely needed half that, but the attack he was about to unleash was his current ace in the hole, and he didn't want to give out its details. It put Alea and Janos in danger for an additional five seconds, but he could only make it up to them later.

Ogras nodded and readjusted his grip on his spear.

"Start charging," the demon said as shadows were starting to gather around him, and his eyes turned completely black. Shadows were soon covering every inch of his body, turning him into a being of darkness. Ogras started emanating a sinister pressure that gave even Zac a hair-raising feeling. Whatever the demon was doing was something Zac had never seen before, and it was likely his strongest attack.

Zac didn't hesitate and started pouring huge amounts of Cosmic Energy into his right forearm. It was time to unleash **[Nature's Punishment]**. The eleven days of mindless killing had been more than enough to finish his quest to decapitate ten thousand enemies. Luckily, the System considered his kills solo battle, even though he was part of the demon army, as long as he was fully responsible for the kills of the insects.

The fractal on his arm was like a bottomless hole, and after seven seconds, he already had poured 80% of his remaining Cosmic Energy into it.

"Get ready," Ogras hissed in a raspy voice, currently looking like a true denizen of darkness. Two ephemeral black wings had sprouted on his back, softly waving back and forth, each reaching over three meters in length. The spear in his hand was throbbing like it possessed a heart, and as the last seconds passed, the heartbeat quickened to a frenzied thumping.

Just before ten seconds passed, Ogras punched off from the ground, a wave of darkness flooding out from him. He turned into a large black beam that shot straight toward the chest of the last royal guard.

There was no impact and no sound from the clash.

Suddenly, there simply was a hole spanning three meters in the last guard's chest, going straight through the beast. The guard's head was only attached to its body with a small string, which broke and fell down onto the floor with a thud where Ogras appeared once again. He stabbed a four-meter-long lance of darkness into the head to make sure it was dead.

Zac didn't hesitate and put **[Verun's Bite]** into his bag. He pushed his hand forward in a grasping motion as though he were trying to grasp the huge crystal from a distance. It felt like he was trying to push through solid matter with his arm, but he only roared and pushed forward with his arm as he poured the last of his energy into the fractal.

With a large dissonant sound, a huge crack appeared in the air as a gigantic rough brown hand emerged out of nowhere. It was quickly evident that the hand was not of a humanoid, at least not one of flesh and blood, as the hand was wrought from tree and roots.

The fingers didn't have any nails, and only got thinner and ended in sharp spikes. Its size was huge, each finger being roughly five meters long, and if one looked closely, one could actually see that many of the roots formed what looked like fractals all across the limb.

The wooden hand mirrored the movement of Zac's hand, grasping toward the crystal. The translucent shield that earlier was somewhat visible around it just gave a bright flash before it winked out of existence, showing that the protective layer that had stopped them earlier was gone.

The core wouldn't simply lie down and give up, and it started to emanate an even greater pressure from before as its green light turned painfully bright. The energy emitted was so great that Zac was starting to get pushed back even though he stood almost fifty meters away, but **[Nature's Punishment]** kept moving forward. As the wooden hand pushed toward the crystal, it started smoking and steaming due to the light. It looked like the light from the core was burning it, and simultaneously, Zac's hand started to blister as well.

Zac only grunted and pushed his hand forward, and the enormous hand gripped the core like a vise and squeezed. A weird screeching echoed throughout the cavern, and the whole structure started to shake, while the large hand actually caught on green fire. However, the power in the hand was enormous, and cracks quickly started to appear on the crystal until it completely crumbled with a huge explosion.

The hand dissipated as an enormous shock wave slammed Zac and his party into the wall of the core room, the force almost enough to knock him unconscious. He shook his head, dizzy from the impact, and looked around. His whole body felt broken, and a stinging pain throbbed from his right arm. When he looked down at it, he saw that it was completely scalded, looking like he had put his arm into boiling water.

The **[Nature's Punishment]** had worked out really well, apart from his blistering hand. The core gave out a force that kept even Zac away, unable to approach, but it managed to push forward without any problem. It was a shame that the core somehow was able to obscure the Dao from him as they fought, since Zac had wanted to try the skill with its full power.

He was pretty sure that the attack would be strengthened with the Seed of Trees, since the hand was made of wood and roots.

Perhaps the attack would be even stronger, or perhaps the hand would have been more resilient, and he wouldn't have ended up with a burned hand.

At least he'd gained another level from the fight, as a huge surge of Cosmic Energy entered him the moment the core shattered, a far larger amount compared to when he killed the Fiend Wolf. That was the third level he gained during the ant waves.

It wasn't the same speed he had during the last waves, but it was still apparently an enormous speed, according to Ogras. The others on top of the Ladder hadn't leveled at all, or maybe gained one level during the same period. He was currently level 54 while Salvation was on the second spot with level 43.

Ten levels might not seem like a lot, but Zac knew the horrifying number of wolves and ants he'd killed to bridge that gap. It would probably take months for the guy or girl to reach Zac's stage, and by then, who knew what level Zac would be. He put those things aside and took stock of his surroundings.

The others were in bad shape too. Ogras was out of his shadow form and coughed some blood as he tried to get back on his feet. Alea and Janos were lying unconscious, blood dripping out of their ears and mouths. One of Janos' legs was at a weird angle, clearly broken.

Zac sat up with a few coughs while he fished out his last E-grade Nexus Crystal and started absorbing. He only managed to absorb a smidgeon before he was interrupted, though. The whole cavern was shaking ominously, some small cracks already starting to appear on the walls.

He hastily got to his feet with a grunt and stumbled to Janos and Alea and flung them over his shoulders. He was only running on fumes at the moment, but with his attributes, it was no real difficulty carrying two people.

"What's going on?" Zac croaked at Ogras, who finally had got to his feet.

"It feels like the hidden space is cracking. We need to get out of here NOW. We don't know what parts will remain and what parts will be sucked into oblivion," Ogras answered while he popped a healing pill into his mouth.

Luckily, the tunnels they entered through once again were opened with the hive queen's death, and they scurried out through one of them. The shaking started to get worse, and there were even cracks in space itself appearing, making the air look like a broken mirror. The two didn't dare go near any of those widening rifts, afraid to be thrown into the void.

They encountered some ants during the mad dash out, but they were completely immobile, blankly standing still, unaware of the surroundings. The two simply ignored them and kept going, the greedy demon not even contemplating stopping to kill the free targets. Ogras usually was in charge of deciding the path, but when he found no clues what to do, they simply trusted Zac's Luck stat, letting him choose at random.

As they ran, the cracks in space only got wider and wider until they feared they might not make it out in time. Luckily, they finally felt the wind and fresh air in the distance, and reinvigorated, they increased their speed. As they turned a corner, they were met with the light of the outside and heedlessly ran out.

The duo stumbled out of the tunnels next to each other, overlooking a vast field of dead ants and panting demons. To Zac's surprise, he saw Sap Trang among the fighters, bloodied but alive. Ilvere and Namys came running up to them and took care of the two unconscious generals, with Namys throwing Zac a baleful glare after seeing Ogras' state.

Finally safe, Zac opened up his quest screen.

Incursion Master (Unique): Close or conquer incursion and protect town from denizens of other alignments for 3 months. Reward: 5 E-Grade Nexus Crystals, Town

upgraded to City, status upgraded to Lord. (2/3) [20:02:32:25]

The second part was completed, though the huge carcass of the hive queen remained. The system never teleported away the corpses of the wolves, so Zac guessed that they would have to deal with the huge hive somehow. That would have to wait a bit until later, though, as Zac was completely spent. Besides, entering that thing right now was to toy with death.

Zac was in no mood to help out with the cleanup and slowly started making his way back to his camp. He had already eaten a healing pill, but his arm was still hurting quite badly.

"Good work, young man," a voice said from his side, and Zac looked up to see Mr. Trang standing some distance.

He was currently using a spear to make sure that the insects on the ground were actually dead. Zac guessed that the experience would be a pretty decent boost if the old fisherman found some live ones still around. Zac didn't have the energy to chat with the old man and only nodded at him as he continued on.

Zac made his way past the wall and the small town and soon found himself in the comfortable stillness of his camp. There were very few who dared to approach this area without invitation, giving it a stillness. But lately, this stillness was starting to get interrupted more and more.

"You're Super Brother-Man, aren't you?" a voice came from the movie-viewing canopy. It was Emily, who was watching a comedy series with a blank face.

Zac sighed and sat down next to her.

110

EXPLORATION

"Why do you say that?" Zac simply asked, taking out a piece of pre-grilled meat from his pouch.

"I have been going over things since you started fighting those insects. There are many things that don't make sense. You're so strong. Like crazy strong. I have never seen or heard anything like it while I traveled with Mom and Dad," she answered as she stared at him. "And while you fought like a madman, Super Brother-Man gained two levels, and a third while you were inside fighting the boss," Emily continued.

Zac said nothing and only continued eating, tired in both body and mind.

"Besides, these demons are weird. They know way too much. Not even the cultivators in the cities know many of the things Alyn explained. And they're way stronger than normal humans. They're not a race that got newly integrated like us. I think you have captured them from an incursion or something,"

"No one can capture this man, little brat," a voice said from behind her as Ogras materialized from the shadows. "We simply came to an agreement with Zac and ended the incursion."

"Whatever," she said with a roll of her eyes.

"What are you doing here?" Zac asked as he turned back to the demon. He didn't bother trying to refute the demon, who'd essentially admitted to being a foreign invader. It was their problem after all, not Zac's.

"I am here to tell you that I'm buying the fruit and will be in seclusion for a while," Ogras answered. Clearly the healing pills that he'd eaten earlier were quite good, since the wound on his chest was largely healed.

"Okay. I might be heading out again soon, just so you know. Take care of things if I'm gone after your seclusion is finished. If you think it will take a longer while, then inform Alea and the others," Zac answered.

Ogras only nodded and disappeared with the shadows.

"It's true, isn't it?"

"Yes," Zac simply said. "Do the other humans know?"

"Maybe not those idiots with Megan. They're too scared to think straight. But I think that old grampa knows," Emily said with a pout.

No one said anything, but as the silence stretched on, Emily's eyes reddened, and two streams of tears started falling down her face. She quickly wiped them as Zac ignored his weary body while getting on his feet and walked over to Emily. He didn't say anything, but only patted her head.

"I was really worried," Emily said with a small voice.

"I know. I'm sorry." Zac sighed.

He sat down next to her as she kept blankly watching the television. He tried to stay up, but between the soft chair and finally being able to relax, he soon fell into a deep slumber.

He woke up some time later and found that Emily wasn't around anymore. There was a package on the coffee table with some bread and meat. The farmers had actually started up some temporary fields within the wall to provide the army with some other food apart from meat, and it looked like it finally had started to pay dividends. Zac was amazed at the speed of the growth of the produce and couldn't wait to set up proper farms as soon as the waves were dealt with.

He had been afraid that the apocalypse would bring with it a lack of food and drink, but it obviously wasn't the case. The beasts were getting more numerous, and farming was getting more efficient. No one should starve to death as long as they controlled some land. Besides, as long as people had access to a System-run shop, they could feed a family for just 10 Nexus Coins a day.

Zac sighed and opened up his status screen.

Name: Zachary Atwood
Level: 54
Class: [F-Rare] Hatchetman
Race: [E] Human
Alignment: [Earth] Human

Titles: Born for Carnage, Ultimate Reaper, Luck of the Draw, Giantsbane, Disciple of David, Overpowered, Slayer of Leviathans, Adventurer, Demon Slayer, Full of Class, Rarified Being, Trailblazer, Child of Dao, The Big 500, Planetary Aegis, One Against Many, Butcher

Dao: Seed of Heaviness – Early, Seed of Trees – Early, Seed of Sharpness – Early

Strength: 279
Dexterity: 140
Endurance: 186
Vitality: 113
Intelligence: 69
Wisdom: 57

Luck: 77

Free Points: 3
Nexus Coins: 21,675,103

Fighting the ant wave the past eleven days gave him 10 million Nexus Coins, covering the cost of building the Teleportation Array earlier. It hadn't given any titles or Dao upgrades either, apart from finishing the quest for his new attack skill. He was very curious about how his new skill would improve when the skill got stronger in the future.

[Nature's Punishment – Proficiency: Early. Awaken the wrath of the world. Upgradeable.]

At Early proficiency, a huge hand had emerged out of the void. He wasn't sure whether he was summoning a living being, or whether the hand just was a copy of his own. Perhaps as he and the skill got stronger, he would be able to summon a huge avatar that could fight in his stead.

He put one point in Strength and two points in Endurance and closed the window. With his race boost, he wouldn't have to worry about attribute caps for a long while, and now that his other stats were in order, he felt he could focus more on his main one once again.

He ate the food left for him by either Alea or Emily and got up and headed to the town. He met a few demons who nodded in respect to him as he walked and gave a simple nod back. His reputation kept increasing among the former invaders as his achievements increased.

As he entered the town, he saw Megan and another tourist scurry about, each carrying a hoe. It looked like they were on farm duty today. They saw Zac's approach but, after a brief hesitation, turned their eyes down and kept moving.

The humans had been horrified when they were taken to the battlefield. Zac's intention was to let them see the reality of the new world, and he made a few warriors escort them to the advance wall while he battled during the fourth day. The sight of a battalion of demons fighting tooth and nail against a horde of mutated ants made them realize that their trials and tribulations on the last island were nothing compared to what they were witnessing.

Since then, they never said anything about fighting or getting stronger and stuck to their daily tasks instead. A few started working on the temporary farms, and others helped with cooking and other tasks around the village. Zac was a bit disappointed, but he also knew that not everyone could become a warrior in this new reality.

The only one from the group of twelve who still wanted a combat class was Sap Trang. Unfortunately for him, he was just too far behind in power at the moment, so he couldn't really partake in the grind fest of the monster hordes. At least it looked like he'd managed to get some kills in at the end of the siege, which should have been quite a boost, since each of the ants gave as much Cosmic Energy as a couple of barghest.

Zac found Ilvere sitting under a canopy, playing an unfamiliar instrument close to the larger tent where they usually held their war meetings. It was a stringed instrument that reminded Zac a bit of a guqin, though the notes generated from the crystalline strings sounded closer to a violin. It was an odd sight, seeing the burly warrior playing such a delicate instrument.

"The triumphant Lord returns," the warrior said as he stopped playing.

"Did you hear about Ogras' seclusion? And what are you doing?" Zac asked after greeting the general with a nod.

"Yes, he will likely be gone for some time," Ilvere answered. "I'm simply relaxing. It's important to properly rest body and mind after an intense battle. Sometimes the tranquility after the battle can give as much or even more insight than the fight itself."

Zac nodded, as it made sense. People couldn't always have a breakthrough in the middle of battle, even though it squeezed out their potential. Sometimes some reflection afterward was all that was needed to take the final step in pushing through a boundary.

"How was the fight yesterday?" Zac asked.

"Four casualties. With Rivea and Herod, it makes six, the worst day since the hordes started," he answered with a sigh.

Zac could only nod, feeling a bit bitter. His army was continuously shrinking. When the wolf hordes started, roughly two hundred warriors had manned the wall, and today, only 160 remained. Twenty percent of his army had died during the last forty days. Of course, some were killed by Ogras and Namys, but the majority died in battle.

Zac had been quite despondent in the beginning, losing one warrior after another, but he was starting to get used to it. People dying while trying to get stronger was the most normal thing in the Multiverse, and no one held any real regrets over it. To cultivate was to defy death. Some did it for the increase in longevity; others for power and wealth. But what all had in common was the knowledge that any day might be their last.

"I plan on sending out expeditions to map the surrounding islands. Please assemble four teams. The goal is reconnaissance, but at least one competent fighter in each team. The team members will be compensated in crystals or Nexus Coins," Zac said.

"You should know that none of us know anything about sailing or naval warfare. There aren't any oceans on our home planet," Ilvere said as he rose to his feet to get to work.

"I know. I will send one of the sailors from the humans with each group. So at least one in each team needs to know the **[Book of Babel]** skill. You people should take advantage of it being available in the contribution store. You are stuck on a foreign planet, after all," Zac answered.

"Many have actually bought it already. Some are just like you, getting antsy from staying on this island for months on end. Most came through the incursion to gain insight and wealth, and that can't be done while staying inside some walls," Ilvere said with half a smile. "I'm sure there will be many willing scouts."

Zac nodded and headed off to find Sap Trang and his fellow villagers. After explaining the situation, the four fishermen agreed to help out after some hesitation.

"If we find some of our lost villagers, can we bring them back?" Mr. Trang asked after some silence.

"Yes, that's okay. You cannot say anything about the situation on the island, though, before they are here. The situation here is… special. If you do, the soldiers have orders to silence you and everyone who heard it," Zac answered. It was extremely strict rules, but he simply couldn't allow any information about his island to leak yet.

He'd learned some things about lordship from Alyn and Ogras while he rested during the ant waves. A Lord held various benefits in controlling a town or even a country, as they gained access to a so-called Lord System. Originally, the system was used as a method for generals of the Ancient Empire to control their armies, but with the Apostate of Order, the System became generalized and gained a host of new features.

As the System evolved over time, various functions were added, and today, many benefits existed. For example, a Lord could automatically enforce a tax on his empire. There were no loopholes either, as the System was in control of the taxation. The only downside was that the System itself took a cut of the taxes.

Lords also got access to more functions on their teleporters and could even get invited to grand happenings such as auctions and special events in the Multiverse that commoners did not have access to.

"Other humans will have to stay put even if they want to come over. Come back and report their situation to me, and I'll decide what to do about it."

"Very well. We understand the importance of discretion. Those who left before us were mainly the younger generation from our village. They risked their lives to find help for us, but we never heard back from them. If we can find them and bring them back here, I'm sure their future will be better than in most parts of the world," the fisherman answered.

"Good. Start preparing; I want the four teams setting out within three days. I'll provide the ships for you," Zac said as he turned to leave.

"One minute, please. I was wondering if I could consult you about my class," Mr. Trang said quickly.

Zac was a bit surprised as he turned around and inspected the fisherman, only to see he was actually level 25. He must have worked quite arduously, since he had been only level 21 when he arrived at Port Atwood. Zac remembered how much work he himself put into finishing those last levels.

"What about it?" Zac asked, a bit curious about what Class the fisherman chose for himself.

111

WAVE WHISPERER

"I haven't actually chosen yet, but I've seen which options I have. They are Fisherman, Dockhand, Marine, Acolyte, and Wave Whisperer," the fisherman began.

The first two were pretty straightforward noncombat classes, whereas the next two were classes Zac knew himself. The old fisherman had likely gotten the option for Acolyte since he'd bought the Water Spear skill earlier. Wave Whisperer was the only one that was unclear to him. It sounded like a water-based class, but more than that he was unsure.

"I am wavering between Marine and Wave Whisperer. Both are Uncommon classes connected to the sea. The Wave Whisperer is connected to taming and controlling aquatic wildlife, which might be very convenient in this new world. We saw fish as large as sharks while sailing here, and who knows what else lurks in the depths. Controlling the giants of the sea might both help with scouting and protection," he continued. "However, my stats are all toward Strength and Endurance so far. It might be a waste to take a mage class after this. What do you think?" he asked Zac.

"The stats you get before your class are insignificant on the road of cultivation. If you believe that Wave Whisperer will be more beneficial, take it. You can make up the missing stats with natural treasures and training in the future," Zac said.

"Sounds reasonable. I will do just that," Sap Trang said with a nod.

Zac nodded and left the living quarters of the fishermen. He knew that the wily old fisherman actually didn't require help but just wanted to show his sincerity to Zac by divulging his future class. He'd already tried to show his worth before the ant waves, and after seeing Zac and the others' power, his desire to pave a path for his villagers only grew.

Next, he went to the Creators' shipyard and ordered four of the small exploratory vessels for a million Nexus Coins each. Karunthel, the spider-foreman, was not around, as Rahm explained that he was currently occupied with some experiments. For people like Karunthel and the Creators, experimentation was in a way cultivation. If they created something functional and new, they would gain a huge surge of experience, maybe to the point of gaining multiple levels.

It was generally the same with many of the noncombat classes. A farmer who reaped a whole field after tending it for months could gain a handful of levels. The higher the difficulty and grade of the herbs or vegetables that were grown, the more energy would be awarded. That was why many blacksmiths and other crafting professions preferred to craft hard and high-grade items rather than mashing together an endless stream of low-grade items. The benefits, both in wealth and levels, if the craft succeeded far outweighed anything low-grade items could compare to.

Other noncombat classes were more of the slow-and-steady type, such as Adran's Administration class, which consistently gained Cosmic Energy while handling town matters. There were certain events, though, that could award large sudden boosts in experience, such as a town upgrade.

Next, he walked over to the small house that Alyn resided in. He found the demoness sitting on the porch in the same comfortable chair she'd used down in the mines.

"How is Emily doing?" he asked.

"She has started following the methods to attain mage classes, but she still insists on training with an axe for a few hours every day," she said as she put down her book with a sigh.

"Well, it's her decision, so let her proceed. Who knows what class she'll be able to get from the combination," Zac said with a shrug.

"I've read that cultivators of newly integrated planets are far more likely to choose unique and unknown classes, but that is a dangerous game to play. You humans will soon see the folly in your ways. I wouldn't be surprised if more than half the people on your so-called Ladder right now will be stuck at F-grade forever. If breaking through to the next levels was that easy, then Clan Azh'Rezak wouldn't only have a handful of D-rank ancestors after thousands of years of accumulation," the teacher said with a serious face.

"You need to have your people choose sensible and Common classes so that you can get some guaranteed E-rank Uncommon underlings. Who knows, perhaps some of them might even be able to evolve into D-rank in the distant future."

"I am not going to tell people what classes they choose. None of the people on the island are really my subjects. Of course, it might change in the future when you create your academy," Zac answered. "Actually, I have a question about class rarities," he said as he changed the subject to the old fisherman. "He is a normal fisherman, but he's got multiple Uncommon skills to choose from when you said that barely one out of a thousand got Uncommon classes after studying at an academy. How is that possible?"

"The first class is mainly based on achievements and experiences, since people rarely are in contact with the Dao at that stage. Someone old will have more of those than a youngster who's only sixteen. However, that doesn't mean one should wait when choosing a class," the demon answered. "The older one is, the harder it gets to improve one's race. I am not sure if Mr. Trang will be able to evolve his race, even with the medicinal baths. The optimal time for evolution has passed. Even if he managed to evolve, it will involve far more resources compared to someone normal," Alyn concluded.

"What about me?" Zac asked curiously.

"Your prime age for evolution had passed, but you sidestepped that with the Fruit of Ascension. Now you're a thirty-year-old whose lifespan is five hundred years; that's almost a baby," she said with a slight smile.

"But generally, it's better to evolve as soon as possible. It will be cheaper, and you will avoid any risk of your body simply not being able to withstand another evolution. If it takes too long, your body might not be able to take that last step, precluding you from evolving. So as soon as you reach E-grade Class, you should start working on your race again," she added.

"On another note. We do not have any cultivation manuals at the moment. Emily is turning sixteen in a month, and she should be using a cultivation manual from the start. It will help her immensely, as reforming pathways at a later date can be quite painful and dangerous," Alyn said. "Using a fitting cultivation manual from level 1 will even adjust the pathways provided by the Class, resulting in a greater synergy."

Zac could only grimace while nodding, remembering his own harrowing experience when he improved his pathways from his initial rudimentary ones. That was likely his first large mistake, and it almost got him killed.

Since there were some pretty good cultivation manuals in the contribution store, he decided to purchase a few of the cheaper ones. It was not only for Emily, but it would be needed if he wanted to create an academy in the future. There were not many other things that grabbed his interest in the shop anyway, and the expenditure seemed acceptable.

There was only one thing he was planning on buying before heading out again, a skill called **[Mental Fortress]**. It was a skill that both protected him from skills like **[Eye of Discernment]** and also boosted the defense against mental attacks and illusions. It cost 10 million contribution points, which made it one of the most expensive skills, but he could afford it. The battle against the ants had given him almost as much as the whole wolf horde, and he currently possessed roughly 34 million points.

Feeling done with everything he needed to do, he walked back to his camper and spent the rest of the day recuperating. His arm was still hurting quite badly, while his feet still had blisters from the acid bath.

Emily came back later that evening, preferring to stay at his camper rather than her assigned housing close to Alyn. He didn't know if it was the familiarity of the camper or the presence of him that made her more comfortable, but he didn't mind, as he had gotten used to falling asleep outside under the moonlight in any case.

"You know, I'm wondering what the world would think if they knew the strongest and the wealthiest man after the apocalypse lives like a hobo outside a camper in the woods," she said with a grin, obviously having recovered from earlier.

Zac only rolled his eyes and motioned her to sit down. He took out his kit for grilling meat and started preparing some food for the evening. Emily sat down and took out something from her backpack. It was a covered tray, and when she lifted the lid, Zac noticed a couple of long pieces of dough.

"Give me two spits," she said, and Zac curiously complied. "Mom made these during the summer. It's really only water, flour, and salt, but it still gets pretty yummy when grilled. It's a shame we don't have butter, though."

She took out one of the pieces of dough from the tray and wrapped it around the spit. She did the same with the second spit, and then she placed them some distance from the fire.

"I think it's called caveman bread? I don't remember anymore," she added as she kept an eye on her spits.

Zac only smiled and salted the large slabs of meat. He made a mental reminder to get some stock of various things when he left next time.

"You're leaving the island again, aren't you?" she said as she kept spinning the spits.

"Yes, in a few days," Zac answered.

"Let me go with you!" Emily immediately burst out, looking up at him.

"You know, I can't go back through the beastman village. They closed their teleporter the moment after we used it. The portal I will use might lead to the opposite side of the planet, far from wherever your siblings might be."

"You don't know that. They might be right where you end up, and you will not be able to recognize them," she retorted, starting to work up a huff.

It was true. One of the things he'd learned from Emily about the Tutorial was that the end-point of the Tutorial sometimes was randomized. Well, not really randomized so much as some were lucky and others weren't.

As the cultivators were undergoing the Tutorial, the world was rearranged, and the System dropped off the cultivators at a spot of its choosing when it was over. Some were lucky that the System chose their own turf when they got returned, like the villagers of Winterleaf Village. But most were dumped at a completely unknown place.

Zac asked the demons about it, and they thought it sounded

like a test. Many would start traveling home, braving dangers to find a way back to their families. Most would likely die, but some would emerge stronger from the experience. Others would give up and hide behind walls, becoming despondent shut-ins like the people of Fort Roger.

That explained why Hannah and the others were never returned, and also meant that Emily's siblings might be anywhere.

"Come on, I will be very helpful. I have visited many towns and know how to find information. I will be useful to you. If you go alone, you might just make a scene and get in all kinds of trouble," she quickly said. "Besides, I'm turning sixteen soon. Traveling might help me get a better class."

Zac kept slowly spinning his spit, mulling things over. He wasn't sure what to expect from his next excursion, and it was a bit troublesome to keep her safe, since she couldn't use the defensive gear yet. However, she might actually be useful.

During the ant waves, there were actually two new choices that cropped up. One was called Cradle of God, and it seemed a bit too weird for Zac's taste, and not somewhere he'd even consider bringing Emily. He actually had a suspicion that it was the home of Salvation, the second-place holder of the Ladder. Judging by the pseudonym he chose, it wouldn't be too far-fetched he'd name his town like that. He knew nothing about that person, and he wouldn't teleport there, since it might get extremely dangerous.

The second option made Zac far more hopeful, as it was called New Washington. It wasn't very imaginative, but it clearly was an American town. The name implied it was government-run as well, and it might be the best bet for him to gain information. He realized it might be a trap, and that was another reason he was hesitant in bringing Emily.

The people who possessed access to an array would generally be elites, and you had to have some balls if you planned on doing something untoward. Besides, he already knew the System restricted the use of the array as some sort of deathtrap. He couldn't place any offensive arrays around it or place it far underground, for example.

Still, he had a very clear goal, and bringing Emily would likely slow him down in addition to putting her in needless danger. He wasn't heading out on a stroll, after all.

"I am sorry. You will have to stay here until you have started cultivating. At that point, you can use defensive treasures and protect yourself. I don't know what I'll encounter when I step out of the teleporter," Zac finally said with a sigh. "But I will ask around for you about your siblings. My main goal is to find my hometown just like you, so I understand your feelings."

Emily didn't seem to care about the promise and angrily huffed as she ran toward the camper, completely forgetting about the bread.

112

BACK TO THE SCENE OF THE CRIME

The next few two days went by excruciatingly slow for Zac, who just wanted to get up and leave. However, there were more and more things to do in order to keep his town running. He couldn't wait for finishing the third horde in a few weeks. When he became a Lord, he'd get a System-trained Administrator, perhaps Abby, who he could leave most of the work to. Adran was a competent worker, but Zac felt it was much too early to start giving the demons real influence in his future town, especially since their alliances mostly lay with Ogras.

Ogras was someone who would take a bit of advantage and run away with it. Zac still believed that the demon would do his best in order to improve the state of Port Atwood, at least for ten years, but he wouldn't lower his guard until he found some real assurances. Therefore, Zac still felt the need to personally oversee some details.

He met up with Alea and Janos, who were mostly fine, with the exception of Janos' leg. The poison mistress looked a bit annoyed upon hearing Zac was leaving once again but didn't say anything. Zac also talked with a few of the mages, who promised to start work on an improved home for him. Emily's comment the other day made him realize he'd forgotten about actually improving his camp. He remembered Ogras' lush palace over at Azh'Rodum, and even a tenth of that would be a nice upgrade to his own living situation.

The second thing he did was to travel to the mountains. He brought only Alea with him this time, pushing his speed to the limit. It wasn't some romantic reasoning behind it; he rather needed her to spot any leftover poison.

Earlier when he'd traveled this distance, he usually had to be careful and moved at a normal walking speed, but now he ran, ignoring the occasional barghest. The trip would take over a day back in the day, but now it only took a couple of hours. Surprisingly, Alea seemed to have no problem keeping up either.

The mountain valley had finally cleared out enough for him to start collecting everything of value from his killing spree. He didn't want to leave this treasure trove as he left the island again. And it was especially nice timing, since Ogras was occupied with absorbing the Fruit of Ascension. Zac learned that it could take weeks to absorb a treasure of that magnitude. A big reason he almost died in the pond was that the mix of Cosmic Water and the Fruit of Ascension made the absorption only take minutes rather than days, which overtaxed his body.

He didn't set about collecting it all in order to hoard the wealth for himself. He planned on using much of it as rewards and salaries for the demons and other citizens in the future, or even stocking stores with the weapons that lay about. Besides, who knew what secret treasures all the elites of the demon army had pocketed for themselves.

They arrived at the mountain slopes at lunch, and after making sure that there wasn't any poison around, they scaled the mountain from the same side as the demon army once did. From there the two followed along the path of the battle, picking up any armor and weapon that seemed useful. The corpses were quite decayed, but at least the scorching sun and blowing winds had caused them to dry out rather than rot, so the stench wasn't as bad as Zac had feared.

Many of them lay in pools of dried but putrid-looking liquid, though, and Alea explained that the poison he'd thrown out would cause them to vacate from every orifice, completely drying them out, as the victims were dying. From that, it was pretty clear which ones died from poison and which ones were dead from the battle before.

The number of demons lying in a pool of waste was quite terrifying, even out at the rim of the valley. Zac mentally shut down and wordlessly kept collecting items. Even Alea seemed subdued by the sight as she helped him out with the collection. They kept moving about for most of the day, finally reaching the epicenter of the poison, the scarlet tree.

The tree still stood up, even though many of its branches were destroyed in the battle. However, its trunk was no longer red, but purple, reminiscent of the poison cloud. The once pristine white leaves were also changed, now having purple veins covering them.

It made a bit of sense, as the closer they got to the tree, it was obvious that the corpses were even more dried out. Perhaps the tree had absorbed the poisoned warriors to heal itself in the same way it had absorbed the trees earlier. From all the poison, it seemed that it mutated somehow.

"How magical! I wonder what kind of fruit a poisoned Tree of Ascension will sprout. I hope it survives its current ordeal," Alea said as she stared at the changed tree in wonder.

"Can we cure it?" Zac asked, more interested in growing normal Fruit of Ascension instead of any weird mutated ones.

"Maybe a skilled botanist could, but the poison has reached its core from absorbing too much of it from the area. It might cleanse it by itself over time, or it might mutate. Or it will simply succumb and die. We'll have to wait and see," she answered with a shrug.

"If it makes a poison version of a Fruit of Ascension, I want it," she added as she stared at him with serious eyes. "It might even give me a poison constitution."

"We'll see what happens with the tree before deciding on any allocation. There is a lot of gear to collect," Zac answered noncommittally.

It was true, the area was packed with elite warriors. Many of those who fought close to the tree even owned their own Cosmos Sacks, making it easier to collect their wealth. They methodically went through the central battlefield, and by the end of it, Zac had another seventy pouches in his possession.

Finally, the two walked over to Rydel, lying close to the tree, a large grisly hole in his chest and a broken arm.

"This wound… Did Ogras do this?" Alea asked with surprise.

"I thought the four of you knew?" Zac retorted, equally surprised. "I battled Rydel and that monkey over there, but I only managed to break his arm and expend most of his aces. He was about to kill me when Ogras attacked."

Zac bent down and grabbed a pouch attached to his belt.

"Wait, check within his clothes as well. Rydel was the unofficial leader of the invasion and a scion of the Azh'Rezak main branch. He should have more than one pouch," Alea interjected.

Zac nodded and, with a grimace, started reaching around within the corpse's clothes. After a while, he actually found another pouch.

Zac inspected the two and was shocked by their quality. The one Rydel wore on his waist was quite large, comprising roughly ten by ten meters of space, far larger compared to his own, which only had two to three meters of space. It mainly contained daily items, such as some foods and clothes. It also contained a couple of thousand crystals and a few other assorted items.

However, the inner one was on another level completely, to the point that Zac suspected that it was an E-grade pouch rather than F-grade. It had a cubic space of roughly fifty meters across, meaning it had a whopping 125,000 cubic meters of space. He would be able to fit a small airplane in it if he found one.

The pouch was mostly empty, but there was a small mountain containing tens of thousands of F-grade crystals. There were also neatly stacked weapons and a huge supply of food. There even were a few siege weapons, looking far more sophisticated compared to the ones the demons built back at Port Atwood. Another corner held a bunch of vials containing pills, labeled and ordered. There also were a couple of ornate boxes, and Zac guessed those things held the real prizes.

The inner pouch held the backup resources of the whole demon invasion, Zac realized as his heartbeat sped up. It was a huge amount of wealth, even for him. He recognized a few of the pills by now, and many of them cost tens of thousands of Nexus Coins per pop. There were over a hundred of each type of those pills.

Zac took out the various boxes and things one by one and together with Alea categorized them. There were certain fruits that could improve the constitution far more efficiently compared to the medicinal bath, and Zac gave a few of them to Alea after seeing her hungry eyes. He didn't need them for himself and felt it was a decent reward for having fought two horde bosses with him. He put aside most of the rest for Janos and the others, though.

The contribution board clearly was an effective method of motivating people, and Zac was thinking of establishing something similar after the beast hordes. If people contributed to Port Atwood, they'd gain contribution points, and with those points, they could buy various things from him.

He immediately consulted Alea about it, and to his embarrassment, learned that such a thing was pretty standard in the Multiverse, and not some novel new idea he concocted. Many of the things in the huge pouch were likely even meant for just that purpose during the invasion.

Done with the looting, they started heading back toward the camp. The amount of wealth he collected was enormous, and including all the armors and tools, Alea and he estimated the value easily surpassed a hundred million Nexus Coins. It was no surprise that war was so common in the Multiverse, as it was extremely lucrative.

Finally, all preparations were done, and Zac prepared to set out. During the return, he transferred most of the wealth to the large pouch, which he now carried hidden under his E-grade robe. He left some of it to Adran so that the warriors could get new gear. Many of the demons were starting to look pretty ragged after battling two beast hordes, so they needed to swap out some of the broken items.

He actually brought a total of ten of the smallest Cosmos Sack with him as well, which he hid in a small travel bag. The reaction from Selas when he realized Zac possessed a Cosmos Sack was quite large, and Zac thought he might be able to sell them for quite a nice profit in a human settlement.

He learned from Calrin and Alea that these smallest Cosmos Sack were worth roughly a million Nexus Coins. Most people in the Multiverse possessed at least one, unless they were young and still needed to spend all their money on medicinal baths. They weren't overly difficult to create for an experienced inscription master. The higher-grade ones required insight into the Dao of Space to create, though, making them far more expensive.

Emily was still angry with him, but she still tried helping out in the end. On her insistence, he carried a large backpack to make it look less suspicious. Zac also wore a new pair of boots, which was actually starting to feel a bit uncomfortable after having adapted to the free feeling of nothing trapping his feet.

Zac gave some final instructions to Adran regarding the scouting missions and some other details before he walked toward the teleportation array. He inserted the crystals and paid the fee, and once again, he disappeared from the island.

From the distance, a pair of eyes was observing everything before receding into the shadows.

The story continues in Defiance of the Fall 2.

113

THANK YOU FOR READING DEFIANCE OF THE FALL

We hope you enjoyed it as much as we enjoyed bringing it to you. We just wanted to take a moment to encourage you to review the book. Follow this link: Defiance of the Fall to be directed to the book's Amazon product page to leave your review.

Every review helps further the author's reach and, ultimately, helps them continue writing fantastic books for us all to enjoy.

DEFIANCE OF THE FALL

BOOK ONE

BOOK TWO

BOOK THREE

BOOK FOUR

BOOK FIVE

BOOK SIX

BOOK SEVEN

BOOK EIGHT

BOOK NINE

BOOK TEN
BOOK ELEVEN

You can also join our non-spam mailing list by visiting www.subscribepage.com/AethonReadersGroup and never miss out on future releases. You'll also receive three full books completely Free as our thanks to you.

Facebook | Instagram | Twitter | Website (www.aethonbooks.com)

Want to discuss our books with other readers and even the authors? Join our Discord server today and be a part of the Aethon community.

Looking for more great books?

Crimefighting is illegal. Punishable by life in prison beneath the ocean. That won't stop Harrier. *Justice—a concept without a universally accepted definition. To some, it means reconciliation, while others deliver it with swift and violent judgment. For me? I just want to not be considered an outlaw for years of serving and protecting New York City. Yep. That's right. Crimefighting is against the law and punishable by life in prison at the bottom of the ocean. It sucks. But that won't stop me from doing what I was born to do: uphold justice and stop good people from being hurt. Even if everyone I once called a friend is against me, I'm not bowing down to the Counter Vigilante Taskforce. My name is Sawyer William Vincent (I know, it's three first names. Think I haven't heard that before?) Once known as Red Raptor, I'm now Black Harrier, one of the world's most famous masked crime-fighters, and this is my city. I think.* ***From #1 Audible & Washington Post Bestseller Jaime Castle and CJ Valin comes a new superhero universe perfect for fans of both DC and Marvel. Actually, its for fans of anything superhero-related. You're gonna like it. Promise.***

Get Harrier: Justice Now!

The Everfail will rise. His enemies will fall. *Hiral is the Everfail, the weakest person on the flying island of Fallen Reach. He trains harder than any warrior. Studies longer than any scholar. But all his people are born with magic powered by the sun, flowing through tattoos on their bodies. Despite having enormous energy within, Hiral is the only one who can't channel it; his hard work is worth nothing. Until it isn't. In a moment of danger, Hiral unlocks an achievement with a special instruction: Access a Dungeon to receive a Class-Specific Reward. It's his first—and maybe last—chance for real power. Just one problem: all dungeons lay in the wilderness below the flying islands that humanity lives on, and there lay secrets and dangers that no one has survived. New powers await, but so do new challenges. If he survives? He could forge his own path to power. If he fails? Death will be the least of his problems.* ***Don't miss the next progression fantasy series from J.M Clarke, bestselling author of Mark of the Fool, along with C.J. Thompson. Unlock a weak-to-strong progression into power and a detailed litRPG system with unique classes, skills, dungeons, achievements, survival and evolution. Explore a mysterious world of fallen civilizations, strange monsters and deadly secrets.***

Get Rune Seeker Now!

The last thing a Necromancer expects is to be brought back from the dead... *After fulfilling the duty all Arch Necromancers are tasked with, the last thing Sylver Sezari expected was to be reborn. He was usually the one reanimating dead things. How ironic. But reborn he was. And after crawling his way back into the land of the living, he finds himself a strange land, a strange time, and with a strange floating screen in front of his new face. Either through plan or chance, he's alive again, and planning to enjoy himself to his heart's content.* ***Don't miss the start of this LitRPG Adventure about a reincarnated necromancer growing in power and finding his way in a new world where the rules have changed vastly since he last "lived."***

Get Sylver Seeker Now!

For all our LitRPG books, visit our website.